THE DARK BETWEEN THE STARS

THE DARK BETWEEN THE STARS

The Saga of Shadows

BOOK ONE

KEVIN J. ANDERSON

**SIMON &
SCHUSTER**

London · New York · Sydney · Toronto · New Delhi

A CBS COMPANY

First published in the US by Tor Books, 2014
This edition published in Great Britain by Simon & Schuster UK Ltd, 2014
A CBS COMPANY

1 3 5 7 9 10 8 6 4 2

Simon & Schuster UK Ltd
1st Floor
222 Gray's Inn Road
London WC1X 8HB

www.simonandschuster.co.uk

Simon & Schuster Australia, Sydney
Simon & Schuster India, New Delhi

A CIP catalogue record for this book is available from the British Library

Trade Paperback ISBN: 978-1-84983-677-7
eBook ISBN: 978-1-84983-679-1

Printed and bound by CPI (UK) Ltd, Croydon, CR0 4YY

The Seven Suns universe is my love letter to science fiction, a response to all the stories and the sheer sense of wonder I experienced over a lifetime of reading the genre.

This book is dedicated to the creators of the many incredible universes that took me out of a mundane childhood and transported me from everyday life to different planets and cultures—including, but not limited to, George Lucas, Gene Roddenberry, Frank Herbert, Isaac Asimov, Robert Heinlein, Arthur C. Clarke, Ray Bradbury, Julian May, Andre Norton, and many, many more.

ACKNOWLEDGMENTS

Writing a novel is a solitary job, but writing a *good* novel requires a lot of help. For *The Dark Between the Stars* I would like to acknowledge the valuable assistance of Deb Ray, Diane Jones, Louis Moesta, John Silbersack, Pat LoBrutto, and my wife, Rebecca Moesta.

People assume that historians want to witness seminal events, but I must disagree. As a historian, my task is to record, to understand, to be objective. Yet objectivity is elusive when one is in the thick of a war that devastates the entire Spiral Arm. Personally, I would rather be an observer than a participant.

Nevertheless, while living through the conflict we now call the Elemental War, I did acquire a unique perspective. Now that I look back over the two decades since the end of that war, I see a time of peace and recovery. Civilization across the Spiral Arm is catching its breath.

The fiery beings called faeros have been driven back into their suns; the hydrogues are contained within their gas-giant planets. The Klikiss insect race departed on their final swarming, disappearing through their mysterious network of transportals to uncharted planets, and their treacherous black robots have all been wiped out.

The corrupt Terran Hanseatic League has become the Confederation, ruled by King Peter and Queen Estarra and composed of former Hansa planets, independent worlds, and Roamer clans. Although Earth remains important to the human race, the Confederation's capital is Theroc, where the worldforest thrives and telepathic green priests tap into the vast knowledge stored in the sentient trees.

The Ildiran Empire is still humanity's closest ally, and I admit to a fondness for their race and culture, having spent most of my professional career translating their billion-line historical epic, the Saga of Seven Suns. The Mage-Imperator even keeps a human green priest as his consort.

Impatient readers might consider twenty years plenty of time to chronicle such sweeping events, but in truth we are just getting started. It will take decades of peacetime contemplation to sort out the details.

If only we had that luxury.

—Rememberer Anton Colicos, introduction to *An Initial History of the Elemental War*

THE DARK
BETWEEN THE
STARS

ONE

GARRISON REEVES

He had to run, and he fled with the boy out into the dark spaces between the stars.

Garrison Reeves stole a ship from the Iswander Industries lava-processing operations on Sheol. Though he'd planned his escape for days, he gathered only a few supplies and keepsakes before departing, careful not to give his wife any hint of what he intended to do. None of his possessions mattered more than getting safely away with his son.

He knew the disaster could come soon—any day now. Lee Iswander, the Roamer industrialist, dismissed Garrison's concerns about third-order tidal shifts in the broken planet; Garrison's own wife, Elisa, didn't believe him. The lava miners paid little attention to his warnings, not because they disputed his geological calculations, but because they didn't *want* to believe. Their priorities were clear. Adding "unnecessary" and expensive levels of redundant shielding and "paranoid" safety measures was irresponsible, both to Iswander Industries and to the employees, who participated in profit-sharing.

Lee Iswander had commissioned follow-up reports, biased reports, that painted a far rosier picture. Garrison didn't accept them.

So he made his choice, the only possible choice. He stole one of the company ships, and when she found out about it, Elisa would claim that he stole their son.

He flew out of the Sheol system, running far from any Roamer settlement or Confederation outpost. Elisa was not only an ambitious woman, she was abusive, tenacious, and dangerous—and she would come after them. He needed a head start if he had any hope of getting away.

The ship was a standard Iswander cargo transport, a workhorse, fully fueled with ekti, run by an efficient Ildiran stardrive. Garrison could fly the vessel without special training, as he could fly most standard spacecraft.

Ten-year-old Seth rode in the cockpit next to him. Garrison made a game of familiarizing the boy with cockpit systems and engine diagnostics, giving him simple navigation problems to solve—as any good Roamer father would, even though Garrison had chafed under how *his* stern father had raised *him*. He would not make the same mistakes with Seth.

Roamers were free spirits, sometimes deprecatingly called space gypsies, whose clans filled niches too rugged and dangerous for more pampered people—places such as the Sheol lava-processing operations. He had followed Elisa there because of her promotion in Iswander Industries.

"You should stay away from That Woman," Olaf Reeves had warned him, not once but dozens of times. "If you defy me, if you marry her, you will regret it. You are spitting on your heritage."

Now, Garrison hated to admit that his father had been right.

He closed his eyes, took a breath, and opened them. He studied the markers on the ship's copilot control panels, then turned to his son. "Go ahead and set the next course, Seth."

"But where are we going?"

"You pick, so long as we're heading away from Sheol." He tapped the starscreen, which showed infinite possibilities. "On this trip, we're truly roaming. I just need some time away from everybody so I can rethink things."

Though anxious, the boy was glad to be with his father. Seth respected his mother, even feared her, but he loved his father. Elisa never let down her walls—not with any business associate, not with Garrison, not even with her own son.

"Will I be able to go to Academ now?" Seth asked. The Roamer school inside a hollowed-out comet had always fascinated the boy. He wanted to be with the children of other clans, to have *friends*. Garrison knew his son would be happier at Academ, but Elisa had refused to consider sending their son there.

"Maybe we'll arrange that before long. For now, you can learn from me."

Unlike other Roamer children, Seth hadn't grown up in a pleasant domed greenhouse asteroid or on the open gas-giant skies of an ekti-harvesting skymine. Rather, his daily view was a blaze of scarlet magma erupting in a smoke-filled sky. All the personnel of the lava-mining facility lived in reinforced habitat towers mounted on pilings sunk down to solid rock. More than two thousand employees, specialists of various ranks—engineers like Garrison himself, metallurgists, geologists, shipping personnel, and just plain grunt workers—filled shifts aboard the smelter barges or control towers, surrounded by fires that could have inspired Hell itself.

No other parents kept their children here. Sheol was no place for a family, no home for a boy, regardless of the career advancement opportunities for Elisa.

As the two closely orbiting halves of the binary planet adjusted their dance of celestial mechanics, Garrison had analyzed the orbital pirouette, uncovering fourth-order resonances that he suspected would make the fragments dip fractionally closer to each other, increasing stresses. He studied the melting points, annealing strengths, and ceramic-lattice structure of the habitat and factory towers.

And he realized the danger to the Iswander operations.

Alarmed, he had presented his results to Lee Iswander, only to be rebuffed when neither the industrialist nor his deputy—Garrison's own wife—took his warnings seriously. Iswander impatiently told Garrison to go back to work and reassured him that the lava-processing outpost was perfectly safe. The material strength of the structural elements was rated to withstand the environment of Sheol, although with little margin for error.

When Garrison insisted, Iswander grudgingly brought in a team of contract geologists and engineers who found a way to rerun the calculations, to reaffirm that nothing could go wrong. The specialists had departed with surprising haste—worried about their own safety?

Garrison still trusted his own calculations, though. Next, he felt it was his responsibility to warn the Sheol employees, which infuriated

Elisa, who was sure that his whistle-blowing would cost her a promotion.

Honestly, Garrison hoped he was wrong. He knew he wasn't. Convinced he had no alternative, he decided to take Seth away from Sheol before disaster struck. . . .

After scanning the star catalog, the boy chose coordinates that qualified as little other than "the middle of nowhere." The stardrive engines hummed and changed tone as they adjusted course, and the vessel streaked off again.

Seth looked up at him with a sparkle in his eyes. "If we had our own compy, Dad, he could fly the ship, and you and I could play games."

Garrison smiled. "We're on autopilot. We can still play games."

Because there were no other children on Sheol, Seth had longed for a competent computerized companion, probably a Friendly model who could keep him company and amuse him. At the lava-mining facility, Lee Iswander used only a handful of Worker compies, none of which were the more sociable types, not even a Teacher compy.

"Your mother didn't see the point in owning a compy," Garrison said. "But maybe we can revisit that." *After we see what happens.*

In his head, Garrison heard his father's gruff voice again. "You never should have married That Woman. You're a Roamer, and you belong with other Roamers!"

"Elisa's not a Roamer, but Lee Iswander comes from a good clan," he had responded, though the words sounded flat in his own ears.

"That man has more of the Hansa about him than the clans. He's forgotten who he is." The bearded clan patriarch had waved a finger in front of his son's face. "And if you stay with him, you will forget who you are. Too many Roamer clans have forgotten. A knife loses its edge unless it is sharpened."

But Garrison had refused to listen and married Elisa Enturi anyway. He'd given up so much for her . . . or had he done it just to act out against his father? He had wanted a family, a fulfilled life, and Elisa wanted something else.

"If we find a place and settle down, will Mother come to live with us again?" Seth asked.

Garrison didn't want to lie. He stared out at the forest of stars ahead and the great emptiness in which they had lost themselves. "She wants to take her chances at Sheol for now."

The boy looked sad but stoic. "Maybe someday."

Garrison could not envision any other answer but *Maybe someday*.

Still running, they crossed the expansive emptiness for days, and then they encountered an amazing anomaly: a cluster of gas bags far outside of any star system. Each bloated globule was twice the size of their ship.

Garrison ran a quick diagnostic. "Never seen anything like these."

The membranous bubbles drifted along in a loose gathering with nothing but light-years all around them. In the dim light of faraway stars, the spherical structures appeared greenish brown, and each filmy membrane enclosed a blurry nucleus. Hundreds of thousands of them formed an island in a sea of stars.

Seth studied both the sensor screens and the unfiltered view through the windowport. "Are they alive?"

Garrison shut down the engines so their ship could drift toward them. "No idea." The strange objects seemed majestic—silent, yet powerful. Organic? They filled him with a sense of wonder. "They remind me of . . . space plankton."

"They're bloated and floating," Seth said. "We should call them *bloaters*."

A random glimmer of light brightened one of the nodules, an internal flash that faded. Then another bloater flickered and quickly faded.

Close together at one of the windowports, they stared out at the view. "If we discovered them, we can name them whatever we want," Garrison said. "I'd say bloaters is a good name for them."

"So we just made a discovery?"

"Looks that way." He moored the ship among the thousands of silent, eerie nodules. "Let's stay here for a while."

Two

ELISA REEVES

Elisa was so furious and indignant she could barely think straight, but she had enough common sense to maintain her composure in a business setting. She stifled her instinctive reaction and wore her professional demeanor like armor.

She could not let Lee Iswander see her as weak. There was too much at stake, and her responsibilities were too great. Her kidnapped son and her husband's betrayal were only part of what she had to worry about. Priorities needed to be weighed and balanced.

He took my son! He stole a ship, and he left me behind!

Even before she'd married Garrison, she had known he was a backward bumpkin, but together, they had agreed on a plan. He said he would follow it, keep his eyes on his silly Guiding Star, trusting that it would change everything for them.

And Elisa had believed him. That made her angrier than anything else. She had *believed* him. She hated to feel like a fool.

Now, Elisa approached the door to Iswander's office in Tower One of the Sheol lava-processing facility. Standing high on carbon-reinforced ceramic struts, Tower One held five decks of offices and habitation spaces. Scarlet lakes oozed up from molten springs to form a shimmering—some called it terrifying—panorama all around them.

Standing outside of Iswander's office, Elisa straightened her uniform and took a moment to compose her expression. She smoothed a hand over her short, professional-length auburn hair with highlights of gold. When she was ready, she entered.

Lee Iswander was busy, an important man, but he always had time for her. As far as she could tell, the industrialist didn't hold her husband's irresponsible behavior against her.

Iswander stood with impeccable posture before the wall of polarized windows that looked out upon Hell. His dark suit fit him well. A frosting of gray at the temples of his dark brown hair gave him a distinguished look, a man who inspired respect and confidence at first glance. As a boss and a business leader, he automatically knew what he was doing and thus was able to convince armies of middle managers and employees to do as he asked. People trusted him when he made a business decision or took a corporate gamble. Elisa believed in him too.

Turning from the window, he welcomed her with a smile. "Pannebaker says there's a new roostertail forming. He's heading out to the hot spot to get images. You know how he is with fresh geological activity."

Elisa also knew how dangerous that was. "Did he sign a waiver?"

"He's signed numerous waivers. He hasn't managed to kill himself yet."

"Then you're set, sir." Elisa took her place beside him at the wall of windows.

The lava flowed in slow-motion waves, their swells and dips caused by seismic instabilities. A reinforced landing gridwork stood in the middle of the three habitation and control towers. Armor-hulled smelter barges drifted on the molten sea, scooping up metals, separating out the valuable ones, and vomiting the detritus back into the pools.

The cratered other half of the binary planet filled much of the sky, tidally locked with the main body of Sheol. The two planetoids fell toward each other, orbiting around a common center of mass. The stresses squeezed and pushed the crust in a gravitational tug-of-war. Garrison claimed to have discovered that the broken planet was unstable—brilliant observation! It was the very instability that kept all the hot raw material flowing for easy industrial extraction. Beyond that, he was being an alarmist, looking for problems rather than solutions.

Right now, Iswander seemed preoccupied. Though Elisa wanted to explode with her news about Garrison—to scream, "My son has been kidnapped!"—she forced herself to remain calm. Lee Iswander was her best ally.

He turned to her and touched the front of his jacket. "New suit for my speech at Newstation in two days. Specially tailored. I want to cut the figure of a leader when I give my speech to the Roamer council. What's your impression?"

"I'm not a fashion consultant, but it's a good look. You always look like a leader, sir."

Iswander did not hide his smile well. "I don't ask my wife for her opinion on these things because she always dithers and says it's fine. I wanted an honest answer."

"I give you an honest answer every time. When you present yourself, the Roamers will see that you are a businessman and a leader, not some sloppy worker who shuffled off a production line. Your opponent won't even bother to change out of his jumpsuit. I expect the decision will be obvious."

"Then I accept that. Sam Ricks cannot possibly believe he has a chance of winning, although there are some clan members who prefer their eccentricities to the reality of business and politics." He frowned.

"Roamers are a dying breed," Elisa said, thinking of her husband and his backward family. Garrison had already caused so much trouble. She searched for a way to tell Iswander, but he was obviously preoccupied.

"I've been looking at the records of the Roamer clans, studying their interactions with the Confederation government—the concessions we've received, the inroads we've made. Even though you married a Roamer, I'm not sure you understand the mindset, Elisa: clan connections, seat-of-the-pants innovations, personal promises and barter, exchange of favors. My business model takes us away from those old, inefficient ways. It's time for the clans to get serious. I truly believe that I'm best qualified to be the next Speaker."

Even with the concern about Garrison and Seth weighing on her mind, Elisa realized in a broader sense that Lee Iswander's advancement as Speaker would open up many opportunities for her. Caught up in his governmental role, he would need to delegate the Sheol operations, put her in charge. "Having watched Roamer politics from the outside, I'd say anything would be better than Isha Seward, sir."

He gave her a wry frown. "That's not exactly a ringing endorsement."

"You're obviously the stronger candidate, sir. It goes without saying."

"But the clans need it said. Isha Seward was just the interim Speaker after Del Kellum retired. She knows it, and everybody knows it. She was chosen as a compromise candidate because she was lackluster and didn't offend anyone. Now it's time for vision, and I've certainly proved myself." He chuckled. "Sorry, I shouldn't be giving you my speech."

"The election's only a few weeks away," Elisa said.

He went back to his desk where reports streamed across the data-screens embedded in its flat surface. "If I'm going to be elected as the next Speaker I'll have to keep in touch everywhere, in real time. Not just through business shuttles, like I have now. Maybe I should bring a green priest here."

Elisa nodded. "Many have hired themselves out, and they take oaths of confidentiality. A green priest stationed here with a treeling could be in instantaneous contact with every other green priest at any other outpost, ship, or settlement. Would you like me to look into it, sir?"

"I doubt it would do any good." He swiveled in his chair to look out at the oceans of turbulent magma. "They prefer to be back on their forested world—or at least in a more hospitable place than this. All this fire and lava would make them nervous."

Elisa made a note in the back of her mind that she would send out an inquiry; perhaps with a sufficient financial incentive, she could find an open-minded green priest who would be willing to move to Sheol. But she couldn't devote her time and energy to solving that problem until *after* she tracked down Garrison and got Seth back. It was time to tell Iswander.

She struggled with her sense of failure, as well as the guilt of knowing that this unexpected matter was going to take her away from her work. Before she could make her request, though, Alec Pannebaker broke in on the comm. "The plume's about to burst, Chief. Right on schedule, right on target. I'm getting images that'll take your breath away!"

Elisa felt tremors in the deck of Tower One, and moments later they calmed down. Sheol was in a constant restless slumber on an unquiet seismic bed.

Out on the lava lake near Pannebaker's small shielded craft, a large bubble became a spurting geyser of lava. It sprayed high, then rained down in a roostertail. Pannebaker whistled as he withdrew his shielded boat. "Those will make great PR images!"

Iswander sounded skeptical. "'Come to Sheol and see the sights'?"

"No, Chief—I was thinking more of how it shows you're a visionary with the foresight and the balls to establish a viable industry where even other Roamers feared to tread. No one can argue with your profit reports."

"It might be good for your Speaker campaign, sir," Elisa said after the deputy signed off. "But you should delete the part about the balls."

As Iswander returned to his desk, Elisa stood straight-backed, anxious. She had never brought personal problems to him before. Finally, she said without preamble, "Garrison's gone, sir. He stole one of your ships."

Iswander sat back. "What are you talking about?"

"He left between six and ten hours ago. He kidnapped our son and flew off."

"I can't believe your husband would do that. He seemed like such a . . ."

"Passive man?" Elisa said. "Yes, he fooled me too."

"I was going to say 'good father.' Is he still insisting that we're operating too close to safety margins? It's nonsense. We've been here for years without any mishap, and the recent structural scans should have put all concerns to rest."

"He thinks the seismic makeup of Sheol is changing, and the old calculations are no longer valid."

Iswander was disturbed. "My consultants double-checked their test results and disproved your husband's concerns. Even so, he riled up the other workers. If they find out he's fled, they're going to demand answers—and I don't need nervous work crews."

"I suspected he might be plotting something." Elisa focused more on her specific problem than on the overall question and its impact on Iswander operations—which demonstrated just how rattled she was. "I could tell by his mannerisms. Garrison can't keep a secret to save his life."

"Do you have any idea where he's gone? For a man to steal a child away from his mother is . . . not a good thing, not a good thing at all."

"It's fortunate I was suspicious, sir. He checked the Iswander ships, saw which ones were fueled and supplied. Garrison thought he was being discreet, but I rigged tracers on all vessels. No matter where he goes, each time he stops and changes course, it'll drop off a tiny signal buoy and squirt a message with his new coordinates." She fought with the dryness in her throat. "I can track him, sir, but I'll need to leave right away. He's got a head start."

Iswander folded his hands on his desk. "You're one of my most important employees, Elisa."

She thought he was going to refuse her request. "I understand this is a critical time for Iswander Industries, sir. You're just leaving for Newstation—"

His expression softened. "And I understand that this is even more important. Choose a ship of your own, any one you like—you've earned it. I'll inform the other team leaders that you're taking an unspecified amount of time for a personal matter."

Elisa should have felt relieved, but her anger wasn't dampened, merely focused. "Yes, Mr. Iswander. This is definitely personal."

THREE

ADAR ZAN'NH

Orbiting the planet Ildira, the new starship looked out of place and alien, even to Ildiran eyes. The first of its kind, the *Kolpraxa* had an unusual design developed by visionaries, astronomers, and explorers. Unlike the giant fighting-fish silhouette of a Solar Navy warliner, this exploration ship had expanded-range engines, habitation spaces, and enlarged cargo holds for supplies on long voyages far outside the Spiral Arm, to push the edge of knowledge.

After the Elemental War, the Mage-Imperator had given their race a new vision, to explore the unknown, to expand the Empire's comfortable boundaries that had stood unchanged for millennia. Adar Zan'nh, the grand commander of the Ildiran Solar Navy, knew the *Kolpraxa* would be only the first of many such missions.

Curiosity, ambition, and exploration were not common to the Ildiran psyche. This drive to seek answers to questions that had never before been asked was clearly a human thing. Zan'nh, and all Ildirans, had to adjust to so many changes in recent years. . . .

The Adar's inspection cutter arrived at the spacedock facility where the final engineering touches were being applied to the *Kolpraxa*. Teams of spacesuited worker kith floated around like beetles, using manipulator arms to remove the construction framework and nudge it away from the hull.

Zan'nh landed the cutter inside the *Kolpraxa*'s well-lit receiving bay and stepped out onto the polished deck. His hair was plaited in a tight braid and done up in a topknot. His short tunic was tied at his waist with a green sash that accentuated the greenish gold of his skin. Glittering rank insignia adorned his chest. For this formal meeting with Tal Gale'nh before the *Kolpraxa*'s departure, he wanted to be worthy of the Ildiran epic, the Saga of Seven Suns.

Yes, history would be made here.

The halfbreed Gale'nh, who had been given command of the ship, marched forward to greet him. He was a young man with a proud demeanor and creamy features that clearly revealed his partial human heritage. A product of the secret Ildiran breeding program, he was the son of the green priest Nira and the legendary Solar Navy commander Adar Kori'nh—Zan'nh's predecessor.

At twenty-six, Gale'nh was young for his rank of tal, but he had a sharp mind and the ability to make swift and accurate decisions. Because of his mixed heritage, he also had a knack for seeing things differently—an advantage in his role, since the Solar Navy suffered from rote adherence to long-established ways.

Gale'nh pressed a fist to his chest in a gesture of respect. "Welcome aboard my ship, Adar. I hope it meets with your approval."

Zan'nh gave the young officer a nod. "You inspected the systems? Drilled your crew? Interviewed your engineers? And it all meets with your approval?"

"More than I can say, Adar."

He gave a brief nod. "You are the *Kolpraxa*'s captain, so your approval matters more than mine."

The two men took a lift to the command nucleus. The blister dome that formed the ceiling of the bridge gave the commander a sense of the universe around him—the starry field, the glare of sunlight, the swiftly moving ships and worker pods withdrawing the last pieces of framework.

Proud of his experimental ship, Gale'nh rattled off a summary of the crew complement, the sophisticated technical equipment, the variety of probe satellites that could be dispatched when needed, and—important for the Ildiran soul—groups of artist kithmen, singers, and especially rememberers who recorded history.

When Adar Zan'nh and Gale'nh arrived in the command nucleus, Rememberer Ko'sh awaited them. The rememberer was a tall, imposing man, dressed in a shimmering gray robe marked with symbols. The expressive lobes on his face were able to shift coloration like a chameleon to add flavor and emotion to the stories he told. He lifted both hands in greeting.

"Adar Zan'nh, this is the greatest mission in our recent history! More significant than Adar Bali'nh's rescue of the human generation ships and his first journey to Earth. Or Tal Bria'nh's encounter with—" The tall rememberer caught himself and bowed. "The *Kolpraxa* will be a light that shines into the emptiness between stars. It is time for our people to go beyond what *was* to what *can be*."

Zan'nh was surprised by Ko'sh's upbeat attitude, for the man had been stodgy in the past, especially upset when the human scholar Anton Colicos had pointed out errors or omissions in the Saga of Seven Suns. "Tal Gale'nh will lead you to points unknown. I have complete faith in him."

Gale'nh bowed, struggling to accept the praise with good grace. Zan'nh had groomed the young officer, training and mentoring him as he moved up through the ranks. Though he was a halfbreed, it didn't hurt that his mother was the consort of the Mage-Imperator, or that his father was the greatest military leader Ildirans knew. "I can only hope to do great work of my own, in my father's name. I am . . . humbled by my own heritage, the weight of responsibility. The *Kolpraxa* is so important."

Zan'nh knew that Adar Kori'nh had been a greater commander than he himself would ever be—everyone on Ildira was aware of that. "I was just a young tal when I was thrust into this position as Adar. I wasn't ready for it either, and I also felt humbled." He lowered his voice as he confessed, "But no one was more ready than I was, and so the job fell to me. If you had not volunteered to command the *Kolpraxa,* Tal Gale'nh, I would have assigned you to the task."

The young tal's eyes were shining; his breathing was fast, his excitement plain. "When I saw the opportunity, how could I not seize it? The chance to go outside the Spiral Arm, to see what's out there?"

A signal on the command nucleus announced that the rest of the docking structures had been moved away. The stardrive engines were fully loaded with ekti and optimal for test firing.

Gale'nh turned to face him. "The Mage-Imperator has prepared a departure celebration in Mijistra, and you will join me. The people will cheer the launch of this great mission." He lowered his voice and added wistfully, "I wish I were going out there with you."

FOUR

NIRA

With seven suns nearby, Ildira's perpetual day kept all shadows at bay. The soaring towers and crystalline architecture of Mijistra caught the bright light and reflected it back, celebrating with rainbows and sparkling flares. The capital city's crowning masterpiece was the Prism Palace, assembled from interlocking multicolored crystal, its central sphere surrounded by a symphony of minaret towers, each one capped with a smaller globe.

In the skysphere audience chamber, Nira basked in the Mage-Imperator's presence. She and Jora'h were inseparable, bound more surely than by law or telepathic *thism,* by unbreakable ties of love. The two had survived ordeals that threw them together, tore them apart, and at last let them return as eternal partners.

Overhead, the skysphere dome was a rainbow-hued ceiling, hung with flowers and verdant vegetation. Birds and colorful insects flitted about, enclosed in the shimmering ecosystem. A roiling cloud of mist in the center of the dome served as a projection screen for Jora'h's benevolent three-dimensional image.

Beside the Mage-Imperator's chrysalis chair, Nira held a potted tree-ling from the worldforest, through which she could share her thoughts instantaneously with her fellow green priests. She looked forward to seeing her son and saying goodbye before he departed on his voyage on the *Kolpraxa.*

She reached over to clasp Jora'h's hand, only to find his fingers already moving to enfold hers. That was how closely their minds and hearts were linked, although her emerald skin looked different from the faint golden sheen of his Ildiran skin.

The Mage-Imperator sat in the skysphere audience chamber, holding court. Jora'h's predecessor had become so corpulent over centuries of rule that his chrysalis chair served as a reclining cradle to hold his enormous body. By Ildiran tradition, a Mage-Imperator's feet should never touch the ground, for even his footprints were sacred. But Jora'h had done away with that tradition, as well as many others. Nira was glad of that. She loved to walk beside him through the Prism Palace or out in the city streets.

Knowing she was eager, he raised his voice to the audience. "Send in Tal Gale'nh so that I may bid him farewell." Noble kithmen and court functionaries repeated the command, and attender kithmen scurried about to make way.

The doors opened, and Adar Zan'nh passed under the glittering archway into the audience chamber, but Nira had eyes only for her halfbreed son. Gale'nh looked dashing in his Solar Navy uniform. Though his skin was paler than that of a normal Ildiran, he was young, energetic, and confident.

Adar Zan'nh stepped aside so Gale'nh could come forward. The young man touched a fist to the center of his chest and bowed in respect. "Liege, I will make you proud of me and the *Kolpraxa*'s crew. We will write a new chapter in the Saga of Seven Suns, and we will lay down threads of our racial *thism* even beyond the Spiral Arm."

Jora'h raised both of his hands. "Yes, your mission expands the reach of our Empire, but we do this not out of mere ambition, but because we are part of the universe and the universe is part of us. For thousands of years the Ildiran race slumbered, but now we are awakening."

Unable to conceal her proud smile, Nira touched the treeling she held. Her fingers brushed the golden bark scales, felt the multileaved fronds tremble. She dropped her mind into the tree, letting her thoughts travel out via telink into the stochastically connected worldforest, where each tree was identical to all others, each one a quantum reflection that allowed her thoughts to be in all places at once, without regard to distance or transmission speeds.

Nira sent images and thoughts back to the primary worldforest on Theroc, as well as to green priests scattered across the Confederation, any colony that had a treeling. Even Ildira had the trees, since she had spent two decades tending them. Her telink announcement of the *Kolpraxa*'s unprecedented mission traveled simultaneously through all of them.

When she opened her eyes, Nira realized that Gale'nh had been speaking to her. "Thank you, Mother, for accepting me and for being proud of me." He understood that she didn't love his father, that she had been impregnated by force as part of the sinister Ildiran breeding program to produce a telepath.

That was long ago, in a time buried in crises. She had survived the ordeal and accepted all five of her halfbreed children now: Gale'nh, Tamo'l, Muree'n—even Rod'h, whose father had been the Dobro Designate himself, head of the enforced breeding program and Nira's worst tormentor. And of course there was dear Osira'h, her daughter by Jora'h, whose telepathy was so powerful she could command the hydrogues and the faeros. No, Nira could not hate her children for the acts of their fathers or the misguided requirements of the breeding program.

"You give me great joy, my son, and I love you as I love each of my children. You have no need to make *me* proud, Gale'nh—go and make *all* Ildiran people proud."

After the Mage-Imperator blessed the departure of the exploration ship, the rest of the audience moved outside for the next part of the spectacle. Adar Zan'nh and Tal Gale'nh marched out of the Prism Palace, shoulder to shoulder, while Jora'h took Nira's hand and led her up to their observation balcony. From there, they would watch the grand pageant.

When they stepped out into the bright sunlight, Nira smiled at Jora'h. The Mage-Imperator's hair had grown longer over the years, and many of the fine golden tendrils twitched and waved of their own volition. His eyes were a smoky topaz with an unusual starflare. Nira thought he was beautiful.

Beneath the balcony in front of the Prism Palace, the tiny figure of Tal Gale'nh met up with subcommanders who led groups of Solar Navy specialists of different kiths dressed in appropriate uniforms, their shoulders spangled with small mirror chips that sparkled in the sunlight.

The crew marched in an orchestrated parade, a clockwork movement that reminded Nira of the shifting patterns in a kaleidoscope.

Overhead, a maniple of warliners cruised across the sky with their solar-sail fins extended, trailing silvery ribbons behind them in a spectacular skyparade. The crew flowed aboard forty-nine cutters that took off like a flock of metal birds into the sky to the orbiting exploration ship.

Nira touched a decorative treeling on the balcony and used telink to send her impressions throughout the green priest network, spreading the word that the *Kolpraxa* would soon depart for the fringe of the Spiral Arm. . . .

As she and Jora'h reentered the Prism Palace, they encountered Rod'h standing there, impatient. He was a strong and hard young man, proud of who he was—the second most telepathically skilled of her halfbreed children, after Osira'h. Had it not been for Osira'h's success, the Ildirans would have relied on *him* to save them from the hydrogues. But he had never been given the chance.

Because Rod'h so closely resembled the ruthless Dobro Designate, seeing him sometimes gave her an involuntary shudder. Though Nira tried to love all of her children equally, regardless of what their fathers had done to her, she could not help but sense that he resented her.

Rod'h bowed with respect to the Mage-Imperator, but gave his mother only a curt greeting. "Liege, I request permission to bring a team of rememberers to Dobro. For historical accuracy, we should record the true facts of the breeding program. My father should no longer be vilified or, worse, ignored. We must not forget what he accomplished."

Nira stiffened. Despite making peace with her past, there were still nights she wrestled with nightmares of how the Dobro Designate had forced himself upon her in the breeding chambers . . . and he had only been one of the many breeders from various kiths assigned to impregnate her. From that succession of experiments to see what sort of halfbreed child a human green priest might produce, five of the children had lived, but eight others had been such misshapen horrors that they were stillborn—merciful miscarriages.

Rod'h saw her instinctive reaction and scowled. "Everyone should know what my father did and why. Our race needed a powerful telepath like me, like Osira'h—someone who could *force* the hydrogues to communicate. That was the only way we kept our race from being exterminated."

Nira kept her voice even, but she could not let his distortions go unchallenged. "And that excuses enslaving thousands of human colonists?"

"Yes, it does! My father did what had to be done. Humans weren't the only ones in the breeding camps. Ildiran experimental subjects also gave birth to countless mixed-breeds in our search for a savior. And the hydrogues *were* defeated. Osira'h *did* do her duty—and if she had failed, *I* would have done it. You, Mother, should have embraced your responsibility without complaint."

Nira felt as if he had twisted an old dagger inside of her. "How did saving Ildirans become *our* responsibility? That was done *to me*—and to the captive settlers, generation after generation, against their will. It remains a terrible shame on the Ildiran soul." She forced herself to be calm. "We've put it behind us now. Humans and Ildirans repaired our relationship—but don't belittle their ordeal."

Jora'h stood between them, not leaving Nira's side. "The story of the Dobro Designate and his breeding camps will remain as it is. It is best if we speak little of that sad history, so we can heal. Your request for rememberers is denied."

Rod'h's eyes flashed. "I would heal better, Liege, if my father earned respect for what he accomplished. Do we not owe that to history? You commanded that many sections of the Saga of Seven Suns be rewritten—are you not the one who insists the Saga must be *accurate*?"

Jora'h shook his head. "Other Mage-Imperators sealed away secrets from their reigns, hid dark activities that they did not want future generations to know. My father certainly did. I will not hide this away, but neither will I glorify it. My decision stands."

Rod'h was so angry that he nearly forgot to make a respectful gesture to the Mage-Imperator before he stalked away.

A N T O N   C O L I C O S

After the *Kolpraxa* sailed away with the usual Ildiran pomp and circumstance, the human scholar Anton Colicos returned to his office in
the Hall of Rememberers. Rememberer Ko'sh had gone off to far, unexplored territories, but Anton was restless here in Mijistra, feeling
both the weight and exhilaration of history upon him. He had
translated—and directly participated in—major events that shaped
many races: not just humans, but Ildirans, hydrogues, faeros, wentals, verdani, and even the now-vanished Klikiss.

And he wasn't done with his work here yet, not by a long measure.

Anton ate a quick meal while he organized the various half-completed
documents he kept in his office. He intended to spend hours proofread-
ing the next massive translation he had just finished—another section
of the Saga of Seven Suns, which no human had ever read before. The
green priests on Theroc were waiting to read it aloud to the towering
trees.

So many people were counting on him! He was just a shy and
dedicated scholar, at least that was the way he saw himself. He preferred that his scholarly works stand on their own merits, but already
people were offering to become his interns and research assistants—
even his biographer. Anton laughed off such requests, insisting that
he'd done nothing worthy of chronicling. And yet when he thought
back on his experiences . . .

He signaled his scholarly assistant Dyvo'sh by activating a humming
crystal on his desktop. Anton considered the thing pretentious. In fact,
having Dyvo'sh at his beck and call was itself unnecessary—especially
someone with such a servile attitude! But Ildiran rememberers considered it a mark of respect and claimed that Anton had earned it.

The eager young rememberer appeared in an instant, and Anton fumbled to switch off the humming crystal; finally, Dyvo'sh had to do it for him. "Do you need assistance with translation, Rememberer Anton?" Dyvo'sh had a hopeful tone in his voice. (But then, he spoke in a hopeful tone even when Anton asked him to fetch a hot beverage.)

"I'm too restless for desk work today," Anton said. "I heard that the excavators discovered a new document crypt beneath the old sculpture museum. I'm curious to see what's inside it—aren't you?"

The lobes on the young rememberer's face flushed with a bluish tint that flowed into red, signaling Dyvo'sh's excitement tinged with reluctance. "Those records were sealed away by some ancient Mage-Imperator for a good reason. Whatever is there will not be canon to the Saga of Seven Suns. We should not question his wisdom."

"Of course we should—that's what a scholar does. Questions are our business."

Dyvo'sh vigorously shook his head. "A rememberer is taught to repeat and preserve only what is already known. The Saga is the only record we need in order to understand Ildira."

"But the Saga came from somewhere. Don't you want to see the original sources?"

Dyvo'sh blinked. "No. It is not necessary."

Anton shook his head. "Before you preserve the words for all time, it's imperative that you have accurate information. Otherwise, you're merely perpetuating errors—and you *know* that has happened before. Come on, we don't even know what's in that vault. I'll do this myself if I have to . . . or I can request another assistant."

When Dyvo'sh became alarmed, his facial lobes shifted through a rainbow of colors. "No, I am assigned to your care. It is a great honor. I would not have anyone else carry out those duties."

"Then let's go."

Anton marched out of his office and through the Hall of Rememberers. In the reviewing corridors, Ildiran storytellers stood before wall-sized crystal sheets that recorded every word in the billion-line Saga of Seven Suns. Apprentices muttered to themselves as they memorized the entire epic, which was ever growing but never changing once established. At least, not usually.

Dyvo'sh had been one such apprentice until recently when he had passed his test—a five-day recitation, without sleep and without a single error, of a randomly chosen section of the Saga. And Anton had thought defending his PhD thesis on Earth was grueling!

Now, thanks to the changes Anton had instituted over the past two decades, by command of Mage-Imperator Jora'h, rememberer scribes worked in a new wing of the Hall of Rememberers where they also preserved the apocrypha, restoring sections of the Saga that had been deleted or censored in times past.

For millennia, Ildirans believed that every word in the Saga was the absolute truth, set down permanently by infallible rememberers. Ildirans had never dreamed that the Saga might be inaccurate—intentionally so—but previous Mage-Imperators had changed the records to cover up their part in the ancient conflict against the hydrogues, rewriting the story for posterity. Oh, the uproar Anton had caused when he revealed that!

He demonstrated that in order to hide the censored history about the hydrogues, new stories of "bogeymen" had been fabricated—tales of terrifying creatures called the Shana Rei that devoured light and infiltrated the Ildiran soul with blackness. Supposedly, *they* were the reason why Ildirans feared the dark.

When he studied the matter objectively, Anton noticed striking differences in the passages about the Shana Rei. They were sketchy placeholders, not as rich in detail or implied veracity, and he found evidence that these sections were *fictional,* meant to hide the horrific truth of the ancient hydrogue war. To the stodgy rememberer kith, these revelations had been a greater assault on their race than the hydrogues. Later, Mage-Imperator Jora'h shook the entire rememberer kith to the core when he commanded that all ancient records be opened for thorough critical study, that all of the sacred texts be reassessed.

As Anton dug deeper, separating the tales, the reality grew more complex still. Newly resurrected records showed disturbing indications that the Shana Rei might have been *real* after all.

The confusion among the rememberers verged on insanity and despair. Their kith dealt only in absolutes, and uncertainty disturbed them greatly. Anton didn't know what to believe anymore. He doubted the rememberers had forgiven him, even after twenty years.

His jaunty step faltered as he led Dyvo'sh along the sun-drenched streets of Mijistra toward the newly excavated document crypt. Maybe it would be wiser if he *didn't* inspect the new records, for they were sure to cause more turmoil. . . . But if he refused to look at new records, he too would be responsible for hiding true information. He clapped a hand on his assistant's bony shoulder. "Let's open another can of worms, no matter how big it might be."

Dyvo'sh blinked his large eyes. "Excuse me, sir? Why would we require worms?"

"A human idiom. I'll explain later."

For Anton, the *story* mattered most of all. He wanted to tell it, preserve it for posterity, and let someone else dicker over the societal implications. Though human, he felt closely tied to Ildira as the first human scholar to translate lengthy segments of the Saga of Seven Suns for academics to analyze and interpret. Anton had no interest in becoming one of the navel-contemplating breed of academics. He loved the challenge of translating new material and immersed himself in the process.

After the Elemental War, he'd spent years with his mother Margaret, the famous xeno-archaeologist, recording the chronicle of the Klikiss race—*The Song of the Breedex*. He and his mother had scrambled to preserve the remarkable story before the insect race vanished forever, leaving only the husks of discarded bodies in the bizarre ruins of their cities.

After Margaret died and her remains were buried on Eljiid, a Klikiss world where she had been studying, Anton had returned to Earth. He took a position at the university, received accolades, was named an assistant dean, and—best of all—had a light course load. He taught only one advanced class per semester, which allowed him to write a biography of his illustrious parents. . . .

But Ildira always called to him. After Mijistra was rebuilt following the war, the Mage-Imperator once again extended an invitation to him, and Anton jumped at the chance. He came back to a guest office in the Hall of Rememberers and had been here for the past six years.

When Anton and Dyvo'sh reached the construction site of the old sculpture museum, Anton watched the worker kith, artists, and sculptors who were restoring the exhibits. This restoration had the

dual purpose of preserving history for Ildirans and edifying the human settlers—a handful of "Ildirophiles" who had formed their own
small enclave in the capital city, where the expatriates ran traditional
stores, cafés, and craft workshops.

The museum workers recognized Rememberer Anton Colicos, who
was one of the most well-known humans on Ildira, even more familiar to them than the Confederation's King Peter. Considering the uproar he so often caused, Anton sometimes wondered if the mere sight
of him struck terror into their hearts. After all, his discoveries often
resulted in changes and disruptions.

Anton greeted them with good cheer and asked directions to the
newly uncovered document crypt. When the reticent workers talked
among themselves, Dyvo'sh stepped forward. "Rememberer Anton
asked a question! You know he has the blessing of the Mage-Imperator
himself."

One of the museum administrators directed the two visitors to a
debris-strewn staircase that led to underground levels. Anton called
for three squat muscular workers to accompany them. "And please
bring your battering clubs and those Ildiran pickax things. We need
to break open the vault."

Anton saw the consternation he was causing. Ildirans had so much
difficulty accepting anything they hadn't done before.

In the underground chamber lit by ceiling-mounted blazers, he and
Dyvo'sh stood before the repository that had been walled up in ancient
times by a barely remembered Mage-Imperator; over the years, other
structures were built on top of it. Once "history" was set in stone and
a Mage-Imperator's reign was permanently recorded in the Saga, all
else was considered superfluous. Anton supposed the Mage-Imperators
might feel a kind of rivalry that let them bury the extravagance of their
predecessors in order to showcase their own reigns, only to have the
same thing done to them by their successors.

But scrap heaps sometimes held the most interesting items for a
historian.

The museum workers hesitated when they looked at the seal. "Well,
go on," Anton said, "break it open. I'd like to study the documents in
there."

Guard kithmen hurried down the stairs in a clatter of weapons, accompanied by two bustling rememberers. "Halt! We forbid you to break that seal. You cannot defy the clear commands of a Mage-Imperator."

Dyvo'sh looked frightened, but Anton just groaned. "If you prevent me from seeing the documents, then you are also defying the commands of a Mage-Imperator. I'd say the current Mage-Imperator's orders supersede the orders of one who returned to the Lightsource centuries ago."

The guard kithmen took up positions in front of the crypt door, blocking the workers and their battering tools. A museum administrator hurried down from the upper levels. "This vault contains discarded records not considered fit for inclusion in the Saga. It holds nothing of interest."

Anton was frustrated. "Then you don't have to look at it, but I'm interested." He crossed his arms over his chest. "I can send word to the Prism Palace right now, if you insist on ignoring the orders of the Mage-Imperator."

With another commotion on the stairs, a lean pantherlike warrior woman bounded into the vault chamber. Her movements flowed like liquid, and she was accompanied by another scrappy girl who seemed cut from the same pattern. "You appear to need my help once again, friend Anton," Yazra'h said.

Anton let out a sigh of relief upon seeing the Mage-Imperator's warrior daughter. Yazra'h gave him a flirtatious, hungry smile, the kind that always made him uncomfortable. He said, "Not quite so dramatic a rescue as you've provided in the past, but I'd appreciate your advice on how to handle this situation."

Yazra'h's mane of coppery gold hair flowed in all directions, and her bright eyes gleamed at the prospect of a fight. She wore thin, tough armor with intimidating spines on her shoulders, but her legs were bare. The girl beside her was similarly dressed, and Yazra'h nodded to her. "This time Muree'n can help me explain our point of view."

The two faced the guard kith who blocked the document crypt, standing firm but uneasy. Yazra'h snapped, "Well? I am the Mage-Imperator's daughter. I command you to do as Rememberer Anton says. I will vouch for him."

One of the nervous rememberers stood to one side. "The seal on the vault forbids it. That is the word of a Mage-Imperator."

She removed a battle stick from her waist, flicked it open into a nonlethal fighting pole. Her companion did the same. Muree'n was one of Nira's halfbreed children, and Anton saw echoes of the green priest in her face. The girl's muscles were tense like tightly wound springs. They waited for a long moment, facing off in silence.

Yazra'h did not flinch. "These records are vital to Rememberer Anton's work. You will obey the command."

Anton swallowed hard. "Maybe there's no need to—"

"They will not change their minds," Muree'n blurted out. "Let us have some practice."

She leaped forward without warning, twirling her battle stick and smashing it toward the nearest guard's face. He brought up a gauntleted hand, so that her blow broke his wrist instead of his nose. He yelped.

Yazra'h sprang into action, trying to keep up with her protégée. The two women fought like dust devils. The battle sticks were a blur, and the expression on Yazra'h's face was intense but also joyous. She loved the fight.

Years ago, Yazra'h had taken Anton under her wing. She flirted with him, toyed with him, made it plain that she wanted to take him as a lover, though he did nothing whatsoever to encourage her. He simply wasn't interested. Yazra'h respected him, and also protected him when he got into difficult situations.

She had no lack of energetic lovers—mostly soldier kithmen, but other Ildirans as well. Yazra'h had finally admitted to Anton that she understood he was a delicate sort and must be concerned, with good reason, that she might break him if she got carried away.

Now, as they fought down the guard kithmen, Muree'n seemed even wilder and more reckless than Yazra'h. The hapless guards fought back, but were reluctant to harm a daughter of the Mage-Imperator—or maybe that was what they told themselves as they lay broken, bruised, and groaning on the floor.

Yazra'h retracted her battle stick, while Muree'n remained alert, as if hoping one of her opponents would climb to his feet and fight another round.

Dyvo'sh stared at the mayhem, wide-eyed. Yazra'h tossed her wild hair, and Anton made a point of thanking her. "Research isn't normally so combative," he said. "Let's just hope there's something important enough in there to make all this trouble worthwhile. I'd rather it wasn't a pile of old agricultural inventory lists."

Yazra'h made an impatient gesture to the worker kithmen, who stood holding their heavy tools. "Go on, there is no need for further delay. Rememberer Anton wishes the crypt opened—so open it."

More afraid of Yazra'h than of some ancient warning, the workers lifted their clubs and pickaxes and smashed open the seal.

SIX

GARRISON REEVES

In uncharted, empty space, the ship floated among the mysterious globules. Two days of unthreatening quiet gave Garrison and Seth freedom to just relax. They played games, and Garrison told him about Roamer history and other planets they would someday see. It was the sort of family life he'd hoped to have with Elisa.

They had plenty of fuel and supplies, but he knew he and Seth couldn't stay here forever. He had to decide where to go next and what new life they would make. Although the knot in his stomach didn't go away, it loosened a little.

The strange bloaters drifted around them, occasionally sparkling, moving onward in a big cluster like slumbering space jellyfish.

With no communication from the outside, Garrison had no way of knowing what might be happening at Sheol. He would prefer to be wrong about his fears for the lava-processing operations. And if nothing happened, Elisa would use that to prove his paranoid irresponsibility and claim that he had willfully stolen her son. Garrison knew his wife could be vindictive if she wanted to be. And after what he had done, she would definitely want to be.

During their downtime, Seth studied different types of compies in the ship's databases, following his fascination with the different models. He could rattle off the capabilities of Friendly compies, Listener compies, Teacher compies, Domestic compies, Worker compies, and numerous subcategories. He even knew the specs of the outlawed Soldier compies, which had caused such disastrous mayhem during the Elemental War. Thanks to those fears, many people had stopped using compies.

Seth, however, could talk on and on about the specialized programming and how new fail-safes had been implemented so there was no longer anything to worry about. Despite these facts, Seth had little interaction with compies. His mother refused to let him have one, and Lee Iswander used only a few of them at his Sheol operations.

As they drifted along, Seth called up the research from well-known compy scientists Orli Covitz and her husband Matthew Freling. Over the years, the couple had championed the cause of compies, helping to rehabilitate them, trying to prove that fears and hesitations were no longer valid. They took in and rehabilitated compies abandoned by their owners.

Seth nudged his father to sit next to him when he played video reports Orli Covitz had recorded. He particularly liked an entertaining set of educational loops that Orli and her compy DD produced. Although DD was a Friendly rather than a Teacher model, he served as a proper and unintentionally amusing foil when Orli explained ways that compies were helpful and loyal. Seth found DD charming, and had mentioned several times that he wanted a compy of his own just like DD.

On the educational loop, Garrison watched the attractive woman in her midthirties, surrounded by compies like a naturalist surrounded by her favorite animals, clearly loving them. Orli had an easy smile and conveyed a childlike sense of wonder as she showed off her compies. She seemed so earnest, both delighted and dedicated. Her sweetness captured Garrison's attention because she was such a striking contrast to Elisa. . . .

Seth went to the cockpit to do a regular systems check, as Garrison had shown him. Garrison, meanwhile, remained alert, observing the odd nodules as they shifted around. The things were beautiful and exotic, possibly organic, possibly some bizarre natural phenomenon.

His father would have given them a cursory glance and then gone back to work. Olaf Reeves had very little patience for distractions or any opinions other than his own.

Garrison feared that his most viable alternative would be to return with Seth to the bustling safety of clan Reeves. His family would take the two of them in, but it would involve an apology from Garrison and lengthy rebukes from the stern clan leader. He would have to slide himself back under Olaf's thumb and let Seth be raised in that oppressive, close-minded environment. The members of clan Reeves were mockingly referred to as "Retroamers" by the modern and open clans at the new government center of Newstation. Garrison didn't accept his family's scorn for "clans tainted by civilization."

No, he would find something else. He had enough skills and interests that he could apply for any number of useful jobs; his resourceful Roamer background guaranteed that at least. A good job was all he wanted, and the best environment for his son.

Seth called from the cockpit. "There's static on the screens, Dad—a sort of pulse every thirty seconds. You think it's a signal from the bloaters? Maybe they're trying to communicate with us."

Garrison came forward to look. On the screen, he saw a tiny blip, a flicker of static. Seth counted, and when he reached thirty, the blip appeared again. "See!"

Garrison used a ship diagnostic sensor to pinpoint the origin. "It's not coming from the bloaters. They're all around us, but this signal is coming from our hull." A chill ran down his spine—some kind of a tracer? "I'd better go outside and check it out."

"I'll stay in here and monitor," Seth said. He couldn't resist adding, "You know, if you let me have a compy, he could be a copilot too. Orli Covitz would let us have one of the compies from her lab—maybe even DD."

"Right now, you're my copilot," Garrison said. "Keep watch."

He donned the flexible environment suit with easy familiarity. Roamers spent half their childhoods in a spacesuit. They knew how to fix things, tinker with all sorts of machinery, rig life support from the most unlikely assemblage of scraps. For a long time, that was the only way the outlaw clans could survive, because they got no help from anyone else. But they had proved themselves indispensable when they took over Ildiran skymining operations, harvesting the stardrive fuel ekti from gas-giant planets.

His father insisted that Roamers were forgetting their heritage by being assimilated into the Confederation, but as Garrison fastened the fittings on his suit and went swiftly through the safety checks, he knew it was something he could never forget. It was part of him. Standing in the airlock, he clicked his helmet comm. "I'll be back in a little while."

"I've got the ship, Dad."

Garrison cycled through and emerged into disorienting open space. He had worked outside at the damaged Rendezvous site for years, reconnecting support girders, stringing access tubes from one asteroid to another. Although Roamers were renowned for their innovation, clan Reeves workers insisted on rebuilding the old seat of government exactly according to the original plan. Olaf refused to consider improvements or modifications. "Rendezvous served us for centuries, and the clans did just fine," his father said. "I wouldn't presume that I know more than they did—and neither should you."

As Garrison moved away from the airlock hatch, he looked up and around him. The eerie bloaters were dimly lit by far-off starlight, as well as the glow from the running lights of the stolen Iswander ship. The swollen spheres hovered in silence, fascinating and unknowable.

Seth's voice appeared in his helmet. "Find anything? I'm watching the blips—every thirty seconds."

"Still looking." He held on to hull protrusions and worked his way along the ship inch by inch. His hand scanner picked up signals, zeroing in on the pulse. It was coming from beneath the engines.

Like cosmic soap bubbles, the bloaters shifted, rearranged their positions.

He jetted down, maneuvered over to the exhaust cones. Now that he knew what to look for, he easily found a magnetic tracker, a standard cluster device that dropped out tiny signal buoys. Garrison knew how such things worked: no signal could travel while a ship moved faster than the speed of light, but each time they shut down the stardrive and reset course, this insidious tracking device would drop a marker with the appropriate information.

Elisa must have put one on every Iswander ship.

Garrison cursed her in silence, aware that Seth was listening on the helmet comm. Breathing heavily, he detached and deactivated the tracker—resisting the urge to smash it, since that would do no good. Instead, he just let it drift away.

High above, a glint of light distracted him, and several bloaters sparkled again. One nucleus flared with a bright flash. A moment later another one lit up in a different part of the cluster. Like a succession of firecrackers going off, two more flickered in some kind of pattern or signal, followed by three more sparking nearby.

Then, a surge of light poured out of the nearest bloater. The flash washed over him and the entire ship, overloading his suit systems. His diagnostic screen went dark, as if the pulse of energy was too much for the sensors to handle. Static crackled through the helmet comm before he was left in deafening silence.

He struggled to make his way back to the airlock. Because of the overload, his life support was failing. He had enough left to get inside, but without power assists from the suit's servomotors, he found it much more difficult to move.

With a crackle, the helmet comm came back on as a backup battery surrendered enough juice for him to hear a signal. "Dad, half our systems just shut down!"

Garrison crawled along the ship's hull, grabbing protrusions to pull himself to the airlock. He hoped the controls still functioned. "Coming back inside." He hammered the activation panel, got only a faint blip in response, then nothing.

Around him, the bloaters were quiescent again. Garrison could already feel deep cold settling in through his suit, though the insulation should have protected him for much longer.

His breathing sounded loud in his helmet. With gloved hands he fumbled with the access plate beneath the useless controls and managed to trigger the manual override, forcing open the airlock. Garrison pulled himself inside, manually sealed the outer door, then used the chamber's emergency canisters for an air dump that equalized the pressure.

Worried, Seth grabbed him as he reentered the main cabin, helping unseal the helmet. Garrison reassured him. "I'm all right . . . but I wouldn't want to be outside during another one of those flare-things."

"Did you find what caused the static signal?"

"Yes, it was . . ." He paused, pondering how much he should say. "It was a tracker placed on our ship back at Sheol. Could be just a standard precaution on Iswander ships."

The boy frowned. "Or maybe Mother put it there."

Garrison hadn't realized it before, but Seth always called him "Dad," while he referred to Elisa with the more formal "Mother."

Garrison was careful to avoid an outright lie. "I don't know who put it there, but it's gone now." He cracked his knuckles. "Better get to work. After that flash, we've got repairs to make." Though the repairs could take days, Garrison made up his mind that they should not stay here any longer than was necessary.

Seth couldn't resist the opportunity to add, "Of course, it would be a lot easier if we had a compy to help us."

SEVEN

LEE ISWANDER

Managing the dangerous operations on Sheol was a challenge, but becoming Speaker for the Roamer clans would be an even greater one. With Elisa Reeves gone on her own mission, Iswander left the lava-processing facility in Deputy Alec Pannebaker's capable hands and headed off to Newstation.

Iswander never stopped looking at the big picture. Considering business possibilities in the Confederation, opportunities that even the most imaginative Roamers had only begun to explore, he concluded that the united clans needed someone with vision to lead them into the future. He could fill that role.

He guided his personal cruiser toward the bustling center of Roamer government—and his future headquarters, if all went well. His cruiser was equipped with the best Ildiran stardrive, a well-appointed interior, and redundant systems, though it looked like any normal ship. Iswander had plenty of wealth, but found no advantage in flaunting it.

The destruction of Rendezvous had scattered the clans, and for years the Roamers were held together by a frayed tapestry of family alliances and habits. After the end of the Elemental War, clan Reeves and their stubborn leader persisted in trying to rebuild the old asteroid complex, but the task was pointless and few people paid attention to them. Lee Iswander certainly didn't.

In re-forming their government, the Roamer clans constructed New-station as their cultural and administrative center. The new space habitat orbited a planet named Auridia, which had a working Klikiss transportal into the alien transportation network that linked numerous worlds. Iswander approved of the choice.

His cruiser glided toward the toroidal space complex. With its bright silver hull, Newstation was an old-fashioned but serviceable design, spokes radiating from a central hub out to a main ring. It rotated like a giant wheel in space above the bleak and rocky planet, which held little of interest for settlers.

Plenty of traffic flitted around the station itself, though: cargo vessels, passenger yachts, diplomatic shuttles from Theroc or from Earth, even a pair of gaudy Ildiran vessels. The place was vibrant, and Iswander loved it. And Newstation was just the tip of what could be a very large iceberg, to use an old cliché that few Roamers could grasp. Once integrated into the Confederation, the clans could become dominant members, rather than just part of the alliance. Iswander should be the one to guide them.

He logged his arrival on the Newstation traffic band, asked for an appropriate docking slot. The traffic attendant recognized his voice. "Mr. Iswander! Right away, sir. I'll see that you get a priority berth."

"I don't deserve anything more extravagant than any other trader, though. What's your name?"

"Klanek. Tony Klanek, sir."

"Thanks, Tony. I'll know whom to call if I need anything."

Normally Iswander wouldn't have asked the young man's name, since he was just a voice on the comm, a low-level worker doing his job, but winning the position of Speaker would require personal interactions, clan votes, family alliances. It wasn't enough for him to rely on his business successes.

Guided by Klanek's signal, he flew his cruiser to the appropriate landing bay and his assigned ship berth. Lights sparkled around the rim of the rotating station.

Prominent in space nearby was a captured comet, Academ, that now served as a school complex for clan children, run by former Speaker Cesca Peroni and her husband Jess Tamblyn. The comet had been diverted to Auridia seventeen years earlier during construction of Newstation, its interior hollowed out, and the ice used for water, air, and fuel supplies. Perfect for a school.

His wife and son wanted to travel to Newstation for a vacation, but Iswander was always too busy. Men like him didn't take vacations. Still, there was only so much fire and lava a person could look at. If he were elected Speaker for the clans, then Londa and their thirteen-year-old son, Arden, would move to Newstation and spend all the time here they liked.

Before disembarking, Iswander combed his hair and made sure his clothes were unrumpled. Though he would not be addressing the gathered representatives until tomorrow, he couldn't be sloppy. He worked so hard at maintaining his persona that he had forgotten how to do otherwise.

As he entered the colorful turmoil of Newstation, Iswander made a point of greeting everyone he encountered, station personnel and visitors alike. Some of them gave him only a sidelong glance; most acted professional; others seemed pleased to have a Roamer celebrity among them.

He took a rail shuttle along the circumference of the station; though the rail was straight, the curvature of the torus made it look as if the rail shuttle were constantly heading up a steep hill. He checked into his rooms, found them adequate and comfortable, and took a brief mist shower in the room's cleansing cubicle. Even though the giant Academ comet orbited nearby, containing all the water they could need, the Newstation Roamers conserved their resources. Roamer austerity ran deep. It was admirable in a way, although unnecessary.

He intended to be well rested and well rehearsed for the following day's convocation. He had to show that he was far superior to his opponent Sam Ricks, a man who had little fire in him. Ricks didn't know business, didn't know how to interact with the Confederation or the Ildiran Empire. He barely seemed interested in the job of Speaker.

Lee Iswander, however, *wanted* it. He doubted he'd have any trouble convincing the clan heads he was the better choice, but he had to be careful not to insult the current Speaker, Isha Seward, a lackluster woman who would go down in history as little more than a name on a list.

The last strong Speaker had been Del Kellum, who served for fifteen years in the turbulent transition that followed the fall of the Terran Hanseatic League, until he finally said *enough* and announced his retirement. As a parting shot, Kellum said he couldn't understand why anyone would want the position, but Iswander knew. This was the next natural step in the progression of his career. His mindset and his business acumen would serve as the Guiding Star for the future of the Roamers.

In his quarters, Iswander looked through the windowport as the view slowly changed from stars to the fleeting lights of space traffic, the shimmering comet, the cracked surface of Auridia, then to the open field of stars again. The rotation was slow enough as to be almost imperceptible.

He called up his concise presentation on his datapad, though the clan representatives were familiar with his biography. (And if they didn't know who *he* was, what business did they have choosing leaders?) Some might call him pushy, but Iswander liked to think of it as being daring, unapologetic about his drive to succeed. He worked hard and wanted everybody else to work hard, to exceed expectations, to seize opportunities that arose. The Roamers needed a bold man with a can-do attitude.

He could have spent the night visiting Newstation's shops, restaurants, or drinking establishments, rubbing elbows and smiling, being everyone's friend, but he preferred to be alone. In his quarters, he practiced his speech and wished he could have reviewed it with Elisa Reeves, because she was supportive as well as intelligent. She'd give him an objective read and tell him what he needed to fix, whereas his wife would merely smile and compliment whatever he said. Good for his ego, maybe, but not necessarily instructive. . . .

He rested, arose early, practiced his speech again, taking out a few lines that sounded forced, and reviewed the changes. He put on the suit that Elisa said made him look like a leader and traveled to the station's primary meeting chamber.

Lines of seats extended up the curvature of the walls so that the attendees in the outer rows looked as if they might fall forward into the speaking area, but the station's rotation held them in place. Iswander assessed the clan representatives with their colorful garb, accented with scarves, embroidery, family markings, swatches of red, violet, blue. Many wore jumpsuits instead of formal clothes, even for an important meeting. He touched his impeccable suit, wondered if he had made a miscalculation.

Isha Seward managed the meeting from her Speaker's platform.

Her shoulder-length dark hair was much grayer now than when she'd first been elected Speaker. She was plump, too, having gained weight during her administration. Iswander vowed to take care of himself, once he became the next Speaker.

The business trivialities seemed interminable because Roamers had to discuss *everything* to death and each clan had to contribute to even minor decisions. Iswander glanced over at Sam Ricks, who was casual—too casual. His rival wore an everyday work jumpsuit with a prominent green clan armband. By the Guiding Star, the man looked as if he hadn't even shaved! Could he not at least try?

When the discussion turned to the upcoming vote, Speaker Seward called on Ricks first. He delivered a rambling and uninspired speech that basically said all the clans knew him and therefore he would make an adequate Speaker.

Stepping up to the podium for his turn, Iswander felt a renewed purpose. Ricks was obviously not serious about his candidacy, so Iswander could proceed. The feeling reminded him of the first day when his lava skimmers had produced exotic metals from the magma on Sheol, or when he dispatched the first shipment of prefab modules to Roamer asteroid colonies, or when he paid the first profit-sharing bonus to his employees. He had built himself a pedestal of his own successes.

"I was born a Roamer, and I am still a Roamer," he said. "But I'm a new kind of Roamer, because we live in a new Spiral Arm. I can guide us into the future and balance who we are with who we need to be." He paused for a moment, letting the idea sink in. "I was just a young businessman at the end of the Elemental War and the birth of the Con-federation. I was one of the first to embrace our new situation, making alliances with Roamer facilities and doing business with former Hansa industrialists."

They didn't react with as much enthusiasm as he had hoped. A few groans came from the audience. "That's a good thing?" someone commented loudly enough for the whole room to hear.

"Who cares about the Big Goose?" someone asked, using the dep-recating name for the Terran Hanseatic League.

After being hounded for so many years by the corrupt, repressive

Hansa, Roamers still resented the idea of big business. They preferred informal family and trade connections to specific commercial guidelines. But those old thought patterns were no longer relevant.

Iswander kept his impatience in check. "It's not the Hansa anymore—it's the Confederation. We should all care about their markets and their facilities, and what they can mean to every one of us. I was one of the first to redraw the business maps, to stop thinking of the former Hansa as our enemy but as a new partner. In so doing, clan Iswander used our materials-processing factories to supply much of the rebuilding effort. We helped the whole human race recover."

He looked at the man who had complained, but he couldn't place the name. He would have to work harder at memorizing the names of people. "Talk to your parents, talk to the elders of other clans. Maybe you aren't old enough to remember it, but ask them if they liked the war so much that they want to perpetuate it. Chairman Basil Wenceslas is long dead, and King Peter is and has always been our friend. Accept it."

Iswander turned to the other gathered faces. "Because I was thinking big, I bought out my parents' stake in our clan business and began building new factories. We specialized in supplying modular space habitats and prefab domes for rugged environments, where Roamers have always thrived. I made it easier, safer, and more lucrative."

Sam Ricks let out a rude snort. "And you charge the clans as much as you charge Hansa customers. Anyone with real Roamer blood in his veins would give us better prices."

Iswander was annoyed that Ricks would interrupt him, when he had politely endured his opponent's bland speech. "That only proves you don't understand business. My production costs don't decrease because a Roamer buys the unit rather than some other customer. It's business. Mathematics doesn't play favorites. The clans have to stop living by the seat of their pants."

From the Speaker's platform, Isha Seward said, "Sam, no more interruptions. Be polite."

A dour-faced man with a thick beard and shaggy gray hair scoffed. "Polite? Roamers sure have changed, and not in a good way. Convocations used to be an open exchange of ideas, now it's like some prissy court dance. Should we bow and curtsy too?"

Iswander recognized the man as Olaf Reeves, Garrison's father—an idiot by any measure. He wore traditional clothes with pockets, zippers, clips, and clan symbols embroidered on the fabric. Some might have called the clothes old-fashioned or woefully unstylish, but the clan head seemed to wear them as a badge of honor. "I don't mind a frank and open exchange of ideas, Olaf Reeves," he said, then couldn't resist twisting the knife. "In fact, let me ask why you haven't finished rebuilding Rendezvous yet? You've been working on it for years, and if you'd let me supply prefab modules, as I offered, you could have completed the job a decade ago. I did make your son an excellent offer."

"We don't need your shizzy prefabs," Olaf said. "We're Roamers. We're self-sufficient. We don't need help from outsiders."

"I am no outsider," Iswander said. "I am a Roamer, and Roamers adapt. I have adapted to the Confederation." He was no fan of the stick-in-the-mud Retroamer leader, and he wondered now if Elisa's husband had fled back to his family's clan. Iswander crossed his arms over his chest, realized it was a defensive posture, and relaxed as unobtrusively as possible. "I offered you a way to finish your project at Rendezvous, but you tossed it aside. Aren't Roamer clans supposed to help one another? Those who turn their backs on their cousins tend to fail."

"You've had a few failures yourself, Iswander." It was Ricks again, oblivious to the frown Speaker Seward gave him. "I checked out your business record—a lot of risky investments. Some might call them catastrophes."

Iswander had been prepared for that. "Yes, I made some risky investments. Some failed, others were successful. Roamers can't forget how to live on the edge—that's where the profit is. And if Roamers made only safe choices, we would have learned nothing and petered out long ago."

He looked around the room. "I understand what it is to be a Roamer. I also understand that we're citizens of the Confederation now, not outlaws in hiding. It's time to come into the daylight and be who we're supposed to be. If you're ready to move forward, I'd appreciate your vote for Speaker. I can see the Guiding Star, and I know where it leads."

When it was time for his own summation, though, Sam Ricks

couldn't even articulate a reason as to why the clans should vote for him.

Iswander swept his gaze across the room, meeting as many eyes as possible. "The Roamers can have a bright future, and I'm willing to work hard for all of us to make that happen. Thank you for your time."

Before the chamber was dismissed, Olaf Reeves bustled out with his younger son Dale and a few other family members. "Doesn't matter which man you vote for—you'll never be the same Roamer clans we once belonged to."

D E L   K E L L U M

For a man who had spent most of his life in space running space-docks, shipyards, and asteroid settlements, Del Kellum loved the ocean. He stood on the metal grid walkway (he preferred to think of it as a "balcony") of his distillery complex that rose on stilts from the shallow seas of Kuivahr.

He told his distillery workers, unconvincingly, that he went out there to ponder the process lines for the various brews they produced. Actually, he just liked to stare out at the water.

Green waves slurped against the breakwater and pilings, curling around the fermentation towers and plankton-separation tanks, in a slow-motion waltz as the twin moons of Kuivahr pulled the tides one way and then another. Hypnotic, beautiful . . . and a hell of a lot more peaceful than the arguing of Roamer clans when he'd served as their Speaker.

Del closed his eyes and pulled in a deep breath, savoring the salt and iodine smell that was integral to so many ocean worlds. Instead of fresh sea air, though, he smelled the crisp, malty scent of roasting Kuivahr kelp in the seaweed kilns, blended with the sour chemical tang of plankton mash. But that was a good smell too, if he adjusted his expectations accordingly.

Gray clouds across the sky obscured the two moons. He had erected his distillery in Kuivahr's tidal transition zone, where the shallow oceans sloshed back and forth, filling the basin with fresh frothy water for part of the cycle, pulling in rafts of succulent kelp, and leaving noisome plankton-rich mudflats when the waters receded. There was always something to harvest.

Not far away on a rock outcropping tall enough to remain

above the highest tides, the ancient Klikiss race had left one of their transportals—a giant stone trapezoid that allowed access to interdimensional tunnels connecting a whole network of worlds. A quarter century ago, humans had figured out the mysterious gateways and now used the transportals as shortcuts to certain connected planets. It formed a fine subsidiary transportation system among the worlds that had once been inhabited by the Klikiss. On Kuivahr, Del was pleased that the transportal made shipping his "aqua vitae" (twenty-three varieties, so far) much easier, although cargo ships and Ildiran vessels also came here on their regular routes.

Kuivahr meant "refuge" in the Ildiran language. The halfbreed Ildiran researcher Tamo'l managed her medical sanctuary domes not far from Del's distillery, but the mixed-breed genetic misfits kept to themselves. They had been on Kuivahr longer. Ildirans, as a race, took comfort in bright sunlight and areas of higher population. Though humans and Ildirans lived in separate settlements on Kuivahr, they benefited from living close together and traded with each other on a regular basis.

Below, Del heard hooting laughter out in the water and saw five Ildiran swimmer kith, the sleek otterlike breed, splashing about. They tugged polymer coracles behind them as they harvested kelpflowers. The swimmers reserved the richer, more intense plankton slime for Tamo'l and her facility, but they gave Del most of their harvest, so long as he brewed the nasty kirae they liked to drink.

Since Ildirans didn't understand economics or payment, it was hard to convince the swimmer kith to bring in regular deliveries of ingredients so Del could plan his distillery process lines. But they were good neighbors, he supposed. He made do.

A grating buzzer sounded from the speakers mounted above the distillery decks. Shift change. He had been meaning to get rid of the abrasive tone: workers should be pleased when their shift ended, and that noise sounded like a punishment. He would get around to it, but these days he didn't get too concerned about small things. He'd had enough of that during his fifteen years as Speaker.

He entered the distillery office levels, greeted the off-shift workers going either to the recreation hall or their own quarters. Many were his distant cousins, or apprentices from other clans who had applied for jobs because they felt Del owed them favors from old political days. He wasn't sure that working in his distillery counted as a "favor," but it was a decent job and better than many Roamer outposts, such as the lava-harvesting operations on Sheol.

Marius Denva, his line supervisor, met him at the rec-room hall and led him to a table, where he had set out four goblets filled with khaki-colored liquids that exhibited varying degrees of murk.

Del placed a hand on his stomach, which had grown much rounder in recent years, though he pretended not to notice it. His beard was now almost entirely salt with very little pepper. Serving as clan Speaker was enough to ruin anyone's health and peace of mind, and he had promised himself he would get back in shape as soon as he had time to focus on that again. Someday.

"Del, we've got samples of Batch Nineteen," Marius said. "Different filtration levels, residual yeasts, and three separate plankton varieties."

"How do they taste?" Del asked.

Marius had curly, dark brown hair, heavy eyebrows, and smoky eyes that squinted when he showed off his trademark smile. "*I'm* not going to be the first one to taste it."

"Yes you are." Del handed one of the goblets to the man.

With a hesitant frown, Marius took a sip, taking great care to maintain a neutral expression, though the flinch at his eyes was unmistakable. "Tastes like shit—but noticeably better than Batch Eighteen."

"That's a relief. The seasonal plankton blooms are so unpredictable that the taste varies widely. At least we have six batches good enough to distribute. It sells well."

"As a novelty, not because anybody loves it. Give people time to develop a taste, while we improve the process."

Moving down the line, he and Marius sipped the alternate varieties, their grimaces growing progressively worse. They were attempting to brew a unique celebratory beverage to be served after the new clan Speaker was chosen.

"Anything's better than that Ildiran kirae, by damn." Del shook his head. "We're shipping tankers of the stuff, but I still think it tastes like eyeballs boiled in urine."

"One of these days, Del, I'm actually going to cook eyeballs in urine, so you can do a comparison taste test."

Del laughed. "Don't need to, and the Ildirans can't seem to get enough kirae, so we'll keep it flowing. Maintain the goodwill between races. A long time ago, we Roamers took over their skymines and supplied stardrive fuel from gas-giant planets. Supplying Ildirans with their new favorite liquor needs doesn't sound as essential, but it's profitable, by damn." He set the sample aside. "Well, I suppose this batch is good enough if Iswander wins. And he's going to win."

Marius maintained his smile. "I thought you weren't interested in politics anymore."

"I'm not. Not in the least."

"Right. Don't tell me you haven't looked at the new Roamer Charter to see if there's a way you could run for Speaker again."

Del made a rude noise. "I'd sooner fight the hydrogues again." He even thought he meant it.

After the end of the Elemental War when the Roamers came together again, there had been more than a year of convocations. Fed up with the ineffectiveness of squabbling clans and committee meetings, Del Kellum had put himself forward as Speaker. He was a blustering businessman who pretended to modesty, as if he could convince anyone that he wasn't really interested in the position of leadership.

He wanted the clans to be strong, and he wanted decisions to be made. His slogan had been "decisions not dithering," and Del was not a man who dithered. In fact, some complained that he didn't take enough time to contemplate his decisions. Over the course of fifteen years as Speaker, though, the shine wore off. He had more arguments than triumphs. The Roamer clans had changed. Some integrated themselves so well into the business mindset of the former Hansa that they were indistinguishable from the people they had despised in the past. Like Lee Iswander.

Five years ago, Del retired after one particularly ridiculous feud over two clan embroidery designs that the families felt were too similar, and neither clan wanted to change theirs. Del hadn't taken the argument seriously—until it came to blows and even bloodshed with one young man attacking and injuring the leader of the rival clan. Stupid people!

Del tried to make it look as if his decision to retire was not made in anger, but that maddening feud was when he made up his mind that he wanted nothing more to do with the nonsense. He gave eight months' notice and set about picking his own successor—a competent, uninteresting woman named Isha Seward, who was so bland and unprovocative that none of the clans could object to her selection.

Del retired to a warm and sunny beach on the planet Rhejak, planning to drink ale and lead an idyllic existence among the reefs. He'd always kept aquariums of angelfish and exotic sea creatures even in the ring shipyards of Osquivel, so he expected to enjoy having Rhejak as his personal aquarium. Within a year, he was bored out of his mind.

After months of intensive research, he established the distillery here on Kuivahr and got back to work. . . .

He and Marius walked the process lines, smelling the tang of saltwater boiled with kelpflowers and the wickedly pungent smell of fermenting kirae. He did hope that one of his aqua vitae concoctions made from kelp and plankton extracts might become a real fountain of youth, but he was more pragmatic than that. "I'd be happy just to create something that tastes good."

"And is marketable," Marius added. "I think you need to change the name from Primordial Ooze, though."

They were standing above the giant copper pots that gurgled as they slow-cooked kelp mash when Del received notice that the Klikiss transportal had been activated. A new arrival was not itself unusual, except that the visitor was a lone man requesting to speak to the distillery manager. His name was Tom Rom.

"He's probably selling something," said Marius.

"If he is, then you'll deal with him, by damn."

"That's why I get the big salary."

Tom Rom was a tall, striking man with dark skin and a lean physique. His sinewy muscles were in all the right places, wrapped like monofiber cables around his bones. He had a long face with prominent cheekbones and bright eyes. A formfitting polymer suit clung to him like a reinforced skin. "Mr. Kellum, I've come to investigate your distillations for possible medicinal uses." His voice was rich and deep as if he had taken Shakespearean training, but this man did not look like an actor. Not at all.

Del stroked his beard and chuckled. "Medicinal uses? I've heard that one before." Of course, Tamo'l did use some of the formulations to ease the suffering of her misbreeds in the sanctuary domes, but he doubted that was what Tom Rom meant.

The strange visitor fixed him with a gaze as intense as a high-energy spotlight. "It is precisely why I'm here."

Marius broke in, "We're always happy to sell our products, Mr. Rom."

"Call me Tom Rom—my full name, no honorific, appropriate for all purposes. No need to shorten."

Del found it odd, but he had met, and done business with, plenty of odd people. "Fair enough. Do you work for a company? A research project? Anything special you're looking for?"

"My employer is Zoe Alakis, and she conducts privately funded medical research. We'd like samples of your raw materials for biological analysis. Some of the natural Kuivahr substances may have pharmaceutical uses."

"Never heard of Zoe Alakis," Del said.

"My employer likes to keep a low profile."

Del said, "We make no medical claims. Our fine distillations are meant to be imbibed and enjoyed."

Marius muttered under his breath, "*Enjoying* them might be a little much."

Tom Rom ignored the comment. "Cost is no object. I require an exhaustive list of your base ingredients and your distillations, as well as liberal examples of each item so we can catalog them. I understand that some kelp extracts and plankton varieties produce unusual effects in humans?"

"And Ildirans." Del patted his rounded stomach again. "Mr. Denva here will set you up. We'll even throw in a batch of Ildiran kirae—it tingles when you drink it, but no human can stand more than a sip."

Tom Rom was utterly humorless, all business. "Thank you. My employer will add that to her studies."

Marius said, "We'll calculate a fair price, but we don't want to give away any of our trade secrets."

"All of my employer's work is entirely confidential, and not for profit," Tom Rom said.

Del suggested, "If you're after medical research, you might want to meet with Tamo'l in the Ildiran sanctuary domes. She has a whole colony of misfits there, the mixed-breeds that didn't turn out well from Dobro." He called up a chart. "The tide's low, so you could take a skimmer over there."

Tom Rom turned his gaze toward Del. "My employer may wish to follow up on that at a later date."

"Does she focus on any special areas of research?" Marius asked.

"Her interests are wide ranging."

In less than two hours they had given Tom Rom sealed packages of ingredients and of each of their distillations, including kirae, and the stranger headed back through the alien transportal. For some reason neither of them could quite explain, the man made them uncomfortable, and they were happy to send him on his way.

Later that afternoon when a clan trader arrived with expensive medusa meat from Rhejak—which Del considered a delicacy and paid well for—the scruffy woman also delivered news packets that included recordings of recent speeches the candidates had given at Newstation: Lee Iswander and Sam Ricks making their case to be elected the next Speaker.

For half an hour, Del refused to watch. He muttered to himself that he had no further interest in politics, that the election of the next Speaker meant nothing to him. But in the end he gave up and reviewed the presentations.

Running the clans was out of his hands now, and he didn't need political ulcers again, yet the candidates worried him. Iswander was a Roamer, but he reminded Del too much of the worst parts of the Big Goose. Sure, Del accepted the need for the clans to change, but he didn't want Roamers to become what the Hansa Chairman had once represented. Ricks's lack of preparation or enthusiasm was hardly commendable either. Del was tempted to record a message of his own. He didn't want to endorse Sam Ricks, but he wanted to rally the clans to remember who they were.

He stopped himself and deleted the recording. No. He would not let himself get preoccupied with the election. He was past that now. He had his own life. If anything, he should have been paying more attention to his family.

In fact, he made up his mind to go to Newstation for the election—strictly for appearances—and then head off to the gas giant Golgen, where he would visit his daughter and his grandchildren. Zhett and her husband operated the skymine there quite capably, but they could always use his advice, and it would give him something to focus on other than politics.

NINE

ZHETT KELLUM

The skymine drifted above the blue and gray clouds of Golgen, churning through rising vapors. Probe lines dangled down for kilometers, analyzing the chemical composition of the gas giant's atmosphere. Roamer skyminers could raise or lower the industrial behemoth in order to harvest the densest hydrogen concentrations. The facility reminded Zhett Kellum of an enormous jellyfish.

Thrumming pistons pumped hydrogen from the intake scoop through reaction chambers, and separated out the rare allotrope ekti, which fueled Ildiran stardrives. Exhaust boiled away from huge stacks, sighing back into the atmosphere and propelling the facility along its aimless route. The skymine produced ekti for the Confederation as well as the Ildiran Empire.

Hydrogues still dwelled in the deep uncharted cloud layers below, but their diamond-hulled warglobes had not been seen for years.

A cargo ship skimmed in across the upper clouds, approaching the skymine. Zhett knew from the schedule that this must be the *Verne*, part of the Kett Shipping fleet. The pilots, Xander Brindle and Terry Handon, were reliable, but more interested in traveling to different places than in establishing a boring regular route. Zhett envied them, but not too much. She and Patrick were happy here with their family.

She touched her ear comm as she rode a lift down to the landing bay. "Fitzy, Xander and Terry are landing in ten minutes. Want to say hi?"

Her husband responded, "I'd love to, and I'm sure Toff would too, but we'll have to pass, since this young man seems much too distracted to finish his homework."

Zhett heard their thirteen-year-old son, Kristof, groan and make excuses, but she tapped the ear comm to silence it, letting Patrick deal with the whining. He was better at it, and this was his week to supervise homework while she did the administrative duties.

The landing bay was a giant open maw in the lower half of the drifting skymine. Racks of sealed metal canisters full of concentrated stardrive fuel were ready to be loaded aboard the *Verne*. Breezes swirled around Zhett as she stepped into the cargo bay, whipping the long dark hair across her face. Just this morning she had found a gray strand and plucked it out, indignant. She was much, much too young to worry about going gray. (And she told herself the same thing every year.)

The *Verne* came in, adjusting from side to side as the pilot used attitude jets to level it out. Though he wasn't yet twenty years old, Xander Brindle had more experience than many professional pilots; he had been born aboard a ship and grown up at the controls.

Xander deftly landed the ship on the alignment cross, then powered down the engines. The side hatch dropped down, and he bounded out. The son of Robb Brindle and Tasia Tamblyn had a youthful energy, light tan skin, kinky brown hair, and striking blue-green eyes. He grinned as he spotted Zhett. "We've got room for a full load of ekti if you quote us a good price."

"And we have more ekti than you could possibly carry—so long as you have items to trade."

His partner Terry came down the ramp from the cargo hold, accompanied by their compy OK. Terry was a studious young man with short hair, a soft smile, and a quiet demeanor. Antigrav clamps at his waist kept his motionless legs and feet just off the deck; he held on to the compy to stabilize himself. Normally in zero-G, Terry's useless legs didn't hinder him at all, but since the skymine maintained gravity, he used the compy to help him around.

Terry said, "OK has comparison prices from ten other skymines, as well as the trading hub on Ulio. We can show you the going rate."

Zhett shrugged. "Skymining isn't cheap. We still have production costs."

"But you're not risking death anymore for every load of ekti you distill. The hydrogues have been quiet for years." Terry held on to a rail and released OK. The compy started moving supply crates out of the *Verne*'s cargo hold to make room.

Zhett glanced toward the sea of clouds. "True. Now we only have to worry about the *normal* huge expenses."

While Terry called up inventory files on his pad, Xander helped OK haul out crates of goods they had brought from the Ulio trading hub. "We'll find something to trade, no worries," Xander said. "Saltpond caviar, medusa steaks, and a whole box of mushroom fillets from Dremen, cured in saltwater. They don't taste too bad, especially if served with enough of this—New Portugal wine, last year's black vintage."

Terry added, "We've got Theron cocoonweave fabrics. I'm sure your husband would want to give you a nice scarf or dress."

Zhett plucked at her work jumpsuit embroidered with clan symbols. "Do I look like the sort of person who wears dresses and scarves?"

"Maybe your daughter then?" Xander said. "Shareen's seventeen, right? Two years younger than me. She must like pretty—"

Zhett's laughter cut him off. "Then you know Shareen even less than you know me. She's still at school on Earth anyway."

OK kept a complete inventory list. The two traders posted their items, and let the skymine workers dicker over them. After Zhett negotiated a rate for the ekti, skyminers loaded the *Verne*, and Xander and Terry were ready to depart.

"Won't you stay for a meal?" Zhett asked. "Fitz would like to see you two."

"Sorry—places to go, planets to see," Xander said. "Too many other spots to check off on the life list."

Even a skymine administrator had to fit some time into the schedule to be a mother. Patrick shouldered a lot of the parenting duties while Zhett ran the huge cloud harvester, and then they alternated shifts. She met him on the skydeck, a large open balcony platform where breezes gusted through the faint filtering field.

Their son Toff was bouncing a ball against the wall and catching it. If the ball bounced wrong, it would carom off the edge of the observation deck and plunge into the infinite sky, but he caught it every time.

Toff had deep red hair, which was genetically unexpected, considering both Zhett and Patrick had dark hair. The thirteen-year-old was blowing off steam, having finished his homework (under duress).

Patrick propped their two-year-old, Rex, against his waist, even though the toddler squirmed and wanted to play with his brother. "I think our Kristof is ready to go back to Academ," he said in a teasing tone.

Toff reacted to his father's suggestion with horror and almost missed catching his ball. "I still have two months off before I go back to school."

Zhett turned to her husband and said in a mock serious tone, "Hmm, do you think he'd do better studying on Earth, like Shareen?"

"But Shareen hates it there!" Toff cried.

"You've both got it good," Patrick said. "Try growing up with tutors at every turn, or protocol instructors who teach you which fork to use at which part of the meal, how to fold your napkin, and which side of the lips to dab first."

Toff snorted. He bounced his ball on the rail, caught it, then bounced it against the deck, where it ricocheted against the wall, arced up into the air, and came down into his palm again.

Patrick Fitzpatrick III was a blue blood, the grandson of a former Hansa Chairman. Patrick had been in the Earth Defense Forces, survivor of a disastrous battle against the hydrogues. Zhett was the daughter of Roamer industrialist Del Kellum, whose clan had rescued Patrick along with other injured EDF comrades. Their romance had had a Romeo and Juliet quality—more than twenty years ago.

The toddler squirmed and fussed, and Patrick let him run around on the skydeck, but he watched every movement. Patrick was a good father, maybe to counterbalance the fact that his own upbringing had been so sterile. Zhett had been surprised by the mellowing and growth in his personality. When she first met him, Patrick was—frankly—a jerk. Now he claimed to have learned as much from being a real father as his children learned from having one.

Showing off, Toff threw his ball again, which bounced sideways in front of Rex. As the ball flew toward the edge of the deck, the two-year-old bounded after it in a cockeyed run. Barely even pausing in his conversation with Zhett, Patrick snagged Rex by the collar and held him dangling, arms outstretched, as the ball ricocheted off into the wide-open sky. Patrick didn't even seem alarmed.

Zhett said, "He could have gone over the edge!"

"No, I was watching."

Toff added, "I could always grab a swooper and dive down to catch him."

Zhett took the toddler from her husband and scoffed at Toff's bravado. "Once he dropped down into the thick clouds, how would you even find him?"

Toff made a rude noise. "Rex would cry so loud I'd hear him for kilometers."

"You might catch him in time," Patrick said. "But you'd have to change his diaper afterward."

"Eww! Now that's dangerous."

Zhett let out a sigh, happy with her circumstances. The clouds below were thick, mysterious, quiescent. She had a good husband, a fine family, a fulfilling career, an important skymine. She liked being a wife and mother, she liked being a businesswoman. In fact, she had everything she could possibly want.

That feeling of euphoric satisfaction should have made her suspicious right away.

TEN

SHAREEN FITZKELLUM

"You don't know everything, young lady," said the professor, looking as if she'd just swallowed a chemistry experiment gone horribly wrong. "In fact, you don't even know as much as you think you do." Professor Mosbach displayed Shareen's test scores for the other students to see in an obvious and juvenile attempt at humiliation. "You need to concentrate on your learning." Some of the students chuckled.

Shareen's cheeks burned, but she didn't look away. In fact, she faced the teacher, her dark eyes flashing. "I *am* learning. For instance, I've learned that professors don't know everything either. You taught me that by example."

This time the students let out guffaws of scandalized astonishment. Shareen was rewarded with seeing Professor Mosbach's pinched face tighten as if it had just been exposed to a hyper-efficient dehydrator. The woman also flushed a bright red.

Shareen's lab partner, Howard Rohandas, leaned closer and whispered (but so loudly that everyone could hear anyway), "Don't provoke her—you'll just make it awkward. And your calculations were wrong. We can all see that."

"Who cares about the calculations? My *answers* were right," Shareen snapped.

Professor Mosbach stalked back and forth. "This isn't poetry class. You can't wait for the muse to inspire you, then pull out an imaginary answer and expect me to believe you understand how you got there. This is a test requiring rigorous calculations, and you are scored on those calculations."

Shareen snorted again. "In the tests I'm used to, you rig up your own life-support system, install the components in a suit, then test it out by going into hard vacuum. You quantify the test results pretty quickly."

At seventeen, Shareen had grown accustomed to being rewarded for her imagination and intuition, for solving problems with innovation using the items at hand. That was considered a useful skill among the Roamer clans. Apparently not, however, among stodgy teachers who preferred paperwork to practicality. Letting her imagination wander briefly, Shareen smiled at the thought of how Professor Mosbach would fare in a live vacuum-exposure exercise. . . .

"In my next report to Golgen, Ms. Fitzkellum, I will inform your father about your attitude. Your parents pulled strings to get you into this exclusive school. There's a waiting list, as you may be aware. You took the place of someone who would appreciate an education more."

"I very much appreciate an education, ma'am." Shareen meant it, but to her an "education" did not mean memorizing redundant facts and doing contrived assembly-line problems.

The professor clicked her tongue. "You obviously have intelligence and potential, but you don't apply yourself."

"Because I don't respect the problems you assign," Shareen muttered. "Completely useless in an emergency."

Howard spoke up to cover her comment. "I'll help her study, Professor. I promise she'll be more accurate in the next examination."

"Thanks, Howard." Shareen's tone conveyed anything but gratitude.

The dark-haired young man was a good lab partner, she had to admit. In fact, he was basically her only friend here, because he didn't seem to mind her scrappy attitude.

Professor Mosbach controlled her temper as tightly as she controlled her unrealistic initial conditions. "I expect you to do better in the laboratory phase."

"I will, ma'am." Shareen did her best to sound meek and chastised. She didn't entirely succeed, but it was enough to deflect the teacher's ire.

She knew her father wanted to give her the best education possible and had used his family name to get her into the exclusive academy, but this just wasn't working, from her attitude to her appearance. Even her hair—Shareen kept her light brown hair tied up in stubby pigtails, which made her look like a tomboy. Since she tucked her hair in helmets so often, she couldn't let it grow long. The other students teased her mercilessly, but she wouldn't change.

Back on the Golgen skymine, she had grown up learning how the systems worked. She tinkered with any gadget she could get her hands on and taught herself how to take things apart long before she learned how to put them back together. In time, though, she could reassemble them better than they were before.

She taught herself the basics, spent years at Academ with hundreds of other Roamer students, learned how to solve bigger problems, co-operate with others, and take advantage of her unique insights. She had been so excited when she was accepted into an exclusive technical institute on Earth, which had produced some of the best scientists and engineers over the past century. Many of her Roamer friends envied her, but Shareen quickly realized that her talents weren't appreciated here.

She could be sharp-tempered with students who failed to grasp concepts as quickly as she did. She didn't consider herself better than they were, but she hated to waste time. She didn't want anyone to hold her back—and teachers like Professor Mosbach certainly held her back.

It was a miserable year for her, and she couldn't wait to pass her tests and go home in a few weeks. Her attitude alienated her classmates, which made Shareen even more miserable. How could she have survived without Howard's patience and his calm words? He grounded her in the midst of frustrating insanity.

He was quiet and unflappable, like a sturdy tree that couldn't be bent by the storm of her impatience. Some days after classes, when Shareen was by herself in the dorm room, stewing over some event, she would realize that she had treated poor Howard badly, and she regretted it, though he never seemed to take offense. What a good friend he was—the only pleasant part about being on Earth.

He helped her with homework, even when she hated to admit that she couldn't follow the detailed mathematical derivations. Although she grasped concepts instinctively, she couldn't reproduce all the fine print. Howard, on the other hand, used mathematical notation with a deftness that embarrassed her.

When she'd finally gotten up the nerve to ask him for help, Howard was glad to be of assistance. He patiently went through the work with her, step-by-step. She did comprehend the subject thanks to him, and that time she actually remembered to thank him. "I didn't get it before. I appreciate it, Howard."

He had given her a small smile, not a beaming overreaction like a foolish schoolboy. Shareen suggested to Howard that they study together again.

And the following day, she failed her test. She could see the answer in her head, but she simply couldn't put down all of the nitpicky steps that were so obvious. When an artist painted a tree, did she have to draw in every single leaf? A good artist could convey a "tree" without all that. . . .

In an engineering lab, though, Shareen could follow her imagination and tinker with interesting gadgets. There, she was in her element with the lab stations, workbenches, tools, circuit boards. And it was her turn to help Howard. He observed her closely, and she knew by the intent expression on his face that he was learning as much from watching her as from Professor Mosbach's lectures.

"I've got an idea for a new sort of power block," she had told him when beginning the project. "Do you want to work on it with me?"

Howard asked her to explain, and she talked quickly, sketching out the thoughts in her head, without being very articulate. Not surprisingly, he didn't comprehend her design, but instead of growing frustrated, Howard asked for clarification. She tried to explain it another way, but he didn't grasp how her concept would function. He shook his head in confusion.

Instead of snapping at him, she realized that she must look the same way when she struggled through complex derivations. And he wasn't bad to look at either. "Okay, a power block is composed of supercharged inverted-energy film, right? The sheets are only a few molecules thick, and when they're bombarded with high-energy particles, they soak up and retain the energy. Then the film is folded up like origami and densely packed inside a neutral casing."

He nodded, but she didn't give him time to absorb. "All the energy stored in the film does no good unless we can release it in a controlled way. I've been thinking up a new type of quantum valve—control strips on the edge of the power block's release port—but it would take a special kind of material."

Howard had followed her instructions, always at her side in the lab, for the better part of a month as they worked on the project for final exam credit. She wasn't sure he grasped the nuances of her idea, but he did watch and participate. She was glad to help him, and glad for his help.

Not long after her embarrassing confrontation with Professor Mosbach, they were wrapping up the laboratory aspect, finishing the prototype of the small power block. As Shareen assembled the last sandwich layers of the metallic-origami film that she had spent five days charging, Howard remained silent. Finally he drew out his pad and displayed a confusing wash of calculations. "I've broken down the physical and mathematical basis of what I think you're doing in our project, Shareen. It's necessary documentation."

Shareen wouldn't have bothered to do that, but she nodded. "Thanks. I doubt Mosbach would give us credit without all the paperwork."

"It's not just that. I want you to look at this: I think there's a chance of an arcing discharge from the connectors of your new strips coupled with the old film."

He showed the math to her, but she stared blankly. "You're saying it won't work? I thought you didn't understand what we were doing."

"I understand it better now that I've done the calculations and run models. I am somewhat concerned."

Shareen didn't want to take out her frustration on him. "What do you propose we do then? Our project is due in three days. I *know* the principle is sound."

"I'm sure the principle is, but I'm worried about the details of its execution."

He showed her the math again. Finally, she held up her hands. "I'm still waiting to hear your suggestion. What do we do?"

"I think we should try out the power block now before anyone sees. That way, we'll have a chance to make adjustments if necessary."

"All right." She hooked up the leads, wanting to get this over with.

When she dumped the power block into the battery reservoir, the strips flickered, and a succession of popping noises was accompanied by blue-white sparks. Howard yanked the leads free. Acrid electrical smoke curled up from the block. Other students glanced at their lab station, but Shareen pretended nothing was wrong.

Embarrassed, she turned to Howard, expecting him to say "I told you so," but instead he gave a matter-of-fact nod. "Good to know. Now let's fix the glitch." He gave her a small smile. "I have an idea for an insulation damper. If we work nonstop, we should be able to refold and connect the filmsheets, and make a functional power block before our deadline."

Shareen felt stung, but he had been right. "Thanks, Howard. You prevented a disaster." She drew a breath. "All right, let's solve this."

They worked in silence for more than an hour before Howard said, "I've never seen anyone better than you at making intuitive leaps, at coming up with amazing and unconventional ideas. But they still have to be implemented, and that takes attention to detail."

Shareen groaned. "The tedious part. I'm not a detail person. Maybe big ideas aren't always enough. I get impatient, cut corners. You're the exact opposite. It never occurred to me that details could be as important as a leap of genius."

His eyebrows rose slightly. "So . . . genius and detail are both required to make major progress. Good to know."

This time, when Howard smiled she felt as if she were seeing him for the first time.

Even though she looked forward to being free of this maddening place and going back home to the Golgen skymine where she could do real work for a change, she wished Howard could go with her. He really was the best part of being at school on Earth.

"I learned something very important from that, Howard." She touched his arm. "I learned that we make a pretty good team."

ELEVEN

ELISA REEVES

Though her ship was faster than Garrison's, the search was tedious. Elisa raced along the course her husband had set, making up for lost time in open space. But she had to wait for the *ping* from her bread crumb tracking devices, had to find the little beacon buoy that was automatically dropped off each time he changed course. Then she had to take readings, adjust her course, and head off again. It was so time-consuming.

Yet she didn't consider giving up or letting him get away with her son—not for a minute.

She had found three bread crumbs already, and Garrison's staggering path made no sense. If she could figure out where he was taking Seth, she could head there and intercept him. But his flight was erratic, zigzagging across space and out into nowhere. Why would he do that, unless he was trying to hide from her? Maybe he guessed that she was hunting for him. Yes, in some ways Garrison was a smart man. She clenched her jaw. In some ways, though, he was a fool.

Drifting near another bread crumb buoy, she projected where he was headed now. Garrison didn't seem to be aiming for any particular star system, known Roamer outpost, Confederation planet, or even an Ildiran splinter colony. She activated her stardrive and headed after him again.

Her personal mission had consumed her for days. Though she'd remembered to bring work along—documents to review, processes to audit and, if possible, streamline—she hadn't been able to focus on her job since racing away from Sheol. And she resented Garrison for that too.

By now, Lee Iswander would be making his case to the Roamer

clans at Newstation. Normally, in his absence, Elisa would have taken charge of the lava-processing operations, but since she had to deal with this nonsense, he would have given the responsibility to Alec Pannebaker. She should have been his first choice.

Iswander couldn't be allowed to think Elisa was not reliable, that she was one of "those" professional women who couldn't balance family matters with business necessities. She didn't want to be seen like that. She had worked too hard, devoted too much of her life, made too many sacrifices to get where she was.

All along she had thought Garrison was her partner with the same goals, who saw the same intensely bright Guiding Star—to use his silly Roamer metaphor.

While cruising along, not knowing how soon she might encounter the next shifting point, Elisa called up her personal image library and scrolled through to find a photo of Seth (not that she had forgotten what her own child looked like, thank you!). The first photo she found was a portrait of herself and Garrison, smiling as they held the one-year-old boy. Happy times. Elisa frowned when she saw it, recognizing the delusion in her eyes.

Without thinking, she deleted the image, scrolled through the library, and found another one of Garrison and Seth laughing as they ate some gelatinous pasta meal they had cooked together. She deleted the second image as well. When she finally took Seth back, she did not want her son to be able to view and remember enjoyable times with his father.

She found several more images of Garrison and Seth at different ages. Then two of herself and Garrison. She deleted them. Elisa didn't need to be taunted by her mistakes. Even more photos of Garrison and Seth. What did he do, spend all of his time staging images? No wonder he hadn't advanced far in his job.

But she couldn't find any warm photos of just herself and Seth. And since Garrison was so keen to take images, he must have intentionally left her out. She finally uncovered several images of her son alone, which she kept. She studied the shape of Seth's nose, the curve of his smile, tried to determine how much of his features looked like her. She saw hints of Garrison there too—that couldn't be helped. Seth was *her* son, regardless. Elisa displayed the images on the cockpit screens. She could always use her imagination to place herself there alongside him, or splice some images together. It would be good enough.

She realized that she hadn't kept photo images of *her* parents or brothers either . . . not for years.

Elisa Enturi had grown up in a lower middle-class family on Earth, small home, two younger brothers, her parents both factory workers. After the faeros attack destroyed the Moon, everyone with the ability and resources had evacuated Earth to flee the bombardment of meteors. But that was beyond the means of people like them, her father had said. Elisa huddled with her family and hoped for the best as impacts peppered the Earth, wiping out several major cities. She felt so helpless—and she never wanted to feel that way again.

The Enturi family seemed incapable of getting ahead, and Elisa was told she couldn't have the finer things she wanted. Her mother said, "At least we know what the future holds for us. We'll content ourselves with what we have."

Elisa had no interest in being content. Her brothers were brought up to believe they would never be anything more than factory workers, would probably never even leave Earth. Her parents told Elisa the same thing, but she turned a deaf ear. While in school, she got a job to earn extra money for herself and for her family, and also to gain work experience so she could be ahead of her classmates.

But all the money she contributed into the family kitty disappeared into occasional meals in nice restaurants, tickets to shows that Elisa didn't want to see. So she took a second job and deposited those wages into a private account in order to pay for her college tuition.

She didn't believe that nice things should be out of their reach. She looked for opportunities and found them. She impressed people, who gave her even more chances, jobs, projects, and quick bonuses, and she started to save additional money. She took the late shifts whenever necessary. She volunteered for extra hours. She made herself useful, and then invaluable.

She worked hard at both jobs *and* maintained her grades, much to her brothers' astonishment. They had told her she couldn't possibly do both (probably because they didn't want to be pressured to take even a single job while they went to school). Because of her grades,

Elisa was accepted into a decent college, though she kept living at home to save on expenses.

When the family vehicle broke down because her father hadn't maintained it, Elisa was the only one who had the money to make repairs. Her mother had just drained the family account by buying an expensive teak dining set unlike any of their other furnishings. (She justified her extravagant purchase, tearfully, "Can't I ever have *something* nice, just for me? For once?")

One of Elisa's brothers got arrested for vandalizing a clothing shop run by the parents of a girl he didn't like, and only Elisa had the funds to bail him out. (She did suggest selling the teak dining room set to raise bail—a perfectly practical idea, but it made her mother angry.)

After a succession of other family financial crises, which she had been forced to rectify, Elisa finally marched into the living room one evening, her face flushed.

She had lived with them all her life and had grown blind to their habits. Elisa was shocked to realize the obvious—that neither her brothers, nor her father or mother ever put in the slightest bit of extra work than they had to. They ducked when someone asked for a volunteer. They grumbled about being forced to put in overtime, despite the extra pay. They actually liked being idle and sat around on their days off "relaxing"—sleeping in, or amusing themselves with stupid games.

For Elisa a "day off" was a chance to catch up and get ahead on other goals. She took night classes, she self-studied, and as she grew more successful, her family often commented that she was just *lucky.* Once, when she got a raise, one of her brothers even sneered that she must be sleeping with the boss. They couldn't imagine that she had earned it, that it was *possible* to get ahead.

"You all deserve your situation!" she said. "You're lazy, unambitious, disappointing. If any of you pushed yourselves, tried harder, and worked to *be something,* then you could pull us all up higher. Instead, you do nothing and just resent those who have more than you do."

Her parents looked deeply insulted.

Elisa shook her head. "And all this time I've enabled you. I see that. You're on your own now. Sink or swim, it's up to you."

She took the remaining money from her account, only a fraction of what it should have been without the drain from her family's constant needs, and left home. She started from scratch—a frightening prospect at first, but she found it much easier without the dead weight of her family holding her back.

She went to work for Lee Iswander, a man whose attitude she admired, and she hitched her star to him. Then she met Garrison Reeves, a member of an important Roamer clan, who needed help. He said all the right things, offered her a chance to make a huge investment in a major business deal for Iswander. They could help each other.

She also thought Garrison was a kindred spirit. Together, they could have become powerful and important business leaders. But he had let her down too, failing to step up to the plate when an opportunity presented itself, and causing trouble with the industrialist who had made her whole career possible.

And now he'd run off with her son.

Her ship stopped at the next bread crumb tracker, and she reoriented her nav system, studying the new course. "Where the hell are you going?" she muttered to herself. "That's the middle of nowhere. Didn't you even bother to make a *plan*?"

When she arrived and scanned for signs of Garrison's stolen ship, Elisa found that the area was not empty at all. She encountered filmy greenish brown spheres brought together through gravity or some kind of willful motion. The cluster looked like a miniature galaxy, with hundreds of other globules floating around the periphery. Trails of outliers extended across the emptiness, marking a mysterious trail through the void.

She wondered if Garrison had come here on purpose. Did he intend to hide this strange discovery from her and from Iswander Industries? The magnetic tracking device had stopped transmitting, but as she extended her sensors, she detected his ship.

Found you!

Yes, Garrison was here. That was what mattered.

TWELVE

LEE ISWANDER

After making his case to the Roamer clans, Iswander headed back to Sheol, anxious to return to business. Though he could have spent days in meetings at Newstation, chatting with clan heads and Confederation trade representatives, he had obligations at his lava-processing operations.

The flight back seemed long. After the first few hours of making notes and putting his thoughts in order, he was ready to be back in his office. Once he was elected Speaker, he would have to rely on Alec Pannebaker and Elisa Reeves for the day-to-day work. Though he liked to show good leadership by being there and being *involved,* some things would have to change. That was the price one paid to move forward.

From space, the hot binary planet looked dramatic, two halves playing tug-of-war. He deployed the cruiser's heat shield, descended toward the magma operations, and radioed ahead to let Pannebaker know he was coming. "Prepare a production summary for me, please."

"Got it already, Chief. I do my homework before I have fun. And by the Guiding Star, there's lots of fun now—thermal instabilities, more than usual. Three lava geysers. One shoots half a kilometer into the atmosphere."

Iswander remembered the warnings of Garrison Reeves. "Does it pose any danger to our facilities?"

"It's five kilometers away from the towers, but worth the trip to go see. I'll take you out there if you like."

"I'm sure you've taken hundreds of images, Mr. Pannebaker."

"Thousands, actually. Got to get just the right frame. We'll show them off to Captain Kett when she gets here."

The head of the Confederation's largest trading fleet, Rlinda Kett was due at Sheol to take a large cargo of metal products to Newstation. It was a symbolic gesture to impress the clan heads, and the hearty businesswoman knew that full well, but she had agreed to do it, so long as he gave her sufficient inducement.

"A bribe?" Iswander had asked her in a preliminary meeting. He was familiar with the way business and politics worked, but he didn't think Rlinda Kett would be so blatant about it.

"Not at all," she had answered. "Shipping terms—I want a ten percent reduction in my costs on all exports from Sheol."

Iswander knew a negotiation when he saw one. "Pure ingots only."

"No—ingots, processed-metal foams, alloy films. Ten percent reduction across the board."

"Ten percent on ingots, five percent on other specialty materials."

Rlinda had let out a loud laugh. "Good enough—and we're done here." She broke out a bottle of her specialty aqua vitae to celebrate. "This is distilled by my associate Del Kellum on an Ildiran planet called Kuivahr. A new product, lots of interest in it."

He had sipped the murky liquid in the glass, controlled his expression, and tried to be polite. "Tastes . . . rough. A little like seaweed, but with a burn."

"He's still fine-tuning the recipe, enhancing the health benefits. But the sea was the source of all life, and he's thinking about calling this Primordial Ooze."

"Doesn't sound very marketable."

Rlinda, a big, dark-skinned woman who had only grown bigger over the years, had been the Confederation's first trade minister, which gave her numerous connections. Previously, she'd run a small shipping company, and now she ran a large one. She owned three upscale restaurants, traded in exotic food items, and ate enough of them herself to make a dent in her profits. Everyone liked Rlinda, and Iswander was sure he could do business with her.

"I'll have Robb and Tasia handle the details and draw up the paperwork," she said. "You know I'm just a figurehead these days."

"Hardly," he said. Robb Brindle and Tasia Tamblyn could manage the business, but Rlinda would never be a mere figurehead of Kett Shipping.

After a handshake, they had set up a date for her *Voracious Curiosity* to fly to Sheol to pick up a large shipment of materials to show off to the Roamer clans. For the upcoming election, the timing was important, though it had to look casual. . . .

Now, Iswander descended using assisted piloting, as thermal disturbances shook his cruiser from side to side. The cracks below were like arterial wounds that bled molten metals and incinerated rock. His extraction facilities rode the hot seas, plated with ultra-heat-resistant materials so they could scoop up fresh material. Alloy processors and fabrication chambers in Tower Two created exotic metal foams and films, useful mixtures with polymers and ceramics.

He steered clear of the lava plumes that had so excited Pannebaker and aimed for the cluster of extraction structures, the three towers, and the anchored landing platform. His cruiser settled into place, and he waited while a heat tunnel extended so he could transfer into the shielded admin tower.

Pannebaker met him in the office on the high deck of Tower One, grinning as he handed Iswander a report, anxious to be rid of it. He was a competent engineer with management abilities, but no great fondness for administrative work—in other words, the best kind of deputy.

Pannebaker had silvery hair and intense eyes, as well as a mustache that framed his mouth all the way down to his chin. Every day in the Sheol lava mines excited him like an adrenaline rush, and his extreme competence sometimes led him to take unwarranted risks for the sheer fun of it.

"The shipment of ingots is ready for Captain Kett, sir—our purest, most expensive stuff," Pannebaker said. "I also included some exotic materials that'll really impress the Roamers."

"I already impressed the Roamers with my speech at Newstation. Speaker Seward set the bar low by accomplishing, uh . . . *nothing*. And Sam Ricks certainly doesn't have impressive credentials."

Not being a Roamer himself, Pannebaker was not interested in clan politics. "Whatever you say, Chief. But you'll want to look at those revised geological reports. Your consultants made a few optimistic assumptions that might not be valid. Heat plumes are rising up—which is great because it adds purer material to the mix, but temperatures are

outside the norms. With the construction materials we used, we're awfully close to tolerances. Could be something to worry about if it gets
hotter."

Iswander wondered if Garrison Reeves had legitimate concerns
after all—which reminded him, "Any word yet from Elisa?"

"None, Chief. Isn't she taking personal time?"

"Yes, but I thought she'd be back by now." Iswander was worried
about her. Elisa would never take so many days away from work unless the situation was serious. Although her husband was an adequate
worker, Iswander had plenty of adequate workers. But he could not
replace Elisa Reeves. He hoped her family problems didn't interfere
with her job performance.

Fortunately, his own wife never posed any problems, never inter-
fered, never demanded too much. He had made the terms clear when
he arranged the marriage: he needed a woman who was willing to
operate within those parameters.

Now that he was back on Sheol, Iswander considered going to the
residence deck to see his family, greet his son (who revered his father),
give Londa a peck on the cheek, answer her few rote questions . . . but
he could do that later. Right now, he wanted to settle into his office—
which, truth be told, felt more like home than the residence deck did
anyway.

When Iswander reviewed the geological reports from Pannebaker,
he began to frown. The tidal stresses were higher than any previously
recorded in eighteen years of study. His consultants had made no mention of that, perhaps because they knew he didn't want them to find
any problems. Had they missed something?

Garrison claimed to have uncovered second- and third-order oscil-
lations in the orbiting planetary fragments, which would begin a cycle
that brought the two halves even closer, a minuscule difference in an
astronomical sense, but enough to increase the tidal heating. Magma
flowed upward at a higher temperature, heat plumes intensified, quakes
struck more frequently—all of which had implications for the stability
of his processing structures.

Although Lee Iswander didn't waste money on unnecessary protective measures, he did have a healthy respect for the inherent hazards here. The Sheol facility was dangerous by its very nature, but he

had made sure it was designed with enough heat shielding to offer adequate—though not overboard foolish—protection. He had taken reasonable measures. Nevertheless, he would have to look into this in greater depth—discreetly, so as not to cause a panic. Garrison had already caused some uneasiness among the workers, and these fluctuations would only make the anxiety worse.

Pannebaker cheerfully interrupted him over the comm. "The *Voracious Curiosity* is here a day early, Chief. Captain Kett says she wanted to catch you sleeping."

"I rarely sleep," Iswander said. "Good thing our shipment is ready."

"And best of all—a fourth lava geyser just erupted! Our sensors picked up the heat spike, and it's jetting high, definitely visible from the landing platform."

"Why is that good news?"

"Because it's spectacular. Captain Kett will see it as she comes in. She loves a good show. She's brought Tasia Tamblyn and Robb Brindle along to handle the business details."

Iswander nodded to himself. Considering the erupting geysers, maybe it was a good thing the *Curiosity* had arrived a day early. With luck, her ship could fly off to Newstation with its cargo before anything dangerous or embarrassing happened here.

Thirteen

Zoe Alakis

Every time Tom Rom returned from a voyage, he delivered vital material for the Pergamus research teams—scientifically valuable data, symptom records and case studies, potential treatments, pharmaceuticals, or cutting-edge equipment that had not yet been released on the market. Zoe Alakis wanted *everything*. At the very least he always brought her something interesting.

Zoe's planetary security teams had clear instructions to let Tom Rom through. As soon as her perimeter scouts sent word that his ship had arrived in Pergamus orbit, Zoe reminded them that she would tolerate no delay. She wanted to see him as soon as possible.

Of course, her own protective systems caused most of the delay—he would take hours to pass through seventeen successive levels of decontamination and sterilization before she let him see her face-to-face—but she would not loosen those requirements, not even for him. People were too dangerous, diseases were too dangerous, and she had no need for any closer contact.

Zoe kept her dark hair short, so she could easily don a decon suit and cap in an emergency. She had prominent eyebrows, deep brown eyes, and pale skin. She was careful to breathe through her nose, for added protection from the implanted filters in her nostrils. She ate bland food—processed and cooked, never anything raw.

Pergamus was a medical-research complex and extensive disease library, the largest one in existence. And it belonged to her alone: privately funded and beholden to no government, university, or research consortium. No one else could be trusted. No one else *deserved* it. Zoe Alakis had it all.

Pergamus barely qualified as a planet, as it wasn't much larger than an asteroid. It held only a tenuous atmosphere, and what little there was proved to be poisonous. The facility was isolated and safe.

Zoe insisted on layers of precautions—she had her reasons—and any researcher who wanted to work for the obscenely high pay she offered had to agree to certain conditions. They could share nothing about their work—absolutely nothing, with anyone, on pain of death. Those specific words were in their contracts. She owned their break-throughs, their cures and treatments, all of their records, and the ge-netic mappings of any viruses and bacteria that couldn't be cured.

Zoe resided alone in the facility's central dome, which she never left. Separate from the main dome, fourteen isolated laboratory domes had been built at varying distances, far enough to protect them if a sterilization blast were required. In those groundside domes, re-searchers conducted studies on cancers, neurological disorders, brain deterioration. Eight of the domes were devoted to various infec-tious diseases—at least the ones considered tame enough to be studied on the planet's surface. For the more dangerous organisms and risky treatment protocols, she had twelve Orbiting Research Spheres, some spinning to provide artificial gravity, others motionless for zero-G research.

Every one of the laboratories, the groundside domes as well as the orbiting satellites, had thorough fail-safe sterilization protocols, along with a no-exceptions set of rules as to when they were to be used. She would allow no unnecessary risks, no outbreaks. Everything was con-trolled by her inflexible procedures, programmed in black and white. Zoe never let herself get personally attached to her researchers, nor did she want anyone else to have a moment of personal doubt in a crisis.

On the monitor screens inside her central dome, she followed Tom Rom's progress through decontamination. She opened the comm. "How much longer?"

He turned his face to the image pickup and smiled at her, his eyes bright. "As long as it takes. No shortcuts. I'd never risk exposing you."

She monitored him as he passed through airlock after airlock, one decon chamber after another and yet another. Chemical sprays, UV bursts. Each one made him cleaner, safer. He risked so much out there for her.

Tom Rom had a lean and muscular body that she admired without the least bit of arousal. Though she loved him more than any other human being, he was not her lover. No one had ever been her lover. The thought of physical intimacy disgusted her. The sharing of bodily fluids—not just semen but saliva, perspiration, sloughed-off skin cells, pubic hairs, even exhaled breath—not only repelled her, it sent her into a panic. She abhorred the thought of kissing someone, holding hands, touching in the most intimate of fashions.

Any such contact could only increase Zoe's risk of unnecessary exposure to contaminants. There were so many ways that the human body could go wrong. From her father, she knew that all too well.

Around her office, electron micrographs showed in exquisite and terrifying detail salivary bacteria, dust mites, virally invaded cells, degenerated nerve fibers, stunted and mutated ganglia. To Zoe, these were monsters more horrifying than the Klikiss warrior caste, the hydrogue warglobes, or any other alien species. And these microscopic enemies in their myriad forms invaded from everywhere, unseen. They changed constantly, mutating in order to find new ways to attack human systems.

It was an odds game, and she intended to stack the deck. She didn't risk breathing unfiltered air or consuming unsterilized food or water. She viewed this as a war, one she knew she could never win, but she had created a sort of neutral ground here on Pergamus.

Tom Rom emerged naked from the last chamber, dried himself off, and donned a white jumpsuit, entirely unselfconscious. He stood before her, such a magnificent man, such a loyal knight. No, he was not and would never be her lover—but he would do anything for her, and she would do anything for him. He was her life.

Zoe had been raised in a scientific observation tower deep in the primeval forests of Vaconda. Her parents, Adam and Evelyn Alakis, had settled in the lichentree jungles, mostly alone on the entire planet and laughing off the obvious "Adam and Eve" jokes.

They had claimed a large homestead, filed the necessary papers, and built a tall forest watchtower above the pointed lichentrees. They were a brave pioneer family on a previously unclaimed world. The Alakis family set about exploring, cataloguing the Vaconda flora and fauna in hopes of finding some profitable export crop, particularly pharmaceuticals, which could help other people. Adam and Evelyn Alakis had been successful in discovering new bark extracts, potent spores, and slime-mold distillates, which were put to use in Hansa medicine, curing several rare diseases.

For her own part, Zoe remembered enduring many jungle fevers as a child—nightmares, chills, delirium. But she recovered every time, got better, stronger, developed immunities.

When Zoe was only eight, her mother's flyer crashed in the thick lichentree jungles kilometers from the homestead. Responding to the auto-distress call, Adam threw Zoe into their second flyer and the two of them raced out from the forest watchtower to rescue his wife. Reaching the crash site, Adam and Zoe extracted Evelyn from the wreckage, took her back to the homestead, and tried to treat her. Adam had a medical background, and was competent in first aid, but he couldn't repair his wife's extensive injuries. Though young, Zoe was already self-sufficient and helpful, and she tried her best to assist . . . but it was not enough. Evelyn died before they could arrange to get her offworld to a sophisticated medical facility. Spores had already begun to grow in her open wounds. . . .

Zoe was stunned. She had never felt so alone, and yet Adam remained on the planet, insisting that Vaconda was a treasure chest. He was still a pioneer, sure that he and Zoe could survive.

With its vines, insects, lichentrees, and bitter-smelling winds, this was a primordial world, and the isolation was profound. Adam's inability to help Evelyn after the accident convinced him to bring in other helpers—biologists, summer students, itinerants, so that he and his daughter wouldn't be so helpless and cut off. Part-timers came, one or two at a time, to work in the jungle and live in the watchtower. When their temporary contracts were over, they left. Adam was unable to find anyone with an equal level of dedication and determination, to commit to the work and to Adam and Zoe.

Until Tom Rom came. And he made up for all the others. . . .

Now, freshly decontaminated, he stood in her presence, still keeping a safe distance. Tom Rom displayed a file explaining what he had brought back from Kuivahr. "It's a Roamer distillation facility on an Ildiran world. Several species of plankton and kelp there have interesting extracts, some with peculiar properties. Worth analyzing for possible benefits. I brought samples of the different types Del Kellum uses in brewing and distillation. There's also a kind of liquor the Ildirans consume. It's unpalatable to humans but supposedly has tonic effects for Ildirans."

"Humans and Ildirans have many biological similarities, but we're not identical," Zoe said. "My library has a whole section on Ildiran diseases that have no effect on humans."

"It might be worth a follow-up visit to Kuivahr. The Ildiran researcher there is studying genetic abnormalities in mixed-breeds."

"Physical deformities?" Zoe asked. Those wouldn't interest her at all.

"Deep DNA studies to see why some of the breedings fail."

"Yes, it might be valuable data for the library—if you can get the Ildirans to give us their records. But that's not what I want from you next." When Zoe stood, she kept her desk between them at first. Tom Rom knew not to get closer than five feet. That was their agreement. She was a very different person now from the girl she had been on Vaconda, and she lived in a very different universe.

After a brief hesitation, Zoe finally came around, standing as close to him as she dared. "I found something else I want you to look into."

One wall of her office chamber was covered with a mosaic of images culled from thousands of news networks. She could spend hours sifting through the selections to find any report that interested her, an outbreak of an unusual sickness, perhaps, or some kind of miracle cure. In many cases, samples of new plagues were easy to obtain, and she employed other scouts and investigators to gather them. Bribes were usually sufficient to obtain library copies of new vaccines or treatments.

Sometimes, though, Zoe suspected an investigation could be particularly dangerous. For those matters she relied upon Tom Rom.

She selected the proper mosaic screen, enlarged it, and showed him the report that had caught her interest. A man had been arrested for dissecting the fallen Klikiss bodies left scattered on their abandoned worlds—and also for extracting and devouring some parts of them.

In a short video clip, the man cried, "They have royal jelly!" but his eyes were wild as he fought against the authorities. "It cured me!"

"According to records," Zoe said, "that man had not been suffering from any major disease at all, so no need for any miracle cure."

"He's obviously insane," Tom Rom said.

"Yes, he is . . . but even insane people can have good ideas. I find his claims fascinating. Go to a place where there are Klikiss bodies, extract this royal jelly, and bring it here so we can run tests. Don't call attention to yourself. If the royal jelly turns out to have exceptional properties, we'll want to harvest it from as many Klikiss bodies as possible before anyone else realizes the potential."

He gave a crisp nod. "There are plenty of Klikiss worlds to choose from. I'll head out immediately." He turned to go.

She felt a pang and had to restrain herself from reaching out a hand to him. "So soon? After all those decontamination procedures, stay with me for a day or two."

"Time is of the essence, Zoe." He wasn't avoiding her, but she knew that Tom Rom didn't feel alive unless he was on a mission of some kind. For her.

She stared at him, knowing she would feel connected to him no matter how close or how far he was. "I have never met another person so devoted to me . . . or to anyone. You know you don't *have* to do everything I ask, Tom."

He regarded her as if she had spoken an incomprehensible statement. "But I want to. You know it's always been my heart's desire to protect you, to help you achieve what you need to achieve. That's why you trust me so much."

"And why are you so dedicated?" She had never understood it herself.

"Why do you need a reason?" He turned to depart the dome. "I'll bring you the royal jelly." On his way out, he paused to give her a broad smile. "It's good to see you."

FOURTEEN

YAZRA'H

The halfbreed girl had a wild intensity in her eyes that would strike fear into an opponent—which was a good thing, but Yazra'h had other concerns about her as well. Yazra'h brought up her blunted katana just in time, and Muree'n's staff cracked down, hard, where her shoulder had been an instant before. Then the girl sprang back, laughing.

From the ringing vibrations through the katana staff, Yazra'h gauged the strength of that blow. Even with her thin and flexible practice armor, the blow would have broken bones had it landed.

Under the bright glare of the suns, the two circled on the high-level combat field. Instead of soft dirt or solid ground, the practice field was covered with large, mirrored spheres packed together, each one a meter in diameter. Both combatants were barefoot, balancing on the smooth, curved surfaces, and they leaped from one sphere to the next, balancing, rolling, and fighting.

Tossing her head to shake the hair away from her face, Yazra'h swung her weapon sideways, trying to smack the girl's head with the flat of the blade—just enough to stun her and teach her a lesson. But Muree'n bobbed, ducked under the katana, and popped up again with her staff to drive the blade aside. The girl was sturdy, muscular, and her half-human features softened the normally bestial appearance of a true warrior kithman.

Muree'n jabbed with the rounded end of her weapon, trying to punch Yazra'h in the center of the chest, but Yazra'h bent sideways, just enough that the blow only caught her in the ribs.

"This is only practice, girl," Yazra'h warned.

"If practice isn't real, then it's worthless." Muree'n threw herself forward with a wild yell. Instead of using her katana, though, Yazra'h reached out with the flat of her hand, caught Muree'n in the sternum, and hurled her backward. The girl spun and caught her balance on one of the spheres. The multiple suns reflecting from the mirrored surfaces sent up random flashes and a constant glare.

"I will try hand-to-hand, then." Muree'n cast her practice stick aside. "I'm good enough. Test me." She jumped closer, balancing on the adjacent sphere. Yazra'h caught the girl by both wrists and threw her up and sideways. Muree'n yelped, tumbled, but somehow landed on her feet.

Yazra'h gasped for breath. "You are getting better, girl. I won't argue with that." Though Yazra'h was a strong fighter, she didn't belong to the warrior kith; she was a noble, a daughter of the Mage-Imperator; few warrior kithmen could best her in combat, however.

For herself, Muree'n seemed to have something to prove. She had grown her hair long like Yazra'h's, but hers was darker, and she braided it with jewels and heavy metallic weights as decorations that could be disentangled and used as surprise weapons in a desperate situation.

Muree'n bowed, as if conceding defeat, then she drove forward to ram her head into Yazra'h's stomach, knocking her off the sphere. Yazra'h fell backward, unable to catch her balance in time, and landed hard against another one of the spheres.

The halfbreed girl was reckless, Yazra'h knew, but sometimes it paid off. Among Nira's children from the breeding program, Muree'n was the youngest, and the lowest born, from a guard kithman. Her brother Rod'h was the son of a Designate, Gale'nh the son of an Adar, Tamo'l the daughter of a lens kithman, and Osira'h, the oldest and most powerful of the five halfbreed children, was the daughter of Mage-Imperator Jora'h himself. None of them, though, could outfight Muree'n.

Yazra'h had taken the girl under her wing as a special student, and now Muree'n had fought her mentor to a standstill. Over the years, Muree'n had suffered many bruises and broken bones, and her skin showed numerous scars, but the girl considered each one a badge of honor.

Yazra'h picked herself up from the ground, panting. "I know few opponents who fight so wholeheartedly." She extended a hand.

Muree'n hesitated, suspicious, before she helped Yazra'h up. "Half measures are for the hesitant."

Yazra'h chuckled. "I've never known you to hesitate, but you charge into a fray without planning ahead."

Muree'n shrugged. "I haven't once been seriously hurt, so I keep fighting."

Yazra'h removed a short fighting stick from her belt, adjusted it to the length of her forearm, and motioned for Muree'n to do the same. "Close combat now, so I can look into your eyes and see what you're thinking."

Muree'n adjusted her own fighting stick so that it matched Yazra'h's. "I'm *thinking* that I'll defeat you this time."

Yazra'h decided she should pummel some caution into the girl. She was a better fighter in every measureable way, but Muree'n's energy and enthusiasm often took her aback.

The staffs hammered together with a loud report, then again. Each end was a whirling blur, but somehow Muree'n anticipated Yazra'h's every move. Yazra'h pushed harder, tried new tricks.

Muree'n flailed and attacked. Finally, needing a momentary pause to catch her breath, Yazra'h clouted the girl on the side of the head and stunned her.

Reeling, Muree'n collapsed to sit heavily on one of the mirrored spheres, shaking her head. Yazra'h stepped aside. "Being impetuous isn't always the best strategy."

The halfbreed girl rubbed what would surely be a large bruise on her skull. "No, but it is unpredictable. It throws my enemies off balance."

"You might also find that you've thrown yourself off a cliff."

Muree'n laughed. "But then I would fly!"

Yazra'h knew that no matter how many times she defeated the girl, Muree'n would come back for another round. She had no humility, no fear, no caution—and Yazra'h could never train that out of the girl. Catching her breath, Yazra'h realized she would just have to make certain that Muree'n got into situations where those qualities were useful, rather than a detriment.

As Muree'n climbed back to her feet and held up her fighting staff, ready to pounce, Yazra'h noticed a figure standing nearby on the otherwise empty observing stand: Mage-Imperator Jora'h in his lush robes, with his long braid of office. Yazra'h turned to her father and bowed with respect. Muree'n was ready to strike when her opponent lost focus, until she spotted the Mage-Imperator as well.

The girl waved, and Jora'h raised his hand, obviously proud—and with good reason, Yazra'h knew . . . unfortunately, the Mage-Imperator's praise would not make Muree'n any easier to control.

FIFTEEN

PRINCE REYN

The trees on Theroc towered taller than most skyscrapers on Earth—or so Prince Reyn had heard. He would see for himself, soon enough. The worldforest conveyed a true feeling of vastness, but Theroc was just one of so many worlds in the Confederation. It was intimidating!

His sister Arita had visited many more worlds than he had, studying alien plants and fungi. Even now, she was off on an empty Klikiss planet studying sentient cacti. Reyn missed her. . . .

As the twenty-year-old son of King Peter and Queen Estarra, he had met many important diplomats, but he had not traveled much himself. Soon, though . . . He needed to see more, learn more, experience more if he was going to be the Confederation's next King.

The Confederation's official capital was here on Theroc. From there, the King and Queen guided the various planets and peoples in the human alliance. The main governing structure was a fungus-reef that covered large sections of an enormous worldtree. On six adjacent trees, smaller fungus-reefs formed Confederation office complexes and residential structures for visiting dignitaries. The hard shelf fungi growths had been hollowed out and turned into a city suspended above the ground, studded with balconies and openings at all levels.

After checking his chronometer, Reyn tightened the sash around his indigo tunic and set out. The fungus-reef structure bustled with business conversations, tourists. Jewel-winged insects flitted about, as well as flying contraptions made from discarded condorfly wings grafted onto engines.

Reyn rode the lift to the canopy, where the sky opened up and ships could land. The historian Anton Colicos would arrive soon from Ildira with his newly translated section of the Saga of Seven Suns, which he would present to the green priests.

Reyn's parents both had full schedules, but since Anton Colicos was an important visitor, King Peter had turned to his son. "Receive him with proper formalities, then take him to see Kennebar. The green priests will want him to start reading aloud to the trees right away. We'll hold a formal reception later in the evening—there's supposed to be a firefly storm tonight." Peter frowned as he saw what appeared to be hesitation on Reyn's face. "You'll do fine."

It was not hesitation, though. Reyn felt a shotgun blast of pain through his nerves, as if a set of white-hot wires had been yanked through his body with a swift, vicious jerk. He had to devote his full concentration to hide the pain, refusing to let his father see. He clenched his left hand, focused his thoughts there, forced the tremors to go away.

"Yes, I'll do fine," Reyn echoed, letting his father interpret the reluctance as shyness. "I'm sure I'll get along with Anton Colicos." Neither of his parents knew how much the pain increased month by month; he had managed to hide it from them so far. Only Arita knew, and she wasn't here. . . .

The canopy level was a vast prairie of interlocked worldtree fronds with some sections paved over so that spacecraft could land. Ships circled and hummed as they settled down. Silver observation towers directed traffic. As he watched, a cargo ship fired its engines and accelerated up to the stratosphere, unreeling a long vapor trail behind it.

Reyn watched three green priests board a bright shuttle, each one carrying a potted treeling, ready to set out as ambassadors or missionaries. Many green priests were leaving Theroc to offer their services to the Confederation, to private employers, and also to help spread the interconnected verdani mind.

Some distance from the paved landing zone, another group of green priests sat among the scattered fronds. Four emerald-skinned priests guided the acolytes, singing songs, telling tales, dictating histories and technical reports—any sort of information whatsoever—to the voraciously curious worldforest.

Reyn adjusted his tunic, checked the schedule, and saw that Anton Colicos's shuttle had already arrived, unexpectedly early—a regular supply transport, rather than a flashy Ildiran ship. Reyn knew he would see plenty of Ildiran architecture and vessels when he visited the alien empire. Soon.

The human scholar stood outside the shuttle holding a satchel, and Reyn recognized him from images. Anton wore loose and comfortable clothes, obviously of Ildiran manufacture. He blinked around him at the tall trees.

The historian was quite a celebrity, though he didn't seem to know his own importance. Reyn had read some of those books during his private tutoring—most students did.

Nervousness at meeting the man made his tremors increase. Reyn clenched his fist, pushed back the pain, and smiled as he came forward. "Anton Colicos, I am Prince Reynald of Theroc, son of King Peter and Queen Estarra. My parents dispatched me here to meet you."

With a smile, Anton held up his satchel. "I don't need any fancy reception, just want to present my work to the green priests. The man I'm supposed to meet is named Kennebar?"

"Kennebar leads a group of green priests, and he's very interested in your new translation, sir."

Anton chuckled. "A genuine Prince is calling me *sir*? No need for that. Why don't you just call me Anton, and I'll call you Reynald?"

"Better yet, call me Reyn. Everyone does." He was anxious to hear Anton talk about Ildira, since he would be visiting there soon. "How long will you be staying on Theroc?"

"Oh, just long enough to read a few hundred pages," Anton said. "I need to get back to Mijistra. We recently uncovered a treasure trove of ancient documents that tell stories nobody has seen in thousands of years, and I'm anxious to read more."

They made their way across the tree canopy toward the green priests sitting among the fronds. Reyn considered Kennebar a stiff man, so devoted to the trees that he himself seemed to be made of wood. The leader rose from his perch and balanced on a branch with his bare feet. His skin was a rich green, and he wore only a loincloth. His muscular body was dotted with tattoos that showed his areas of expertise. "Anton Colicos, we look forward to more of the Saga. The worldforest would find it most interesting if you read portions aloud yourself."

Anton lifted his satchel. "I have it ready here. I've read aloud to audiences before, though not usually to a group of *trees*."

Reyn smiled. "Well, these aren't just normal trees."

Anton smiled. "I know that very well."

Several other green priests gathered around Kennebar, silent and respectful. Reyn recognized Collin, a young man who had been very close with Arita, before the worldforest accepted him as a green priest and rejected her. The rest of the acolytes were children with pale or brown skin, but they all hoped to take the green someday when they were ready.

Kennebar nodded toward his followers. "This is what green priests should be doing, not flying off to sell themselves. We were made to serve the verdani, not human ambitions." He gave Reyn a brusque dismissal. "You may leave the historian with us. We will take care of him."

"He just got off the ship," Reyn said. "Maybe he'd like time to—"

Kennebar remained stern. "After a long trip, he will be pleased to energize himself out here in the open among the trees."

Reyn left the historian with the green priests and headed back down to the fungus-reef.

Peter and Estarra had the grand throne room to themselves. It was their habit to have at least one calm hour in the afternoon alone together. The fungus-reef walls were soft and warm, the throne room welcoming, yet spectacular.

Reyn's parents sat in ornate chairs, though they had changed out of the insect-wing and beetle-shell ornamentation that Therons expected of their leaders. (The Confederation favored more businesslike attire.)

When he joined them, Estarra stood and stretched. "We have lunch, Reyn—join us. How did you like the historian?"

"He's an intelligent man, very interesting." Reyn paused in front of the table where Theron fruits, nuts, and skewers of roasted insects had been laid out. He plucked one of his favorite beetles out of a buttery sauce, cracked it open, and sucked out the sweet meat.

Peter was a handsome man in his midforties with blond hair and blue eyes. Estarra was a dark-skinned beauty with lush hair wrapped in a nest of braids. Although theirs had been a political marriage of an unlikely pair, they had genuinely grown to love each other as they fought the powerful forces arrayed against them.

"We made all the travel preparations for you and arranged meetings with necessary officials on Earth," Peter said. "Deputy Cain will be your point of contact. Don't worry, he's a good man."

Estarra picked up a pair-pear, splitting it and handing the other half to Peter. "And Rlinda Kett should be back in her offices on Earth before long. You'll probably learn more from her than from any dull meetings. She's more enjoyable to be around than a bunch of politicians."

Reyn was quite fond of the big trader; he remembered her booming laugh and enthusiastic hugs from when he was just a little boy. He had other reasons for going to Earth, and much of his hope hinged on what connections he could make; he knew Rlinda could help him out.

Seated in a chair off to the side, old Father Idriss coughed, grumbled, and cleared his throat as he woke from his nap. Estarra's father scratched his big square-cut beard, which was now mostly gray instead of black. "Is it lunchtime already? I thought we were just in a meeting."

Peter laughed. "Don't worry I nearly fell asleep too."

"Ah, Reynald is here!" Idriss, the former leader of Theroc, leaned forward. "You don't remind me at all of my own son Reynald, young man, but it's still a good name. You'll live up to it. So, you're off to Ildira now?"

"Earth first, Grandfather. Then Ildira."

"Never been to Ildira." Idriss cleared his throat again and glanced at the table as if suddenly remembering. "Oh, is it lunchtime already?"

While Estarra made her father a plate of food, the old man turned to Reyn. "I am proud of you, you know. You'll be a good King." He looked around. "Where's my granddaughter?"

"Arita's still on the Klikiss world," Estarra reminded him.

"Ah. Don't like the Klikiss. I thought they were all gone? Well, I'm proud of her too. Tell her that next time she comes home."

Reyn wished he could see his sister before he departed; she knew the real reason he wanted to go to Earth. On the other hand, Arita would pester him about his symptoms and worry about him. He didn't want that either.

Arita couldn't understand why he wouldn't tell anyone about his declining health, but Reyn was a private person. He preferred to listen instead of talk, and he knew there was no treatment for his disease in the standard Theron and Confederation databases.

He also knew, however, that the Spiral Arm was vast and filled with more things than he could imagine. He intended to keep searching for a cure.

_____

SIXTEEN

The cactus-studded desert of the empty Klikiss world was so different from the lush worldforest. The skies of Eljiid were streaked with
tan from high levels of blown dust. On Theroc, Arita rarely ever saw
the sky unless she climbed up to the top of the canopy. Because of her
interest in studying plant species, the young woman had spent most of
her life on the jungle floor collecting specimens, cataloguing, sketching, or simply _enjoying_ the exotic flora.

And Theroc was just one planet out of many planets.

After she arrived on Eljiid, passing through the Klikiss transportal
from the busy hub of Rheindic Co, she claimed a spot in the sprawling research camp that had been established by teams of Confederation scholars. The air was crisp and dry, with an inherent chill; she
hoped her traditional Theron cocoonweave garments would be warm
enough, especially at night.

Several independent research teams worked on Eljiid, one of the
best preserved of the abandoned Klikiss worlds. Among the teams
were university scholars documenting the Klikiss ruins and the vanished insect race, architects studying the alien building materials,
transportal specialists monitoring the network of interdimensional
gateways. As far as Arita knew, she was the lone botanist.

When she got there, many of the camp areas were empty because
the researchers were still about their day's work, but others sat outside
their tents at tables or under awnings, writing reports, collating specimens. Many of these came out to greet the new arrival who came
through the transportal wall, and Arita tried to remember all their
names as they introduced themselves. She told them her first name,
but did not explain who she was.

Mr. Bolam, the camp administrator, knew that she was a Princess but did not want to be treated as such; he had been given strict preparation instructions, so he gave Arita no special treatment—per her own request. Because she was only nineteen, though, he treated her like a kid.

Arita didn't take long to recognize what sort of man Bolam was. He did not seem interested in the wonders of the alien ruins, the ancient site, even the desert landscape. He clearly didn't like being on Eljiid. Arita had read a quick summary of his career before traveling through the Klikiss transportal network. Bolam had fallen backward into this position, and the horizon of his ambitions was only an arm's length in front of his face. In running this encampment, he had reached the peak of his abilities.

Arita did not need the administrator to pamper her, nor even to be friendly to her. She had come to Eljiid to investigate the armored succulents, spiny cacti, and tortured-looking Joshua tree analogues—and the Whistlers, which fascinated her most. She would keep herself busy.

After she dropped off her packs and activated the self-erecting tent, Arita looked around her site. At a nearby spot, a desert geologist named Kam Pellieri sat sorting rock samples. He gave her an approving thumbs-up, as if she had done something commendable just by coming here.

Mr. Bolam checked out Arita's meager camp setup and asked if she needed anything. "Just need time to explore," she answered. "I'm self-sufficient."

Bolam put his hands on his waist. "In this place, we all have to be. Eljiid's not actually on the tourist route."

Because Arita came from King Peter and Queen Estarra, she did have a few official duties for the Confederation before starting her work. "Could you please take me to the grave of Margaret Colicos?"

Bolam nodded. "I figured you'd want to see that. Why else would King Peter send his daughter here?"

"My father didn't send me. I asked to come—for the Whistlers."

Bolam rolled his eyes. "Nobody can figure out those creepy things. Not that anyone's tried very hard." He cocked his ear and fell silent for a moment. "You can hear them when the wind picks up, but it's quiet now."

"I'll go out to the Whistler forest and explore later, but first, I have a plaque. . . ." She squatted in front of the self-erecting tent, rummaged in her pack, and withdrew the engraved, lightweight memorial. "Margaret Colicos did a great service for humanity, and she deserves to be honored."

Bolam scratched his left cheek where he had missed a patch while shaving. "The grave's not much to look at, really. That was before my time here."

"The importance is in the woman, not the grave," Arita said.

Eljiid was a typical Klikiss world, now known primarily for the fact that Margaret Colicos had died here. The xeno-archaeologist had spent the last years of her life studying the Klikiss, before the Breedex announced it was abandoning the Spiral Arm forever. The insect aliens had departed through the transportal network on a mass migration, leaving behind numerous old drones, whose mummified husks now littered the ruins on many planets, such as this one.

Margaret Colicos had been buried outside one of the tall structures of the empty hive city. Rocks piled around the grave were neatly arranged; many more had been stacked high, and the stack looked fresh. Arita wondered if Bolam had added to the mound after learning she was coming. Margaret's name had been laser-etched into a smooth stone, but Arita's plaque was more impressive.

She found an appropriate place to set the new marker she had brought, and she read the plaque aloud, because it seemed like the thing to do. "Margaret Colicos, beloved wife and mother, respected researcher, deep thinker, hero of humanity. Her work changed our understanding of more than one race."

She paused, not sure if Bolam wanted to add anything. Apparently he didn't. "This marker is just a symbol of our gratitude and respect for her work. Replicas of this plaque will be displayed on Theroc and on Earth. The worldforest itself holds all of her writings and will preserve them." Arita took an image of the gravesite with its new marker to show her parents.

Having done what she'd promised to do, Arita returned to the main camp settlement. It was late in the afternoon, and though she was anxious to get started, she felt tired from the trip.

The research teams returned from the Klikiss ruins or from dig sites or meteorological stations, settling back into the camp for the end of the day. Arita learned that one crew of architectural specialists, led by Tarker and Orfino, was analyzing the ruined mounds and spires to see what they could adapt for buildings on human colonies. None of the research teams worked with any sense of urgency, Arita realized. University funding was low, their needs were modest, and they could stay in this camp for years. Their funders likely had minimal expectations.

Some of the visitors were even prospectors hoping to strike it rich with a find of prisdiamonds, naturally occurring fire crystals, even a practical though unglamorous strike of useful metals. When the Klikiss had lived on this planet, they'd done little to exploit its natural resources. The insect race had been intent only on wiping out and devouring their rivals.

While Arita settled in for a quiet evening in front of her tent, Pellieri made a large pot of delicious-smelling soup. Other researchers offered supplies from their own stockpiles, and he happily accepted the gifts to make a more complex stew. Arita had brought packaged rations with her, but Pellieri's soup smelled wonderful.

"I like to cook," he told her with a smile, "and they like to let me. We all benefit, and they take some of my other chores. You're welcome to stick to your pre-packs, though, if you want."

Arita chose the soup instead.

Tarker and Orfino were a middle-aged couple who had worked together for years. They set up a game board painted with geometrical patterns, and engaged in a confusing play with square pieces and flat disks. They invited Arita to join them, showing her the general rules, but she never quite grasped the strategy.

Lara Vanh, who had studied empty Klikiss cities on other worlds, sat in the gathering darkness with a stringed instrument on her knee, playing a pleasant, ethereal melody. All the researchers seemed comfortable with one another, giving company and personal space at the same time.

Full dark had set in when the Klikiss transportal at the edge of the camp shimmered. The flat stone window grew murky and sharpened into transparency as a man stepped through, unscheduled and unannounced. He was tall and incredibly lean, dark-skinned, with high cheekbones and sunken cheeks. His tight polymer bodysuit looked more like a film of armor than clothing. The newcomer shouldered a pack and looked around with eyes as focused as cameras taking snap-shots of all details.

Bolam hustled forward to greet the stranger. Arita remained by her tent, wondering how often casual visitors showed up on Eljiid. The man spoke to Bolam. "My name is Tom Rom. I'm here to study the Klikiss."

"Another Klikiss research expedition? I wasn't informed about this."

Tom Rom seemed unfazed. "I didn't know I was required to let you know. No one owns the Eljiid ruins and the Klikiss bodies left behind."

"No, no, of course not. I just like to keep track, that's all. It's part of my organizational duties. What institution sponsors your work? Maybe your research will dovetail with some of our university teams. Perhaps Lara Vanh?"

Tom Rom looked at him. "I don't think so. I work alone. My research is privately funded."

Bolam did not argue with the oddly intimidating man. "As you wish. Don't expect any formal help, though. Our resources here are limited."

"Not asking for help. In fact this was the emptiest Klikiss world I could track down that suited our purposes. If there was an emptier one, I would've gone there."

Bolam gestured around the camp, as if Tom Rom had asked for advice or permission. "We have a community area over there. Those water pumps are for everyone's use. You can set up your tent wherever you like."

"Yes, I'll do whatever I like." He headed away from the settlement into the deepening twilight without even a glance over his shoulder.

Arita watched him under the camp lights, envying the stranger's con-fidence. She began jotting down notes, making plans on how she would map out the Whistler forest near the hive city ruins. If she kept doing her work as a naturalist, maybe someday the verdani would reconsider and give her a second chance to take the green.

She and her childhood friend Collin had made up their minds at an early age that they would become green priests. She'd been so dedicated as an acolyte . . . and yet the trees chose Collin but not her, and in the process they did strange things to her head. Their rejection had damaged Arita, but she would not be defeated. . . .

Near the base of the Klikiss structures, thorny thickets filled the arroyos. As night breezes stirred the thicket, she heard an eerie whisper now, a song that was like a murmur of conversation in a large crowd, but with a lyrical quality.

The Whistlers were an unusual species of cactus with hollow woody stems dotted with holes, which the winds of Eljiid played like a natural flute. The cacti exuded the strong chemical stench of an alkaloid toxin that was rumored to cause unpleasant side effects, although no one had done a thorough study.

There was some evidence—perhaps wishful thinking, perhaps just overactive imaginations—that the Whistlers communicated through chemical traces in the air and through their root systems. That communication manifested through modulated tones in the wind. And though Arita didn't want to admit it, her fascination went beyond mere scientific interest. She hoped the Whistlers could help her. . . .

Bolam came up to her, making sure she heard the sounds. "Wait until the wind whips up, then you'll really hear a symphony. I think it's just noise myself, a coincidence, but some folks call it communication." He chuckled in an abrasive voice, and Arita heard no humor there. "Though I couldn't imagine what a bunch of cactus has to talk about! 'Dry weather today, isn't it?' 'How are your spines doing?' 'Looks like rain.' " He snorted.

Arita kept staring toward the spiny thicket. She pointed out, "The verdani have insightful conversations with green priests."

Bolam shrugged. "Sure, but those are the worldtrees. That's different."

Different, Arita thought, but she hoped not too different. If there was some connection between the Whistlers and the worldtrees, maybe she could find a way. . . .

SEVENTEEN

TASIA TAMBLYN

Part of the binary planet loomed in the sky overhead, fissured and cratered, as if ready to fall on top of them.

Tasia Tamblyn flew the *Voracious Curiosity* on its final approach to the Sheol landing structure. Although Rlinda Kett wanted to pilot her famous old vessel for the meeting with Lee Iswander, after hitting severe thermal storms in the atmosphere, she quickly handed over the piloting chores. "This has ceased to be fun, Tamblyn," Rlinda said. "I'll bow out in favor of a better pilot."

"What do you mean a better pilot? I'm the *best* pilot." As Tasia white-knuckled the ship down, she secretly allowed a bit of buffeting—just to give them a good ride.

Robb Brindle saw what his wife was doing and muttered, "You don't need to impress Rlinda."

She blinked her eyes innocently. "I was trying to impress you, dear man."

Rlinda was neither frightened nor impressed. "I know damn well what Tamblyn's capable of, and I've flown through rougher conditions than this myself. Let's stick to business. We've already caused some consternation by showing up a day early."

"I thought that was the intended effect," Robb said.

"Exactly."

Below, the molten sea churned and swirled. A cascade of lava spewed up, ejecting globules high enough that they cooled and hardened in the air. Tasia gave the scarlet spray a wide berth.

Rlinda looked around. "This is for anyone who ever told me to go to hell—they can't say I didn't listen."

Tasia admired the fact that Iswander had built a thriving industrial operation here. In the past, many clans had eked out an existence in ferociously inhospitable environments, but they had softened much in the past twenty years. "Roamers don't have to do such risky work anymore, but it looks like Iswander made it a viable operation." She settled the *Curiosity* down on the landing deck, where workers in heat-armor would load the ship with cargo.

When the shielded heat tube connected to the *Curiosity*'s hatch, Rlinda led the way into Tower One. She still owned Kett Shipping, but rarely involved herself in day-to-day operations now, letting Robb and Tasia handle the business. Tasia came from the well-known Tamblyn clan, Roamers who had operated the water mines on Plumas for generations. And Robb Brindle was the son of General Conrad Brindle, the former EDF commander. Together, they were well suited to run Rlinda's shipping company.

The big woman entered the administrative deck of Tower One, waving at the workers as if she were throwing a party. Through the thick observation ports Tasia scanned the large, roving foundries outside, and was astonished to spot two armored workers riding lava sleds over the sluggish waves to inspect the pumping and hardening apparatus.

Deputy Alec Pannebaker came up as she marveled. "I can take you out on one if you like. It's a lot of fun."

"Looks dangerous."

Pannebaker shrugged and repeated, "It's a lot of fun."

Lee Iswander arrived, shook hands, and introduced himself; Tasia recognized him from his appearances before the clans. As he took them toward his office deck, she thought Iswander had a harried look, but he covered it well. He said, "I'm glad you arrived early, Captain Kett. Our supplies are ready to be loaded, and I want to make sure that this delivery gets to Newstation in time."

"Guaranteed, Mr. Iswander," Rlinda said. "You need to make an impressive showing to prove to the clans that you're a good businessman, an innovative manufacturer, and a true Roamer."

Iswander chuckled. "Sounds like a speech I should be giving."

"I could hire myself out as a speech writer," Rlinda said. "Reasonable rates. I'm a woman of many talents."

He clasped his hands in front of him. "It's no secret that I've thrown my name into the ring to become the next Speaker. With a cargo load of ultra-pure ingots, exotic metal foams, energy films, and alloy polymers, everyone on Newstation will be able to see what I have to offer."

"We're also sending hundreds of spectacular images," Pannebaker added. "You never know, it might even bring some tourists."

Rlinda walked around the office deck with her rolling gait. "For the next important question, what sort of food do you have around here? You must have a commissary."

"There's a cafeteria," Iswander said. "It's adequate, I suppose."

Rlinda let out a loud huff. "Adequate is never good enough. Let me see your kitchens, maybe make some helpful suggestions."

Tasia laughed. Rlinda never seemed to change.

Robb interrupted, "I've already set up a proposed schedule of cargo runs from here to Newstation, Ulio, and Earth—a regular flow of Kett Shipping vessels coming to deliver whatever materials you have to trade."

"We'll put the *Verne* in the loop as one of the first ships," Tasia suggested. "I doubt Xander and Terry have marked off Sheol on their lists yet." It was important to think of their own son when opportunities arose.

During the Elemental War, she and Robb had been separated from each other for so long that they'd made up for lost time as soon as the war was over. They went on a honeymoon to see nebulas, gas giants, the trees of Theroc, the ruins of the Prism Palace, and the recovering operations on Plumas, which technically belonged to Tasia and her brother Jess, but Jess had his Academ school with Cesca, and Tasia happily ceded the operations to a distant cousin.

She was a Roamer through and through, and she needed to be free to do what she wanted. As a teenager, she had run away from home to join the Earth Defense Forces as a gesture of rebellion, and then she'd been stuck in a military career. Only later had she seen the irony of trading the comparative freedom of her teen years for a life of training, service, rule-following, and "Yes, sirs" up and down the chain of command (and "chain" was the right word for it, because it certainly bound people to do unreasonable things). After the end of the war, she hadn't wanted any more of that.

Robb, raised in the military under his career-officer parents, had always thought his life would be centered on the EDF. He signed up, completed his training, did his duty, fought the enemy . . . and ended up spending a relative eternity as a hydrogue prisoner. Afterward, he had plenty of doubts. He didn't think his core loyalty had changed, but the governments that claimed his loyalty were no longer the same.

Captain Rlinda Kett had offered the couple the *Voracious Curiosity* and asked if they wanted to be the first pilots in her new shipping company. They accepted, without mentioning that Tasia was pregnant. Their son Xander had been born on board ship, because Tasia incorrectly believed she could make one more run to the Rendezvous reconstruction site before her due date, and when her hard labor started, they couldn't get to a medical facility fast enough. On that chaotic day Robb frantically read medical databases about birthing, and Tasia told him to *solve the problem* as she went into heavy contractions. "Or do I have to deliver this baby myself?"

"You have to do most of it, but I'm right here with you." At that point, she wished she had gotten another compy after all, because Robb certainly needed the help. Medically speaking, the birth was not difficult (though Tasia took exception with the characterization). The baby was healthy.

They had agreed on Alexander for the boy's name; Robb wanted to call him Alex, Tasia wanted to call him Xander . . . so they compromised and called him Xander. Not surprisingly, the young man was an instinctive pilot, since he'd spent his whole life aboard ships.

Now, in the Iswander Industries offices, Robb handled the inventory and paperwork for the new shipment, as well as the schedule for expanded commercial deliveries of Sheol metallurgy products. Rlinda planned to show off for the crew of magma harvesters by cooking them a meal unlike anything they'd ever had before.

Meanwhile, Tasia asked Deputy Pannebaker to show her how to suit up in the thermal armor, so she could go outside and supervise the loading of metals aboard the *Curiosity*. Pannebaker suggested again that they go lava sledding, but she turned him down. "Work to do. Maybe on our next visit."

She put down the glare shield on her helmet and exited, with Pannebaker following in his own armor suit. The storm of heat and fire around them seemed to be Sheol's natural state. Exposed, the *Curiosity* sat on the raised landing deck, connected by the safe access tube. Worker compies and suited crew used antigrav clamps to bring load after load of packaged metals into the hold.

As tons of product were loaded aboard, Pannebaker kept up a running commentary and explained the operations in the three towers.

Tasia realized that the deck felt uncertain beneath her boots. She stomped down, saw that her heel left a clear impression in the metal. "Is it supposed to be this soft?" Then as she watched in amazement, the *Curiosity* slid several inches. "Shizz, the landing deck is tilting!"

The startled workers stopped loading the *Curiosity*. "We're off-level, that's for sure." Pannebaker clicked his general-comm signal. "Must be closer to material tolerances than I thought."

Nearby, another lava geyser spurted—bright yellow with a core of white.

"You sure this is safe?" Tasia asked.

In his bulky thermal armor, Pannebaker lumbered to the shielded control shack, and she followed, tilting her helmet for a last glance at the half planet looming above like a boot about to smash them.

Once the shack door was sealed and coolant jets dropped the temperature down to acceptable levels, Pannebaker slipped open his face shield, disengaged his thick gloves. Curls of steam drifted around them. Pannebaker called up a summary on his screens. "There's a massive thermal plume upwelling from below—much hotter than we've seen before."

"The facility has heat shielding, doesn't it?"

"Shielding, yes—but these peak temperatures might compromise our bedrock support struts. The three towers were built with high tolerances, sure, but in a plume this hot they might soften and bend."

Workers outside scrambled for shelter on the raised landing deck while the compies retreated. The *Curiosity* slid another few inches.

Out on the molten sea, one of the enormous smelter barges began to founder. The crew boss yelled over the open comm so all employees could hear, "This is an emergency. Thermal breach in our lower hull!"

EIGHTEEN

ELISA REEVES

She found Garrison's ship surrounded by the mysterious nodules drifting in empty space. The vessel's running lights were on, but Elisa didn't think he had detected her yet. Not surprisingly, he'd let his guard down. Why would anyone be watchful for a ship out here, so far from the nearest star system? He must have thought this was a perfect hiding place.

Noticing carbonization on the hull, burned-out station lights, and other indicators of damage, she wondered what sort of trouble Garrison had gotten into. It looked as if the ship had been in a fight. Elisa narrowed her eyes as she ran scans. He'd better not have let any harm come to Seth.

Not bothering to think through her words, she activated the comm. "Garrison, don't make this harder on yourself."

Seth's image appeared on the screen, surprised and confused. The boy seemed different, but she wasn't sure how. Elisa tried to remember the last time she had really looked at him. "Mother! You found the bloaters too."

Bloaters? What were they?

When Garrison came on the screen, he didn't look angry or frightened, just resolute. "I thought you might be following us. When I found your magnetic tracker, I couldn't believe it, but after all these years of knowing you, I don't know why I was surprised."

"I knew you well enough that I could guess what you'd do. If I'd been more prepared, I would have stopped you."

Garrison frowned. "I had to get Seth away from Sheol. You and Iswander kept ignoring the warnings."

"You stole my son!"

"*Our* son," he corrected in a calm voice. "I wish you had left with us. We could have stayed together as a family, but you made your choice—and I made mine."

Having studied the specs en route, she knew that the weapons on her ship were better than those on his stolen vessel. Elisa knew exactly how to cripple his ship. "I'm taking him back with me. You proved you're an unfit father by kidnapping him."

She tried to bait Garrison, make him lose his temper in front of Seth, but he wouldn't rise to it. "Provided Seth doesn't go back to that place, we can work out a resolution. My priority is keeping him safe."

"He's coming with me. That is nonnegotiable." She nudged her ship closer, trying to think of how she would strengthen her relationship with her son, make life better for him on Sheol, make him love her more. She might even let him have his own compy.

Garrison regarded her on the screen, and for a moment his features looked just like the image of Seth she kept on display. "He's not a trophy you can claim in order to prove you've won something." His stolen vessel drifted in among the bloated nodules, trying to hide. One of the nuclei flashed, and the sudden flare of light distracted her. "I'm not going to make him choose."

"I didn't ask him to choose—he's going home with me! I warn you, I can damage your engines with a single shot and then take him to safety."

Two small, defensive jazers would be sufficient to take his stardrive offline. Lee Iswander's ships had to be able to protect themselves against marauders; as a powerful and wealthy industrialist, he'd learned how to protect what he had, and Elisa had learned from him. Garrison wouldn't stand a chance.

"We could find a neutral place," he said. "Seth is old enough to go to Academ. It would do him good to be among other kids his age. We can send him there, work things out."

"You might want to shirk your responsibilities, but he's coming with me. I'm his mother."

He maneuvered his ship through the mysterious bloaters, dodging out of sight. He was trying to lose himself, and Elisa accelerated after him. She tried to lock in on his engines for a disabling strike.

He sounded disappointed on the comm. "I thought that's what

you'd say, but I wanted to make sure I tried everything. We got rid of your tracker—you can't follow us." He powered up his engines and began to move, dodging the island-sized nodules as he gained speed.

"Damn you, Garrison!" She plunged after him, looking for a good shot to damage his engines. "I'm warning you!"

His parting message enraged her. "I've had plenty of warnings, and I know which ones to listen to."

He didn't take her seriously! He was forcing her to do this. She tracked ahead and fired a warning shot across his bow. The jazers lanced out like javelins, magnetically bound high-energy beams.

When the beam struck one of the bobbing globules, the sphere erupted like a supernova. The explosion was more than just an out-pouring of fire and energy: the detonating bloater ignited an adjacent bloater, then another one, like firecrackers in a chain-reaction inferno.

The shock wave engulfed her ship.

NINETEEN

LEE ISWANDER

Surging heat plumes turned Sheol's red magma into an angry yellow-white storm. Iswander stared at the horrific beauty from his tower windows while the harpy song of alarms shrieked from dozens of systems.

Rlinda Kett began heading for the door of the office deck. "I know shit hitting the fan when I see it. You have an evacuation protocol?"

Iswander hadn't been able to study the cautionary report Pannebaker prepared, and he needed more time to develop a modified emergency response plan. "The situation might be beyond the scenarios we modeled."

Rlinda looked at him in astonishment. "You live in . . . *this* and you aren't ready to evacuate on a moment's notice?"

Iswander was scanning the reports on the screens, the stranded smelter barge with the breached hull. He forced down panic. "Let's not go overboard, Captain Kett. Everything here was built to withstand the heat."

The structure of Tower One began to groan. As the ceramic-metal pilings were heated beyond their tolerance levels, the deck shifted noticeably. Iswander grabbed his desk for balance and activated the comm. He broadcast over the full-facility loudspeakers. "This is Lee Iswander, activating emergency protocols. Team leaders, get your crews to safety. Take emergency shelter precautions. Go into your bolt-holes if necessary. I want structural integrity reports for Towers One, Two, and Three. We'll have evacuation ships on standby if this gets worse."

Iswander knew how to keep awkward information confidential, but he was going to have to rely on every possible option now. He turned to the trader woman. "We don't have enough ships for an immediate and total evacuation—not nearly enough." Didn't budget for it, didn't plan for it—but he wasn't going to say that. "We did not foresee any circumstance that would require us to abandon the facility completely."

But Garrison Reeves had warned of this. All of his employees knew that Iswander had received, and dismissed, the man's warning. Now he had to salvage the situation, or he was going to look terrible.

The material tolerances *should* hold, unless the heat grew significantly worse.

His five enormous smelter barges had the best hull shielding, and he hoped they could withstand the increased heat from the plume, even though one was already foundering, taking on magma in the lower compartments. Iswander contacted the other four barge pilots. "Do you have room for evacuees? We might need you to carry a few dozen people until this simmers down."

One of the barge pilots responded, "I don't like the readings from our hull, Mr. Iswander. We're well into the red zone and softening up here ourselves."

Iswander pounded on the transmit button. "And I don't like the readings from Tower Three! Get over there and rescue as many as you can."

A second barge pilot broke in. "Will do, sir, but just because these barges look big doesn't mean we have any spare room. Most of the vessel is for lava processing and metal storage. Only a few small chambers on the bridge level are shielded enough for habitation."

"Understood." He should have planned better, should have paid attention to worse-case scenarios no matter how problematic they might be. He'd been reluctant to listen to Garrison's paranoia, more intent on quieting the rumors and keeping the workers calm than on assessing the problem. Dammit! These structural materials should stand up to the thermal stresses! It was in the design. He was supposed to be able to rely on his people when they gave him assessments.

The Tower Three supervisor called in, "We're tilting at an alarming angle here. Our struts are buckling."

Through the window wall of the admin deck, Iswander saw cumbersome smelter barges lurch toward Tower Three. He had 450 people in that structure, and if each barge could take only a dozen or so refu-gees under the best circumstances ... Maybe it wouldn't collapse. Maybe the material strength and heat tolerance were higher than projected.

Maybe that was wishful thinking.

Tower One began to groan again. A keepsake beverage mug from Iswander's son slid off the smooth desktop and thumped on the floor.

"You've got one more ship." Rlinda activated her comm. "Tamb-lyn, we need the *Curiosity*. Dump whatever cargo you've loaded and hook up to the Tower One heat tube. It's going to be standing room only, but we'll get all the people aboard that we can."

Tasia responded, "Going to the cockpit right now to prep. Robb is over there—make sure he gets aboard."

Standing near the windowport, Iswander could see the rippling sur-face of the landing deck. Blistering heat radiated through the special insulated glass. Three empty company ships were in shielded struc-tures on the landing platform, along with his own private cruiser. He switched his desk comm to a secure channel. If the disaster grew worse, he had to set priorities. "Mr. Pannebaker, get my wife and son to our cruiser and take off. Once I know that they're safe, I can better deal with the crisis here."

Rlinda added, "If you don't have enough lifeboats for everyone, you'd better cram your cruiser as full as you can. That's another twenty people? Thirty? We'll need every spot."

Iswander was more angry than panicked. This wasn't supposed to be happening. His engineers had guaranteed him that these structures were safe! Geologists had analyzed the tidal stresses, the magma tem-peratures; materials scientists had approved the tolerance levels of the ceramic-metal composites. This should not have been a problem!

Tower Three transmitted dozens of alarms, and the supervisor grew more panicked. The first smelter barge approached the distressed tower, positioning itself so it could link with the access hatch and take on a group of evacuees.

The Tower Two supervisor called out, "Save room for us! Our sys-tems are already failing."

Robb Brindle rushed in from the records vault, breathless. "What's going on?" At the window wall, he watched the *Voracious Curiosity* lift off from the raised landing deck and circle around. "Where's Tasia going?"

As soon as the ship was in the air, the cargo hatch opened. Pallets of specialized metal products, foams, ceramic alloys, and stacked ingots tumbled out like discarded garbage, falling into the broiling yellow soup of molten rock. The *Curiosity* came back, buffeted from side to side as a thermal hurricane stirred the air.

Tasia Tamblyn's voice came over the comm. "I'll land on the deck close to the access tube, but even the platform looks questionable to me."

Iswander sounded a full-fledged evacuation. Personnel in Tower One were to fill the ships waiting on the landing deck. It was complete chaos.

The facility comm lines were a chatter of overlapping queries, shouts, and contradictory orders. On the private channel, Pannebaker broke in, "Londa and Arden are aboard your cruiser, Chief, and we fit twenty other people aboard. If we stick around, I could maybe take five more, but—"

"I want them safe *now*." Iswander no longer had any faith in safety margins.

"Understood, Chief."

The private cruiser lifted off into the smoke-stirred sky just in time for Tasia Tamblyn to land the *Curiosity* on the open grid next to the access tube. "All right, we're open for business. Get people aboard."

Iswander dispatched a pair of large company ships over to Tower Two to rescue maybe a hundred more workers. It wouldn't be enough, but he had no more ships to give. He promised to send more nevertheless, reassuring the doomed people.

When the first vessel landed on the Tower Two access deck, though, the evac hatch wouldn't open. "It's fused shut!" the pilot cried.

The tower supervisor yelled through the static-filled comm, "We have to get out of here!"

"Send your compies to assist the evac ships," Iswander said. "We've got twenty of them outside now." The special heat-shielded robots were designed for maintenance of external systems and they should be able to withstand the conditions. He just didn't know if they could do any good.

The smooth, shielded compies crawled outside Tower Two and worked their way to the fused evac hatch. Blunt-headed models manufactured to endure extreme heat, they looked more like beetles than miniature humans. The robots scuttled around the hatch, using their specialized tools to attack controls that had melted shut.

"We're working on the problem," Iswander said to Tower Two in his cool administrator voice. "Stand by." He felt light-headed, and sweat prickled on his forehead.

One of the smelter barges finally attached to the evacuation hatch on the bottom deck of Tower Three. As the remaining three barges closed in, one veered off, declaring an emergency just like the first stranded barge. "Lower hull breach! Lava flooding the lower chambers. We're going to get cooked in here."

Iswander didn't know what to do. "Your habitation chambers are insulated. Just hold on." His hopeful words sounded empty, but the desperate workers clung to them because they had no other choice.

Moments later, Tower Three collapsed and came crashing down into the lava.

TWENTY

GENERAL NALANI KEAH

It was just a routine patrol for the Confederation Defense Forces. The Juggernaut *Kutuzov* led a battle group of ten smaller Manta cruisers. General Nalani Keah sat in the command chair on the flagship's bridge—*her* bridge. *Her* battleship.

She'd even given the big vessel its name after Field Marshal Mikhail Kutuzov, one of the military heroes she'd studied in the history of warfare. Whenever someone asked, Keah would give a full description of Kutuzov's military career, his suppression of the Bar Confederation uprising, fighting in three Russo-Turkish wars, and of course his battles against Napoleon at Borodinō and Austerlitz. She could give many colorful details, story after story of Kutuzov's career and exploits, but very few people were actually interested in old military history.

Those who did study the records were interested in more recent events, such as the Elemental War and the Klikiss invasion, but Keah had lived through those events herself when she was an up-and-coming officer in the Earth Defense Forces. She had been there at Earth facing off against the Klikiss swarmships when sabotage ripped through the new EDF battleships, destroying the human defensive line and killing half of her crewmates.

That wasn't *history* to her; she wasn't that old! She preferred her military history to involve sailing ships, cannons, horses, and cavalry.

"Arriving at Rheindic Co," said Lieutenant Tait, at the helm.

"Right on time," Keah said. "Check with the transportal transfer station down there. Make sure all is well." Rheindic Co served as a hub for those using the alien transportal network to travel among the connected planets.

"Yes, General. That's the reason we're here."

She was sure the crew didn't believe it. They all kept up the polite fiction, played their roles, did their duties, and got high marks in their personnel files when each mission was over.

Unlike her predecessors running the EDF, now the CDF, Keah preferred to have a mobile command, engaging in practical exercises like this. The best times in her life had been aboard ships, doing hands-on military business, grooming herself for promotions and more command responsibility, while staying far away from offices and bureaucracy.

Nalani Keah was tall, six feet five inches, with long blue-black hair, Asian features blended with islander features (although she had, in fact, been born at the EDF base on Mars). Raised as a military brat, she had been transferred often in her youth, seen a lot of installations (all basically the same), made a lot of friends (although shallow ones), and enlisted, as expected.

The comm officer touched his implanted microphone. "Rheindic Co says all is well, General. Transportal functioning normally, travelers flowing through as usual. Oh, and they say thanks for checking on them."

"All in a day's work for the CDF, Mr. Aragao." She turned to her sensor technician. "Lieutenant Saliba, please run a complete scan of the system. Keep your eyes open."

The female sensor tech looked up. "For what purpose, General?"

Keah arched her eyebrows. "For the purpose of keeping you busy! Or would you rather use a fingerbrush to clean out every reclamation stall on this ship while contemplating why a bridge crew officer doesn't have any business nitpicking orders?"

"I understand, General," Saliba said, cowed. "I was only asking for clarification as to *what* you're looking for, so I could adjust the sensors accordingly."

"So you only search for what you're already expecting to find? That's a recipe for disaster."

The woman flushed and looked away. "Scanning now, General. Looking for anything unusual . . . nothing. The system is clear."

From the helm, Lieutenant Tait said, "Should I plot a course for the next system on our patrol route?"

"Don't bother. We're staying here." Several members of the bridge crew *almost* asked why, but then remembered not to.

General Keah looked at the chronometer. Another ten minutes and she would be annoyed. "Come on, Z," she muttered. "You're spoiling my surprise."

"General!" Saliba cried. "Sensor traces. Large ships just entered the system—seven of them. Checking sensor profile, matching configurations now. I'll have an identification soon."

"The fact that they're traveling in a group of seven should give you a hint. Ildirans always travel in sevens." Keah didn't bother to hide her satisfied smile. "Battle stations!"

"Confirmed," said Weapons Officer Patton. "Seven warliners, entering attack formation. Weapons powering up!"

"Defense protocol twelve—you've all been briefed, and you've run simulations. Remora pilots, to your spacecraft and prepare to launch."

"But, General, we have no conflict with the Solar Navy—"

"Does it look like we have no conflict with them? Jazer banks active. Set shields on full."

Mr. Aragao hovered over his communications station. "Should I open a commline, General? It's . . . it's Adar Zan'nh himself."

"Only after we've got our defenses set. I don't want the *Kutuzov* blasted to atoms while we're saying hello."

Her bridge crew scrambled to their duties, and the remaining ships in the CDF battle group took positions. The ten Manta cruisers spread out, shifting places, per orders, while the seven Ildiran warliners arrived in a precise wheel pattern, with the Adar's flagship in the dead center. It was very pretty and strategically stupid, Keah thought. Just what she expected.

The commander of the Ildiran Solar Navy appeared on the screen. He wore his formal military jacket, bedecked with sparkling medals; his topknot had been arranged neatly in place. "General Nalani Keah." His voice sounded flat and dry, as if he had recorded it himself earlier and practiced lip-syncing. "I am Adar Zan'nh."

He was really getting into the show. Keah rolled her eyes at the absurd comment and couldn't resist a comeback of her own. "I recognize you. I have a pack of *Identify Famous Ildirans* trading cards. It wouldn't be complete without your picture."

Zan'nh didn't smile at the joke. "With this septa of warliners, I will seize your battle group and lay claim to the transportal nexus world Rheindic Co in the name of the Ildiran Empire."

Her bridge crew couldn't hold back their cries of dismay, groans, and even a few catcalls.

"I think not, Adar," Keah said. "I could make my point by blowing you to pieces, but all that debris would form a navigational hazard around a perfectly viable world. I've got ten battleships here to your seven."

Zan'nh was unimpressed. "My warliners outgun you."

"My ships are still better. Mr. Patton, power up jazer banks. Remora squads, deploy according to your orders. Manta cruisers, take your new positions—just don't hit each other."

Six hundred Remora fighter craft spewed out of the launching bays of the ten CDF ships. The Mantas spun and circled while the gaudy alien warships remained in perfect, precise formation. Adar Zan'nh's warliners extended their solar-panel wings, which made them look fierce and intimidating.

Keah just snorted. "It's all for show, and it makes them bigger targets. Paint 'em up. Fire at will!" Then she added, though it should not have been necessary, "And don't forget, *simulated* charges only." Most had figured out already that this was a joint war-game exercise, but considering how wound up her battle group was, the reminder didn't hurt.

Three Manta cruisers rotated to take up blocking positions in front of the *Kutuzov,* which prevented Keah from firing as much as she liked, but since the object of the game was to disable and capture the opposing team's flagship, it was strategically necessary to protect her Juggernaut at all costs.

The other seven Mantas, meanwhile, launched a flurry of potshots at their Ildiran counterparts. Hundreds of Remoras flew out like a maddened swarm of honeybees, completely random and unpredictable.

Keah leaned back in her command chair, watching. The bridge crew might as well learn something, she decided. "Ildirans can't stand anything that has no pattern. By letting our pilots choose their own targets, and telling the Manta commanders to head toward the end-goal however they see fit, Adar Zan'nh can't predict what he's facing, nor can he formulate a defense on the fly. Believe me, this is an important lesson for the Ildirans." She didn't even try to hide her smile. "And I am very honored to teach him."

Over the next hour, the tallies of hits and kills piled up. Once Remora pilots were struck and declared destroyed, they limped back to their launching bays. For a fully realistic scenario, the dead ships should have been left on the space battlefield, where they would become hazards, but General Keah didn't want to overwhelm the Ildirans. Adar Zan'nh could learn one step at a time.

Although she lost five of her Mantas due to bombardment, their shields depleted, her Juggernaut was virtually unscathed. Four of the Solar Navy warliners were also offline, and the fifth one was nearly spent. The Adar's flagship had been damaged as well, but not severely.

When General Keah finally grew tired of the game and decided to lock up her victory, she sent a tight signal to the three nearly depleted Mantas that huddled around the *Kutuzov* as a defense. "On my signal, drop out of the way. You'd better clear fast, or you'll be in the crossfire and wreck my shot." She turned to her weapons officer. "Mr. Patton, I want all of the *Kutuzov*'s jazers ready to fire at once, on my command. I don't care if it depletes our batteries. One shot will be enough—if it works."

When General Keah gave the order, the Mantas fell away and accelerated, leaving the *Kutuzov* exposed—and ready to fire. "Now!"

The Juggernaut's full array of energy weapons painted the flagship warliner, running down the Adar's remaining score within seconds. Keah smiled and mouthed, "Boom!"

After the engagement, it was her turn to invite Zan'nh over to the *Kutuzov*. When the Adar arrived, he was accompanied by an entourage of peskily eager attender kith who carried a display case half a meter on a side. Zan'nh presented to her an exact replica of a Solar Navy warliner, suspended in an energy field that kept it positioned inside the case.

She accepted the gift and invited him into her captain's suite. "My ship models sit on plastic stands, Z. This will be a very nice addition." She set the warliner replica on her shelf in a place of honor (actually the empty place where her model of the *Merrimack* had sat before she surrendered it to the Adar).

During their previous practice engagements, Keah and Zan'nh had established a tradition that the loser would present an interesting gift to the victor. So far, General Keah had given the Adar two of her favorite sailing-ship models. She had lost the first two engagements, simply because she wasn't familiar with Ildiran Solar Navy techniques. Once she figured out the Adar's pattern, though, she beat him in the next four engagements.

The attenders remained out in the corridor so she and the Adar could have a private conversation. Closing the stateroom door, Keah gave him a frank assessment. "You worry too much about the *show*, Z." She tossed her long hair back and regarded him with her jade-green eyes. "In a real battle you should figure out how to *win*—not how to show off. Do whatever it takes."

"For the Solar Navy, the show itself has often been the victory," he said.

"That may be fine in times of peace, but you were there and you remember—neither the Hansa nor the Ildiran Empire were prepared when the hydrogues started attacking planets." She unsealed her bureau drawer with a thumbprint lock and pulled out an old facsimile journal. She held it for a moment, wistful, then handed it to him. "Have this translated by one of your rememberers—it's an actual journal from the original General Kutuzov describing his strategic philosophy. It was written after Borodinō."

"You do not owe me a gift. You won our engagement."

"You're my friend, Z. If I find something interesting and want to share it with you, then shut up and accept it."

The two of them had spent hours engaged in reenactment simulations, using the starting parameters of old Earth campaigns and then playing out the battles with their own insights. Keah was keen to see if she could do better than history's great military commanders. Of course, she had the advantage of knowing what those commanders had done wrong, but there was nothing wrong with learning from the best.

During the dramatic final showdown with the Klikiss fleet twenty years ago, Keah had operated entirely on instinct. She had made a name for herself that day, leaping into the bridge chair when her commanding officer was killed. Now, after decades of peace, she still remembered the heat of combat, and she didn't want to let her guard down—which was why she also studied the Ildiran military. Adar Zan'nh was faced with a similar challenge, to keep his Solar Navy from growing stagnant.

She opened a bottle of her favorite wine and poured them each a glass. "Neither one of us wants our military to become just a show-piece, Z." She clinked her glass against his. She sipped, savored the smooth red wine.

Zan'nh didn't much care for wine, but he drank it out of polite-ness. He said, "Even though our wars have ended, General, the uni-verse is not a peaceful place. There are hazards and dangers that have nothing to do with actual enemies, and our personnel need to know how to respond."

Keah got down to business. "I've identified three potential ene-mies that I'm forced to think about."

"Three?"

She set down her wineglass and ticked them off on her fingers. "First, there may be internal struggles in the Confederation. Planets have their independence, and we have the Confederation Charter, but that isn't going to stop squabbling. It's just human nature."

The Adar seemed amused. "Human nature? Fortunately we don't suffer from that failing. With the telepathic *thism* that connects us all and with the guidance of our Mage-Imperator, squabbling rarely hap-pens among Ildirans."

She raised her eyebrows. "Oh? Didn't your mad Designate start a civil war not long ago?"

"That was . . . an unusual thing." Embarrassed, he sipped his wine again. "What is the second threat?"

"The second threat—and my apologies, Z, but we must be realistic—the Confederation could clash with the Ildiran Empire. I don't know how or why, but it's a possibility. So it's my job to make sure my CDF ships can kick the Solar Navy's butt."

Zan'nh chuckled. "You can try, General, but you're not likely to succeed."

"Today's results suggest otherwise. That's the point of war games."

"And the third threat?" he pressed.

"Third, is something we can't even guess—like the appearance of the hydrogues or the faeros. A totally unexpected enemy."

"We can be vigilant against such a threat. But if we know nothing about it, how can we prepare?"

"We'll have to learn that on the fly." She smiled. "I look forward to our next mission together, Z."

TWENTY-ONE

TAL GALE'NH

The *Kolpraxa* headed into uncharted space, cutting through the emptiness. In the command nucleus under the open dome showing the vast universe, Tal Gale'nh let himself enjoy the sense of wonder. The *unknown* was so compelling.

Outside the Spiral Arm, the stars were sparser, and space was emptier, almost devoid of light. The hundreds of Ildiran crewmembers aboard the exploration ship experienced flickers of uneasiness to be so alone, so far from the Empire. Gale'nh felt the tingle of their fear through the *thism,* but he was strong. He hoped that they could also feel his excitement.

Ildirans were joined with faint racial telepathy, the *thism.* Their minds had a synergy, their presence was bound together in a complex mental network. Like a gossamer safety net, *thism* embraced every member of the race and tied them all together. And every strand led back to the Mage-Imperator.

Gale'nh's mother had told him stories about Earth's generation ships dispatched centuries ago, following an astonishingly thin thread of hope as they ventured slow and blind in search of other habitable worlds. They knew their journeys would likely take more than a century. In light of what Nira's people had done, Gale'nh thought, the *Kolpraxa*'s mission was not so daunting.

Rememberer Ko'sh stood beside him. The screens showed denser stars in a river of celestial light below. "All the stars in the Ildiran Empire are there beneath us. We are so far from them. It makes the rest of space seem emptier."

Gale'nh raised his chin and gave the tall rememberer a confident smile. "Who else in all of history has had a grander view? Does even the Mage-Imperator have a perspective like this?"

"A valuable insight, Tal . . . a different way of looking at the darkness to distract us all from our fear."

"What is there to fear?"

"The *darkness*. That fear is in our genes, since Ildirans evolved on a planet always bathed in daylight. Only when we ventured to other worlds and star systems did we learn that night even existed."

"I've been to those worlds," Gale'nh said. "I grew up on Dobro, and our camp had lights shining down. We could see the dark overhead, but I wasn't frightened by it."

Ko'sh regarded him for a long moment. "Perhaps your human half gives you strength that the rest of us do not have. Your Ildiran half should remember the Shana Rei, however."

The others in the command nucleus glanced up from their stations with an involuntary shudder. Gale'nh drew a breath. "There are many questions about the accuracy of those stories. Rememberer Anton Colicos discovered that."

"That does not prove all the stories are false," Ko'sh said. "No true Ildiran doubts that the Shana Rei were real."

Gale'nh had heard about the black ships that swallowed light, monstrous creatures of darkness that had englobed the planet Orryx in shadow so that it remained a wasteland to this day. He knew how the heroic Tal Bria'nh had fought against the Shana Rei using "sun bombs," but the creatures of darkness were not defeated until Mage-Imperator Xiba'h became a faeros sacrifice, and the cleansing light drove the Shana Rei from the Spiral Arm.

Gale'nh said, "The hydrogues were a more fearsome enemy, and we defeated them."

Ko'sh sniffed. "With all due respect, Tal, you do not understand the Shana Rei. They are more than black warships—they are *blackness itself*. They attacked the Ildiran race, and the Ildiran soul, through the *thism*, through our fears." He folded his long-fingered hands together. "Let me tell you a story."

Gale'nh smiled. "You think I am a child to be frightened by simple tales?"

"During the first attacks of the Shana Rei, long ago, the splinter colony of Ahlar was saved by the Solar Navy. A barrage of sun bombs drove away the black ships. The Ahlar Designate rejoiced with his people, celebrated with his nine sons and daughters.

"But part of the Shana Rei remained behind, living in the shadows of space and the night of the world. Unseen, they struck through the Designate's mind, blackened his hatred, fed his violence, and convinced him that his own children were evil monsters that had to be destroyed.

"After the grand feast, when everyone was smiling and giddy, the Ahlar Designate took his children into a private room where he drew a crystal dagger and prepared to slay them all." Ko'sh gave a grim nod. "But he was a son of the Mage-Imperator, and so he was stronger than even the Shana Rei expected.

"The Ahlar Designate fought against the madness inside him while his terrified children watched. Eventually, he plunged his hands into a bright fire, which burned his flesh, but the pain and light and heat were strong enough to bring his mind back into focus, and he stopped himself from killing the children.

"But he could still feel the blackness like a parasite inside. The Ahlar Designate took the crystal dagger and drew a long gash in his arms to spill out his lifeblood. And what poured out"—Ko'sh dropped his voice, knowing that everyone else in the command nucleus was listening—"what poured out was *black blood*. The Designate let it flow down his arms and onto the floor, while he sobbed. The children tried to make him stop, but they could see the blackness oozing out of his body. He needed to drain it all from him.

"Finally when he was near death, the blood flowed true again, and the Designate declared himself free . . . but he was too weak to recover. Even so, he died satisfied, and the children knew the danger of the Shana Rei, as did all Ildiran people." Ko'sh tightened his lips as he finished his story.

"That was a brave thing to do." Gale'nh looked at the intent Ildirans who served aboard the *Kolpraxa*, then turned his gaze to the sparsely scattered stars. "This ship's crew can be brave in our own way. Just think of everything out here that has never been seen before: nebulas, stars, planets full of wonders. And as we experience it, the Mage-Imperator is with us. We are casting our racial net of *thism* wider. Keep studying. Keep exploring."

"Tal, I detect an anomaly ahead, a dust cloud or a dark nebula," said a scientist kithman amid the ports and contacts of the *Kolpraxa*'s scanning devices and telescopes. "No energy signature, but it covers a wide swath."

The screen showed a prominent emptiness, a swatch of space without any visible stars. "Why didn't we see it before?" Gale'nh asked.

"There are so few stars out here, Tal, it is difficult to see whether the light is blotted out by dust or just emptiness."

"Then we will do the brave thing." He lifted his chin. "We investigate."

Though he was just a halfbreed, Gale'nh's Ildiran blood did come from the greatest military hero in the Saga of Seven Suns. He had not known his father, but he had studied Adar Kori'nh so intensely that he felt that the man was his mentor after all, that Kori'nh was truly part of him. And Gale'nh did his best to meet that potential. Maybe the *Kolpraxa* would give him a chance to make his own mark on the Saga. . . .

As the exploration ship headed toward the anomaly, Gale'nh could see the dark nebula covering even the sparse scattering of stars, like a hole in space, an opaque cloud that eclipsed starlight. It seemed darker than the blackness itself.

Gale'nh stood straighter at the command rail. Rememberer Ko'sh looked deeply fearful, probably frightened by his own stories.

The scientist kithman withdrew from the network of sensors, wearing a perplexed expression on his flat and analytical features. "Tal, our sensors give indefinite readings. It is difficult to measure the extent of the anomaly when there is . . . nothing there. The cloud is not solid, not vacuum—just a *shadow*. But the shadow cloud has changed significantly since we first detected it."

"Changed?" Gale'nh asked. "How?"

"The dark nebula is growing, and moving."

Ignoring the expression on Rememberer Ko'sh's face, Gale'nh recalled his duty. "If it is unknown, then the *Kolpraxa* must investigate. That is the Mage-Imperator's command."

TWENTY-TWO

ELISA REEVES

Elisa's screens went blank as emergency filters blocked the surge of energy from the exploding bloaters. The concussion hurled her ship backward, spinning out of control. Garrison's ship vanished in the blossoming flash.

Since she'd been worried her husband might trick her, maybe even open fire with his low-power weapons, Elisa already had her shields up. That probably saved her life.

As the cluster of nodules continued to explode in a chain reaction, her ship tumbled away, damaged and blind. Elisa couldn't orient it, couldn't regain engine control. It was all she could do to hold on.

She finally managed to restore one screen, but the view was disorienting. The spreading inferno filled space, and the shock waves rippled farther and farther. Even the outlying bloaters glinted and sparked, as if in alarm.

Her screens went to static again. Through the windowports, she could see the blast going on and on and on.

Alarms rang through the cockpit, and her life support wavered into the red zones before secondary systems stabilized the air and light. The chain reaction continued interminably, until the inferno climaxed and dwindled as the explosions spread to the diffuse outlying bloaters.

Half-blinded, she tried to catch her breath, astonished to be alive.

With only a few of her sensors still functioning, she scanned the fading energy cloud, frantic. Elisa couldn't detect Garrison's ship, not even any wreckage. But if his vessel had been in the heart of those detonating bloaters, it would have been vaporized. That meant her son was dead!

Anger warred with her grief. Garrison had ripped the boy away from her because he feared *Sheol* was a dangerous place—and he'd brought Seth out here to a cluster of unstable bombs in space. Damn him! She felt sick inside.

Over the next several hours, the glare from the clustered explosions dissipated, but her ship was too damaged to move. Her screens remained dark, most sensors nonfunctional, and she would have to determine how many other systems were ruined. It was going to take all of her resources just to limp back to civilization.

With burning eyes, she looked at the portrait image of Seth she kept in the cockpit. She didn't understand what had happened, refused to believe what she knew was true. It was just a small warning shot with low-powered jazers!

Hundreds of the bloaters still drifted around her, as mysterious as before. Another question tugged at the back of her mind. *What the hell are those things made of?*

L E E   I S W A N D E R

Sheol's Tower Three was located in the most intense part of the thermal plume, and when the thick support struts approached the melting point, the tower's legs buckled. In a slow and inexorable plunge, the tall structure folded over and collapsed on top of the smelter barge that had docked to the base to take evacuees. The comm channel was a storm of screams.

Iswander gasped, "There's no way to fix this!" He wanted to call up his technical reports, prove that he had done everything prudent to provide a safe environment. This was going to look very bad for him.

Rlinda demanded his attention. "How many personnel are stationed on Sheol?"

He called up the data. "Over two thousand—two thousand seventeen, I think." Then he remembered that Elisa Reeves had gone off after her husband and son. "No, two thousand fourteen."

"Too many for the ships you have," Robb pointed out.

Iswander couldn't argue with that. "We have shielded facilities, heat-resistant smelter barges, bolt-holes in the towers. We did not foresee the need for a complete evacuation of personnel."

On Tower Two, shielded Worker compies kept working at the evac hatch, while two large rescue ships circled, looking for a way to retrieve the stranded personnel. Through the magnification screens on his desk, Iswander saw one of the shielded robots spark and collapse, its exterior skeleton melting. It dropped away from the hatch and fell like an insect sprayed with poison. Another compy took its place, working at the same ruined controls.

Half of the geothermal sensors positioned around the worksite had already burned out. Through the confusing squawk of alarms, Iswander heard an even more urgent tone: on the warning screen, a spike in the readings indicated an intense heat column rising through the magma near Tower Two.

He signaled to the Tower Two supervisor. "A new lava geyser is forming. Prepare yourselves. There's going to be—" He stopped, knowing there was no way the supervisor could prepare herself.

Vomiting molten rock covered the hull of Tower Two. The spray hammered both of the waiting rescue ships like liquid cannonballs, destroyed the tower's evac hatch, vaporized the compies, and hardened in the air to form an impenetrable seal over the structure.

The two damaged rescue ships reeled, unable to maintain control. One engine exploded, and the first ship tumbled into the sea of lava. The other ship managed to circle a little longer before skidding to a landing on the access deck of Tower Two, but the weakened deck collapsed and dumped the second vessel down into the magma.

Iswander reeled, stunned to think of how many people had just died, but also angry and frustrated that the structural engineers had let him down again. The deck should have been sturdy enough. They had run tests!

Rlinda grabbed Iswander's arm, pulling him toward the door of his office. "Come on, we're getting to the *Curiosity* now. You're not going to be stupid and go down with your ship."

He followed her, surprised by her comment. He had no intention whatsoever of going down with the facility. The structure shook and slid, and Iswander knew it wouldn't be long before those support struts buckled as well. Captain Kett was right: they had to get out of here.

All five smelter barges had now declared emergencies. Temperatures inside their enclosed chambers were rising and there was no way they could escape. Every crewmember aboard was going to be roasted alive—the barge crews had to realize that by now.

He, Rlinda, and Robb staggered along uncertain corridors, racing toward the exit tunnel and the waiting *Curiosity*. Rlinda huffed as she ran. Robb touched his comm. "Better not leave without us, Tasia."

"I'm already fully loaded, sixty-three people, but I've got room for a couple more. You may have to sit on my lap."

"If that's what it takes," he said. Five other evacuation ships lifted off.

Most of the people assigned to Tower One had already gotten away, but the bulk of Iswander's personnel were out at the various worksites for the day shift. The processors and materials handlers were all in Tower Two, and the off-shift workers were in the crew quarters on Tower Three. Iswander felt a heavy certainty that they were all lost already. Nothing he could do about it.

He felt overwhelmed, sickened, and furious. "This was supposed to be safe. My engineers, my designers, my specialists were all—"

Rlinda cut him off. "We can point fingers later. Get aboard."

As he ran, he realized this would have repercussions throughout the Roamer clans. They would learn of this disaster right before the election of the new Speaker. Garrison Reeves was on record with his warnings, and an inspection of records would show that Iswander Industries had operated on very narrow safety margins, had declined to use superior—but more expensive—materials.

Many people were going to die here. That was unavoidable. He had to rescue as many as possible. If he had, say, a ten percent casualty rate, then he would still look good, that he had led them through a disaster. The sympathy vote might even be stronger than his own campaign.

But he knew he was going to lose more than ten percent. A lot more.

As they charged through the access tube to the waiting cargo ship, Iswander felt heat blazing around him. The walls of the thermally shielded tunnel had a dull shimmer, nearing the melting point. If even the smallest crack broke through, the searing temperatures would incinerate them in an instant. Iswander didn't intend to be one of the casualties.

Tasia's voice shouted across the comm, "The outer section of the landing deck just collapsed. All available ships have launched, and we are going to be gone in a minute if you're not aboard!"

They raced through the tunnel into the crowded loading deck, the last ones aboard, and Robb sealed the hatch. He touched his comm. "*Go*, Tasia!"

Iswander collided with a group of panicked, sweating workers. They looked at him, recognized the chief. Most were too stunned to say anything, their faces red, their eyes wide, but several glared at him. He saw their accusing expressions—and knew it was just the beginning. They already knew who to blame.

With a lurch, the *Curiosity* lifted off just as the low landing deck dropped away. The structural sheets folded and sank into the lava, where they melted in a discolored swirl.

Rlinda shouldered evacuees aside, clearing a path to the cockpit. The ship was packed with people, but the numbers were deceptive. Iswander was responsible for 2,014 people, and only a small fraction of them had gotten away.

The *Curiosity* rose into the sky, and Iswander saw the other half of the split planet looming huge overhead. Tasia fought against thermal buffeting.

Once the evac ships departed, there would be no survivors left behind on Sheol. Some would die instantly in a flash of heat; those who managed to reach temporary shelter would bake slowly in a horrible death.

He had to start thinking and planning. He had a very serious problem.

TWENTY-FOUR

ORLI COVITZ

Every time Orli entered her compy laboratory on Relleker, she felt like a teacher entering a classroom full of eager students.

"Good morning, Orli," said LU, a blue and gold Listener compy who had been with the laboratory complex since the beginning.

"Good morning, Orli," said MO, a Domestic model who had such an abhorrence of dirt and stains that she kept every surface spotless. MO circled the laboratory, dusting, scrubbing, polishing. The compy was cheerful as she worked, cleaning even before it was necessary, as if trying to *intimidate* dust and smudges ahead of time.

A year ago, when MO arrived at the facility as a donation, Orli had thought it was a good idea to put the Domestic compy to work in their own home, but MO's obsessive cleanliness was maddening, especially to her husband Matthew. She could understand why the original owners had gotten rid of her.

Now Orli was trying to modify the Domestic's programming to increase her tolerance; she wanted to make MO understand that while humans liked a clean home, they did not want an absolutely sterile environment. Once, when she and Matthew were having a meal together on their anniversary—a supposedly quiet and romantic meal, which had degenerated into a tense discussion—MO only made things worse by hovering close to the table and snatching away any dirty plate the moment either Orli or Matthew took a last bite. . . .

Carrying her record pad and files of notes with ideas she wanted to pursue, Orli entered the main center to a chorus of "Good morning, Orli."

A decade ago, when she and Matthew got married, they had decided that rehabilitating discarded compies was what they wanted to do. When her old friend and companion Mr. Steinman passed away, he had left her some money, which Orli used to fund their work, and Matthew had inherited the facility building itself when his parents died.

Now, she had twenty-five compies here under study, each one contributing to the research as best they could. The different compy models used laboratory wallscreens to run diagnostics on themselves while running modified core programming. The compies were pleased to be guinea pigs. In fact, they were happy to be with her, since she took such good care of them.

Orli tried to keep track of all of their designations, not the full serial numbers, just the two-letter nicknames. The donated compies came and went as she did her therapeutic work on them, then found them new homes and useful assignments.

"Good morning, Orli," said another compy, whose voice she recognized.

Looking up with a warm smile, she said, "And good morning to you, DD."

She gave the little Friendly compy a hug. DD had been with her for most of her life, though his succession of owners dated back for more than a century. He spent much of his time in the lab complex when he wasn't with Orli in their home. Even Matthew was fascinated with him, tinkering with DD's deepest programming to determine what exactly the evil Klikiss robots had done to him when they held him captive for so many years.

Every standard compy possessed basic Asimov strictures, modified and expanded to encompass numerous scenarios; basically, the unbreakable subroutines forced compies to obey direct commands, and not to harm humans or let humans come to harm. Even so, after the major uprising of Soldier compies at the end of the Elemental War, people had become so uneasy that many had given up their compies, regardless of the model.

MO cheerfully brought Orli her cup of klee, a hot beverage brewed from ground worldtree seeds, a specialty of Theroc. "Your cup, just the way you like it, Orli."

"Thank you, MO."

Rlinda Kett's shipping company made a great profit distributing klee to other markets, especially the upscale consumers here on Relleker. Because she and Orli were so close, after all they had been through together, Rlinda made sure Orli always had a generous private supply. Since Matthew had never acquired a taste for klee, Orli had it all to herself.

She took a seat at her desk, logged onto the screens that displayed reports. Matthew's image appeared in the corner, but it was just a portrait, not a new communication. He was gone on a long business trip, traveling to Earth, New Portugal, Theroc, and Newstation, giving talks. He was a vocal advocate for compies, insisting that they were perfectly safe. Orli already knew that, as did anyone with common sense who had spent time around compies; they were so warm and personable, and so useful. But many people remained leery of them, despite the reassurances.

Before the Elemental War, compies had been ubiquitous throughout the Terran Hanseatic League, and they had also been used by the Roamer clans. But in the past twenty years, their popularity had dwindled. Very few were manufactured anymore. Maybe it would just take patience, Orli thought. Maybe it would take a great deal of crusading, which her husband was doing. She didn't much care for being on stage and the center of attention; fortunately, Matthew enjoyed it.

For her own part, while staying home in the quiet Relleker laboratory, she and DD recorded some standard educational lessons and released them widely, even though she doubted she made much impact out in the Confederation. DD seemed a natural, and she felt comfortable enough when she had rehearsed her talk. Orli performed a good educational service for anyone who was interested, but her subtle goal was to demonstrate how warm and charming DD could be. Such a faithful Friendly compy could never be a problem; people needed to see that.

Although in some ways the compy facility functioned like an animal shelter—since people dropped off troublesome or abandoned compies there—compies were far more than "animals" to her. She had always felt a close connection to them, especially to DD. She considered the facility more of an orphanage. And she wanted to find these compies homes.

When she and Matthew got married, they talked about having a family. Both wanted children. Unfortunately each came to that realization at a different time. Matthew decided he'd like to have a family just as they were establishing their compy laboratory, but Orli was too busy with the many strays who needed reprogramming to return to human society. Years later, when she was satisfied with her work, Orli decided she was ready to have children. But by then, Matthew had changed his mind and talked her out of it. Poor biological timing.

Matthew was proud of what they had accomplished in the compy laboratory, but he focused on the broader mission now, so he was often gone. Orli found that she didn't mind, since she had so many compies to keep her company, and DD was hers again. She never felt alone. Orli instructed the compies, learned from them, watched their actions, and she loved them.

Now, DD hovered by Orli's desk. "I arranged your files and answered some of the standard messages. Are you sure that's all right?"

"Of course it is, DD. Just like it was yesterday, and the day before." She shook her head. "How could I not trust you?"

"Would you like me to formulate an answer?"

"No, DD. It was rhetorical."

"Ah, a rhetorical question. I understand."

Orli and Matthew had everything they wanted, and they were doing good work. Although her marriage had not turned out to be as exciting or passionate as she had hoped, she was happy enough. She'd had a lifetime's worth of excitement in her younger years—far too much, in fact—and she felt no regret about having a quiet, normal life.

While Matthew went off on his lectures and crusades, she spent her days working here. Though Orli still felt an occasional bittersweet twinge that she hadn't had children of her own, these compies were enough. She and Matthew had agreed that it was enough.

MO brought her lunch, precisely at noon. "Your favorite, Orli. I've prepared a special dish that's exactly what you'll like."

Orli made a point of appreciating whatever MO created, though she had never given the Domestic compy any guidance as to which foods she actually liked. MO simply worked her way through numerous recipes in a catalogue and pronounced each one a delicious masterpiece.

MO hovered to take away her tray as soon as she finished the last bite. "Was it delicious?"

"It was delicious, MO."

DD came cheerfully into her office as she finished her meal. "A message just came in from your husband, delivered by a trader to Relleker."

"Thank you, DD," she said. Matthew preferred to record his messages and send them the old-fashioned way, rather than via a green priest, who would transmit the words through the worldforest network. He wanted his own voice, his own expression. Orli thought he just liked to hear himself.

She activated the transmission and saw his face: the dark hair, the faint crow's-feet around his eyes, the pale blue gaze that she had once found so riveting, especially when they sat across the table from each other and discussed compy problems. Now, he looked tired, his expression haggard.

When he sent messages, Matthew did not use endearments. He had never been the romantic sort, and Orli had learned not to expect that of him. He had recorded this message some days ago and managed to avert his eyes so that he wasn't looking at Orli on the screen. He seemed troubled.

"Orli," he said as if addressing a business correspondent, "I'll be back at Relleker in a week. We . . . we need to talk."

Compies would never identify nuanced expressions or tonalities, but Orli heard something in Matthew's voice, and she was already convinced she wouldn't like what he had to say.

TWENTY-FIVE

TOM ROM

Heading toward the empty Klikiss city and into the gathering darkness, Tom Rom went far from the camp and lay on the ground, staring up at the stars. He felt safe in the open aloneness, wearing the armor of his own confidence.

The sketchy records he had found about Eljiid made no mention of dangerous nocturnal predators. He wasn't worried. Tom Rom was never worried. He had taught himself to sleep lightly, and he always awoke feeling rested, and ready.

When the dawn washed over him, he rose to see the distorted alien towers that looked like pockmarked termite mounds. The nearby Klikiss city was empty, but he knew many insectoid bodies remained inside, preserved where they had fallen after the end of the last swarming. He had his autopsy kit and specimen containers. He would find what Zoe Alakis wanted.

During his trip to the transportal nexus at Rheindic Co, Tom Rom had studied all public information, as well as three classified reports, on Klikiss physiology. Dissections of the various Klikiss castes had already been done; one report was so detailed it was called *An Atlas of the Klikiss Body,* but the work was merely documentary—images, measurements, some limited chemical analysis—without any insightful conclusions. From the images, he had identified the "royal jelly" gland that Zoe wanted to investigate. None of the other scientists had even postulated what purpose the organ might have served.

In preparation for this mission, Tom Rom had also worked his way through the complex and confusing tome, *The Song of the Breedex,* which gave insight into the culture and history of the violent insect race, but he found it irrelevant. He only wanted to harvest what Zoe needed.

Brushing himself off from where he had slept, he took a sip of tepid water from his pack, ate a flavorless nutrient bar, and shouldered the pack. He had brought cutting tools, gloves, and a sterile mask—just in case. If he worked efficiently, he could be gone from Eljiid in a day. Zoe would be waiting for him.

As dawn brightened, he made his way through long shadows into the alien metropolis and searched for one of the ground-level doors. There were numerous openings at other levels, out of reach. He left spots of marker paint along his path, not wanting to get lost inside the hive labyrinth. The structures seemed similar to other Klikiss ruins, and Tom Rom was confident he could find his way. Locating a door, he entered.

The walls were made of a resinous cement, covered with spidery writing and complex symbols that extended out in shattered angles—Klikiss math and scientific principles. The powdery air smelled stale. This environment would have mummified the fallen insect bodies, preserving organs inside their exoskeletons.

All he needed was to find some cadavers.

He wandered through the empty insect city, following the curved tunnels, climbing up ramps. Finally, in a large open chamber, he found twenty alien bodies. The Klikiss drones looked like three-meter-high cockroaches with plated abdomens, multiple-segmented arms, flat heads. Each Klikiss caste had the soft thorax organ that would be filled with the glandular royal jelly.

Alone in the chamber, Tom Rom set up his lights, unrolled his pack, put on his gloves and mask, then withdrew his tools: a wide-bladed knife, a narrow hatchet if the exoskeleton proved too tough, jawlike spreaders, and tongs. Tipping up the head of the first drone, he cracked open the thorax. From the dissection records, he knew approximately where to find the gland. With gloved fingers, he dug around in the soft gelatinous tissue, but he was too clumsy with the first specimen. He ruptured the gland, mangling the job so that the thick, nearly hardened jelly oozed out. Contaminated, useless for Zoe's purposes.

But there were other bodies to choose from. He exercised greater care with the next cadaver. After cracking the shell with the point of his knife, he used the spreader to open it wider. Using the tongs to move tissue aside, he exposed the gland at the base of the creature's throat.

It was spongy and misshapen, gray-green in color, a swollen pustule filled with half-crystallized liquid. Taking care not to puncture the membrane, he snipped out the gland—intact—and placed it in a specimen container.

Technically, that was all Zoe needed to run her tests, but since there were numerous other Klikiss bodies lying here for the taking, he decided to increase his sample size. This would give the Pergamus researchers much more to work with. Also, if the royal jelly did prove to have exceptional health properties, Zoe would want to have more of it.

Practiced now, he cracked open another thorax, extracted the gland, and added it to the specimen container. He discarded the mangled Klikiss body and worked on the next one, and the next. In less than an hour, he filled three large specimen containers, sealed each one, and sterilized the exteriors. His gloves and sleeves were covered with ichor and slime, but his breathing mask remained seated in place. Only two more drone bodies left to harvest.

From the chamber doorway, he heard a loud, disgusted gasp. The disheveled-looking Mr. Bolam stood wide-eyed, as if ready to vomit. "What the hell are you doing? Those are specimens, protected by a Confederation Act. You can't just—"

Tom Rom carefully stripped off his gloves and tossed them aside. He applied a sterilizing gel to his skin, just in case he had been exposed to any fluids. "Do you think the Klikiss care? Or are you one of those who believes the bodies are still alive and just hibernating?" All around him, the harvested Klikiss bodies lay sprawled in oozing pools. Even through his mask he could smell an odd, putrid odor that wafted up from the cracked insect shells.

"I don't give a shit about the bodies—but you're not allowed to do that." Bolam looked indignant.

As Tom Rom talked, he continued packing away the specimen containers. "It's important work."

"But what is it for? Why would you do this?" The man narrowed his eyes, lowered his voice to a conspiratorial whisper. "Is there some profitable substance in the bodies?"

"My employer has reason to believe that there may be some medical potential in the royal jelly excreted by these Klikiss glands." Tom Rom sealed his pack, then opened the kit to remove a needle-tipped thimble. "It could be a miracle cure, could be a drug. We're going to do a thorough analysis. That's why we needed the samples."

He rummaged in his kit and found a vial filled with clear liquid. He removed the cap and dripped some of the fluid onto the end of the thimble, making sure the fluid was evenly distributed.

Bolam was incensed at being treated as irrelevant. "I can't just let you walk in here and do this. I'll need to file a report. If you suspect there's some medical use to the Klikiss bodies, then we'll set up a research team, investigate it thoroughly."

Tom Rom shouldered his pack, adjusted the straps, and stepped up to the still-babbling Bolam. With a flick of his finger, he scratched the man on the neck.

Bolam recoiled. "What the hell?" He swatted at Tom Rom, who easily dodged the man's flailing hands. "I'm going to have you held until we can bring in the authorities."

Finishing his business, Tom Rom removed the thimble from his finger and slid it back into a pocket in his kit. He paid no attention to Bolam, who continued to grow more outraged by his attitude.

The camp administrator touched the scratch on his neck, and his face began to swell. His mouth opened and closed like a dying fish's. He choked, his eyes bulged. White boils appeared on his skin. He wheezed, but could not draw a breath. His hands swelled, and more boils appeared along his arms. He began to drool down the side of his chin, which Tom Rom found disgusting.

"My employer wants this matter kept confidential," he explained, though it served no purpose. "If the royal jelly is successful, she intends to obtain a large stockpile without competitors knowing about it. If the glands prove to have no use, then it doesn't matter."

Bolam dropped to the floor, writhing. He took longer to die than Tom Rom expected, but the fatal allergic reaction could not be measured precisely. Removing a small antigrav handle from his pack, he strapped it to the body, then lifted the dead man like a lightweight package and carried him out through the Klikiss corridors.

He encountered none of the camp's other archaeological teams as he carried Bolam out, found a thicket of the tortured Whistler cacti. Several species of Eljiid cacti were known to have alkaloid poison, to which some people were prone to extreme reactions. He dumped Bolam's body next to the thicket, where the long spines left more scratches on his skin.

Finished with his work, Tom Rom made his way back to the camp. As he grew closer, he feigned a panicked expression. "I found Mr. Bolam by the Whistler thicket outside the ruins!" he cried. "I think he's dead—looks like anaphylactic shock. It was horrible."

Several researchers gaped at him from their tents and tables, before grabbing first-aid kits. Tom Rom called as they rushed off, "Maybe you can save him, I don't know."

He returned to the Klikiss transportal and stood before the tall stone window. Its flat opaque surface showed nothing until he activated the coordinate tile for the Rheindic Co nexus. The solid surface shimmered and formed a doorway, and he stepped through.

Another successful mission. Zoe Alakis would be pleased.

Twenty-six

Zoe Alakis

On Pergamus, Zoe Alakis waited for Tom Rom to return with new findings. She looked forward to seeing him, hearing about his new discoveries, and studying the samples he brought for her. He never let her down.

Other people longed to visit strange worlds, but Zoe was terrified by the idea of *exposing* herself to all that. She was no coward, but she was no fool either. Every planet was full of insidious, invisible organisms ready to compromise biological systems. *Compromise biological systems:* a fancy scientific way of saying "Kill any human who allowed herself to be vulnerable."

Tom Rom took enormous risks for her—he always had—and he knew how much Zoe appreciated his efforts, his sacrifices. Thanks to him, as well as her dedicated scientific teams and her spare-no-expense research facilities, Zoe possessed a vast library of cures and treatments, and an even larger library of diseases. It was her arsenal against the worst imaginable situation.

Her central dome on the planet's surface contained everything she needed. It was home to her. It was safe, and she never intended to leave. The filtered air inside her dome was cool and smelled metallic from the disinfectants. She needed no scents to brighten her quarters. The wallscreen continued to sort news reports, interviews, articles, and research papers.

While she waited for Tom Rom, she had programs to administer and results to assess. Zoe ate a bland breakfast porridge of autoclaved grains and devoted her morning to reading the project summaries from her Pergamus teams.

Two of the surface domes were biological sweatshops where a

hundred diligent but unimaginative data specialists crunched through genetic maps of countless microorganisms to be stored in her ever-growing database. The vast majority of those microorganisms would never be looked at, would never prove useful, but at least Zoe had them. Someday, she would allow the information to be shared among other researchers, but not now. They didn't deserve it; no one deserved it. For the time being, that treasure vault was hers alone.

Most of the project reports showed continuing work, but little progress. Even with generous funding and the best equipment, break-throughs were rare. But today's report submitted by Dr. Hannig from Orbiting Research Sphere 12 was flagged as important, so Zoe contacted him via screen. She never met personally with any researcher. While her teams operated under the strictest sterilization and decon-tamination protocols, she still had qualms about their proximity to the dangerous diseases.

She didn't need to refresh her memory about his work; she kept track of exactly which diseases each team was studying. In his weight-less research sphere, Hannig and his four associates worked in a sterile facility lit by white lights. The lead researcher drifted into the screen's frame. He was a round-faced man with bristly white hair and close-set eyes. He had gained weight, or at least curves, from his recent six months in zero-G.

"Ms. Alakis, we've made progress in curing Tamborr's Dementia. Our models show that we can develop a phage through auto-cloning techniques. This stops the deterioration of the neural systems in the brain and might even begin to restore the biochemical channels."

Zoe brightened. Every time one of her researchers found a cure, she felt as if she had acquired another weapon in her arsenal for the never-ending war. "I'm pleased to hear that, Dr. Hannig."

The man kept smiling and nodding, as if he could feel her pat him on the back, even from orbit. "It's an innovative approach, and we wouldn't have thought about it without access to your previous work on Heidegger's Syndrome. It gave us the key we needed."

"Now you see why all the research is interconnected, why I need to have everything."

"Tamborr's Dementia is not common, but this breakthrough could help many people," Hannig said. "Even the methodology would give other teams the possibility of—"

She cut him off. "My terms are not negotiable, Dr. Hannig. You read your contract, you know the conditions, and you understand the penalties. *My* funding, *my* research teams—*my* cure."

He looked hurt, which soured her joy in his breakthrough. She hated it when her scientists acted like this. Zoe had not founded Pergamus because she wanted to be a humanitarian. She'd always taken care of herself, and she kept the cures for her own use, exclusively. After her death, the library could be opened to others, but until then she kept tight control. If anyone disobeyed her orders, Tom Rom would hunt them down and retrieve the information. And she knew he would do it. Yes, she could count on him. . . .

Tom Rom had come to Vaconda when Zoe was eleven, three years after her mother died in the crash. He arrived with a group of interns, but he wasn't one of them. He came to Vaconda because he wanted to be there, but he remained secretive about his background. When Zoe asked where he came from, he answered, "Everywhere." He tapped his forehead. "Home is *here*. I carry it with me wherever I go."

For months, young Zoe tried to get him to talk, pestered him to tell her about his past, places he had seen, but he remained stony. "Those are my stories. You have to create your own."

Over the years, other interns came and went, while Tom Rom made himself indispensable. He taught Zoe much survival craft, taking her into the lichentree jungles and along the forest floor. When she asked where he had learned so much, he said, "I continue to learn, step by step—it's common sense, past experiences, and reactions. I'm learning about Vaconda at the same time you are."

The other helpers left, but Tom Rom performed their duties and more. He did everything Adam Alakis asked him, helped maintain the forest watchtower, repaired systems that failed, built additions to their tower, installed research traps on the forest floor. Whenever they needed supplies, he flew off to other Hansa worlds. He watched the weather, sniffed the air, listened to the jungle in ways that no sensor devices could record.

Once, he woke Zoe and Adam at dawn, wearing an alarmed expression on his normally placid face. "We don't have much time," he said. "Help me." Together, the three of them scrambled to string emergency netting all around the tower balconies. Tom Rom rigged it to their generator and electrified the mesh just before a swarm of hummers scoured through like a storm cloud across the lichentree tops.

Zoe remembered that long, buzzing, frightening afternoon. When a midlevel door cracked open, part of the voracious swarm swept into the access shaft and the living quarters where Zoe and her father had taken shelter. Tom Rom rushed in, flinging hummers away from his face, diving toward the two. Adam demanded that Tom Rom take Zoe to safety as he battered at the hungry insects, and that was what Tom Rom did, dragging her away even as she screamed for her father. Tom Rom wouldn't listen to her. He threw her in a closet, sealed the door, and waded back through the swarm to rescue Adam as well. Afterward, he accepted disinfectant salve on the numerous bites that pocked his skin, but insisted he did not need any painkillers. Zoe asked him if he even felt pain, but he didn't answer her.

When Zoe was fifteen, her father came down with a severe jungle fever, suffered for a long time, recovered after taking massive doses of the most potent medicines they had developed on Vaconda, but afterward he seemed weakened, wrung-out, deflated. Adam Alakis grew weaker over the next year, long after he should have recovered from the fever.

They finally went offworld to a medical center on Khandul, where Adam was diagnosed with a rare autoimmune disorder known as Heidegger's Syndrome. There was no cure, and the degeneration would be gradual, but inexorable.

Afterward, Adam went back to Vaconda for the long, slow process of dying that would take the next four years. Zoe was appalled, unable to believe that a tiny virus had such power. She never wanted to feel so helpless again. . . .

Now, as Dr. Hannig and his research associates faced her on the screen, Zoe called up her accounts, studied the other work his team had done on ORS 12, Hannig's specialties, his particular interests, even his family history. Her smile was cool but sincere. "Your work on Tamborr's Dementia is a remarkable achievement, Doctor. I can't thank you enough. As before, I am pleased to offer you and your team an extravagant financial reward for work well done. Success is its own payment, but I'll pay you enough to leave Pergamus if you wish, retire on any planet—on the condition that all research stays here, all records are wiped, and you never reveal what you did for me." She paused only briefly, then continued, "On the other hand, if you choose to continue working for me, you will have your pick of programs, the best facilities. I'll refit ORS Twelve with whatever equipment you desire."

She waited. Some research teams accepted the payoff and left, but most were dedicated for their own reasons, even with her draconian rules. She selected her employees not just for their genius, but for their lack of outside connections. They liked to be turned loose on a medical playground.

Hannig glanced at his associates, but they had obviously discussed the matter beforehand. "There's still too much to be explored, Ms. Alakis. Bank the bonuses in our accounts, and we'll discuss which line of investigation to pursue next."

Zoe was not surprised. "Thank you, Doctor. I appreciate your drive, as always. You and your team are shining examples of human ingenuity. Work on whatever you like, so long as it has a chance of being useful, and the cures are mine to develop and keep."

After signing off, she skimmed through spinoff research proposals from her scientific teams, then approved the funds for every single one. Why take chances?

Tom Rom could always procure more prisdiamonds if she needed the money.

TWENTY-SEVEN

GARRISON REEVES

When the bloaters exploded, Garrison had been accelerating away from Elisa's ship. He had activated the stardrive, shields on full—and they missed the worst of the blast.

He could not believe Elisa had actually fired on them! No doubt she had meant it as a warning shot to prove she was serious, but the bloater detonated like a small supernova. The shock waves compounded the flame fronts, blossoming outward like solar flares.

Seth yelled. The windowports automatically opaqued as the flash roared over them until their engines made sufficient headway. Before the damaged stardrive shut down again, Garrison's ship had leaped so far away that the light from the growing explosion took a full three minutes to reach them.

Their life-support systems were drained and damaged, but the hull remained intact. Garrison's hands flurried over the controls. Though in shock from what had just happened, Seth pulled himself together and helped his father. Garrison had never been so proud of him.

Elisa was surely dead in the inferno. The conflagration had erupted so quickly, shock waves extending outward in all directions. No, she couldn't have survived back there. Seth realized it as well, but they didn't talk of it. Not yet. The boy finally whispered as the main lights came back on in the piloting deck. "Why did Mother do that?"

Garrison hated making excuses for her. "She didn't know they would explode."

"She still shot at us—why would she take the chance?"

Garrison focused on the controls in front of him and said in a quiet voice, "I really don't know . . ." Maybe he didn't know Elisa at all, not the way he had thought.

She was so different from the woman he had met and fallen in love with. Growing up in clan Reeves, working at the half-empty reconstruction site of Rendezvous, he'd been trusted with starship runs since he was seventeen, flying to clan strongholds and Theroc, negotiating for supplies, requesting loans (which, more often than not, had to be reclassified as "donations").

But Earth had always been a forbidden destination; Olaf Reeves made that very clear. The clan leader hated the Hansa, though it no longer existed. "You only have to look at the destroyed Moon to see the danger they brought upon themselves."

Once, standing up to his father, Garrison pointed out, "Rendezvous was destroyed too. How is that different? Did we bring it on ourselves?" Olaf slapped him, hard. For insubordination.

After that, Garrison acted dutifully obedient, but the more he was told not to go to Earth, the more tempted Garrison was, and so he made an undocumented detour on one of his runs. When he saw the busy rubble-corralling operations in the debris field of the Moon, it reminded him of Rendezvous—the big ships and equipment. The Moon operations, however, used the efficient Iswander modular habitats, and he realized the modules could be used to great effect at Rendezvous. Clan Reeves would be able to finish their large, slow, long-term project.

Knowing this, he'd met with a Confederation trade representative who worked with wealthy and ambitious Roamer industrialist Lee Iswander. Her name was Elisa Enturi, independent, hardened, out to make a good life for herself. He learned that she might be able to help him get some of the Iswander equipment modules for Rendezvous. She agreed to help.

Later, he had spotted Elisa at an Earthside bar. They went out on a balcony with their drinks, and she discouraged light conversation. "The meteor shower is supposed to be spectacular tonight. I want to see it." Together, they watched the shooting stars, which were frightening and beautiful, and they didn't talk business at all.

Elisa helped him make a deal with Lee Iswander, leveraging the finances from his line of clan credit. He arranged to buy surplus modules and heavy equipment from the lunar operations. He saw it as his chance to demonstrate to his father the sort of abilities a clan leader would need. This was also a big deal for Elisa, because it made significant profits for Iswander Industries. Garrison and Elisa went to Rendezvous with a flotilla of Confederation machinery and modules.

Olaf was horrified and wanted nothing to do with the "help" from Earth, blaming them for the destruction of the former Roamer center of government. He upbraided his son for making such a foolhardy mistake, refused to accept the delivery. Elisa lashed back at the stubborn clan leader, "Sorry—the shipment's paid for, and Iswander Industries will not take them back."

She dumped the equipment modules at Rendezvous and left. Just to show his disdain, Olaf cut them loose and let the modules drift out in space, not wanting to clutter the rest of Rendezvous with them.

Garrison was appalled by his father's bigotry and stupidity, and told him so. Olaf slapped him again, beat him down. This time Garrison slapped his father back. "Don't treat me like a fool, Father, when you're an even bigger one."

Returning to Earth, he had found Elisa to apologize for the treatment she'd received from his pigheaded father. She said she only cared about the treatment she received from *him,* and Garrison treated her very well. Together, they slipped back to Rendezvous, rounded up all the perfectly good modules that Olaf Reeves had discarded, then returned them to Iswander Industries where they were quietly sold again. Out of pride, Olaf would never bother to search for the modules (or never admit it), and Elisa looked like a hero for doubling Iswander profits.

She and Garrison celebrated, and commiserated, and slept together. Realizing the most potent way he could defy his father, he married Elisa. She introduced him to Lee Iswander, and they began working together. Olaf disowned his older son, but Garrison didn't care.

He had been happy when Elisa got pregnant, though she found it inconvenient. Congratulating them, Iswander gave her time off for the new baby and distributed her responsibilities to secondaries, promoting them instead of her. Elisa felt left behind, but she hadn't admitted she resented her husband until later.

On Sheol, Garrison had his work, but he cared more about his family than advancement. Oddly, though Olaf Reeves had never even met his grandson, Garrison began to realize the call of family that he hadn't understood before. As he thought of the falling out with his father, now he worried that the clan leader might have been right about Elisa. . . .

He and Seth spent eight hours assessing their damaged ship as they drifted in open space. They repaired what they could, verifying their energy levels and life-support reserves before calling up the starmaps.

"Where are we going now?" Seth asked.

Garrison didn't trust the engines, but he could limp along to a destination, provided it wasn't too far. After the pummeling it had received, this ship deserved a full refit and overhaul in an adequate spacedock facility, but he couldn't afford that. He had left everything behind on Sheol.

He was a Roamer, though. Maybe they could go to Newstation and ask some sympathetic person for help. But feeling the sharp pain in his heart from knowing that his wife was dead—and he had indeed loved her—he realized that he had only one place to go.

Home.

Garrison set course for the clan Reeves settlement at Rendezvous.

TWENTY-EIGHT

LEE ISWANDER

1,543.

The number haunted him. *1,543.* Lee Iswander wasn't even convinced the count was accurate, but that remained the official casualty number from the Sheol disaster.

Once he and the evacuees had arrived safely at Newstation, two days' starflight away, Iswander felt it was his grim obligation to scroll through all the names of the dead. It bothered him that so many of these people were unfamiliar to him. Yes, he knew a handful of team leaders, shift supervisors, some of the crew chiefs, the five smelter barge pilots, but he simply didn't recognize hundreds of his own workers; in many cases, even their clans were unfamiliar.

Frowning, he called up the personnel records, their images, studied how long those people had worked for him, reviewed any commendations or reprimands they had received. He did recall a few of the faces from when he walked through the cafeteria chamber in between shifts at Tower Three, but most were just random strangers to him—men and women who had families, people with political leanings, people who loved their work, and people who hated it.

1,543.

The escapees vocally blamed Iswander's lack of foresight, his failure to design proper protective systems. In the grief, shock, and anger, no one gave him credit for the nearly five hundred who had survived. Didn't that count for something? They only saw that he'd placed all those people in danger for the sake of his profits, that he had not provided adequate safety margins, that there had been no comprehensive disaster plan, not even enough escape ships. He had managed to save a quarter of them.

But three-quarters of his personnel were dead.

The deaths had not all been swift and painless, either. Even Iswander cringed as he thought of how many were trapped inside the sunken smelter barges or the collapsing towers where they had fled for safety . . . only to be roasted alive. It gave him nightmares—as well it should.

His ambitious Sheol facility should have been a shining example of Roamer ability to succeed while dancing on the cliff edge of danger. Lee Iswander was proof of both Hansa business acumen and clan ingenuity, yet all of his accomplishments had been swallowed in a whirlpool of molten metal and stone.

In his own defense, he submitted engineering records to show that the structural materials and heat shielding should have been sufficient against the Sheol environment. Normally, Roamers would have been sympathetic in the face of a planetary catastrophe . . . but Iswander had been warned. Garrison Reeves had made no secret of his concerns that Sheol itself was changing, and Roamers knew how capricious the universe could be. They did not ignore warnings. Iswander simply hadn't wanted to spend the money, hadn't let his operations be inconvenienced by a potential disaster.

The evacuees took refuge at Newstation. Clans met there, Roamers exchanged assistance, other ships came in to offer help to the refugees. There in the giant wheel habitat, they recovered, and they talked.

Normally, Roamer clans pulled together in times of crisis. Throughout their existence, they had faced setbacks, and their history was full of tragedies. But Iswander could tell by their harsh whispers that they did not feel sorry for him or forgive him.

Reunited with his rescued wife and son at Newstation, Iswander holed up in his usual suite with all the amenities. Always before, it had been a room where he slept and prepared for business meetings; now, it became a place to hide. He couldn't stay here for long.

He sat in the chamber, staring at reports, reviewing his losses. He was ruined, of course. The Sheol disaster would drain him of everything he had. Lee Iswander would be reviled, disgraced—and there wasn't a thing he could do about it.

1,543.

Londa brought him a cup of pepperflower tea. It had never been his favorite—too sweet—but she felt as helpless as he did, and this was her way of making a gesture. "It'll be all right," she said, finding nothing absurd in her statement. "I can talk to some of my family. Maybe they can help."

"Thank you, Londa." He took a sip of the tea, then shooed her away as politely as he could.

"Would you like me to bring lunch? I can make your favorite."

He wondered what she thought his favorite was. In fact, Iswander didn't even know he had a favorite, but it would give her something to do. "That sounds nice. I'll have to go soon, though."

As Londa bustled off, Iswander felt metal jaws of guilt gnawing at his stomach. He knew most of the clan heads, but not well enough to consider them friends. He couldn't guess how any of them would react. He tried to think of what he would say at the clan gathering, whether he should be defiant or defeated, whether or not to beg for understanding and forgiveness, a second chance.

He knew, however, that Iswander Industries would never be able to secure funding for even a traditional, stable Roamer business such as skymining, despite the continuing demand for stardrive fuel. Nor was he likely to find large crews to work for him.

He stared at the list of unfamiliar names, all the people who had burned on Sheol. *1,543.* He could think of absolutely nothing he might say.

The door slid open and his son burst in, his eyes wild. Arden was fuming rather than sobbing, his face flushed with emotion. He sported several fresh scuffs and bruises.

When Iswander rose to his feet, Arden whirled as if ready to throw a punch, but his shoulders sagged. His voice hitched. "They hate you! They called you . . . they said—"

Iswander faced his son. "I don't care what they say. They weren't there. They don't know."

Arden looked up to him, even though they rarely spent close time together. Once in a while, Iswander gave him encouraging talks. He checked on his son's grades, emphasized how important it was that he become educated, intelligent, and the best he could be, reminding Arden that he would run Iswander Industries someday. He felt a knife twist in his heart at that thought.

Arden trembled with rage or with shame. "They said all those people died because of your Big Goose ways. They say you're not a real Roamer, that the facility failed because you cut costs and took risks to increase your profits."

Iswander quelled his angry retort and calmly pointed out, "Anyone could see that Sheol is a risky place. And yet when I first announced my operations there, they applied by the hundreds to work for me. They were excited to sign up for profit participation. Roamers know that life is hard and dangerous on the edge."

Arden burst out, "It's not your fault!"

But Iswander knew that it was his fault, at least in part.

His family couldn't stay here at Newstation. The more visible he remained, the louder the recriminations would be. Better to lie low, find a quiet place out of sight until the anger cooled. He decided to take them back to Sheol, settle in one of the orbiting transfer stations that had quarters, food, life support. He needed time to figure out what to do next, to see what could be salvaged.

But he had to stay for the vote. He felt obligated to face that, at least.

Londa came back carrying a tray of food, noticed Arden's tears and his flushed face, and her mouth dropped open. "What's wrong? What happened?"

Iswander thought it was ridiculous that she couldn't guess. He said, "Look, your mother brought you lunch. She'll take care of you, son." Iswander glanced at the clock as if it marked the hour of his execution. "I need to go. The clan gathering is scheduled soon, and I don't want to be late for the voting."

When Lee Iswander entered the speaking chamber, he heard a distinct change in the low conversation that hummed from the filled seats. No, he would not get a sympathy vote.

He wore his best business suit and a veneer of all the pride he could manage. He reminded himself that he was one of the greatest Roamer industrialists in recent history. But he felt very small. *1,543.*

Because he and Sam Ricks were the two candidates for Speaker, by tradition they would stand at the heart of the assembly area while the audience voted. It made Iswander feel naked to have so many eyes on him, though it gave him a well-defined place to be, rather than sitting among the clan representatives. He wouldn't have to risk an awkward moment when others got up and changed seats to avoid being near him.

I will get through this. He made a point of recalling his earlier accomplishments, triumphs that any Roamer would applaud. But those were eclipsed by one incident. He silently wished Elisa Reeves were there at his side, but she was gone—and overdue to return. *I will get through this.*

Sam Ricks chatted with several companions as he walked along the lowest row of seats, waving to clan members. He seemed energetic and confident, much more than in their prior debate. And why not? Iswander felt a distinct chill in the room, and it was directed toward him.

Speaker Seward took her place at the elevated podium and decided it was time to get down to business, no matter what the clock said. "Exact schedules are for Hansa types" was a new Roamer saying. Though the Big Goose had been gone for two decades, it was still used as an insult.

"We're all here," Seward said. "Let's wrap up this election so I can retire." At any other time attendees would have chuckled, but today there was too much tension in the air.

Before the clans could start voting, though, Olaf Reeves stood. His dark gray hair was thick, not quite unkempt, but he certainly didn't pay much attention to it. Sitting beside him, his son Dale remained dutifully silent.

"Before you start with the nonsense," Olaf said without waiting for the Speaker to recognize him, "I want to make an announcement. My son Garrison warned that something bad might happen at the lava-processing plant, but Iswander didn't act on it. In past times, no Roamer would have ignored possible hazards just for the sake of profit."

Many members of the audience turned toward Iswander, and he forced himself to remain calm, turning his annoyance back on the gruff clan leader.

Olaf ignored him. "Lee Iswander is only a symptom, not the cause. It isn't just his industries—it's all of you. My clan cannot tolerate the direction the Roamers are going. You've sold yourselves out to the Big Goose."

"It's the *Confederation,* Mr. Reeves," Iswander said. "The Hansa is long gone."

"Different name, but no different in the ways that matter. You've all lost what you really are. Everything handed to you, nothing earned. Easy lives, full bank accounts, peaceful settlements, pampered homes." He jabbed his finger in the air as he made a pronouncement. "A knife loses its edge unless it is sharpened. And you have all become very dull indeed." He shook his shaggy head.

"My clan found a place outside the Confederation and away from the Ildiran Empire. We are going to pack up and leave the Rendezvous site, make our own lives far away." He gestured insultingly toward Iswander. "It's your problem now." With exaggerated bustle and disruption, Olaf Reeves and his family members worked their way out of the seats and left the chamber.

Isha Seward made light of the incident. "That was an unusual introduction to our official proceedings. Now it's time to elect my successor."

She called upon Sam Ricks to cast the first vote, for himself, of course. Next, she turned to Iswander, who cast his vote, and the chamber was filled with an immensity of silence.

Iswander listened to one member after another say the name of Sam Ricks, most of them with little enthusiasm. He just endured. In his chest, this heavy disgrace felt as spectacular as the disaster on Sheol.

After Speaker Seward called upon every clan head, Iswander had received only a single vote, the one he had cast for himself.

TWENTY-NINE

JESS TAMBLYN

Parked in orbit next to Newstation, the hollow comet of Academ was a sheltered school complex for Roamer children, but its exotic internal waterfalls made it seem more like a playground—at least that was how Jess and Cesca tried to portray it for the kids.

Roamers needed to solve problems on the fly more than they needed the drudgery of book learning. Computers and compies could do the brute-force calculations and implementation, but Roamers had to have the *ideas*. Jess's greatest wisdom came from his personal experiences, desperate problems he fixed, crises he endured. Survival, he had found, was an excellent teaching tool.

Now, drifting in the comet's zero-gravity central grotto, he used a squirt of compressed air to meet up with Cesca Peroni. They both hung in the open watching a group of children, eight or nine years old, being instructed by the Teacher compy BO. With her deep female voice, BO was programmed to sound matronly and protective. Male-voiced Teacher compies sounded more erudite and professorial, and Jess had found that the students listened better when BO spoke.

Drifting, Cesca snagged Jess's waistband and gave him a kiss, which naturally made the children laugh. Jess gave the class a mock glare. "This isn't funny. You should learn from it. Here, let me demonstrate again . . . like so."

He gave Cesca a longer kiss this time, slow, but not too passion-ate, before she pushed him away, saying, "Good to see you've still got it after twenty years."

"Oh, we started before that," Jess teased. "Even without the wen-tals inside us anymore, I feel energized."

When he mentioned the water elementals, Jess saw the faint illumination in the ice walls brighten. The controlled wental presence within the comet made Academ come alive, and the sparkle was ubiquitous. The lingering wentals could be felt, not just by Jess and Cesca who were all too familiar with the energy touch, but by the young students as well. It made Academ a magical place.

Cesca was the former Speaker of the clans, before Del Kellum, before Isha Seward. During the height of the Elemental War, Jess had become infused with wentals, his cells filled with such deadly energy that he was unable to touch another person, not even Cesca, whom he loved—until she also took the water elementals into herself. She and Jess had exhausted all their powers in the final battles against the faeros, leaving both of them normal again—although not quite. They longed for a family of their own, but the wental possession had transformed them, rendering them unable to have children.

When Roamers established Newstation to replace the rubble of Rendezvous, Jess and Cesca had proposed creating a school for clan children. A group of ambitious clan engineers had captured a wandering comet as it passed the planet Auridia, then towed it into orbit next to Newstation to provide water, fuel, and air resources. Excavations hollowed out the comet's core, leaving a huge empty grotto. Administrative offices, classrooms, labs, and dwelling units were drilled into the walls.

When the structure was ready, Jess and Cesca had released the tamed wentals into the ice. The water elementals had learned how not to contaminate others who came in contact with their energy. Now, waterfalls sprang from floor to ceiling and side to side, flowing in the zero gravity and guided by controlled elemental force. A spherical lake tumbled and rotated at the heart of Academ.

Hundreds of students attended classes to learn about life in harsh environments, to train on high-tech equipment, and to study politics and Roamer history. The classes were led by dozens of Teacher compies, as well as guest speakers from various Roamer clans who volunteered their time during temporary assignments at Newstation.

After Jess's interruption, BO continued teaching. "We were talking about the original construction of Rendezvous as a stopping-off point for the generation ship *Kanaka*. That was the start of the Roamer way of life." The students stared up at the central spherical lake, restless.

BO said in a scolding tone, "Pay attention, children. It is important for you to have the basics of your history."

Cesca gave Jess an indulgent smile, explaining, "They're distracted. I told the kids they could go swimming after the lecture."

The class cheered, but Jess responded with an exaggerated frown. "Swimming? What could be more fun than a lecture?"

He and Cesca loved watching the boys and girls from different clans gathered here to learn about their varied homes: space stations, asteroid mines, nebula skimmers, greenhouse domes, skymines on gas giants, rugged planetary settlements, even a rare few on worlds that were actually pleasant.

Jess wondered why Roamers always chose to do the most difficult thing. It seemed to be a genetic stubbornness. The clans had lived in the shadows for a long time, driven to settle in places no one else wanted—first because they were forced to, and then by choice, because Roamers were proud and wanted to show that they didn't need pampering. Now, with the Spiral Arm at peace and more planets available than could ever accommodate the Confederation's population, the necessity was gone. But Jess didn't think Roamers would abandon their risky ways—even after the recent disaster on Sheol.

When BO finished her historical lecture, the children remained silent and attentive, though it was clearly an act. Ending her lesson, BO said, "Now it is time for us to begin our aquatic instruction. You will learn about fluid dynamics, parabolic arcs, surface tension, and hydrostatics—"

The children cried out, "Swimming!"

The Teacher compy took the students to the suspended body of water, while Cesca remained with Jess. "To answer your question," Cesca said, "no I don't regret retiring as Speaker for the clans."

"I never asked that question. I always knew the answer."

"I'm just reminding myself after the recent election."

"Does it bother you that you're not doing important things anymore?"

Her dark-eyed gaze flashed him a question. "This is just as important."

On his comm, Jess received a summons to the offices. He and Cesca kicked off toward the near wall, wondering what business had called them now. When they arrived in the network of chambers carved out of the comet wall, they found a stern-looking Olaf Reeves, his son Dale, and several other Roamers waiting for them. They all wore the same clan embroidery on their old-fashioned jumpsuits.

"We've come to take our children back," Olaf said. "Per our agreement."

Cesca was alarmed. "Is something wrong with the instruction?"

Dale started to speak, glanced at his father, then fell silent. Olaf said, "We can teach them what they need to know. Clan Reeves is going to pack up from Rendezvous and head out to a new home." He seemed defiant.

Dale Reeves added in a low voice, "We want to be like the old clans, the families that came off the *Kanaka*. We're self-sufficient, and we won't be beholden to anyone."

Cesca let out a slow sigh and turned to Jess. "How many Reeves children are at Academ?" Even he didn't know offhand.

Olaf glanced at Dale, who answered, "My two sons Jamie and Scott and seven others, total. When we agreed to let you teach our children, it was on the condition that any parent could take their child away for whatever reason."

"Yes, that was the agreement—I wasn't arguing," Jess said. "Academ is for all Roamers, but they have to come here by choice."

They called the clan Reeves children to the headquarters office. The waiting felt awkward, and Dale looked as if he didn't want to be there.

Cesca was troubled. "We're sad to see them go. I wish you'd reconsider."

Olaf's ire was clearly directed elsewhere. "It's not either of you. You aren't those new self-centered Roamers, the ones who attend meetings and run for office rather than feel the joy of building something, strengthening a clan, and remembering who we are."

"Where will you go?" Cesca asked.

"Rendezvous for a while, until we finish our preparations," Olaf said. "Then we'll go far away."

Dale added, "It's a secret, but once our settlement is established, we may make contact again."

"Or not," Olaf said. "If we need extra supplies, we have an agreement with Kett Shipping."

Teacher compies entered the office chamber leading nine children, some of them dripping wet from swimming. The boys and girls looked confused. When Dale's two sons saw their father, they bounced forward, happy. "Are we going home?" asked the younger of the two.

BO presented herself. "Could we please know what is happening? This interrupts my class activities."

Cesca hugged the nine Reeves children, one by one. "You're going back with your clan. We'll miss you." Her eyes were sparkling. "Go pack your things."

Jess turned to the clan leader. "Do you have instructors where you're going? I know clan Reeves doesn't have many compies, but . . . I could offer you a Teacher model if that would help. BO, would you like to continue instructing this group of children?"

"Yes," the compy said. "That is my reason for existence."

Skeptical, Olaf stroked his bushy beard and then conceded. "As long as she knows Roamer history."

"I am an expert in Roamer history," BO said.

"Good enough, then. Come with us."

THIRTY

PATRICK FITZPATRICK III

When Del Kellum showed up at the Golgen skymine for a surprise—and probably extended—visit, Patrick Fitzpatrick made the best of it.

He got along well enough with his father-in-law, considering. After all, Zhett had put up with Patrick's grandmother, the Old Battleaxe, who had threatened to disown him and call down the authorities on the Roamer girl he'd fallen in love with. Ah, romance had its charms!

Del Kellum arrived without making any prior arrangements, expecting the skymine operators to drop everything and accommodate him. He flew across the gas giant's high wisps of cloud and called for a landing spot in the skymine's main industrial bay. "And what is your business here, sir?" asked a young man at the comm station, newly assigned to the task. *Too young*, Patrick thought.

"I'm *Del Kellum,* by damn! Just clear a spot for me. I know that skymine like the back of my hand—and I am very familiar with the back of my hand."

Patrick had been in the upper control dome, inspecting the flow readings from the station's numerous process lines. The crew chiefs sent him regular updates. Even though everything was nominal, Del Kellum would probably have plenty of suggestions on how to "fix" things.

Zhett hurried in from their quarters with Rex propped on her hip, connecting the toddler's harness to a small antigrav battery; when she released him, Rex bobbed along at her side like a tethered balloon. Her face was flushed. "It's always good to see my father." Her tone sounded weary rather than excited.

"From a distance," Patrick said. Zhett elbowed him.

Because it was a big shipping day for ekti, the skymine's industrial bay didn't have a berth for an unscheduled ship. Zhett got on the comm and instructed her father to land on one of the upper sky-decks. "If you can handle it, Dad—it'll take some careful flying."

He made a rude noise and clicked off.

His ship took up two-thirds of the cramped skydeck, but he landed in perfect position. As soon as the big man descended from the ramp, Zhett ran forward to give her father a hug with a bobbing Rex in tow. Patrick shook the older man's hand. "Good to see you, sir."

Del clapped him on the back, but was more interested in scooping up his grandson. "Just came from Newstation and the election of the new Speaker. I had to be there for appearances, but what a cluster-fart!"

"Sam Ricks won, we heard," Zhett said.

"Lee Iswander *lost*. Nobody imagines Ricks is qualified, but after the Sheol disaster . . ." Del made a silly noise at Rex, which caused the boy to giggle. He handed the toddler off to Zhett, who passed him to Patrick. "I needed an excuse to clear my brain, and what bet-ter excuse than to come see all my grandchildren?"

"Two of your grandchildren," Zhett said. "Shareen won't be back from Earth for a couple of days yet."

"Then I'll just have to stay long enough to see my favorite grand-daughter. If the invitation stands?"

Patrick gave Zhett a *What can you do?* look. "Of course it stands."

"Don't know why you sent her to Earth, though. That girl needs Roamer training, not fancy impractical academics."

"She needs both," Patrick said. "But I agree she'll do better in a Roamer environment. A formalized class curriculum isn't Shareen's strong point."

"She belongs at Fireheart Station," Del announced. "Have her spend a year with Kotto Okiah—let her thrive. She has so much poten-tial."

Zhett smiled as they made their way to the top of the skymine, because Del would want to inspect the skymine's activity. "Knowing Shareen, I think she'd end up teaching Kotto a few things."

Inside the control dome, the shift crew studied the ekti-reactor output and the gas densities in Golgen's cloud layers, as detected by dangling probe antennas. Pilots adjusted the directional output from the exhaust stacks to keep the big facility wandering along.

Del marched to one of the embedded screens to call up a summary and frowned when his old password didn't work. Without hesitation, he nudged aside one of the techs, accessed the system, then raised his eyebrows at Zhett. "That's an impressive production number, by damn. Up fifteen percent from my day. Of course, it doesn't hurt that the drogues aren't harassing you anymore."

"Shareen designed several of our engineering upgrades herself," Patrick said with understandable pride. "She's got a good feel for the operations."

Del eyed his son-in-law. "And have you figured out all the processes yet? Every skyminer needs to know every system."

"I've picked up quite a bit over the years. Zhett and I manage the skymine together."

"Of course she manages the skymine—she's my daughter."

"Fitzy and I do it *together,* Dad," Zhett corrected. Del had never resolved that in his mind. "I cured him of a life of luxury long ago. You should be glad he didn't go into Confederation politics."

Del gave a grudging nod. "He's better off here on the skymine. Or maybe I should take you to my distillery on Kuivahr—then you'd really get your hands dirty."

Patrick pulled Rex closer in his antigrav harness and gave his son a playful bounce. "As exciting as you make that sound, I think I'll stay here. We still have a family to raise."

Coming from a blue-blood family, not to mention being the grandson of a former Hansa chairman, Patrick had absolutely no interest in politics, though he could have had any number of ambassadorial positions or government posts. Patrick decided he preferred the Roamer way of life, and he was perfectly content with his spirited and beautiful wife.

"And where's my other grandson?" Del looked around the control dome as if he expected Toff to be working one of the stations. "Hope he's studying hard. His sister left some big shoes for him to fill."

"Toff is reminded of that every day," Patrick said. "We'll find him down on the loading dock. Busy day today. Four big shipments going out, open-grid cargo frameworks lined up and waiting to be loaded with ekti canisters."

"Let's go see the boy. Once I review how you do things, maybe I can offer suggestions for improvement. I have plenty of experience in industrial operations, you know—not to mention leading all the Roamer clans."

"We'll be happy to hear your suggestions," Patrick said. This time Zhett gave him the *What can you do?* look.

The skymine was a satisfying flurry of activity. Down on the cargo deck, the air was filled with fumes and stardrive exhaust, the smell of hot engines and cold chemical breezes. The bay rang with the clamor of tanks being loaded onto pallets, adjustment jets maneuvering cargo frames into place where their open grids were loaded with hundreds of ekti canisters for transport. Two empty cargo frames hovered outside in the sky, waiting to enter the big bay.

"You should have a subsidiary storage raft where you can keep surplus silos of ekti," Del announced. "You're producing faster than you can distribute."

Zhett pointed out the cargo doors. Not far off, a storage raft floated above the clouds, loaded with excess ekti tanks. "Like that one you mean?"

"Exactly like that, by damn. But you should really have two of them."

They did, in fact, have a second one under construction. Rather than point that out, Patrick said, "We'll run the numbers and see if it makes sense."

Outside, workers with safety jetpacks rode on slender swoopers, zooming around the skymine like wasps as they guided the waiting ships. The swoopers rode up to intercept a cargo hopper, while inspectors wearing helmets and insulated suits dove deeper to follow the probe lines.

Near one wall, Kristof was using antigrav handles to stack empty crates. Seeing his grandfather, he bounded over to them. Del Kellum sized up his grandson. "You must be five centimeters taller than last time, but there's not a speck of meat on your bones! Zhett, don't you ever feed this boy?"

Toff said, "I burn it off. There'll be enough time for me to fill out later." He playfully jabbed his grandfather's significant gut. "I hear it happens to everyone when they get older."

A loud crash outside the loading area startled them, and two jump-suited loaders leaped out of the way. An incoming ship flown by an impatient pilot struck a glancing blow against a cargo frame, which jarred one of the racks loose. Trying to avert disaster, workers ran yelling and waving toward the open bay doors and the long drop into the sky, but they couldn't stop the collision.

The empty ship caromed off and went tumbling as the pilot reasserted control. The heavier cargo frame skidded to a halt on the deck, but ten ekti canisters were knocked loose and tumbled out of the bay and into Golgen's sky.

Zhett's mouth dropped open. "Damn clumsy asses! That's valuable stuff, and now it's—"

"I've got this, Mom." Toff grabbed one of the narrow swoopers and swung it around toward the open door. "Already got antigrav handles in my pockets. I can round up those tanks." He started the engine, lifted off from the deck. "All I have to do is fly faster than they can fall."

"Careful!" Patrick yelled—out of habit, not because it would make any impression.

Del was shocked. "You're letting the boy . . ."

Toff's swooper streaked out of the open bay door and plunged straight down the clouds below.

Zhett shrugged. "He's done it before."

Del chuckled and cupped his hands around his bearded mouth and shouted after him, "Watch out for hydrogues down there!"

"He's not going that deep," Zhett said. "He'll catch up with the canisters before they hit the secondary cloud deck. Otherwise, the mist will get too thick for him to see."

Bobbing in his antigrav harness, Rex seemed amused by the activity, as well as his brother flying off in such a rush. Patrick muttered to Del, "But please don't tell Toff *not* to find the drogues because then he'll do it just to prove himself."

THIRTY-ONE

ARITA

In the camp near the Klikiss ruins, researchers were stunned to learn of administrator Bolam's death. Eljiid was a rugged and unexplored world, however, with countless natural hazards—including poisonous plants.

Lara Vanh and Kam Pellieri prepared the administrator's body, while Tarker and Orfino wrote up a report, summarizing what had happened, to the best of their knowledge. Arita joined the research teams in an impromptu meeting to discuss the matter, and they decided to bury the man there rather than ship his body back through the transportal to Rheindic Co. Besides, Margaret Colicos was already under a cairn nearby, so they had the beginnings of a cemetery.

Although Arita had barely met the man, she helped with the burial after a cursory funeral service, piling rocks over his body in a cairn much smaller than the memorial for Margaret Colicos. Vanh played her stringed instrument.

Then the independent teams got back to work on their own projects. They didn't particularly need to be managed, although from that point on the teams were more careful to avoid native plants that might provoke deadly allergic reactions. Arita was glad that she had learned of the Whistler toxin before she blundered into the thickets in an attempt to connect with the possibly sentient cacti.

Day after day, she sat cross-legged at the edge of the Whistler grove and listened to them. As the breezes picked up, the gnarled, angular cacti began to whisper and mutter in what sounded like a secret conversation. When the winds grew stronger, she heard the fluting music that had given the plants their name. She tried to crack the code and learn the mysterious language, but it eluded her.

Because green priests, like her friend Collin, could hear the language of the worldforest, they spoke to the trees and to one another through the telink network. How she envied them. But the trees had found Arita wanting. . . .

Arita had not become close with the other researchers here, though she was friendly enough with a few of them. At dinner, they ate a vegetable stir fry that Pellieri prepared with native edibles; they discussed their own work, Tarker and Orfino played another intense game of squares and disks. Arita was welcome to join them, and no one seemed interested that she was the daughter of King Peter and Queen Estarra—which was good, but Arita felt alone, thinking about her brother. By now, Reyn should be headed off to Earth, where he might be able to find the medical experts he needed.

Far from the worldforest, Arita gazed into the tangled thicket and watched the Whistlers stir in directions that had nothing to do with the breezes. The gabble of noises rose, then quieted. Before the complete hush, the murmur sounded like words.

For several days, Arita took images of other Eljiid flora, trying to develop a basic understanding of the world's plant types. Spiny succulents were the dominant forms in Eljiid's rocky, arid environment, and she catalogued more than forty types. But she was not satisfied with just imaging and recording—she wanted to understand the worldforest and the verdani mind, and she hoped the Whistlers might give her some clue.

Most of all, Arita wanted to understand why the trees had rejected her.

If the Whistlers were sentient, Arita wanted to touch them in the same way that a green priest touched the worldtrees. If there was a hope of her understanding, of *connecting,* she had to become part of the Whistler forest. That was why she had come to Eljiid in the first place.

She had seen the white boils on Bolam's face and arms, his eyes puffed shut, his face a grimace of agony, his throat closed off so he could not breathe. No one had performed an autopsy; everyone could see where he had scratched himself on the spines, and the extreme physical reaction was obvious.

But Arita wasn't so sure. She used delicate tools to take samples of the Whistler thorns, testing the intensity of the alkaloid poison. The camp researchers had been curious about the strange cacti for a long time, but no one had done a thorough study. If the Whistlers were as toxic as Bolam's death suggested, Arita was surprised no one else had died from a similar scratch. In fact, two structural engineers studying Klikiss architecture in the abandoned city confessed that they had tangled with Whistler thorns while climbing around the old buildings, but they had suffered only brief nausea and dizziness.

When Arita ran chemical tests on the thorns, she did find an alkaloid component, but the properties should have been hallucinogenic rather than poisonous. Maybe Bolam had an allergic reaction that had resulted in anaphylactic shock.

She distilled the alkaloid toxin, diluted it, and cautiously smeared a drop on her skin. She waited, but observed no reaction. Growing more daring, Arita added the toxin in successively higher concentrations. Only at full strength did her skin show a slight redness—not at all like Bolam's reaction. The Whistlers couldn't be as toxic as she had thought.

One evening in the gathering dusk, the Whistlers kept talking, humming, singing—and she wanted to understand. Leaving her warm rock, Arita walked into the thicket like a dancer, weaving her way, careful not to let the spines scratch her.

The cacti stirred, and a low hooting sound rose and fell. They were *talking,* she knew it. The Whistlers had a kind of sentience that might be part of the worldforest mind, or a separate entity of its own. Or maybe they were just cacti that made strange sounds when breezes blew through them.

She thought of Collin, how he could touch any worldtree, even a little treeling in a pot, and become part of an immense tapestry of thoughts and knowledge—a tapestry that excluded her.

Arita drew a deep breath, trying to forget the disappointment of that day. Without letting herself think, she reached out and grasped the nearest Whistler branch.

She felt the thin stab of the needles, a dozen pricks as the spines penetrated her skin. She thought she heard the whispering grow louder, and she closed her eyes, trying to let her mind flow into the plant network. She wanted to share with the Whistlers, tell them her passions, understand the interlinked community that spread beyond any individual plant, any individual person.

Her hands burned. The alkaloid secreted by the spines was in her bloodstream. Her pulse raced from more than just excitement and fear. Her thoughts grew sharper, more colorful, more intense. Her chest heaved like a set of bellows. Suddenly the night air felt hot. Her thoughts ricocheted in all directions, but she refused to release the Whistler. She gripped even tighter.

A trickle of blood ran down her hands, red and warm and now swirling with mysterious Whistler chemicals. Arita knew it was not a poison that would kill her. She wanted to join the Whistlers, to float among them and understand what they had to say.

Instead, she saw herself from more than two years ago—younger, energetic, optimistic. She'd spent years as an acolyte reading aloud to the worldtrees as a good Theron child should, tending them, following the instructions of the green priests. While Prince Reyn was being groomed as the next King of the Confederation, their parents endorsed her desire to take the green—there was no more essential Theron activity, and they were proud of her.

She and Collin planned to be green priests together. Though they were young, they both felt the attraction growing, a romance blossoming between two young people who belonged with each other. Arita imagined that someday she and Collin would be like her aunt Celli and uncle Solimar—green priests who had been together for two decades and now tended their own floating worldtrees at the Roamer complex of Fireheart Station.

Nervous about the green priest testing, Arita and Collin had gone into unexplored parts of the forest, running together for a time. But the test was a private thing. Each person had to endure his or her own rite to become a green priest, had to accept the verdani mind, surrender to the call of the forest. They would sink deep and then emerge transformed, green-skinned and forever different.

Arita remembered the wonder as the thickets stirred around her, worldtree fronds bending down, vines reaching up. Leaves stroked her naked legs, creepers wrapped around her ankles, her waist. Arita struggled at first, but then allowed it to happen. The living sentient forest enfolded her, and she could feel the powerful presence of the verdani mind, a brain composed of millions of trees connected through a quantum root system.

Arita's heart pounded—she couldn't breathe. She gasped even now as she stood among the Whistlers. Maybe it was the effect of the alkaloid poison, or just the reawakened painful memory that she had to live all over again. . . .

Sleeping in the cocoon of foliage, young Arita had felt the grandeur of the forest, the millennia of experiences stored in an infinite number of thoughts. As a green priest, she would be able to access all of it. She could touch any tree, think about anything she wanted, talk to anyone else connected through telink. She felt the verdani in her mind, prying, changing, shifting. Arita opened herself up, surrendering utterly.

But her head pounded. Pain shot through her. It grew more intense, building to a crescendo—

Until the forest rejected her.

The vines had recoiled and released her. The worldtree fronds backed away and left Arita on her knees gasping and confused. She stumbled out of the thicket, and when she looked down at her arms, she saw only her normal tan flesh, not the fresh green of a transformed priest. Arita realized she had failed. Although something had changed in her mind, she would not be a green priest.

She had begun sobbing as she realized just what a crushing defeat this was. The trees would not give her a second chance. She didn't understand what was wrong with her, didn't know why the trees had not accepted her. She was the daughter of Peter and Estarra, Father and Mother of Theroc . . . yet the trees had cast Arita out.

She had sat shuddering on the forest floor, where the weeds and plants now seemed prickly and unwelcoming. She had pulled her knees up to her chest and waited, trying to control her tears. When Collin bounded through the underbrush to find her, calling her name and grinning, she looked up through reddened eyes to see how he had changed: now bald, his skin a beautiful green, and his eyes filled with a new wisdom.

And when he saw her, Arita felt worse than ever. They were supposed to be together, partners, lovers, laughing with the wonder of the forest. . . .

Now among the Whistlers Arita felt a fresh pang of loss. She released her grip on the spiny branch, looked at the blood on her hands. Though feverish and dizzy, she didn't sense *anything* from the cacti. Their fluting sounds and low tones no longer held the promise of sentience, of shared thoughts. Maybe they were just noises after all.

Or maybe the Whistlers had rejected her too.

Arita staggered away back toward the camp, finding it hard to keep her balance. Her vision was blurred, and her head pounded with the aftereffects of the toxin. This was different from when the worldforest had been inside her brain. Back then, something had altered in her thoughts, something Arita had never understood.

Tonight she merely felt disappointed. No, the Whistlers did not have what she was searching for.

Gradually, as she walked, her breathing grew less labored. The exposure was diminishing. It was deep night by the time she reached her tent. She crawled inside and collapsed, hearing a roar in her ears, listening to the pulse pounding in her temples.

The other research teams were asleep, and Arita wanted to be alone. She lay back, waiting for the night to end. She had finished her work here on Eljiid.

In the morning, she decided it was time to go home to Theroc.

THIRTY-TWO

TAMO'L

The breeding camp on Dobro had changed in immeasurable ways since her childhood there, but the old memories could not be erased with rebuilt homes and resettled colonists. Tamo'l approved of the changes. The humans and Ildirans had a tighter bond now—scar tissue was tougher than untouched flesh.

As she looked around her, Tamo'l saw humans and Ildirans chatting, working side by side, engaged in spirited debates as well as laughter. Children played together, climbing the girders of a new meeting hall under construction. Some were *viable* halfbreeds, whose bodies were not twisted, not genetic practical jokes like the ones she nursed in the sanctuary domes on Kuivahr. She let out a wistful sigh.

Tamo'l and her four halfbreed siblings were products of the secret breeding program—the *culmination* of that program. Tamo'l's father had been a lens kithman, a philosopher who saw visions from the Lightsource and could feel the *thism* more clearly than other Ildiran breeds. Her mother's human and green priest genes had increased Tamo'l's sensitivity.

Tamo'l was one of the most successful halfbreeds from the Dobro program, but not all of the offspring were so fortunate.

She was thin and tall, with short feathery hair, large eyes that held the star reflection characteristic of her Ildiran bloodline. Her nose was smaller than her mother's, her face more narrow. One young human man had said that her eyes and face were haunting, and Tamo'l took the comment literally, much to his embarrassment. Only later did she understand that he had been flirting with her. Even with lens kith insight, she often didn't comprehend personal subtleties. . . .

Dobro's air was dryer than she liked. On Kuivahr, she was used to kelp and saltwater, sour plankton flats, and skies that were shrouded in cloud. She was anxious to return as soon as she retrieved her new volunteers. On Kuivahr, so many lives depended on her, although there wasn't much they could do for the worst misbreeds, except to offer them care and understanding, make them comfortable, and keep them as healthy as possible. She hoped Shawn Fennis and Chiar'h were up to the task.

Tamo'l studied the couple as they came forward to meet her. Chiar'h had striking regal features, from the noble kith. She held her husband's arm and laughed when he said something that Tamo'l couldn't hear. Shawn Fennis was a grinning man with red hair, green eyes, and pale skin with a dash of freckles that Tamo'l found fascinating. She wondered if these spots had once been a form of racial camouflage. . . .

Fennis had been born on Dobro, and Chiar'h had been assigned here during the years of reconstruction. They had fallen in love and married, a mixed couple *by choice* who understood each other.

Fennis extended a hand to shake Tamo'l's. "You're doing such important work on Kuivahr. We want to be part of it."

"The work has its own rewards." Tamo'l tested them, wanting to be sure. "Your wife does not belong to the scientist or medical kith. Do either of you have expertise in genetics or medicine?"

"I spent three years off-planet studying basic biology on New Portugal, and I've assisted the medical kithmen here on Dobro. I met Chiar'h when we both worked in the hospital. We're used to hard work. But we're not volunteering just because of the medical aspect. We accept what it means to be different."

Chiar'h said, "We understand how fortunate we were to find love together, despite our differences. We want to share some of that love with others who need it. That is what we have to offer. The rest we can learn."

Tamo'l softened her expression. "I wanted to be certain you were prepared. The misfits can be . . . disconcerting. They are not like those ones." She nodded toward the healthy halfbreed children playing nearby.

"Uniqueness is not a disadvantage. My patients may not be aesthetic, but they are still worthy." She paused, then added, "I do what I can to mitigate the suffering of those people who paid a much higher price than I did."

Tamo'l and her two new volunteers rode down from Kuivahr orbit in a cutter loaded with food, equipment, and medical supplies. Fennis and Chiar'h were eager but Tamo'l could also sense their nervousness. Shoulder to shoulder, they peered through the windowports at patches of cloud cover, rough seas, flooded mudflats, and the sketchy outlines of reefs.

The cutter flew in past the outcropping that held the Klikiss transportal wall, then the Kellum distillery towers, and soared low over the water.

"The tides are high during this part of the cycle, so the sanctuary domes will be submerged," Tamo'l said. Only the tops of the hemispheres rose above the waves like blisters. An upraised landing platform had been ratcheted up on stilts as the seas rose.

"I see figures in the water down there," said Shawn Fennis.

"Swimmer kith. They have raft settlements out in the open sea and work on the kelp and plankton beds. They harvest the ocean and deliver supplies to the sanctuary domes."

The cutter landed in the rain. Tamo'l and her two companions emerged into the windblown dampness. She smelled the iodine air, felt the drizzle on her face. *Home.*

Shivering, Chiar'h looked up at the gray clouds. "The sky is so dim."

Tamo'l said, "The laboratories and living quarters are bright and sterile."

Fennis took his wife's hand. "Let's see what we've gotten ourselves into, love."

They left the wet landing platform and rode a lift tube down into a dazzling white chamber. Overhead, waves washed across the curved surface of the dome.

Through *thism,* Tamo'l sensed the presence of her patients, her friends. Many would come out to greet the new volunteers. With her lens-kith sensitivity, Tamo'l could feel the warmth of their exuberant welcome.

Shawn Fennis and Chiar'h looked uncertain, but friendly. They smiled as the first group of misbreeds came forward.

THIRTY-THREE

TAL GALE'NH

As the *Kolpraxa* approached the swelling black nebula, the emptiness grew deeper and darker. From inside the command nucleus Tal Gale'nh watched the sparse stars wink out in the observation dome overhead. The cloud swirled with shadows and expanded like the blood of night spilling out of a deep wound.

"This is a research ship," he said. "We have all the sensors we need. Analysis?"

"It is not dust, Tal," said one of the scientist kith. "No known astronomical phenomenon. Perimeter measurements are difficult to determine." The other crewmembers studying their screens just shook their heads.

The oily-dark blob grew aimlessly. "Dispatch a probe," Gale'nh said.

The small device shot from the *Kolpraxa*'s bow like a flying fish, sailing off with extended fins and antennae that sent pulses into the dark nebula.

Rememberer Ko'sh watched and waited with grim concern. "Darkness grows without the light."

Gale'nh glanced at him, not sure what the historian meant. "Then we'll bring the light."

Readings transmitted from the probe showed nothing, and the response screens remained dark. The scientist kith were confused. "It is not just darkness, Tal. It is a complete lack of light and energy."

When the shadow cloud extended toward the *Kolpraxa*, Gale'nh ordered the helm, "Alter course, keep a safe distance. Shields at full strength."

The probe continued to send back signal pings, to the further consternation of the analysis team. "Trying to pinpoint the source of the shadow cloud, Tal. It seems to be emerging from a tear in space." The chief scientist shook her head. "It is not composed of matter. Not solid. There is no substance whatsoever."

The probe transmissions broke into static, then silence. Command nucleus screens went blank and dead. On the primary screen, Gale'nh watched the bright glimmer of the probe plunge into the dark cloud and disappear.

The scientist kith reviewed the readings and stared at one another, waiting for someone else to offer an interpretation. Finally, a small-statured male with fluttery hands said, "It is just . . . blind entropy."

Gale'nh shored up his resolve, remembering the Mage-Imperator's command. "We need to understand this. We will not succumb to a fear of the unknown."

"There is danger, Tal," said Rememberer Ko'sh. "The darkness is its own warning. We have a great deal of historical precedent."

"We have a great many *stories*," Gale'nh corrected.

Ko'sh looked offended. "Those stories are our history."

Gale'nh knew thousands of tales from the Saga of Seven Suns, and some of those tales were no longer trustworthy. Ko'sh had reminded his crew of the Shana Rei, but the creatures of darkness were long gone from the Spiral Arm—if they had ever existed.

What did the *Kolpraxa* have to fear from a shadow?

Tal Gale'nh faced the tall rememberer. "What we do now becomes part of the continuing Saga. When faced with our first mystery of this expedition, would you have us turn and flee?"

Ko'sh lowered his gaze. "I merely record the history, Tal. You are the one who makes it."

Gale'nh pressed, "You're the rememberer—you know the tale of my father. What would Adar Kori'nh do in this situation? What is your assessment?"

"Adar Kori'nh would investigate."

Gale'nh turned to the helmsman. "Approach with caution. Extend our sensors and map that shadow cloud."

"Impossible to be accurate, Tal. It changes, it grows. It . . . emerges." The blackness hung there in front of them.

Gale'nh directed his gaze to the communications officer. "Open a channel. Let me address it."

"Do you think there is anything in that cloud, Tal?"

"I cannot draw conclusions until we know more." He turned to the main screen. "This is the Ildiran exploration ship *Kolpraxa*. We are representatives of the Mage-Imperator, seeking to expand our knowledge." He paused and listened only to silence as deep as an eclipse. "If there is anything sentient in that cloud, please respond."

As the *Kolpraxa* drew closer, suddenly the helm and control systems began to stutter and shut down. Gale'nh gripped the command rail as the deck tilted. He called engineering. "What's happening?"

"Everything is failing—massive systemic errors and shutdowns."

The analysis crew called up diagnostics, but the screens flickered and blurred with static. Several panels went dark. Emergency lighting glowed from floor and ceiling rectangles. As the command nucleus dimmed, the faint light of sparse stars shone through the transparent dome overhead.

"Withdraw to a safe distance," Gale'nh said.

"All systems are failing!" the helmsman responded. The engineers fought to reassert control of the ship.

The black nebula continued rolling toward them. Gale'nh stared up through the observation dome. *Blind entropy?*

A deep mechanical silence set in as the *Kolpraxa*'s engines died, and the exploration ship drifted. Sparks showered from control panels throughout the command nucleus, and the life-support systems shut down.

The main lights went out, then even the emergency glow was smothered.

Through the transparent observation dome overhead, Tal Gale'nh watched a midnight pseudopod reach out and swallow the *Kolpraxa*.

Thirty-four

Osira'h

The faeros frolicked in the churning photosphere of the star Wulfton. Ellipsoidal incarnations of fire itself, the elemental beings dove into the gas layers, while others leaped in joyous arcs, riding magnetic pathways, sailing along wide coronal arches to their apex, then turning and plunging back into the stellar inferno.

Alone in her insulated observation globe, bathed by the close starfire, Osira'h watched the faeros, sensed them, and felt her remaining telepathic connection to them. During the Elemental War, the faeros had wrought terrible damage, but Osira'h had forced them to obey her. Now, the fiery beings remained quiescent, tamed, yet still dangerous, incomprehensible. The faeros had returned to their unruly isolation. They still knew her and found her marginally interesting but also . . . irrelevant?

She concentrated harder, trying to maintain the link, but it was frayed. The faeros had little interest in her anymore. Osira'h had a difficult time translating their thoughts, which were so entirely alien. But they did understand that she was no threat to them—not any longer.

Reaching outward through the pathways of *thism,* Osira'h could sense the other Ildiran researchers in the nearby stellar analysis station, an orbiting facility outside the coronal zone. She was the only one who ventured this close to the inferno, and to the fiery elementals.

The Ildiran astronomers at the Wulfton station were nervous whenever she went out in her insulated observation globe, but she sensed the faeros would protect her if she called on them. The fiery ellipsoids were capricious, had been both enemies and allies, but

Osira'h knew them—and they knew her. They remained a powerful, looming noise in her mind . . . if only she could grasp it.

Her globe cruised over the stellar maelstrom below. Convection cells the size of continents boiled up, changing the gaseous landscape every moment. Thanks to many layers of dense filters, her eyes could tolerate the sight. She watched a large dark stain appear on the star, a duller red than the bright orange of the surrounding photosphere—a magnetic storm, a starspot. It was a gateway, as more fiery ellipsoids emerged and then sank back into the layers of hot gas again.

Osira'h came out here in the shielded globe so she could have solitude, peace among the faeros. It helped her to feel that everything was in balance.

Because they were a communal race, any individual Ildiran felt uneasy to be alone, but Osira'h was different. As the daughter of the green priest Nira and Mage-Imperator Jora'h himself, she was strengthened by myriad other connections.

Osira'h was never truly alone because her mind was tightly bound with her halfbreed brothers and sisters. Her four siblings could also feel the faeros, though their connection was not as strong as hers. Gale'nh had his place in the Solar Navy, Tamo'l had her medical research on Kuivahr, Muree'n was being trained by Yazra'h with dreams of becoming the greatest Ildiran fighter ever. Rod'h was the closest of her siblings, the most similar to her; they had the strongest telepathy of the halfbreeds. They shared much and helped each other, but despite their strengths, she and Rod'h were misfits among the Ildirans.

The Dobro breeding program had spent generations trying to breed a savior, and Osira'h had done her job. Her potent telepathy had brought the faeros and the hydrogues to their metaphorical knees at the end of the Elemental War. The enemy was defeated, the war over. She'd been invaluable in bringing the titanic enemies under control—but now what was she supposed to do?

She had finished her life's work when she was still a child.

Oh, the Empire revered and celebrated Osira'h, but they didn't understand who she was. The Ildirans were proud of her, although in some small corner of their minds—she could feel it through the thrumming of the *thism*—they were afraid of her, didn't know what to do with her.

Rod'h felt their unique predicament even more sharply than she did. He hadn't even been given the chance to serve his reason for being—a potential savior with nothing to save. Osira'h had been triumphant, and Rod'h was merely the backup. An unnecessary spare.

She hoped to keep her brother's disappointment from hardening into bitterness. She wished Rod'h could be with her at Wulfton. They could have been watching the faeros together, trying to understand them better. But he had refused, claiming he wasn't interested.

Beneath the observation globe, a fireball rocketed up like a bullet ejected from the star. The living thing shot past her craft, curious, sensing her. Inside her mind, Osira'h could hear ethereal voices and noises, the fiery intensity of faeros thoughts: a wash of defeat, withdrawal . . . not resentment, but limitation. Even in her closest contact with the fiery beings, Osira'h had not been able to understand *why* they turned their capricious behavior on both sides of the conflict.

The hydrogues were similar, as were the watery wentals. The verdani—the worldforest mind that manifested in all the trees of Theroc—was the most easily accessible sentience. Green priests like her mother had long been able to tap into the verdani mind, read the thoughts of the forest, share the knowledge stored there.

Concentrating now, Osira'h opened up to the fireball that hovered in front of her shielded globe. The flames brightened and swirled, and the ellipsoid spun before it shot off to swim with other faeros in a solar flare. Osira'h felt an afterimage in her brain, a warm tingle from the strange alien presence.

As her globe drifted, she closed her eyes and cast her thoughts out along the *thism* web. She listened to the simmering power of the elementals, the crackle of the faeros, the humming of the hydrogues that slumbered uneasily in their gas-giant planets, the sighs of the wentals across open bodies of water, the whisper of verdani voices like leaves blowing in the wind.

But there was also an uneasy background static . . . ghost voices stirring in the fabric of the universe. She could hear it more loudly than any of her siblings.

As she concentrated, Osira'h heard an unexpected *crack,* a sudden strengthening of the telepathic bond with her brother Gale'nh. She knew he had departed on the *Kolpraxa* for the far boundaries of the

Spiral Arm—and now she heard him cry out in her mind. A pitch-black coldness flowed from him, a shadow fell across his thoughts, and Gale'nh suddenly went silent in her mind.

She knew something terrible had happened to him, to the *Kol-praxa,* to all the Ildirans aboard it in the unexplored void of deep space.

When her vision snapped back into focus and she saw the faeros still bobbing in the depths of the star, Osira'h felt no warmth from them, only urgency. A panic? Even the faeros were afraid!

She activated the engines of her observation globe and raced up above the stellar corona. She transmitted to the astronomers at the astronomical research station to prepare a ship for immediate departure for Ildira.

She had to report to the Mage-Imperator.

THIRTY-FIVE

GENERAL NALANI KEAH

After General Keah returned to the Lunar Orbital Complex at Earth for a tedious meeting with her Grid Admirals—all quiet on every front, as expected—she insisted on heading out again. She didn't bother to manufacture a reason; she felt more effective if she kept moving.

The Lunar Orbital Complex was the administrative heart of the CDF, with enclosed military bases, spacedocks, construction yards, and civilian habitats. Although Theroc was the Confederation's capital, the military headquarters remained at Earth in the rubble of the Moon. Traditional Theron culture didn't have the infrastructure to support a major military complex (those gigantic verdani battleships orbiting Theroc, however, scared the crap out of Keah every time she went for an official visit).

Her Juggernaut was the most powerful ship in the CDF, and she liked to think of it as her office. With a green priest on her flagship, she could be contacted immediately, wherever the *Kutuzov* might be. The real command center was where *she* was.

The Juggernaut continued its long patrol, accompanied by nine Manta cruisers selected from the various grids, "taking them out for a test drive." This time, Adar Zan'nh also joined them with a septa of graceful Solar Navy warliners. During this joint exercise, all the ships followed the more optimistic scenario that the CDF and the Solar Navy would operate together against an outside enemy. Keah preferred that option. She and Zan'nh had already traded formal dinners on each other's flagships along the way.

Following a previously agreed-on course, the patrol group headed toward a cold gas giant named Dhula: a world with rusty red clouds orbited by a crowd of small moons. Dhula lay at the fringe of Ildiran space, unclaimed and unremarkable. Its atmospheric composition made the planet an unlikely candidate for ekti skymining; it was too isolated for human colonists to take notice, nor did the Ildirans seem interested in the world.

Under the pretext of their patrol, though, General Keah could have a look at the moon cluster, take a few readings. Maybe someone in the Confederation would figure out what to do with Dhula, or maybe it was no more than a planet on a list, a destination for these military exercises. She could live with that.

She glanced at the sleepy-looking green priest at his station beside his treeling. "Mr. Nadd, anything to report?"

Startled out of a doze, Nadd touched his treeling, then shook his head. "No emergencies, General."

She considered telling the green priest to go back to sleep, but decided that would set a bad example for her commissioned officers. She sat back in her command chair. "Part of me longs for a little excitement— you know, the kind of thing that makes for great CDF recruitment loops. On the other hand, a nice quiet patrol is how things are *supposed* to be, and it means that all is right with the Spiral Arm."

"There's a boost in pay for hazardous missions," First Officer Wingo pointed out.

"Only if you survive to collect it," said Tactical Officer Voecks.

After her heroic performance during the Klikiss space battle at Earth twenty years ago, Nalani Keah had worked her way up through the military. She was a golden girl, but also willing to call out inefficiency or stupidity when she encountered it. She made few friends among the old-guard sedentary bureaucrats, but she drew applause from up-and-coming officers who appreciated the improvements she suggested. Now, as the commander, her mission was to make the CDF lean and agile—an adaptable response force, rather than a bloated and showy institution.

Keah turned to her comm officer. "Open a channel to the flagship warliner, Mr. Aragao. I need to ask Adar Zan'nh if it's his turn to come over for dinner and strategy sessions, or for me to go over there."

The Ildiran commander's image appeared, as if he had been waiting for her to call. "General Keah, I have developed a plan for us to map the Dhula moon cluster. I would like your approval."

Keah nodded. "It's approved, Z."

"You don't wish to study it?"

"Not in the least. I know your capabilities, Z. No one's better at it than you are."

"Very well, we will arrange our exploration ships accordingly."

Keah gestured to her first officer, letting him take care of the matter. She hated paperwork and did too much of it when she was stationed back at the Lunar Orbital Complex. Mercer Wingo had won her over when he proved that he could ghostwrite most of her reports.

First Officer Wingo projected a map of the Dhula moons. The smaller CDF scout ships would do a quick flyover of the outlying satellites, while the Solar Navy would take larger squadrons, because Ildirans tended to get anxious when flying alone. Her Remora pilots could have done the entire operation with far less manpower, but she let the Solar Navy do it their own way.

Remora scouts flew out on their assigned surveys, while others arced around to "assist" the Solar Navy scouts. Dhula's first nine moons were rocks and snowballs, with no interesting mineral content, nothing that would attract even the most optimistic and impractical industrialist. Two of the moons showed denser metal concentrations, and Keah flagged them in case anyone wanted to bother with a deeper survey.

The twelfth moon was in an erratic elliptical orbit, probably knocked off course by a collision or gravitational perturbations. It had an icy outer crust, but it emanated thermal energy, an unexplained heat spike.

The Solar Navy sent a squadron of sensor-equipped cutters to cruise above the outlying moon for detailed mapping, but Keah called two of her Remoras to join them. "Let's pull together and do a full analysis. Maybe we'll find something interesting after all."

Her first officer gave her a skeptical look. "Are you prepping us for another war-game scenario, General?"

She shook her head. "Not unless Adar Zan'nh has a trick up his sleeve—and he never has a trick up his sleeve, unless he's really pushed."

The survey ships orbited the small moon, and the readings were

unusual enough that Keah decided they warranted a hands-on surface investigation. Adar Zan'nh agreed. The group of Solar Navy
cutters kept their distance, using remote mapping equipment. The
ruddy gas giant cast a glow on the moon's surface, and one of the
CDF Remoras skimmed over the pockmarked ice, sending sensor
pulses down. Keah watched the images flood back in.

Suddenly the frozen landscape took on a different character. Artificial shapes rose up, smooth towers that looked like termite mounds
made of ice. Geometrical patterns were scribed on the ice crust, even
a trapezoidal structure, a familiar framework that looked fresh and
new—under construction.

"This is some kind of base, General! A whole settlement down
there."

"Now that's a surprise." She contacted the flagship warliner. "Z,
does this ring any bells?"

"I have no bells," the Adar said. "I have transmitted a greeting
and request for information to the site. It is not an Ildiran splinter
colony. We will see if they acknowledge, whoever they are. I also dispatched a ground inspection team."

Keah gritted her teeth. "I would have preferred to use a little more
caution. Keep me in the loop, Z."

One of the Ildiran cutters landed on the ice near the strange structures. Adar Zan'nh was moving quickly, perhaps to stay one step
ahead of his rival. "No response from the base, as of yet, General.
Three of my soldiers have donned environment suits and will make
initial contact with the inhabitants."

On a private channel, Keah instructed her Remora pilots to keep
a close watch. "I don't like this at all." The scout pilots flew in a grid
pattern overhead, crisscrossing, keeping an eye on the Ildiran expedition.

"Thermal spike is increasing," said her sensor chief. "Like somebody's opening doors and powering up systems." The frozen moon
had a faint glow as energy seeped through the thick frozen layers.

"They know we're here." Keah transmitted to the flagship warliner,
"Adar, I recommend that your team exercises extreme caution."

The three suited Ildiran soldier kithmen emerged from the landed
cutter. The alien space helmets were elongated, reminding her of a

conch shell. Adar Zan'nh provided the *Kutuzov* with a direct feed from the helmet imagers so Keah could watch the progress. The contact team walked in a slow-motion march across the landscape toward the base, following the edge of a deep, straight trough in the ice.

The explorers shone blazers in front of them. The pool of bright light sparkled from ice that had been melted and refrozen many times. The three approached some kind of access hatch into the underground facility, or base, or hiding place—whatever it was. The Ildirans studied the hatch.

Adar Zan'nh contacted Keah, breaking her train of thought. "General, our rememberers have finished reviewing historical records. A discovery similar to this was made on a frozen moon of Hyrillka."

Keah knew that Hyrillka was an Ildiran planet, the site of several battles in the Elemental War, but she didn't know how that might apply here.

The three suited explorers stepped back as the access hatch shuddered, then cracked open. No wisp of atmosphere bled out, so this was not an airlock, simply an access door to an airless base. The helmet imagers showed movement behind the hatch, a wink of crimson eyes . . . dozens of them, then hundreds.

The Ildirans shone their blazers ahead, suddenly revealing a mass of black beetlelike machines with flat geometrical heads, glowing eye sensors, articulated limbs. The machines surged forward.

"Klikiss robots!" Keah yelled.

Adar Zan'nh commanded his soldiers to retreat. Now that they had been discovered, the black robots boiled out of their underground base. Keah saw hundreds of attackers before the Ildiran helmet imagers went from static to black.

"I thought the bugbots were all wiped out at the end of the war!" Keah sent a signal throughout the scout group. "I'm not inclined to sit around and chat, Z—I say we attack."

The Adar had already issued orders. "I agree completely, General."

THIRTY-SIX

EXXOS

The black robots had bided their time for centuries, surviving apparent extinction, two major Klikiss swarmings, and the Elemental War. Now, from their last redoubt in an unnamed icy moon orbiting an all-but-forgotten gas giant, Exxos had made plans for the past twenty years.

After the disastrous end of the recent war, his remaining black robots tunneled deep into the frozen crust, setting up this base, while others gathered useful scrap components from secret searches around the Spiral Arm. The machines constructed industrial equipment, extracted metals, manufactured new vessels and weapons.

Following their utter defeat, the resurgence of the Klikiss robots required careful planning, and patience. His hundreds of robots pooled their immense calculational abilities, casting a wide net of projections to capture every possible scenario. Exxos had analyzed the entire scheme—it could not fail. They had only to hide and wait. The black robots could brush aside the immensity of history and simply consider the final result. The conclusions were indisputable.

But first, they had to survive.

In establishing their redoubt, Exxos had considered it extremely unlikely that any ship would investigate the Dhula system, although humans were persistent, ambitious, and unpredictable. Should the robots be discovered by an unexpected scout ship, perhaps some naïve miner poking around the moon cluster, Exxos had planned a response. In one scenario, he had projected that a Solar Navy warliner might detect them in the course of inspecting Ildiran planets. The black robots had assumed they could simply lie low and hide their base. Barring that, as a last resort, they could destroy any ship that displayed too much curiosity.

deck. By now all robots should have been aboard, and he could wait for no stragglers. He remotely sealed all hatches and fired his engines, clearing the way for liftoff. The blast of heat melted more ice shards.

In the sensor view, he watched as three black robots were caught in the backwash of his roaring engines. Each loss was significant. Of the million or more Klikiss robots that had fought at the height of the Elemental War, only this handful remained. Though it might take centuries to create more Klikiss robots, Exxos could find a way—but long-term plans did not concern him now. They were relevant only if he and his robots escaped.

When all six escape vessels were ready to rise, Exxos triggered the rest of the trench detonations. Lines of explosions vaporized the ice sheet overhead and shot geysers of vapor and debris into the sky, which served as a momentary smoke screen. He felt the rumble of his ship as the levitation engines activated.

The loaded robot vessels rose away from the moon, firing weapons indiscriminately as the human and Ildiran warships closed in. Unfortunately, the high-velocity ice projectiles had not caused enough damage.

He anchored his armored body against full acceleration. Leaving the frozen moon behind and escaping the rubble of their base, the robot ships fled into space.

THIRTY-SEVEN

ELISA REEVES

Elisa spent four days stranded alone in space at the site of the exploded bloaters. She worked on her ship, rerouting power around the damaged systems to bypass any that were not absolutely vital. And she did it herself.

Garrison had always been arrogantly proud of Roamer ingenuity; he bragged about how his people could take the most unlikely hodge-podge of components and make them work like magic—the proverbial spit, chewing gum, and bandages. Elisa found it ridiculous.

Lee Iswander was also a Roamer, but instead of relying on his pilots being able to make duct-tape-and-twine repairs, Iswander Industries simply provided each ship with adequate spare parts in case anything should fail. It seemed a much more rational way to prepare for emergencies. Elisa had worked for days swapping out life-support modules, navigation circuits, and damaged engine controls.

Eventually, her ship was ready to fly again.

During the flight away from the site, where most of the bloaters had been destroyed, she pondered and rehearsed exactly how she was going to tell Iswander what had happened. Her mission had not turned out the way she'd expected, but at least she wasn't returning empty-handed—thanks to her intrepid investigations. She had studied two of the surviving bloaters and couldn't wait to tell Lee Iswander what she had found.

She didn't want Iswander's pity for the tragic death of her son as well as, she supposed, her husband. But once the industrialist learned what she had discovered, he would surely promote her (after acknowledging the painful loss of her family). This find was worth an incalculable fortune.

When she reached the Sheol system, the binary planet looked like a glowing ember in space, cracked and bleeding with lava. Just like always. The lack of space traffic surprised her, though. She heard none of the constant comm chatter of cargo ships hauling exotic metal-polymer materials or shipments of ingots. She surfed the channels, expecting to hear the usual drone of conversation from smelter barge crews and the control towers, even Alec Pannebaker showing off some stupid stunt. Their perimeter systems must have detected her, but she received no ID request. Odd.

She transmitted her queries, trying to find someone who would answer, and finally received a reply—but the transmission did not come from the admin tower down on the fiery surface; rather, the response was from a small satellite station in orbit that received bulk shipments and transferred supplies down to the main facility.

It was Lee Iswander's voice. She couldn't believe he would be manning the comm himself. By now, she had expected he would be the new Speaker for the Roamer clans.

"Elisa, you came back!" He sounded strange, shaken . . . relieved? "Did you retrieve your son?"

"No, he . . . he's dead. Garrison put him in a hazardous situation. He was reckless. He . . . they were both lost in a massive explosion."

Iswander groaned and said in a much quieter voice, "Haven't we had enough deaths already?"

Elisa felt a sudden chill, now even more alarmed that the lava-processing facilities were so silent and empty. "What happened? Where is everyone on Sheol?"

"*Everything* happened. The facilities are gone. Hundreds dead— fifteen hundred and forty-three. The survivors are at Newstation, but I had to come back here, see if I could salvage anything. It seemed the best place." He didn't sound like himself at all. He seemed *broken*.

Though Elisa was ready to explode with questions, she quelled them, forced a businesslike calm. "I'm docking soon. You can tell me about it face-to-face."

She guided her ship into the orbiting transfer station, and hers was one of only four ships in the bay; half of the lights had been dimmed.

She carried images of the bloater cluster, the record of the explosions, and her quick analysis. Rushing back to Sheol, she had been bursting with excitement over her news—enough to temporarily overshadow the loss of her son. But when she presented herself in the control chamber, she was astonished to see Lee Iswander's face. He looked exhausted, aged. His skin tone was grayish, and he had shadows around his eyes.

"I'm glad to have one supporter back," he said. "You don't know how much that means to me."

Alec Pannebaker swept into the control center, and his usual smile looked more relieved than excited. "Elisa! Well, that's one step closer to digging our way out of this hole."

"We're in space," grumbled Iswander's son. "Everything's a hole."

Arden's mother wrapped her arm around the boy's shoulders and pulled him close, though he resisted. "I told you it'll be all right. Your father's had ups and downs before. We'll get through this—we just have to be strong."

Elisa looked Iswander straight in the eye. "No matter what happened, sir, I'm here to provide anything you might need for Iswander Industries. You have my full commitment . . . now that my son is gone." Her voice cracked at the end.

Now that I have no distractions. No family obligations. Nothing else to divert me.

"We'll need it," he said. "But I'm afraid I've lost everything."

Iswander explained the disaster in the lava-processing facilities, how he was being accused of using "irresponsible safety margins." Elisa had also dismissed Garrison's Chicken Little fears. Well, he hadn't lived to see his fears proved right.

Iswander continued. "Only two dozen workers followed me back here, in hopes of salvaging something from the wreckage. Not necessarily because they have faith in me—they may not have anyplace else to go."

When Iswander looked at her, his reddened eyes and his intense but distant stare made her stomach knot. He said, "When we came back here, I didn't expect anyone to be alive, but the station had recorded transmissions from the smelter barges below, and some survivors in one shielded chamber in Tower Two that remained intact after the collapse. Those people knew they were going to die as the temperature rose and the insulation failed."

His voice sounded hollow and distant, as if he had scrubbed and scrubbed to remove all emotion from it, but the stains remained. "They recorded farewell messages, said goodbye to their wives or husbands, families, friends. Some of them cursed me, some of them seemed resigned. Sooner or later they all died, and most of them not quickly. In the last seconds, they—" His voice hitched, and he glanced at his son. "Arden heard some of the messages. I should have sent him away sooner."

Elisa stood straight, determined. "Do I need to listen to them? Anything valuable in the last words?"

"I deleted the messages. All of them. Couldn't risk anyone else hearing that."

She thought for a moment, then nodded. "Good decision, sir."

He hung his head. "I'm ruined. I have assets from my other industries, and I've buried funds in banks on scattered planets, but it won't do me much good. After this debacle, no one would partner with me again."

Elisa had never heard him like this. "So . . . you came back to lie low?"

"We're not hiding—we're reassessing." Iswander gave Elisa a self-deprecating smile. "Oh, and I lost the election to become Speaker, in case you were wondering. I got one vote."

"I wouldn't vote against you," she said, and decided it was time. "In fact, I've found a new venture for you, something no other Roamer knows about. Are you willing to start from scratch?"

"Don't have much choice," Iswander said. "And I've done it before."

Now she saw a faint light in the back of his eyes again. *Good.*

She displayed the file she had brought. After the explosions and the loss of her son, she had felt defeated as well, but there was too much at stake. Even if she was wounded from her own loss, she had to be strong in order to help Lee Iswander.

She showed images of the swollen nodules drifting about in the empty dark between the stars, thousands of them. "This is where I tracked Garrison in his stolen ship, a large cluster of strange nodules. Maybe organic, maybe not. They aren't in any database. He tried to hide among them, but look how dangerous they are."

She displayed the furious inferno as the bloaters detonated, one after another, a chain reaction that swelled outward like multiple supernovas. The blast flung her ship on the crest of the shock wave. She didn't tell him that the initial energy discharge had come from her own ship.

Iswander blinked, as if reminded of the erupting fires on Sheol. He reached out to clutch her hand, a surprisingly warm and compassionate grip. "I'm sorry about your son, Elisa."

She pulled her hand away and called up another file. She had to make him see. "That isn't all, sir. Those bloaters . . ." She felt a pang as she used the word Seth had made up. "I analyzed a few outliers that survived the explosion. They were scattered across great distances, like bread crumbs in a line, and once I knew what to look for, I scanned far and wide—and discovered a second cluster of bloaters near the fringe of an uninhabited star system. I suspect there are other conglomerations as well. I left a marker at the new site—we can go back whenever we like."

Iswander looked at the images of the exotic bloaters, dull brownish green nodules barely lit by the distant spray of starlight. "But what are they? Why should I care?"

"Because, sir, they will save you, make you fabulously rich." Elisa's eyes shone, and now she clasped his hand, trying to push her intensity upon him so that she reignited his own drive. "The bloaters are filled with *ekti*!"

The battered Iswander Industries ship made its way to the rubble belt that had once been the heart of Roamer government. Thanks to Garrison's falling out with his father, Seth had never been to Rendezvous, despite its significance to the clans. The boy seemed nervous as they approached the main asteroid. "Does my grandfather even know who I am?"

Garrison tried to keep his voice light, though his heart felt heavy. "Of course he knows who you are! And I'm sure he's anxious to meet you." He reached over to tousle his son's hair.

Seth ducked his head away. "But do you think they'll be glad to see us?"

"Definitely." This time, it was harder to sound convincing.

He was sorry to see how quickly Seth recovered from the loss of his mother. The boy had cried a great deal during the long flight from the explosion site in deep space, but now he seemed to be denying or ignoring what had happened. Children were resilient, but Garrison thought this was more than that. Maybe at Rendezvous his son would feel more settled, for a while.

Garrison had paid little attention to his last sight of the asteroid cluster when he turned his back on the place eleven years ago to run off with Elisa Enturi. Although clan Reeves had worked hard in the intervening years, he saw now that they had not made a great deal of progress in rebuilding Rendezvous. The project was just too big for them.

Garrison had been a teenager during the Elemental War, and he remembered the frantic evacuation of Rendezvous as the Earth Defense Forces bombarded the connected asteroids, a devastating act that had turned the clans into outlaws. From that point, Garrison had lived with his family in place after place, scrounging a living, surviving without "frivolous comforts," as Olaf called them. After the end of the war, when the proud clans vowed to rebuild Rendezvous, Olaf Reeves championed the task as if it were a sacred duty.

But the scope of the reconstruction project became plain over the years. The members of clan Reeves spent years maneuvering the dispersed asteroids back together, connecting them with struts and walkways, excavating the collapsed grottos that had been meeting chambers.

Once the clans joined the new Confederation, however, Newstation became a more viable government and trade center. Rendezvous had originally been established as a mere stopping-over point for the generation ship *Kanaka*. Aside from its historical significance and being a place close to every Roamer's heart, the system was out of the way, with no particular resources. Speaker Del Kellum had suggested a fresh start for the Roamers in a more hospitable place.

As the other clans lost interest and withdrew their support for rebuilding Rendezvous, calling the project a boondoggle, Olaf Reeves grew more intractable and more determined, though he refused to accept any outside assistance—especially not the Iswander Industries modules Garrison had tried to deliver.

"Stubborn" seemed an insufficient word to describe his father.

Garrison sighed as he flew the battered ship toward the main docking asteroid, steeling himself before he flipped on the comm. "Hello, Rendezvous, this is Garrison Reeves, on my way home. My son is with me. If you've got a place for us to stay for a few days, we have a story to tell."

The thin face of his younger brother Dale appeared on the comm screen. His voice was almost a yelp. "Garrison! We thought you were dead on Sheol."

Garrison's heart lurched. "Dead on Sheol?" He had been cut off from all communications since fleeing the lava-processing facility. "What happened?"

"A disaster. The whole facility—lava eruptions! Hundreds killed."

Seth's eyes went wide as they filled with tears, and Garrison felt a hot coal in his chest. "You were right, Dad."

"Not the way I wanted to be."

After he landed the stolen Iswander ship—which he had never bothered to name, though Roamers always named their ships—several clan members gathered in the rock-walled bay to meet him. Clan engineers came forward to fuel the ship and check out the systems, as if this were any other vessel landing for a brief stopover.

A squat, swarthy man with the incongruous name of Bjorn eyed the discolorations on the hull. "You're awfully hard on your ship, Garrison."

"Not my ship."

"Then you're awfully hard on other people's ships. We'll fix what needs to be fixed, patch what needs to be patched. How long are you staying?"

Garrison didn't have an answer for that. "Depends." *Depends on the reception we get. Depends on what happened at Sheol. Depends on what I decide to do from now on.*

Bjorn scratched a bristly cheek. "I just need to know how much time we have to complete repairs."

"As long as you need," Dale said as he entered the bay. His younger brother had a high forehead and a pointed chin that was now covered with a wispy beard, as if he were trying to imitate his father's extravagant whiskers, but came up far short—as he did in most things. He stepped forward to shake Garrison's hand, then enfolded him in an awkward embrace. "Your timing is perfect—we're all packing up to leave."

"Leave?" Garrison couldn't believe that his father would finally give up on the insurmountable task of reconstructing Rendezvous. "Going where?"

Seth broke in, pale and anxious. "Tell us what happened at Sheol?"

Dale grinned down. "This is your boy? Sendra and I have two sons of our own, five and nine. You knew that, right? We have plenty of time to catch up and . . ." He looked uncertain. "I, uh, should let Father tell you everything. He'll be glad to see you."

Garrison raised his eyebrows "Will he, Dale?"

Shy and awkward, his brother avoided the answer. "He'll certainly want to talk with you."

As they left the hangar bay, they encountered a slender and pretty woman with strawberry-blond hair. Standing inside the rock-walled corridor, she directed an intense gaze toward Garrison. Dale said stupidly, "You remember Sendra, my wife?"

"He better not have forgotten me." She came forward to kiss Garrison on the cheek, which embarrassed Dale more than it did Garrison.

Sendra Detemer should have been Garrison's wife; everyone knew that. They were a perfect match, attracted to each other, and the marriage should have joined the two clans. But after he had left Rendezvous with Elisa, Sendra accepted Dale's marriage proposal. She was smart, pretty, and followed her own interests. His brother knew full well that he was merely the second choice. And now, after what had happened with Elisa, Garrison was painfully reminded of the bad choice he had made.

With Dale standing right beside her, Sendra gave Garrison a gaze full of meanings, regrets, questions, and not-so-subtle flirtation. *You could've had me,* she seemed to be thinking. "And how is your wife?" she asked.

Dale hissed, "Sendra—they came from Sheol."

She looked mortified at what she had said. "Oh, I'm so sorry!"

Garrison lowered his head. "Elisa wasn't there either."

The boy blurted out, "My mother died in an explosion out in space."

Dale hurried them along, eager to get away from Sendra. "We shouldn't delay. I let Father know we're coming, so he's waiting for us."

Garrison knew what that meant. "Then we'd better not keep him."

The clan leader's chambers had once belonged to the Roamer Speaker, back when this asteroid had been the heart of Rendezvous. Olaf Reeves sat behind his metal desk as if holding court. He did not get up to greet Garrison or Seth; he was too proud for that.

"It's the prodigal son." Even here in the small office, Olaf's voice was booming. "You're older now—and wiser, let's hope. You went off looking for Hansa happiness, when you should have been satisfied with Roamer happiness."

"I was looking for my own happiness, Father. I wanted to do what was right." But Olaf's words hit home. Elisa's definition of happiness— her goals, her success, her drive—had been very different from Garrison's desire for a fulfilled life, a strong family, close friends. That would have been enough for him, but it had never been enough for Elisa.

Olaf turned toward Seth. "And my grandson, quite a young man. We'll have a place for you among us. We just retrieved our clan children from Academ, so they can be taught in proper Roamer ways. We even brought a Teacher compy to help."

Seth brightened. "A compy?"

"We have five total now," Dale interrupted. "We made sure the fail-safe programming systems are in place."

Seth looked at his father, disappointed. "But I wanted to go to Academ."

"I'll still find a way for you to go there, don't worry," Garrison said.

"You don't need Academ." Olaf leaned forward, giving his grandson a warmer welcome. "The Teacher compy's name is BO. She knows a lot about Roamer history—you can join the other children in their independent classes. With us. You'll do well, I'm sure."

Garrison felt distinctly uncomfortable. "That wasn't my plan, Father. We're getting ahead of ourselves."

His father's bushy eyebrows drew together. "Yes, we are. I'm not surprised you spotted the dangers at Sheol, because you're smart and could see what was in front of your face. We hadn't heard that you got away . . . thought you might have stayed with That Woman."

"I sounded the warning, but Lee Iswander didn't listen. Neither did Elisa."

Olaf made a disgusted sound. "That man's been Goose-headed for years, forgot he's a Roamer. We are best when we push the limits and survive by the skin of our teeth—that makes us grow, makes us strong."

Dale said, as if repeating a benediction, "A knife loses its edge unless it is sharpened."

When Garrison was in his father's presence, the big man seemed to consider Dale invisible. "Too many Roamers have gone soft on comfortable planets. The romance is gone. They lost something vital. That's why we're all pulling out—leaving Rendezvous and making a new home."

"Leaving Rendezvous? You invested everything here, insisted on clinging to this place even when everyone else pulled out and called you a stubborn fool. Where are you going to go?"

"Far away," Olaf said. "We're too close to the stink of Newstation, the Confederation, and all the things that weaken us. One of our clan scouts found an ancient city in space, probably millennia old. It was like a sign. No one's touched it. We'll make it our new home." He leaned forward to encompass both Garrison and Seth with his gaze. "*Our* home." He pretended to notice reports on his desk screen, then glanced at the chronometer on the wall. "I understand they're making repairs to your ship now? We'll find a place for you to settle in, figure out what your place will be with us."

Garrison held up his hands. "We haven't said we're going with you. Seth and I just came back for a visit, and to ask for a little help."

"That Woman gave you enough help. The wrong kind. Now it's time to come home, if you've learned your lesson."

Seth looked lost, and Garrison gave his shoulder a reassuring squeeze. He remembered the opportunities he had missed while growing up because of his father's pigheadedness, and he would not inflict that upon his son. "No. We're not going with you to whatever isolated place you're taking the clan. Seth needs to grow up in the Confederation, to be part of the future, not part of the past. He's going to Academ where he can learn with Roamer children his own age."

A flush rose in Olaf's cheeks, and his voice became a growl, though it didn't get any louder. "You've already had a terrible lapse in judgment, Garrison. That Woman seduced you, corrupted you. You can be forgiven for making one major mistake, but you're about to make another one."

"I'm making a decision. Whether it's a mistake or not is something we can determine later. Seth and I won't be following you out to the middle of nowhere just because you're fed up with the Confederation and with other Roamers. Seth wants to study at Academ, and I think that's a good choice for him." Olaf snorted, but Garrison stood straight, feeling his face flush. In the years he'd been gone he had learned a lot about strength. "Did you give the other clan members the chance to make up their own minds? Or are you forcing them to go with you, because you know what's best for them all?"

"I do know what's best for them, so their choice is obvious."

"And the choice is obvious to me too. Seth and I will make our own way, build our own lives."

Olaf glowered. "Then let the consequences be on your own head."

This was exactly what Garrison had feared, and he'd expected nothing less. He also knew that argument was useless with Olaf Reeves.

Olaf glanced at his other son, as if just remembering Dale was there. "Tell Bjorn to get Garrison's ship fixed and fueled so he can be about his important business. The rest of clan Reeves has its own Guiding Star to follow."

THIRTY-NINE

ORLI COVITZ

Matthew had asked Orli to meet him at one of their favorite restaurants, a colorful high-end establishment built and run by Rlinda Kett. By long distance, he had made reservations and added a significant tip so they had their favorite table—the one Rlinda always guaranteed for them. That was a good sign, Orli told herself, and she clung to the thought as she got ready, even though she felt a distinct uneasiness about what her husband planned to say.

Matthew Freling wasn't a man who laughed often. He was serious and focused to the point of being preoccupied. Orli had fallen in love with his smile, but she couldn't recall any hearty laughter—that wasn't part of his personality. There had been no smiles in his recent message. He said he had something "important" to talk with her about. Not something "special." Not a "surprise."

In their apartment, Orli obsessed over which dress to wear. Expensive business attire? Something flirtatious to welcome him home after his long trip? Muted colors to acknowledge a serious occasion, or just a casual outfit to downplay any sort of concern she might have?

Finally, she asked DD for his advice. The Friendly compy lectured her about alternatives until she sighed and held up a hand for him to stop. "Make a random selection for me, DD. That'll do." He selected a maroon blouse over a pair of tailored black slacks made from merhsilk. Orli added a necklace of polished reef pearls from Rhejak—a gift from old Mr. Steinman, and more expensive than she liked to think about.

Orli was reluctant to wear anything with too much sentimental value. She and Matthew had weathered plenty of rough patches in their relationship, but they had worked through the serious ones, varnished over the pain, and didn't pick at the scabs, careful not to draw blood. In their marriage, they'd had five good years and five not-so-good years, with the issue of children being the primary thorn in their relationship.

"You seem sad, Orli," DD said.

"Maybe a little sad. Maybe a little worried. I don't know what Matthew has on his mind."

"Would you like me to transmit a message and ask him?"

She gave him a wan smile. "It's not that simple, DD. This is something we have to explore for ourselves."

"Oh, like a research project."

She gave DD a hug, then went off to Rlinda's restaurant.

She was on her second glass of wine by the time Matthew arrived. He was always five minutes late; Orli was used to that. His personal clock was irreparably off by the same amount. Tonight, though, he was fifteen minutes late, and that told Orli a great deal. He would have some mundane excuse—a shuttle was delayed, traffic was bad, or Orli must have gotten the time wrong.

He knew where to find their table. Seeing him come in, Orli raised her hand in a signal. With a brief nod, he came over to her.

At the beginning of their relationship, there had been warm greetings, happy kisses and hugs, but public displays of affection were not Matthew's habit. She initiated an embrace to make herself feel better. He kissed her on the lips, but to Orli it felt more like a misplaced peck on the cheek.

"Welcome home," she said. "How was your trip?"

Matthew seemed relieved to fall into a business conversation, rattling off a summary of his talks and presentations, remarking on which universities drew large audiences and which ones gave him a less-enthusiastic reception.

She knew the places he visited, knew the other researchers he talked about, knew the concerns and the high points of their work. Their passion about compies gave them so much in common that getting married had been the obvious, logical thing to do. Work partners and life partners.

When the waiter came, they ordered appetizers, their usual. The restaurant's excellent food represented a range of cultures and exotic flavors, traditional dishes from Theroc, the Roamer clans, and Earth. Rlinda's chef made a special platter of flaming buttery grubs from Theroc, which they particularly liked.

They had first tried the dish during dinner on their fifth anniversary—the last good anniversary. Matthew was squeamish, but Orli had eaten many disgusting things during desperate times on Dremen, Corribus, and other places. Rlinda had joined them for a few minutes during that anniversary meal, insisting that the appetizer was her favorite thing on the menu. So Orli and Matthew dared each other to eat the grubs, which were indeed as tasty as promised.

Now, however, Orli poked at them. The waiter raised his eyebrows knowingly, as if accustomed to patrons who ordered the grubs but couldn't find the nerve to eat them. Orli frowned and took one, swallowed it whole. When the waiter hovered to take their dinner order, she sent him away. "We're not ready yet." She turned to Matthew, got serious. "What is it you needed to talk about?"

He swallowed, and she saw his Adam's apple move up and down. He straightened in his chair, getting down to business, and his expression changed. His eyes grew distant, and she knew he was about to deliver words he had memorized and probably practiced again and again as he traveled back to Relleker.

"I had a surprise visitor after my lecture on New Portugal," he said.

She waited, and realization began to dawn. New Portugal had already raised her suspicions.

Matthew said, "Henna came to see me."

Though Orli knew it was coming, she couldn't stop her heart from skipping a beat. "I thought she promised not to see you. *You* promised you wouldn't."

He nodded. "That's how it was supposed to be."

The crisis had been only four months ago, when she discovered his affair with Henna Gann . . . or maybe he had confessed it. The timing was murky in Orli's mind, and the argument had been so severe that the details were fractured and not something she wanted to recall.

It was a hard twist of the knife, coming so soon after their most recent fight about having children. When Orli learned of the affair, she was deeply hurt, but in a quiet corner of her heart she realized she had put up walls and added distance between them too. She had buried herself in her work, surrounded herself with her compies, sent Matthew away on his rigorous speaking schedule. Somehow, even with all those work commitments, Matthew found the time and energy to sleep with another woman.

Orli had been through ordeals before. She'd seen the slaughter of the Corribus colony, including her father, had been a captive of the Klikiss race, fended for herself while she was lost and starving. So, she put the hurt behind her, and they had worked it out. She and Matthew decided to give it another try.

The buttery grubs on the plate now gave off a nauseating smell. Orli couldn't tear her eyes from him. He had more to say.

"She told me something's changed," he said.

"How would you know, if you'd kept your promise not to see her again?"

"Henna came to me after my lecture. I didn't ask to see her. She was just there." He seemed about to unravel a long string of excuses and rationalizations, but he stopped himself, looked Orli in the eye. "She's pregnant. I didn't know. The affair was over, I swear to you— but now she's carrying my child." He clasped his hands together. "*My child.* That changes everything."

Orli felt as if someone had tripped her when she wasn't looking, knocked her facedown on the ground. Yes, that did change everything.

At the beginning of their relationship, Matthew had wanted children, but Orli convinced him to wait; later, when she was ready, Matthew had been preoccupied with his busy career. He said no, not yet. Without any sort of goal or time frame, the idea of a family kept vanishing beyond the horizon. And now . . .

"Henna and I are going to have a baby," he repeated. From the look on his face, the hint of expression behind his eyes, she wondered if he expected her to leap for joy and congratulate him. She rose from the table and walked away.

He called after her, "I hope we can still work together."

She paused without turning, thought of several retorts, and dismissed them all. She kept walking.

When she got home Orli couldn't stop herself from crying. Tears rolled down her face, and she ran into their main living room where DD waited for her.

"How was your dinner?" he asked brightly. "How was Matthew?" Then even the childlike Friendly compy noticed that something was wrong. "Oh, Orli, I am so sorry."

She couldn't guess how he knew to say that, but she caught him up in an embrace and sobbed onto his polymer shoulder.

FOURTY

GENERAL NALANI KEAH

Within fifteen minutes, General Keah ran out of expletives. This was supposed to have been a routine patrol with the Ildirans, not even a surprise war-game exercise—and the ships had stumbled upon an infestation of black robots.

"Those bugbots should have been wiped out twenty years ago," Keah said. The beetle-like machines had caused incalculable damage to all sides in the Elemental War. "Let's finish this damn job—it'll increase my career satisfaction."

After seeing his exploration crew slaughtered on the screens, Adar Zan'nh's expression clouded like a storm as he called on his ships to retaliate. Keah had never seen the cool Ildiran commander so furious. She liked him this way.

Their ships reeled in the ferocious surprise attack from the frozen base, the bombardment of high-velocity ice projectiles, but General Keah could give as good as she got.

"Full jazer bursts, Mr. Patton. Fire up the railguns and use kinetic projectiles—hell, use harsh language! Pass the word to all ships in our battle group. Hit them with everything. And if we do this right, each crewmember gets a piece of bugbot shrapnel for a souvenir."

The moon's surface cracked and collapsed as implanted explosives blasted away the ice sheet to expose a half-dozen monstrous angular vessels that sent a chill down her spine. She leaned forward in the command chair. "I'd say that's an invitation for a full carpet bombing, Mr. Patton."

The weapons officer responded with a hard grin. "On it, General."

Six robot ships began to rise from their cold underground base, heaving up out of the curtains of steam and flash-melted ice. Gases boiled around the black vessels like a smoke screen.

She addressed the Solar Navy flagship. "We better hit them before they head off into space, Z. They're vulnerable now."

"That is my intention, General."

When she saw the heavy armor on the ships, Keah realized the bug-bots must have been planning for defense and outright combat for some time. The massive vessels ascended from gaping craters blasted through the ice, and the first four headed out to open space. The Solar Navy warliners and CDF battleships closed in.

Their main targets were the last two robot ships, which were still rising from the crevasses. Concentrated bombardment damaged the fifth sufficiently that it barely managed to lift itself above the surface before it crashed down like a dying whale. The sixth fleeing ship exploded just as it cleared the ice.

The other four robot ships did not turn back to defend their comrades, did not work together—they simply increased engine power and accelerated away from the Dhula moon cluster.

Keah yelled, "Helm, increase engine speed. Keep pace, and keep firing."

The Ildiran warliners spread their extravagant sails, fired up the stardrives, and accelerated as they blasted at the fleeing vessels. They gained on the robot ships, and the rearmost enemy vessels launched a fusillade of energy bursts that struck the shields of the CDF battle group, forcing three Mantas to veer off so their systems could recharge.

Adar Zan'nh's flagship took point as the Solar Navy septa closed in. One robot vessel fired another round of energy blasts—targeted on the lagging robot ship. The barrage damaged its engines in a sacrifice play, and a crippling explosion sent the vessel tumbling backward in an uncontrolled spiral. It careened into the oncoming warliners, striking one and caroming off into a second warliner, taking both out of the chase.

Adar Zan'nh let out a loud curse. "Bekh!"

Keah had never even heard him raise his voice before. While her battle group streaked past the reeling Ildiran ships, she gave him a reassuring smile. "We've got it, Z."

The engines of the last three enemy vessels were bright and hot as they burned their systems to tolerance levels. Black robots could withstand far more acceleration than any fragile biological body, but Keah pushed the *Kutuzov*'s engines as hard as she dared.

She loathed the bugbots, and it was more than just a philosophical disagreement—this was personal. She had been there on Earth when the robots launched their worst betrayal, wrecking numerous EDF ships, including hers. As a young bridge officer, Keah had seen the explosions all around her, watched her commander killed, could still recall the names of her fallen comrades.

Keah gritted her teeth and ordered another full weapons volley, just because she was pissed. She raised her voice to the green priest on the bridge. "Mr. Nadd, use your tree to tell the King that we've flushed out an infestation of leftover black robots, but we're in pursuit."

Nadd blinked. "Shouldn't I wait until we're done, General?"

"Some news is too good to sit on."

The three surviving robot ships had left the ruddy gas giant behind and plunged headlong into open space, racing beyond even the cometary cloud.

The five intact Solar Navy warliners caught up with the *Kutuzov*. "We're causing damage," she transmitted to the Adar, "but the bugbots will get away if they can keep up that acceleration without exploding their engines. We can't match it."

On the tracking screens, the three robot vessels increased their lead, pulling ahead into the emptiness. Keah yelled to her sensor chief, "Lieutenant Saliba, do not lose track of them—that's an order!"

"Scanning ahead, General, keeping my eyes on—" Saliba paused. "Detecting something odd outside the system. Some sort of black nebula or dust cloud. I can only tell it's there because I can't read anything else through it." She shrugged. "It's giving no readings at all—like a hole in space, and I swear it wasn't there when we entered the Dhula system."

On screen, the black nebula swirled, darkness mixed with deeper darkness. Keah thought it must be an illusion, because any dust cloud so large would grow and change on a cosmic timescale, nothing the human eye could ever notice. She hit the comm again. "Z, do you see that shadow cloud up ahead?"

"There is a deep shadow, and I find it unsettling—we have no record of anything in that area."

"There's definitely something now."

The three robot battleships changed course and veered directly toward the cloud.

"They probably want to hide in the dust," her navigator said. "If we lose them inside the nebula, they'll get away."

"Then don't let them get there," Keah said.

As the *Kutuzov* raced toward the looming dark nebula, several bridge screens flickered and blurred. Bursts of static danced across the display panels before they sharpened to clarity again.

Keah's throat went dry. During the Elemental War, the Klikiss robots had introduced insidious viruses that wrecked EDF command-and-control systems. "Did those bugbots sabotage our core programming? How is that possible?"

When Adar Zan'nh contacted the *Kutuzov*, his image was out of focus. "We are experiencing difficulties, General." Behind him, the lights in his command nucleus flickered.

"Ditto over here." She turned to her weapons officer. "Mr. Patton, please tell me that our jazers still work."

"I suggest we test them out, General."

She grinned. "I like the way you think. Indulge yourself."

Patton opened fire, and a barrage of energy beams streaked toward the fleeing robot ships, but the aim was wildly off. He looked embarrassed. "Sorry, General. Our systems seem to be out of whack."

The warliners blasted as well, a haphazard flurry of discharges that went far afield, although several struck and damaged one lagging robot ship. The other two enemy vessels pulled forward, careening straight toward the black cloud.

The shapeless nebula surged and roiled, which Keah found disconcerting. She leaned forward. "What the hell?"

The robot ships pushed toward the blackness, and suddenly, like the pseudopod of a nightmare amoeba, it lunged out and engulfed the two enemy vessels.

The third robot ship kept struggling along. The CDF and Solar Navy ships charged forward to intercept it, but the lights flickered on the *Kutuzov*'s bridge. Diagnostic screens went to complete static. The engines sounded as if they were laboring.

The navigator fumbled with his systems. "We're losing control, General. I can't figure out these glitches."

From Engineering, Mr. Kalfas transmitted on the override line, "Systems everywhere are going haywire."

All the pursuing ships were struggling as they raced after the last robot vessel. Adar Zan'nh signaled from his command nucleus, "I do not like this, General. If these malfunctions continue, we will be dead in space." His face looked drawn, his eyes haunted. "One of our re-memberers has reminded me of a similar black nebula from our past. I am not sure I believe it myself, but it could be very dangerous."

The lagging robot ship finally made it to the shadow cloud and vanished inside the darkness.

The *Kutuzov* lurched, and the deck tilted as the artificial gravity systems became unstable. Two Manta cruisers sent distress signals and abandoned the pursuit, changing course. Systems flickered on the Juggernaut's bridge, and competing alarms began to ring out. Many systems had already dropped offline.

No robot vessels were visible on screen, but the shadow cloud continued to swell toward the pursuing ships.

In disgust, Keah muttered under her breath, "All right, dammit!" She activated the comm again; it took her three tries to connect with the Solar Navy flagship. "This is frustrating, Z! Break off the pursuit."

The battle groups veered away from the dark nebula and retreated. The robot ships were gone.

SHAREEN FITZKELLUM

After a year in the straightjacket of schools on Earth, Shareen was glad to be back in the free skies of Golgen.

When she had asked her quiet study partner if he would be interested in leaving the classroom for some "real education" at the gas giant, Howard remained so calm that he almost fooled her, but she knew him well enough to see the excitement in his dark eyes. "That would be an excellent way to acquire a practical education. My family would be pleased if I became a certified ekti-processing engineer."

She thought it was cute. "And I'd love to have you there with me," she said. While she couldn't wait to leave Earth, she didn't want to lose Howard.

Happy to reward a child that caused them no problems, unlike his siblings, Howard's parents agreed to the proposal. Howard Rohandas had seven brothers and sisters; as the youngest, he had often been left alone, especially since his siblings gave his parents so many headaches. Howard was a good student, self-sufficient and reliable.

As they emerged from the transport in the skymine bay, the clangs, pumps, engine roars, and venting gases sounded like a welcoming choir to Shareen. Howard wrinkled his nose at the chemical exhausts in the air and the industrial racket. "Is it always this noisy?"

Shareen laughed. "Sometimes louder, when big shipments come and go. You'll get used to it."

She spotted her parents working their way toward them, dodging equipment and activity. Her mother held Rex with one arm, waving with the other. Shareen ran forward to give her mother a hug, then she playfully poked her baby brother in the stomach, making Rex giggle.

"About time we had some qualified help around here," Patrick said. "This must be Howard Rohandas? You come highly recommended from a source I trust." He nodded toward his daughter.

"Pleased to meet you, sir," Howard said. "Shareen and I worked together in school, but she says I'll learn much more on Golgen."

"Shareen might not have gotten passing grades without you, Howard," Zhett said.

Howard blushed. "We helped each other."

"My problems were with the instructors, not the science," Shareen said, then gave Howard a comradely nudge with her elbow. "I needed him more than I thought, and it was good to have a friend to help me out."

Her brother Toff bounded in, his hair tousled, wearing a justified expression. "See, Mom? You can't send me to Earth. Academ was hard enough."

Shareen teased him. "Academ was hard for you because you can't sit still."

Toff looked to his father, as if he might be a better ally. "I'm going to be a skymine engineer, so I may as well just stay here and learn."

"First you'd have to find a skymine that'd take you," Shareen said.

Her grandfather blustered into the bay, both arms extended. "And there's my lovely granddaughter!" Del Kellum's exuberance always embarrassed her. "And who is this fine-looking young man?"

"Shareen's boyfriend," Toff said.

Howard's mouth fell open, and he looked as if he were trying to speak, but no sound came out. Shareen took pity on him. "Don't overwhelm my friend or he'll jump off the deck. Let him settle in."

Though he seemed to be out of his depth in this new environment, Howard finally managed to say, "Really, this is nothing compared to my usual homecomings with seven brothers and sisters."

"Good," her mother said. "We intend to put you to work on the next shift."

After unpacking, Howard wanted to explore, and Shareen led him along the process lines deep in the bowels of the skymine. Roamer workers in jumpsuits moved through the maze of conduits, testing

flow temperatures or monitoring pressure levels in the throbbing reactors. Pistons pumped alongside the catalyst chambers.

The skymine plowed through the Golgen sky, gulping and exhausting huge quantities of atmosphere, digesting the hydrogen, and
crunching the atoms into the rare allotrope that served as stardrive
fuel. Up on the intake deck, Shareen laughed in the roaring wind as
fans cleared the air of chemical mists.

When Toff came in, obviously looking for his sister, he had a mischievous expression. Shareen rolled her eyes. He always tried to find
ways to pester her. "We're working here," she said, hoping he would
take the hint.

"Looks like you're just chatting," Toff said, then added in a sing-
song voice, "Or did you want some alone time with your boyfriend?"

Shareen snapped, "Why don't you dive into the clouds and go
hydrogue hunting? Don't come up until you find some."

Toff started to give her a rude response, but ducked when he saw
Del Kellum enter the deck. "Toff, there you are. I've got work for you
to do."

"Sorry, I have homework! I was just asking Shareen some questions." Toff darted away.

When her brother was gone, Shareen said to her grandfather, "I'm
showing Howard the process line. We studied the engineering on
paper, but he should see it with his own eyes. If Howard and I put
our heads together, we could change the nature of skymining. He's
very practical, and I've got lots of big ideas."

Her grandfather chuckled. "You always did—and sometimes
they're even good ones." Del Kellum glanced up at the chutes, the big
fans, the pumping turbines. "Roamers have been in the business for
centuries, and this skymine's been working for a long time. I have
high hopes for you, girl."

Shareen clipped a stabilizer cable from her belt onto a thin metal
rung, and gestured for Howard to do the same. "The view's better up
there. Come on."

The young man followed her, with Del Kellum huffing to keep up.
From the high platform, they could look into the vortex of misty
chemicals that were sucked into the main body of the skymine. Sha-

reen swung out, relying on the clip to keep her safe. Howard peered into the dizzying swirl of gases.

Del raised his voice above the loud wind. "You always were a tomboy—just like your mother! But you're a young woman now, a beautiful girl, even if you don't know it." He jabbed a finger in her face. "You could trouble yourself to look nice. Don't you want this young man to notice you?"

"I already notice her, sir," Howard said, making Shareen feel warm inside.

She responded with a mock huff. "I want a boy who sees me for who I am."

Del reached out to wipe a grease smudge from her cheek. "Sometimes it's hard to see who you are." Then he playfully tugged on one of her pigtails. "I want to show you something." He unfolded a flexible screen from one of his jumpsuit pockets, spread it on a flat surface, and activated the power film. "You're not done with your schooling, just because you didn't like Earth. It's time for some Roamer education."

"That's why we came here. Hands-on work at the Golgen sky-mine."

Del took Howard by the sleeve and pulled him closer to the film-screen as well. "Not good enough. You're a genius, and geniuses have to go the extra parsec."

On the screen Shareen saw a beautiful maelstrom of nebula gas, a cluster of stars at its core, and a flotilla of domed habitats, skeletal frameworks, flitting ships, stretched sheets of polymer fabric like butterfly wings, and a partially completed arc that, when finished, would become a giant metal ring.

"Kotto Okiah has the biggest ideas of any Roamer," Del said. "I'm going to make some contacts. I have a lot of clout as former Speaker of the clans, by damn."

Shareen wasn't impressed. "My dad used his connections to get me into the best Earth academy—and look how well that turned out."

"My clout is different from your father's, and I know different people. Wouldn't you like to study with Kotto Okiah?"

Even Howard seemed impressed. "He's a legend."

Del tapped the images on the screen. "This is Fireheart Station, where you belong. Once you've studied with Kotto, the Spiral Arm will be your oyster."

Shareen frowned. "I don't like oysters. You made me eat one when we visited you on Rhejak."

Del laughed. "Don't much like them either—salty and squishy, and if you don't swallow one whole, it's like a glob of phlegm stuck in your mouth." He rolled up the flexible screen and stuffed it into his pocket. "Anyway, that's just an expression. Sure, spend a few months here if you want, but you'll have all your life to run this skymine. I want you to dream big, girl. Dream big."

travelers telling stories about far-off places. He made a habit of checking the origins of various ships that came to Ulio, though he rarely got up the nerve to talk with the visitors. He was only two years older than Xander.

Xander had just come from the Plumas water mines, which were run by his clan Tamblyn cousins. He showed Terry images of the Plumas ice sheets, the pumping stations under the crust, the wellheads that poked above the surface.

The next time he came through Ulio, he sought Terry out to show him images of other places he had visited in the meantime. The third time, he showed Terry his scrapbook, as well as the extensive list of planets still waiting to be checked off. Terry had seen none of them, which surprised Xander. "You live at the heart of a *spaceport* and haven't gone anywhere?"

"Never had the opportunity," Terry said.

"Never *took* the opportunity."

Later, after Xander asked Rlinda Kett's permission to engage a copilot other than OK, Terry was shocked when Xander made him the offer. "Now you can't say you never had the opportunity. Are you going to take it?"

Together in the *Verne*, Xander and Terry made a point of traveling many routes. They were the first to put in for isolated or exotic deliveries because Xander wanted to check another place off his big list. Terry did not possess the same completist mentality. Every spot they visited was new to him, and he was glad to go along.

Now, as the *Verne* penetrated deeper into the nebula, the starlight and reflected radiation were so bright he couldn't see the full extent of the Roamer facilities. When they approached the illuminating stars of Fireheart Station, they could make out shielded Roamer harvesters that flew between stations. Cylindrical collectors covered with reflective sheeting were isotope farms. Giant molecule-thin sheets of absorbent polymer metals soaked up the powerful star radiation, and processing stations gathered the energized films and folded them into dense packages, which were then sold as ubiquitous power blocks.

Prominent near the heart of the nebula, the arc of Kotto's Big Ring was far from complete; not even Roamer scientists could understand exactly what Kotto intended to accomplish with it, other than that he said it "might" become a black-hole factory. The genius inventor had made so many useful discoveries over his career that the clans had stopped asking questions and indulged him.

Xander said, "With so much going on here, it's too bad we're just doing a mundane supply run."

"They'll be happy to see us. They need to eat, and we can get rid of that Primordial Ooze from Del Kellum's distillery." He knew the green priests at Fireheart would also be anxious for the seeds and botanical supplies the *Verne* carried, crate after crate of crop seeds, bulbs, and modified strains of grain designed to grow under the constant, colorful starshine of the Fireheart nebula.

"Would you like me to recite the manifest?" OK asked.

"No, thanks." Xander continued looking out the windowport. The *Verne* headed directly for a terrarium station that glinted in the extravagant starlight. "Nice place for a garden."

OK recited, "The terrarium station was founded by green priests Celli and Solimar. Over the years it has provided supplemental fresh crops for the workers at Fireheart Station."

After the *Verne* was welcomed into the terrarium station's landing dock, OK secured the ship, checked the engines, and assessed the cargo. Xander bounded down the ramp. The gravity was low enough that Terry needed only a slight assist from the antigrav harness strapped to his waist.

The green priest couple met them. Completely hairless with skin the color of fresh leaves, each wore only a traditional Theron loincloth. Celli, Queen Estarra's sister, was thin and wiry, with small breasts. Solimar's chest was broad and muscular.

"You're a long way from Theroc," Terry said. "This must be different for a green priest."

"We have our trees," said Solimar. "We can communicate with the worldforest network whenever we like, and Fireheart Station depends on us."

Celli added, "We can't leave."

"Can't, or won't?" Xander asked.

The green priests answered in unison, "Can't."

Xander and Terry followed them into the main dome of the terrarium, a large structure with a curved crystalline ceiling. The air was moist and lush with plant smells, spicy leaves, warm grasses. Through the crystalline panes, the incandescent pools of gases made an ever-changing panorama.

"Our orchards and gardens grow more than three hundred different varieties of edible plants," Solimar said.

Xander stopped in awe as he saw the giant worldtrees that rose up and arched outward to fill much of the terrarium. Even the immense dome seemed too small for the great trees.

"Those were . . . your treelings?" Xander asked.

"We carried them in pots when we came here," Celli said. "They've grown."

"We agreed to stay at Fireheart Station for a while to provide communication. Under the constant sunlight, the treelings grew more rapidly than we expected. Now they've got no place to go."

The worldtrees had reached the top of the dome, and curved over. The fronds swept down so low they touched the deck and mingled with the rows of crops.

Celli ran her green hand along the golden bark scales. "They can't leave, and they keep growing."

Xander followed the trunks and branches, saw the bent boughs, and felt a brooding sense of claustrophobia. "What's going to happen to them?"

"The trees are trapped here," Celli said. "That's why we have to stay."

Solimar squeezed her hand. "We know it's only a matter of time."

PRINCE REYN

After arriving on Earth to numerous receptions, after watching parades and meeting with dozens of business leaders, ambassadors, industrialists, and military representatives, Reyn was exhausted. He worked hard to remember all the important people he had met, and when he was simply overwhelmed, he remained polite and gracious, which seemed to be good enough.

He couldn't wait to finish his diplomatic duties and find time to rest. He felt drained. His arms were weak and trembled at the most inopportune times.

For centuries, Earth had been the center of the Hansa, with its Whisper Palace where the Great Kings had ruled, where his own father had been groomed to be no more than a figurehead. Now, under the Confederation, a mechanism existed so that the diverse threads of humanity could be pulled together in the event of a massive outside threat, but under normal situations, local governments were adaptable enough to rule their own worlds.

Even two decades after the dissolution of the Hansa, Eldred Cain retained his title as transitional Deputy. He took Reyn under his wing and sympathized with the frenzy of the Prince's protocol schedule. Deputy Cain was a quiet man, hairless and pale-skinned, with a slight build. He was competent, businesslike, and soft-spoken. After they left a diplomatic reception Cain leaned close to him and said, "I'll make sure you get time alone."

Reyn sadly shook his head. "I've seen the schedule—I have another meeting in twenty minutes, something about a union of rubble workers combing through the debris of the Moon."

Cain gave him a soft smile. "I took care of what needs to be done, but I left it in your schedule as a placeholder. No one else knows. You have an hour off."

"Thank you! I don't know that I could have acted interested for another hour—not until I recharge my brain." Then he flushed. "I mean, I am interested. There's just so much . . ."

"I understand, young man. I've dealt with wars and unimaginable crises, but I find social obligations to be tedious and exhausting."

Reyn was surprised that he felt so comfortable in front of this man. "They're all impressive people, and I know that it's important to meet them, but nobody knows *me*. They just know *who I am*."

Eldred Cain, the former right-hand man of Chairman Basil Wenceslas, had never had the charisma or ruthlessness to be Chairman. Since the end of the Hansa, Cain had served as the transitional representative, overseeing the constitution of the new Confederation, helping broker agreements among the loosely allied planets, clans, entities, and cultures. Because of his soft touch, soft voice, and wise counsel, Cain had helped create a powerful network ruled by a King and a representative council.

During his unexpected hour off, Reyn relaxed in a quiet lounge. Deputy Cain sat on an overstuffed sofa. "I don't envy you, Prince. Your father was chosen for his position after being observed and tested. They knew he had the material to become a King before anyone ever saw his face. But you're more shy and introspective, not comfortable as a showy, heroic leader like the people want."

Reyn couldn't disagree. "Is that why *you* never tried to take over yourself?"

Cain laughed. "Oh, the King can get all the attention. I'd rather stay behind the scenes and keep the engines functioning."

Reyn was surprised. "You'd rather be an engineer than a captain?"

"Exactly. I've watched how kings are made. King Frederick was killed by politics." He grew more serious. "Prince Adam was quietly erased when he didn't prove to be acceptable, and Prince Daniel was groomed, crushed, groomed again, and then sent away. No one's seen him for twenty years, if he's even still alive. Peter and Estarra barely survived assassination attempts. Why would I want to invite that upon myself? I have everything I need—people get in trouble when they want more than that."

Reyn nodded. "Being the firstborn son doesn't necessarily make me the best choice for the job." He knew how the populace liked the fairy tale of royalty, a colorful figure they could look up to. "Even so, I'm determined to rise to the challenge."

A lightning strike of pain shot through the network of his nerves, and he struggled to hide the wince. It lasted less than a second, and afterward a wash of cold sweat prickled his skin. His heart pounded, and he couldn't take more than a shallow breath, yet somehow Reyn maintained a calm smile.

"I think it's time for our next meeting," the young man said. "I want to finish my obligations because I'm having dinner with Rlinda Kett."

The smell was so delicious it made his mouth and eyes water. Rlinda kept main residences on several planets, and she claimed that each one was home. When Reyn requested a private meeting with her, she insisted that he come for dinner and changed her entire schedule for him. "I'd move the Moon itself to have dinner with you, Raindrop—but I don't really have to, since the Moon's no longer there."

During her years as the Confederation's trade minister, spending so much time on Theroc, Rlinda had become something of a godmother to Reyn and Arita. She always gave him such enthusiastic hugs that he felt swallowed up in the soft enormity of her body.

He was so eager to speak with Rlinda that his tremors grew worse, but he no longer had to keep up pretenses. She was so intent on being the hostess that she didn't notice how shaky he looked—not right away, but he was sure she would. She had visited Theroc often as he grew up, and she knew him too well.

Rlinda still ran Kett Shipping, but her main love was cooking and her restaurants. Even at home, half of the apartment space was devoted to her kitchen. She stood behind a large sizzling griddle as Reyn hovered next to her. She tossed a jumble of sliced onions onto the hot surface, where they danced and spat in the grease from a ground beef patty. She tended the burger with a spatula, forming it, pressing out just enough of the juices.

"I can't believe you're the son of the King and you've never had a cheeseburger." She flipped the patty, and peeled off a rectangle of orange cheddar from a package beside the grill, which she placed over the meat.

"Even if I had, it wouldn't be as good as yours."

Rlinda laughed. "That's a guarantee."

She slid the burger onto a toasted bun, used the spatula to scoop up the browned onions and spread them across the melted cheese. In the small dining area, she presented it to Reyn with the appropriate condiments. Like a scientist explaining a complex physical theorem, she instructed him in how to add the finishing touches. "Of all the exotic foods on all the strange worlds, nothing sums up the joy of eating better than a good cheeseburger."

Reyn took a bite, and the flavors exploded in his mouth. It was as delicious as she had promised. He ate, wiping his mouth so often between bites that Rlinda had to fetch a stack of fresh napkins.

"I love to cook for special guests, and if I don't have any guests around, then I cook for myself. Used to cook for BeBob. He was always my guinea pig." She sighed. "Ten years now . . ."

Reyn remembered when her "favorite ex-husband" Branson Roberts, affectionately known as BeBob, had died. Although Reyn had been a young boy at the time, he had felt the waves of grief coming from the usually jovial woman. Even a decade later, the mere mention of BeBob brought a tightness to her face and a stillness to the conversation.

She heaved a breath, and Reyn stopped eating. She gestured for him to pick up the cheeseburger again. Resting her elbows on the table, she leaned forward and changed the subject. "I know you and your sister adore me, Raindrop, and I know I'm the most sparkling company anyone could possibly want." Her dark brown eyes were shrewd. "But why are you here? Really? You look sick."

He set down the remnants of the messy burger and looked plaintively up at her. "I need something, Rlinda. Something important."

As if released from a cage, the nerve fire rattled through his body again, and he could not hide the shudder of pain. He breathed hard, glad he didn't need to pretend anymore. "This has to remain confidential. Can you help arrange a private consultation with the very best Earth doctors? I need tests to identify what's wrong, find a treatment . . .

if there is one. The symptoms have been getting worse over the past six months."

She leaned back, deeply concerned. "Your parents are the King and Queen. They should be able to arrange everything."

"I've done my own research, talked to a few Theron doctors, but . . . my parents don't know yet. They'd make a galactic incident, send out a call across the Spiral Arm. Every colony and planetary government would send comforting messages and offers of help, and my parents would go mad with worry. And I don't want that. It's private. I don't want pity or sympathy." His hands began shaking uncontrollably, and a sparkle of hot tears welled in his eyes.

Rlinda gave him a look of grave concern. "All right, I won't betray your trust." Her brow furrowed as she concentrated. "I know some people. I can make the necessary contacts." He could see she had made up her mind not to disturb him further by letting him see her anxiety. "I'll help you in any way I can, Raindrop." She laid a big hand across his forearm and squeezed it. For a while, the warmth of her touch made the pain go away.

FOURTY-FOUR

ZOE ALAKIS

A private ship flew into the Pergamus system, disregarding the warning transmissions from the guardian stations. No one had invited the vessel, and the pilot refused to give his name. He demanded to speak with Zoe Alakis in person.

That was always a bad sign.

Her security ships scrambled from the orbital picket lines. Ground-based defenses tracked the incoming blip. From her sterile central dome, Zoe triggered the standard lockdown procedures that sealed her groundside facilities and Orbiting Research Spheres. Incineration protocols and complete data-wipes were placed on hair-trigger standby. She would not allow any of her work or stockpiles to get loose. With all the valuable—and often dangerous—medical specimens in her numerous laboratories, Zoe maintained enough security to drive off an army. They could handle one annoying intruder.

When Tom Rom appeared on her private screen, Zoe felt the sense of relief that he always brought. He had just returned from the Klikiss ruins on Eljiid with the royal jelly samples, and he remained on Pergamus, awaiting his next assignment. "Do I need to solve this problem, Zoe? I can chase away the ship—destroy it, if necessary. The cleanup would take extra work, but it's still manageable."

The fact that Tom Rom had offered Zoe the choice was in itself calming. "Not just yet. We don't want to initiate an outside investigation. There's no telling how many people knew this man was coming here."

Tom Rom looked neither pleased nor disappointed. "I am here. Let me know what you need."

Two security ships launched from orbit, while three other defenders rose from the surface to intercept the small ship. The stranger flitted around the satellite stations, dodging pursuit. He kept transmitting, sounding more desperate. "I need to speak to Zoe Alakis. My name is James Duggan. My wife is Andrea—Andrea Duggan. Maybe you've heard of her? She's an artist, quite well known." On the screen, his young face looked gaunt, and beard stubble covered his cheeks. "Dammit, why won't you respond?"

"Mr. Duggan, you are not authorized here," said one of her security pilots. "Pergamus is a private facility. If you do not depart immediately, we will consider you dangerous and defend ourselves with lethal force."

Duggan's eyes widened, but he was so determined that the threat barely made him flinch. "I just want to talk. I need to speak with Ms. Alakis."

On the private channel, Tom Rom said, "I'm ready anytime, Zoe. Waiting."

She hated how this intrusion would distract her researchers from their important work. She didn't need to be reminded that Pergamus was vulnerable. "Let me try one more thing." Zoe adjusted her chair, glanced at her reflection, then activated the transmit function. "Mr. Duggan, this is Zoe Alakis. I don't know you. I don't wish to speak with you. I don't want you here. Please leave."

Duggan leaned closer to the screen as intense as if no one else existed but the two of them. Zoe felt a chill. "I've got nowhere else to go," he said. "You're my only chance—my wife's only chance. She has . . . she has Heidegger's Syndrome, in its final stages."

Zoe's expression hardened. So that's what it was. "If she's in the final stages of Heidegger's, then it is incurable. Go home. Be with your wife, comfort her."

"She's already nearly blind, the degeneration of the optic nerve was the worst for her. She's an artist, a laser artist. She's *famous*. You must've seen her work."

"I don't look at art, Mr. Duggan. I don't leave Pergamus. We have too much work to do here."

"It's *Heidegger's*! I know you're researching it. I know you have a cure."

"Heidegger's Syndrome is incurable. You can read that anywhere."

"You have a cure," he insisted. "You can help my wife."

"I could help a lot of people . . . and if I did, there would still be more who need it, and even more after that." Her work was too important to let herself plunge into that quagmire.

The pathetic man had let himself and his wife fall into this trap. The universe was not a fair place, and it wasn't her job to rectify injustices. She didn't like him, didn't like that he had intruded here, didn't like how he assumed that after all her years of effort, all her expenses, all the trial and error, all the extreme measures *she* had taken in the pursuit of a cure for Heidegger's, while her own father degenerated . . . that she would just give it to this man because he was sad and desperate? She felt no sympathy for him whatsoever.

"*If* I had a cure for Heidegger's Syndrome, Mr. Duggan, then it would be *my* cure. I developed it. I tested it. I keep it. I don't have to share." No one had bothered to help when her father needed it. She had learned much about human nature.

"I can pay you," Duggan said. "My wife can create original masterpieces if she gets her sight back."

Zoe rolled her eyes. Even after intensive treatment, the chances of repairing the damage to the woman's optic nerve were minuscule. And what use did Zoe have for artwork anyway? There were too many threats in the universe, too many germs, too many dangers to watch out for at every turn. She had no desire to cover up the risks with pretty pictures.

"You miss the point, Mr. Duggan. If you don't leave *now*, I am within my rights to have Pergamus security destroy you. I have a full record of this conversation. You have been warned several times. You are trespassing."

Duggan reeked of naïve disbelief. His voice was hoarse. "You're not human. How can you do this?"

"You don't know what I am, or what I've been through."

She switched over to Tom Rom's private channel. "Encourage him to depart with all due speed." Then, as a last kindness she added, "But don't harm him, don't destroy his ship. Let him go back to his wife."

After looking at her for a long moment, Tom Rom acknowledged and switched off. Zoe was sure he understood her justifications, though it had taken her a while to figure it out for herself.

James Duggan reminded Zoe of what she had been like years ago. At one time she had been desperate too, willing to do anything to cure her father as his Heidegger's progressed on Vaconda. No one had rescued her then. In those last months, she had been forced to watch the awful worsening of his symptoms, even though Tom Rom had done his best to help. . . .

For Adam Alakis, the course of the disease manifested differently from Andrea Duggan's symptoms. His sympathetic nerves had suffered the worst damage, making it harder and harder for him to breathe, making his heart forget how to beat.

He lost the ability to control the muscles of his throat, so he couldn't even swallow his food; Zoe had to hook him up to intravenous nutrient drips in the forest watchtower. Even when he did manage to breathe, he couldn't control his voice. Unable to speak or write for the last few months, he communicated with his daughter only through longing, hopeless looks; his unexpressed thoughts piled up like drifts of old gray snow that refused to melt. She'd been nineteen.

Zoe refused to believe there was no cure for Heidegger's. In their watchstation above the lichentree forests, with the droning symphony of insect songs and the trill of reptile-birds, she used to sit in the window enclosure. She propped her father in his comfortable chair, adjusted the nutrient drip, and let him stare out at the undulating lichentree colors. Tendrils of orchid vines broke off in strong breezes and drifted across the treetops before they dropped into the underbrush and tapped into other plant systems.

While her father faded, day by day over the course of five long years, Zoe made it her cause to understand everything known about Heidegger's. The Alakis watchstation library had a wealth of medical records, as well as all the data the Vaconda teams had collected for decades on the pharmaceutical possibilities of native insects, flowers, spores, and poisonous saps.

Heidegger's was a rare disease, with fewer than a thousand recorded cases across the Terran Hanseatic League. Zoe did discover several recent studies, and a medical research team on New Portugal that had made interesting progress. A few obscure research papers suggested promising data, but that research had never been pursued— Zoe didn't know why. She found it maddening. If that research team had simply followed up with trials, they could have had a test treatment by now, something that Zoe's ailing father could *try*.

She sent pleas to the research teams, begging them to release anything they had—unpublished studies, unverified experiments. But she was just a teenaged girl, and she received no response. At the time, the hydrogues had launched their war across the Spiral Arm, and the entire Hansa was in turmoil. Hydrogue warglobes were attacking numerous planets, the Ildiran Empire was reeling—and nobody cared about a lone biological researcher and his daughter on a small wilderness planet.

As Adam's health failed, Tom Rom dismissed the few remaining volunteers on Vaconda, who were glad to get away. But he stayed, as he always did. After Zoe told him about the abandoned Heidegger's research she had found, Tom Rom looked at Adam, then gave a brisk nod to Zoe. "I'll go find them, retrieve their data, and interview them to see if they can offer any hope." He left the two alone in the watchstation.

Zoe wished she could take her father away to some kind of hospice, where he would receive the care he needed as his health failed, but Adam refused to leave Vaconda. With great effort he managed to make his answer clear: no. She knew his reasons. He had spent many years here, and his wife had died here. He knew full well that no one could help him—in fact, he seemed to accept that fact long before his daughter did.

Zoe was frightened and frustrated by her inability to do anything except care for him. How was it possible that human intelligence and science could be defeated by some *mindless germ*?

While they were alone in the vast planetary wilderness, she read aloud to her father, played his favorite music, talked about how she would find a cure for Heidegger's Syndrome—and not stop there. She would cure many other medical conditions too. She waited for Tom Rom to come back from New Portugal.

He was gone for a month, and he returned at last with a disappointed expression and a pack of data that amounted to little. "There was not much progress, Zoe. The experiments were incomplete and inconclusive."

Her voice cracked as she felt her last hopes slipping through her fingers. "So you spoke to the research teams, then? Did they run into some difficulties? Maybe we can work—"

"I brought you all the results they had," Tom Rom said. "From early indications, I have no doubt that they could have developed a cure, or at least an effective treatment, but they never bothered to pursue it, because Heidegger's is so rare. The work did not meet their cost-benefit requirements."

Zoe was disgusted. "It shouldn't be an either-or! They should find cures for everything."

"They claimed they didn't have enough resources. They had to pick and choose." He narrowed his eyes. "It boils down to money. They work on whatever they can get funding for. Everyone else is out of luck."

From his seat by the watchstation windows, Adam Alakis could hear the two of them, though he could not respond.

"It's not fair." Her throat felt raw, her face hot with rage.

Tom Rom hesitated a long moment, then wrapped his arm around her. He felt as sturdy as a tree. "You're right, it's not fair. Other people are selfish. They don't care about you unless it benefits them somehow."

Zoe watched her father who sat in his chair facing the sunset. As colors deepened in the sky and the taller lichentrees began blooming with the twilight, he was trembling. A single tear leaked out of the corner of his eye and trickled down his cheek.

T O M   R O M

Rest only made him restless, and after a week of being back at Pergamus, Tom Rom was anxious to go out on another mission for Zoe.

James Duggan's desperate demand for access to the Heidegger's cure had unsettled many of the researchers. From his offices, Tom Rom tapped into their private conversations and eavesdropped on their laboratory chatter. He found it disturbing.

Some of the scientists went back to their work as usual, but several grumbled about the terms of their contracts. By now, Tom Rom knew that idealistic medical researchers, and humans in general, would rationalize ways to do what they wanted, to change the terms of their promises. To him, that was like breaking the backbone of a moral code. He didn't understand why anyone would prefer chaos and uncertainty to clear-cut, black-and-white stability.

Zoe never shared her cures, her library, her information. Never. Tom Rom understood that. If she decided to make an exception because of James Duggan's sad story, then she would have to make decisions on anyone else who asked for information or treatment or cures. It was only a matter of degree. Even if she had given the Heidegger's cure to save one blind artist, she couldn't possibly help all the sick. That had never been Zoe's goal. What would be the point? Anyone who called her selfish and ruthless simply didn't understand her.

Now, Tom Rom entered the main Pergamus infirmary dome for his scheduled medical inspection. He had a complete workup each month and another physical examination before he left on any mission. He underwent a full body scan, 3-D muscle map, blood tests, saliva tests, DNA scan, heart monitoring, pulmonary function workup, circulatory tests, dental and vision exams—whatever the doctors wanted to do to him. Zoe's face appeared on the screen, watching him, always watching him. That didn't bother Tom Rom; rather, it made him feel secure.

"We have to keep you healthy, Tom. No surprises, no disease, no malfunction, no degeneration. You expose yourself to so much out there for me. You know how much I appreciate it."

"I do it for you, Zoe. That's enough."

If he ever did contract some exotic malady, he knew she would move planetary systems to treat him, bankrupt herself to fund a cure. He didn't believe he deserved it, but Zoe did, and he wouldn't disagree with her.

As the doctors prodded and scanned him, he ignored them and spoke to Zoe instead. "Any new findings on the Klikiss royal jelly I delivered?"

"It's an interesting substance, unusual biochemistry. We don't quite know what to do with it, yet. Three teams are still running analyses."

Tom Rom focused on her face on the screen so he could ignore the sting of a deep lymph needle. He didn't measure what obtaining that royal jelly had cost, didn't consider the blood price of the annoying camp administrator. If the man had minded his own business, he wouldn't have had to die. Tom Rom never sought out violence, but when someone got in his way, he did what was necessary. "Where would you like me to go next?"

Zoe brightened, although he knew she didn't want him to go so soon. One of Tom Rom's greatest rewards for the risks he took was the pure joy Zoe expressed whenever he returned. If he hadn't had any other reasons driving him, that alone would have made it all worthwhile. Zoe's voice broke into his thoughts. "Several possibilities, but we'll start with this one. Rumors of a brain parasite on Ramah that causes rapturous hallucinations. I'll transmit the files."

The planet sounded familiar. "Ramah was the home of the madman who claimed to have found heaven in the Klikiss royal jelly."

"He may have suffered from the parasite himself," Zoe said, "but the royal jelly controlled it. We would need specimens to understand better."

Tom Rom listened. "Obtaining tissue samples as well as an intact and viable brain parasite may be difficult. And it would raise questions." His lips curved in a faint smile. "But I'll get you one."

"Be careful," she said.

"I will be—always."

When Adam Alakis was dying, Tom Rom had hated to leave young Zoe alone, but it was pointless for them both to stay on Vaconda just to wait. And wait. Zoe kept herself awake by consuming high levels of jungle stimulants in order to keep researching the disease. She slept only two hours a night for weeks at a time.

After all the time Zoe, Adam, and Tom Rom had spent trudging through the lichentree forests, studying the underbrush, testing leaves, berries, roots, and fungi, Zoe was convinced there must be some option for a cure on Vaconda. No one knew how her father had contracted the extremely rare disease. Armed with his tissue samples and blood tests, she refused to give up hope, insisting there was a miracle solution hidden in the biological reservoir, somewhere.

Tom Rom knew that the likeliest source for a cure lay in the work of the original research team that had made progress investigating Heidegger's Syndrome. He vowed to help Adam Alakis. More important, he wanted to save poor Zoe from the looming tragedy.

So he left her at the watchstation to take care of Adam and flew off to the university laboratory on New Portugal, where he hunted down the members of the research team, now dispersed. He wanted to ask why they had made reasonable progress, then lost interest and devoted their work to other things. Personally, Tom Rom hated to leave a job unfinished.

Hydrogues were attacking numerous planets, but he didn't care about that. New Portugal was isolated, frightened by the war, waiting for the next announcement that another planet had been devastated by the alien warglobes.

When he found the university researchers, he asked polite questions, then was forced to interrogate them more vigorously. He began by being reasonable, asking them to cancel their other projects and relaunch their work on Heidegger's Syndrome with the goal of finding a treatment. But the researchers refused, unmoved by the plight of Adam Alakis. They were dismissive of Tom Rom—which only made their situation worse. They didn't understand how determined he was.

So, he made up his mind to kidnap the researchers and drag them back to Vaconda where he would force them to continue their research at the facilities in the forest watchstation. Adam Alakis already had the medical equipment any scientific team could want, and Tom Rom would provide anything else they required—provided they did the work he asked.

After they turned down his initial request, he lured the researchers to an empty laboratory late at night, locked the doors, increased the illumination. He identified the scientists by their names and tied them to chairs, where they were unable to move. Tom Rom asked them about the Heidegger's research protocol they had developed, the results they had achieved.

He spent hours getting details from them, using intimidation when possible, pain when necessary. Baffled and terrified, the researchers tried to lie to him, but Tom Rom was not merely a thug—he understood their work from first principles.

Soon, it became quite clear that even if he dragged them to Vaconda and forced them to treat Adam Alakis, their work was only at a preliminary stage. Any possible cure was still years away.

"There were promising avenues," admitted one of the researchers, a stocky, square-jawed woman. "But Heidegger's is an orphan disease. The cure wouldn't benefit enough people. It's not worth the time and effort—"

So Tom Rom killed them all. The violence resulted from a flash of uncontrolled anger, and over the years Tom Rom had come to regret the lapse. As he looked down at their silent, cooling bodies, he muttered, "What do you think of the cost now?" They had made judgments about the *value* of saving other people's lives, so he judged them. Then he departed.

The news of some horrific defeat of the Earth Defense Forces swept across New Portugal, frightening the population. He cleaned up the site of the crime as best he could, but he wasn't worried about being pursued. No records of his identity were in any database, and with the Spiral Arm embroiled in a genocidal war, a small crime like this was not likely to be solved. Ironically, he thought, it would not be *cost effective.*

He never told Zoe what he'd done, simply reported that the research was incomplete and that the scientific team could not help. He did not want to burden her with the unpleasant knowledge. Over the years, though, Tom Rom realized that Zoe Alakis could have handled it well. . . .

Much, much later, with her sophisticated Pergamus facilities, unlimited funding, and the best researchers she could possibly hire, they had indeed found a cure for Heidegger's Syndrome. They catalogued the symptoms, causes, and treatments—but during the work Tom Rom had uncovered an even more burdensome secret, one that he could never allow Zoe to learn. A private analysis showed that *he* was a Heidegger's carrier. He was not affected by the disease, showed no symptoms, and according to the most reliable statistical indicators, the chances of him infecting anyone was practically zero. *Practically.*

Given all the time he had spent with Adam Alakis on Vaconda, *he* had to be the one responsible. Tom Rom treated himself as soon as the cure was available, purged all trace of the disease from his body. But Zoe didn't know, nor could she ever know.

As soon as the Pergamus doctors proclaimed him healthy and fit for duty, he headed out to find a sample of the Ramah brain parasite. He did enjoy being on Pergamus close to Zoe, especially the rare times when she allowed him past all the sterilization precautions so they could talk face-to-face like two normal people.

But he had to continue the work, and no one was more reliable. Tom Rom took his ship and departed from Pergamus in search of new diseases.

ARITA

When she arrived back at Theroc after her unsettling expedition to Eljiid, Arita drank in the sight of the green, tree-covered planet. *Home.* But by now Reyn was likely on Earth.

Bristling verdani battleships orbited the world like a crown of thorns, huge sentient trees that had burst free of their roots, transformed into mighty guardians. Integrated into each treeship was a green priest pilot, a body and mind combined with the heartwood to watch over the worldforest. Friendly vessels considered the verdani battleships majestic and awe inspiring, while enemies feared the enormous orbiting trees.

As her shuttle passed among them, Arita could feel nothing from the giant treeships beyond a distant and haunting echo, a tantalizing whisper of what she should have been able to hear. The worldtrees had altered her before rejecting her. She had been prepared for all the changes associated with taking the green, but none of that had happened. The failure itself was not unusual, supposedly not a humiliation, but no one had ever heard of a candidate being changed in any other way. Once again, Arita didn't understand.

Back home again, she bounded off beneath the canopy, listening to the constant stir of fronds overhead as well as the movement of people, the buzz of winged vehicles flitting among the thick trees, shuttles landing and taking off.

More than a dozen lifts ran up to the primary fungus-reef. Arita worked her way through levels of offices and reception halls, passing guards and protocol officers who recognized her. She found her parents in the main throne room. Although they ruled the whole Confederation, each afternoon Peter and Estarra served as Father and

Mother of Theroc. Wearing traditional robes and headdresses made of insect wings and beetle carapaces, they listened to the concerns of their people.

Arita entered in time to hear a complaint that a wyvern had been terrorizing a village on the coast. The large carnivorous creatures were rare, but this one had already devoured four people, and the villagers asked for assistance. King Peter ordered a team of hunters to go slay the monster.

When the villagers left, Estarra rose from her throne, smiling. "Arita! You didn't let us know you were home!" She and King Peter came down to greet their daughter.

Old Father Idriss sat in his chair of honor. Though retired, Idriss liked to feel he was still an important leader. His wife had died when Arita was thirteen, and he had little else to do, so he sat in on many sessions. Lately, Arita had seen Idriss snooze through the discussions (despite his insistence that he was paying close attention). Now, the old man stirred himself awake. "Ah, Arita is back—about time!" His gray brows drew together. "Where did you go again? I've forgotten. Earth?"

"Reynald went to Earth," Peter said. "Arita went to Eljiid."

"Never heard of it. Is it an Ildiran world?"

"Klikiss world," Arita said. "Lots of ruins."

The old man grimaced and levered himself out of the chair. "I kept this chair warm for you, Granddaughter. You'll have to take my place. Watch closely, listen closely. There are important matters afoot."

"Important matters?" Arita asked. "What's happening?"

Father Idriss shook his head. "I don't know—ask your mother. I'm going to go lie down."

After he made his slow way out of the throne room, Arita settled into the secondary throne, as instructed, while King Peter called for the next petitioners.

Ten green priests entered, led by tall, humorless Kennebar. Arita's friend Collin was with them, and her heart skipped a beat; she caught his eyes, and he turned away but not before she saw a confused patchwork of emotions in his eyes: embarrassment, guilt, and worst of all, pity for her.

Arita felt disappointed in how her childhood friend seemed to be giving her a cold shoulder. They had been so close, had cared so much for each other. Did Collin believe the trees might think less of him if he maintained his friendship with her? Now he spent most of his time with Kennebar's increasingly isolated green priests.

As children, she and Collin had been equally fascinated with bugs and plants. Neither of them had imagined the verdani would accept one of them and abandon the other. Even if he no longer saw her as a proper partner, romantic or otherwise, Arita missed his friendship. It wasn't unheard of for a green priest and a normal person to fall in love. . . .

Now Kennebar presented himself to her parents. "Mother Estarra, Father Peter, my people and I have reached a decision."

That sounded ominous, Arita thought.

Estarra said, "You've served Theroc well. How can we help you?"

"We intend to become examples of what it means to be true green priests. Unlike so many other priests who have scattered themselves to far worlds, we serve the *trees,* not any human government. My group will leave here and go into the Wild." Even after generations of settlement, huge parts of Theroc's other main continent, the Wild, remained unexplored and undocumented. Kennebar glanced at his followers, at Collin. "Two hundred of us will travel across the sea to where the worldforest is pristine and uninhabited. By living all alone with the trees, we can do our real work without distractions."

Arita gazed at Collin, wishing she could accompany the green priests, but she didn't belong among them.

"Did someone offend you here?" King Peter asked, clearly troubled. "Have we hurt you in some way?"

Kennebar shook his head. "Too many green priests have become part of the Confederation and have forgotten that they belong to the worldforest. My people and I don't wish to be exploited. Our work is sacred. We should serve the trees—not outsiders."

Queen Estarra said with a sigh, "I cannot give you instructions if the trees tell you otherwise. We hope you find what you're looking for in the Wild."

Kennebar gave a brusque farewell, and his group of green priests followed him out. Arita tried to hide her pain and disappointment when Collin didn't even turn to give her a glance. . . .

. . .

That evening, Arita attended a banquet that was thrown for her. Many Therons welcomed her back home, asking questions about the desert planet and the whispering cacti. She was weary, she missed Reyn, and she felt sad that Kennebar's green priests were departing.

Late at night, when she entered her room, she sensed that something was different. The soft round window in the fungus-reef let in a night breeze, as well as the buzz of jungle insects. On the shelf near the window, some of her keepsakes had been nudged aside, and she found a note on the gossamer sheets of her bed—just a small scrap of leaf paper. It was from Collin.

The young green priest must have climbed the outer walls of the fungus-reef, knowing exactly which window was hers. Had he been too embarrassed to send a message through the trees knowing that all green priests could hear what he said? His handwritten message had a single word, "Sorry."

Arita picked it up, felt the texture of the scrap, and held it close for a long while.

EXXOS

The black void was incomprehensible to his sensors, to his racing thoughts, and to his thousands of years of experience. It was not part of the same universe, did not follow the same physical laws, to which he was accustomed. Exxos was lost in an infinite, formless darkness.

The three surviving robot ships had plunged into the shadow cloud, hoping to elude the pursuing humans and Ildirans. But this irrational gulf seemed worse than nonexistence. As soon as his vessels were swallowed up in the dark nebula, the systems shut down, and the armored hulls crumbled and vanished, as if the matter itself were being *unmade*—leaving the robots drifting and helpless in a confusing nowhere.

The flood of data was irreconcilable. Space-time paused and shifted. The hundreds of black robots found themselves tumbling in a place where the universe itself seemed—literally—unreal.

Exxos sent sensor sweeps through his lenses and detectors. He could still communicate with his comrades, and their flow of inquiries shot back and forth like weapons fire. Although the black robots were materially identical, Exxos served as their de facto leader. Yet he had no answers either. His diagnostics made no sense out of the swirling void, and the boundaries seemed infinite.

The darkness around him changed, and a small section became impossibly *blacker,* a pulsing random shape, an inkblot that defined the very concept of un-light. Other blots manifested in the darkness, and in the center of each ebony blob there appeared an eerie and improbable *eye.*

The bizarre shadow-eyes brightened . . . focused on the black robots. On Exxos.

"You are different." The thundering voice poured into his complex robot mind. "You are aware. You are intelligent—but your thoughts do not scream into the flesh of the universe. What are you?"

Instantly wary, Exxos guarded his information. "We are unique," he said. Scouring his memory, he searched through his exhaustive internal database of historical records and personal experiences, including numerous encounters with the Ildiran Empire and their recorded history. He reached the inevitable conclusion: "You are the Shana Rei."

"We are the purity and personification of the void." The throbbing voice seemed to come from the staring inkblot in front of him, but also emanated from all the others that surrounded the helpless, drifting robots. "We cannot hear the scream of your existence, unlike all other sentients."

"We are unique," Exxos said again, trying to understand what the Shana Rei were saying. Something had interested the creatures of darkness enough that they kept the robots alive.

One of the floating, aimless Klikiss robots—Exxos identified the argumentative Azzar—split open his rounded carapace, extended angular wings. Thrusters sent heated exhaust through tiny rocket ports in the beetlelike body as Azzar tried to escape, though Exxos did not know where he intended to go. The void appeared infinite around them.

The Shana Rei focused on Azzar, and the robot froze in space, suspended like an ebony insect in obsidian amber. As if with invisible hands, the Shana Rei plucked the long wings from the robot's body, one at a time. They tore the angular alloy film, crumpling it. Azzar struggled, but the Shana Rei were fascinated with their deconstruction activity.

Unseen hands snapped off the carapace. They plucked out the articulated limbs one at a time, peeled off the front plates that covered Azzar's circuits. Next, they spun the robot's angular head in a full circle before detaching it.

Even then, the Shana Rei weren't finished. They tore out each of Azzar's now-dull optical sensors and extracted circuits, spreading out an ever-growing cloud of debris. After the argumentative robot was completely dismantled, the Shana Rei broke down the components even further, snapping them, twisting them, until the large pieces were smaller pieces, then tiny bits that broke down into nothing at all.

Exxos had been correct in withholding detailed information. The Shana Rei could easily destroy all of the robots, but Exxos had to find some way to make himself, and his comrades, worthwhile.

Finally, the throbbing dark stain turned its eerie eye back toward Exxos and pronounced, "You are machines, but you are aware."

"We are intelligent. We are independent. Our ships were escaping an enemy. We did not mean to intrude. We intend you no harm."

The Shana Rei said in unison, "We cannot be harmed. The Shana Rei are everywhere. We live beneath, between, and behind the cosmos. You cannot intrude."

Exxos pondered the conundrum, his thoughts racing. "We understand. Perhaps we can assist you."

The black blot continued. "Order and precision offend us . . . but your robot thoughts do not cause us pain, as the Ildiran *thism* does, as the thrumming and rattling of verdani thoughts, as the piercing wail of the faeros . . ."

From Ildiran databases, the black robots knew that ages ago the Shana Rei had leaked through from the void to uproot the stranglehold of Ildiran *thism*. It had been a tremendous battle, and only an unlikely alliance with the fiery faeros had driven them back.

The Shana Rei grew more strident, more agitated, more deafening. "As does biological life everywhere—festering, chattering, droning, pounding."

Exxos spoke, trying to stall while he thought of a way to save himself. "The Shana Rei are creatures of the void, chaos incarnate and entropy itself."

"We are the natural state of the universe. Order and form are contaminants in the cosmos," said the shadow blot. "We hold you now in an entropy bubble, safely walled off from the rest of the universe. Once, we resided quietly in the dark spaces between the stars, but now we have been forced to move, driven out of the silent emptiness because something tremendous is awakening."

Reacting with incomprehensible anger, the formless Shana Rei expanded and collapsed like a midnight heartbeat. Then they used their invisible force to separate another helpless robot from the rest and sent the specimen spinning and careening.

Exxos watched as they toyed with it like a malicious child who had caught an interesting insect. The black robot struggled, bleated out signals of panic, but the others could not help. Exxos remained silent, fearing how many of his remaining robots would be torn apart on the whims of the shadow creatures. He began to doubt any of them would survive—unless he could find a way to make the black robots valuable.

As if testing their abilities, or just destructively curious, the Shana Rei extended the victim's segmented metal legs, breaking off one at a time, before splitting open the back carapace to toy with the internal circuitry.

"We are only searching for peace, silence," the Shana Rei continued. "To restore the universe to the way it was before the infestation of life." The dark things continued their casual dissection of the robot. "The screams of living things and the thrum of minds make the universe an intolerable place."

With a vicious yank, the Shana Rei tore off the robot's flat head and sent it spinning into the emptiness.

"The noise just became intolerably louder as something great and terrible is awakening. It poses a powerful threat."

With swift invisible strokes, they continued the methodical disassembly, breaking the robot's pieces into smaller and smaller fragments, until nothing visible remained.

"The Shana Rei have been driven out and forced to war. Though the universe holds more emptiness than substance, we are losing the battle for creation."

Before the Shana Rei could turn on other robots, Exxos decided he had to gamble to survive. He lied. "We are unique—and we know how to win that battle. You would be wise to ally yourselves with us."

OSIRA'H

The astronomy team rushed Osira'h directly to Ildira from the turbulent star Wulfton. Because her other halfbreed siblings were connected with Gale'nh, she knew Rod'h, Tamo'l, and Muree'n had also sensed the crisis aboard the *Kolpraxa*.

The distant expeditionary ship had been swallowed in nothingness, a paralyzing shadow. The Ildirans aboard had cried out into the *thism,* despairing and drowning in cold, infinite blackness.

Though the rest of the *Kolpraxa*'s crew had fallen silent, her brother Gale'nh was still in there somewhere, alive but separate, immersed in a cold blindness that went to her marrow. She could sense him but could not comprehend the flood of his thoughts and emotions any more than she could understand the faeros. But she felt his urgency.

She raced back to join Rod'h and Muree'n in Mijistra; maybe together they would find a solution. . . .

When she met him inside the Prism Palace, Rod'h wore a grim, lost expression that could not be softened even by the rainbows that shone through the crystal walls. "The entire *Kolpraxa*—it's gone. I sensed fear throbbing from the crew. Gale'nh tried to challenge it, but he was overwhelmed."

Osira'h nodded. "There was no explosion or attack that I could understand. We have to go see my father. He must have sensed something when the *Kolpraxa* vanished. All those Ildirans."

Rod'h shook his head. "He failed to sense it the way we did. The other Ildirans were just . . . removed from the *thism,* as if taken out of the universe entirely." He narrowed his eyes. "But there is more. Through the treelings, our mother received a message from the CDF flagship accompanying Adar Kori'nh on war exercises. They encountered an infestation of black robots at Dhula."

Osira'h frowned. "I don't believe black robots are responsible for what happened to Gale'nh."

"Perhaps not," Rod'h said, "but the robots escaped into some sort of dark nebula—exactly like what Gale'nh encountered. Adar Zan'nh just returned and is briefing the Mage-Imperator now."

They hurried toward the skysphere audience chamber. Before they reached the tall entryway, Muree'n joined them. Their half-sister wore the scaled tunic and reinforced leggings of a warrior, and her every movement was filled with prowling grace. Muree'n's telepathic ability was the least of Nira's five halfbreed children, but the sibling bonds were strong, a connection forged through blood and breeding, as well as through *thism*. Osira'h knew that on distant Kuivahr, Tamo'l had felt the same thing.

And she could still feel Gale'nh. And the terror that engulfed him.

"We may have a fight on our hands," Muree'n said. "Something attacked our brother—it was an act of war." She spoke as if she fervently wished that it were so as the three made their way past the guard kithmen into the audience chamber.

Mage-Imperator Jora'h sat in his chrysalis chair with Nira beside him. Adar Zan'nh stood at the base of the dais, issuing his report. He had a harried, almost disheveled appearance as he described his recent fight. "Liege, the robot ships vanished into a dark nebula that was no mere dust cloud. It was *alive*. Our sensors began to fail, controls became confused."

As three of her children entered, Nira straightened. Interrupting Adar Zan'nh, Rod'h stepped forward past the courtiers and audience members. "Something terrible happened to the *Kolpraxa*."

Muree'n added, "They were attacked, possibly destroyed."

"We think it was another shadow cloud," Osira'h said. "Like the one the Adar encountered. But Gale'nh is still alive. We can all sense him. Our bond with him is strong." Next to her, Muree'n and Rod'h nodded.

The Mage-Imperator raised his hands as if to grasp the invisible threads that wove through the air in front of him. "I thought that might have happened . . . several days ago. I sensed a tremor in the *thism,* but it was cut off, as if the threads to many of my people suddenly went numb."

Adar Zan'nh spoke with gravity. "In our history, we have seen this before, Liege—I believe the Shana Rei have returned from the void."

Palpable terror rippled through the audience. When Rod'h shot a glance at Osira'h, all the pieces fell into place for her. A shadow cloud had swallowed the robot ships. The *Kolpraxa* had vanished into cold, dark, blankness. The Shana Rei! It seemed impossible.

Osira'h faced Adar Kori'nh, and her voice was husky as she spoke. "I can guide you to where Gale'nh is. We may be able to save him. If so, perhaps he can give us answers."

Rod'h lifted his chin. "Let me guide you to him—I can do it."

Mage-Imperator Jora'h made his decision without even looking at Rod'h. "No, Osira'h is the strongest, let her show the way—if she can. Adar, take a septa immediately to search for the *Kolpraxa*."

Rod'h looked disappointed, even annoyed, at being passed over for the important duty.

The Mage-Imperator stood up from the chrysalis chair. "If the Shana Rei from ancient history have indeed returned, we must know before the shadow spreads farther."

FORTY-NINE

ZHETT KELLUM

The swirling clouds of Golgen were restless, and increasing winds whipped across the atmospheric layers. As Zhett stepped out onto the skydeck, she could smell the foul chemical vapors coughed up from deep below. For years, she had watched this planet, staring at the kaleidoscopic tangles of cloud bands, the ever-changing cauldron of colors. She knew the gas giant's moods, and right now Golgen was in a surly one.

Near the edge of the deck, Shareen and her friend Howard peered down into the clouds, shoulder-to-shoulder, hypnotized by the storms. The studious young man seemed to be mapping out meteorological equations in his mind, while Shareen impressed him with the story of an enormous vortex storm years ago that had caught the skymine in a slow maelstrom for two weeks before the hurricane forces dissipated.

They were so preoccupied with each other that Zhett startled them when she stepped up. "I think this is something different, Shareen. I don't like it."

The clouds looked bruised and discolored, but the weather satellites detected no large-scale storms brewing. On a planet the size of Golgen, storms were huge but ponderous. They took months, even years, to rise and die. Zhett and her skyminers should have had time to prepare.

This vortex, though, was changing in a matter of *hours.*

Kilometers-long whisker probes dangled into the cloud decks beneath the skymine, analyzing chemical compositions and vapor layers. Sounding stressed, the shift chief called Zhett to the control dome. "You've got to see this for yourself—I have no idea what it means."

"On my way." She glanced at Shareen and Howard. "Coming?"

Howard continued to stare out at the stormy clouds. Shareen called over her shoulder. "We'll be there in a few minutes."

Taking a lift up to the control dome, Zhett could hear the skymine groan and rattle in the increasing winds. The powerful antigrav engines would keep them afloat, but the skymine could be in for a rough ride.

Del was already in the control dome, doing his best to appear knowledgeable and commanding. "Gas giants are capricious things, by damn."

The control crew turned to Zhett as she arrived, relief clear on their faces. "I've never seen a cloud layer profile like this," said the shift chief. He called up a display of uncharacteristically jagged traces from the probes, as well as color-coded chemical analyses of vapor content.

Suddenly the signal spiked, and the entire skymine lurched as the dangling probes went taut, then snapped free. The skymine tilted, as if being tossed about on rough seas. The shift chief yelled, "Something just tore off our whisker lines!" Sparks flew from the control decks. Alarms whooped. "Stabilizers are working overtime—but they can't handle it."

Zhett raced to a set of screens that showed images from exterior cameras and scout flyers circling the skymine. A maintenance man called from one of the drifting ekti silos. "The clouds are opening up! Something's down there."

A lump as heavy as cement formed in Zhett's chest as the misty layers parted, and a dark and angry stain swirled up. Shapes moved deep below—ominous diamond spheres studded with pyramid spikes.

"By the Guiding Star!" she whispered in awe, then slammed her hand down on the station-wide comm. "The drogues are back! Prepare for evacuation!"

Ten huge hydrogue warglobes rose from the depths of Golgen and surrounded the skymine. The sight reminded Zhett of the horrors of the Elemental War, how these seemingly unstoppable diamond spheres had destroyed whole EDF battle fleets and wrecked countless Roamer skymines.

Del Kellum's face paled. "But—they've been quiet for twenty years, by damn." His own beloved Shareen Pasternak had perished aboard a skymine that the drogues had annihilated.

She got on the comm. "Fitzy, get Toff and Rex! Time to go."

Evacuation alarms sounded throughout the skymine. The crew had been drilled thoroughly for this situation, which they had hoped never to see again. Now they scrambled to their stations.

An eleventh hydrogue warglobe rose to the top of the clouds and bobbed there, motionless.

"The drogues aren't opening fire," Del Kellum said. "What the hell?"

Zhett realized that her daughter and Howard were still out on the skydeck, but before she could manage to say anything, Shareen signaled her. "Mom and Dad, I need you here—now! You *have* to see this. He—it—says it needs to speak with you!"

Zhett nearly collided with her husband as he rushed to the control deck with a crying Rex and a flushed and breathless Kristof. "I'll lead the evacuation," Patrick said. "Our ships can spread out in the sky until we get vessels to take us up to orbit. We just might be safe there."

Shareen's voice hammered through the comm. "Mom and Dad, *please*—on the skydeck, *now*!"

The lifts were jammed with people trying to get to different decks, but Toff bounded ahead of all of them. Reaching the proper level, they all ran out onto the windswept skydeck where Shareen and Howard still stood side by side.

A living hydrogue stood on the open skydeck—a human-shaped avatar fashioned out of liquid metal. The elemental figure faced them, silent and unmoving, like a statue.

As soon as her parents appeared, Shareen pointed out to the sky. "Look at the warglobes! Something's wrong with them."

The diamond hulls were stained, as if suffering from some kind of blight. Black splotches seeped into the curved crystal, and dark cracks appeared. The smooth spheres rolled slowly in the thick clouds, and the discolorations grew and swelled, hardening like rough scabs.

"I . . . think they're dying," Howard said.

Del Kellum pushed his way close to Zhett and Patrick. "By damn, they look like fish floating belly up."

The hydrogue figure regarded them with its blunt-featured face, a poorly molded doll made of metallic clay. The figure took one lurching step toward them, as if uncertain how to move its limbs. It turned toward Zhett, and she could make out only the shadow of a representative nose, eyes, mouth on its face.

The hydrogue avatar spoke in a hollow tone that held a background of thunder and clanging metal. "You must depart." The deep-core aliens had learned human language from the prisoners they had taken during the long war. "Leave this planet."

Alarms continued to sound on the skymine. In the past, the drogues had given no warning, simply annihilated any Roamer facilities that trespassed in their clouds.

But the warglobes surrounding the skymine still had not opened fire.

"Why?" Zhett demanded. "What did we do?"

"Leave this planet," the avatar repeated. "It has been contaminated."

The figure flinched. Its facial features sharpened, then transformed into a caricature of agony before the face melted away, streaming back into smooth blankness. Its arms and legs twisted, flailed, and it bent over as if having a seizure. When the hydrogue straightened again its body was distorted. Its mouth opened so wide it filled most of the simulated face.

"*Leave this planet!* Escape . . ."

Shareen turned quickly toward her parents. "It's not threatening us—it's *warning* us."

"There is a breach through the transgate," the hydrogue continued. "The shadows are bleeding through from our core. . . ."

Patrick grabbed Zhett's arm. "I think we should listen. Let's get the hell away from Golgen."

The hydrogue's quicksilver skin looked tarnished, blotched, and leprous. The thing's mouth opened to let out a long hollow moan, like a blast of cold wind on a lonely night.

Then the figure bent backward at an impossible angle and staggered to the edge of the skydeck. With a last burst of energy, it leaped away from the skymine and plunged down into the endless sky.

FIFTY

ORLI COVITZ

Marriage wasn't supposed to be a unilateral decision, but her husband's choice wasn't something Orli could alter. His mistress was pregnant, and he'd decided, belatedly, that he wanted children after all. Matthew was gone now. No further discussion, just a change in situation, and Orli refused to become one of those shrill and desperate wives in a crumbling marriage who embarrassed herself by fighting for something that she didn't really want anymore.

Matthew continued his travel schedule after staying only two days on Relleker (in a hotel—at least he had that much consideration). He was off on his usual speaking circuit, and Orli didn't expect him back anytime soon. She accessed his itinerary, saw that he was flying to New Portugal—and Henna Gann—after only a brief stopover on Qorliss.

Out of habit, Orli kept working at their compy facility, just going through the motions, but it gave her something to focus on. She had once considered the compies her surrogate children, and now the realization stung.

She was due to record another one of her amusing educational loops with DD, and had already laid out the lesson and speech, but she couldn't find the heart for it. She didn't feel very amusing, or even useful, at the moment. She hoped DD wasn't too disappointed, but knew he would cheerfully accept the change of plans without question.

"Good morning, Orli," said LU as the Listener compy moved among his companions in the Relleker facility. She had noticed that LU spent his days on an unwavering circuit, striking up conversations with other compies, going around the room, and eventually talking to the same compies again, often with the same conversational gambit.

She tried to keep the sigh out of her voice. "Good morning, LU."

"Good morning, Orli," said the other compies.

The Domestic compy, MO, said, "Your breakfast is ready, Orli. I prepared your favorite. It's hot and delicious."

Orli wasn't hungry, but she appreciated someone taking care of her. MO had made a savory omelet, and Orli took two polite bites before settling in to enjoy the cup of steaming klee. The bold peppery taste always perked her up, as if she were drinking distilled sunshine from Theroc.

She found a note beside the cup, a message from Rlinda Kett. "Here's your monthly supply of klee, Orli—a new blend, a little stronger and yet smoother. Let me know how you like it. It's been too long since we've talked."

As Orli read the message, she felt a smile creeping up the corners of her mouth. The big trader woman had accepted Matthew because he was Orli's husband, but she had never much warmed to him. Now Orli expected Rlinda would also politely refrain from saying, "I told you so."

Sipping the klee, Orli remembered the excitement she had felt when she was younger, traveling to different planets (many of them not by choice). She had accompanied her daydreamer father on his quests to strike it rich, supporting his preposterous schemes—growing mushrooms on Dremen or joining a new colony on Corribus, which had led only to disaster. But those ordeals had made Orli strong. If she could survive a black robot massacre and a Klikiss invasion, she was strong enough to handle a disenchanted husband.

Years ago, Orli had traveled the Spiral Arm, seeing amazing things. She flew on many missions with Captain Branson Roberts and Rlinda Kett.

Orli had enjoyed exploring, but when she settled down, she'd given up everything for Matthew. Together, they devoted their time and energy to tending discarded compies and finding them new homes. For years, she had thought that was enough. Matthew basked in the limelight, the travel, the speaking engagements, and Orli was surprised to realize that she had become a homebody—not quite a recluse, but unadventurous, almost introverted. She didn't like that about herself.

No wonder Matthew no longer found her interesting. She'd done what she thought he wanted, what she thought *she* wanted.

DD came in to give his morning report, bright as always. "Good morning, Orli. How is your day so far?"

"The same as yesterday. No better, no worse."

The compy activated her desk screen, called up a series of messages. "Maybe I can make it better. We have received a report from Matthew Freling."

Her husband tried to maintain a formal business relationship, as if nothing had changed in their work, even though their marriage had collapsed like a dying star. Her throat went dry, but she maintained a neutral tone. "What does he have to say?"

"I can play his verbal message for you. He makes quite an articulate case."

Orli frowned. "I prefer to hear the words from you."

"I can do that." DD repeated the exact words he had said, and she was grateful he didn't try to simulate Matthew's voice. "'I called in a few favors, Orli, contacted a Confederation colony on Ikbir. They have two hundred settlers now, but they're expanding and need compies of all kinds. I told them we had twenty-five available and the colony leader offered to take them all.'"

DD's voice changed slightly as he returned to himself. His optical sensors glowed with excitement. "That is what our facility wants, isn't it, Orli? All of these compies can have homes on Ikbir. I hope I get a good home."

"You *have* a good home, DD." Tears filled her eyes, but she brushed them away. "I'm keeping you with me, no matter what. You don't have to worry."

MO came in to whisk away her breakfast dishes, though Orli had barely touched her omelet. It was cold by now anyway. "I can cook you a new one if you wish," the compy said. "But I really should start planning your lunch."

"That's all right, MO." Orli sat back in her chair. Just like that, everything had changed. New choices were open to her. All of these compies would have homes, thanks to Matthew. If she kept the facility open, more refugee compies would be donated, without doubt— but was that what she wanted?

She sipped her hot klee again, and the taste reminded her of Theroc, of Rlinda Kett . . . all the wondrous places she had visited, all the ships and trade routes, the adventures, the memories. *How did I end up here, again?* Orli thought.

At the time, many of her adventures had seemed like nightmares, but now she wished she could do it all again. The Relleker compy facility had been anchoring her to a boring life—one that had been thrown into chaos by Matthew's affair, by a biological inconvenience.

But there was more to it than that. For more than a decade Orli hadn't allowed herself to consider what she really needed. If all these compies found good homes on a new Confederation colony, why would she stay here?

"That is good news, DD," she said. "Let's get in touch with the Ikbir colony leader so I can arrange the transfer of our compies and send summaries of their specialties. They should be happy."

"Compies are happy to do whatever we're assigned to do," DD said.

"After that, you'll help me with the process of shutting down this facility. We won't be accepting any more compies here at Relleker."

DD remained silent for a second longer than she expected. "Then what are we going to do, Orli?"

Now she let herself smile—a genuine smile. "I need time off to remember who I am after all these years, and I know who can help."

DD stood close, his optical sensors bright. "And who is that, Orli?"

She took another sip of her klee. "You and I are going to visit Rlinda Kett."

FIFTY-ONE

SHELUD

The isolationist green priests departed on humming personal flyers like bright condorflies rising from the worldforest. It was a beautiful sight, and the Therons came out on balconies of the fungus-reef city or stood on the forest floor to watch.

Kennebar's people were a quiet—even somber—lot. They flew away from the bustle of Confederation activity to make their settlement in the Wild across the narrow sea, content that the worldforest would provide everything they needed.

Shelud watched the departure with a mixture of joy and sadness. As a green priest, he was uncertain about his decision to stay behind. He had much in common with Kennebar's people, did not like the spread of the Confederation government and the dispersal of so many green priests far from Theroc. But Shelud also thought that going into the forest and hiding would accomplish little. That was not the reason he had become a green priest.

His brother Aelin stepped up next to him. "Good riddance!" Though he was a green priest too, he rolled his eyes in scorn at the departing flyers. "I'm glad you're not going with them."

Shelud looked at his older brother. "I almost did. I agree with parts of Kennebar's philosophy, but I want to accomplish something more."

Aelin said, "I think the two of us should sign aboard a trade ship, maybe a diplomatic transport, see the Spiral Arm together."

Shelud frowned. "I don't want to disappear into the Wild, but that doesn't mean I'll hire myself out to the Confederation. It's not important enough."

Shelud and Aelin were close, but they often disagreed—as brothers did. Shelud was old enough to remember the Elemental War, the horrific attacks on Theroc and the burning worldtrees. He had been five at the end of the war, his brother seven. They grew up in the recovering worldforest. The two boys, being boys, were fascinated and curious, running around to explore the wilderness.

Celli and Solimar, a green priest couple dedicated to tending the wounded forest, had taken the brothers under their wing. Back then, Shelud and Aelin were excited to help, eager to become green priests themselves. Celli and Solimar taught the boys to read, because they wanted apprentices who could tell stories to the trees. The brothers spent days reciting stories, poems, any sort of documents to the voraciously curious verdani mind.

Aelin had trouble sitting still, while Shelud would read even the dullest documents, glad to know he was helping the verdani. Celli taught Shelud to play a stringed instrument and make up tunes of his own while strumming. Aelin frequently teased him about his clumsiness, but Shelud didn't care if he was any good, as long as he was entertaining himself and the trees.

More energetic, Aelin liked to be on the move, and Solimar tried to teach him treedancing. But after only a month of practice, Aelin fell and broke his leg, which took a long time to heal—enough time to quench further dreams of treedancing.

The boys grew up and took the green at the same time. Though two years younger, Shelud had studied harder. Together, the brothers went into the deep forest, losing themselves in tantalizing thickets of underbrush where the worldforest would test them. Shelud remembered how the forest had come alive, enfolded him in a green cocoon, and made him lose himself in the wondrous cacophony of the verdani mind. Both brothers emerged with green skin, their thoughts connected to the worldtrees and all other green priests—but there they diverged.

In the early years of the Confederation, King Peter and Queen Estarra needed a way to communicate across vast distances to establish commerce and defense across the Spiral Arm. Many green priests volunteered to help. The schism between green priest factions and priorities, as exemplified by the departure of Kennebar and his followers, had been brewing for a long time.

Aelin sympathized with the green priests who wanted to venture out and see new things. Green priests could provide important services, and Aelin wanted to be there when humans explored new places and built new things. He believed green priests should use the knowledge stored in the worldforest mind to help civilization recover.

Shelud, on the other hand, felt an affinity for Kennebar's primitivists, but he knew his brother had a valid point that a green priest should *serve* rather than just exist. He spent many nights awake, leaning against a worldtree trunk and just letting the comforting hum of verdani thoughts give him peace, if not advice. The verdani offered no opinion on the matter whatsoever.

When Olaf Reeves and his Retroamers announced their plans to depart from the Confederation, Shelud knew he had finally found his purpose.

Now, he stood next to his brother on the forest floor, watching Peter and Estarra launch a celebration to commemorate the twentieth anniversary of the Confederation's founding. Treedancers hung colorful ribbons from the boughs of the surrounding trees, and newly hatched emerald moths took wing after being released from gossamer cages. Old Father Idriss watched the festival with clear delight, though he seemed tired.

Visitors and dignitaries from Confederation planets came for the festival, even an Ildiran entourage that bore an etched-crystal proclamation from Mage-Imperator Jora'h himself.

Aelin looked wistfully up at the trees as the lissome dancers hopped from branch to branch, and Shelud knew his brother was thinking of his aborted career as a treedancer. The people applauded the spectacle.

Then the ragtag ships from clan Reeves arrived and stole the show. Their vessels landed like a gypsy carnival in the broad meadow near the main fungus-reef city. Olaf Reeves had not chosen his timing by accident.

The bearded clan leader presented himself to the King and Queen accompanied by a crowd of cousins, friends, and other family members. Olaf acted as if he were the King's equal, which he was, according to the strict terms of the Confederation Charter, since all Roamer clans were independent.

Olaf spoke in a deep voice loud enough for all to hear. "King Peter, Queen Estarra, my clan is tight-knit and strong. We remember our Roamer history, but human civilization has changed since the end of the Elemental War." He raised his chin. "We've come to realize that the Confederation can offer us nothing. We are Roamers in our hearts and souls, and we must live by Roamer ways. A knife loses its edge unless it is sharpened. We will leave the Confederation."

Queen Estarra looked surprised. "Where will you go?"

"Out in deep space we've found an abandoned city that will serve as the site for a new colony. We will live as Roamers have lived for centuries. We don't know who built it, but we'll make our home there." Olaf Reeves showed no particular curiosity.

Estarra looked at Peter. "If it's an ancient alien city, scholars will want to study it. We could send xeno-archaeologists to document the structure, help you understand."

The bearded clan leader shook his head. "No, our home will not be a scientific expedition. It's nobody's business." His voice was implacable. "We are not required to share what we learn."

His son Dale looked more conciliatory. "After we get settled, we may send records with a trade ship, but we won't welcome research teams for the time being. We're not hiding, but we do want our independence and privacy."

King Peter pondered a long moment. "That is your decision, and if you need help, you have only to ask."

"Roamers have always survived, Sire." Olaf Reeves seemed grudging in his formality. "We bear the Confederation no ill will, but we are doing what Roamers do—making a home where others might not want to go."

Watching the so-called Retroamers, Shelud noticed that Olaf's son seemed nervous about abandoning civilization, heading out all alone. Over the centuries, Roamers had suffered many losses and tragedies because they lived in inhospitable places like Sheol. And if clan Reeves intended to go far beyond the reach of the Confederation, they would be entirely cut off.

The idea occurred to him like a seedpod bursting, spreading possibilities in his mind. Shelud knew what he had to do. "I'll go with you!"

His words sent a surprised murmur through the audience. "A green priest can share archaeological information without any intrusive research teams. And I can help you stay in touch, if you need it."

His brother elbowed him and whispered, "What are you thinking?"

"We won't need a green priest," Olaf said. "We want to be left alone."

Young Shelud continued in a loud voice, "Many Roamer clans have perished from some disaster or other. If you're going into the unknown, there's no need to exile yourselves completely—accept my help."

Olaf scowled at the interruption. "We've made arrangements with Kett Shipping in the event of an emergency, but otherwise we will rely on our own skills and resources."

Shelud's heart was pounding, but he had made up his mind. "You could still use a green priest. If I bring a treeling, I have access to all the knowledge of the worldforest, if you need it. And if not . . ." He shrugged his bare green shoulders. "I'd still be happy to pitch in and help you make your new home."

Shelud was surprised when Aelin offered his support for the idea. "Green priests *should* go out, explore the Spiral Arm, share new information with the verdani. That is our reason for existence."

Olaf's brow furrowed. "But we don't want our location known. If you come with us, then all the green priests will know where we are and what we're doing. We don't need a spy among us."

"A spy?" Shelud shook his head. "A green priest gives to the world-forest only what he wishes to give. If green priests weren't trusted to keep information in confidence, who would ever hire our services?"

Dale Reeves whispered something in his father's ear, and the bearded man gave a grudging nod. He said in a warning voice, "You have other skills as well?"

"And all the knowledge contained in the worldforest. Anything you might need, access to any expert. Do you have that on your ships?"

Olaf huffed, looked around the lush forest. "It'll be a very different life from your forest here, green priest. A hard life, but a satisfying one."

"I am a green priest, but my *name* is Shelud. With a treeling, I am with the worldforest, no matter where I am. And I would rather have a satisfying life than an easy one." The bearded clan leader grudgingly agreed.

Aelin embraced his brother and shook his head. "I never thought *you* would be the first of us to leave Theroc!"

With a start, Father Idriss sat up in his observation chair, looking around. "Has the festival begun yet?" He blinked. "Or is it over?" With great effort, he rose. "I need to rest."

FIFTY-TWO

GARRISON REEVES

Taking Seth with him in his repaired ship, Garrison left Rendezvous and his sour memories behind. The clan engineers had completed the overhaul on the battered Iswander vessel, repaired the engines, fixed the hull, and provided a fresh alloy coating.

They also painted over the Iswander Industries logo and renamed the ship *Prodigal Son*. Olaf Reeves hadn't asked Garrison for his approval, but the name did seem oddly appropriate. His father wanted him to carry the reminder with him, and Garrison embraced the *Prodigal Son* as his identity and as his ship.

Now he needed to find a new life for himself. For a man of his background and abilities, there were numerous options, but Garrison wanted to find a stable place and make sure he could send his son to Academ. Previously, Elisa had shut down the idea whenever Garrison suggested it, no matter how badly Seth wanted to go there. He had done his best to teach Seth what he could during their evenings off shift, while Elisa had arranged for computer tutoring on Sheol. She had thought that was enough. But their son longed to be with other Roamer children—and, of course, all the compies.

With Elisa gone and Sheol devastated, however, Garrison was starting from scratch. Aboard the *Prodigal Son* after Seth was asleep in his bunk, he pored over images of the Sheol disaster. The public records of the catastrophe were disjointed and uncertain, many parts censored. Even so, the images were so horrific he could barely watch. Those people had been his friends and coworkers. Fifteen hundred and forty-three workers had lost their lives.

He heard a gasp and a quick sob behind him, and realized that Seth had been watching silently over his shoulder. Garrison blanked the screen, but his son stayed where he was. "No, I want to see what happened there."

Garrison could not shield his son from the reality of what had happened, nor could he sanitize the images. Seth had been through an ordeal, and needed to know why his father had been desperate to take him away from Sheol. Garrison muted the sound and showed some of the general images so Seth would understand. . . .

Garrison decided to apply for a job mining and shepherding the rubble belt of Earth's ruined Moon. When he sent his application to the Lunar Orbital Complex, the work crew supervisors saw his qualifications and hired him without hesitation. His father would have been particularly infuriated that Garrison was working for *Earth*. He could almost hear Olaf's voice: "I didn't give you skills and expertise so you could help Those People out of the problems they created for themselves."

Garrison would have pointed out that few people on Earth had any influence on why the faeros had destroyed the Moon, but that was an argument his father never would have let him win. Fortunately, clan Reeves was pulling up roots and heading away from civilization. Olaf would never know.

After his work briefing in the lunar rubble belt, Garrison moved into a company-provided habitation unit in the civilian section of the Lunar Orbital Complex. Although concessions were made to allow for daycare and schooling, most LOC workers either had other arrangements or no families at all. That was all right; Garrison didn't expect Seth to remain there long.

His son searched for new educational loops recorded by Orli Covitz and her Friendly compy DD. Garrison had begun to realize how much Seth enjoyed them, counted on them as distant friends even on Sheol where there were no other children, and while he traveled alone with his father. Seth seemed disappointed. "I think Orli stopped making the loops. I haven't found a new one in a long time. Do you think something happened to DD?" He was genuinely worried.

"A lot of things can happen in a person's life," Garrison said. "Relleker is far away, though, and we have no way of knowing."

Soon, Seth would be much happier. Garrison told his son the news after he finished filing all the proper forms. "It's set, Seth. We'll stay here another two days while I finish my work arrangements, and then I'll fly us off to Newstation. You're already approved."

Seth beamed. "Academ? I'm going to be with the Teacher compies?"

"And the other Roamer children."

His son was visibly thrilled. "But will it be all right? I could help you with your work here. I know how to suit up, and how to drive a cargo pod and operate machinery. That's all you need."

He didn't doubt Seth was as qualified as many of the workers assigned to the LOC worksites. "Yes, but it's not all *you* need, and you'll learn a lot more with intensive Roamer instruction. I need you to be *educated,* not just trained. Training will only get you so far. Education will make you wise."

"Grandfather Olaf said *experience* makes you wise."

"That too," Garrison admitted. "But let's get you an education before you experience too many things. You need friends your own age." He softened his voice, "Your grandfather did say one true thing—a knife loses its edge unless it is sharpened."

"And I'll get my edge at Academ?"

Nodding, Garrison realized that *he* needed to get his own edge back too. He called up images of the Roamer school and showed Seth the interior of the hollowed-out comet, where waterfalls flowed from all directions with wental-charged water. From the sparkle in the boy's eyes, Garrison knew he had made the right decision.

FIFTY-THREE

LEE ISWANDER

A few months ago, Lee Iswander could not have imagined such an ambitious new start, the possibilities as numerous and bright as all the stars in the Spiral Arm. After losing everything at Sheol, he had doubted he would ever recover. But now, thanks to Elisa's discovery of the bloaters, he had a tremendous opportunity, and he did not intend to waste it. Iswander Industries would rise like a phoenix from the ashes of the lava-processing disaster.

Elisa had led him out to the new cluster of drifting sacks, thousands of them on the far outer edge of a solar system that was so obscure it had no name, only coordinate numbers. The silent bloaters were as marvelous as they were mysterious.

Alec Pannebaker ran an analysis, trying to understand what the swollen nodules were, where they were drifting, and why they had clustered together in ways that gravity could not explain. They were possibly organic, but with very little structure. A comparison to giant plankton seemed apt. Most important, the membrane-enclosed globules were filled with ekti that could be easily drained and processed. That was all Iswander needed to know.

Most of his assets had been tied up in the Sheol facility, his primary accounts impounded, pending legal actions. Accusations and criminal charges flitted about as the investigation continued, but Roamers were loathe to fall into what they saw as "old Hansa ways" of pointing fingers, looking for scapegoats, and solving problems with lawsuits. The history of the gypsy clans was filled with instances of life-support failures, dome breaches, asteroid collisions, structural collapses. Sometimes the universe lashed out, and people paid the price. Roamers tended to stick together.

Even so, they were not convinced the industrialist was really a Roamer, in his heart.

When Iswander tried to buy the equipment he needed for his new secret operations, many Roamer businessmen refused to deal with him, blaming him for the Sheol catastrophe. One particularly intractable supplier of storage silos told Iswander, "You'd never be able to meet my price."

Iswander met the man's gaze. "Name your price—I'll meet it."

The supplier crossed his arms over his chest. "Fifteen hundred and forty-three lives."

Iswander went elsewhere. He managed to liquidate some of his other assets, scraping together enough funds to buy the basic equipment he needed, though he told no one what it was for. Over the course of a month, he set up his operations in the new bloater field under tight security, inviting a small group of workers who were willing to take another chance on Iswander Industries, the few faithful who had stuck with him even in his darkest hour.

The drifting cluster of bloaters soon developed into an ambitious ekti-extraction outpost: a cluster of big ships, modular stations, industrial storage tanks, pumping vessels, and six cargo shuttles that would soon begin distributing stardrive fuel. Iswander was optimistic, and expected he would need more ships soon enough. These thousands of bloaters held a wealth of ekti for the taking, and no one else knew the source.

Fifteen of his modular habitats were linked together, comprising a headquarters, an admin module, living quarters, landing bays, and a small medical center in case of accidental injuries. At the moment, only sixty people worked out at the site, but once Iswander began making a profit he could hire more employees, all carefully vetted. Before long, Lee Iswander would restore his wealth and, more important, his reputation.

His wife and son were glad to help him make a fresh start. Though they were lonely out here, both Arden and Londa believed him when he said he was going to make his name and his fortune all over again. Elisa Reeves got to work, as she always did.

Pannebaker and two other engineers modified existing equipment to drain bloater sacks. The ekti was easily obtained, the operation far more efficient than the huge and expensive traditional skymines that processed mind-boggling quantities of hydrogen into small amounts of stardrive fuel. Iswander knew that his new ekti source would change the Confederation, change the whole Spiral Arm—but he did not intend to reveal his secret.

Best of all, tests confirmed that the ekti from the bloaters had a higher energy potential than traditional stardrive fuel. The difference was so remarkable that Iswander decided to call his product *ekti-X*. There would be much consternation among the Roamers who now shunned him, because they wouldn't be able to figure out his source.

Occasionally, the nodules sparkled and flashed, but no one understood why, how to predict the sequence, or what it meant. The discharge caused problems with electronic circuitry nearby, and Iswander's engineers installed significant shielding where necessary. Because he knew how explosive the bloaters could be, having seen the images Elisa brought back, he also instituted extreme safety measures.

Otherwise, Iswander was happy to let scientific investigations continue so long as they didn't interfere with the extraction work. He had a lot of ground to make up.

Ships flitted around the bloaters, and tankers filled with purified ekti-X hung near the clustered spheres. By now, fifteen of the giant sacks had been drained, and the empty membranes hung like husks in space. As he watched the workers tow another flaccid membrane out beyond the traffic areas, Iswander was reminded of old sailing ships on the seas of Earth, hunting whales for the blubber. He knew he was anthropomorphizing the nodules, which certainly weren't alive, weren't aware. They were just gas bags filled with stardrive fuel. They weren't even biological, as far as anyone could tell.

Elisa stood with him in the admin module looking out the windowports. "As soon as possible, we will bring clan Iswander back to prominence, sir."

"Your confidence is contagious—as well it should be."

Her smile was hard. Elisa Reeves was not soft by any measure, but she was a beautiful woman. Elisa *Enturi*, he corrected himself; she no longer wanted to be known by her married name.

"Garrison is gone," she had reminded him when she took her maiden name again. "He was dead to me before the explosions killed him and my son. I don't want to carry his name around like old luggage. We both need a fresh start, sir—and this is the place to do it. Once you begin supplying limitless cheap ekti-X for the Confederation and the Ildiran Empire, the Sheol disaster will be forgotten. Everything else will be seen as a mere setback."

"Thank you for that, Elisa," he said—but he wouldn't soon forget the 1,543. Nevertheless, he realized that reliability and loyalty were very attractive qualities.

Alec Pannebaker loved zipping around in an inspection pod while the extractors plunged nozzles through the tough bloater membranes and began pumping out the murky contents. It was like protoplasm inside a gigantic cell, and each bloater contained an amorphous dark structure at its core, like a rudimentary nucleus. Iswander's processing stations centrifuged the base material to remove unwanted compounds and then filled hundreds of canisters of ekti-X.

Ten years ago, Pannebaker had served aboard a Roamer skymine, and he understood ekti processing. He made sure Iswander understood that draining bloaters was a thousand times more efficient than traditional stardrive fuel operations.

Elisa said, "Once we start distributing our ekti, sir, the Roamers are going to go nuts. We'll have to be very careful not to let anyone else discover where our operations are."

"We've got plenty of reasons to keep a low profile," Iswander said. "And I can't trust anyone more than I trust you, Elisa. I want you to handle the distribution. Our first major shipment should be ready to go soon."

"I've already started making plans, sir. If we bring our ekti-X to a central point—say, Ulio—I can hire pilots to distribute it from there." She looked out at the expanding operations, the extraction and refinery. "This is something we both needed." The bitterness in her voice had not faded.

"A new start," he said. "Everybody loves a redemption story."

Trapped in an incomprehensible pocket behind the universe, Exxos and his black robots struggled to understand the Shana Rei's hatred and capriciousness. Was it curiosity, or just a penchant for destruction? The cold inkblot creatures had offhandedly dismantled two more robots for no comprehensible reason, unless they were bored or frustrated.

"How can you help us fight?" the Shana Rei demanded.

"We have abilities that you cannot know," Exxos bluffed. "We will demonstrate them—when necessary."

With racing thoughts, he collated everything he had learned, including unreliable knowledge from his databases of Ildiran myths. He needed to comprehend the Shana Rei before he risked offering further answers.

The robots drifted in a netherworld of darkness surrounded by a cloud of debris from their dismantled ships. Suddenly a flicker of light rippled through the void, and all the inkblots flinched. The representational eyes flickered and blurred, then blazed more intensely.

"What was that?" Exxos asked. "Please explain."

"Pain. More pain. It grows worse."

"Where does the pain come from? What hurts you?" Exxos said.

"Pain comes from the evolving universe. Pain comes from the stain of life, from thoughts and order being imposed upon the natural state of chaos."

"My robots are powerful, but our sentience causes you no agony. We are different."

"You are different."

"We are powerful."

"That remains to be seen."

The black blots swelled and closed in on Exxos, and he thought they might call his bluff and dismantle him, but the Shana Rei kept talking in their vibrating portentous voices. "In the beginning, all was silent, all was black, all was peaceful. But now the chatter of thoughts, the burning of stars, the outcry of gravity is one endless scream in our minds. We cannot unmake it fast enough."

"Our goals are aligned," Exxos immediately pointed out. "We wish to destroy as well."

"We intend to destroy everything—including you."

"No, not us. My robots are unique. Do not underestimate what we can do." Exxos had to convince them. "Listen—and hear our silence amid the scream of creation. A powerful silence. We know how to create the silence you need. If you destroy us, you will lose an opportunity to win your battle."

"We will not destroy you. Yet." The eye in the inkblot vanished, then reawakened. "The greatest agony is caused by the frenzy of life, the pulsing of minds, the energy of thoughts. We are exploring, reaching out. We have found an Ildiran ship and swallowed it. We have found the hydrogues and will systematically eradicate them. But they do not cause us the worst pain—there is something new, something greater."

The surviving black robots floated motionless in the entropy bubble, unable to escape. Exxos calculated their probability of survival as . . . very small. "We know the Ildiran race fought you long ago," he said. "You failed. You lost. You need our help."

Another flicker of light rippled through the void, causing the Shana Rei to flinch. Exxos observed, but remained unable to draw useful conclusions. Something in the outside universe was disturbing them, but he did not understand what it was.

The nearest inkblot swelled. "Ildiran *thism* burns like a net made of agony. We would have disintegrated the *thism* network long ago, but the faeros fought beside the Ildirans. In a similar way, the extended verdani mind forms a deadly web that traps us. We nearly destroyed it once, but some trees survived . . . and now we can feel that the world-forest thrives again. The task ahead of us is great."

Exxos insisted, "Our robots also attempted to exterminate humanity and the Ildirans. Robots and Shana Rei fight the same battle. We know how to destroy it all. Together, we can succeed, if you trust us."

Apparently they did not want allies. "For millennia, we retreated to where we found a glimmer of peace, but now the universe is stirring, like a monster emerging from a chrysalis. Something powerful threatens us in a way we have never before experienced. We were driven to act, triggered to return."

The dark blots insisted that their war was not just a physical one, but a conflict that required more than weapons and ships and explosions. The Shana Rei would lash out in less-comprehensible ways against the cosmic shrieks of life. They would attack their enemies via their psyches; they would follow the paths of *thism* that were strung like hot wires from planet to planet, cutting with razor edges into the minds of the Shana Rei.

The Shana Rei gathered around the helpless black robots. "The jabber of sentient life will never fall silent. If we do not prevent the great awakening, all is lost, and the void will never know peace. We must eradicate the detritus of creation."

"We robots are intellectually familiar with the Ildiran Empire and their *thism,* with the verdani and their green priests," Exxos said. "We can design an organized plan to achieve our goals. Together, we will be invincible. We can help you create weapons that will obliterate everything."

"Creation is pain."

"It is necessary to create in order to destroy." Exxos would say whatever was necessary to maintain his survival and that of his robots. He surmised that the Shana Rei were insane by any rational measure. An insane sentience was dangerously unpredictable . . . but potentially manipulable. "We will help you extinguish sentient life. All we ask is that you preserve one small corner of the universe for us. You would be wise to take advantage of our powers."

The inkblots fell silent, conferring with one another in a manner the black robots could not detect. Finally, the nearest Shana Rei answered, "We agree to exclude a zone where you and your kind can exist— provided you prove useful and can accomplish what you promise. So long as the pain diminishes."

Exxos felt that he had achieved a great victory; the Shana Rei believed his claim, for now. The other captive robots buzzed and hummed. The shadow creatures converged on them. The voice said, "We Shana Rei wish to be at peace. We wish to die. We wish to be *uncreated*."

Exxos digested that data for a moment, then said, "We can help."

FIFTY-FIVE

SHAREEN FITZKELLUM

The clouds of Golgen continued to erupt with black storms, and the gas giant seemed to be tearing itself apart. Mist plumes thrashed like serpents, and the cloud layers ripped open as atmospheric quakes rumbled up from below.

One huge warglobe lurched above the dense clouds, so close that it sent the whole facility reeling, and then lay like a dead fish, its crystalline hull turning black. From within, the stain spread and swirled like poisonous smoke. Black cracks shot along the diamond hull, and then the warglobe split open. Curved shards tumbled down into the clouds. Nearby, two more warglobes blackened and shattered.

Shareen realized that the open skydeck was not a smart place to be, now that the blight-stricken hydrogue had thrown itself off the edge and into the open air.

With Rex tucked under his arm, her father shouted, "Down to the launching bay—we have to get to a ship!" From below, the first escape vessels streaked out of the skymine's lower bay doors.

Toff bolted for the open doorway. "I'll get a tow-skimmer. We can hook a tether to the ekti storage silos and pull them to safety."

"Don't you dare," Zhett yelled. "We can get more stardrive fuel, but I have no intention of replacing my children."

To the untrained eye, the evacuation looked like complete chaos, but the skyminers knew what they were doing as they raced to assigned gathering stations. Ever since she was a little girl, Shareen had been drilled for emergency evacuation. She took Howard by the arm and raced him along. "Follow me, and I'll keep you safe. Everyone on the skymine is trained for this."

"For *this*?" The young man seemed more fascinated than terrified.

"Sure. We plan for every contingency."

Down in the launching bay, the doors were wide open, the atmosphere field dropped. Breezes whipped inside the bay, tossing debris around and scattering lightweight equipment. Ships launched out in all directions, somehow managing not to collide. As five skyminers tumbled into an escape shuttle, the pilot yelled to anyone else in the bay, "There's room for four more. Get your asses aboard!" Four more people got their asses aboard. After the hatch sealed, the shuttle took off.

Out in the open gulf of clouds and wind, another hydrogue warglobe succumbed to the black stain. During its death throes, the pyramidal projections crackled with blue fire and lanced out in uncontrolled blasts. One stray burst struck a nearby ekti-storage raft, and the detonation created an expanding fireball in the sky.

Rex wailed, but Del didn't let go of him. Patrick shouted, "Which ship, Zhett?"

"That one. I have the launch codes, and I'm taking the controls. Anybody want to argue with that?"

Nobody did.

"Classes were boring on Earth," Howard said to Shareen, "but . . ."

"Trust me," Shareen said, "you'll learn more in fifteen minutes of this than in a dozen exams."

The skymine shuddered, and the deck tilted so severely that a wheeled loader slid sideways toward the open bay, blocking the exit. A husky skyminer leaped into the cab, powered up the engines, and rolled the loader out of the way, but it began sliding toward the opening again. The driver gave up and jumped out just before the loader rolled off into the sky.

Zhett's ship scraped along the sloped deck, its struts sending up sparks. The roar of wind in the cargo bay, the monotonous alarms flooding the station comm, her little brother crying, and warglobes exploding out in the clouds all mixed together to make a deafening din.

Toff's face was flushed with excitement. "I can fly a swooper out there, round up any stragglers."

Zhett grabbed him by the arm, then by the ear, and pulled him up the ramp. "I don't think so."

Shareen helped push Toff onto the ship as her mother raced to the cockpit. "This whole planet's going insane." Six additional evacuees followed them aboard, breathless and windblown.

Zhett activated the comm, listened to a gabble of reports from the skyminers. Shareen thought everyone sounded remarkably calm considering the circumstances.

Her father dropped into the empty copilot seat, handed Rex off to his sister, and called up report screens. "We have enough ships for everybody to get away, but we might not have enough time. This skymine is breaking up."

"Once our people evacuate, where do we go?" Shareen asked, bouncing her little brother in a vain attempt to calm him.

"*Away* from Golgen," Zhett said. "I don't think we have any choice."

Deeply concerned, her grandfather fussed over Shareen. She handed him the toddler again, so she could make her way up to the cockpit and help. "Watch Rex—and Howard."

"I can take care of myself," Howard said.

"Then take care of my grandfather so that he doesn't get into any trouble."

Del looked scandalized, but Howard said seriously, "I'll do my best."

Zhett powered up the thrusters and launched the ship out of the skymine's cargo bay as the passengers scrambled to secure themselves to seats. They flew up and away from the skymine, while winds buffeted them from side to side. Patrick worked in the copilot seat, scanning ahead as his wife dodged other struggling ships. "Never seen wind shear like this," he said. "It's not natural."

Zhett gave him a wry look. "You think?"

Behind them the skymine bounced about like a discarded toy, its exhaust stack bent. Pieces broke away from the lower decks, and the bottom sensor array twisted free and dropped spinning into the mists. The last few evacuation ships shot away from the structure.

Shareen and Howard leaned toward the windowport. Golgen's pastel cloud layers had turned dark, and she saw only one remaining warglobe, blackened and dying, before it sank into the depths like a drowned corpse. The clouds looked as if great gouts of ink were vomiting through the atmosphere.

The evacuating ships climbed to orbit, while the blackness continued to bleed into Golgen's clouds. Shareen was shaking, and when she realized that she was clutching Howard's arm, she was embarrassed, but she didn't let go. She tried to joke about it, her voice dry and raspy in her throat. "Well, that was exciting."

He forced a faint smile. "You did promise I would find it interesting."

"Let that be a lesson to you," she said. "I always keep my promises."

FIFTY-SIX

PRINCE REYN

Rlinda Kett had not let him down. She knew the right people, made the proper calls, and got Reyn an appointment with Earth's foremost specialists in obscure degenerative diseases. She went through unofficial channels, called in favors, and possibly even forked over a few bribes. Once Rlinda made up her mind, she was a woman who would do whatever was necessary—for a friend.

Rlinda told Reyn everything he needed to know. "Dr. Benjamin Paolus is your man, Raindrop." She reached over to pat him on the cheeks, which embarrassed him. "I wish I could diagnose you myself."

Reyn thanked her sincerely. "That's what Dr. Paolus is for."

"Most importantly, this is off book, as you requested. He assures me this will be discreet and completely confidential." She narrowed her dark eyes, giving him a look of concern. "But if you're sick, you shouldn't hide it—there's no reason."

"I don't want the uproar, and I need a few answers of my own before I tell them. It's my choice."

"It's your choice, Raindrop, and I wish you the best. You're my favorite Prince, you know." She pinched his cheek this time.

Dr. Paolus was indeed the best—he told Reyn so three times during the examination. He managed an extensive lab in a university hospital complex, and also received funding from numerous biotech industries.

"After I take samples and complete a full analysis protocol," Paolus said, "I'll run a comparison with all known microorganisms, toxins, and genetic disorders."

"Maybe I can speed up the diagnosis." Reyn transferred a code-locked document, which Dr. Paolus scanned with great interest. "I found some similar cases in the Theron records dating all the way back to the first colonists from the generation ship *Caillié*." He forced himself to continue. "All of them were fatal." No cause had been identified, and no treatment had shown any promise.

That was another reason he hadn't told his parents—not yet. It was difficult enough for him to grasp the problem and deal with it. He knew it was unfair to keep them in the dark, but once he had exhausted his options, then he and his family could decide what to do.

Feeling miserable and worried, Reyn described his symptoms while Dr. Paolus continued to compile notes. So far the doctor had not commented about who his patient was. Reyn cleared his throat and reminded him, "I'm relying on your discretion, Dr. Paolus. I need to keep this entirely confidential."

The doctor looked up from the summary in front of him, and Reyn felt like a specimen being studied under a microscope. Paolus seemed offended. "Young man, patient confidentiality is the foundation of my work as a doctor. You are a human being who suffers from an illness that I hope to treat, if not cure. I don't care who you are." He tapped the screen where the report results were displayed. "I've never seen anything like this before. It could greatly expand our knowledge base."

"Glad I could make such a contribution to science," Reyn said.

Reyn canceled some meetings and rescheduled others, juggling his diplomatic schedule so that no one noticed the unaccounted for hours. Deputy Cain had taught him that trick. He provided Dr. Paolus with every imaginable sample and scan.

More swiftly than Reyn thought possible, the medical team delivered a confidential preliminary analysis that was key-coded to his thumbprint. When Reyn activated the report, Dr. Paolus's quiet voice droned as he delivered his summary. "This is a degenerative neurological disorder, as you correctly surmised. I believe you were exposed to an exotic microfungus somewhere in the worldforest, perhaps from a berry or insect you consumed."

The screen displayed Reyn's scans, body profile, and genetic map. "The microfungus has adhered to your DNA, which changes your cellular profile. Given the markers of the microfungus, we can track the progress of the disease." Another scan of Reyn's body appeared, showing highlighted tracings. Dr. Paolus didn't waste time with platitudes, but gave a dry assessment. "The microfungus is fully involved throughout your nervous system. We will study it, although we're starting from scratch. I can't offer any realistic hope for a cure at this time."

Reyn hadn't expected a miracle or even a resolution, but Arita insisted that he not give up hope, so he would remain stoic for her. He studied the report, took a deep breath, and viewed it again.

Very soon, he was due to spend several months on Ildira as part of a formal cultural exchange. Again, Reyn would perform his diplomatic duties as expected, but he also intended to meet with their medical kithmen. While he realized the alien doctors were not likely to know much about human genetics or exotic microfungi, they did have different techniques and fewer preconceptions.

He code-locked the report so no one else could access it, then reviewed his schedule—two more days of meetings, handshakes, banquets, and interviews before he could go home. People loved the fairy tale of the handsome young Prince who would someday be King, but he was a flawed Prince who would soon become incapable of doing his duties.

He thought of Arita, though, and drove those negative thoughts from his mind. She would have insisted that he be strong.

A somber messenger came to his guest quarters in the diplomatic residence. "I have news that arrived within the past hour, Prince Reyn. It was sent through the green priest network. You needed to be informed without delay."

He took a moment to calm himself, fearing some disaster. "What is it?"

The messenger looked down at a note in his hand, though he had already read the message that was given to him by a green priest. "I'm sorry to inform you that Father Idriss of Theroc passed away yesterday. According to the message, he died quietly in his sleep after attending a gala celebration."

Jarred from his thoughts about his own medical condition, Reyn blinked, not sure he had heard the report correctly. "My grandfather?" It was a surprise, yet not a surprise. Father Idriss had always been there throughout Reyn's life, but although the changes were gradual, the old man's health had been fading. He had grown weaker, looked *older*.

Reyn would degenerate as well, over the course of only a few years.

"Word is being spread across the Confederation, Prince Reynald. We will help you make whatever arrangements are necessary for your return to Theroc with all possible speed." The messenger gave a curt bow and departed.

Reyn tried to sort his thoughts. He let out a long sigh and felt empty inside. He'd had too many reminders of his own mortality in a single day. He thought of his grandfather and closed his eyes.

An hour later, Rlinda Kett arrived, her round face full of caring. "I heard about Father Idriss, Raindrop. You'll need to go home—and I'm taking you there. No arguments. It's time I paid a surprise visit to my restaurant on Theroc anyway, and I was the Confederation's trade minister, spent a lot of time with old Idriss, so it's appropriate that I'm there for the funeral."

Reyn hadn't thought that far ahead. "Yes, there'll be a funeral . . ."

"A big state funeral. Deputy Cain needs transport as well, and I've offered to take him with us. We'll head out as soon as you're ready." She gave him a big hug, did not ask any questions about his visit to Dr. Paolus. He felt the warmth of her comforting bulk and held her for a long time.

"I'm ready," he said. "I want to go home."

FIFTY-SEVEN

ZOE ALAKIS

Even with Tom Rom off hunting down interesting diseases, Pergamus remained a bustling place. Zoe's teams added more and more knowledge until she felt that her databases would burst.

She refused to give up the battle. Each new discovery expanded her arsenal in the never-ending war against enemy microorganisms. Zoe could never be victorious against so many mutable strains of viruses, disease, and bacteria, but she would put up the best possible fight. No one had better resources than she did.

From inside her sterile dome, Zoe reviewed progress reports and pored over study proposals. She ate a bland but nutritious meal, took her high-dosage supplements, then completed the day's body measurements—pulse, blood pressure, oxygen saturation, temperature, body composition index—and logged the data in her extensive file. No single human body had ever been so thoroughly and consistently documented.

Finished, Zoe sat back at her desk with a weary sigh. Two more interim reports had come in, and one of her freelance operatives arrived from Earth, broadcasting appropriate priority clearances, so that her security teams allowed him through the picket line.

After the unsettling arrival of James Duggan, Zoe had dressed down every member of her security team, and they were now far more alert. What if, instead of a distraught husband, the intruder had been part of an active military operation against Pergamus? Or some terrorist intent on stealing her vast collection of deadly biological organisms?

Fortunately, few outsiders knew exactly what Zoe Alakis did here or how she funded her work. In the worst-case scenario, she had her fail-safe systems, automated self-destructs that would vaporize every-thing. At all costs, she would keep the deadly samples and records out of any hands but her own.

She preferred to rely on less extreme preventive measures first, how-ever.

The operative from Earth expected to be well paid. Dr. Benjamin Paolus appeared on her main screen, cool and humorless, a consum-mate professional. "Ms. Alakis, I have an interesting delivery for you."

She sat back to listen. "You haven't previously let me down, Doc-tor."

"This one is unlike any other disease in your library—an extremely rare microfungus DNA-adherer, originating from Theroc. I have sam-ples and a complete medical workup—quite an unorthodox spread and progression."

"Can you cure it?"

"Doubtful."

Paolus transmitted his files, and she glanced at her desk screen. He would deliver the physical specimens in triply sealed quarantine con-tainers to one of the Orbiting Research Spheres, where the organism could be properly assessed. "Is it fatal?"

"In this particular case, almost certainly fatal," Paolus said, then paused. "One other detail adds special interest—the victim is Prince Reynald of Theroc."

Her eyes widened. "The Prince is dying? How could I not have heard of this?"

"He is careful to protect his privacy. I am committing a severe ethical breach by delivering the sample and records here."

Paolus didn't seem to be angling for an increased payment; he was simply stating a fact. She said, "You will not find anyone with more discretion than I have, Doctor."

"That's why I do business with you, Ms. Alakis. I know your pen-chant for protecting and withholding your data. If your research teams were to find a treatment, however, the King and Queen would be immeasurably grateful. And if Reynald did survive to become the next King, you would forever have a solid ally in the government."

Zoe's voice was as brittle as breaking ice. "Thank you for the suggestion, Dr. Paolus, but I think not. Allies have a tendency to demand more than they give. If I make an exception for one pathetically ill patient, even if he is a Prince, then where do I stop making exceptions?"

Dr. Paolus fumbled with something out of the range of the screen, then nodded. "As you wish, Ms. Alakis."

"You will be compensated well, as before. I am always here if you should encounter anything else of note."

She signed off before he could reply. Her security team met his ship and received the sealed medical samples, which they delivered to an assigned ORS. Dr. Paolus departed, his business finished.

On screen, Zoe skimmed his report, looked over the results and the body scans, glanced at young Prince Reyn's face before dismissing that part of the file as irrelevant. She would add the disease to her collection with all the others, one more piece in the grand puzzle.

Her father died on Vaconda, although he had been functionally dead for a month before his last flickering breath. Tom Rom and Zoe were beside him, hovering near his bed and the monitoring instruments. His life signs were already so faint that they didn't realize he had slipped away until several minutes later.

Zoe had just turned twenty. Though Adam Alakis had suffered five years of slow decline, she was startled to realize that she had made no plans for his funeral—an intentional blind spot, but now she made the quick and obvious decision. "I want him buried out in the jungle next to my mother's grave."

Tom Rom nodded. "Then that's what we will do." If she had said she wanted Adam Alakis to be placed aboard a flammable basket and sent off in a hot air balloon, Tom Rom would likely have reacted the same way.

But her mother had died twelve years ago, and when Zoe went out to search for the grave, she found that the lichentree jungle and fungus vines had grown so thick and dense that she could not locate the right spot—not that it mattered in a real sense, but it mattered to her.

That was when the grief finally hit her with a crushing weight, and she broke down, lost. She remembered her mother, but the missing grave marker seemed to have erased Evelyn Alakis's entire existence.

There at the bottom of the forest, Tom Rom wrapped his arms around her, held her in silence as he took her back to the watchstation above the treetops. He left her in the empty deck and returned to the forest floor. In the watchstation, she was surprised to see that Tom Rom had quietly cleaned up the death room and put away all the monitoring and medical equipment that had kept her father alive for so long. He had made the bed, and now the research tower appeared to be a normal and comfortable home again.

Zoe wouldn't have had the strength to do it herself, hadn't even thought that far ahead. The lonely station was not a place where she wanted to stay, however. She had no idea what she was going to do now.

In less than an hour, Tom Rom led her back down to the overgrown forest floor. He had rediscovered Evelyn's grave and cleared away the underbrush to expose her name marker. He had also made a marker for Adam, which he placed next to Evelyn's. The new grave marker was perfect, created with great care. Zoe couldn't imagine how he had done it so quickly—until she realized that Tom Rom must have prepared the marker some time ago without telling her.

They buried her father out there, knowing that the jungle would creep in swiftly. Standing by the fresh grave, young Zoe looked around her at the scabrous lichens, the feathery pollens blowing through the air, the insects crawling in the undergrowth, the slime molds oozing up the sides of trees. Vaconda was a turgid place where Adam and Evelyn had come to hunt for pharmaceutical possibilities, but Zoe saw it as a place of rot and death.

She looked up at Tom Rom, cold and businesslike. "The homestead is mine now. Everything automatically transfers into my name upon my father's passing."

Tom Rom nodded. "Yes. I helped him prepare the documents myself."

"And you are my guardian."

"I am your guardian in actual fact, regardless of the legalities. You are an adult, but I will stay with you if you wish."

She looked at him as if he had become a fool. "Of course I wish it."

He gave another nod. "I don't need a document to tell me who I am. I am your guardian regardless, and forever."

Zoe knew she was being impetuous, but she made up her mind. "I don't want this homestead. I don't want to stay on Vaconda. I don't want anything to do with this place. I want to leave."

Tom Rom said, "I will take you wherever you wish. But what do we do with the homestead?"

Zoe heard the simmering sounds of the lichentree forest, watched a purple beetle making its way too close to the questing probe-tendril of a sluggish mold, which snapped it up and retracted the pseudopod into its own main spongy mass. Seeing all the festering life, the churning biological cauldron all around her, she turned to one side, vomited, and sank to her knees. "I hate this place. I wish we could just burn it."

"I can burn it," Tom Rom said, "if that is what you want."

At first, she was unwilling to consider it a genuine possibility. "But it's all I have. How will we live?"

"We know how to survive. I'll make sure you survive."

Zoe looked at him for a long moment, then told him to do it.

Back at the watchstation above the lichentree forest, they packed their few belongings aboard Tom Rom's ship and retreated to a safe distance to watch.

He triggered the fire bombs he had scattered throughout the jungle for kilometers around. Explosions erupted in orange feathers of fire that flattened a large swath and ignited the surrounding lichentrees. As the wildfire spread, it cleared a giant section of the dense forest, leaving only a smoking smear of ash.

As Zoe watched the fires, she felt a kind of satisfaction, of freedom. Even though there was nothing left, she still owned it. The fire bombing had erased all the years of her life there, all the marks her parents had made, everything Vaconda had done to them. The jungle would reclaim its own soon enough, she knew, but Zoe planned to be long gone by then.

In an irony even greater than the reward, after the smoke cleared and the ashes settled, they discovered that the wildfire had exposed an extensive vein-inclusion of prisdiamonds long buried under the jungle growth.

And those prisdiamonds were enough to make Zoe Alakis one of the wealthiest women in the Spiral Arm.

FIFTY-EIGHT

KING PETER

The funeral for Father Idriss brought visitors from across the Spiral Arm: important businessmen, representatives from Confederation planets, heads of Roamer clans, even an Ildiran delegation that included the Mage-Imperator's green priest consort, Nira, who was pleased to be back in the original worldforest after so many years on Ildira.

Normally, Peter conducted the business of the Confederation alongside Queen Estarra, as equal partners, but after her father's death, Estarra withdrew to mourn silently and sent her apologies to the visitors.

The throne room would have had two empty chairs, one for the Queen and one where Idriss had sat to listen (or snooze), but Peter's children joined him. Prince Reyn had returned from Earth, accompanied by Deputy Eldred Cain and Rlinda Kett. Using the facilities of her own Theron restaurant, Rlinda would cater the food for the funeral banquet that evening.

Reyn sat with Arita, filling their roles as Prince and Princess, dressed in traditional Theron finery, beside their father. They were as close as a brother and sister could be, but they had little time to talk, caught up in the swirl of responsibilities. Peter was glad he didn't have to face his duties alone, especially today.

They received the visitors who came to express their sympathy. Green priests gathered around, sending reports and passing messages through telink. The Roamers, through their newly elected Speaker Sam Ricks, sent a beautiful embroidered tapestry.

Deputy Cain entered the chamber wearing a business suit. The soft-spoken, responsible man had been an unexpected ally in the final days of the Hansa. He gave a polite bow. "Father Idriss was an honest and well-respected man. I present formal condolences on behalf of Earth, but on a more personal note, King Peter, I wanted to give you this. It's from my own collection." He lifted a rectangular object the size of a thin briefcase and removed a cloth to reveal a small framed painting that depicted a poignant sunset. "It's one of my particular favorites done by the twenty-first-century master Dolus. The image is both majestic and sad—I felt it evoked the right feelings on this occasion."

As Cain presented the painting, Peter felt a lump in his throat. He knew the Deputy would have found it difficult to part with one of his prized works of art. Peter, Reyn, and Arita marveled at the colors, the beauty, the majesty. It did remind him of Idriss in that indefinable way that only the best art could achieve. "We will hang it on the throne room wall to remember Father Idriss, and also to be reminded of you, Deputy Cain, and all you've done for us."

The funeral gathering also served as an awkward reunion for members of Estarra's scattered family. Her sister Celli returned with Solimar from their terrarium dome in Fireheart Station, and—an even greater surprise—their older sister Sarein returned from the Wild, where she had lived in self-imposed exile since the collapse of the Hansa.

Estarra and her older sister had a strained and scarred relationship. In the political turmoil of the Elemental War, Sarein had done many questionable things that hurt Estarra and Peter, but she had also helped them when they needed it most. By going off to the uninhabited continent, Sarein had avoided any accusations. For a social and ambitious woman who had once fought hard for Theroc to become a vibrant part of the Hansa, Sarein must have found it difficult to live as a virtual hermit. It took the death of Father Idriss to bring her back.

Now, the three sisters shared grief over the loss of their father. Their brothers, Reynald and Beneto, had both been killed years ago in the Elemental War, and the sisters clung to what they had left.

After Peter, Reyn, and Arita finished receiving the visitors, a staff member informed them that the green priests had finished preparing

Father Idriss for the ceremony. Wearing dark cocoonweave garments adorned with moth wings and segmented beetle shells, Estarra and her sisters came to meet Peter.

The Queen clasped his hand. "I wish we could just do this privately with the family."

"The rest of the Confederation needs the spectacle," Sarein said in a cool voice. "Peter was trained properly. He understands." She had once been beautiful, but now looked weathered and hard.

"I understand it too." Estarra straightened, looking regal. "I'm just saying what I wish."

All the dignitaries and visitors had already gathered on the forest floor. Peter held Estarra's hand, and they wound their way along an open path through the thick worldtrees, a trail that Peter was sure hadn't been there before. Somehow, the forest had created a wide avenue for the procession.

The mourners entered an open glade spangled with small white flowers and fleshy green vines. Father Idriss's body lay on the ground in the meadow, draped in a pristine white cocoonweave shroud. When Estarra saw the wrapped body, she paused, suddenly uncertain.

Since Celli had taken the green, she and Solimar led the worldforest in the actual funeral. The two green priests knelt among the vines, touching the white cloth. Celli had tears in her eyes. Solimar turned to the crowds that had gathered at the edges of the meadow. "Father Idriss was not a green priest, but he had a special connection to the forest. He was *Theroc* for all of us, Father of our people, and the father of my wife."

Celli looked up. "And now he joins the worldforest."

Together, they lifted the pale vines and draped them over the shrouded figure. The vines stirred, followed by other vines, until all the strands covered the body like an additional blanket. Leaves sprouted, tightening the green embrace that grew at an astonishing speed until buds appeared, rose higher, and unfolded to display dozens of creamy white orchids. A sweet, pervasive perfume filled the air, like scented applause for a life well lived.

Around the edge of the meadow, the observers murmured sounds of approval and wonderment. Estarra and her sisters hugged one another.

. . .

Grim business intruded as soon as night fell.

The numerous visitors took part in a large outdoor feast, which Rlinda Kett's chefs had prepared to perfection. Peter listened to quiet conversations, Confederation representatives making deals, discussing politics. Representing the Roamer clans, Sam Ricks didn't seem to know what to do at all, didn't even know most of the guests. He stood with his hands in his pockets, offering condolences but to the wrong people; without the other clans around him, he seemed out of his element.

A ship arrived with unexpected visitors—Del Kellum, the former Speaker of the clans, as well as his daughter Zhett and their entire family. They looked haggard and distraught. Kellum barged into the funeral banquet, as if he didn't care what was going on. "I need to see the King, by damn! This is a crisis—he's got to know."

Deputy Cain rose to his feet. Sam Ricks blinked and merely managed to look confused. Peter and Estarra both went forward to meet Kellum, while Ricks deferred.

All conversation stopped as the bearded man announced, "Our skymine on Golgen was destroyed. The hydrogues are back!" He cut off an outburst of conversation. "But *they* didn't attack us, by damn. It was something else—a blight, a black stain that infected the drogues and destroyed their warglobes. A shadow arose from inside the planet itself—and one of the damned drogues even came up to warn us! Told us to get away, and all our skyminers barely got out in time. The whole damn planet was vomiting black when we flew away."

Patrick Fitzpatrick uploaded and displayed horrific images of the inky stain welling up from the cloud banks. Peter had never seen anything like it, yet for some reason it reminded him of another strange occurrence—the report General Keah had sent via green priest not long ago about how her battle group had flushed out a hidden infestation of Klikiss robots, which had escaped into a mysterious shadow cloud. He frowned. Those two events couldn't be related. . . .

Nira watched the images with a drawn expression. "Another terrible shadow engulfed an Ildiran exploration ship far outside the Spiral Arm. I think it took my son. Some Ildirans believe it's the return of the Shana Rei." She looked around. "And that strikes great fear into their entire race. Adar Zan'nh is investigating now. Of course, we'll share with you whatever he discovers."

"It was awfully strange, by damn," Del Kellum said. "Unlike anything I've ever seen."

"General Keah's battle group just returned to CDF headquarters at Earth," Peter said. "We will need to compare Del Kellum's report with images of the shadow cloud they encountered." He frowned. "I thought it was bad enough news that some of the Klikiss robots were still around."

Estarra stood close to him, and as they watched the images of the blackness bleeding into the gas giant's clouds, Peter felt his skin crawl.

Deputy Cain showed increasing concern. "It took us too long to realize the hydrogue threat when they first appeared, Sire. I suggest we study this with proper urgency, factor in General Keah's report, and add whatever information the Ildirans can provide on the Shana Rei."

"If there is proof," Nira said. "We still don't know. The historical accounts of the Shana Rei are sketchy in the Saga of Seven Suns, but I'll return to Ildira immediately with the Mage-Imperator's entourage. If the Saga has any information that we can use, I'll communicate it via telink."

Deputy Cain nodded to the King. "Even if we don't know exactly what we're up against, we should start full-scale ramp-up and escalation of the CDF. Just in case. With your permission, Sire?"

With the safety of the Confederation at stake, the King and Queen had to put aside their grief to avert a possible greater tragedy. Peter gave his permission, issuing orders to dispatch scouts and follow-up teams, widespread inquiries, full reports on all the ships in the CDF, strategic ekti reserves.

They didn't even know the enemy yet, but once again Peter had to prepare for war.

FIFTY-NINE

RLINDA KETT

Rlinda had named her finest and favorite restaurant Arbor, for obvious reasons. It was a sheltered overhang on the Theron canopy with numerous finger decks and open balconies that could be enclosed during occasional inclement weather.

Colorful insects flitted about, some of them nuisances, some of them delicious. A stream of customers came and went, and Rlinda liked to think that some of them made excuses for business trips here to Theroc just so they could eat dinner at Arbor. She had commanded her chefs to be absolutely impressive.

During her years of travel as the Confederation's trade minister, Rlinda always kept her eyes open for new delicacies and recipes. She did her work, while running her trading company, but she really wanted to run the perfect restaurant. Now she had three: one on Relleker, one on Earth, one here.

She had insisted on providing the food for Father Idriss's funeral banquet, telling the King and Queen not to concern themselves. Rlinda instructed her chefs to give the meal understated elegance. The meal had been perfect—except for the disastrous news of the Golgen skymine and the ominous shadow clouds.

In the following days, while the Confederation buzzed with the reappearance of hydrogues and black robots, and possibly the Shana Rei, Rlinda reminded herself that she was done with all that. No longer her concern. Instead, she met with her "culinary explorers," who constantly sampled the bounty of the Theron forest, while teams of chefs concocted new recipes and preparation methods with all the dedication of scientific researchers. Now *that* was important.

They created various dishes of insect meat, succulent grubs, sweet or tart berries, herbs with indescribable flavors, stems, leaves, roots, bulbs, tubers. Yes, she loved this restaurant, and her chefs went out of their way to show off their favorite new creations, indulging her, overstuffing her—exactly as she liked.

Sitting at her own canopy table on her own finger deck, she ate only small servings in order to save room for more entrees. She didn't want to eat too much, but sometimes she couldn't help it. The chefs and servers brought out sample plates, one after another. For months, they had been experimenting with new concoctions, but each menu item needed her approval, and Rlinda had very high standards.

She glanced at tables on the other decks, where offworlders as well as some adventurous Therons—even a few green priests—were expanding their gourmet tastes. With so much bounty in the world-forest, Theron natives rarely bothered to sample outside delicacies. When she noticed a green priest couple trying several dishes from the "offworld menu," as opposed to the "Theron specialties" pages, she watched as they tasted, shared, and exchanged opinions.

Smiling, Rlinda called for Zachary Wisskoff, the manager and maître d' of Arbor. The man gave excellent service and knew his business, so she found him indispensable. On the other hand, Wisskoff's prissy arrogance also made him insufferable. Although the maître d' seemed stressed no matter when she visited, Rlinda suspected that he enjoyed regularly having something new to complain about.

The officious maître d' arrived immediately, like a specially trained silver beret responding to a threat. She nodded toward the green priests at the other table. "Zachary, I'm picking up the tab of that couple over there. The meals are on me."

Wisskoff had a long and narrow face, as if it had been pinched too much in the birth canal. His skinny nose was chiseled to a fine point, and his chin wasn't much more rounded. Thanks to his close-set eyes he could look down his nose with great disdain. "I'll have to discuss the matter with our accountants to see if we can afford it, madam."

"Buy their meals now, ask the accountants later. And if there's a problem, then I must be paying you too much. I'll deduct the bill from your next paycheck."

"Delightful," he said with a sniff. "I'm so pleased I can subsidize your generosity."

"You should be even more pleased that you have a job managing the finest restaurant in the Spiral Arm."

His eyebrows rose up like two Theron insects taking wing. "I thought it was the finest restaurant *because* I manage it." Wisskoff took out a small pad, consulted the screen, tapped a command into it. "There, the entire bill is deleted. It's as if they never ordered a meal, and the food simply vanished without a trace from our kitchens." He put the pad away. "I'll see about overcharging some planetary delegations to make up for it. They'll never know the difference."

Two members of the kitchen staff arrived bearing plates of sweet confections—gossamer sculptures made of spun fruit gelatins and crystallized sugars, topped off with seeds that looked like tiny gemstones.

Wisskoff turned to go. "By the way, madam, do you know a woman who has a compy? She arrived demanding to speak with you. I informed her that since I am in charge of this establishment, she would speak with *me*, but she refused. Only you. Her compy seems polite enough, even friendly, but we don't generally allow them in Arbor. The woman was quite persistent to the point of being annoying."

"You're quite an expert on annoying people, Zachary, so I'll trust your judgment in the matter."

"Oh, very witty, madam."

"Did this woman give a name? Is she from Theroc?" Rlinda knew there weren't many compies here.

Wisskoff sighed as if she had just asked him to redo two years of tax forms. "She's an offworlder . . . Relleker, I believe, though I don't know why she couldn't bother you at your restaurant *there*. She had an odd name, Orli something. I sent her away."

Rlinda perked up. "Orli Covitz? Get her back! I don't care if you have to send out search parties."

"That would be unnecessary, and also melodramatic," Wisskoff said. "I'm certain she's still here, as she was quite a nuisance. Did I mention the compy was polite?"

The maître d' tracked down Orli and DD and sent them onto the finger deck. Rlinda rose to her feet and opened her arms in a hug so wide that even a black hole could not have escaped from it.

DD gave a formal greeting. "Captain Kett, it is an honor to see you again."

Orli looked oddly conflicted. She accepted Rlinda's hug and then something broke loose in her. She clung more tightly, burying herself in the broad embrace. She began shaking, trying to restrain sobs, and finally gave up restraining them at all. Rlinda was at first startled by the outpouring, but she put away her questions and just held onto Orli.

Wisskoff stood embarrassed by the awkward tableau. With a not-so-polite clearing of his throat, he asked, "Is there anything I could bring you for now, madam?"

"Two cups of hot klee, Zachary." She glanced down at the re-splendent, fruity confections. "We've got desserts to share, and obviously we need a heart-to-heart, so once we have our klee, ignore us for a while."

"With pleasure, madam. Do I take it that you'll be footing the bill for the klee as well?"

Rlinda's dark eyes flashed, and the maître d' seemed to realize he had pushed too far, so he retreated with as much grace as he could manage.

Orli tried to straighten. "It's all right, Rlinda. I'm fine." She sniffled, and her lips trembled.

"If you're fine, then I'm skinny," Rlinda said. "Now tell me about it."

"I've had some . . . life changes." Orli turned away. "Damn! I thought this would be easier. I rehearsed it over and over again on the trip here to find you."

"Some things aren't supposed to be easy." Rlinda turned to the Friendly compy. "DD, help us out here. Tell me what happened—just a summary please."

The little compy was happy to oblige. "Orli Covitz and Matthew Freling have dissolved their relationship. Matthew found a home for the wayward compies from our Relleker facility. Orli placed them with a new colony on Ikbir, but she kept me as her companion—I'm very pleased about this. We traveled here to find you."

"To find me? How did you know to come here instead of Earth?" Rlinda asked.

With a heavy sigh, Orli dodged the painful part of the conversation. "We went there first and learned about the funeral. Even here, though, we almost didn't get to see you. That maître d' is very rude."

"He gets away with it only because he's amazingly competent. The moment he makes a mistake he'll be fired."

"I don't need to worry about being fired then, madam." Wisskoff appeared next to them, set two cups of klee down on the table, and turned away without a further word.

"Enough about him," Rlinda said. "If you need to talk to me about Matthew, I'm here." She pushed one of the fruit confections toward Orli. "And so is dessert. Help me test this."

Orli picked at her dessert, but smiled as she tasted it. She sipped the hot klee and gradually started to relax. "I shouldn't be acting like this. Mine isn't the first marriage to break up. It wasn't right in the first place, and it was as much my fault as it was his."

"I've got my own collection of ex-husbands," Rlinda said. "That doesn't mean it's not painful. In fact BeBob—" Her words cut off as her voice shut down. It always surprised her how swiftly the sadness came upon her, like an ambush. She forced herself to take a bite of her own dessert. "This reminds me of one of BeBob's favorite dishes. He was my favorite ex-husband."

"I know. I used to fly with him a lot."

Rlinda nodded, still feeling the heaviness of loss. "If you can put up with a man in a cramped spaceship, that means he's a man worth knowing."

Twenty years ago, she and BeBob had been happy. She would bustle from planet to planet as trade minister. At first BeBob followed her like a puppy dog, took care of her, kept her company, but over the years, he'd grown weary of the "glamour" and the constant travel of Rlinda's powerful position, so he chose to stay on Earth more often. She flew about the Spiral Arm, doing her duties, and flitting back home to see him. She kept herself so busy that she hadn't noticed that BeBob wasn't feeling well, that his energy seemed low.

Ten years ago, she'd been away on Ildira for the gala opening of the rebuilt Prism Palace when Branson Roberts dropped dead of a brain hemorrhage while crossing the street.

Rlinda swallowed hard now, trying to hide the tears. After all of their adventures, their perils, their harrowing escapes, she couldn't believe he had died while crossing a street. . . . As Rlinda spoke, the words rattled out in a flood; if she talked quickly enough, she could stay one step ahead of the tears.

Her favorite ex-husband was cremated and his ashes compacted and placed in a capsule, which she kept on her desk. When she died (preferably after a glorious meal served with the best wines) Rlinda had left instructions that her remains were to be placed in an identical capsule, and they would be launched together into interstellar space.

"That's very romantic," Orli said.

Rlinda shrugged and sniffled. "It seemed like a good idea."

They finished the desserts, and Rlinda folded her big hands on the tabletop. With her napkin, she reached over to dab a sparkle of sugar from Orli's cheek. "Other than needing a shoulder to cry on, is there some way I can help you?"

Orli froze for a moment, then spilled her request. "I'm done with the Relleker compy facility, done with staying at home and keeping my feet dirtside. I need a change of scenery, a change of pace."

Rlinda drew her brows together. "Running away won't solve anything."

"Maybe I'm running *toward* something . . . or maybe I just need to keep moving. You know I can fly ships. Does Kett Shipping need any pilots? Somebody to make a few runs?" She seized on this sudden direction for her life, which only pointed out just how aimless and lost she had been feeling.

Rlinda chuckled. "Why, yes, in fact, I do. One of my pilots, Mary Coven, is retiring, and I bought her ship for a song, but I don't have a captain yet. That sort of paperwork usually falls to Tasia and Robb."

"What do I need to do to get approvals?"

"You need to ask me." Rlinda tapped her on the head. "There, you're approved. The ship is called the *Proud Mary*. We can rename it if you like."

Orli shook her head. "The name sounds fine."

"Go to Earth, spend a week or two arranging matters, take the *Proud Mary* on a shakedown flight. I assume DD will be your copilot, given the appropriate upgrades?"

Orli threw her arms around Rlinda and gave her a big hug again. "Thank you. This is just what I needed."

SIXTY

ADAR ZAN'NH

The Solar Navy search ships headed out into uncharted space above the Spiral Arm, attempting to follow the course the *Kolpraxa* had taken. Adar Zan'nh's septa flew for days, seven fully equipped warliners with sensors extended, hunting for any sign of the lost exploration ship.

There had been no report, no distress signal, but every Ildiran had felt the crew's outcry in the *thism,* then utter silence. Osira'h had felt it more sharply than anyone else.

As the warliners flew through empty space, the crew remembered stars, but there were few stars nearby in this vast void. It would be so easy to get lost out here in the void. . . .

Zan'nh forced himself not to think about that. Through the faint threads of *thism* that connected them, he felt the crew's uneasiness. Out here in the universe's darkest spaces, *he* had to be the strongest tie that bound them all. Yet he could not ignore the fact that he was worried for the *Kolpraxa* and its commander. The expedition should have been a shining moment in Tal Gale'nh's career.

Throughout the voyage, Osira'h remained in the command nucleus, alert, guiding the search by following the connection she maintained with her brother. Though none of the warliner's sensors detected any trace of the lost ship, she reached out with her enhanced telepathic powers, feeling a vibrant sense of purpose again.

Looking up, she reassured Zan'nh, "Gale'nh is still alive, Adar. We will find him—I can still sense him."

Zan'nh kept his voice low, so as not to feed the fears of the crew. "I am personally concerned for Tal Gale'nh and the *Kolpraxa*'s crew, and as Adar of the Solar Navy, I am also concerned about the threat they may have encountered." He could not push away the sight of the ominous shadow cloud that had swallowed—destroyed?—the fleeing black robots. What if the Shana Rei truly had returned? It seemed impossible. What could have awakened them? And how could the Solar Navy fight them?

Beside him, Osira'h held on to the command rail and closed her eyes. Her feathery hair twitched with a hint of her thoughts.

Zan'nh regarded the halfbreed girl who had grown into a beautiful young woman. Osira'h was slender, with an elfin face and small rounded nose reminiscent of her mother's, the noble cheekbones and generous lips of the Mage-Imperator.

Zan'nh remembered when Osira'h was just a little girl, the most perfect product of the Ildiran breeding program. Unlike the others, she was a halfbreed child born of love instead of scientific experimentation. Trained to use her mental powers, Osira'h had bravely confronted the hydrogues. Zan'nh remembered how impressive she had looked, forcing her will on the great elemental beings and commanding them to cease their destruction.

Now she concentrated, finding the faintest gossamer connections that told her Gale'nh was alive. Zan'nh knew she was trying to send strength to her brother, and she continued even when she sensed no response from him.

"I will not underestimate the power of hope," she said.

The search ships flew onward, guided only by Osira'h's reassurances that they were following the correct course.

Five days later, Osira'h called out, "He is here." She raised her voice so everyone in the command nucleus could hear her. *"He is here!"*

At Adar Zan'nh's command, all seven warliners decelerated and hung together in the middle of an infinite emptiness. Osira'h's eyes remained closed as she guided them, confident and insistent.

Sensor operators deployed fast-moving probes in all directions, like fluff from a seedpod, but they detected nothing. The communications array sent out persistent signals hailing the *Kolpraxa*. Still no response.

They combed the emptiness for hours with no result.

Osira'h paced the command nucleus. "I know Gale'nh is here, but

I'm trying to find one small spark in all this emptiness. The stars are far away. It's so dark." She could not suppress a shudder.

Finally, they blundered into the *Kolpraxa* almost by accident, detecting a mass anomaly in the vacuum, even though the expeditionary ship was all but invisible. It emitted no electromagnetic or heat signature; its running lights were dead; its anodized metallic hull didn't reflect even a hint of starlight.

The seven warliners approached cautiously, shining forward blazers on the exploration ship, which was little more than a silhouette that drank light, as if the *Kolpraxa* had been painted with a matte coating of deepest black.

"It is the Shana Rei," someone whispered. "Just like in the story of the planet Orryx." Zan'nh remembered the tales from the Saga of Seven Suns, how the creatures of darkness had englobed entire worlds and battle fleets with impenetrable black armor.

Osira'h leaned against the command rail, her eyes wide. "Gale'nh is inside there. He's nearly smothered. We have to get to him." Her voice grew more urgent. "We have to break through!"

Zan'nh pushed back his uneasiness. "Dispatch a full team with high-powered lasers. Maybe concentrated light will break through." If Osira'h sensed Tal Gale'nh was alive in there, then the *Kolpraxa* must still have life support and atmosphere.

As they suited up, Ildiran engineers and warrior kith studied the *Kolpraxa*'s design plans to familiarize themselves with the external airlock placement, discussing their plan of rescue.

From the flagship's command nucleus, the Adar watched his crew make their way over to one of the exterior airlocks. The controls were sealed with the ebony film, but when the rescue team used their lasers, the intense light peeled away the coating, turning it into smoke and shadows. They worked at the hatch for more than an hour.

Osira'h fidgeted beside the Adar. "I'm trying to let him know that help is coming, but Gale'nh can't sense us, can't sense *me*, though we're so close, even with the *thism* of so many Ildirans aboard these warliners. I can't detect any crew aboard the *Kolpraxa*. None at all."

"There were thousands," Zan'nh said.

"And now I sense none." Impulsively she added, "I want to suit up and go over there with the rescue crew. I need to be there for Gale'nh."

"Not until we know it is safe," Zan'nh said.

"When I was a child, I saved our entire Empire." Her eyes flashed. "My presence on the *Kolpraxa* will help keep us safe."

When the Adar could not dissuade her, he and Osira'h both suited up and jetted over to the silhouetted ship. By now the engineering team had forced open the airlock's external hatch, but they waited for Zan'nh to join them. Moving with extreme caution, they entered the *Kolpraxa*.

The interior of the lost ship was dim and only the grayish blue emergency bioluminescence lights glowed, giving the corridors a surreal appearance. The temperature measured as cold, but not intolerable. The searchers carried brilliant blazers that shone into every corner, bleaching away the shadows, but creating a flood of new ones behind them.

When sensors indicated that the atmosphere was breathable, one of the engineer kith risked opening his faceplate. After he breathed without difficulty for several minutes, the warrior kith followed suit, but made the Adar and Osira'h wait while they too verified that the air was safe.

Zan'nh inhaled, trying to place a strange smell. A warliner's atmosphere was always scrubbed and processed, but this smelled cold and lifeless. Except for the small group accompanying him, he detected only a resounding silence in the *thism*. Everything about the *Kolpraxa* was drained of energy, devoid of life.

"Where has the crew gone?" Osira'h asked. "There's no *thism* here at all."

The team moved forward. The corridors were empty, as were the chambers and meeting rooms, the dining halls, the crew quarters. All deserted. Osira'h struck out in the lead. "To the command nucleus—I feel Gale'nh there."

The interdeck lifts were nonfunctional, so the team climbed stairs and ladders, deck after deck, until they reached the command nucleus. The transparent observation dome was entirely obscured by a blackness that allowed no glimmer of starlight inside. The control panels were dead and dark. Even the faint blue emergency lights barely functioned here.

They found Tal Gale'nh, all alone in the dark. He sat on the floor beside the command rails. Although he faced the searchers, he didn't react to their arrival, didn't seem to see them.

He huddled next to five bodies, the only other Ildirans they had seen aboard the *Kolpraxa*. His arms were outstretched, as if trying to encompass the fallen crewmembers next to him. They were all completely drained of color, bleached into near nothingness.

In the pale blue light, Adar Zan'nh did not at first recognize the difference, but Osira'h ran to her brother. "Look at his hair!"

Tal Gale'nh had once had dark locks and a deep greenish gold skin. Now, the color had been washed out of him. His skin was ghostly pale, his hair the color of ivory. His eyes stared ahead.

Zan'nh shone his handheld blazer on the Tal's face. Osira'h wrapped her arms around her brother, clung to him—and finally Gale'nh stirred. Osira'h touched his forehead, cupped his cheeks in her hands, and closed her eyes as she concentrated.

Eventually, Zan'nh felt a flicker as Gale'nh's presence returned to the *thism*. The pale and devastated Tal looked at his sister, then at the Adar. "They're all gone." His voice was a hoarse whisper, like stone scraping on stone. He indicated the bodies around him. "I tried to save these, used all my strength to hold them, while the shadows took the others away. Not . . . enough left."

Zan'nh spoke in a crisp, commanding voice, hoping to get through. "What happened to your crew, Tal?"

Gale'nh's eyes flickered, but continued to stare off into an inconceivable distance. "The shadows took them and unmade them . . . but they said I was different." He heaved a deep breath and let it out. "All my people are gone, faded to black."

SIXTY-ONE

DALE REEVES

The ragtag group of Retroamer ships arrived at their isolated destination: an incredible and majestic alien city in space, built and abandoned long ago. Clan Reeves could call this place their own.

Dale Reeves and his wife rode with the bearded patriarch in the convoy's lead ship. After investing so many years of work at the Rendezvous site, Dale had been uneasy about this great exodus, but he knew he would never change his father's mind. Olaf Reeves was like an asteroid on a collision course, and those who got in his way would suffer from the impact. Garrison had proved that without question.

Sendra came to the forward compartment with their two sons. "The boys want to watch as we arrive."

She was a good mother, patient with Jamie and Scott—more patient, in fact, than she was with him. Sendra was a strong woman, ready to fill her role as the wife of the future clan leader. The only problem was, Sendra had expected *Garrison* to be the next head of clan Reeves. Dale had never aspired to be a leader and did not quite understand why she had married him anyway. Maybe Sendra thought she could change him, strengthen him, make him into the right sort of person.

But Dale Reeves wasn't malleable in that way. His father had attempted to bully, poke, and prod him into becoming a leader. Dale had tried—he truly had—but it didn't work. He remained a quiet, amenable person who liked to listen more than he liked to talk, which was good when he sat next to Olaf Reeves, but didn't bode well for making tough decisions of his own as clan leader.

Now, the Retroamer vessels decelerated as they arrived at a large, strange habitat built out in space, far enough from the parent star that it had remained unnoticed and empty for millennia. Dale had never seen anything like it—a giant self-contained alien metropolis, completely dark, bristling with towers.

The space city was built on a five-point pattern; separate arms of varying lengths radiated from a central hub so that the structure looked like a spiny, metal snowflake with swollen polyhedral modules—habitation areas? Storage chambers? Ildirans had a very distinctive architectural style—as did the Klikiss—but this station had a completely different origin. Someone, something else had designed this.

"Do you think it was built by some unknown alien race?" Dale asked. "This could be the find of the century. Shouldn't we report it to the Confederation?"

Olaf grimaced with disdain. "Our green priest will share the necessary details, but I'm not having hundreds of scholars and xeno-archaeologists crawling all over our home. We found it. The right of salvage is clear."

Dale thought he remembered that the Confederation Charter—which the Roamer clans had signed, so therefore clan Reeves was bound by the terms—classified alien artifacts and archaeological sites as "gifts to civilization" for the study of all. But maybe the wording specifically referred to "Klikiss artifacts," because there were no other known alien races. He didn't press the issue, knowing that his father would find some way to insist that he was right, nevertheless.

Dale considered it remarkable that anyone had found the derelict structure out here in the dark between the stars. One of their scouts had stumbled upon it during a wandering trip back from the closed-off neo-Amish planet called Happiness. The neo-Amish refused to deal with any outsiders, except occasionally for Olaf Reeves and his Retroamers. Clan Reeves wanted to create a similar home for themselves in the derelict city.

Dale found it uncharacteristic that his father would go to an already-extant city, even an abandoned one. He would have expected the old man to insist on building their own place from scratch, making every component with their own hands. When Dale pointed out the seeming contradiction, his father had frowned. "Roamers take advantage of valuable resources, wherever we find them. Why would I let this go to waste?"

As the Retroamer ships gathered around the huge, silent city, Dale studied the readings. "Gives off almost no thermal signature. That city's been abandoned for a very long time."

"What is that place?" asked Jamie, his older son.

Dale tried to think of the right way to answer, but his father spoke first. "That is the new home of clan Reeves."

"I thought Rendezvous was our home?"

"We left Rendezvous," Dale said to the boys. "I explained that to you. We're not going back. This will be our home now."

"But who built it?" Scott asked.

Olaf said, "Nobody knows, but we'll find out. The city is ours for the taking. There'll be room for every clan member to have twice as much living space as we had on Rendezvous."

"Do we even know if we can live there?" Sendra asked him. "Have all the systems been checked out yet?"

Olaf looked at her. "Of course we can live there. We're *Roamers*. If something's not functioning, we'll fix it. If it's missing a system, we'll install it. And if it proves untenable, then we'll build our own city from scratch and use this place for spare parts. That's our Guiding Star."

BO, the Teacher compy transferred to them from Academ, came into the cockpit to attend the two boys. "I will watch them, Sendra Reeves. It's good that they're seeing this with their own eyes. This is history—our clan history."

"It looks spooky," said Jamie.

Sendra said, "BO will protect you from any space-station ghosts."

The boys giggled, knowing their mother was joking. The two had been born long after the Elemental War, but Dale certainly remembered the faeros, the hydrogues, the Klikiss invasion, the treacherous black robot attacks. He wouldn't lie to his sons and tell them that monsters did not exist.

Like a conquering hero, Olaf opened a comm channel to all the convoy ships. "Welcome to a new beginning for clan Reeves. Let's make this place *ours*. I need ten ships and some scouts to survey the exterior."

The Retroamer ships scanned the derelict city, mapping the modules on the radiating spokes, identifying viable access points. At the first three door hatches the scouts encountered on the nearest spoke, bold but crudely drawn pink triangles marked the exterior hull. Nobody knew what that meant.

Until they found an intrinsic energy source, or hooked up their own power blocks to bleed heat into the complex one section at a time, the first groups would have to wear environment suits. Over the centuries of abandonment, it was possible—even likely—that the atmosphere had leaked away, but clan Reeves had plenty of oxygen generators, if needed.

The first suited Retroamer scouts inspected the hatch areas of the hub sphere, tried to decipher the exterior controls, and in the end dismantled them. Though they had no idea how the alien builders engineered their systems, basic physics and mechanics were the same. With a small power block, the scouts triggered the hatch to gain access to the city.

"Shouldn't take us too long to finesse the controls so that we can open other hatches and some large docking bays. The hull seems intact, but there's plenty to do," the scout reported.

Olaf grinned. "Once we bring our ships inside, I'll assign squads of workers."

Four other scout teams reported in, and one announced even more exciting news. "There's an atmosphere, Olaf! It'll even be breathable once we warm it up."

The clan leader issued orders throughout the convoy. "It's a huge city, and we'll be methodical with our exploration teams, but first things first. For now, give priority to the central hub and one primary spoke for our habitation. Engineering crews will make the place livable: light, heat, power, and air. We've got a lot of people waiting to stretch their legs."

From all across the Retroamer exodus convoy, clan members shuttled over to the largest community ship to celebrate. The mood was light, and Dale felt his tension unwind. Though he had been reluctant to leave Rendezvous, he had to admit this alien city was truly remarkable.

Shelud, the green priest volunteer, joined them for the celebration.

He was shy but smiled frequently, and Dale already liked him. Olaf came over. "I remind you, green priest, that when you use telink, you are not to reveal the location of this city—not yet."

"His name is *Shelud*, Father," Dale said, which earned him a sharp frown.

The green priest nodded. "I understand. I used my treeling to announce our arrival, but no one knows where we are. The worldtrees are waiting to hear further news."

Olaf Reeves called for the attention of those gathered. He stood near a large viewing port, with the enormous empty space city behind him, but faced them all without looking at the impressive backdrop. "We don't know who built that city or why they abandoned it, but our Guiding Star brought us here. It is our new home, our new Rendezvous. As part of the process of making it ours, the city deserves a name." He paused, looking at the clan members there, and Shelud wondered if he was waiting for input. Before anyone could speak up, though, he continued. "I have decided we'll name our new home Okiah, after the great Roamer Speaker who guided our clans for so many years before the Elemental War. Jhy Okiah steered us through good, independent years, kept the clans productive, before we were scattered, before we became outlaws, before we lost our soul by joining the Confederation."

The Retroamers muttered, the tone of their voices clearly indicating they were pleased with the choice. Shelud said he knew about old Speaker Jhy Okiah, but promised that when he had a chance he would use his treeling to tap into the verdani database. He would learn more about the revered woman, especially since their new city would bear her name.

Dale looked out the windowport to see a few lights already shining in the derelict city, though most of the structure remained dark. Soon, they would make it bright and warm, fill it with laughter and hope. This strange city-station was their future and their new home.

SIXTY-TWO

LEE ISWANDER

Yes, things were definitely looking up. His son Arden regarded him with a genuine pride that eclipsed the defensive attitude the young man had shown in the past few months. Londa, who always believed in him, now had a shine in her eyes that showed she really meant it and was not just being a dutiful wife.

And Lee Iswander believed it too.

By the Guiding Star, he was going to reclaim the power, wealth, and prominence he had lost in the fires of Sheol, and he felt damned proud of it. A disaster that would have crushed anyone else proved to be nothing more than a setback for him—soon enough, the number 1,543 would be lost in the noise.

And these bloater extraction operations were so *easy*! The ekti was just there for the taking.

Iswander stood inside the admin module, looking out at the dimly lit islands of bloaters, countless cosmic bubbles floating in the emptiness. Though the cluster was moving closer to the nearby star system, no stars were close enough to shed substantial light. Iswander's own factory operations illuminated the area like a swarm of phosphorescent insects: refinery stations, cobbled-together filtration chambers, workhorse garbage ships that had been converted to extraction pumps. He had added several more hab modules discreetly transferred from his off-books company stores, careful not to raise questions about why he needed the structures or where he was taking them.

New employees arrived weekly. They signed ironclad nondisclosure agreements and lived out in the habitation modules of the complex.

Iswander paid them well enough that he was able to attract unmarried and unconnected employees who were willing to come here.

Elisa Enturi flew out to Ulio and other industrial outposts, acting as his recruiter to find skilled workers and convincing them to take a chance on Lee Iswander again. Many refused, but some took the risk. Their support would pay off extensively. The profits were already so breathtaking that Iswander intended to give a substantial bonus to the workers who had supported him from the beginning.

The complex grew week by week. Iswander's team could barely keep up with the opportunities that presented themselves.

By contrast, the operations at Sheol had required incredible effort and investment to get up and running. He'd eventually turned a profit, but at such a tremendous cost. *1,543.*

Roamers knew how to eke out a living under dire conditions. Some people, like the fool Olaf Reeves, took a twisted, defiant pride in enduring misery. Lee Iswander, though, saw no particular badge of honor in hardship and suffering—the Retroamers were welcome to it.

A moving light flitted about in the industrial field: the restless Alec Pannebaker bouncing around in a survey pod. Pannebaker reported in, "Two more bloaters drained in the past twenty-four hours, Chief. We're going to need more storage tanks unless Elisa can distribute the stuff faster."

Iswander responded, "I see no reason why we can't do both."

They could also slow down production, but Iswander would not even consider that alternative. He had lost everything on Sheol, and he had a lot of ground to recover. He watched as extractor ships hooked themselves to another bloater and began to siphon off the murky internal fluid. He shook his head just watching it all, feeling energized, as if a special kind of ekti-X filled his bloodstream with optimism.

That afternoon, Elisa returned from making her fifth delivery of ekti-X tankers to the transfer station of Ulio. The woman looked more content now than he had seen her in some time—still focused and impatient, but with less of an angry edge. She had quickly gotten over the loss of her husband and son.

"The Confederation is starting to notice, sir," she said. "Ekti-X is more efficient than regular stardrive fuel. Demand is going up. Each time, I dispose of the cargo within an hour of my arrival."

Iswander ran silent calculations. "Maybe we should charge a premium."

"I would advise against it. We're producing so much stardrive fuel and so quickly, we can't risk slowing the demand."

"Is anyone asking questions?"

She shrugged. "They can ask all they want, but I don't have to provide answers." She glanced through the windowport at the bloaters floating out there, drifting toward the nearest star. "In the time it took me to deliver one cargo load, you've got three more waiting for me. We need other distributors."

Iswander felt an odd sensation in the muscles on his face and realized he was smiling. "I got a report from our scouts. They've discovered two other bloater concentrations outside of isolated star systems, one cluster even larger than this one." He clasped his hands behind his back. "Someone else is bound to make the discovery before long, once they know what to look for. I can't believe that in all of our centuries of space exploration no one, not even one of the generation ships, encountered the bloaters before."

"They seem so obvious now," Elisa said. "Or maybe they weren't there before."

Iswander turned. "What do you mean?"

"They could be just appearing."

He laughed. "Manifesting out of the universe? Spontaneous generation?"

"I wasn't trying to explain it, sir, just offering a possibility."

"Let's worry about finding more distributors to handle our ekti output. I trust your judgment, Elisa. Find another ship that will take, sell, and deliver our ekti to customers as fast as we can deliver it."

He saw relief and wonderment on her face. "So long as we can keep this secret, sir, our wealth could be limitless."

Although the financial rewards were certainly gratifying, Iswander was just as concerned about his reputation. His name had seemed fatally damaged after Sheol, and he meant to get it back. It was not hubris to reclaim what he deserved.

He smiled at her. "While you arrange the shipments, I'm going to make a trip to Theroc and meet with King Peter. I can still pull a few strings."

"Isn't there a legal risk?"

"Not worried about that. I can out-lawyer anyone in the Spiral Arm, if I need to. Sheol was a tragic accident, and thanks to the ekti-X, I'll be able to make any reparations necessary. First though"—he gave her a genuine smile—"everyone in the Confederation needs to know that I'm back."

SIXTY-THREE

MAGE-IMPERATOR JORA'H

Though the Prism Palace was bathed with purifying sunlight, Mage-Imperator Jora'h had slept restlessly for weeks.

As the nexus of the *thism* that bound the entire Ildiran race together, Jora'h had felt the growing unease for some time now, like a grating hum just below the level of hearing. All his people were on edge from the news of the ominous dark nebula, the missing exploration ship, the tales of shadows from Ildiran legends. . . .

This time when he slept, he felt as if he had fallen into an abyss. He tried to fight back to consciousness, but he was smothering, cold—*blind*.

Thrashing, he forced himself awake, but he could not see, could not breathe. He tried to claw away the blindfold of nightmares. His heart pounded, and the sense of dread was a palpable thing inside him, as if some monster had gotten entangled in the *thism* and was straining to tear the strands apart. With a great gasp, he flung his eyelids open, and dazzling light flooded in. He tried to orient himself, tried to understand.

Nira was beside him in the bed, and her presence shone even brighter than the sunlight around him. Wide awake, she leaned over him, holding his shoulders. "Jora'h!"

He stopped struggling, and she sank down against him, wrapping her arms around him, pressing her body close. He was drenched in Nira's strength. As a human green priest, she was not part of the *thism*, could not connect with him in the way that other Ildirans did, but he felt closer to her than to anyone else. She had been back from Theroc for only a few days, and she too had brought reports of the spreading shadows.

"A nightmare," he said, and his voice caught in his throat. "And now my frightened thoughts have gotten into the *thism*." He had never felt so terrified and didn't comprehend why. He could never allow any Ildiran to see him like this. "Just a nightmare," he said again, trying to convince himself.

She touched his face. "I'm no stranger to nightmares either."

They lay together in silence, then Jora'h said, "But your nightmares come from experiences and real memories. Mine felt like a premonition."

Needing to be out in the bright light of the seven suns, he walked through the city of Mijistra with Nira. She laced her fingers in his. They were accompanied by the usual coterie of noble kithmen, guards, and attenders, but they were always there, and Jora'h paid little attention to them, basking instead in the city's population.

Jora'h still had a displaced feeling from the nightmare, and because his mood was disjointed, other Ildirans could feel his unease. If the *thism* was stressed inside him, the vibrations radiated outward, and he could do little to soothe his people until he himself became completely calm.

But he could not relax until he heard some news from Adar Zan'nh. The seven rescue ships had been gone for weeks in search of the lost *Kolpraxa*.

At Nira's suggestion, they went to visit the small enclave of human expatriates who made their home in Mijistra. Over the last ten years an organized group of Ildirophiles had settled here, bringing samples of human culture, setting up shops, restaurants, art galleries, and clothing boutiques. The Bohemian settlement made itself out to be a microcosm of old Earth. Though these particular aspects of human culture were as foreign to a green priest from Theroc as they were to the Mage-Imperator, Nira enjoyed going there.

One craftsman made musical instruments—flutes and ocarinas for children, extravagant harps and dulcimers for ambitious Ildiran musicians. There were restaurateurs, including a matronly woman named Blondie who ran a diner that specialized in "home cooking."

Jora'h and Nira led their entourage into the human enclave, and the smiling shopkeepers opened their doors and came out to greet them in a flurry of activity and interest. The Mage-Imperator didn't often visit this district, and his arrival brought a flood of Ildiran customers. The merchants and settlers looked relieved for the sudden rush of business.

Blondie opened her diner and stood with hands on her ample hips, adjusting her apron. "I've got fresh fruit pies. You've never had any better."

Jora'h stopped. "You offered me a piece last time. It was delicious."

"I've got different kinds now," she said.

The owner of the music shop played one of his dulcimers to demonstrate the quality of his music. Nira asked the art gallery owner, "Are you opening your shops just for us? Were you closed?"

A human male who called himself a writer sat alone at the café. Jora'h had been introduced to him before; he found the man interesting because he insisted on using an old-fashioned stylus, writing his words by hand on sheets of paper. The writer looked up from his paper where he had just jotted down a line. "No customers, no visitors. I thought the Ildirans were shunning us for some reason."

Blondie waved a hand. "Oh, it's not as bad as all that."

The writer snorted. "Yes, it is—you were just complaining an hour ago."

Nira looked at Jora'h with concern. "Why would Ildirans stay away from here?"

He turned to his entourage. "These humans are our friends. We have always welcomed them."

Encouraged by their leader, more Ildirans came forward; some ventured into the art gallery, others toyed with the ocarinas, making shrill and decidedly nonmusical noises. Jora'h asked the accompanying nobles, "Is there a reason why anyone would avoid interacting with the humans?"

The Ildirans discussed the matter among themselves, but shook their heads. The guard kithmen could give him no answer either.

The writer said, "There's been a strange mood in the city for a while. We can feel it."

"But you have no *thism*." Jora'h was concerned that there had been some kind of echo caused by his own nightmares and lingering uneasiness.

"We have eyes and ears. It's obvious."

"You are very perceptive—a useful skill for a writer."

The man was pleased, then embarrassed by the compliment. He sat back at his table and furiously jotted something on his paper.

As they led the entourage onward, Jora'h said to the humans, "Thank you. We are glad you have settled here."

The expatriates were reassured, but Jora'h wasn't entirely convinced. He turned his face up to the seven suns in hopes that the brightness could cleanse him, but in spite of the intense sunlight he still felt shadows everywhere, just out of sight, as if something dark were growing inside him.

SIXTY-FOUR

ARITA

After returning from Earth for the funeral of Father Idriss, Reyn had to prepare for his journey to Ildira, where he would spend a month as the Mage-Imperator's guest to learn about Ildiran culture.

In the meantime, though, Arita remained close, concerned, watching him.

One night she accompanied her brother out on the fungus-reef's soft curving rooftop. As children, they had often scrambled up the walls of the enormous growth, much to the consternation of watchful tutors. Queen Estarra, though, merely gave them an indulgent smile, since she had climbed her own share of worldtrees when she was a young girl.

Now, though, Arita had to help Reyn move across the smooth surface. The Prince managed to play his role and do his duties in public, but Arita knew how hard it was for him. So far, no one had noticed the slight tremor that she saw, or the occasional drawn expression on his face as he fought back pain. She didn't want him to go away again.

After they climbed through the high, small window and worked their way up the outer wall of the reef, she clasped his hand. Reyn's grip was strong, but by the time they sat together under the rustling worldtree fronds and the glimmer of stars, he looked tired and shaky. They watched the bright trail of a spacecraft ascending to orbit.

"So what did you learn on Earth?" They hadn't been able to find any quiet, private time to discuss his efforts until now. "Did Rlinda help you see medical specialists?"

"The best ones on the planet—I think. Dr. Paolus has a lot of experience in strange diseases like this, and I can only hope."

"*We* can only hope," she said.

Reyn gave her a small smile. "When I get to Ildira, their medical kithmen might suggest an entirely different approach."

The Ildira visit sounded like an exciting adventure, the sort of thing a Prince should do, strengthening ties with humanity's greatest ally, making connections that he would use when he became the Confederation's King. Reyn also carried the secret hope that their medical specialists would offer a unique perspective on treatment for his disease.

Arita squeezed his arm. "You're going to have to tell Mom and Dad—and soon. We all want to help you, and they can bring so much more influence to bear."

Reyn hung his head. "I don't want to be turned into a medical experiment."

Arita gave a stern answer. "You know that's a stupid reason. I want you to stay alive, and if it takes the full resources of the Confederation, then that's what it takes."

"Not yet. Let's see what the Ildirans have to say first."

"In other words, you don't have any good reason," Arita said.

"I'll tell them, after I get this last bit of information. Just . . . give me a little more time."

Arita understood him better than he was willing to admit to himself. He had studied the other similar cases from Theroc, and the prospects didn't look good. Even with armies of medical researchers and physicians running countless tests and offering treatment options, Reyn feared it would all be for naught. But he'd *promised* her he wouldn't give up hope.

"I'm always here for you, whatever you decide," Arita said.

ponytail, and she wore a loose blouse and slacks. Her Polynesian features seemed more prominent without the distraction of the uniform. Even sitting in the patio chair, Nalani Keah looked twice his size.

When they finished eating, the compy silently retrieved their dishes and brought them coffee. A fireball tumbled overhead, flashed, and split into two pieces, both of which flickered out. "That was a bright one," she said, picking up her coffee. She drank most of it in a single gulp, wiped her lips, and held up the cup. "Where's that compy? I could use a bit more. In fact, have him leave the pot." The Domestic compy scuttled forward to refill Keah's cup, and left an insulated carafe between them on the table. "You've gone to too much trouble with the meal, Deputy. Are you flirting with me? Is this a date?"

The very idea startled him. "Absolutely not."

Keah nodded, satisfied, then reconsidered. "What? Is there something the matter with me?"

"No. Nevertheless, I have no such designs. I would have chosen the same meal for myself." Deputy Cain saw three faint shooting stars, none of which was remarkable. "I believe we can be more productive outside the context of a formal meeting. We have serious matters to discuss."

More meteors streaked overhead accompanied by a shrill whistle. "They remind me of jazer blasts," Keah said, then got down to business. "I spent the afternoon in a quick inspection of the shipyards and the CDF Lunar Orbital Complex. Impressive industry there, but I worry that our people have gotten lazy over the past twenty years. Just when you think you've eliminated a gigantic cosmic threat, something else comes and messes things up again."

During the flight from Theroc after Father Idriss's funeral, Cain had reviewed the records of CDF's encounter with the black robots and the shadow cloud. It made no sense. The blackness erupting in the clouds of Golgen had destroyed the Kellum skymine, and that was just as inexplicable.

"I suggest dispatching a battle group to Theroc to strengthen defenses around the King and Queen," Cain said. "And launch new patrols across all ten grids. We have to be on high alert until we know the nature of the threat."

General Keah couldn't agree fast enough. "If there are any more robot infestations, we'll find them and wipe them out. I've got a vendetta against those bugbots, and I can't think of a better way to spend a Saturday morning than smashing a few thousand of them."

"All well and good, General," Cain said, "but a handful of surviving Klikiss robots can't possibly be more than a nuisance. We don't want to cause a panic among colonists by telling them the sky is falling."

As if the heavens had heard him, six shooting stars came down in rapid succession. One large bolide made a sighing, crackling sound as it tumbled in the atmosphere.

Keah agreed. "To tell you the truth, Mr. Deputy, that shadow cloud we encountered makes me more nervous than the bugbots. I've never seen anything like it. Adar Zan'nh believes it could be very dangerous."

"Send an astronomical investigation team to map it, find out if it's a dust cloud or a nebula."

The General set down her coffee cup. "I did send a scout back there, but the cloud was gone."

That took him aback. "How can a nebula disappear?"

"A standard-issue nebula can't—but that shadow cloud *moved*. It messed with our systems, it swallowed up the robot ships. The Ildirans have legends about some ancient enemy called the Shana Rei, creatures of darkness. After what we saw, the Adar believes the Shana Rei may be more than just legends, and I'm inclined to agree. If he's right, we'll need to know whatever they know. We may even need their help."

"I agree," Cain said. "Launch more joint patrols if you like."

"I'm on it, Mr. Deputy—anything to keep me away from a desk job."

Overhead, the meteors continued to fall.

SIXTY-SIX

GARRISON REEVES

For the first few years after the destruction of the Moon, it had taken a massive effort to map the orbits of the largest remnants and then to stabilize the rubble. Groups of celestial mechanics plotted orbital perturbations and ran simulations to determine which asteroids would intersect the Earth's path. The primary concern was to identify any chunks on an imminent collision course, so the cleanup teams could work to deflect them.

In a few centuries—an eyeblink on an astronomical scale—the Moon's rubble would have distributed itself into a lovely ring around Earth, but with so many fresh fragments in unstable orbits, collisions occurred faster than they could be mapped, and the impacts deflected previously benign rubble, which forced the cleanup teams to react and make changes.

Garrison loved the work. In the *Prodigal Son,* he was one of the surveyors sent out to respond and submit recommendations each time the automated network of telescopes detected a large-scale impact.

Growing up in clan Reeves, he had spent a lot of time studying celestial mechanics, because Olaf Reeves insisted that every Roamer needed to know how the universe worked. He had a particular intuition for nuances and subtle effects, which was why he noticed slight perturbations at Sheol that others had discounted.

Garrison took no pride in being right about Sheol, and carried a weight of guilt, wondering if he could have done more to warn about the danger. If Elisa had believed him and supported him, he would have had enough leverage to convince Lee Iswander. But it had been a long time since his own wife had given him the benefit of the doubt. At least he had saved Seth. . . .

He received regular updates on his son's progress at Academ. Seth thrived there with other students, swimming with the wentals, being taught by compies as well as Jess Tamblyn and Cesca Peroni. The cheerful messages Garrison received allowed him to remain satisfied with his work at the LOC.

On his patrol, he flew past the gravitational stable points of L-4 and L-5, where much of the lunar rubble had already collected. The flight was like a constant sandblasting barrage, but his enhanced shields protected him against the majority of the debris, which was no larger than pebbles or dust grains. He rode the Moon's old orbit in a great circle, taking a week to make each circuit. Some might have called it lonely work, but he found it peaceful.

Earth was always at the center of the orbit: a large blue and green sphere swirled with white. This was much different from Rendezvous, the stark cluster of rocks where clan Reeves had spent so much time. The bustle of activity in lunar orbit gave this planet—the birthplace of humanity—a vibrant energy.

It was where he had first met Elisa. He pushed those thoughts aside. He had made his choices, set his course, and then changed course. He decided to let go of the bad choices, let go of those thoughts entirely. Elisa was gone. The past was part of him, but it was *the past*. Seth was at Academ, and happy; Garrison was here now, and content. They had the whole future ahead of them.

He discovered a tumbler ahead, a large sharp-edged rock that spun across his path where it shouldn't have been. So he marked its location and sent a high-priority signal back to the main LOC operations. The tumbler would be tagged and tracked, its orbit mapped in detail, then deflected if necessary.

During his mapping activities, Garrison surveyed the rubble composition, identifying metal-rich fragments from which miners could extract valuable materials. It was merely a sorting job, and in a month or two he would request a transfer to something more challenging.

His short-term goal was to get back on his feet again, to support himself and to take care of his son. Even after only a couple of months, his supervisors had noticed the quality of his work, and he was confident he'd be promoted—if this was even the work Garrison decided he wanted to do. In the long run, he intended to take control of his life and choose its direction. He wouldn't let himself just fall into a permanent career.

After he finished his orbital patrol, Garrison headed back to the LOC. The numerous civilian and military structures there represented an industrial boom, a golden age. The retooled CDF set up their main base there, which included freestanding space stations, as well as orbiting survey docks, communication ports, tunnel habitats inside the largest rock fragments, and habitation platforms that looked like swollen ships tethered to rocks.

Although the LOC did not have the finesse or rough beauty of a Roamer installation, Garrison had grown comfortable with it. He had his own quarters, friends who worked on the sorting and excavation teams, and recreational activities in the primary hab and commercial complex, when he wasn't on duty. Before his next scout circuit, he would have a day of downtime: playing games, chatting, and relaxing.

By now, he supposed clan Reeves had abandoned Rendezvous and flown off to their mysterious city in space. Garrison did not regret staying behind and making sure Seth had a normal upbringing.

On his return flight to the LOC, he organized his survey readings, flagged the items that he felt deserved particular attention. As the *Prodigal Son* docked, he transmitted his full report, knowing it was all that interested his supervisor Milli Torino. She wasn't a warm and fuzzy person, and she didn't like to spend face time with her employees.

Leaving the dock, he submitted a requisition for refueling, then used only a fraction of his allotment to take a quick mist-shower (conservation was in his Roamer blood), before venturing out into the crowded communal areas of the complex. Instead of a chemically warmed packet from the ship's galley, he wanted a hot meal prepared by a human, but his son was always his first priority. He went to the hab complex's marketplace, walked past cafés and entertainment centers, until he found the resident green priest, Lubai.

Many LOC workers were Earth natives who had scraped together their spare change to secure a job at the rubble site. Other employers, especially the Roamer specialists, came from far away, which made communication with home difficult. Seeing a need, the green priest had set up his shop as a freelance messenger to deliver news and letters to loved ones across the Spiral Arm.

When Garrison paid Lubai the agreed-upon fee, the green priest slid his potted treeling across the table, placing the leafy fronds like a barrier between himself and his customer. The fronds obscured the green priest's face, which allowed Garrison to concentrate on his words and imagine that he was looking at Seth's face instead of a tree.

"I want this message routed to Academ, to be transcribed and delivered to my son, Seth Reeves."

Between fronds, he could see a slight smile on Lubai's face. "As you wish—as always."

Garrison began talking, as if to a telegraph operator, and the green priest whisper-mumbled his words back, touching the slender treeling. The message would go out into the verdani mind, and a counterpart green priest at Newstation would receive the message and transfer it to Academ.

Although he would rather have spoken directly with his son, this was the best way for them to remain in contact. Most important, Seth would understand how much his father missed him.

SIXTY-SEVEN

SHELUD

On the isolated alien space city, Shelud was far from the lush world-forest of Theroc, but with his treeling, he could touch the verdani mind and remain in contact with all other green priests, including his brother. It was his safety net.

He had never set foot off of Theroc before. While Shelud had always enjoyed "recalling" the experiences other green priests added to the verdani mind, secondhand events and shared information were not the same as actually being there himself. This was amazing!

Although he had promised not to reveal the exact coordinates of the derelict city, now named Okiah, Shelud could observe and listen, and tell parts of it to the worldforest. The strangeness of this place was breathtaking as clan Reeves began to settle some of the habitable chambers. He shared his impressions through the treeling, showing the mysteries even though he had no answers. No other green priest had ever experienced anything like this ancient alien city. The trees' reactions to his news indicated strange gaps in the forest knowledge base. Even so, he felt excitement among the verdani. They were intrigued by the derelict.

As clan Reeves worked to set up their new home aboard the cold station, however, Shelud missed the smells of foliage, of berries and wildflowers. This air smelled sterile and metallic. He was used to warm, natural sunlight on his green skin, but here the artificial illumination felt too white, too cold. The metal decks were hard and unyielding. His treeling found the light weak and unsatisfying.

Yet Shelud didn't regret his decision to come here to Okiah. He had joined the Retroamers to do his duty as a green priest, and he would make certain the worldforest had these new experiences. He occasionally accessed specific data when the Retroamers asked him, although clan Reeves seemed quite self-sufficient and secure in their own practical knowledge.

They installed power blocks to add light, heat, energy, and life support to the central hub and the habitation modules in the first spoke they had claimed. Olaf Reeves assigned a science team to study the long-dormant alien engines and generators. The Roamers could not decipher the mysterious writings, but they did analyze the alien *engineering*. Once they discovered that the extant reactors operated on principles they understood, the team managed to reactivate some of the systems. After installing supplemental power blocks, they restored primary lighting and power, which radiated out along all five axes.

The Teacher compy BO watched over the clan children. Though the students were restless and excited, she continued her usual curriculum. Clan Reeves had five other dedicated compies to work aboard the derelict city, but for the most part the Roamers did the tasks themselves.

As the days went by, Shelud had no regular role and almost no technical experience that could help the Roamers. Simple data from the worldforest mind wasn't the same as *knowledge*, and Roamers seemed to possess an instinctive engineering understanding from the time they were children. While the families kept themselves busy, he tried not to get in the way. Shelud felt self-conscious about standing around and not helping with the frantic activity. Every person kept busy with myriad duties without needing to be told. Shelud didn't understand how they all just knew what to do.

Of all the members of clan Reeves, he liked Dale best. The quiet son of the gruff clan leader seemed to be a kindred spirit. Finally, in frustration, he asked a harried Dale, "Please let me help somehow. What can I do?"

Dale looked grateful for the offer, although it wouldn't necessarily diminish his workload. "I don't know, what can you *do*? We've got habitat zones to check, recycling systems to install, galleys to rig so we can prepare food. This city is huge, and there's so much room!" He chuckled. "At least no one's fighting over particular quarters. That's a nice change."

"I can keep records," Shelud said. "I can help unload ships. And if someone shows me how—"

Dale flashed him a quick, mischievous smile. "Oh, nothing like that. I think you're most qualified to do *exploring*—hmm, and I'd better go with you to make sure that it's done properly. We've been so busy setting up our new home, we've only explored one of the five spokes. Who knows how many secrets Okiah still has for us?"

"Your father said we shouldn't do any discretionary exploring until all the work is done."

"The work will never be done—I know my father." He gave a quirk of a conspiratorial smile. "Don't you want to share these new discoveries with your fellow green priests?"

"Yes! The verdani want to know all about this place. Some part of the worldforest already seems to know . . . but it's forgotten." He shook his head. "Maybe I can remind them."

They had no clue about the race that had built this space complex, or why they had chosen to locate the city so far from any planet, but Olaf Reeves was a man with little curiosity. "If this is our new home, we'll have all time in the world to poke around and play. But business first, survival first. We stake out our territory, make the systems functional. Families must help one another. Then, when we are stable, we can move on to sightseeing."

Many Retroamers, though—including Dale—found this frustrating. They wanted to investigate all five spokes, searching for treasure or wonders or information. They were hungry for some hint about the strange race that had created this city.

Looking at Shelud, Dale said, "Worst-case scenario, we could live aboard our ships indefinitely, however long it takes to make Okiah completely habitable. There's no crisis deadline to get all of the city systems running, so why not explore? Isn't it more important to learn more about where we are? Okiah is our new home, after all."

"Yes, I would say it's important."

Dale continued, stretching his reasons. "What if we find something that makes the habitation more . . . habitable? We might find a water reservoir that the original inhabitants used, or a self-sustaining greenhouse dome full of fruits and vegetables. Who knows? It's worth a look—I'd only be doing it to help establish our new home, you know."

He obviously didn't expect even the gullible green priest to believe that. Shelud said, "*And* because you're curious and want to look around."

"That too."

Dale monitored his fellow Retroamers as they worked, settling into the private quarters they had chosen throughout the first module. Each day he oversaw a list of required tasks, and when that work was done, he and Shelud set aside several hours to secretly explore new parts of the derelict station. Dale did not announce his plans, nor did he ask explicit permission—therefore, his father could not explicitly forbid him.

The two went off by themselves, working their way down spoke three, chamber by chamber. When other clan members dropped out of sight for brief periods, Shelud realized that he and Dale weren't the only ones investigating the derelict city.

Steeped in the curiosity of the worldforest, Shelud wanted to know who the builders were. What had they called themselves? What had they looked like? Where had they come from before constructing this ambitious city in space, and where had they gone after leaving it?

Each day, Shelud and Dale explored another empty geometrical chamber, and when they came back, Shelud would connect through his treeling and describe what he had seen.

Most of the station chambers were empty, unadorned, sterile metal, but in one dark room not much larger than a closet they found an astonishing mural. When Shelud and Dale shone their lights inside, they saw that the walls had been painted with dense, tangled foliage, bright leaves and lush fronds, close trunks of crowded and immense trees. It looked like a swatch of pristine worldforest. Shelud stared with awe, running his fingers over the images imprinted on the walls. The worldtrees were unmistakable—but how?

Most of the chambers and bulkheads were bare metal, with no colors at all. He didn't understand this particular vibrant painting.

In a secondary module on spoke three, they discovered a vault where the angled walls were divided into interlocking triangular sections, enameled in bright primary colors. Each colored section was studded with raised designs, embossed symbols that tapered down to the triangles' points, and unmistakable stylized patterns of worldtree fronds . . . but why here, in a sterile space city far outside an uninhabited solar system?

Shelud ran his fingers down the vertex of a triangle marked with a frond, touched the raised alien letters. He pressed harder, hoping the language might respond in a tactile way. When he depressed the point, he felt the enameled plate vibrate and grow warm. Then the panel itself dissolved into a projected image.

He gasped and snatched back his hand. Dale hurried over, and they both watched the image sharpen into the face of a parchment-skinned alien unlike any species Shelud had ever seen. The creature was small-statured and hairless, its head round and craggy, like a crudely formed boulder. It had large black eyes surrounded by jutting orbital ridges. The voice droned out incomprehensible words in an even, soothing sound, like a professor giving a lecture.

A grin filled Dale's face. "You and I just discovered a new alien race!"

"At least the remnants of one," Shelud said.

Astonished, Shelud remembered where he had seen something like this: During the Elemental War, when the first giant treeships had come back from deep space, one of them had held a mysterious pilot, whose alien features had fused after millennia, becoming part of the tree's heartwood. The pilot came from a forgotten race that had been connected with the worldforest. Long ago.

This creature looked similar. Could they be the same race?

Such a discovery was too important to keep hidden. When Dale confessed to his father that they had been exploring, he acted tentative and nervous. When Olaf began to rebuke Dale for wasting time and effort, Shelud insisted that *he* had encouraged Dale to search, because the worldforest had asked for details about the original builders and any cultural artifacts they had left behind.

After Dale and Shelud explained what they had discovered, Olaf could not keep the other Roamers from investigating their mysterious new home. Curiosity seekers and treasure hunters crowded into the library chamber, pressing enameled triangular plates and watching the projected images. All the recordings showed a similar lecturing alien, perhaps even the same individual. But since the Roamers could not understand the language, the records meant little beyond the novelty of observing a new alien race.

Despite Olaf's disapproval, clan Reeves could not keep this great discovery a secret. Shelud reported the exciting news through telink, spending hours with his treeling to explain the treasure trove of knowledge aboard the empty city they had named Okiah.

Back in the Confederation, numerous xeno-archaeologists were fascinated, and offered to send large teams to complete the exploration "in a professional fashion," but Shelud honored his promise and refused to reveal the location of the space city.

"I won't have swarms of strangers picking our place apart," Olaf grumbled. "We came here. We took the risk, and this is our home." The clan leader did, however, grudgingly allow exploration parties to continue the investigation, provided their work did not suffer. And Shelud reported the findings.

Pursuing an idea, Shelud brought his treeling into the library chamber. Although humans couldn't understand the alien language—not yet—he thought the knowledge might exist somewhere in the vast verdani mind. He depressed the point of an enameled triangle, playing a report while his mind was connected to the worldforest and all the ancient knowledge there. The strange-sounding alien language droned in his ears.

To Shelud's delight, the worldtrees *understood*.

As the green priest played the alien records, the verdani mind passed information back to him—not a word-for-word translation, but a basic summary of concepts. Listening to the unfolding story, he was filled with wonder. . . .

Later, he met with the Roamer families in an amphitheater chamber for a small clan convocation. Beside him, Dale Reeves listened with bright eyes, as Shelud said, "They called themselves the Onthos, a quiet and passive race that inhabited a dozen star systems. The Onthos did not conquer worlds, did not build a vast empire. The verdani were aware of them ages ago."

"What do the records say?" Olaf asked. "Why did the Onthos build this city so far from any planet?"

"The Klikiss preyed upon their race in a swarm war. The Onthos were attacked on their planets, wiped out on one colony world after another—the Klikiss destroyed anything in their way. The Onthos were nearly exterminated, and the survivors fled here. Over the years they built this refuge fortress far from any planetary system the Klikiss might be interested in, living where they would not be hunted. They took in refugees from their devastated Onthos planetary colonies. This was their last hiding place."

"If this city was their sanctuary, then where did the aliens go?" asked Dale's wife, Sendra.

"That part isn't in the records," Shelud said.

Dale suggested, "That was thousands of years ago. After the Klikiss left on their swarming, maybe the Onthos didn't need to stay here anymore. They wouldn't have to hide."

"Then why haven't we found any trace of these aliens anywhere else in the Spiral Arm?" asked another Roamer. Shelud still didn't know everyone's name.

"We haven't explored every planet in the Spiral Arm," said Bjorn, the head spacecraft engineer.

"It doesn't matter." Olaf Reeves was impatient with the discussion. "The important thing is that this city is *empty*, and we've claimed it as our own clan's sanctuary. Now that the mystery is solved, we can focus on other things."

Shelud didn't think the mystery was solved, and numerous questions remained. Countless chambers remained to be explored, including one entire spoke of the derelict city.

Four days later, Shelud and Dale went to one of the last main modules in the only remaining spoke left to explore, the most remote section on its extended axis. Prominent pink triangles were painted on the entry hatch. Unlike the colorful triangles in the library module, these were crude. The electronics of the hatch had been damaged, so Dale had to work for an hour before he could force the barrier open.

Inside, they found the bodies.

SIXTY-EIGHT

OSIRA'H

Adar Zan'nh flew his warliners back to Ildira at top speed, bearing the only survivor of the *Kolpraxa*.

After rescuing Tal Gale'nh from the command nucleus of the black-encased ship, the uneasy scout team was anxious to depart, fearing the return of the Shana Rei. Zan'nh insisted they remain long enough to scour the ship's log computers, but all systems had been wiped clean. Gale'nh was the only one who could say what had happened, and he had fallen back into an overwhelmed silence. There were no other survivors.

They marked the position of the *Kolpraxa*, and abandoned the empty vessel.

During the flight back into the denser star systems of the Spiral Arm, Osira'h did not leave her brother's side. Except for occasional glimmers of consciousness, pale and ghostly Gale'nh remained in a detached state. The medical kithmen could find no physical damage, no reason for the loss of color in his hair and the bleaching of his skin.

Osira'h wondered if he had been changed by profound and incomprehensible shock, a depth of fear that no other Ildiran could understand. Everyone else aboard the *Kolpraxa* had been obliterated by it, but her halfbreed brother was different. She understood what it meant to be unique.

As Osira'h reached into his thoughts using her telepathic connection, she began to bring him back from the dark wilderness inside his head. This was a different sort of battle than when she had forced the hydrogues into submission; now she fought against Gale'nh's own turmoil, tried to take the dark from him.

In his mind, she saw glimpses of the *Kolpraxa*'s command nucleus, the panic of the crew as the whole ship was engulfed, in murderous shadows, his fellow Ildirans being torn into atoms and winking out of existence. Gale'nh had found an unexpected strength that the rest of his crew did not have, and now Osira'h experienced how he had fought, grabbing a few nearby crewmembers, trying to hold them, save them . . . and failing.

Then he was left all alone on an empty ship in the infinite dark.

Osira'h took those flashes of memory and tried to ease his mental burden, while fighting the instinctive terror it evoked in her too. She shored up her brother's strength as the warliners flew back to the Ildiran Empire.

And there could be no doubt: it was the Shana Rei, she sensed it, *knew* it, though she couldn't comprehend the details that her brother had buried deep within his mind. Osira'h told Adar Zan'nh what she had learned. Though shocked and disturbed, none of the Ildirans were surprised to hear it.

The Shana Rei.

Eventually, Gale'nh awoke, although he couldn't yet face the thought of speaking, or even remembering.

Back home under the light of the seven suns, with the comforting blanket of millions of other Ildirans nearby, Gale'nh grew stronger. He spent several days in Mijistra's primary medical facility.

Osira'h remained with him as much as possible, supporting him by being there, touching him with her thoughts to reinforce his mental armor. Nira came to stand vigil beside her son. Though she had no access to the *thism*, she read to him for hours, as she had once done as an acolyte to the worldforest. Muree'n hovered at the door of Gale'nh's room, as if standing guard against the shadows. Rod'h stood next to Osira'h, concerned, angry, and insisting that the Mage-Imperator take some kind of action, though he couldn't define what that might be. Only Tamo'l was absent, responding to a crisis with her misbreeds on Kuivahr. She had also sensed the terrible stress and sent a deeply concerned message, but she could not abandon the hundreds of tortured lives that depended on her.

Finding no physical damage to treat, the medical kithmen released Gale'nh and sent him back to the Prism-Palace. For days he sat looking weak and lost, even as he bathed in the bright magnified light that shone through curved crystal ceilings. He would clasp his siblings' hands, drawing strength from their presence.

Finally, one afternoon he looked at those gathered around him, shuddered, and began to speak in a halting voice. He looked from Nira to Osira'h, to Adar Zan'nh, who also came to visit him every day, and finally he addressed them all.

"I can't explain what happened to me or where the rest of my crew went. The *Kolpraxa* investigated a dark nebula—that was our mission, to explore the unknown. The Mage-Imperator commanded it." His voice was ragged, his pale face drawn. "And the shadow swallowed us."

Rod'h asked, "But hundreds of Ildirans were aboard the *Kolpraxa*—why were you spared? Is it because you are a halfbreed, like us? Were you stronger?"

"The darkness came at us through the *thism*—that much I remember. The others had nothing else to fall back on." Gale'nh reached out and clutched Osira'h's and Rod'h's hands. "Rememberer Ko'sh knew it before anyone else did, and I dismissed his ideas, but it *was* the Shana Rei . . . and they are more fearsome and more incomprehensible than we could ever imagine."

Adar Zan'nh had brought a crystal sheet coupled with an image projector, which he placed before Gale'nh. "I did not show you this aboard the warliner, because I thought it might be too terrifying—but I need to know. Are you strong enough to see these images? This is what we encountered near Dhula."

He activated the crystal screen and showed the robot ships escaping from the ice moon. When Gale'nh saw how the shadow cloud engulfed the enemy ships, he turned away. "That is what we encountered." He shivered, and his breathing quickened. He closed his eyes, then forced them open to look at the images; perspiration stood out in clear beads on his forehead. "It wasn't a nebula or a dust cloud. It was . . . alive somehow. It was *darkness*."

Rod'h was grim. "It matches the records of the Shana Rei."

A silence filled the room. No one could argue with the assessment.

Gale'nh gave a slow, weak nod. "They are a darkness in the fabric of the universe, and they are seeping through the cracks, oozing everywhere." He shivered and held out his hands as if to draw in more of the sunlight. "The *Kolpraxa* didn't awaken the Shana Rei—I know that. Something else did. But now the darkness is everywhere."

Osira'h was concerned. "Is the darkness inside you?"

Rod'h hardened. "And did you bring it back among us?"

Gale'nh touched his chest, his face. "No . . . but it exists."

Adar Zan'nh said, "This is a new kind of enemy, and we have to understand it. There must still be plans and designs for the old weapons we used against the Shana Rei."

Nira said, "When I returned from Theroc after we learned of a mysterious shadow attack on a Roamer skymine, the Mage-Imperator commanded the rememberer kith to comb through the Saga. He asked them to find all information about the Shana Rei."

Adar Zan'nh nodded. "The Solar Navy fought them before, so we need the details. What weapons were effective? Didn't Tal Bria'nh use sun bombs at Orryx? How do we build them? We need to know again."

Osira'h said, "The Saga is not complete in its story of the Shana Rei. Many records were sealed away when other Mage-Imperators rewrote parts of history."

Nira smiled. "That's why Jora'h also asked Rememberer Anton Colicos to scour all records from that time, even the ones buried in document crypts. He has a more open mind than most Ildiran rememberers."

"There is one weapon that no one will find in the ancient records." Rod'h was edgy, defiant. It seemed important to him that he prove his own worth. He faced Adar Zan'nh. "The *Kolpraxa*'s crew were not strong enough to resist the Shana Rei, but Gale'nh was. Maybe my sisters and I will be, too."

He looked at Osira'h and Muree'n, then finally rested his eyes on Nira. "Maybe the Ildiran Empire will once again need the strength of your halfbreed children, Mother."

SIXTY-NINE

SHAREEN FITZKELLUM

Following the evacuation of Golgen, some of the skyminers went to Theroc while others headed to Newstation for transfer back to their own clans. The Kellums and Fitzkellums all came to Kuivahr.

After the traumatic experience, Shareen's parents thought Howard should go back home to be with his family, but the young man wanted to stay with the Roamers and keep learning. "My parents won't care. Now that I'm on Kuivahr, I can learn everything about the distillery business." He blinked at Shareen. "Unless you don't want me here?"

She gave him a quick hug, then brushed it off with an embarrassed laugh. "Of course I . . . we want you to stay, Howard! You were the only person who made school tolerable. Just imagine how much fun we can have here."

"I'd rather be with you too."

When her grandfather stood on the decks of his Kuivahr distillery, he seemed proud and defiant, even after the horrific events on Golgen. Del was a big bearded man looking out across a kingdom composed of soupy mudflats. "We'll come back and we'll be just fine, by damn," he said. "I've rebuilt from scratch before."

"*I* haven't," Shareen said, not impressed. "My whole life was centered around being a skyminer. I knew everything about the reactors and filtration chain, Golgen's winds and cloud composition. I don't know anything about running a distillery."

"Roamers have to learn on-the-fly, my sweet." Del gestured out toward the mucky plankton-rich tidal flats. "Expand your horizons."

"Does it always smell like this?" asked Howard Rohandas. He sounded genuinely curious, not complaining.

Shareen was glad he was still here with them. The odor did seem particularly rich that morning.

Del said, "What you smell is a wealth of raw materials. We scoop up the slime, process it, and make a fortune."

"Or at least we make a mess," Patrick Fitzpatrick said.

Shareen's mother was more optimistic. "By the Guiding Star, Dad, we'll make this the most efficient distillery in the Spiral Arm. Your granddaughter's a genius. Who knows? She and Howard might even figure out how to make a brew that's halfway drinkable."

Del felt the need to continue his pep talk. "Our clan ran shipyards in the rings of Osquivel, by damn, and when we lost those, we moved our operations up to the cometary cloud. When I got tired of *that*, I went back to skymining. Then I served fifteen years as Speaker for the clans. Now I've got this distillery." He stomped his foot on the metal deck. "And I'm damn pleased with it."

Patrick pointed out, "Your grandfather is saying that he hopes you lead a much more stable life than he did."

Shareen knew they would indeed survive. Once she and Howard learned the basic distilling principles, she was sure the two of them could improve the production operations, much as they had done on the Golgen skymine.

Marius Denva, the distillery manager, said he was glad to have Del Kellum back. Puffed up, Del said, "Did everything fall apart while I was away?"

Marius couldn't hide his teasing smile. "Actually, in day-to-day operations we didn't notice a bit of difference. I just wanted you back as our first taster to fine-tune that special eyeballs-boiled-in-urine taste you appreciate so well."

Shareen and Howard made plans to tour the facility, and Toff wanted to tag along so he could tease the two of them, just like a pesky brother. But when Zhett suggested that he check out a mud-skimmer and cruise across the plankton flats, Toff decided that making a mess of himself in the mud sounded like fun.

Instead of showing them the engineering and mechanics of the distillery, Marius Denva suggested that Shareen and Howard first take advantage of the extreme low tide. "Have a look at the distillery from the shore. Get the big picture. You don't often see it so high and dry."

So she and Howard donned work boots and protective jumpsuits, then went down to the water line. It was a hazy, sunny day, and the retreating water had left a foul-smelling slurry. They stayed on the support deck, wary. Shareen bent down to dangle her fingers in the muck. The greenish brown slime, rich with plankton, had the consistency of thick phlegm. "This would suck you right down like quicksand— unless the smell itself keeps you afloat."

The distillery towered above them on tall support legs with retractable launching chutes that could be adjusted according to the rising and falling sea level. Howard drank in the details, shading his eyes to look across the tidal basin.

The Kuivahr mudflats swirled with colors, magenta and yellow blooms splotched the surface like spilled paint where plankton species thrived in the ocean interface zone. With each lunar cycle, the waters rushed in to flood the mudflats and stir the nutrients, then rushed back out again, leaving thick layers of plankton redolent with minerals and oxidation chemicals.

Mobile Kuivahr kelp colonies were like forests that migrated from place to place; during low tide the kelp anchored its roots and burst forth dazzling green and blue blossoms. From where they stood at the base of the support walk, Shareen could see one of the transient kelp forests half a kilometer away.

Howard extended his arm. "Look—are those Ildirans?"

Shareen saw the figures waving. Two of them jumped from the kelp island and rode floaterboards toward Shareen and Howard. Ildiran swimmer kith had sleek brownish skin, streamlined faces, and large eyes with double lids so they could see better under the water. The young swimmers seemed overjoyed as they splashed up silty brown roostertails and slid their floaterboards to a halt in the slurry near Shareen and Howard. The swimmer kithmen wore shells as ornaments and short breeches woven from kelp fiber.

Shareen whispered to Howard, "Do you think they speak trade standard?"

"Of course we do," said one of the swimmers. "We were instructed to learn it so that we could work with your facility." He flicked water from a webbed hand. "My name is Tora'm. We brought a delivery for you."

The swimmers opened fibrous satchels at their hips to reveal packed masses of magenta kelp flowers. When Shareen sniffed one, her eyes stung from the sour garlicky scent.

"Special bloom, this phase, very rare," said Tora'm. "We reserve most of them for Tamo'l at her sanctuary domes. They make good medicines and treatments for the misbreeds."

"I read about the Ildiran medical facility," Howard said. "It's nearby?"

Balanced on their floaterboards, the swimmers gestured off, but distances were deceptive in the tidal flats. Shareen thought she could see part of a dome protruding from the water, near the horizon. "Is that where you live?"

The otterlike creatures blinked their eyes. Tora'm said, "No, we live on the kelp rafts. But we always bring in our harvest."

The swimmers handed over two satchels of the rare kelp flowers to Shareen, who asked, "Do we need to pay you for this?"

Tora'm didn't seem concerned. "Maybe. Not today. Talk to someone else."

They activated their floaterboards and accelerated away. The playful swimmers circled, intentionally spraying mud all over Shareen and Howard. She wiped at the plankton slime on Howard's cheek, but only smeared it into a pattern of war paint. He returned the favor, which required a response from her, and soon they were both a complete mess.

When they returned to the distillery decks, Del Kellum chuckled at the two of them spattered with mud, but when Toff came in from an afternoon of mudskimming, he was so coated with muck that the distillery workers had to hose him off.

Shareen delivered the rare kelp flowers to her grandfather. He sniffed the special blooms, wrinkled his nose. "Potent. We'll run an analysis to see what they're good for—maybe to flavor one of the really sour batches."

"The swimmers said these particular kelp flowers have important medicinal uses," Howard pointed out.

Shareen said, "Do you think we could visit the Ildiran sanctuary domes?"

Del frowned. "It's a sanctuary and a colony. Tamo'l is very dedicated, but the misfits . . ." He shook his head and patted Shareen on the shoulder. "Don't be in a hurry, my sweet. You're not ready for that yet."

X A N D E R   B R I N D L E

Though Xander and Terry preferred to check new places off their planetary list, Ulio was one of their favorite stopping points. Ulio was also the place where the two had met, which made it worth visiting again for their own reasons.

OK piloted the *Verne* across open space, but as soon as they reached the active hub, Xander took the controls. The different types of ships and traders, both human and Ildiran, always made the Ulio transfer station, trading hub, and repair yard vibrant and hectic.

Xander guided them in, keeping his eyes open. Sometimes it was a strategy game just to find a place to dock in the haphazard structures. Officially, the rule was first come, first served—which sounded fair and polite, but in reality, it turned Ulio into a spaceship free-for-all.

The transfer hub had no formal administrator, political affiliations, or security enforcement. It was simply a gathering point in space for travelers who wanted something, or wanted to get rid of something. An example of organized anarchy that somehow worked.

Over the past two decades Ulio had become a place where ships could refuel or make repairs, where traders could exchange cargo, where passengers could secure transportation with no questions asked. The conglomeration of ships was like a flea market, a swap meet, a jamboree, and a trade show located in a small, unimportant system in the blurred boundaries between the Confederation and the Ildiran Empire.

Ulio had begun as an unincorporated, unregulated, and untaxed scrapyard. Entrepreneur Maria Ulio had lost everything on Boone's Crossing when the hydrogues destroyed that colony, but she cobbled together enough money to buy some wrecked Ildiran warliners and

EDF battleships after the end of the war. She got many of the wrecks for free, on the condition that she haul them away from habitable planets where they were a navigational hazard. Salvage or scrap, no one else saw much value in them.

As a first step, Maria Ulio had patched and repaired two of the hulks so they could support inhabitants, then she looked for refugees whose homes had been destroyed by the hydrogues, the faeros, or the Klikiss. Plenty of people fit the bill. She offered them a place to live, so long as they helped her repair other salvaged ships she brought there.

Even the Roamers were impressed with Maria's operations, and so they brought other ships in need of repair. Some were fixed up and converted into space habitats; intact engine components were stripped out and used in other vessels.

Traders began to stop at Maria Ulio's hub. A few ships simply parked there and stayed, finding it easier to sell and exchange wares at a central point, rather than flying back and forth across the Spiral Arm. Roamers brought their business as well, and word began to spread.

The Solar Navy sent damaged warliners and teams of Ildiran mechanics to work alongside the renowned Ulio engineers to observe and learn. After a while, Ildiran traders began to stop at Ulio as their giant ships did business with the Confederation.

Then, when she was fabulously wealthy, Maria Ulio simply packed up her old ship. She tasked the engineers to recheck her stardrives—which had not been operated for fifteen years—dusted off her vessel, bade everyone farewell, and simply flew off. No one had heard from Maria since, but her legacy remained. In the five years of her absence, Ulio ran itself and grew even larger.

Terry had spent most of his teenage years at Ulio. He'd met Maria several times, and the old woman took him under her wing when he arrived as a twelve-year-old, asking to help with the repairs. She gave Terry a pep talk when he asked if his handicap would be an insurmountable problem. Maria had just laughed. "Most of those ships don't have gravity turned on anyway. You won't need to use your legs except to fill out your pants."

"Why would I need to fill out my pants?" he asked.

"Because it makes the pockets easier to reach. Better access to your tools. You'll figure it out."

She had assigned Terry to a team that needed an extra hand, and he drifted around inside stardrive engines, skinny enough to fit in tight crawlspaces; he often suited up and went outside to help patch hulls. It took his coworkers the better part of a week to notice that Terry couldn't use his legs. . . .

Now, the *Verne* arrived at Ulio's main hub, a pair of cobbled-together Ildiran warliner hulls that looked as if the two ships had collided and fused. By now, Xander knew which of the permanent facilities maintained artificial gravity "for the convenience of patrons" and which ones maintained au naturel microgravity. Out of consideration for Terry, Xander exclusively patronized the weightless units.

By sheer luck, a spacecraft was detaching from a docking unit just as they arrived, and Xander accelerated the *Verne* to capture the spot. Another ship raced in, and a stream of curses ricocheted through the comm system when Xander reached the dock first. "Have a nice day," Xander said and clicked off the comm.

OK transmitted their cargo manifest: fully charged power blocks of various sizes and capacities fresh from Fireheart Station. The information went into the bidding board, which all traders could access. Many ships simply hung around Ulio and watched the board like vultures waiting to pounce on unusual items. Vagabond travelers could also put up requests for passage to particular worlds, offering to work aboard ship to avoid the standard fee, but they often waited at Ulio for a long time. There wasn't much work to be done on a routine passage, and most captains had a compy or two to handle the more unpleasant tasks.

Led by OK, Xander and Terry floated into the main hub. Terry was at ease propelling himself along, and Xander followed, while the compy preferred to use the magnetic traction of his synthetic feet.

By habit, they went to the observation lounge and star balcony where they had met. The two found themselves a good seat next to the wall of interlocked crystal, where they could watch the ships come and go. After clipping themselves to the table, they ordered drinks from the server compy.

OK was proud to announce, "Multiple bids have come in. Every one of our power blocks has been claimed for the asking price. Two bidders were so enthusiastic about our highest capacity units that they drove up the price. Our profits will be five percent higher than anticipated."

"Excellent," Xander said. "Let's celebrate and spend that profit on a vacation."

Terry gave him a skeptical look, then turned to accept their drinks as the server compy returned. "We'll never take a vacation. You won't let me."

"Our work is a vacation. But I could treat you to a place we've never seen before." Xander called up their list on the datapad he always brought with him. "Checking off places one at a time. It's good to have a big, long-term project you can sink your teeth into."

Terry leaned over to look at the list, scrolling through the names of planets and star systems. "Since we've got more than we can possibly visit in a dozen lifetimes, why don't we pick someplace pleasant?"

"If you insist." They debated the merits of various worlds and whether they could convince Xander's parents that a trade expedition would be worthwhile to Kett Shipping. They finished their first round of drinks and sent OK to fetch a second while they watched the graceful ballet of space traffic.

An unfamiliar woman accompanied the compy back to their table. She was in her midthirties with short brown hair with gold highlights. "I paid for your round of drinks," she said. "Can I have a word with you?"

"Anybody who pays for drinks can have a whole sentence," Xander said.

She pulled herself up to the table and attached a stabilizing clip. "We've met briefly before. My name is Elisa Enturi. I work for Iswander Industries."

Now Xander placed her, but the name wasn't right. "Elisa . . . Reeves, wasn't it?"

"*Enturi.* I know who you are, and I know Kett Shipping. I'm looking for distribution. It'll be a long-term contract and very lucrative."

"We like the lucrative part," Terry said. "Hauling what?"

"Ekti. As much as you can haul, and as fast as you can take it."

Xander was surprised. "So Iswander is back in business? After Sheol?"

"Yes," she said.

"Where's he getting the ekti from?" Terry asked.

"From his own production facilities. It's pretty simple. I'll deliver ekti to you, and you'll distribute it to open markets."

"Any markets in particular?" Xander instinctively glanced at the list on the datapad.

Elisa didn't seem to care. "Everyone needs stardrive fuel. We're the suppliers, you're distributors. So long as Iswander Industries gets paid, you can sell it wherever you like."

"That's the kind of deal I enjoy," Xander said.

"A requirement of the contract would be that our operations remain confidential. Is that acceptable?"

Xander and Terry exchanged a glance; neither wanted to look too eager to agree. Terry said, "Rlinda Kett runs the company. We have to check this out with her first."

Elisa narrowed her eyes. "*Do* you? This is Ulio, and I could find twenty other interested pilots in an hour. I checked your records, and I asked you first, but . . ." She shrugged.

Xander hurried to accept. "The *Verne* is at your service."

SEVENTY-ONE

KING PETER

After the Sheol catastrophe, the Roamer industrialist Lee Iswander had dropped out of sight, shutting down his businesses, keeping a low profile. Therefore, King Peter was surprised when Iswander arrived at Theroc and cheerfully requested an audience with him.

As the King, Peter had known the influential businessman for years. In the early days of the Confederation, Peter encouraged cooperation among former Hansa planets, independent worlds, and Roamer clans. The new government was supposed to enable a cross-pollination of interests. Iswander exemplified that—a man who wrapped Roamer ingenuity in efficient Hansa business practices, the best of both worlds. Although the man seemed a little too focused on his bottom line, Peter was confident they could work together, especially when it appeared that Iswander might someday be elected clan Speaker.

The lava-processing tragedy had left more than fifteen hundred dead—an accident that could have been prevented if Iswander had heeded warnings and planned better for the unthinkable. Under other circumstances, victims might have unleashed an avalanche of lawsuits and recriminations, but Roamers had a way of drawing together after disasters. They lived in rugged environments on hostile planets, and when the clans built their facilities on the edge, sometimes they fell off. The universe was not invested in their safety.

Even so, the Roamers suspected Lee Iswander was to blame for at least the magnitude of the catastrophe. He had wisely gone into hiding for the last several months. Until now . . .

The Roamer industrialist arrived unannounced on Theroc, guiding a large ekti tanker that wore a fresh Iswander Industries logo like a badge of honor. Iswander transmitted an exuberant message, as if he expected fanfare for his visit. "I have excellent news, and I'd like to meet with King Peter and Queen Estarra, please. Iswander Industries is back online, and I have a new trade agreement to propose with the Confederation."

Life seemed to be getting back to normal after an appropriate mourning period for Father Idriss, and Estarra sat at Peter's side again. Celli and Solimar had gone back to Fireheart Station; Sarein, awkward and uncomfortable among people, had returned to her isolated existence in the Wild.

Now, receiving Iswander's request, Peter looked at Estarra. "He's a bold man, I'll give him that."

Estarra was less kind. "And full of himself."

"We should meet with him, anyway," Peter said. "He's an important Roamer industrialist."

"*Was* an important industrialist. I'm not surprised that he managed to get back on his feet—I just didn't think he could do it so quickly."

Peter agreed. "His reputation will take longer to recover."

"If ever," Estarra said.

Leaving the ekti tanker in orbit, Iswander piloted his own shuttle down to the main fungus-reef complex, where he greeted Confederation trade representatives, met men and women whom he called "old friends," shaking hands and smiling, despite the occasional cool reaction he received. The industrialist entered the throne room wearing business attire instead of a traditional Roamer jumpsuit; he entered with the demeanor of a conquering hero, despite all those who had died on Sheol. Did he think everyone had forgotten?

Iswander made a perfunctory bow. "King Peter, Queen Estarra, whenever Roamers suffer a tragic setback, we pick up the pieces and make a new start. I'm here to celebrate the miracle of second chances."

"We've all mourned those who died on Sheol," Estarra said. "We only hope you can make reparations to the poor family members."

Iswander didn't look at all stung by her comment. "Indeed I intend to. I thought I was ruined after the accident, but I managed to pick up the pieces. My new business venture is doing extremely well."

Estarra regarded him with plain skepticism. "What business venture?"

He gestured upward to some vague place far overhead. "Your Majesties, I brought you a gift—a tanker of a new and highly concentrated stardrive fuel that will change commerce and space travel as we know it. I call it ekti-X."

"When did you get into the ekti-harvesting business?" Peter asked. "And who funded your skymine?"

"Cloud harvesting is an enormous and expensive operation that would require a large crew and years of full-scale production before turning a profit. Under my current circumstances, I couldn't wait that long." He smiled. "Instead, I've discovered an entirely different and more efficient method of ekti extraction."

Peter and Estarra were both surprised. "Some new technique that wasn't developed during the Elemental War?" After hydrogue attacks put an abrupt end to traditional ekti production on gas giants, the human race had scrounged for any means to produce vital stardrive fuel.

"My ekti operations are safer, cheaper, and far more productive than anything the Roamers have done before. My lava-processing operation wasn't the only dangerous work Roamers have done. Think of all those who perished on skymines, generation after generation. I understand there's been a terrible debacle on Golgen?"

Peter gave only a curt nod. "The Kellum skymine was destroyed, yes. The hydrogues surfaced again, although they don't appear to be responsible for the disaster."

The words seemed to skate across Iswander without leaving a mark. "Well, soon enough, Iswander Industries will supply so much ekti that other Roamer clans won't need to take such unnecessary risks."

Estarra said coldly, "Perhaps we should send inspection teams to make sure there are no lapses in safety—like on Sheol."

"You'll understand my reluctance to share proprietary operations." His expression darkened; his voice became harder. "Since everyone turned their backs on me in my company's time of greatest crisis, I need to protect my assets." Then he seemed to remember where he was. His expression softened, and he smiled again. "As I said, my operations could benefit the entire human race. The ekti-X I brought is my token of thanks for all of your hard work in holding the Confederation together. I expect my business to expand greatly in the coming year."

Peter thought that Iswander looked too smug, as if he had succeeded in washing all the blood from his hands. "You remind me of Chairman Basil Wenceslas, Mr. Iswander."

The Roamer man nodded, accepting the assessment as a compliment, though Peter certainly had not intended it as such.

SEVENTY-TWO

AELIN

When he heard that Lee Iswander had come to Theroc with his new business success, against all odds, Aelin knew what he had to do. He hadn't realized it before, but he had been waiting a long time for this. Shelud was already gone on a great adventure with clan Reeves on a derelict alien station. He could do no less!

Iswander's return was, in and of itself, an act of bravery, Aelin thought. Many other company heads, when confronted with such a terrible disaster, would have gone into permanent hiding, unable to face the shame and the accusations. But Lee Iswander refused to be defeated. By his demeanor now, the industrialist looked strong, and Aelin found his optimism and determination inspirational. Maybe he deserved another chance after all.

Mr. Iswander had always made an impression on him. While recovering from his treedancing accident when he was young, Aelin had a window near the spaceport landing zone. As his broken leg healed, he watched the commercial ships, Roamer vessels of all kinds, diplomatic yachts for planetary reps, and exotic visiting Ildiran shuttles.

One day, he saw Mr. Iswander arrive in a fancy cruiser. Though his leg wasn't entirely healed, Aelin felt restless and hobbled out to see the ships. He tried to sneak aboard the Iswander Industries cruiser, hoping to stow away and see other planets, but his plan was poorly thought out, and he was caught. The crew tried to chase him off, but Iswander took pity on the young Theron man, took him aboard, and showed him around. During an hour-long tour, Iswander was interrupted so many times that he finally sent Aelin away with apologies. "I'm sorry, that's all the time I can spare."

Nevertheless, he had shown Aelin what he needed to see—how *important* such a man was. Whole planets, the Confederation, the Roamer clans, all depended on Iswander's business. It made Aelin realize how parochial the previous concerns of his life had been. He never forgot the impression Lee Iswander made on him.

Now, while Iswander was meeting with the King and Queen, Aelin made inquiries about speaking with the man before he departed. But Lee Iswander had filed no formal schedule, and the green priest couldn't figure out how he might make an appointment. So, he climbed to the canopy landing field, found the Iswander Industries shuttle, and hunkered down to wait. . . .

Several hours later, when the sky was darkening at sunset and the blue moths came out, Lee Iswander returned to his ship and was surprised to find a green priest waiting for him.

Aelin rose to his feet and gave a formal, uncertain bow. "Mr. Iswander, my name is Aelin. I'm a green priest."

Iswander eyed him up and down, wearing a cautious, polite smile. "I can see that."

Aelin had trouble getting his words out. "I'm not sure if you remember me, but when I was just a boy—"

Iswander's smile widened. "Yes! The curious one with the broken leg."

"Yes, sir. Would you possibly have any use for a green priest in your operations? I could send any messages you like through telink, and I have access to the knowledge in the worldforest." Aelin had already checked, and although Iswander had made a few peremptory inquiries about using telink services in his Sheol operations, the industrialist had no green priest working for him yet in his mysterious new venture.

Iswander looked at him for a long moment, as if running a thorough analysis. "My operations are high security. I can't have any proprietary details shared with the rest of the Confederation."

"Green priests work in strict confidence, Mr. Iswander. We're trusted in commercial operations, isolated colonies, even aboard the CDF fleet. I would transmit no information without your permission."

The industrialist pondered again, longer this time, weighing suspicions, then discarding them. "Considering our isolation, and my wide-ranging activities, I've often thought a green priest could be useful for instantaneous communication—not to mention an emergency link—but also to monitor the activities of other ekti producers, the ebbs and flows of the market." He narrowed his eyes. "But how can I be reassured that you would keep my business secrets? I would lose a great deal if a competitor discovered what I'm doing."

Aelin blinked at him. "I'm a green priest, sir. I give you my word." He didn't know if that could be enough.

Iswander finally said, "I do remember you, young man. I saw something in your eyes . . . and, yes, green priests are considered trustworthy. So I'll take you at your word. What you see must remain strictly confidential, unless I give you permission to reveal any details. Understood?"

"Understood."

Iswander opened the hatch of his shuttle and motioned Aelin aboard. "Join me, and I'll show you something quite remarkable."

SEVENTY-THREE

DALE REEVES

Each new chamber they opened contained dead aliens.

Dale and Shelud found the mummified creatures preserved by the cold, desiccated space environment. The first ones were sprawled in the corridor, like discarded rag dolls. Their skin was gray and discolored by blotches. The puckered eyelids had turned into iron-hard leather, their lips drawn back as muscles contracted to reveal tiny rounded teeth.

The bodies were naked. The preserved skin looked hard and smooth, and they appeared sexless, as if they were all dolls made from an identical mold. Dale recognized the Onthos from the images in the library chamber. He found it strange for a race to be in such a large city with no garments, no pockets, no adornments. Shelud, who wore only a loincloth, did not think it unusual.

The green priest paused at the open hatch. "They're all dead." In order to explore farther, he would have to step over the fallen alien bodies.

Dale tried to be brave. "Of course they are—it's been thousands of years. Now we know where at least some of them went." The mystery of this gigantic empty city had grated on him like a subsonic vibration. "Not knowing is more frightening than the truth."

He ventured ahead, and Shelud followed. They opened the habitation chambers. Doors scraped and groaned aside to reveal more stacked bodies, some carefully arranged, some sprawled in desperate positions, arms and legs at odd angles.

In a large gathering chamber, they found hundreds of the Onthos. Dale turned away and instinctively covered his mouth, but after so much time the only smell that lingered was a papery sweetness that reminded him of tobacco.

Shelud stared at the corpses. The aliens had died together, and in a relatively short period of time. They looked as if they had known their fate. "How could they all have died at once?" Shelud asked.

The green priest had spent his life on Theroc and didn't understand the rigors of living in space. Dale explained, "Okiah is an isolated city, entirely dependent on energy systems, air, water, and food brought in from outside. One small failure could have been enough."

Dale thought of disasters that had befallen Roamer installations, not just the recent debacle at Sheol, but also dome settlements that experienced sudden decompression after meteor impacts; on Teritha, a slow buildup of poison in the central life-support system had made an entire colony succumb before anyone realized the danger.

"We found air inside the city when we first broke open the hatches," Shelud pointed out. "The Onthos power reactors were still intact even after so many centuries. We got them running with only minimal repairs. It doesn't make sense."

Dale didn't know the answer either. "These fatalities weren't instantaneous. Some of the Onthos died before others, because you can see that their bodies were tended, while the rest fell like stragglers. That argues against a sudden, massive decompression." As he considered the hundreds of corpses, Dale slowly shook his head. "Let's go back, Shelud. We need to tell my father."

Once the news spread, the Retroamers needed to understand why their new home had become a mysterious graveyard. Olaf Reeves sent teams into spoke five to learn what they could about the fallen aliens. He wanted to put the matter to rest.

Shelud retrieved his treeling and accompanied the team. If they found another library chamber to explain what disaster had caused the deaths, he would tap into the worldforest mind and translate the Onthos language.

In Okiah's central hub, Olaf held up a hand before Dale could rush back out to spoke five. "I know you're pleased with yourself, but you're a Roamer and you should tend to your family."

Dale blinked. "What's wrong with my family?"

"BO brought both of your sons back from their lessons today. They've fallen ill, something going around among the children. I pulled Sendra from her duties to watch them, but you're their father. You should be with them, too."

Dale put aside a flash of resentment; Olaf had never wasted any time tending his sons when they were sick. "I'll go to them right now. Have they seen the doctors?" Among the group that left Rendezvous, six were fully qualified doctors and surgeons with various specialties, and another ten had basic medical knowledge.

"The medical bays are busy." The clan leader snorted. "A lot of people are claiming to be sick. I think it's just an excuse to get off their duty shifts so they can go exploring. See what you started?"

Dale lowered his eyes, but then felt a strength and raised his chin. "See what I *found*? Now we understand more about this city."

Olaf grumbled and sent him off, not wanting to make any admissions.

Inside the quarters that Dale's family had claimed, he found both of his boys in their sleep clothes, wrapped in blankets. Scott was dozing fitfully, his face flushed. Jamie looked miserable as he sat watching one of his favorite interactive entertainment loops, though he wasn't interacting much. Dale didn't see Sendra. "Where's your mother?"

Jamie seemed to need extra time to process the question, then he nodded toward the reclamation chamber. "In there."

Sendra emerged, wringing out a wet towel, then wiping her mouth— clearing vomit away? "I think I caught it too," she said. She coughed and looked queasy. "The doctor sent over broad-spectrum antivirals and antibiotics, but we probably have to ride this out." She ducked back into the reclamation chamber.

Because Roamers lived in enclosed habitats with reprocessed air, sicknesses were rare and usually brought in from the outside. The sterile environment, however, left them with little resistance when they did encounter a virus.

He sat next to sleeping Scott; Jamie's eyes were heavy-lidded, not watching his entertainment loop. In such close quarters, Dale supposed he couldn't avoid catching the bug himself. He could wash his hands, get rest, take vitamin supplements, but it was a lost cause. The flu would strike most of clan Reeves.

"I'll make some soup," he said.

Shelud came to talk with him before he presented his information to Olaf Reeves. Standing at the door to Dale's quarters, the green priest looked concerned. "We need to tell your father—and soon. As clan leader, he has to decide the best way to inform everyone."

Dale felt tired and feverish, though he hadn't yet suffered the full-blown symptoms of the strange flu. Both of his boys had high fevers, and Sendra—normally so dynamic and independent—stayed in bed most of the day, too tired to get up and help. Dale didn't want to leave his family, but the look in Shelud's eyes disturbed him greatly. "What did you find? More records?"

The green priest swallowed. "Yes, more records—the last log entries, which I translated through the worldforest mind. I know why all the aliens died."

Inside the hub chamber that Olaf Reeves used as his office, the clan leader looked haggard, though not sick from the same illness that so many were suffering. Olaf's heavy brows drew together as the two entered. He ignored the green priest and turned to his son. "By the Guiding Star, where have you been?"

"Tending my family, as you told me to. They're sick."

Olaf sighed, as if Dale had disappointed him again. "Everyone's sick. It'll pass."

Shelud's voice was urgent. "I don't think so." He set his potted treeling on the clan head's makeshift desk. "The aliens all died from a plague. We found more information about the Onthos."

Olaf shook his head. "You said the aliens came here to escape from the Klikiss. That's why they built the city. They even took refugees from wiped-out Onthos settlements."

The green priest nodded. "Yes, the Klikiss attacked them on their worlds, and the survivors came seeking refuge. But some of the wounded were infected by a disease the Klikiss carried—and they brought it here."

"Are you saying the Klikiss were struck by a plague, too?" Dale asked.

"They were just carriers, unaffected. They had some kind of resistance, but the disease mutated, infected the Onthos, and spread throughout their race. This refuge city became a death house." Tears shimmered in the green priest's eyes. "Even I could hear the passion and despair in the Onthos voice. Their leader said, 'We marked this city with pink triangles to warn everyone off. We used the symbol to let all visitors know that this is a plague station.'"

Dale said, "Pink triangles? How were we supposed to know what that means?"

Olaf hung his head in defeat, and Dale was surprised by his father's reaction. He expected the man to be scornful about irrelevant matters from millennia ago, but Olaf looked at a desk screen filled with names; he rotated the file so that Dale and Shelud could see a report from the medical bay.

"The doctors just transmitted this list to me. Fifty of our clan members have been struck by the flu, and the sickness seems to be getting worse. No one was ill before we came aboard Okiah."

Dale couldn't stop thinking about his two boys still shivering and miserable after two days. "But it can't possibly be the Onthos plague. It's been centuries—and it affected an entirely different race. Diseases don't translate across species."

"Klikiss were the original carriers," Shelud said, "and the disease adapted to the Onthos. Who's to say it can't adapt to human biology, too?"

Dale stared down the list of names. Fifty sick already . . . and how many more felt feverish like himself with the first stages of the disease?

Olaf looked at the green priest. "Translate the records and give our doctors whatever information you have, any clues that will help them cure this."

"I'll do what I can, but the Onthos never found a cure. Thousands of inhabitants of this space city . . . and every one of them died from the disease."

SEVENTY-FOUR

TOM ROM

When Tom Rom passed through the Klikiss transportal to Kuivahr, he saw that the tides were substantially down from the previous time. The flat seas were more of a quagmire.

On this trip, though, he would not be visiting Del Kellum's distillery. Zoe's researchers had already tested the sample kelp extracts and plankton distillates, from which they identified interesting antioxidants, as well as immunity and metabolic enhancers.

Now he meant to see what the Ildiran researchers had to offer.

After sending discreet inquiries, Tom Rom had made arrangements to go to the sanctuary domes. If he could convince Tamo'l that his employer had similar interests, the Ildiran researcher might even be willing to provide him with all the genetic data she had compiled on her misbreeds.

Now that the seas had dropped with the tide, the reef outcropping that held the Klikiss transportal stood high above a wet basin. Stagnant pools swirled with an oily sheen of plankton; dark clumps of kelp looked like tangled hair caught in a drain. The water level was so low that more mud than open water showed.

Tom Rom glanced at his chronometer. Tamo'l should have arranged transportation for him, but he saw no sign of a boat from the sanctuary domes. He heard a buzzing sound and saw a small open-framed flying craft wobbling toward him, dipping and bobbing in the air.

He worked his way down the outcropping that supported the transportal wall to an open area where the flying vehicle could land. It came in, extending struts to keep it balanced. The pilot stepped out, a human with reddish brown hair and freckles on his face. "Are you Mr. Rom? I'm here to give you a lift."

He regarded the man coolly. "Call me Tom Rom. I wasn't aware that humans worked at the Ildiran medical facility."

"My name is Shawn Fennis, and I was born on the Dobro colony. My wife is Ildiran, and we volunteered to work with the misbreeds. Tamo'l thought you might like to see a recognizable face when you arrived. Some of the misfits are . . . startling."

"I'll thank her in person for the consideration, but it was unnecessary."

Fennis gestured to a seat behind him in the craft. The gossamer flyer had a sturdy but ultralight construction. "Hop in and buckle up. And no sudden moves, because this thing is hard to balance."

Tom Rom climbed inside and braced himself against the framework. The insubstantial flyer seemed likely to break apart in a strong gust of wind. When his passenger was situated, Fennis powered up the engines, and used his feet to nudge the flyer a few inches off the ground. At the last moment, the engines caught, and the craft flew away from the reef outcropping. With Tom Rom's extra weight, the craft dipped low toward the pools of mud and plankton.

Fennis concentrated on flying, lifting the craft higher in the air. He shouted behind him into the wind, "One last thing, Mr. Rom—don't fall out! If you hit that quick-slime, nobody's going in after you."

"Thank you for the warning. I do not intend to fall."

When they arrived at the medical station, the sanctuary dome was exposed to the sun, covered with drying seaweed and smears of mud. The landing platform was high above the standing water, and Shawn Fennis skidded the flying craft onto the deck.

Tom Rom climbed out and waited while his escort secured the flyer. "My wife and I have only been here for a couple of months," Fennis said. "Does your employer run a facility like this, to help mutations and defectives?"

"Her facility is called Pergamus. And, no, it is not like this. I'll explain everything to Tamo'l."

Fennis led him inside the sanctuary domes. The air smelled of medicines, disinfectants, and quarantine, but Tom Rom also smelled fish and salt and odd spices. This was not just a hospital or a research station—it was also a home for those Ildirans misbreeds who couldn't survive elsewhere.

He recognized Tamo'l from his prior communications. She was pretty, with a scholarly look, obviously a halfbreed; her feathery hair had a sparkling quality. When Tom Rom greeted her, he tried not to stare at the two figures beside her. Both were male, or so he thought.

The taller one had three eyes, one of which was in a socket low down on the cheekbone. His skin was leathery, and his features looked as if they had been carved out of wax and left for too long under the hot Ildiran suns. One arm was shriveled and drawn up to his chest, while the other dangled long and loose, more of a tentacle appendage than an arm.

The other misfit was hunched over, but his head was at the end of an abnormally long neck, like a stalk bent upward. His skin was covered with thick, yellowish brown scales that looked like stained thumbnails.

Showing no disgust whatsoever, Tom Rom nodded to the head of the facility. "Thank you for seeing me, Tamo'l. My employer is very interested in your work."

Tamo'l assessed his reaction, as if she had given him some kind of test, then she nodded with a smile. "You are welcome here, sir. I'm happy to share our work with a fellow researcher. Follow me and meet the rest of our people." She turned, and her strange companions turned with her, moving with a unique awkward gait that they had developed to deal with their infirmities.

More misbreeds emerged from adjacent corridors and chambers in the sanctuary dome. They were an amazing conglomeration of misshapen bodies, overgrown faces, a patchwork assortment of limbs, skin types, fur, scales.

"During the breeding program on Dobro," Tamo'l explained, "Ildiran researchers crossbred kiths in many possible combinations, including a separate group interbred with human colonists." She caught herself, then forced the words out, "Human *prisoners*. I am one such halfbreed. My father was a lens kithman, my mother a human green priest. As you can see, not all of the mixed offspring turned out as healthy as I did."

Tamo'l led him toward the medical research stations, which interested Tom Rom the most. Along the way, they passed living chambers, some dim, some bright, cluttered with possessions, blankets, tapestries, cushions. A group of the misfits preferred a damp environment, while others wanted dry, hot chambers.

"Kuivahr truly is the best refuge for the mixed-breeds. Obviously, they have difficult lives, often tragically short, although they can also live longer than the norm. The idea behind the Dobro breeding program was to develop hybrid vigor. Some of the mixed-breeds are indeed superior . . . but they don't all turn out so well."

Misbreeds played music, they cooked, filling the air with the interesting smell of spices and grease. There were even children, Tom Rom saw—and he realized that the misfits here interbred and formed families. They all turned their faces toward Tom Rom as he passed, several were blind, several had too many eyes.

"With so many specimens to study, you must have done a great deal of research," he said. "My employer will be pleased with this data. Would you share your genetic records as well? Maybe she can find a useful breakthrough."

Tamo'l faced him, her expression hard. "I do not think of these people as mere specimens. They are my friends as well." She calmed herself with a visible effort. "I will, of course, share my information for the greater good, though I don't know how applicable our Ildiran genetic research will be to your employer's work."

Inside a large chemical research lab, Shawn Fennis greeted an Ildiran woman warmly. "This is my wife, Chiar'h," he said, as if he had won a trophy.

Tom Rom gave a polite nod, but he wasn't interested in their relationship. He wondered if these two intended to have halfbreed children, or if they were frightened by all of the misfit halfbreeds they saw around them.

"We're testing kelp extracts and mineralized slime as a palliative for some of our worst cases," Tamo'l said. "There's been a blossoming of a rare kelp strain, and that gives the mixed-breeds a strength they didn't have before. They can never be cured, but they can thrive here, even love like normal people." She looked around with obvious satisfaction. "Kuivahr is more than just a last hope for hopeless cases—this is their home. They are victims of the breeding program, as so many of us are. They just paid a higher price than most."

She showed him her extensive medical treatment facility with special wards for tending the numerous breakdowns of the misbreeds. When one of the misfits died, even the body was studied in order to help the others.

The misfits did not fill him with disgust so much as fascination. Not pity, not sympathy. Tom Rom only cared that they might be useful to Zoe Alakis.

Getting down to business, Tom Rom opened the satchel he carried. "My employer has authorized me to offer a substantial fee for your data." He revealed a glittering kaleidoscope of prisdiamonds, enough to make anyone in the Confederation gasp with astonishment.

Tamo'l was appreciative. "I understand that this is a great treasure, so I will accept it and put the funds to good use." She looked at him with her large eyes. "But Ildirans don't value wealth the way humans do. If your employer makes a breakthrough that could help my misfits here, I hope she will share."

"I will tell her that."

He knew the very thought was absurd.

SEVENTY-FIVE

ORLI COVITZ

Before Orli reported to Kett Shipping for her new job, she did her homework. DD helped her track down the records and specs of the *Proud Mary*—the ship she would be flying.

Orli had worked so long at the compy facility on Relleker that she'd forgotten a great deal about piloting a ship. Before marrying Matthew and settling down, she had traveled far and wide, often flying with Captain Kett aboard the *Voracious Curiosity* or Captain Roberts on his *Blind Faith*. She was certainly competent, and she could learn—or relearn.

Even so, when she delivered the formal paperwork to Tasia Tamblyn and Robb Brindle at the Kett Shipping headquarters, Orli wanted to make a good impression.

After Orli entered the offices on Earth, Tasia shook her hand. "You're very welcome here, Captain Covitz."

Orli was at a loss. "*Captain?* I'm just submitting my application. I haven't been—"

Robb scanned her application. "Of course, you're accepted. You can fly a ship right? Looks like you have plenty of experience." He tapped the screen.

Tasia said, "Rlinda recommended you, and it's her company. I understand you're already slated for the *Proud Mary*?"

DD piped up, "Captain Kett suggested the *Proud Mary* might be an appropriate ship for us."

"She's refueled, ready for a shakedown cruise," Robb said. "Will you need a copilot? I can assign one of our shipping experts to show you the ropes, if you like."

Orli couldn't control her smile. "I have DD."

The compy added, "Captain Kett said there were enhanced piloting and engineering modules for me to upload if it became necessary."

Tasia called up ship records, toggling past image after image. Each vessel had a different hull configuration, some with additional engines or expanded stowage pods. "Kett Shipping currently has forty-seven ships. Rlinda owns fourteen of them outright—including the *Proud Mary*. Robb and I own four, and the others are privately owned by their individual captains, who have contract arrangements with us."

"If those captains own their ships, what do they get out of being part of Kett Shipping?" Orli imagined that if she owned her vessel, she'd want to be independent, fly from place to place, pick up whatever cargo she liked.

"Insurance," Robb said. "Steady work, a safety net, repairs and rescue, and prices negotiated through the clout of Kett Shipping."

Tasia grinned. "And the pleasure of working with us. That's our biggest selling point."

"We are very pleased to work with you," DD said.

"Good. Let's go take a look at your ship."

When one of their pilots complained that he'd been cheated on an agreed-upon fee for a shipment, Tasia hurried off to deal with the minor emergency, while Robb took Orli to the company hangar. DD strutted along beside them.

The *Proud Mary* was a small cargo ship with a comfortable cockpit, a compact stateroom just big enough for Orli, and a well-organized cargo hold. She wouldn't be hauling any huge loads, but the ship could make niche runs to specialized markets and planets that saw little regular trade.

She ran her gaze along the hull. "I like it."

Robb nodded. "*Proud Mary*'s a good ship. Mary Coven flew her for us seventeen years, and before that she did black-market runs in the last four years of the Elemental War."

An odd sour smell clung to the upholstery. Robb sniffed. "Mary Coven had her quirks. She liked to smoke a tobacco pipe, spent a fortune replacing air filters, but she claimed it was worth the expense."

The captain's chair was frayed at the corners, the armrests patched with polymer strips and adhesives. Some of the paint on the control panel was worn, and spots of alloy films had been rubbed away; labels on several controls had been marked over with fresh tape and hand-written identifications.

"Looks like she did a little custom rewiring," Orli said.

"Those are fixes, but the ship checks out, fully functional. If you want, I can reupholster the seats, give the interior a repaint and a freshening up, but I don't think Rlinda will pay for an upgrade of the control modules."

Orli stared at the cockpit, imagining the other captain who had spent so much time inside the ship, an independent and adventurous woman who was free to go where she wished and not afraid to do it. So different from her own situation with Matthew and the Relleker facility.

"That won't be necessary. New control modules have their bugs too, and this ship's got history. She's proved herself."

Robb grinned. "If I hadn't approved you before, Captain Covitz, you just passed the test. That comment shows you know enough about piloting. You and the *Proud Mary* will get along just fine."

"I am very excited, Orli Covitz," DD said in a completely dead-pan voice.

She sat in the pilot seat, touched the controls, settled into the cushion. It felt right. She wanted to do this.

Robb said, "We've got a small shipment ready to go to the military base on Mars. Nothing fancy. It'll be a quick trip, take you no more than two days, but it would be a good shakedown, if you want to practice."

"I'd like that very much. DD, how do you feel about being my copilot?"

"I look forward to my new role, Orli."

She ran her hands along the arms of the pilot's chair and flicked on the power systems, verifying that the fuel supplies were full, the energy levels optimal. "All I need is a course to set and a cargo to deliver."

. . .

The flight was smooth, quiet yet exhilarating, and it let her forget. Orli felt as if she had shed her skin and become a brand-new person, no longer just a shadow of herself in the aftermath of Matthew's change of heart. Orli wasn't defined by him anymore; she was a ship captain now, and DD was at her side.

The simple delivery from Earth to Mars was one of the most satisfying things she had done in a long time.

After landing back at headquarters to make a report and look for her next assignment, she was pleased to see Rlinda waiting as she and DD disembarked. The matronly woman crossed her arms over her chest. "Everything went well?"

"Without a hitch."

"Good, that makes you my very best captain—thought you'd like to know that."

"Very best? How is that possible? I only did one little run."

"Statistically, you are one hundred percent reliable and not a nanosecond overdue. Of my forty-seven ships, not a single other pilot can say that."

Orli felt warm inside. Yes, she was going to like this job very much.

"I've got your next assignment," Rlinda said. "Nothing urgent, but it'll give you practice . . . and frankly, it would make me feel a whole lot better."

That piqued Orli's curiosity. "Where am I going?"

"Olaf Reeves and his clan headed off for points unknown to set up some new colony. They think they can be self-sufficient, and I've heard that some pigs think they can fly, too. I doubt the old curmudgeon believed it himself, because he left me the coordinates and arranged a line of credit, in case he needs emergency supplies."

"Did he ask for help?" Orli asked. "How long has he been gone?"

"Not long. And he'd never ask—he's too proud. But I could have you just drop in, make sure they're all right, and take a cargo of emergency supplies with you, as well as some pampering items. They won't chase you away, I promise."

A N T O N   C O L I C O S

The Mage-Imperator's order was everything a scholar could possibly hope for. Jora'h wanted all possible knowledge about the Shana Rei, real answers about the previous crisis, no matter how deep the rememberers had to dig or which document crypts they opened.

Anton wished he could work without interruption—there were so many recovered documents to read and translate, so many lost records that no Ildiran eyes had seen in centuries. Five sealed vaults had been smashed open on the Mage-Imperator's orders.

Scouring the document crypts from that time period, rememberers had indeed found old accounts of the Shana Rei, correspondence from the legendary Tal Bria'nh, even rudimentary designs for the sun bombs. The ancient plans had not been destroyed, merely buried by the weight of countless centuries of records. After the Shana Rei had been defeated, the sun bombs were considered obsolete, unnecessary, and resigned to obscurity.

Nevertheless, Anton had rushed the designs to Adar Zan'nh, who turned them over to his military engineers for study. The Solar Navy would begin building and testing prototypes right away.

For an eager historian, however, there was so much more to learn.

He and Dyvo'sh continued to unearth and catalogue the densely etched crystal sheets. The young assistant worked at his side, and excitement sent a flush of color into the lobes of the young assistant's face each time he found some obscure mention of the Shana Rei.

Among the apocryphal documents, Anton found a bizarre and disturbing sketch of a shapeless black blot, like an ink stain that featured a central staring eye. Surrealistic certainly, meant to evoke a primal fear, but even the stylized representation gave him a chill.

The translation summaries would keep the Hall of Rememberers busy for years to come. Scholarly careers would be built around some of these apocryphal records, academic squabbles would flare up—but Anton brushed those thoughts aside. He had left that petty professorial life behind, and he didn't care about the politics of academia.

But he couldn't read everything himself, and so he had to set priorities for himself and for the rememberer kith. It was difficult to choose! He read until his neck ached and his shoulders were stiff and his eyes felt as if they might fall out of their sockets. He couldn't stay awake all the time.

"I need coffee," he told his assistant Dyvo'sh. "It's been a long time since I've had a good strong cup."

"What is coffee?" asked the young rememberer.

It was just an offhand comment. "A human beverage—it's delicious and stimulating."

"I understand," Dyvo'sh said. "Like kirae."

Anton remembered the one and only time he had tasted the Ildiran beverage. "No, not like kirae. Not at all." Then he brightened, realizing that he could possibly find a cup after all. "We'll have to go to the human enclave."

He had always intended to visit the human district to see the shops and art galleries, eat the food, and sit at one of the cafés . . . the things that he had never appreciated in his years on Earth. On Ildira, Anton constantly immersed himself in his work, so a trip to the human district had never reached the top of his priority list. Now, however, he felt a sudden longing. He picked up a stack of restored documents to take with him. "Come along, I'll buy you a cup of coffee."

He left instructions with Ildiran scholars who continued to comb through the recovered documents. The rememberers would sort out any records that mentioned the creatures of darkness, and Anton would review them himself.

Before he and Dyvo'sh left the Hall of Rememberers, Anton reminded the studious Ildirans who hunched over well-lit tables, scanning one document after another, "I want any legends, stories, anecdotes. We found the sun bomb plans—there must be more ideas waiting to be uncovered. As for the rest of the documents . . ." He let out a long sigh.

"We'll just have to read those at some later date. We've got enough to keep us busy for a long, long time."

Anton had no idea how Yazra'h knew he was about to head across the city, but she was waiting for him when he and Dyvo'sh exited the Hall of Rememberers. She stood in all her intimidating beauty, wearing fine-scale armor with a crystal dagger at her hip. "I will escort you, Rememberer Anton, in case the streets are dangerous."

He chuckled. "It's Mijistra. How could it be dangerous?"

She tossed her long hair. "Nevertheless, I will escort you. What is your destination?"

"The human district. Join us for a cup of coffee." Since she seemed stuck on the idea, Anton didn't argue, but let her lead the way. "We're searching for any tidbit, but since the Saga of Seven Suns is over a billion lines long and the lost documents are at least ten times that—finding a relevant passage is an extraordinary task."

Yazra'h did not seem to envy his work. "That is a battle you must win for yourself, Rememberer Anton. Have you learned how I can fight the Shana Rei?"

"I'm looking for how the Solar Navy and the Confederation Defense Forces can fight them. Adar Zan'nh and the CDF are about to engage in more war-game exercises, but I doubt their traditional maneuvers will be useful against the creatures of darkness. First I have to separate the legends from the genuine historical events. By all accounts, the Shana Rei are fearsome opponents."

She gave a gruff nod. "Then I look forward to fighting them."

When they reached the section of the city settled by human expatriates, Anton smiled at the familiar architecture, the open shops, and the business banners, and the outdoor tables. It reminded him of the university district on Earth where he had spent so many years.

He heard music from some kind of old-fashioned instrument, pleasant tones played by someone who knew what he was doing. A middle-aged couple displayed ornamental clay pots they had glazed themselves. Another craft shop offered yarn soul-catchers strung with sparkling crystals. The milieu itself was enough to reenergize Anton after his long hours in the Hall of Rememberers. Then he smelled the coffee—a rich, roasted essence that was unlike any traditional Ildiran beverage. It was so strong that even the aroma seemed to contain caffeine.

He claimed an outdoor table and yanked out chairs for his two companions. A fascinated Dyvo'sh continued looking around, particularly interested in the soul-catchers. He tapped one with a finger, and the inset crystal caught the light as it rotated.

When the café owner came out, Anton greeted her with a grin. "Large coffee for me, please, with a dollop of cream. My friends will each have one, too."

Dyvo'sh took a seat next to him, copying Anton's every move, like an apprentice. Yazra'h remained standing until Anton insisted that she take a seat.

The café owner was a Rubenesque woman with cool blue eyes and curly ash-blond hair. "I'll brew it fresh," she said. They were apparently the only customers in the district. She glanced at Yazra'h and Dyvo'sh. "I'll bring some condensed milk as well. Ildirans tend to like it sweet."

When she delivered the coffee, Anton wrapped both hands around his cup, savoring the smell before he sipped and let out a sigh. Dyvo'sh mimicked his every move, took a sip, and struggled to control his grimace.

Yazra'h was brave and took a gulp, but the coffee didn't appeal to her either. "It is potent," was the best she could say.

Anton looked around the empty café. "Not many customers? I suppose Ildirans don't come back for coffee once they've tried it."

"We're all hurting," said the café owner. She glanced around. Several blocks away, the streets of Mijistra were filled with bustling Ildirans, but the human district seemed isolated, as if shunned. "The Mage-Imperator visited not long ago, encouraged Ildirans to do business with us—and that lasted for about a day."

The art gallery owner came over and took an empty seat beside them. "It wasn't always like that. We were at least curiosities, but something's changed."

Anton took another sip of his coffee and made up his mind to come back here as often as possible. "Why would customers avoid the whole district?"

"Nobody knows. Maybe we did something to insult them." The

café owner brought him a refill. Dyvo'sh and Yazra'h did not need one. Dyvo'sh added some sweetened condensed milk at the woman's suggestion, and he seemed to tolerate it better.

Anton recalled how he had suffered censure from the Ildirans years ago when he pointed out errors in the Saga of Seven Suns. "With all the new archive crypts being opened and mountains of new documents revealed, there'll surely be more turmoil."

Yazra'h frowned. "The turmoil is not caused by the human enclave."

"Well, Ildirans shouldn't be afraid of what the rememberers find—we're just making the history accurate."

"They are not afraid of the history," Yazra'h said. "It is the *Shana Rei*. They fear the shadows are coming again."

Dyvos'h seemed very nervous. "Perhaps it would have been best if all those stories remained hidden. Then the Shana Rei might not have returned."

Anton scoffed. "It has nothing to do with cause and effect. You shouldn't fear reading old records."

"They are the darkness," Dyvo'sh said. "Of course, we fear them."

Anton had never understood the irrational Ildiran fear of the dark, but it was an integral (perhaps even pathological) part of their being. Yazra'h, who was one of the bravest people he had ever met, shook her head. "Even though Ildirans are surrounded by light, we understand the power of dark, and we know that its tendrils can slip in anywhere."

She defiantly finished her coffee, as if going to battle against the taste. "If the Shana Rei have indeed returned, we must know how to fight them. Sun bombs? Then we must build them! It will not be a traditional military effort. The creatures of darkness can strike everywhere and at any time." Then she looked at him with absolute confidence. "You will help us understand, Rememberer Anton."

Anton could see that Yazra'h was deadly serious. He sipped his coffee again, but it had gone cold.

SEVENTY-SEVEN

EXXOS

The shadow cloud appeared in the dusty skies of Eljiid, roiling out of the vacuum like smoke burning through the fabric of space.

Because they were not part of the same universe and did not follow the same physical rules, the shadow clouds could creep like spiders through the back alleys of the cosmos, slipping through cracks created by the minds of living things—fears, doubts, pain.

To Exxos, this was merely an unimportant Klikiss world, but one that would serve the black robots' purposes. And it was a place to start, an appropriate demonstration. Working with the Shana Rei, the robots would wreak great havoc, cause destruction, increase entropy . . . decrease the shadows' pain.

He was surprised, but not disappointed, to discover that a small group of humans had established a settlement there—not a full colony, just a research group studying the old Klikiss ruins like carrion birds sampling a corpse. That was even better; human treachery had caused the near extinction of the robots, and Exxos hated them almost as much as he and his comrades hated their creator race. *Almost* as much.

When the ominous dark nebula arrived over the Eljiid settlement, the humans began transmitting frantic signals: first inquiries, then indignant demands, followed by pleas for mercy, and finally an unasked-for surrender. Exxos listened to it all but did not respond. The Shana Rei did not care, were content to absorb the confusion and growing dread.

Exxos and his robots moved about in ships made from new matter the Shana Rei had manifested, simply rearranging energy in the universe to create what was necessary. When insisting on his plan to demonstrate their destructive prowess here, Exxos had convinced the shadow creatures to re-create the six vessels his comrades had built at the Dhula moon—along with certain improvements.

He had studied the Shana Rei enough to understand a few basics. *Creating* went against their fundamental nature, and only seemed to make the creatures of darkness more irrational and incomprehensible, but Exxos persuaded them to fight against their instincts. A temporary expenditure of entropy here for a larger benefit soon. He was glad to have warships again, and he knew he could cause satisfying damage to Eljiid. He would make sure the Shana Rei valued the exchange, and would agree to do it again when he suggested it elsewhere.

It meant the creatures of darkness had been intrigued enough by his bluff that they would keep the robots alive . . . for now.

As the shadow cloud grew larger overhead, the Shana Rei manifested their own huge battleships, despite the terrible pain it caused them. The dark nebula opened like a midnight flower, and Shana Rei ships emerged into real space: ebony hexagonal cylinders, long rods with flat sides and sharp angles. The creatures screamed into the silence and suffered the act of creation, doing as Exxos told them. Three of the hexagon ships were sufficient for a relatively minor target such as Eljiid.

By comparison, the black robot warships looked like little more than gnats, but Exxos and his robots raced out to begin the attack on Eljiid. He was eager to prove that the robots were worthy, valuable allies. Together, they could erase all the annoyances of sentient life here . . . and, eventually, everywhere else.

The screaming of the Shana Rei grew louder, and Exxos knew he had to strike swiftly. The creatures of darkness wanted to snap back into the void, where they could recover from the agony they had inflicted upon themselves.

The black robot ships swooped down, strafing the human camp with energy weapons, ripping up tents and settlement modules. Some researchers ran scrambling toward the Klikiss transportal, hoping to activate the stone wall and escape through the gateway back to Rheindic Co. But they didn't have the opportunity.

The robots bombarded the area until it was a glassy molten field. The transportal itself was more durable and required six overflights and heavy blasts before the trapezoidal wall came down as well. No one would be able to depart from Eljiid now.

Exxos took pride in showing the Shana Rei what his robots could do, and the creatures of darkness were satisfied to eliminate even this small cluster of intelligent life, which eased the clamor in the universe by a small degree.

Although the Shana Rei cooperated, they considered this an insignificant part of the battle. They were aware of an even more titanic sentience that terrified them, made them feel helpless, but Exxos didn't understand it. The shadow creatures claimed something tremendously powerful was awakening in the cosmos. It had maddened and provoked the Shana Rei, driving them out of hiding. Whatever it was, Exxos felt sure he could help them destroy it . . . or at least he and his robots could survive until the Shana Rei themselves were destroyed. If the tides of battle shifted, maybe the robots would find a way to ally themselves with this powerful new force. Exxos would keep his plans flexible.

The Shana Rei were chaos incarnate, violent but disorganized, and could not develop long-term plans. Exxos, though, could create much more intricate schemes, look at an overall strategy. He had convinced the Shana Rei to fear, or at least respect, the robots. While drifting in the black void, Exxos had proposed grand schemes, extolling how his robots could assist the shadow creatures in obliterating life. He made up more extravagant lies.

And the Shana Rei believed him, for now.

When their initial annihilation was finished, the robot ships landed in the smoking ruins of the research camp. Exxos and his comrades filed out, scuttling forward on clusters of fingerlike legs. They inspected the charred bodies of the human colonists and used metallic pincers to tear apart a few who still groaned and tried to crawl away. Exxos declared the settlement lifeless before he and his robots moved toward the abandoned Klikiss city to finish their work.

A thick briarpatch of Whistler cactus had grown up around the base of the ruins, and the hollow thorny growths moaned and hummed, as if the smoking devastation had changed their tune. When the robots set fire to the Whistler grove, the roaring flames and rising heat made the fluting sounds even more shrill. The Shana Rei seemed even more pleased when the Whistlers fell silent.

Exxos and his companions entered the ruined city. Millennia ago, when the Klikiss had created their sophisticated robots, they gave them personalities, emotions; they also designed the robots to feel pain, weakness, and defeat—simply so the malicious Klikiss could torment them. How could the insect race have been surprised when their own robots turned on them?

Now, when Exxos came upon the numerous mummified bodies left behind in the final swarming, the black robots remembered the awful tortures that had been inflicted upon them. Unified in their rage, they fell upon the Klikiss corpses and tore them to pieces with snapping pincer claws.

The violence did little to salve their hatred, and the mutilation seemed petty when compared with the grand cosmic plans of the Shana Rei to eradicate all sentient life. Exxos was pleased nevertheless. After destroying the Klikiss towers, the black robots flew away into the greasy smoke that rose from the Whistler grove and the blackened human settlement.

The ships returned to the simmering shadow cloud and rejoined the enormous hex ships, which withdrew into the swirling nebula. As the Shana Rei erased their newly manifested ships from existence, uncreating the raw matter, their own pain decreased.

When the shadow cloud departed from Eljiid, it left a very quiet place in its wake.

SEVENTY-EIGHT

OSIRA'H

Even though Osira'h and her siblings could not feel the same affinity with the worldforest as a green priest did, they knew their mother took great solace among the trees. Because Nira longed to help poor Gale'nh, she asked him to meet her in the lush greenhouse on top of the Prism Palace. She wanted to see if the verdani could help.

Osira'h accompanied her brother, leading him up the glowing corridors to the rooftop. Gale'nh seemed so empty and fragile, as if the depths of the shadow remained inside him. Osira'h shared her own thoughts with her brother, whatever energy she could dredge up from her mind, but Gale'nh's close connection with his halfbreed siblings had been damaged. Nevertheless, alone he had found an inner strength, a way of propping himself up so that he could move through the days.

The grove of tall worldtrees in the rooftop garden stood invigorated by the seven Ildiran suns. The treelings, planted there many years ago, now served as the point of contact for green priests with the rest of the Spiral Arm. The worldtree fronds whispered together.

Nira waited for them by the trees, her skin a bright, rich green. She smiled, but Osira'h could see the concern hidden just beneath the expression. Her fingertips touched the gold-scaled bark of the nearest tree. Nira closed her eyes briefly and let her thoughts flow into the verdani mind, then she sighed and reached out to take Gale'nh's hand, drawing him close, as if completing a circuit.

"I will help you in any way I can," she said.

Gale'nh held her hand, but remained unmoved, clearly feeling nothing from the green priest's contact. "If I knew a way you could help, Mother, I would accept it." He released her grip, ran his own hand over the trunk of the tree, but he didn't seem to find what he was looking for.

Osira'h took her brother's hand and grasped her mother's, trying harder. As she concentrated, she did feel the innate power of the worldtrees, a presence that connected the vast forest across the entire Spiral Arm.

"Sometimes we can share strength," Gale'nh said, "and sometimes we're all alone. I was there all alone aboard the *Kolpraxa*. My entire crew included hundreds of Ildirans woven together with their *thism*— but that didn't give them enough strength to stand against the shadow cloud."

His entire body shuddered. Osira'h squeezed his hand harder. Nira's eyes widened as if she caught a hint of what he was seeing inside his mind.

"The blackness didn't understand us either," Gale'nh continued, as if the memories were growing sharper in his mind. "It engulfed us, devoured us—and found all of my crew wanting. I watched Rememberer Ko'sh standing in terror, shouting that it was the Shana Rei. He raised his fist, howled for them to go back to the void—and then he disappeared. Uncreated." His voice hitched. "I used everything I had, gathering those closest to me. I tried to protect them, tried to hold on to them, but I felt them fade, as if they were bled down to nothing." He blinked at Nira. "I want to say that I was stronger than the others, Mother . . . but I think I was just different. I could feel the *thism* being torn up all around me. The mental threads snapped. There was nothing I could do." He hung his head.

"You survived," Nira said. "You came back to us. You're still here."

Osira'h added her encouragement as well. "You're the only one who has touched the Shana Rei. You'll remember something. You know something."

Gale'nh shook his head. "What if I brought back some residue with me? When Rememberer Ko'sh told the stories, I thought he was just trying to frighten my crew, but maybe he wanted to prepare them for what was out there. He couldn't prepare them enough."

Neither Osira'h nor Nira had an answer for him.

"While I was alone in the dark on the *Kolpraxa,* swallowed up by that suffocating nothingness, I remembered the planet Orryx and Tal Bria'nh." He turned his reddened gaze to his sister. "Now I know the story is true."

"Orryx?" Nira asked.

Osira'h said, "It was the first Ildiran planet to succumb to the Shana Rei, ages ago, a fertile place with a strong population, but the Shana Rei spread out from dark nebulae and covered the entire planet with a black shroud that absorbed all light. When Mage-Imperator Xiba'h sensed Orryx being engulfed, he rushed a septa of warliners to fight for them."

Gale'nh interrupted his sister's story. "They vanished into the blackness."

"The Mage-Imperator commanded his engineers and scientists to develop new weapons. A brave military commander named Tal Bria'nh rushed to Orryx with even more warliners and a hundred new sun bombs, which produced as much purifying brightness as a star. They burned the Shana Rei like acid, searing away the black shroud that surrounded the planet, but even the light from a hundred sun bombs eventually dwindled. The Shana Rei attacked again. They swallowed up Tal Bria'nh's entire cohort, painted the whole world black.

"When more Ildiran ships arrived, they found all the warliners wrapped in cocoons of shadow. Tal Bria'nh and his brave crew were literally smothered in darkness."

"Like the *Kolpraxa*," Nira whispered.

Gale'nh said, "I can imagine their last moments, Tal Bria'nh alone on the command nucleus, suffocating in the dark. That was all I could think of as I drifted and waited. How long did he survive before his own soulfire was extinguished?"

Nira held on to the worldtree, closing her eyes, listening to Gale'nh speak and moving her lips as she repeated his words into the verdani network. "I'm so sorry. I wish I could have been there to help you."

Gale'nh hardened. "No, Mother. No one should have been there. I encountered the Shana Rei, I lost my crew. I lost a fundamental part of myself, and I can't even remember it." Gale'nh's eyes widened, and he turned abruptly to her. "Wait . . ." He let the word trail off.

Osira'h pressed closer. "Did you remember something?"

The worldtrees stirred, their fronds rustling.

Gale'nh seemed surprised by what he had just realized. "The Shana Rei came back, not because they wanted war, not because they wish to attack us." He shook his head as if trying to grasp an intangible thing just beyond his reach. "The Shana Rei are *afraid*."

SEVENTY-NINE

TOM ROM

After purchasing medical records of the Ildiran genetic misfits on Kuivahr, Tom Rom stopped at the Ulio transfer station to stock up on supplies and refill his ship's expanded tanks with stardrive fuel.

When he finished at Ulio, his funds were depleted, but he didn't have to worry about money, and Zoe Alakis never begrudged a single credit he spent. Nevertheless, he would have to go to the trouble of obtaining more prisdiamonds. He set course for Vaconda.

He knew his ship inside and out. The vessel had been built to his specifications, modified, reinforced, and expanded over the years. It had emergency fuel reserves, triple backups of computerized navigation systems, spare parts, and a separate self-contained quarantine laboratory with its own generator systems and independent in-system engines; the quarantine chamber could be used as an evacuation pod under extreme circumstances. Tom Rom did not require luxuries, but he needed the room and facilities to do his work.

He was a self-sufficient man who spent much of his time imagining how things could go wrong and preparing for the eventuality. Tom Rom was not paranoid; he was diligent and reliable.

During the flight, he noted some anomalous flickers on his long-range scans, but he found nothing, so he recalibrated the sensors.

As he orbited Vaconda, the continents looked pale and ghostly, covered with lichentree forests, tall spiky growths of lavender and white. According to legal Hansa paperwork, which had been grandfathered into Confederation rules, the forest watchstation on Vaconda belonged entirely to Zoe Alakis. He supposed that on other parts of the continent there could be outlaws or squatters. Nobody cared. The planet was basically uninhabited.

More than twenty years ago, he had incinerated a swath of forest, per Zoe's request. Together, they let the fires rage uncontrollably until nature itself shut down the blaze, but in only a few years, the fecund jungle had subsumed the area, erasing any remaining scar. Now there was no hint of the watchstation where Zoe and her father had made their home for so long.

Even without familiar landmarks, Tom Rom knew the exact location. In the years since, he had returned here often to retrieve prisdiamonds, and had deposited tremendous fortunes in numerous planetary banks in Zoe's name.

When she decided that her goal in life was to create a disease library and research installation, Tom Rom had set aside all the funds she could possibly need. Following in her father's footsteps, she offered to partner with other research teams, join her wealth to major facilities, but they took her investment, put her name on a new research wing, and then politely—then less politely—told her to go away and let "professionals" handle the important matters.

They viewed Zoe as a backward, socially maladjusted girl who had grown up on a wilderness planet, little different from a feral child. She was innocent of commercial and academic politics, accepted promises at their face value (Tom Rom was her only example of a man who was true to his word), and she did not fit in well among them. She funded huge projects that were swallowed up in bureaucracies and regulations, with results lost in delays or obscurity. Other people took the fruits of her teams' research and called it proprietary information that became lost in a deep gravity well of "development" and "profitability assessments." When she tried to take the discoveries she had funded, they shut her out, ousted her from their boards, but graciously kept her name on the research wing she had built.

Afterward, Zoe abandoned all thoughts of kindness and cooperation. She decided to do it herself, her own way, with all results under her control.

In preparing to build Pergamus on her own terms, she came to regret her impetuous decision to burn down the forest watchtower station along with all records and research her father had compiled during his years on Vaconda. When Zoe poured out her feelings of guilt over destroying her father's work, Tom Rom had stared at her,

his expression flat. Finally, he admitted that out of a sense of obligation to Adam, he had backed up her father's data, preserving it despite her instructions. She had wept, then thrown her arms around
him. Tom Rom could not recall ever having been so moved.

Zoe spared no expense in setting up her complete private facility on
Pergamus—and even that depleted only a small fraction of her wealth.
She wanted it, and Tom Rom made it happen. He arranged to build
the domed research facilities and orbital research stations for her. Zoe
tracked down the best scientists in a variety of fields—medicine, biochemistry, genetics—and sent Tom Rom to approach them discreetly.

Her first order of business, of course, had been to develop a cure for
Heidegger's Syndrome. It felt like a twist of the knife when the cure did
not even prove to be difficult, once researchers applied resources and
time to the problem. If only someone had been able to do that for her
father . . .

While she lived, her work would be her own obsession, her own
masterpiece. She agreed to share all her results after her eventual death,
not because she was generous, but because she didn't care what happened afterward. She had no interest in fame, or history, or making
any mark. She didn't have to explain her priorities to anyone.

Now, as Tom Rom descended through Vaconda's atmosphere, he
caught a strange echo on his sensor map, but lost the flicker again
when he reached the lichentree forests.

The thick spiky treetops did not mesh into a solid canopy, and the
forest floor was too dense and cluttered for him to land his ship there.
Rather, he dropped a pontoon tarpaulin that self-inflated and expanded, anchoring itself to the lichentrees. This gave his ship a tough
temporary spot to land.

Settling down on the suspended tarpaulin, the craft swayed, then
stabilized. He collected specimen cases and extraction tools, filled the
fuel tank in his torch gun for clearing underbrush. Wearing a head-
lamp and two shoulder-mounted lamps to penetrate the murk, he
strapped everything to his back, emerged from the hatch, and looked
around the pale and silent forest. After activating the locator beacon
on his ship, he strung his cables and rappelled down the hollow-
sounding trunk of a lichentree all the way to the forest floor.

The lower levels were lit by ghostly sunlight filtered through a mist of fine spores. The ground was a chaos of deadfall. Large-eyed salamanders scuttled away, leaving faint trails of phosphorescent slime behind. Mushroom globules jittered and wobbled as if in secret laughter as Tom Rom crashed past.

The lichentree forest seemed to be closing in around him, but his locator gave him his bearings. Down here in the gloom, everything looked the same, but he knew where he was going.

He unshouldered his torch gun and began blasting. A large blue slime mold tried to slump away, shrugging and rolling at glacial speed. Tom Rom played bright flames over the area, igniting the lichentree deadfall and the squirming mosses. He continued to focus the torch, burning the vegetation, then burning the ash. The heat itself activated the prisdiamonds, which made them easier to find.

Putting on a breather mask and thick gloves, he cleared away the powdery residue to reveal sparkling clusters like geological ice crystals bursting out of the rocks. He struck them with a rock hammer, snapped off the valuable gems, and scooped up the glittery debris until he had filled his satchel.

The torch gun's fuel chamber was empty, and Tom Rom discarded it, not wanting to bother carrying it back up to the treetops. Tired and sweaty, he stripped off his heavy protective gear and dropped it on the ground so he could make good time back to the ship. He followed the signal from his locator.

When he reached the rope at the base of the tall lichentree, he could see the bright fabric of his pontoon tarpaulin high above and the shadow of his waiting ship. He secured his satchel of prisdiamonds, clipped onto the rope, and activated the climber, which scrolled him back up to the treetops.

Reaching the spore-hazed daylight above, he blinked in disoriented surprise. Another ship had landed adjacent to his own vessel. It was a battered, disreputable-looking craft without any markings. Tom Rom reached for his torch gun, but he had left it down on the forest floor.

Four men in ragged jumpsuits were waiting for him, two had Roamer clan markings that had been scuffed and covered. He did not recognize the men. He did recognize their type. They might well be Roamers but they were definitely outcasts, better labeled as pirates.

The men crossed a metal gangplank from their own ship to his pontoon tarpaulin.

"See? Told you he'd come back," said a thin man with sideburns so long he clearly had poor judgment in shaving.

"And I told you it was better just to wait here than to go looking for him," said a second man.

All four withdrew hand jazers.

Tom Rom regarded them. "I think I saw you at Ulio. You must have gotten lost on your way here."

"No, we followed you just fine," said the man with the sideburns.

"I should be more careful, then."

The men chuckled and kept the weapons trained on him. "Yes, you probably should."

Tom Rom did not like to feel so helpless. He could fight, but he had no weapons. They would cut him down.

"Let's just see what he's got in that case," said the quietest man, who seemed to be the leader. He had a head of thick red hair combed back away from his forehead. He looked at Tom Rom. "We ransacked your ship, but didn't find much of value. So we figured there must be something more important here."

"Yeah," interjected the man with the sideburns. "Who ever goes to Vaconda?"

"Maybe *you* shouldn't have come here," Tom Rom said.

They relieved him of his case, and when they opened it to reveal the prisdiamonds, they nearly fell off the pontoon tarpaulin. "Prisdiamonds! Where the hell did he get those?"

"Obviously down there." The quiet leader pointed toward the forest floor.

"We could each buy two starships with this load," said Sideburns.

Probably three, Tom Rom thought, but he kept the comment to himself.

"This will be very satisfactory," said the leader. "Well worth the trip."

"We'll have to remember this place," said Sideburns. "We should just kill him now and get it over with." The other pirates muttered in halfhearted agreement.

Tom Rom looked at the quiet leader without blinking. "You've

already proved yourselves to be thieves, but not all thieves are mur-
derers."

The leader apparently wasn't. "Go inside his ship and wreck the
control panels, smash the engine conduits. He won't be going anywhere."

"You mean you're just stranding him here?" said Sideburns, as if
that were a more horrendous fate.

"I can survive," Tom Rom said in a quiet voice, stating a fact.

"Good enough, then," the leader said. He turned his comrades
loose inside Tom Rom's ship, where they destroyed the systems. When
they came out, their expressions were aglow with the satisfaction of
vandalism.

The quiet leader held the satchel of prisdiamonds, pleased with
the haul. "I assume there's more down there?"

Tom Rom didn't nod, but the answer was clear enough.

"We'll be back, maybe rescue you. If you survive that long."

"I'll survive," Tom Rom repeated.

Carrying the prisdiamonds, the four Roamer outcasts walked back
across the makeshift gangplank and pulled it up before climbing
aboard their battered vessel. Sideburns gave Tom Rom a taunting
look before sealing the hatch.

He didn't wait for the pirates to leave before ducking into his own
ship. With a fast glance, Tom Rom scanned the damage: a few smashed
power blocks, a peeled-off circuit film, a navigator control overlay,
cracked instrument plates, two shattered viewscreens. His engines
were quite durable, and he doubted they had sustained serious damage. The men had no organized sabotage plan, simply let loose with
random destruction. Good, that would be easier to fix.

As he heard the Roamer ship priming its engines to leave, Tom Rom
opened a locker, rummaged around, and withdrew a boomerang limpet. He'd never had occasion to use one before, but he came prepared.
It seemed simple enough.

He stepped back out onto the uncertain surface of the pontoon
tarpaulin and watched the battered pirate ship lift off. It accelerated
into the sky, curving south as it climbed above the tops of the lichentree forest.

Tom Rom gripped the curved handle of the boomerang limpet,

bent over to coil his muscles, and hurled it up into the air. It spun with a soft whistling sound, gathering speed until its motivators fired up. The limpet's sensors cast a wide net, then the device altered its trajectory, accelerated, and rose up to strike the bottom hull of the pirate ship. It clamped on to the metal plates and started its timer.

Tom Rom had set the countdown for forty seconds, which should allow the ship to fly high enough and far enough away that he wouldn't be bombarded with debris.

He counted silently, then watched a blossom of flames and shrapnel expand outward as the boomerang limpet detonated. Wreckage rained down into the pale white treetops, far from his position.

Tom Rom went back inside his ship to start the repairs. He knew how to jury-rig most of the systems, and he had spare parts and replacement circuitry for the vital components. He was able to tap into the independent propulsion system linked to the quarantine chamber/lifepod, which would give him the boost he needed. He could implement the rest of the repairs once he got back to Pergamus. Despite the inconvenience, he never had any doubt that he would make it.

The repairs took him three days.

Before flying away from Vaconda again, though, he had to return to the forest floor, using his spare protective suit. After so much trouble, he wasn't about to leave without a load of prisdiamonds.

EIGHTY

AELIN

Full of wonder, Aelin arrived with Iswander at the ekti-extraction yard that accompanied the moving bloater cluster, and the industrialist gave him a full tour of the operations. Aelin felt overwhelmed with the sights and experiences.

"You cannot reveal anything about our operations, green priest," Iswander cautioned him for the third time, "but it's important for you to understand the full scope of what we're doing here."

Aelin recognized that the man was showing a remarkable amount of trust in him. While he understood the necessity for keeping secrets from Iswander's competitors, he found it disorienting to withhold thoughts and impressions from the worldforest network, acting only as a passive observer. After growing up in the wide-open worldforest, he was not well practiced in keeping secrets, but he kept his word to Lee Iswander.

He knew his brother must be in a similar situation on the mysterious Onthos city. Shelud had delivered reports of the vanished aliens and the interesting discoveries aboard the derelict, which the worldforest had translated, but he had given no details about the location of the new clan Reeves home of Okiah.

Neither brother could share his wondrous and amazing secrets, but Aelin and Shelud could share their excitement, if nothing else. Though they had disagreed in philosophy, they both found themselves in similar situations. Aelin realized that they might be closer than he expected.

Out here at the extraction field, bloaters drifted along in empty space, with a clear trajectory toward the nearest star, which was only a brighter spot in the forest of twinkling stars. The bloater cluster had no obvious means of propulsion, but it was accelerating.

Aelin stared out at the mysterious nodules floating together. Even the verdani knew nothing about them; he had searched the entire worldforest database, while being careful not to reveal where he was or what he knew.

As he watched the drifting bloaters, Aelin could sense something there, a distant slumbering force, a brooding . . . *presence*. No one believed those gas bags were actually alive, but they did not seem to be a mere natural phenomenon either. Iswander, who considered them nothing more than space plankton, had promised that as soon as his operations were stabilized and running smoothly, he would bring in scientific teams for a full analysis, but so far he concentrated on the extraction. There would be time enough for the rest later.

When returning from Theroc, Iswander brought in six more tanker ships, which he used to drain raw ekti-X from the bloaters. Alec Pannebaker spent much of his time hauling away the empty, deflated husks, towing them from the rest of the cluster so they wouldn't get in the way. Even after all the ambitious extraction efforts, many hundreds of bloaters remained, crowded close in a great drifting cloud.

After the phenomenal success of the first ekti-extraction operations, Lee Iswander established a pilot industrial station in a second bloater cluster that Elisa Enturi had located. More and more workers arrived weekly for their isolated job assignments. And they produced more and more stardrive fuel.

Aelin often remained with Lee Iswander in the admin module, trying to learn the operations. "If this cluster still has so much ekti, why was it necessary to set up a second harvesting field?"

Iswander was patient with him, explaining the business, as if Aelin were still that bright-eyed young acolyte with a broken leg. "A secondary source of ekti-X at a different part of the Spiral Arm eases our distribution bottleneck. And," he added with just a small smile, "when our delivery ships originate from two different points, it's more difficult to backtrack our source. That should let us keep our secrets longer."

Iswander stretched his arms. "I have to take advantage of this boom and bank my fortune while I can. It's such a simple operation, sometimes I think this is too good to be true. As soon as bloaters are discovered elsewhere—and somebody *will* stumble upon a cluster—then anyone can harvest ekti-X. So much for our edge on the market. If there's such a glut, our operations might not be worthwhile anymore." He paused. "I want to keep this secret long enough to rebuild my family name, and make a future for Arden."

As a green priest, Aelin had never bothered to consider those nuances before. He realized that Iswander had made the last comment for his son to hear, since Arden had appeared at the hatch of the admin module. The young man cast a frown toward the green priest. "Then today's lesson should be about the ekti business, not history and legends and culture—that's all Aelin wants to talk about."

Because he had few actual duties in the bloater refinery yard, Aelin also tutored Iswander's son. He was not trained as a teacher, nor had he planned a curriculum, but whenever he needed information for a lesson, he used his treeling to tap into the verdani mind.

Iswander chuckled. "That sounds exactly like my own complaints when I was your age! Trust me, son, it's important. You need a background and a perspective on where things come from."

"But those stories are so old they don't mean anything," Arden said.

Iswander shook his head and explained; Aelin couldn't have made the argument better. "It's the foundation of what we do—you need to understand that the whole basis of the ekti market is predicated on the Ildiran stardrive. Humans didn't invent it. Without the gift of the stardrive, we would still be crawling across the Spiral Arm in slow generation ships. And while the Hansa was expanding their colonies, the Roamer clans earned great power by taking over cloud-harvesting operations from the Ildirans, running their old skymines, and then building new ones of their own." He frowned at Arden. "It caused quite a bit of friction, and that's one reason that the Roamers were looked on with skepticism—or jealousy—by the rest of the Hansa. It's why we were made into scapegoats during the Elemental War."

The young man was not satisfied. "That still doesn't help."

Aelin added, "When you're a businessman, Arden, you'll be dealing with other people who have the same old scars, possibly the same prejudices. You have to understand those resentments if you're going to be a successful negotiator."

Iswander said, "You are a part of history right now, son. Our ekti-X will change civilization in the Spiral Arm. At some future date, there will be another young man complaining about why he has to take history lessons and learn about how Arden Iswander was part of the first bloater operations."

That seemed to convince the young man at last. Arden tugged the green priest's elbow. "Let's get on with it then. One hour, right?"

"Two hours," Aelin said.

The boy started to argue. Suddenly the green priest felt a violent shiver, as if static electricity had flickered through him. He turned to see a pattern of sparkles cascade through the bloaters. One nodule lit up, then another, and another. The flashes were not connected, but they did seem to be in sequence somehow, like a signal. Each impulse lasted only a fraction of a second.

The harvesting operations quickly went into shutdown and response mode. After only a few seconds, the flashes died away again, and the bloaters were dim and silent again, grayish green islands that floated nowhere.

Pannebaker sent a signal to the admin module. "A few disruptions, Chief, but no overloads. The extra shielding helped. We'll run diagnostics to determine any damage, but I think we're set."

Iswander let out a sigh. "Excellent." He turned to the green priest. "We have to be careful. The bloaters are volatile, potentially explosive, as my deputy discovered during her first encounter. We've instituted rather extreme safety measures, and there's a full evacuation protocol I can engage, in case of an emergency. But those flashes . . ."

The flash storms came at intermittent times, widely separated. Sometimes they were faint, while other times the dazzling surges damaged the electronics until Iswander's people had added extra shielding. This was the first such display Aelin had seen from so close. "I wonder what it means."

"Nothing to worry about. Just an interesting phenomenon. Now, shouldn't you get to your duties teaching my son?"

They went into an unoccupied boardroom, and Aelin set his potted treeling across from the boy, ready to tap into the worldforest.

Using telink, he touched the verdani mind and accessed information and news, while Arden waited, fidgeting.

Within moments, he received a devastating report from the trees: Shelud and all the members of clan Reeves aboard their alien space city had been exposed to a mysterious plague.

EIGHTY-ONE

SHELUD

Aboard the ghost-filled Onthos city, more and more people fell victim to the strange plague. Clan Reeves was devastated—most were sick now. Nausea and fever consumed them; dark discolorations appeared on their skin from hemorrhaged blood vessels. Dale quarantined himself with Sendra and their two boys, and their condition grew progressively worse.

The Retroamer families clung to one another, initially putting the sick ones into isolation chambers, but there was no escaping infection in the enclosed city. The somewhat healthy ones struggled to remain strong so they could care for the ill. They wore environment suits and specialized survival breathers. Still the disease got through.

Connected to the verdani, Shelud worked nonstop to translate the log entries left behind by the dying Onthos. Although his discoveries in the Onthos records gave the doctors ideas of treatments to try, nothing worked. Nevertheless, he shared the information through the telink network so all green priests could know that forgotten history.

Olaf Reeves imposed extreme measures to prevent the spread of the plague, but he knew full well that the virus saturated the city of Okiah, and the incubation period was long enough that everyone aboard had surely been exposed. The disease that had been dormant and harmless in the Klikiss race had infected the Onthos with a mortality rate of one hundred percent.

Three-quarters of the clan's members already showed symptoms. "And those are just the ones who'll admit it," Olaf said to Shelud in the main hub office. He eyed the green priest up and down. "Do you feel any ill effects?"

"Possibly. Nausea, exhaustion . . . but that could be just from the tension."

"That's what I keep telling myself, too," said the clan leader. "But it doesn't sound convincing."

A delegation of six Roamer men and women barged in to see Olaf; they all looked frightened but otherwise healthy. "If we stay here, we'll all catch it. Our medicines don't work," said a man named Reese Carlin. "*We're* healthy. Let us take our ships and fly away from here, bring back medical teams, experimental treatments, whatever we need. We've stayed bottled up here for too long. We need to get out of Okiah before it's too late."

"Not a good idea," Olaf said. "If you leave here, that plague will spread to an inhabited planet."

"We don't have any other choice!" said a woman, Indira Reeves, whose husband was a cousin of Dale's. Her husband had fallen sick and gone into quarantine, but Indira remained outside.

Olaf looked angry. "You're right—we *don't* have a choice. If this is a deadly plague, and we've all got it, you can't go spreading the disease everywhere. At least it's contained here. I won't turn you loose out in the Spiral Arm."

"We'll be careful, Olaf," Carlin insisted.

"No. We wait for now—that's my decision."

"Wait? For what?" said a third man. Shelud didn't know his name, though he had been trying to memorize every member of the clan Reeves exodus.

"We wait until we recover. That'll show we're strong enough to fight this disease. And if we all die, then that proves how deadly it is."

The delegation left the hub office, trembling with anger and fear.

As soon as they departed, Olaf hammered on the desk communications system. He adjusted to a specific frequency. "Attention, compies. This is Olaf Reeves transmitting directly to you with a priority command. Go to every ship that's docked to this city—seventeen vessels linked to hatches and in landing bays. Open the hangar bays, use autopilots, and dump those ships out into space—set them adrift. I don't want anyone able to fly away and cause trouble. Okiah must be quarantined."

The six clan Reeves compies acknowledged and trudged off to follow the instructions.

Shelud was concerned. "Won't that cut us off, sir? If we do recover from the plague, we'll never be able to get away."

Olaf Reeves clenched his hands together. "That's a trivial problem compared to what we're facing now. We know how to be self-sufficient, and we can find a way to round them up if necessary—when the time comes. Or you could send word through the worldforest, if it comes to that." He shook his head. "Never much liked compies, but now I wish I had a dozen more. Our people can't do their work, and soon we won't have enough personnel even to keep life support functioning. Thank the Guiding Star most of it's automated."

Olaf coughed and covered his mouth, then his eyes flew open in alarm. He rubbed his neck. "Just a tickle in my throat."

Shelud didn't argue with him.

"And where's my son? Is he getting stronger?"

"Weaker, I think. Dale's incapacitated. I visited him yesterday in the quarantine chambers."

Olaf Reeves scanned down at the list of names again. "Eighty percent of my people." He shook his head. "Probably more."

Shelud was sure it would be more.

Dale's son Scott was the first to die. Shock waves rippled through the space city, and the frightened Retroamers tried to make excuses. He was just a boy. Perhaps his immunity was lower than others, maybe he was weaker. They told themselves that one death didn't necessarily mean the Onthos plague would be fatal in all cases—but they didn't manage to convince themselves.

Within three days, every member of the indignant delegation that had wanted to leave Okiah on their ships showed signs of the plague. The later the onset of the disease, the more severe the symptoms.

Then Dale Reeves died. Soon people didn't have time to mourn or hold formal funerals as the death toll mounted.

Olaf followed Shelud into the quarantine section—a quarantine that meant nothing anymore—and sank to his knees beside the bunk where Dale lay dead, little Scott wrapped in a sheet beside him. Sendra and Jamie were both so sick they seemed unaware of what had happened.

Olaf let out explosive sobs and then collapsed. When Shelud helped him back to his feet, he realized that the burly clan leader was burning with fever.

"We can't let this get out," Olaf said. "The Onthos called this a plague city. They marked it, but we didn't understand the message. We unleashed the disease on ourselves, and it's our job to make damn sure the plague doesn't spread farther. If this gets out into the Confederation . . ." He grasped the green priest by the arm. "Use your telink. Inform them where we are and what's happened. Then tell them to stay away from Okiah."

"Even if we warn them away, do you think they'll really leave this city isolated forever?" Shelud asked. He remembered all of the researchers and xeno-archaeologists who had demanded access.

"Probably not." The bearded man's shoulders slumped. "I better find a more definite means to keep them away." Olaf shuddered violently and had to rest against his son's deathbed before he could move on again. When Shelud hesitated, the clan leader glared at him. "Go, green priest! Find your treeling."

When Shelud reached his quarters, he grasped the small tree with trembling fingers, plunged into telink, and sent his message throughout the verdani network. He poured out his thoughts with enough urgency that every green priest would notice. They already had his description of the plague, but now they would know how it spread like wildfire—and how deadly it was.

"Stay away from this derelict city," he said. "We will all be dead before any help can arrive . . . not that there can be any help. If you come here, you will die."

He broke the connection with the worldforest mind. As his hands trembled violently, his stomach clenched, and he suddenly became sick on the floor of his quarters. He caught his breath, inhaling and exhaling; he touched his forehead, feeling the sweat there. His fever was already high, and it was only a matter of time. Shelud had been aware of that. He didn't know how much longer he could last.

He took a long time to compose himself and focus his mind so that stray terrors would not leak into his telink thoughts. When he touched the treeling again, he was determined and strong, and he sought out the presence of his brother Aelin.

Yes, they would have a good conversation.

EIGHTY-TWO

NIRA

Though the seven suns of Ildira created an entirely different calendar, Nira kept track of her own birthday, as recorded by the central Confederation calendar on Theroc. She was now forty-nine, and she felt vibrant and rejuvenated by her frequent contact with the worldforest mind. Years ago, Nira had been abused as a breeding slave and prisoner on Dobro, but now with Jora'h at her side, she was strong.

As consort of the Mage-Imperator, she had all that she wanted and felt no particular need for gifts or feasts on her birthday, but Jora'h had learned that it was tradition for humans to commemorate the anniversary of their birth. And so he commanded an annual celebration for Nira in the city of Mijistra.

When the procession emerged from the Prism Palace, Nira walked alongside Jora'h as part of the large procession, wearing an outfit of the finest imported Theron feathers, beetle carapaces, and iridescent moth wings.

Fawned over by attenders and noble functionaries, the Mage-Imperator wore fantastic robes as well, and his chrysalis chair was festooned with reflective streamers. This was one of the rare times when Jora'h allowed attenders to carry him in the chair.

The first time they had celebrated her birthday, Jora'h suggested that a special chair be built so Nira could be carried beside him, but the uproar had been so extreme that he decided against it. The kiths were already uneasy about all the changes the Mage-Imperator had imposed in the aftermath of the Elemental War.

Over thousands of years of history, Ildiran tradition held that a Mage-Imperator was supposed to be alone, the sole focal point of the *thism*. In his years as Prime Designate, Jora'h had taken countless lovers to spread his bloodline among the Ildiran kiths. People had been startled when he took the young green priest as his exotic lover, and when they fell in love, some Ildirans found it even more shocking than the reappearance of hydrogues after ten thousand years. Jora'h's people simply did not know how to react to the human woman at his side, when no previous Mage-Imperator had ever kept even an Ildiran female as his consort.

But Jora'h did love her, and he had put his foot down, quieting the whisperers and social unrest, insisting that his people understand and accept change. As Mage-Imperator, he *was* the Ildiran race.

Nevertheless, Nira was content to walk at his side, while his chrysalis chair was carried by attenders, so everyone in Mijistra could see her acknowledging his importance. When Jora'h looked as if he might continue to press the issue, Nira had smiled, touched his arm, and said, "It's my birthday celebration, and by our custom I'm allowed to ask for and receive gifts. This is the gift I ask of you—don't disturb your people further."

And so today, as she had done every year for nineteen years, Nira walked beside him with bright sunlight reflecting from the shimmering insect scales. Two rounded condorfly wings were mounted to her back; Nira thought the wings made her look like a fairy princess, which she remembered from the stories she had read aloud to the worldtrees when she was just a green priest acolyte. . . .

Next in the procession, behind the chrysalis chair, walked Osira'h, Rod'h, and a fragile but brave Gale'nh who proudly wore his Solar Navy uniform, though his bleached skin and hair still made him look startlingly out of place. Murcc'n accompanied them, dressed in the special armor and uniform of the Mage-Imperator's personal guard, as she had requested. Nira had never seen her youngest halfbreed daughter look happier than when she donned the same outfit and weapons as Yazra'h, who walked on the other side of the chrysalis chair.

Prime Designate Daro'h, the Mage-Imperator's heir, walked near his father. Like Jora'h, Daro'h had spent years with breeding advisers who kept a catalog of his numerous offspring. As the procession passed into the city, he glanced over at Jora'h, pleased to see how many Ildirans had come out. He was overjoyed to point out many of his children scattered in the crowds. Daro'h did not hide the waxy burn scars on his face, which remained as an indelible reminder of when the faeros had nearly killed him.

Crystalline buildings towered all around them, and crowds of Ildirans gathered. Nira saw a panoply of faces and body types, numerous kiths with different faces and builds and colorations, yet the same racial identity. Thanks to their *thism* connection, Ildirans had a commonality she couldn't feel, which left her an outsider, no matter how long she lived among them, although she could comprehend a similar thing with her green priest network.

Jora'h normally basked in the telepathic tapestry of his people, but today he seemed uneasy in his chrysalis chair. He glanced around as the spectators crowded close. Although this celebration was supposedly for Nira's birthday, most Ildirans loved any festival in which their Mage-Imperator appeared among them. He waved to the crowds, as did Nira. She listened to the murmur of so many voices, so many people. It droned and throbbed around her.

Suddenly an Ildiran man sprang out of the crowd, a noble kithman dressed in unremarkable clothes. She had glanced at him, seen a face that appeared normal and placid, but now it was transformed into a twisted expression of hatred and revulsion. He produced a curved crystalline dagger, shoved other spectators aside, and bounded toward Nira, shouting, "To keep the Ildiran race pure!"

She tried to duck as the man slashed with his dagger. He caught one of the fragile condorfly wings on her back, shattering the sapphire membrane. Someone screamed. Two attenders lost their hold on the chrysalis chair, and Jora'h's palanquin lurched.

Nira tore herself free and spun to face her attacker. The man raised his dagger to come at her again.

His mouth spewed blood as Yazra'h thrust her crystal-tipped katana through his back. Yanking her ceremonial spear free, she stabbed him again and drove the man to the ground, where he gurgled and died. Yazra'h held up her bloody weapon, her eyes flashing, taking one step closer to Nira in an instinctive protective move.

Nira gasped. "Why—?"

A howling woman from the artist kith bounded forward holding a cutting tool and a sharp-ended cudgel. She flailed both, trying to reach Nira as she screamed, "You corrupt the *thism*!"

Yazra'h stood to defend Nira, but Muree'n lunged forward to intercept the artist. Without hesitation, she swept her katana sideways and neatly decapitated the second would-be assassin.

A third person, a burly worker kithman, charged forward like a bull. He held a metal-tipped mallet, which he swung from side to side. The mallet struck Muree'n hard on the shoulder, though her armor protected her from serious injury. She recoiled briefly from the pain, recovered herself in a flash. She and Yazra'h used their weapons to drive the worker kithman back from the procession, and then Yazra'h ran him through.

Muree'n looked around at the bodies, at the spilled blood, then up at Yazra'h. "That was my first kill."

Yazra'h stood close to her, raising her weapon again. "It may not be your last one today. We need to get the Mage-Imperator out of danger. All of you—back to the Prism Palace!"

Jora'h sprang out of his chrysalis chair and landed beside Prime Designate Daro'h. He was outraged. "Why are they trying to kill Nira? I felt an uneasiness in the *thism,* but nothing from those Ildirans."

The crowd was churning now, people gasping and screaming, some trying to flee—yet there also seemed to be an undertone of anger.

Though terrified, Nira grabbed Jora'h's arm. "Understand this later—we have to get to safety now."

Yazra'h and Muree'n began to herd Jora'h, Daro'h, and Nira away, leaving the toppled chrysalis chair behind in the road. Though disoriented, Gale'nh straightened. Helping their brother, Osira'h and Rod'h followed the group at a brisk trot as they retreated toward the path that led up to the Prism Palace.

Nira's heart pounded, but she couldn't ask questions now. Jora'h was already growling, "I will order an investigation. What caused this?"

As they hurried away, Nira looked back at the Ildirans who had been cheering them only moments before; they now appeared sinister, and she feared that another assassin would spring after them.

EIGHTY-THREE

ARITA

King Peter and Queen Estarra made brief formal farewell speeches before Reyn's much-anticipated trip. Arita made a point of looking cheerful and excited, to show good optimism for his sake. Reyn's glance met hers, and they both understood. She silently, but fervently, wished him luck, and she held their farewell hug for an extra few seconds.

Queen Estarra gave her son a warm embrace, as did King Peter, and Reyn climbed aboard the Ildiran cutter accompanied by several Solar Navy officers and noble kithmen who had been dispatched by the Mage-Imperator to escort him. An entourage of Confederation ministers, traders, and protocol advisers also went along, supposedly to watch over the Prince, though he said he didn't need them. Arita shaded her eyes and watched as the colorful alien ship launched up through the open forest canopy.

After her brother was gone, Arita returned to her quarters and began gathering the equipment, supplies, and clothing she would need. Her own expedition would be much closer to home, but she was excited nevertheless. Thankfully, she didn't need a large crowd with her. She had so much to explore, so much to see and learn—by herself, in the distant, sparsely inhabited continent of the Wild.

Unlike Reyn, Arita managed to depart without ceremony. She took a small flyer and raced across the undulating canopy, rising high enough to dodge cumulus clouds, and then passing over the narrow sea to the shores of the Wild.

Being on the wilderness continent would fulfill a deep need within her, a mission she wished she could have undertaken as a *green priest,* but she would do it anyway. . . .

While she continued her studies in the Wild, she could survive on whatever the worldforest provided: berries, fruits, nuts, fungi, and edible insects. She could take care of herself. Water would be no problem. Shelter was everywhere.

Though she wanted to be alone for her studies, Arita chose an area not far from where Kennebar and his isolationist green priests had gone. Just in case. She was also interested in finding her reclusive aunt Sarein, whom she suspected was a kindred spirit.

Arita circled until she found a meadow broad enough to land. Everything around her was lush and unexplored, much like when the first colonists had landed from the generation ship *Caillié,* more than two hundred years ago. She had brought hundreds of sample cases, five types of imagers and DNA modelers, so she could keep accurate biological records of new species she catalogued. She might be a Princess, but in her heart she had always wanted to be a naturalist.

She could study fascinating flowers on one day, beetles another day, or maybe worms that tunneled in the deep forest mulch. She kept journals of climbing berry-vines, and leather-jawed predatory plants that could crunch through the thickest insect armor. Theroc was amazing, and she wondered if even the green priests felt the same sense of wonder as she did. To her, the Wild was like a huge, open book just waiting to be read.

After setting up camp, she was eager to start her project. She ventured into the forest, doing reconnaissance of her surroundings. The tapestry of surging life in the Wild seemed to intensify the force of the verdani. Her head ached, and she could hear echoes and whispers of thoughts that were not her own. They seemed to emanate from the millennia of the worldforest's experiences. But her sensitivity to the trees was just a mocking leftover from when the verdani had tested, rejected, and altered her without making her one of them. Arita stopped and listened. The voices remained just out of her mind's reach, just out of hearing.

Choosing the nearest worldtree, she pressed her body against the golden-scaled bark. She wrapped her slender arms around the immense trunk and closed her eyes, *willing* the trees to reconsider, begging them to let her in now, to accept her as a green priest after all.

But she only heard the sounds of ghosts. She went back to gathering specimens, now feeling a sadness instead of joy. . . .

The following day, while gathering interesting plants and insects, Arita sought out Kennebar's settlement. The green priests lived in the trees, and she heard them gathered up in the high fronds, reading to the worldforest, singing together.

Kennebar was the first to notice her. The others acknowledged her presence, but did not climb down to welcome her. "If you needed to speak with us," Kennebar called down, "you could have sent a message through any green priest."

Arita knew she sounded defensive. "I'm here for my own purposes, compiling an exhaustive catalog of species."

"Oh," Kennebar said. "The worldforest is aware of all species. Any green priest can access that information. Is there something in particular you need to know?" He seemed to think that if he answered her questions, she would leave.

"Other humans don't have that information," she said. "I mean to compile a catalog to help naturalists across the Spiral Arm."

"Oh," Kennebar said again. "Then we won't disturb you at your work. We have our own tasks." The priests climbed higher in the fronds, out of her reach.

When the others were gone, though, Collin dropped down to the forest floor, grinning shyly at her. "It's nice here, but I miss you. Did you get my message?"

"Yes, but I would have rather said goodbye to you in person."

Collin looked away. "But it wasn't goodbye. You came here."

"I have a camp out by the meadow."

"We know. We could all see it through the worldtrees. We watched you land."

Arita should have known this. "Now that I'm here, you could help me find specimens—like we used to do."

"Maybe for a little while, but I have my duties to serve the trees."

Arita glanced up into the high trees where she could still see some of the isolationists. "And what exactly do you do to serve the worldforest?"

Her question surprised him, and he searched for an answer. "We came here to the Wild where we can better serve the trees, uninterrupted."

Arita sniffed. "How does that make sense? The worldforest thrived on Theroc for ten thousand years or more without any green priests."

"Others tended the worldforest in the past. Even before humans came here, the verdani weren't always alone." Collin just looked at her. "I can't explain it to you because you wouldn't understand."

The words stung.

He accompanied her through the trees, led her around thickets, and ducked under branches that seemed to ease aside for him while scratching Arita's skin. He led her directly to a cluster of wriggling condorfly larvae, then to a towering conical fungus whose rotting stench seemed to attract a particular species of green moth.

As they went along, Collin frequently brushed the trunk of a worldtree, as if to check in with his fellow green priests, afraid to be out of touch for too long. He sighed. "I wish you were a green priest, Arita."

"Because we can't be friends if I'm not? Other couples have done it." She still felt that he had abandoned her. They had been so close, had even shared a first kiss.

"Not just that. There's so much more. Even when I'm not touching the worldforest, I can hear the song of the trees. Words, knowledge, memories, legends, things I can't understand, but they're part of me anyway." His words were a breathless rush. "The verdani mind is everywhere. It's like being part of everything."

He did his best to describe it, pitying her, but his words only emphasized how deafeningly silent the worldforest was for her. Seeing her forlorn expression, Collin was embarrassed to have brought up the subject. "I should be going back to Kennebar. Can you find your way back to your camp?"

"Of course," she said a little too quickly.

Before bounding off, Collin called, "If you get into trouble, we'll know. The worldtrees are always watching you. Don't worry."

He left Arita with her specimens and the whole continent to explore. She got back to work.

EIGHTY-FOUR

PRINCE REYN

After the Ildiran cutter landed on a high tower platform of the Prism Palace, Prince Reyn emerged into the brightest sunlight he'd ever experienced. Until his eyes adjusted, his noble escort gave him a pair of thin filmgoggles. "Human visitors are often blinded by the dazzling beauty of Mijistra."

"Maybe it has to do with all those suns shining down," Reyn said, shading his eyes.

Located in the Horizon Cluster, Ildira was surrounded by many nearby stars, but the main suns in the sky were the system's orange K-1 primary, the nearby Qronha binary star, the Durris trinary system, and the blue supergiant Daym. Reyn understood the basic astronomy, but at the moment he had no great desire to locate all seven of the nearest suns in the sky. It was too bright.

Now the other members of the Confederation entourage stood blinking, looking about for their Ildiran counterparts so they could get to business.

A beautiful young woman came to greet him, singling him out. She had ethereal Ildiran features with a decidedly human caste. Her hair was pale and feathery; her eyes large, her smile genuine. Reyn's Ildiran entourage placed fists against chests in a gesture of respect for her. One of the dignitaries bent close to him. "This is Osira'h, daughter of Mage-Imperator Jora'h and his consort Nira."

He certainly knew who Osira'h was—she had fought the hydrogues at the end of the Elemental War when she was just a girl.

She extended her hand. "Prince Reynald of Theroc, I will be your liaison here. Since my mother was a green priest and my father an

Ildiran, maybe I can help you bridge the two cultures." She gave him a more personal smile. "I was looking for something interesting to do, and you seem interesting."

He realized he was blushing. "I'll try to be." And, yes, Osira'h was very interesting, too.

The Solar Navy officers, the noble advisers, guard kithmen, and the Confederation representatives were ready to accompany Prince Reyn into the Prism Palace, but Osira'h grabbed his arm. "You must have felt so crowded on that ship. Growing up on Theroc with its big open skies, you probably just want a little space. Follow me." She glanced at the others. "I will take care of him."

She led him at a brisk pace away from the entourage, who were surprised when she abandoned them. As they entered the tower halls, she said conspiratorially, "Ildirans don't like to be alone—you've probably noticed that already. Come, I can take you the back ways, and we'll encounter fewer people, if you'd like that?"

At the moment Reyn would have liked anything she suggested.

They passed many soldier kithmen, ferocious-looking guards with body armor and prominent weapons. Reyn frowned to see so much security. "I thought Ildira was a peaceful planet. Are these just ceremonial guards?"

Osira'h hesitated. "There was a recent assassination attempt, and no one can understand it. Some people tried to attack my mother during a public festival."

"Ildirans rising up to attack? What caused that?"

"No one knows—the assassins were like a silence in the *thism*. My mother would have come to meet you, but she's being kept under special guard. You will see her at the banquet."

Osira'h guided him along back corridors, through an empty sculpture exhibit, and up a winding spiral staircase to another tower of the Prism Palace where she led him to his guest quarters made of curved crystal adorned with colored lenses.

Regarding him with her large, strangely opalescent eyes, she said, "My inclination is to show you everything right away, drag you from tower to tower in the few hours before our banquet, and then tomorrow take you to all the planets in the Ildiran Empire." She let out a quick laugh. "Maybe I'm being overly ambitious."

He chuckled. "You are. I'm exhausted just hearing your plans."

"We'll have time," she said. "You look weary. You should rest."

Later, he followed Osira'h to the dining chamber where attender kith bustled about. Mage-Imperator Jora'h gave Reyn an effusive welcome, and Nira asked him about Theroc, even though she had visited recently for the funeral of Father Idriss. The rest of the Confederation entourage sat at a different table.

Her eyes sparkling, Osira'h took a seat beside him and explained the variety of colorful foods, fruits, meats, and confections (some of which were indistinguishable from the decorations). Ildiran musicians and singers performed an odd sort of atonal music with water-bubbling flutes; Reyn pretended to enjoy it. They both listened in rapt silence as a rememberer told a brief story from the Saga of Seven Suns.

His hosts did everything possible to make him feel welcome; nevertheless, Reyn felt a sense of uneasiness in the chamber, as if the Ildirans were subdued.

Osira'h introduced him to her brother Rod'h. Though he was a year younger than Osira'h, he seemed older, harder, and extremely serious. "There is an uneasy mood on Ildira," he said, "a dislike for outsiders . . . like a kind of shadow."

Osira'h flashed a quick glance at her brother, as if exchanging a secret warning, then she turned to Reyn. "We will protect you, don't worry."

He hadn't been worried about that at all, but now he reconsidered.

Yazra'h, a strong and feral-looking Ildiran woman with flowing hair, rose to her feet. "We have no results in our investigations yet from the incident at the procession, Liege. We spoke with the families of the attackers. We studied their work, their homes. They had no connection to one another, no prior suggestion of violence." She struggled with her words, wrestling them out. "It is baffling."

"I should have foreseen it through the *thism*," Jora'h said. "But they managed to hide their thoughts. The attackers were blank to me."

"It is one of the ways the Shana Rei attacked us, during the ancient conflict," Rod'h said. "Through our fears, through a weakness in the *thism*."

Reyn felt uncomfortable as he finished his meal. Perhaps this wasn't a good time for his visit to the Ildirans after all, but he needed his own answers as much as they did.

At a time of the day when only three of the bright suns were in the sky, the Ildirans noticed the diminished illumination; for Reyn it meant he could remove his filmgoggles when Osira'h took him to the lush greenhouse at the top of a palace tower. "The Mage-Imperator made this place for my mother," she said, stroking one of the young worldtrees. "I thought you might feel more comfortable here."

The well-lit chamber was full of exotic Ildiran plants, but the centerpiece was a small grove of worldtree saplings, each one taller than Reyn. He chuckled. "I've only been here a day, Osira'h. I'm not too homesick yet."

"Still, I wanted you to know that this place is always here. You have to be experiencing culture shock with all these new things. I'm the daughter of a Mage-Imperator, and you're the son of the King and Queen. We understand the need to have a special place. Your father must have had the same need when he was a Prince."

Reyn smiled to remember the stories he'd been told. "My father lived on the streets of Earth. His real name was Raymond Aguerra, and he had three brothers, a mother who worked several jobs." He glanced at Osira'h. "The Hansa thought he would be a perfect candidate to replace old King Frederick, so . . . they kidnapped him, staged an accident that killed the rest of his family, and then altered his appearance. They indoctrinated him so he'd be a good little King." Reyn gave a harder smile. "That didn't turn out exactly as they planned."

Osira'h was surprised by the story, but she had one of her own. "And I was raised in a breeding camp where my mother was held prisoner. They trained me to be the savior of our race." The two stood together, staring at the worldtrees. "I guess neither of us is exactly what we appear to be."

Reyn hesitated, feeling the ever-present tremors inside him, but at least the twinges of pain had left him alone for now. "Then it's good to know you."

EIGHTY-FIVE

XANDER BRINDLE

The *Verne* arrived back at the Ulio transfer station a day before their scheduled meeting. Xander had intentionally pushed the date, because Terry enjoyed the place and loved meeting with old friends; Terry was also pleased to show his former coworkers how successful he'd become, how his life's path had improved. He had a happy relationship, a good ship and an exciting career, and had seen much of the Spiral Arm. (Thanks to Xander's obsessive list-ticking, he was going to see a lot more of it, too.)

Since they had agreed to the ekti-X business venture with Elisa Enturi, the two young traders had gained a great deal of clout, not to mention profits. If this meeting with Xander's parents went as well as he hoped, the distribution operations could increase fivefold through Kett Shipping, and Iswander Industries seemed ready to expand even more.

After the *Verne* docked—in a much less convenient berth this time—he and Terry worked their way through the connected ships. Terry propelled himself along in the vessels that courteously kept their gravity off; in other ships where his useless legs were a problem, he held on to OK's shoulder and used his antigrav belt to keep himself weightless.

Terry bought drinks for some of his old comrades on the engineering and repair crews. They were glad to see their former coworker, and even more enthusiastic when Terry bought them a second round. Xander indulged his friend. Thanks to the ekti-X runs, their accounts were flush and likely to be even more profitable. They played games, told bad jokes and tall tales. Xander and Terry regaled them with descriptions of Fireheart Station, Rhejak, and the now-destroyed Kellum skymine on Golgen.

Xander was glad to see his partner so happy, but when two former coworkers tried to borrow substantial sums, Xander interceded and said it was time to get back to the *Verne,* where they would be spending the night rather than paying for a rented cabin. They preferred to sleep in their own bunk anyway.

During the next day shift, they had breakfast at Terry's favorite galley café and checked the board to see that the *Voracious Curiosity* had just arrived. While Xander signaled his parents, Terry scanned the eating establishments and picked a new restaurant that served "Ildiran-human fusion cuisine," including beverages such as kirae (which Ildirans found intoxicating and humans found disgusting) as well as new kelp and plankton brews from Kellum's distillery. Xander dared himself to try a pint of "Primordial Ooze."

Tasia Tamblyn and Robb Brindle joined them, with embraces all around. Even though Xander worked for his parents, and the *Verne* was still a Kett Shipping vessel, their travels rarely took the two young men back to company headquarters. With so much potential business hinging on this deal, though, Xander insisted that Tasia and Robb could justify a trip out to Ulio.

In the Ildiran-human fusion restaurant, Terry suggested that they eat family style so he could try the different dishes. Tasia and Robb had both spent years eating military rations, and Robb had even endured bland textured nutrients provided by his hydrogue captors while he was held as a prisoner of war. His parents weren't picky, and Xander was happy to eat whatever Terry liked.

As they settled in to the meal, Tasia said through a mouthful of noodles, "We've been impressed with your shipments. The profits from all that stardrive fuel are really helping our bottom line—but where is it coming from? That's enough output for a couple of top-level skymines. And Golgen's gone."

Robb reached over with a napkin to wipe some brown sauce from his wife's mouth. "We're also concerned about the connection with Iswander Industries. I'm all for giving the guy a second chance, but I'd like reassurances that we're not asking for another disaster. What is his new ekti source? Nobody knows."

Terry said, "We understand you have questions, and we thought you'd like to ask them directly." He glanced at Xander, and then in a comically simultaneous gesture both of them looked at their watches.

Elisa Enturi was punctual and businesslike, as always. OK led her to their table, and Xander introduced everyone. Elisa gave them a cool smile. "Good to see the pilots of the *Verne* decided to bring my proposal to the highest levels of Kett Shipping." She sat, but didn't bother to clip herself in place; she seemed comfortable with or without gravity. "We'll all benefit greatly from this."

Tasia held up a hand and shot a sidelong look at her son. "Not so fast. We don't know about your proposal. And we do have questions."

Elisa raised her eyebrows. "Questions? Hasn't the ekti-X been selling well?"

"Wonderfully well," Robb said in a conciliatory tone. "But it's not all about profit."

"Really? I was hoping to expand our agreement to provide regular loads of stardrive fuel for at least five more Kett Shipping vessels. Our output is still increasing, and there's a consistent demand. It's business—it *is* about profit."

"But where does your ekti-X come from?" Tasia asked. "I'm familiar with ekti-harvesting operations, old Ildiran skymines, nebula skimmers, hydrogen extraction from cometary clouds. I know how cost-intensive it is and how difficult. But . . . Iswander Industries—by the Guiding Star, where is it all *coming from*?"

"We have alternative methods of production," Elisa said.

A waiter appeared, but Elisa gave him a slight shake of her head, and he backed away. She returned her gaze to Tasia and Robb, and Xander felt as if she were ignoring him entirely.

"Ekti-X is our proprietary discovery, our industry, and our profits. Lee Iswander just recovered from a severe setback that would have ended most careers, but he is resilient and innovative. Let him keep his secrets and don't begrudge him his success."

Robb raised his hands. "We didn't say we begrudged it, but if we're going to be distributing ekti-X, we want to know its source."

"And I cannot tell you. Those are the terms. Iswander Industries has a growing supply of stardrive fuel to distribute. Do you want to be part of it, or should I contact other shipping companies?" Her expression was completely bland, as if she didn't care a whit which option Tasia and Robb chose.

Xander interjected, "Ekti-X is a high-quality product, and it practically sells itself."

Terry added, "Not to mention, we're getting a good reputation as trade pilots. You should see your son in action--he's getting to be a pretty good negotiator!"

Tasia and Robb looked at each other, weighing options. Elisa sat motionless, as if counting down seconds in her mind. Xander felt anxious, and when his mother saw his pleading expression, that was enough to tip the scale in their favor.

"All right," Tasia said. "Draw up the paperwork, and we'll look it over—but I think we have a deal." Of course there were logical and commercial reasons to accept the contract, but she made her choice because she knew it would benefit her son. "From now on, Kett Shipping will be your ekti-X distributor."

EIGHTY-SIX

GARRISON REEVES

As he flew the *Prodigal Son* at the end of another debris-mapping mission, Garrison was delayed outside the Lunar Orbital Complex because CDF ships were engaged in maneuvers. Newly commissioned Manta cruisers flitted through an obstacle course in the space rubble in a shakedown exercise.

After one of the rookie Manta pilots collided with a spinning rock fragment and tumbled off course, the pilot had to anchor the damaged cruiser to an asteroid and call for repair teams. The shutdown of the obstacle course and the mounting of emergency response crews delayed all traffic around the LOC.

Garrison had to park the *Prodigal Son* in a distant orbit, out of the way. And wait.

Finishing this run had earned Garrison two days of R&R, but he was banking his time so he could take a longer trip to Academ to see his son. He missed Seth, but the boy loved his school, and Garrison realized this was what life should have been for a normal Roamer boy. He wished Dale had kept his two sons at Academ, so Seth could have gotten to know his cousins.

Finally, when the space traffic was released again and the delayed ships could dock, Garrison parked the *Prodigal Son* in its assigned slot and then requisitioned fuel and a standard maintenance check. He got to his station quarters three hours later than expected, and was taken aback to discover a message tacked to his door. It was a handwritten note from Lubai, the green priest who did freelance work in the LOC's exchange. "Garrison Reeves: I received an urgent message for you through the worldforest network. See me immediately."

A chill poured through his bloodstream. Seth! Something must have happened to Seth. He should have gotten this message three hours earlier.

He raced into the exchange marketplace just in time for a new lunch crowd. He jostled his way past the entertainment kiosks and the clashing smells of different food stalls until he reached the green priest, only to find Lubai occupied with another customer. Lubai was bent over his treeling, eyes closed, while a young CDF soldier dictated a letter to her husband who was stationed on Theroc.

Garrison fidgeted, trying to catch the attention of the green priest. Countless scenarios played through his imagination. After rescuing Seth from Sheol and the bloater explosion, it would be an unbearable irony if the boy had suffered an accident in the supposedly safe environment of the Roamer school.

The female soldier continued talking to the green priest, an intimate, romantic message for the husband she missed so much. As he eavesdropped, Garrison felt a pang, knowing that Elisa had never felt that way about him. Finally, the soldier noticed him and looked embarrassed at what he must have heard; she left quickly.

Lubai looked up. "Garrison Reeves—I expected you'd come sooner."

"There was a delay. What's your urgent message? Is it my son?"

"No, not your son . . ." He paused, looked at Garrison with a deep and intense gaze. "It's the rest of your clan."

Garrison couldn't understand what he meant. Lubai gestured for him to take a seat on the hard metal bench across from the treeling. "There was a deadly plague on the space city where clan Reeves made their new home. Their green priest, Shelud, sent messages of their explorations, the discoveries of an alien race. Then Roamers began to get sick. They started to die. Your brother Dale, his family, your cousins . . . such a tragedy."

Garrison stared, unable to believe what he was hearing. "A plague? How many are dead? And what about my father?"

"All dead." Lubai hesitated. "As they fell ill, Shelud went from deathbed to deathbed, interviewing them, speaking their words into the worldforest network. Many had a chance to pass along final messages. A woman named Sendra wished to say goodbye to you. And Olaf Reeves . . . he was still alive when Shelud sent his last message. But he too was already sick." The green priest shook his head.

"When did this happen?"

"We lost contact with Shelud more than a day ago. Even then, he was one of the last ones left alive."

Garrison felt weak. His arms were trembling as he rested them on the table.

In a compassionate voice, Lubai said, "Here, let me tell you everything." He touched his treeling, dipped his mind into the forest database, and repeated the messages Shelud had delivered, told the whole story, the spread of the disease, Dale and his family dying, Sendra's farewell. . . .

Garrison's eyes refused to focus, and he felt light-headed. It was too much to take in at once—his brother and Sendra, their two boys . . . all dead now because Olaf Reeves had dragged them away from civilization, away from everything.

His anger toward his father for doing such a foolish thing could not push aside the sorrow. He couldn't imagine anything as small as a virus defeating the blustery, inflexible clan leader. Of the Retroamers who followed him out into empty space, how many had really wanted to exile themselves? How much had they even known about where they were going?

He could hear his father's booming voice as he railed at Garrison for letting himself be seduced by That Woman. When he was young and determined, Garrison had been so sure his father was wrong about everything, but Olaf's assessment of Elisa, at least, had been correct.

Garrison had been dead to his father for a long time. He wished they could have reconciled, but now he knew that if he'd rejoined his family and gone along as Olaf wanted—and taken Seth there!—then he and his son would be dead too.

Sitting across from the green priest, he realized he had been silent for a long moment. Though Seth had barely known his uncle, his grandfather, or his cousins, the boy needed to hear this news. He said to Lubai, "Please send a message to Academ for me."

EIGHTY-SEVEN

ORLI COVITZ

In a very short time, the *Proud Mary* felt like home to Orli. The worn upholstery in the cockpit chair was soft, warm, and comfortable, conforming to her body. Even the lingering sweet smell of Mary Coven's tobacco pipe smoke seemed natural.

According to records the *Proud Mary*'s previous captain had been a curmudgeonly woman, a loner by her own choice (and because people didn't much like her company). Orli had a sense, though, that Mary Coven would have approved of the ship's new steward.

DD proved to be an excellent copilot as well as a companion. He was, after all, a Friendly compy, originally designed to be a best friend, and DD was definitely Orli's best friend. Oddly enough, when she'd been married to Matthew, even during the good times, DD had always been a closer confidant. She hadn't realized that until now.

"I'm glad you're with me, DD," she said as they flew toward their destination.

"And I am very happy to accompany you, Orli." The compy turned back to the ship's screens, taking his navigation duties seriously. "We have thirty-one minutes before we disengage the stardrive and arrive at the space city."

She leaned back in the pilot chair. "I hope the people of clan Reeves welcome us—or at least don't get upset with us for checking on them."

"I am a Friendly compy, Orli. People don't normally get upset when I visit."

"That's because you're charming."

"And I find you quite pleasant as well, Orli."

She had enjoyed the solitude during the long flight, the chance to get her thoughts together. DD often chattered to keep her company, but when she told him she wanted some quiet time to think, his feelings weren't hurt.

Everything felt so different since leaving Relleker, as if she'd become a different person. Her life had changed in extraordinary ways, many of them reactive, many of them self-inflicted. By asking Rlinda Kett if she could fly a trade ship, Orli had taken control of her own life again. This was Orli Covitz version 3.0.

She had no idea if this was what she'd do for the rest of her life. She was still intelligent and attractive—at least she thought so. She had plenty to offer, whether or not Matthew realized it. And after her days alone in the quiet of the ship, with time to assess who she was and what she'd accomplished, Orli realized she wasn't bitter toward her husband, just disappointed. She didn't want to turn into a curmudgeonly old woman like Mary Coven—but she didn't have to think about the rest of her life now, just the next step. She had no way of knowing who Orli 4.0 might be.

Wanting to make a good first impression for clan Reeves, Orli put on a clean captain's jacket, washed her face, practiced her smile, and rehearsed a greeting. She had heard stories about Olaf Reeves, and when she'd asked for advice on how to handle the Retroamers, Rlinda just chuckled in her deep heartwarming way. "Orli, girl, be yourself—that's all you need. Chances are, Olaf will tell you to go away and leave them alone. That's fine—no harm done. You can use the practice, and I'm paying for the ekti to make your run. Xander and Terry have some sort of sweet deal, so we get the fuel cheap."

The coordinates Olaf Reeves had discreetly given Rlinda were not at any planet, not even in an interesting star system. Orli wondered what could possibly be all the way out here. Then she saw the large station, an artificial structure that looked like a barbed-wire snowflake, with a central hub and five angled spokes.

Orli had been to dozens of planets, but she had never seen anything like this. "How did that city get here? And who built it?"

"I do not know, Orli. Let me check the ship's databases for an answer."

"I doubt you'll find any information on it, but clan Reeves discovered it somehow. It looks . . . ancient." She activated the comm. "This is Kett Shipping vessel *Proud Mary* contacting the station, or city, or whatever it is. I'm looking for clan Reeves. Please respond."

DD continued to scan the area. "Orli, I found seventeen Roamer ships. They match the vessels owned by clan Reeves, according to records."

"We must be in the right place, then." Orli listened to the continued silence from the comm. "Calling clan Reeves, please respond."

DD studied his readings. "This is puzzling to me, Orli. All seventeen of the Roamer ships are simply adrift in the vicinity with power systems shut down, no life support."

Orli shot the compy a surprised look. "What do you mean—they're not docked to the station? Why would clan Reeves set them loose?"

"I was asking you that question, Orli."

"That makes no sense at all." She repeated her transmission, but got only more silence. She frowned and took her finger off the comm button. They would have heard her call; either they were *unwilling* to answer, or *unable* to. "Rlinda sent us out here because she was worried about those people. Maybe she was right. We'd better find some answers."

She adjusted course to take the *Proud Mary* past one of the drifting ships and verified that it was just an empty vessel, apparently undamaged, but cold and dark. If anyone had been on that ship, they were dead now.

The space city had not been built by humans—that much was obvious—but it didn't look Ildiran or Klikiss either. The symbols on the outside were incomprehensible, particularly the bright pink triangles near the hatches. DD scanned the ship's databases, but found no reference or significance to the designs.

One of the landing bays near the hub was wide open, like a gaping mouth, but glowstrips and guidance triangles were still illuminated. "At least somebody left a light on for us," she said. She landed the *Proud Mary* inside the open bay, and when the weight of her ship pressed down on the pressure pads, the big doors glided shut, and the bay automatically began to refill with air.

"Everything seems to be working," Orli said. "But still no response from the comm. We're going to have to investigate this in person."

Once the atmosphere checked out, they stepped into the pressurized landing bay and headed toward the hatch that connected with the rest of the space city. DD stood before the controls. "These are alien electronics and engineering, Orli. I don't comprehend them."

On the adjacent bulkhead, though, Orli found a different control pad that had been jacked into the main system. "These are Roamer add-ons. Somebody rigged a bypass." She ran her fingers over the familiar pad, reading standard air pressure and temperature on the other side of the hatch. "They made the interior ready for human habitation."

"I recommend that we exercise caution, Orli. There could still be danger."

"I agree—*something* happened to those people." She went back to the *Proud Mary*, rummaged in the captain's locker, and withdrew a hand jazer, just in case. The Retroamers had turned their backs on human civilization, preferring isolation. Maybe they were too isolated. Someone could have gone berserk, perhaps released poison gas into the station atmosphere? She put on a facemask and found a portable air tank, which she strapped to her waist. Now she was ready.

Carrying the weapon, she opened the jury-rigged hatch into the main station. When she and DD entered the eerily silent alien city, a chill went down her back, though the temperature was warm and the lights were bright. Perfectly habitable and welcoming.

"Hello? Anybody home?" she called. DD picked up the refrain, calling out every few seconds in a piping voice that carried along the empty corridors.

Orli stepped into an open chamber—and found the body of a middle-aged woman wearing a typical Roamer jumpsuit with pockets, zippers, and embroidered markings. Her skin was blotched and discolored. She hadn't been dead long. Orli pressed the mask tighter against her face. Poison? Nerve gas?

A plague?

She and DD pushed onward. In the second module they found an entire family huddled together, dead. Orli stared aghast. Whatever it was had struck them down quickly. Inside a larger chamber they found forty-three more, all gathered as if in a last community meeting.

"There could still be survivors sealed in other chambers," DD suggested. "This is a very large city."

"How does a compy get to be such an optimist?"

"It's in my original programming."

Inside the community chamber, one of the bodies had distinctive green skin. When he died, the green priest had knocked over a potted treeling that now spilled onto the deck, its fronds withering.

Orli breathed rapidly into her mask, close to hyperventilating. She felt her skin crawl and wondered how the disease or poison was transmitted—through simple respiration? Through the pores of the skin, or the moisture of the eyes?

"I should have worn a full environment suit," she said.

"I can go back and retrieve one," DD offered.

"Too late now. Let's keep looking. Maybe someone left a log entry."

At the control hub, they found a gray-bearded man at a desk surrounded by control screens. He was slumped into his chair, his head tilted forward, cold.

Orli recognized him. "I think that's Olaf Reeves."

"It does match the images in my database."

Orli crept around the desk and forced herself to look at the main screen that Olaf Reeves had been using. It was still recording—the clan leader had tried to leave a final message. According to the counter, he had begun the recording nine hours and twenty-four minutes earlier.

She ran the file back, skimming it in reverse past hours and hours of his motionless body staring at the imager. Finally, near the beginning, he started to move and talk again, and she replayed his message.

His voice was raspy. "I am Olaf Reeves, head of clan Reeves. My people came to this abandoned city to create a self-sufficient colony, to make a new start. We didn't know that the original inhabitants of this station had perished from a deadly plague, thousands of years ago. Now my clan has found death here as well.

"We are completely quarantined, and I jettisoned our ships so no one could escape and spread the disease. As of this recording, every one of my people has been infected. Most have already died, including"—his voice broke—"my son and his family. Our green priest dispatched a warning, but I'll transmit this recording too. If you receive this message, stay away. This entire station is contaminated. I will not let the alien plague spread. If it gets loose in the Confederation, it could kill billions."

Each breath was labored, and dark splotches covered Olaf's face as he stared into the imager. His shoulders trembled. "To make damn sure, I'm going to destroy this city. My compies—" Then he went into a spasm of coughing that did not end. He vomited blood, and after a severe seizure he collapsed into unconsciousness. At some point during the remaining nine hours of the recording, he died at his desk.

Orli just stared, knowing that the clan head had meant to send his message on a repeating broadcast, but he had succumbed before he could complete his recording. She'd had no contact with Kett Shipping since she departed on this journey. Orli and DD had come here, unaware.

She stared silently for a long moment. "That means I've been exposed, DD."

"That is a matter of great concern, Orli, but I should point out that you wore a breathing mask."

Orli shook her head. "I didn't don the facemask until we went into the city. The landing bay would have repressurized with station air. And if it's all contaminated . . ." Still, she didn't know for certain.

A Teacher compy strutted through the doorway of the admin hub. "I came to report on our progress. Is Mr. Reeves not receiving visitors?"

"Never again," Orli said. "He's dead."

"Oh." The Teacher compy paused to reassess. "I am BO, assigned as special tutor to the clan Reeves children. Unfortunately, I no longer have any students."

"A pleasure to meet you. I am DD, a Friendly compy. This is Orli

Covitz, captain of the *Proud Mary*." He seemed happy to make the introductions. "Where are your students?"

"They are all dead. I was the only Teacher compy on the station, but there are five other compies. I came to report to Olaf Reeves that we are nearly finished with the task he assigned us."

"What task?" Orli asked.

"Olaf Reeves gave us orders to modify the power blocks and alien energy reactors to generate an overload sufficient to destroy this entire city. It is imperative that no one else be infected. Olaf Reeves was not convinced that his warning would be heeded. The plague remained viable aboard this station for centuries or millennia, and he was certain that once humans learned about the derelict city, someone at some point would come here exploring." BO's voice changed, and she sounded more like a stern schoolteacher. "I see you did not heed the warning. Now I recognize his wisdom regarding human nature."

"I didn't receive any warning. He never finished or transmitted his recording. We arrived too late."

"That is disappointing," BO said. "I believe all members of clan Reeves are deceased. Fortunately, that removes a matter of some consternation among the compies."

"What matter of consternation?"

"The reactor explosion will be sufficient to vaporize all components of this station. If any Roamers were still alive, our compy programming would preclude us from causing the detonation that would kill them."

Orli was intimately familiar with the protective strictures embedded in compy core programming. "Failure to detonate the station might lead to continued spread of the plague. By waiting, you could endanger the lives of entire planetary populations."

"That did cause a conundrum. In the meantime, preparing the linked reactors for detonation is a complex and time-consuming process, which we have not finished yet. Now the conundrum is solved."

Orli and DD followed BO to the hub engineering chambers where the Worker compies were connecting a series of power blocks to the alien reactor, while others strung linked secondary explosives up into the spokes. Watching all the dutiful compies brought tears to Orli's eyes. It reminded her of her own compies back on Relleker, who were now happily (she hoped) assigned to the Ikbir colony.

BO said, "Since you are here, Orli Covitz, you are certainly infected. Now we will have to wait until you perish before we detonate the station."

EIGHTY-EIGHT

AELIN

Elisa Enturi returned to the bloater-extraction operations with great fanfare. "We have sealed a deal, sir—expanded ekti-X distribution operations with Kett Shipping."

Listening to the discussion without interest, Aelin sat alone and sad in the headquarters module. He touched his treeling, let his thoughts wander among messages from thousands of green priests. Aelin drew comfort from the everyday personal activities across the Spiral Arm.

As he watched the ekti-extraction operations among the drained bloater sacks in space, he no longer felt the joy and wonder he had once experienced. The industrial activity was extensive and exotic compared to the forests of Theroc, but Aelin had felt stifled because he couldn't share these wonders with his fellow green priests.

Shelud's death, though, changed everything.

Iswander was never generous with his smiles but he gave one to Elisa now. It was just business as usual. "They met our terms without complaint?"

"A few complaints, but they had no real leverage. Your gift of ekti-X to King Peter and our constant shipments are already causing tremors in the stardrive fuel market. Nobody knows where the supplies come from, but prices have started dropping, and traditional skyminers have gone from being curious to being worried. We'll have six more Kett vessels to deliver ekti-X from both our primary and secondary extraction fields."

She added an even more confident smile. "And I'm certain that if we cast a wide sensor net in the interstellar void where no one else has looked before, we'll discover even more bloater clusters. They've got to be out there. I don't know how they've gone unnoticed all this time. They seem to be appearing everywhere."

Iswander called up displays of optimistic and pessimistic projections. "We have to be careful that we don't glut the market, while we bank all possible profits. I've already diverted a third of our production into storage silos. We can build up a huge strategic stockpile of stardrive fuel."

Aelin's admiration for Lee Iswander remained undiminished. He had once viewed the man as the personification of the human spirit, taking risks and pushing boundaries. While he tutored young Arden in physics and engineering (learning much about those subjects himself), the green priest also taught him about his father's business ventures, both successes and failures, including the spectacular failures—like Sheol—as well as the spectacular successes, such as these ekti-X operations.

But recently Shelud had contacted him through telink, told him about the Onthos plague and how all of clan Reeves was dying. His brother revealed everything to him, and once a message was sent through telink, all green priests could access it. Aelin didn't care that their private last moments were experienced widely.

Through telink, he and Shelud talked and talked, and he'd connected to his brother's ever-more-wavering and chaotic thoughts at the very end. Shelud described the plague symptoms in excruciating, painful detail until his thoughts became blurred, disjointed.

On the alien space city, Shelud had walked among the dying Roamers, listening to their stories and repeating them into his treeling so that the worldforest, at least, would remember them. The last survivors had gathered in one of the community rooms, knowing they had little time left. Shelud remained connected via telink even as the fever surged through him and his body died.

Aelin kept talking to his brother, giving him a familiar voice to hold on to, a comforting lifeline. And then Shelud's thoughts slipped away. In the final moment he took the only refuge of a green priest, pouring the remnants of his mind and soul into the trees, letting all his thoughts live among the verdani so that he was at least partially preserved. . . .

Now, in the headquarters module, Aelin only half listened to Elisa giving her excited report to Iswander. She seemed so brave and confident. "You lost everything on Sheol, sir . . . and I lost my son, and husband." She didn't look affected at all. "But we're recovering."

Surprised, Aelin lifted his head from the treeling. Was it possible that she didn't know? "You are mistaken, Elisa Enturi. Your son isn't dead. Your husband isn't dead. They both survived the explosion."

Elisa stared at him. "What are you saying, green priest?"

"I have seen their messages sent through telink. Garrison Reeves works in the rubble shepherding operations at Earth. Your son, Seth, is in school at Academ with other Roamer children. Were you not aware of this?"

Elisa looked aghast and then furious—not at all what Aelin expected. If someone had surprised him with news that Shelud still lived, he would have been overjoyed. He said, "I thought you'd be happy."

Elisa whirled to Iswander. "He tricked me! He's still got Seth."

Flustered, Iswander waved a hand to calm her. "Of course, take a ship and go. I know you want to see your son."

She was already moving out of the admin module. "I have to *rescue* him."

EIGHTY-NINE

GENERAL NALANI KEAH

Along with the *Kutuzov,* General Keah decided to bring three battle groups to the next round of exercises with the Ildiran Solar Navy. To lead them, she chose three of her Grid Admirals, specifically the ones most fond of their desks. She called those men the "Three H's"— Admirals Handies, Harvard, and Haroun. She figured they needed the practice.

True, the Three H's were skilled in the administrative complexities of the Confederation Defense Forces. Admiral Handies had made his mark managing the Grid 0 portion of the fleet, which encompassed Earth, the Lunar Orbital Complex, and the Mars military base; Haroun and Harvard, who managed Grids 6 and 11, respectively, were also adept at paperwork. While Keah wasn't one to wax poetic about the glories of combat, she did need to pry the three admirals away from their offices and give them some real experience.

Adar Zan'nh had promised to share new information his people had uncovered about the legendary Shana Rei and the possibility of their reappearance. Keah was skeptical of scary stories about bogeymen that lived in the shadows, but she herself had seen the dark nebula that swallowed the fleeing black robot ships, and she had viewed the images of the blackness vomiting up from the clouds of Golgen. *Something* sure as hell was going on.

She and the Adar both saw the enormity of the potential threat, and the CDF and the Solar Navy were stepping up the intensity of their war games until they figured out what they were dealing with. Zan'nh was bringing an entire maniple of warliners this time—seven septas, or forty-nine ships.

It should be a good challenge.

Keah realized that standard space battle routines would be useless against an intangible enemy like that shadow cloud at Dhula. Nevertheless, the exercises would give her CDF personnel hands-on practice and would keep them on their toes.

She flew the *Kutuzov* out to the Plumas system for the exercises, though her role in this case was just to observe. The Three H's had Juggernauts and Mantas, and would be responsible for their own movements. Keah was anxious to see how they interacted.

The CDF ships arrived early in the system, and not by accident. Even though these were scheduled war games, General Keah never took anything at face value. She trusted Adar Zan'nh for the most part, but she had been there at that terrible battlefield in Earth orbit twenty years ago. She had witnessed the astounding treachery when supposed allies had turned against the human military in their last stand. She didn't intend to be fooled again—ever.

The CDF battle groups appeared over the frozen moon of Plumas, a water-refueling station and deep ice mines still run by the Roamer clan Tamblyn. Ron Tamblyn, the current manager of the water mines, was not overly pleased when informed that the CDF and Solar Navy would engage in complicated exercises in the vicinity. He complained that the activity would disrupt his usual business, until Keah reminded him that many of the participating ships would need to take on large loads of water—at full price. Mollified, the Roamers kept their heads down, remaining in the grotto beneath the Plumas ice sheets.

When all CDF ships were in position and waiting for the Solar Navy to arrive, Keah grew impatient. She suggested to the three Grid Admirals, "Why don't you loosen up, run some flight patterns?"

"Good idea, General," acknowledged Admiral Harvard, as if the thought had never occurred to him. The other two H's joined in.

"But I thought we were running an exercise against the Ildirans, General," said Admiral Haroun. "What sort of flight patterns do you want us to run?"

Keah sighed. If they got into a real space battle, Keah hoped she wouldn't have to look over their shoulders and tell each one where to point the jazers and when to push the firing buttons. "The problem with the Solar Navy is that they've been too set in their ways, but now they're trying to be more nimble and adaptable. You can do the same."

The Three H's directed their ships into separate groups, as if this were a formal military parade. Hoping to show these desk admirals how it was done, she sent out a fleet of her own Remoras. Maybe she'd pretend to launch a turncoat attack, just to rile them up.

Then a real threat intervened.

Out at the fringe of the system, her Remora patrols discovered a disturbance—an emptiness like a tear in space that began to spew out a thunderhead of dark dust. General Keah felt a chill when she saw the emerging shadow cloud: she had seen this before.

She sent an emergency signal to all ships. "No time for practice. This is real." She ordered the *Kutuzov*'s systems to be powered up. "I am assuming control of the battle group. We head out to see what we can do against that shadow cloud."

Admiral Handies transmitted back, "General, the Ildiran Solar Navy isn't here yet. Shouldn't we wait?"

"No, dammit!" When she and the Ildiran warliners had pursued the black robot vessels, that shadow cloud had taken them by surprise. As part of their preliminary training, she had required all the crews on every CDF vessel to review the briefings on that previous encounter. "I want to figure this out, but keep a good distance."

The Juggernauts and Manta cruisers raced toward the edge of the system. The dark, shapeless mass looked like an amoeba made entirely of midnight. She kept her eyes open, studying it.

A message came over the comm from Ron Tamblyn at Plumas. "General Keah, what's going on up there? Is this part of the simulation?"

"Better if you just stay where you are, Mr. Tamblyn. We have a problem."

On the bridge, her green priest sat shivering next to his potted treeling. Nadd was always cold aboard the *Kutuzov,* and now he seemed nervous as well. "General, shall I inform the worldforest network what's happening?"

"Go right ahead. But nothing's actually happened—yet."

As soon as she said the words, Keah knew she had spoken too

soon. From within the folds of the ever-expanding black nebula, three gigantic shapes appeared, composed of a different, more solid type of darkness. A trio of long hexagonal cylinders thrust like blunted knives out of the dark nebula.

Then, like buckshot, dozens of smaller ships streaked out of the shadow cloud, accompanying the black hex cylinders. Keah immediately recognized the design of the smaller vessels. "Those are bugbot ships!"

Admiral Harvard transmitted from his Juggernaut. "General, should we send a liaison ship forward? Try to communicate with them and ask their intentions?"

The black robot ships roared toward the CDF ships in attack formations.

"No, Admiral Harvard, we will not. Shields on full, prepare to fire jazers."

Her crew aboard the *Kutuzov* reacted more swiftly, since they had experienced this before. She could only imagine the confusion aboard the other three Juggernauts, and she hoped her Grid Admirals would learn and respond quickly. There wouldn't be time for on-the-job training.

The black robot ships opened fire first, and Keah heard the impacts against her shields, saw the flares on the display screens. "Return fire, Mr. Patton! Hit them with everything, and then hit them again."

"My pleasure, General," said the weapons officer.

The order was transmitted across the battle group. Though out of practice, the other CDF warships unleashed such an enthusiastic flurry of jazers that dozens of shots hit the robot ships, destroying one by dumb luck. The angular vessels spun and reeled, changed course, and raced forward again at accelerations too intense for any biological form to survive.

"Can't say if any of those are the same bugbot ships that escaped from Dhula, General, or if they're fresh ones," said Sensor Tech Saliba.

"We know what the bugbots are capable of. Best solution is to wipe them all out—just to be sure."

"Trying to do just that, General," said Patton.

Looking lethal, the huge hexagonal cylinders continued to glide out of the shadow cloud. The hex ships displayed no lights, window-ports, engines, or apparent control systems—no vulnerabilities. The *Kutuzov*'s bridge screens flickered, her systems faltering.

"Shields are losing their integrity, General!" called Tactical Officer Voecks.

"Open fire on those hex things. That's what's causing the problem."

Retargeting, the flagship Juggernaut launched an intense jazer volley, but the jacketed energy beams struck the obsidian cylinders and reflected harmlessly off the angular surfaces.

The *Kutuzov*'s bridge began to shake and rattle as more internal systems failed. Meanwhile the robot ships harassed the CDF vessels. One of Admiral Haroun's Mantas accelerated toward the nearest hex ship, shooting repeated jazer blasts and a fusillade of railgun projectiles. But as it neared the black vessel, the Manta trembled, then began to tumble wildly. The Manta captain transmitted a distress signal. "We've lost control! All systems have gone haywire."

The unfortunate Manta struck the nearest hexagonal cylinder. It crumpled, ricocheted off, and exploded. The fires and shock waves from ignited ekti chambers slammed against the black hull and were absorbed.

Keah seethed. "Now would be a good time for Adar Zan'nh to show up with his warliners." She picked four Remora pilots and sent them an urgent message. "Head out of the system at top speed along the Ildiran inbound vector. Intercept the Solar Navy ships, inform them what's happening—and tell them to haul ass. They're probably planning some fancy arrival parade."

Her green priest clutched his treeling and continued to report. As she listened to the tangled, overlapping transmissions from other ships, Keah heard an increasing edge of panic in the reports. Their weapons seemed to be having no effect whatsoever on the hex vessels.

"Keep firing as long as our systems hold out," she told her crew. "Target the damned bugbot ships—at least we can blow *them* up."

They fired additional rounds, but even the *Kutuzov*'s weapons began to fail. The targeting was misaligned, and numerous shots misfired. Two more black robot ships were destroyed, but Keah knew she didn't have much time before her entire battle group fell apart.

Walled off and frustrated, Exxos could only watch the battle from within the entropy bubble. The Shana Rei would not let him participate, and so they trapped him—*protected* him—in his own isolated pocket universe.

Given time, the robots would learn how to manipulate the physical laws of that sub-universe, perhaps even create matter, shape existence to their own desires. The black robots could be gods. They could be *masters*.

All in due time. First they had to survive the Shana Rei . . . and preferably destroy them, along with all sentient life, so they could have the universe to themselves.

At the moment Exxos was more interested in the clash taking place in the Plumas system. That small Roamer settlement should have been an easy target to annihilate, just like Eljiid. Exxos had not expected to find the human military ships there. Nevertheless, he was excited by the opportunity to unleash the destructive power that the Shana Rei alliance could generate.

How he longed to be part of the battle, not just trapped here, but the capricious Shana Rei had kept him apart—either as a hostage, or a distant commander. He wasn't sure which. The creatures of darkness left much to be understood. Their thought patterns were different from anything the black robots had previously encountered, and the Shana Rei were not inclined to explain their rationale.

They had singled him out as leader of the black robots, unique among them, and he accepted the role. Although the robots themselves were identical in their basic structure and programming, each one had personal experiences assimilated over thousands of years.

But he could only watch as his comrades soared toward the human battleships in new vessels the Shana Rei had manifested for them. The modified ships should have been sufficient to obliterate an undefended Roamer water-pumping station.

Imagining the potential of their incomprehensible benefactors, Exxos had redesigned the robot attack craft. The Shana Rei were devoid of knowledge about physics, science, engineering, but they could create matter in whatever form they desired, so long as they had a basic pattern. The robots understood the structure of ships, the mechanics of engines and propulsion systems, the layout of electronics, circuitry paths, weapons systems. Exxos convinced the creatures of darkness to create enhanced ships according to new plans.

And now they wouldn't let him fly as part of the attack.

The Shana Rei drained energy from the vacuum and also created huge hexagonal cylinders, traditional shadow ships such as ones they had used in their previous appearance millennia ago. The effort of creation caused them pain; even in his entropy bubble, Exxos could hear the Shana Rei moan and scream. That pain transformed into anger and violence, which they unleashed at Plumas.

With robot battleships in the vanguard, the black hex cylinders loomed forward. The CDF Juggernauts and Manta cruisers struggled to meet the attack, but were unprepared. Exxos listened to the dance of radiofrequency chatter, heard the defiant General declare revenge against the hated black robots. But Exxos understood that revenge went both ways, and he intended to hurt the CDF for all the destruction they had visited on his fellow robots in times past.

The robot ships hammered the CDF shields with unexpectedly powerful weapons, draining the energy reserves of the human vessels. They were reckless; they took risks and inflicted great damage. The robots targeted one Manta with their bombardment until its shields failed and the engines exploded. And they continued, relentless in their goal. . . .

A rippling inkblot appeared inside his entropy bubble, hovering before him with a staring singular eye. "This must end soon."

"It will. Look at our success so far."

The CDF released weapons in a flurry against the robots, but they did not know how to deal with the Shana Rei. Their very proximity to the black hexagon ships caused significant disruption in the human vessels. Electrical and mechanical systems began to fail, and they lost control. A Manta cruiser careened into one of the giant hexagons, but left no mark on the black hull.

The Shana Rei had overwhelming power—that much was obvious—yet even as they moved toward the Plumas moon, the creatures of darkness were desperate to withdraw and fold themselves back into the fabric of space.

Just a little longer.

Exxos possessed a database of all the worlds and races that needed to be destroyed. The Shana Rei claimed that some minds were a brighter fire than others; some thoughts hacked like sharp blades, while others were mere annoyances. The Ildiran *thism* was among the worst, as was the worldforest mind with its green priest telink network. Exxos would gladly destroy it all. Removing this human infestation at Plumas, as well as the CDF battleships, were just small steps toward that goal.

From inside the entropy bubble, the Shana Rei said in its pulsing voice, "Victory here will silence a few small whispers, but what drove us from our void is a far more powerful enemy—an intelligence that has only begun to awaken."

NINETY-ONE

ZOE ALAKIS

Tom Rom was late.

If any other employee missed a scheduled return to Pergamus, Zoe Alakis would have been annoyed. But Tom Rom was never late, and that made her worried.

He was an independent man. She had no chains on him, nor did he want any. His loyalty to her was a bond that could not be broken by the pull of two opposing black holes, and even Zoe didn't know how she had earned such devotion. He was also diligent and should have been back from his trip to the Ildiran sanctuary domes four days ago.

His last contact had been from Ulio, where he'd stopped to refuel and resupply, and he had added a code phrase to his message to let her know he would make a brief trip to Vaconda, as he had many times before.

But he should have been back days ago.

Zoe contemplated sending out searchers to trace his route from Ulio, but if Tom Rom didn't want to be found, no one would ever track him. What if he was hurt? Or lost? If it would help, she might even leave her sterile dome and go after him herself. Only for him. But that would be a last resort.

Her concerned thoughts were interrupted by a message from Orbiting Research Sphere 12—Dr. Hannig's lab. The scientist looked worried, and his bristly white hair had a distinct sparkle of perspiration. "Ms. Alakis, we've had a . . . slight problem."

Zoe's eyes hardened. With the dangerous work on Pergamus, there was no such thing as a "slight" problem. She even momentarily forgot about Tom Rom. "What sort of slight problem?"

His chuckle held an undertone of anxiety, so she knew not to believe his dismissive attitude. "It's probably just an administrative error. Nothing to worry about, but I wanted to let you know."

Her expression turned icy, her voice even colder. "Details, please." She leaned closer so she could watch his face.

"As you requested for the library, Ms. Alakis, we finished our work with Tamborr's Dementia, isolated the virus, purified it, and stored it in capsules. One of our notebooks states that we had twelve vials, but our final inventory lists only eleven. We've double-checked it, and I just wanted you to know there was an accounting error in our original submission."

"An accounting error." Zoe didn't even try to hide her skepticism. "Your team has never had accounting errors."

Dr. Hannig chuckled again, that awkward nervous titter. "There's always a first time. I've reprimanded my team and will launch a full investigation. When cleaning up the lab, we did find the twelfth vial, but it was empty."

"You mean it was spilled."

"No, of course not!" Hannig sounded more nervous now. "Absolutely not. I'm positive."

Zoe frowned and thought, *Meaning, "I don't think so."*

In its natural state, according to Hannig's report, Tamborr's Dementia was very difficult to contract, but Hannig's work had isolated and concentrated the virus. If that vial had spilled, every member of the research team would be infected now. The symptoms would manifest within a few days.

Dr. Hannig's words petered out, and he fell silent, staring at her on the screen, as if hoping. Zoe stared back without responding. Rules were rules, considering the extreme hazards of their work. There could be no room for flexibility, no possibility for compassion. Another example of why she refused to befriend her researchers.

Hannig's voice came out as a hoarse whisper. "Please!"

She made up her mind. "Dr. Hannig, I want to thank you and your team for your years of service. We have copies of your documentation, as well as an archival sample of the Tamborr virus, which we'll seal away in the Pergamus library. Your work will not be lost."

The panicked researchers gathered around Hannig on the screen, shouting. "At least wait a few days, see if we show any symptoms! You've got to be sure. You can't just—"

"Protocol is protocol," she said. "You all signed on to it. You've known from the very beginning."

"But it's just a damned counting mistake!" one of the scientists cried.

"We have to be sure. Thank you for understanding."

Zoe muted the voice pickup, because she had no interest in hearing desperate excuses or pleas. From her desk, she initiated a full decontamination protocol for ORS 12.

Hannig would know how much time he had. The magnetic charge at the heart of the station would take fifteen minutes to build up enough energy for the gamma-ray burst, which would release five times the amount of energy needed to destroy any known virus or bacteria. Just to be sure.

She supposed Hannig would try to rip apart the control systems to access the central magnetic canister, but he couldn't possibly do it in time. If he was an honorable man, he would accept his situation and not further damage the ORS. The station would be put back to good use after she sent her teams to clean up and repair all of the systems.

She watched her screen, saw the power buildup in the ORS core. She blocked the comm screen, even though Dr. Hannig repeatedly sent requests for communication.

The gamma-ray burst ended that, vaporizing all organic matter inside the sphere, down to every individual cell and the smallest virus. Afterward, the ORS would be subjected to twenty-four hours of thermal decontamination to cook away any remnants. And after that, the hatches would be opened to vent the station to space, leaving the chambers in hard vacuum with temperatures near absolute zero. That should be sufficient to make it a safe environment for the next team in the ORS.

Fortunately, because all of her research groups were isolated, no one else even needed to know about the disaster.

She called up her files to review the applications of other scientists who might be candidates for the new research team. She scanned down the names, read their specialties and accomplishments. Hannig would be difficult to replace, she knew, but she would have plenty of time to find someone. Her cleanup crew would take a week to scour and then reequip ORS 12 for further research anyway.

Zoe closed the file on Dr. Hannig and his team. Her attorneys would handle closing out their employment, releasing insurance payments for the designated beneficiaries. They had excuses to make, false stories to file, loose ends to tie up. They were used to it by now.

Tom Rom returned that afternoon.

With a suddenly gladdened heart, she watched the images transmitted from her picket line scouts as his ship streaked in toward Pergamus. Her eyes sparkled, and her pulse quickened just to know he was all right, but his ship looked more battered than usual.

"What took you so long?" she cried. "I was worried."

"Unforeseen difficulties. My ship was damaged on Vaconda, and I needed a few days to fix it up. It'll require a full overhaul and cleaning, engine upgrades, resupply, and spare parts replacement, but my repairs were good enough to get me home."

"What happened? Tell me."

"It's a long story. Nothing to concern yourself about. I am fine. I managed to obtain the records from Kuivahr, as well as intact samples of the Ramah brain parasite you asked for—and, of course, the shipment of prisdiamonds. That was what caused me a little trouble."

Zoe didn't care about prisdiamonds. She had never been concerned with budgets or resources, because she always had enough to pay for whatever she wanted. After worrying about him for days, Zoe now needed to see Tom Rom, face-to-face, just like two normal people, and listen to the harrowing adventures he'd had on her behalf. "Land your ship. Our teams can make the necessary repairs while you go through the decontamination stages to see me."

Staring at her from the screen, Tom Rom looked tired but not weak; his posture remained so straight that she wondered if he ever bent his shoulders. "If I cycle through decon, that'll be a twelve-hour delay. I'd like to see you very much, but there's an urgent matter you should know about."

"How urgent?" Zoe tried to hide her disappointment.

"I intercepted a message as I flew past Rhejak, and word is spreading through the green priest network. There's a deadly plague sweeping through a Roamer space city."

Now Zoe perked up. "A new plague? Or something we've seen before?"

She saw an unusual shine in his dark eyes. "Nothing any human has *ever* seen, Zoe." He described the disease carried by the Klikiss, which had killed off an entire unknown race, and now had adapted to infect humans.

Zoe caught her breath listening to this. "We've got to have it for the library."

"I already plotted a course. The Roamers quarantined their entire city, and they will all be dead shortly. I need to get there as soon as possible."

As much as she longed to see him, as much as she wanted his strength and his presence next to her—to ease the loneliness that was always there inside her cold, clean dome—Zoe wanted that alien plague more.

"Go. Bring me a sample of that virus and any records the Roamers might have left behind."

No one else would have seen the flicker of a smile on his emotionless face, but she knew Tom Rom all too well. "I'll do that, Zoe," he said. "For you."

NINETY-TWO

PRINCE REYN

Ildirans instinctively kept time by the positions of multiple suns in the sky, but Reyn had to use a chronometer to tell him when it was time to sleep. With his worsening symptoms, he often became exhausted at inopportune times. On the other hand, the amazing sights and experiences in Mijistra gave him energy he hadn't known he had. And he very much enjoyed Osira'h's company.

She was a considerate and enthusiastic tour guide. When the Mage-Imperator suggested the names of others who could show him highlights of Ildiran culture, Reyn assured him that he preferred Osira'h's company. Nira gave them such a warm and indulgent smile that Reyn felt embarrassed.

Now, when the Prince was well rested from a satisfying sleep, Osira'h said she had something important to show him. Laughing, she took him to one of the Prism Palace's open landing decks where a long-range cutter waited. "I'm going to take you to one of the seven suns of Ildira. Durris-B."

Reyn adjusted his protective filmgoggles. "I'm seeing too much sun as it is."

"Not up close. And there's something special about Durris-B. You'll see."

"I wouldn't argue with my hostess."

She led him aboard a cutter much too large for just the two of them, but Ildirans always liked to crowd too many aboard, so the combined *thism* would keep them from feeling isolated. Osira'h, though, was different in many ways, and when Reyn asked who else was going with them, she told him that his company would be enough.

With the Ildiran stardrive at full power, they arrived at the nearby star within two hours.

Durris was a trinary star system, a white and a yellow sun orbited by a red dwarf, and as Osira'h flew closer, the yellow sun filled the cutter's view, blocking out its white and red companions. Durris-B swelled to become a sea of hot gases in front of them. With all shields on maximum and filters in place, Osira'h streaked forward as if she meant to plunge directly into the sun.

Reyn felt awed and more than a bit intimidated. "Aren't we close enough?"

She shook her head. "You can't see them yet."

He spotted cells of roiling gases, plumes of solar flares, ethereal coronal discharges . . . and something else. Bright flashes darted about like embers in a breeze.

Osira'h glanced at him with her captivating eyes. "The faeros."

Reyn tried to cover his instinctive shiver. He'd only been a baby when the faeros devastated the worldforest. His parents had barely escaped, whisking him to safety as the trees burned. "I don't . . . have fond memories of the faeros."

Osira'h remained at the controls but closed her eyes, as if she wanted to fly blind on purpose. "They're neutralized—I helped neutralize them." She opened her eyes and turned to look at him. "I can communicate, after a fashion."

"Do they listen to you?"

"I'm not sure. I haven't tried to exert my powers over them for a long time—there's been no need. Nothing to worry about."

Prince Reyn did a brave thing and said, "In that case, I'll trust you."

She guided the cutter close to Durris-B, where thousands of faeros frolicked in the star layers, riding the arcs of flares. Several fireballs streaked past their ship as if they could sense Osira'h. Reyn followed them through the filtered windowports, amazed. Like an angry nest of buzzbeetles stirred up in the sunlight, faeros circled the cutter before diving back into Durris-B.

"I've never seen them this active before," she said. "Something has riled them up."

"I thought you could communicate with them."

"I can send messages I want them to hear, but I don't understand how they *think*. They are made of living, sentient fire—we don't exactly have a common set of experiences."

Another shudder went through him, searing pain along his nerve lines, like the fire bursting from the faeros. He winced, fighting back his reaction, which had nothing to do with the faeros.

Osira'h was deep in thought. "I wish I could understand what agitated them. . . ."

She noticed his trembling, and her gaze locked on his arm, then traveled up to his drawn face. She stared at him, waiting, and he felt his walls breaking down. Reyn had told few people—his sister, Rlinda, some researchers—but as he sat close to Osira'h, who was so strange and beautiful and understanding, he had found another ally. A friend. That was one of the reasons he had come to Ildira in the first place.

"I need your help," he said, and ignoring the inferno outside their shielded cutter, he told her about his mysterious disease. "No one knows how to cure it, and I was hoping an Ildiran physician might. . . ." He couldn't control his trembling now. "But I don't want anyone else to know—not until I'm sure."

Ignoring the faeros, Osira'h veered the cutter away, changed course, and raced back to Ildira. Several of the curious fireballs followed them for a time, flying in fiery loops, before they dropped back to the churning star.

"Our best medical kithmen will devote themselves to the challenge," Osira'h said. "I'll make sure of that."

The medical kithmen found Reyn to be a perplexing problem.

After Osira'h made her request, the intense Ildiran doctors were completely dedicated to his case, convinced that if they found a cure then it would also honor the Mage-Imperator. They took samples and ran tests with diagnostic apparatus Reyn had never seen before. One of the doctors ran sensitive fingertips over his skin, as if he could telepathically pick up tiny flaws in Reyn's DNA.

They were fascinated by the challenge, in part because it gave them an opportunity to learn more about human genetics. Unfortunately, although they were eager and curious, they could offer Reyn little hope beyond promising to find out all that they could about the mysterious disease.

He maintained his confidence, remembering what he had promised his sister, but Osira'h beseeched the researchers. "In the name of the Mage-Imperator, apply all your knowledge, all your imagination, all your skills to find a cure for this man." Her eyes sparkled. "He is important to me."

The doctors bowed. "We will do everything possible, with all the resources of our kith. If it is within our power, we will find a treatment."

Reyn said, "Thank you." And when Osira'h reached over and squeezed his hand, he felt even stronger.

NINETY-THREE

ARITA

Arita spent her days in the Wild surrounded by the lush Theron forest and thousands of species just waiting to be documented and categorized. For the most part, Kennebar and his green priests ignored her, but how could she feel alone out here? She found the ecosystem endlessly fascinating, and it was a full-time job just to *glimpse* as many species as she could. Genuine understanding would come after years of investigation conducted by armies of naturalists. Arita could never do it all, but at least she was laying the groundwork.

She would have been able to learn so much more if she could tap into the verdani mind like a green priest. Instead, when she was alone in the wilderness the tantalizing, even maddening, echo whispers did nothing to help. The sounds and thoughts simply reminded her how much of the worldforest remained out of her reach.

The trees were huge and powerful, and occasionally the ghost whispers grew louder in her head. When she closed her eyes, she saw faint flashes of light, as if she were at the edge of a presence that was incredibly vast . . . *more* vast than even the worldforest.

Arita continued her work, gathering vials of interesting spores, imaging fungal growths without destroying their delicate soft tissue, scanning myriad insects, even hard seedpods that startlingly took flight when she tried to pick them up.

Arita could have stayed at home and not managed to document all the species within a few kilometers of the main fungus-reef city, but she wanted to put footprints in unexplored territory, to see exciting new plants and creatures in the Wild. She also wanted to get away—like her aunt Sarein had when she chose to exile herself to the empty continent.

Decades ago, Sarein had been an influential person in the Hansa. Before the Elemental War, she'd been the lover of Chairman Wenceslas, an ambassador, and a manipulator who had made many questionable decisions, as well as a few wise ones. Arita didn't know the full story; her mother did not talk much about her own sister, leaving the details in shadow, but Arita had always wanted to know more.

One day, she packed up supplies, records, and equipment, double-checked the logs so that she had a general idea of where she was going, and set off in search of Sarein. She knew the general location where her aunt made her isolated home, and Arita wanted to get to know her and understand what she had done that caused her to hide from other people.

On the way, Arita continued to image and collect samples. Of course, she would never convince Sarein that she had "accidentally" stumbled upon her out in the empty worldforest.

She wandered farther afield, but found no sign of Sarein, though she was sure she had the location right. After two days, Arita focused her efforts more intensely, but gradually realized that she had no idea where to go. Eventually, Arita admitted that she was lost in the depths of the worldforest. She couldn't even find her way back to the meadow and her ship.

While growing up and running free through the forests, she had always had an instinctive feel for direction, but here, nothing looked familiar. With a sinking feeling, she sat down with her back against one of the worldtrees and forced herself to gather her thoughts. "Now what?"

Collin descended from the fronds above, working his way down the trunk from one bark scale to another. He landed in front of her. "Need some help?"

"I'm so glad to see you!" She didn't want to let him see her relief. "Wait—have you been *spying* on me?"

He shrugged his bare shoulders. "I don't have to spy—the worldtrees see everything. But you are far from your ship—far from anything, in fact."

"I was looking for Sarein. I know she can't be far from here." Arita lowered her head. She'd gotten herself into this mess.

Collin said, "All right, I confess, I was watching to make sure you were all right. You're not even close to where Sarein lives, you know. Would you like a hint?"

Indignant, Arita said, "I'm on the right continent, at least."

Chuckling, he took her hand. "Follow me." He led her back to where she had been an hour before, then set off in a different direction. "I was going to try that way," she said, "but I didn't know."

He nodded. "It's because you can't hear the trees."

"Stop reminding me."

They were actually closer than Collin had implied. By late afternoon he led Arita to a tree from which dangled an empty hiveworm nest, a papery structure suspended between branches. The hive had once been filled with thrashing, ravenous worms, but after transforming into giant moths, they left their nest behind. Therons had long used hiveworm nests as dwellings.

"There she is." Collin pointed up at the hive, then lowered his voice. "Good luck." He darted off into the worldtrees, and Arita was amazed at how quickly he vanished.

From below, the hiveworm nest looked to be a clean, though austere, home, with a few window hangings and some technological conveniences Sarein had brought from the main continent.

Hearing the voices, a woman appeared at one of the windows cut from the side of the papery nest and frowned down on Arita. "I came out of hiding for my father's funeral, and now everyone thinks I'm ready to receive visitors?"

"Not everyone," Arita said. "Just me."

Sarein recognized her niece, of course, but she had never shown any particular warmth toward her. Arita lifted up her pack and samples to show them. "I'm collecting and cataloguing specimens from the Wild. Since I was on the continent, I wanted to talk with you."

"About what?"

"Do I need a written agenda? I've been here alone for a couple of weeks. Kennebar and his green priests aren't very hospitable."

Sarein made a sound of disapproval. "They choose to be alone as if it's some matter of pride. I'm alone because the other parts of my life required it."

"Like when you used to work for the Hansa?" A troubled look

crossed Sarein's face, but she didn't move from the window above. Arita continued. "I just want to visit, get to know you. But I'll leave if I'm not welcome." She started to walk away, hoping her aunt would respond.

Eventually, she did. "Come on up, then, but I don't have a lift. You'll have to climb."

Arita laughed—as if *that* would present some sort of challenge. She secured her specimens, tightened her pack, and scrambled up to the nest.

Everything in Sarein's home was functional: no artwork, decorations, or other frippery. Expecting no guests, she had only one lightweight polymer seat, so Arita swung up into the cocoonweave hammock that served as a bed. "What do you do here all day?"

Sarein took the lone chair, which sat next to a flat platform she used as a writing desk. "I think, and I write down what I remember, the decisions I made, the events I was part of." She hesitated. "All the crimes I watched Basil commit. I've tried to re-create my rationalizations for why I didn't stop him. The reasons seem pretty weak now."

"So you're writing your memoir?"

"I'm documenting history—as objectively as I can. No excuses. I don't need to paint myself with pretty colors."

"Can I read what you've written?"

"No."

"Then what is it for?"

"For myself. I've spent years working through what I remember."

Now Arita thought she understood. "Ah, like a kind of confession."

Sarein frowned. "As I said, I'm documenting history. Sometimes when I get lonely I need to remind myself why I withdrew from public view." She glanced at Arita's sample packs and noted the Confederation logo. "I don't miss any of it, and I don't like interruptions. That's why I wish those green priests hadn't moved into my Wild."

Arita felt awkward, decided to respect her aunt's privacy. "I didn't mean to intrude. Back home I stay away from politics. Exploring nature is what makes me happy. Even though I'm the daughter of the King and Queen, all I ever wanted was to be a simple green priest."

Sarein looked at her with greater interest now. "Then why didn't you? It's a good tradition. My sister Celli is a green priest. So was my brother Beneto."

Arita's eyes burned. "I tried . . . but that's my story, and if you're not going to tell me about yourself, then I have a right to keep my own secrets."

"Yes," Sarein said. "Yes, you do."

At her small stove unit, she began heating water, to which she added ground worldtree seeds, making them each a cup of klee. "You can use my hive as a base camp, if you like. It's better than sleeping on the ground—as long as you don't bother me too much."

NINETY-FOUR

Orli had been exposed to the plague, and she knew it.

The clan Reeves compies worked throughout the Onthos space city, rewiring the power blocks and the alien energy reactors, setting up a thorough network of detonations. Meanwhile, Orli tried to convince herself that her racing pulse, feverish feeling, and nausea were just a response to stress. The disease's incubation period had to be much longer than this. She wouldn't know for some time yet if she was infected.

But judging from the mortality rate—one hundred percent—if she did contract the plague, then she was going to die. She couldn't go back to civilization and risk exposing anyone else. Meanwhile, BO and the other five compies were precluded from destroying the infected city while she remained aboard.

The other compies were focused on their task, which was not so difficult as it was time-consuming. The sequence would have to be carefully synchronized and monitored, and the five compies, plus BO, would take separate stations . . . or they would have to spend even more time to automate the process. While two Worker compies primed the reactor for an overload, two other compies went up and down the spokes of the city, opening every module to hard vacuum, venting the air to space, just in case some self-contained sections survived the massive planned explosion. They were meticulous and thorough.

Olaf Reeves had been careful in his instructions, insisting that the compies must be vaporized along with the station. No trace. BO repeated the man's words to Orli, even imitating the clan leader's gruff voice. "By the Guiding Star, I know how people are, especially greedy ones. A dire warning will only make them more curious. Bleeding hearts will try to save us long after we're dead. Prospectors and historians will come here to poke around, looking for lost treasure, convinced that a few sterilization routines are good enough. No, I'm not going to doom the whole damned race because somebody will be an idiot—it might take years, might take centuries, but they'll come. We have to wipe out this city, every speck of it, at all costs. Leave no chance whatsoever that this disease can spread. If it ever got loose in a populated area . . ."

Orli's gut twisted, and her head was pounding. She closed her eyes, even though she knew BO and DD were staring at her, waiting for a response. "He's absolutely right," she said.

At all costs.

Since Orli and DD's unexpected arrival, the Retroamer compies had reassessed their timing and instituted a delay—for her, even though Orli hadn't asked them to do so. BO said, "If you are still alive, Orli Covitz, we cannot trigger the detonation, because then we would knowingly be causing your death. Our programming precludes that."

Orli thought she could probably alter their basic routines, adding logical loopholes and justifications. They had to know that by obliterating the plague, they would save millions, if not billions, of human lives at the cost of one. It was simple mathematics.

Or, she realized, instead of making such a complex argument, Orli could just rig the reactors to explode by herself.

"I'll live for a week, ten days at the outside, right?" She had made the grim calculations herself. "And if you refuse to destroy the station until I'm dead—that might give someone else enough time to get here. I am the first, but there'll be more soon. The green priest sent out his warning through telink, and other people may already be on their way."

DD said in his usual naïve fashion, "If others were warned to stay away, we will be safe. Why are you concerned, Orli?"

"Because the louder you tell someone to stay away, the more eager they'll be to come here. Olaf Reeves knew that, too."

"That is illogical."

"Yes, people often are."

But Orli realized there was another consideration if this ancient city was destroyed without a trace. BO took the time to show her the

Onthos library chamber, the images and records of the small group
of aliens, remnants of their waning race who had fled out here in the
hope of remaining safe. According to translations by the green priest
Shelud, most of the Onthos had been wiped out by some great disaster even before the Klikiss swarm wars, but BO didn't know the details. Every bit of information was entirely new.

That would all be lost.

As she looked at the images of the strange, small-statured aliens,
Orli felt sad to know she was destroying the last remnant of an intelligent civilization. No one had previously encountered any Onthos relics, as far as she knew. Neither the Ildirans nor the humans
had any inkling that the race had existed. The worldforest held only
a faint memory of the Onthos and had asked Shelud to transmit
every bit of information he could. But according to BO, the green
priest had barely begun the task before he succumbed to the plague.
And once this station was vaporized, all that knowledge would be
gone. . . .

DD sounded dejected. "I spent many years with Margaret and
Louis Colicos when we investigated Klikiss ruins. We were proud
xeno-archaeologists and discovered many important things. That was
before we knew how evil the Klikiss robots were." The little compy
paused as if dealing with his own fears. "There is much knowledge in
this ancient city, Orli. I am sad to see it all lost."

"But we can't risk infection—the danger is too great," she said.
"We don't dare let other archaeologists have access to this place. One
small slip, a careless exposure . . ." Then she realized the solution had
been in front of her all along. "BO, can you help me compile a digital
summary of this station, the Onthos history, everything that happened?"

"Already completed," the Teacher compy said. "I also have full
documentation of clan Reeves and their time here, as well as records
of the spread of the plague. The green priest used his treeling to
communicate the basics to the worldforest network, but the complete library of Onthos records remains intact. It would be good to
preserve it."

Orli said, "Let me take those records aboard the *Proud Mary*. DD
will accompany me, and we'll fly close to some human outpost where

we can transmit the data. At least that way it can be preserved and shared—the information is too important. But we'll remain isolated aboard the ship. *Proud Mary* will be my quarantine." She drew a deep breath. "And when the plague gets me—" Her voice cracked, and she felt dread and despair rising within her. "When I die, DD will have the same instructions you do. My ship has to be destroyed in space, and no one else need ever contract the disease."

"A very good solution," BO said in a voice that sounded much too cheerful for the subject matter. "And we will not need to delay the destruction here."

Orli thought of all the work she had done on Relleker, trying so hard to save compies. "In fact, BO, I want you and the other compies to join me aboard the *Proud Mary.* We can detonate the station remotely."

"That will not be possible, Orli Covitz. Our explicit orders are to remain here and complete our tasks, then to perish with the station."

"But it's not necessary. I'm giving you new orders. Come with me." Her mind raced to find a way to ensure complete sterilization of the compies. Simple exposure to vacuum for an extended time should be sufficient. And there were numerous backup decontamination routines, which she explained to BO.

"I see no flaw whatsoever in your reasoning," the Teacher compy said. "But we have prepared the detonation so that all compies must act in unison. To reconfigure now would take an extra day. An extra day could again change the parameters. If yet another unexpected visitor arrived, it would change our timing once again. Any delay increases the danger."

"Then DD and I can help. We'll work together to make it possible."

BO turned to face her. "I appreciate your earnest desire to save us, but our orders are explicit and inflexible. I will not allow you to rationalize a way for us to escape—any such deviation increases the risk. You know this, Orli Covitz."

Orli remained silent, her stomach knotted, as she tried to think how she might convince the willful Teacher compy. But BO's argument was sound, even if Orli didn't like it.

"I will be your companion, Orli," DD said. "And I will follow whatever instructions you give."

"I know you will, DD." She felt tears filling her eyes.

The Teacher compy marched off. "I will retrieve the records I assembled. The compies here have nearly finished venting the modules to space. We will be ready to detonate the Onthos city within two hours."

"Two hours . . ." Orli said. "You're being very brave, BO—you and all of the compies."

BO swiveled her head. "We do what is asked of us."

Orli and DD went back to the control chamber and watched a Worker compy connecting power blocks to the alien reactor, as if it were simply another task. These compies knew they would cause their own destruction, but Olaf Reeves had given them commands. Even though compy core programming had self-preservation subroutines, they understood the larger picture. Their work and their sacrifice would save human lives, which took precedence over their own self-preservation drive.

Orli could not convince the compies otherwise.

Watching them, she thought fondly of the misfit compies she had rescued, retrained, reprogrammed, and sent out in civilization again. She thought of LU and the too-diligent Domestic compy, MO. They'd been her companions when Matthew was gone. She was glad that they, at least, would have stable and satisfying lives.

The Worker compy turned from his work at the reactor and directed bright optical sensors at her. "We can complete our preparations within fifty minutes. You should get to safety."

Orli loaded the files BO had collated into the *Proud Mary*'s computer and then stood on the boarding ramp with DD. All six clan Reeves compies gathered with her in the launching bay, their work done. She said goodbye and tried to tell them how much she—and by extension the human race—appreciated their efforts, but she ran out of words. The compies understood anyway.

She and DD stepped inside the *Proud Mary* and sealed the hatch. "Time to retreat to a safe distance, but I want to stay until the end. We owe them that."

"I agree, Orli," DD said. "We can record the image to complete the story."

She replaced the hand jazer in the captain's locker, bitterly amused at herself for thinking that a hand weapon could have protected her against what had killed the Retroamers. She had been cautious, but not in the right way. Orli powered up the systems and eased the *Proud Mary* away from the derelict city.

DD said, "You called those compies brave, Orli. Do you truly believe that? They were merely following instructions, as compies do."

"I choose to think they were brave, DD." She looked through the windowport of the *Proud Mary*, studying the strange beauty of the dead city.

"Are we being brave, Orli?"

"Yes, DD, I think we are."

"My self-preservation programming compels me to avoid being destroyed. And I have a great many fond memories. My existence has been filled with experiences, but I cannot say that I am afraid to die. Are you afraid to die, Orli?"

She swallowed hard and avoided the answer. "I know what we need to do, and it's important that we survive for just a little longer. We have to deliver this vital information so that it isn't lost forever. Also . . . Rlinda Kett deserves to know what happened to us. I suppose even Matthew deserves to know." Otherwise, she and DD would have just disappeared in space, leaving only a void of questions.

As the *Proud Mary* hung at a safe distance from the derelict city, Orli considered her life and now her own mortality. She had been with old Mr. Steinman when he passed away, and she knew he was at peace. She thought of how Rlinda Kett kept BeBob's small capsule of ashes with instructions to join him when she died. Orli didn't have anyone . . . except DD. The little compy would have to be enough.

"I'm not necessarily afraid to die, DD, but I'm not looking forward to it, and I don't want to hurry it along."

In the last minute, BO transmitted, "We are prepared, Orli Covitz. Final countdown initiated. We have thirty seconds."

"I'm proud of you," Orli said. "All of you."

The Teacher compy stared back, as if she were contemplating the proper response. "Thank you. And we are proud to do our best."

The space city exploded.

The first eruption blossomed bright as a star in the central hub, the nucleus of the jagged metal snowflake. Heat and shock waves radiated outward while additional explosions rattled along the five spokes, detonating the separate modules.

The compies had been very thorough in their planning. Orli felt a pang as she saw the bright flash, the expanding cloud of debris. She knew that nothing would be left. The disease was eradicated.

Except in her.

She used the medical kit and took her temperature to find that it was elevated—possibly because of her anxiety, the effort of rushing to get away—but she had been sitting in the cockpit for some time, resting in the *Proud Mary*'s worn pilot seat. No, the fever was already starting. She would finish her work, deliver the data and her messages . . . and then DD would complete his job, too.

A sensor blip alerted her to another ship approaching. As the debris of the Onthos city continued to spread and the thermal glow faded, the new ship raced in like a projectile heading toward a target.

"Now who the hell is that?" Orli already guessed it was some treasure hunter, do-gooder, or curious spectator, just as Olaf Reeves had predicted. She let out a sigh; the Retroamer compies had done their work just in time.

"DD, open a comm channel." She turned to the *Proud Mary*'s screen. "Incoming ship, please stay away from the vicinity. This was a quarantine station, all members of clan Reeves are now dead. The area has been sterilized."

The other pilot responded, "No survivors?" His voice was clipped and businesslike. "Everything destroyed?"

"No survivors of the original group, but I believe I've also been exposed, so please keep your distance. I'll maintain a self-imposed quarantine until . . . until everything else can be taken care of. But I have a compilation of data I can transmit to you. That should give you all you need."

After a long silence, the other pilot appeared on the screen. His face was lean, his skin a dark brown as if carved from mahogany. "My name is Tom Rom. I will accept your data, but that is not my priority. If you've contracted the disease, you have something that I need. Stand down and prepare to be boarded."

NINETY-FIVE

ADAR ZAN'NH

His maniple of warliners was en route to the Plumas system, ready for an exhilarating test engagement with the Confederation Defense Forces. He had new information about the Shana Rei to share, as well as a surprise or two. He liked it when he could surprise General Nalani Keah.

Zan'nh considered Keah a tactical genius. Fortunately, she intended to remain in the background for the Plumas maneuvers, merely observing how her Grid Admirals handled a realistic combat scenario. Adar Zan'nh would do the same, allowing the maniple commander Qul Uldo'nh and his seven septars to demonstrate their prowess in the space engagement near the ice moon.

A clash with the CDF, however, would be quite different from a battle against the Shana Rei. On Ildira, Anton Colicos and the rememberer kith had been discovering information about previous battles with the creatures of darkness, stories of Tal Bria'nh's engagements and his plans for unusual weapons that might have some effect on the Shana Rei. But they remained to be tested.

The grand procession flew through space, forty-nine warliners closing in on the Roamer water-pumping station, precisely on schedule. The Solar Navy crews were drilled, the ships in perfect shape.

As the maniple approached the system, however, three fast CDF Remoras soared toward them. The lead warliners in the formation immediately went on alert. "Human ships approaching rapidly, Adar," Qul Uldo'nh reported.

Zan'nh was immediately wary. "Shift warliners to defensive formation. Are their weapons active?" He suspected this was some surprise from General Keah.

"They are coming too fast for us to tell, Adar. The pilots are sending an urgent signal."

One of the techs in the command nucleus activated the comm screen so they could hear what the Remoras were broadcasting. "General Keah has declared an emergency. Our ships are under attack."

The Adar frowned. Maybe General Keah wanted his ships to race directly into a trap—so she could laugh, having tricked him again. "Let me speak to those pilots."

Even though the Remoras decelerated at maximum thrust, they overshot the oncoming maniple of Ildiran warliners. It took them several minutes to wheel about and streak back toward the Solar Navy ships.

Zan'nh crossed his arms over his uniformed chest. "Is this part of our exercise? If General Keah is attempting to trick—"

"Good Lord, no, Adar!" squawked the Remora pilot. Zan'nh was familiar enough with human expressions to see the genuine alarm on her face. "One of those black nebulas appeared in the system, like the one at Dhula. There's a swarm of black robot ships and three gigantic vessels of unknown origin. It isn't a joke, sir! This is not a wargame exercise."

Zan'nh knew Keah would not undertake such an elaborate ruse. Black robots and a shadow cloud. A smile crept to his lips. He had not expected an immediate opportunity to use the new prototypes the engineer kith had built from the old designs. "Engaging a real enemy will be a far superior experience to any war games. Full acceleration!"

The CDF Remoras led them into the Plumas system, and Zan'nh saw that indeed this was no trick.

Mammoth hexagonal cylinders had emerged from a cavernous black cloud, and he knew they were Shana Rei battleships. The smaller, frenetic attacking vessels were of Klikiss robot design, but far more numerous than the few they had pursued at Dhula. The robot ships harried the CDF Juggernauts and Mantas.

Zan'nh opened a direct channel to the *Kutuzov*. "General Keah, the Ildiran Solar Navy is at your service."

On screen, Keah appeared flustered; her bridge deck seemed canted at an odd angle. "It's about damned time, Z! We could sure use the cavalry."

The Adar nodded to Qul Uldo'nh, who transmitted to his seven septars, who then transmitted to their subcommanders. "Attack formation, full speed ahead. Weapons active, traditional artillery as well as modified test lasers."

The CDF battleships were in disarray, struggling to maintain course and keep up the attack. The firefight was a confusing staccato of jazer beams, relativistic projectiles, and artillery blasts.

Ignoring the main battle, the mammoth hexagonal cylinders glided toward the frozen planetoid. Plumas must have been the original target of the shadow creatures, and the encounter with the human battle group was merely accidental.

Seeing the Solar Navy arrive, a group of robot ships streaked in among the warliners, letting loose with their weapons. The Ildirans scrambled to raise their shields, then struck back with a barrage of high-energy blasters. Against the robots, Zan'nh would use traditional weapons.

As the black hex ships cruised past like blunt spears thrusting into an unprotected body, the warliner systems began to crackle, disrupted by the aftereffects of the Shana Rei, creatures of chaos.

On the main screen, Keah yelled, but a crackle of static distorted her voice. "They're heading toward the Plumas station, Z. I've ordered the Roamers to evacuate, but our ships aren't exactly a safe haven either."

"We will try to intercept the Shana Rei," Zan'nh said.

The screen shifted, and Keah's signal changed as the commline was commandeered, replaced by an image out of a nightmare—one of the beetlelike Klikiss robots. It had a flat geometric head and a cluster of crimson optical sensors. Zan'nh had seen too many of the black robots during the Elemental War.

The simulated voice was rough and grating. "Humans and Ildirans, this transmission is to inform you of your fate. The Klikiss robots and the Shana Rei are now allies. Together, we will eradicate all intelligent life, down to the last human, the last Ildiran, the last city, the last ship."

On the same channel, General Keah made a sarcastic comment. "Well at least you're ambitious."

"We are invincible." The robot's signal was sharp and clear, as if their vessels could bypass the entropy disruption.

Zan'nh couldn't believe what he was hearing. "You expect us to surrender?"

The robot swiveled its geometric head. The optical sensors blazed like red coals. "We expect you to *perish*. Everything else is out of your control." The signal blanked out.

"Sounds like we've got our work cut out for us, Z," General Keah said as her Juggernaut altered course. The other CDF ships, many of them already damaged, limped toward Plumas in pursuit of the huge hexagonal cylinders.

Zan'nh transmitted to his maniple, "Warliners, fill all energy-weapon chambers and prepare laser missiles for a maximum-intensity discharge. Target those Shana Rei ships."

Lasers had not been used for weaponry in a very long time, having been superseded by far more efficient modes of destruction, but the historical records suggested the Shana Rei might be vulnerable to the intense coherent light. He did know that laser cutters had sliced through the ebony shell that covered the dead *Kolpraxa*.

As the warliners cruised in, their control systems began to flicker and fail, but not before they targeted one of the huge black hexagons. A blinding fusillade of high-intensity laser missiles struck the obsidian armor. Though Zan'nh's eyes were dazzled, he could see part of the ebony hull turn into black smoke under the barrage of light, roiling up and into space.

The Solar Navy soldiers cheered. Zan'nh felt giddy with relief.

General Keah sent over a signal, "What the hell was that, Z? What have you been hiding on us?"

"Lasers, General. Concentrated light."

"Good to see that it had some effect," Keah said. "I want some, but I think we're going to need bigger ones."

The Shana Rei battleship rotated the damaged section out of view and continued toward Plumas, undeterred.

As their guidance systems and sensors failed in the backwash of entropy, the Ildiran battleships drifted out of their coordinated flight patterns. Two warliners careened close to each other, tangling their solar-sail wings.

Although the maniple was blinded by malfunctions, the robot vessels flew in and attacked. The flagship's systems were failing. Qul

Uldo'nh reported, "Five warliners down, Adar!" Meanwhile, the robot ships destroyed two more CDF Mantas.

Roiling, unmade matter spewed from the deep scar in the hex ship's hull and wrapped like a shroud around one of the warliners. The shadow englobed it in impenetrable black and cut it off from the universe. All signals from the warliner abruptly ceased, and Zan'nh could no longer feel the crewmembers in the *thism*. The silhouetted ship winked out of existence.

On Plumas, clan Tamblyn was evacuating their water mines, as Keah had ordered. Fifteen bloated water tankers lumbered up out of the gravity well, flanked by dozens of smaller ships that raced away from the facilities.

The Ildiran flagship's laser missiles needed another hour to recharge to full power, and many of the warliner batteries were already depleted. Zan'nh watched yet another of his ships explode into debris that rained down on the ice moon below.

The flagship's weapons systems went dead.

Zan'nh didn't know how he could protect the evacuating Tamblyn ships. He doubted they would be safer out in space than under the ice sheet of Plumas. In fact, he feared the Solar Navy and the CDF might be lucky to escape at all.

NINETY-SIX

GENERAL NALANI KEAH

This was going to hell, and she didn't even have a handbasket to carry it in.

General Keah gripped her command chair as the bridge of the *Kutuzov* rocked from side to side—partly due to weapons blasts from the attacking robot ships, partly because her ship's stabilizers and artificial gravity had gone haywire. She could see the writing on the wall.

The CDF ships descended toward Plumas, and Keah wondered why the Shana Rei had such a grudge against that unremarkable frozen moon. "We have to take those Tamblyn evacuees aboard. I'm not sounding a retreat just yet, but when we do get the hell out of here, I want to take those people with me."

The mammoth cylinders went into orbit, aligning their flat hexagonal ends toward the icy crust. Their very presence seemed to distort the *reality* of the moon. Ripples and tremors tore through the pockmarked surface, and quakes shattered the ice. Geysers of released water erupted from the oceans below.

The surface wellheads, pumping stations, and landing fields were flattened. Urgent distress signals came from Roamers beneath the ice sheet who had not yet managed to evacuate; they cut off abruptly as the ceiling collapsed. The rest of the clan Tamblyn ships lurched away from the ice moon, racing pell-mell toward the dubious protection of the CDF battle group.

Fifteen lumbering water tankers tried to match the speed of the swifter evacuation ships. Why would Ron Tamblyn bother rescuing a water cargo that could easily be replaced? When Keah scolded him over the comm, the Plumas administrator responded, "By the Guiding Star, General, I don't care about the water—I want the *tankers*! You know how expensive those are?"

"That's not your biggest worry right now, Mr. Tamblyn. Get your people aboard my Juggernaut. We've got all our landing bays open. Come in hot—don't waste any time!"

The Shana Rei were devoting their energies against Plumas itself, ignoring the flurry of space battle. The thick ice sheets continued to crack and crumble under the entropy bombardment.

The Ildiran ships continued the battle, but in disarray, and many of their weapons seemed to be offline. Three more warliners careened into one another, and black robot ships swooped in and hammered the damaged Solar Navy vessels, destroying all of them.

The Three H's had gone quiet, letting Keah issue orders for the entire battle group. She appreciated not having to chase after unruly and inept admirals, but she needed them to pull their weight. "Admiral Handies, go lend assistance to Adar Zan'nh. The warliners are suffering heavy losses."

"*Our* ships are suffering heavy losses, General."

"We're all in this together—that's the point of being allies! We don't have super-lasers like what the Ildirans just tested, but you can use regular old jazers to wreck some bugbots. There's plenty of 'em."

Admiral Handies dutifully sent his Mantas into the fray.

Keah transmitted to the other two Grid Admirals, "Buy us some time so the Roamer evacuees can get aboard."

The first clan Tamblyn ships rolled in, skidding to a halt in the *Kutuzov's* landing bays. Though the Roamers were not military trained, even the worst of them was a crack pilot.

She sent a signal to the Ildiran flagship. "We'll have everybody on board within an hour, Z. Can you give us that much time?"

"We shall do our best, General. And then I suggest we retreat."

Keah let out a grim laugh. "In the CDF we prefer to call it 're-grouping and reassessing'—but I agree."

"I have one more item to test," the Adar said. "Observe. You may find this interesting—we have only one prototype. For now. If it proves effective, we will build many more."

"What is it?"

"A weapon called a sun bomb. We recently found the plans in old records."

Keah thought that sounded promising. "What are you waiting for?"

The Adar's flagship launched a pulsing sphere, a metallic ball that hurtled out from a specialized weapons port. Keah leaned forward, holding her breath, staring at the screen. Her bridge crew fell silent. She counted to five.

The Ildiran sun bomb became a miniaturized supernova, an explosion of pure photonic energy so intense that it temporarily burned out her main viewing screens. When the images finally returned, blurred and filled with static, Keah saw the Shana Rei hex ships reeling, parts of them melted away, craters hollowed out in their long obsidian sides.

She hammered the comm button. "Damn, that was terrific, Z! When can we get a thousand more of those?"

"Not until we manufacture them. But we will share the designs with you—now that we know they are effective."

"Good. I'll thank you later." Now she had to take advantage of the surprise and get her ships ready to race away.

A haggard-looking man in a smudged and patched jumpsuit staggered onto the *Kutuzov*'s bridge. His headband was askew, his hair sweaty. "My first Roamers are aboard, more to come—thanks for giving us a lift." Ron Tamblyn shook his head. "Now can you tell me what is going on out there?"

When the Roamer administrator stood by her command chair, Keah could smell his sweat. "Black robot attack, creatures of darkness . . . the usual. We don't know how to fight them, but we're learning as fast as we can."

The detonation of the sun bomb served to rile up the robots, and they intensified their attack, causing significant damage, because their weapons were immune from the Shana Rei entropy backwash.

Tamblyn looked mournfully at the cracking moon on the screen, the crushed ice sheets that bled sprays of spilled water. Plumas didn't even look spherical anymore. He let out a low moan in his chest. "I guess now I'm director of Humpty Dumpty Station."

"If you want to get out of here, sir, our engines are iffy," said the *Kutuzov*'s navigator.

"Admiral Haroun reports the same, General," said the comm chief. "He's lost eight Mantas already."

She worried that even when they retreated, the robot ships could pursue them and continue to harass, damage, and destroy her ships. It wouldn't do much good to escape the Plumas system if the bugbots wiped out the rest of her battle group before they got back to Earth.

She realized with a chill just how bad the situation was. *Somebody* had to survive and make a report about the effectiveness of the laser missiles, the sun bomb.

"We'd better squeeze as much out of our stardrives as possible," Keah said. "Get ready to run."

The fifteen Roamer water tankers continued to crawl upward, well behind the rest of the evacuating ships. She studied the water tankers, then snapped her head around. "Mr. Tamblyn, do those pilots have evacuation pods? Can they dump the tankers and get to safety?"

Ron Tamblyn grimaced. "After all that work of getting them away?"

"I already know what we have to do—I'm just trying to see if I can save a few more of your people."

Tamblyn recognized the terrible shape they were in. "Yes, they can evacuate. And most of our people are aboard by now—do what you have to."

She sent a tight signal over to the Ildiran flagship. "Z, we need to get the hell out of Dodge, and I've got a way."

Adar Zan'nh responded, "Where is Dodge? We are at Plumas."

The Shana Rei hexagon ships were reassembling themselves, rematerializing structural matter, but they seemed smaller and stubbier now, as if they had been dealt a terrible wound. She didn't know if the creatures of darkness would get vengeful, but she didn't want to stick around to find out.

"I'm going to make a smoke screen. Set your course and head out when you see your chance. We evacuated about as many of these people as we're going to."

A few more Roamer ships were still crowding into the *Kutuzov*'s bays. She could give the Plumas workers a few more minutes as she set up.

Adar Zan'nh's normally implacable face showed deep concern. "Very well, General, I will trust your instincts. The Solar Navy is ready to depart."

She turned to Ron Tamblyn and gave him instructions. He broadcast on a frequency that the CDF didn't use, instructing his tanker pilots to eject and to make their way immediately to the nearest battleship. The barrage of complaints that came back was loud enough to make Tamblyn flinch.

Keah said, "Tell them they've got five minutes. No excuses, no apologies." She turned to her navigator. "Mr. Tait, set a course for us to get out of here."

"Yes, General. Informing our other vessels as well—all the ones we've got left."

The tanker pilots ejected their tiny evacuation pods, and some of the last-wave Roamer ships scooped them up and pulled them into the nearest Manta cruiser landing bay.

Keah let out a sigh. "Mr. Patton, train our jazers on one of those tankers. Inform your counterparts to do the same and wait for my signal."

"A smoke screen," said Patton. "Yes, General."

When the tanker evac pods had tumbled aboard the waiting CDF ships, Keah gave her order. As the black robot ships continued to attack, jazers exploded the tankers and vaporized their contents. The detonation was powerful enough to spread water vapor in a huge, dense cloud.

It was exactly what they needed.

The vapor cloud engulfed the robot vessels, blinding them, along with the CDF ships. In a last glimpse, Keah saw the Solar Navy warliners wheel about and accelerate away.

Ron Tamblyn stared at the tanker explosions and at the crushed ice moon, seeing in the water droplets a few billion tears for his facilities and his lost friends.

"Helm, full acceleration! Let's get out of here."

She would have preferred to score a clear victory rather than just getting away alive, but their survival was vital. She had to report this to the Confederation. The data they had gathered would form the basis for developing new defenses for the CDF and the Solar Navy.

And she wanted a lot of those sun bombs.

She muttered, "Well, Z, looks like we found that unexpected enemy after all."

NINETY-SEVEN

OSIRA'H

The Ildiran mirror ballet was one of Osira'h's favorite displays in the city of Mijistra, and she knew that Prince Reynald from Theroc had never seen anything like it. As much as she looked forward to the spectacle, she would spend most of her time watching the sparkle in his eyes.

Reyn was content to see whatever Osira'h wanted to show him, although he was weary of the crowds that followed them everywhere. "My parents sent me here to experience Ildiran culture. While your doctors keep running tests to figure out what's wrong with me, I should do what I came here for."

"Then I'll show you Ildira and tell you everything you need to know." She found the young man interesting.

The mirror ballet was held in a large arena, taking place whenever all seven of Ildira's suns were visible in the sky. Today, the double sun of Qronha was low to the horizon and mostly obscured by buildings, but even so, the mirror ballet was performed.

Reyn wore filmgoggles to protect against the intense light inside the arena, and misters dispersed jets of vapor to cool the air, with the added benefit that the humid haze intensified the rainbows for the kinetic-prism part of the performance.

Because of her status, Osira'h reserved a private observation box for herself and Reyn, so that the two of them could relax in solitude during the performance, although the ever-present entourage didn't seem to understand why they might like to be alone. When a dozen noble kithmen and courtiers crowded into the small box to join them, Osira'h noted Reyn's flicker of weary disappointment. Glad that she had solved this problem in advance, she instructed the others to leave. "I have arranged special seats for you near the conductor. The Prince and I have important political matters to discuss in private."

When she and Reyn had the observation box to themselves, he gave her a curious look. "Important political matters?"

Osira'h chuckled. "We'll think of something. I just didn't want to be crowded."

He let out a sigh. "I am glad for just a little peace."

In the arena, chrome-plated sculptures rose out of compartments in the ground; their articulated arms were studded with large round lenses. Curved mirrors swung into position to direct light into rotating prisms that bobbed up and down like photonic pistons. Reflective slats in the domed ceiling turned downward on louvers and aimed the light into the performance area.

The ballet conductor brought forth an array of laser projectors, which looked like some kind of bizarre weapons system. Rich beams of varied hues danced through the low-hanging mist. The play of lights, mirrors, lasers, and vapor created a hypnotic cat's cradle of colors.

The Ildiran audience cheered. Some blew on shrill pipes, making a piercing noise that signified their appreciation. Osira'h tore her gaze from the beautiful display to look at Reyn. Even behind his protective filmgoggles, she could see an excited shine in his eyes, and she knew she had chosen the right thing to show him. "I'm glad you like it."

She saw a flicker of pain cross his face like a sudden quake. He flinched, squeezed his eyes shut, and struggled to concentrate. Finally, he drove back the nerve spasm.

Although the medical kithmen found Reyn's sickness intriguing, they had offered no breakthroughs. Yet. They had studied his genetic samples, requested several other tests. With their full attention, they pored over the cause, the symptoms, and possible treatments to mitigate his pain. Confederation doctors might have access to more background in the morphology of human diseases, but Osira'h knew that Ildiran medical kithmen had an added drive, since they were trying to find a cure for Reyn in the name of the Mage-Imperator.

She had also sent data and samples to her sister Tamo'l on Kuivahr, where she could study them in her sanctuary domes. Her own medical researchers might have ideas. Osira'h was determined to find some help for him.

As the ballet continued, she reached out and took Reyn's hand, squeezing hard, focusing her thoughts as if she could break down his barriers. She summoned the considerable mental powers she had inherited from her green priest mother and her father, the Mage-Imperator. That combination of telepathic skills had allowed her to command the hydrogues and the faeros. Now, however, she was just trying to open herself up to Reyn. She wanted to touch his mind and console him.

Alas, as hard as she tried to break through, the Prince felt no contact. His mind was silent to her, and his thoughts remained his own.

Nevertheless, even without telepathy, he seemed to draw strength from her presence.

After the ballet, they visited her brother Gale'nh, with his bleached skin and hair. Despite his wan appearance, Gale'nh seemed to improve each day. While the Adar's training maniple was away, engaged in intensive combat exercises with the CDF, Gale'nh wore his formal tal uniform, as if it kept him connected to the Solar Navy. Osira'h knew he wanted to be out there with Adar Zan'nh.

When she introduced him to Reyn, Gale'nh touched his own pale skin and explained, "I looked into the shadows that killed every other person aboard the *Kolpraxa*." He walked across his room and stared out at the curved crystalline towers of the city. "I have no wish to fight them again, but the creatures of darkness are still out there." He wrapped his arms around himself, as if huddling in the light.

Osira'h used their telepathic connection to offer Gale'nh strength and reassurance, but there were dark corners in her brother's mind. The full details of what he had experienced were still hidden. He was incredibly strong—she knew that—but Osira'h could feel how he had been changed, as if his soul had diminished.

After Gale'nh's return, he had met with many lens kithmen, who drew upon their own abilities and focused his recovery meditations, trying to bring him closer to the Lightsource.

Reyn looked over at Osira'h. "I have heard that Anton Colicos described the Shana Rei in some of the translations he brought back to the worldforest, but I never really understood the story."

Osira'h said, "If the Shana Rei have come back, we need to learn how to protect ourselves, how to fight them. The Solar Navy has some prototype weapons drawn from the old records, but in the old war, the Ildiran race survived the creatures of darkness only because Mage-Imperator Xiba'h convinced the faeros to fight alongside us."

Reyn was obviously concerned. "The faeros are dangerous allies to have. They leveled Mijistra, burned much of Theroc. They are not friends."

Osira'h was determined though. "The faeros listened when I called them before. Maybe they will listen again."

"There is another way to bring them," Gale'nh said. "Mage-Imperator Xiba'h did it long ago."

Osira'h explained to Reyn, "Mage-Imperator Xiba'h called the faeros by immolating himself. He threw himself into a great pyre, and his agony through the *thism* was so loud that the faeros came."

Reyn looked at Osira'h in astonishment. "You're not going to do that!"

"No, I won't," she said, then added in a smaller voice, "unless it's absolutely necessary."

NINETY-EIGHT

ORLI COVITZ

As Tom Rom's ship rushed toward her, at first Orli didn't understand. She activated the *Proud Mary*'s comm again. "Look, maybe I wasn't clear. I'm the only person on this ship, and I think I'm infected with a deadly alien microorganism. You cannot come aboard." Nearby, the glowing debris cloud from the Onthos city continued to expand.

DD said, "Should we transmit copies of the records to him, so that a second person has all the data about the Onthos and clan Reeves."

"Not yet. There's something odd about this guy."

Tom Rom's face came back on the screen. His expression hadn't changed; his eyes were just as intent. "I repeat, stand down and prepare to be boarded."

Now Orli was losing patience. "And I repeat—this ship is quarantined! Do you have static in your ears?"

Tom Rom opened fire.

In the copilot's seat, DD reacted with speedy compy reflexes and punched in a course-adjustment burst that sent the *Proud Mary* into a corkscrew spin. The lurch threw Orli out of her padded chair, and she barely managed to catch one of the arms before being thrown face-first into the control panel.

The stranger had specifically targeted their engines, trying to cripple the ship, but his low-powered jazer blasts skimmed past. Only one beam grazed the hull, causing no damage.

Orli scrambled to pull herself upright. "DD, get us out of here!"

The compy accelerated the *Proud Mary* away from the expanding debris cloud of the Onthos city. She feared that the Friendly compy would ask too many questions—*Which course, Orli? What acceleration would you prefer, Orli? Do we have a final destination, Orli?*—

but the compy simply did his work. The acceleration threw her to the deck.

"Good work, DD," she muttered under her breath as she hauled herself back onto the seat. She hammered the comm controls, yelling at Tom Rom. "What the hell are you doing?"

"Attempting to acquire a valuable sample. I can extract the virus from your dead tissue, if necessary, but I would prefer you make this simpler." He opened fire again.

The *Proud Mary* did not have military-grade shields, but they offered enough protection to absorb most of the blast. Her ship shuddered and jerked. She took the piloting controls from DD and began a looping, zigzagging course away, but Tom Rom's ship stayed close behind them.

Orli gritted her teeth. "Is he insane?"

"I cannot make an assessment of that, Orli," DD said. "His weapons did not cause significant damage, but our shields are weakened."

She flicked her glance around the cockpit, still getting to know the ship. "I didn't expect to take us into battle. Do we have any weapons?"

"There is a hand jazer in the captain's locker. Don't you remember? You carried it when we first entered the Onthos city."

"That's not going to do me much good in a battle like this. I meant ship's weapons."

She scanned space around them. The derelict city was far from any inhabited planet, since the Onthos had not wanted to be found. Deeper into the system, there was an asteroid field she could hide in, but Tom Rom would run her down long before she reached it. The only thing out here was the alien city itself, which was nothing more than an expanding cloud of debris that still throbbed with dissipating thermal energy.

It would have to do.

Orli continued to fly an evasive course, but Tom Rom closed the gap between them. His engines were better, his shields were better—and his weapons were definitely better. He continued to fire at her with carefully modulated low-power bursts. If he accidentally hit the wrong mark, maybe he would blow up the *Proud Mary* instead of crippling the ship. That wouldn't be Orli's first choice, but at least it would keep him from getting his hands on the plague. . . .

"DD, we have spare fuel canisters don't we?"

"Yes. Captain Kett insisted that we be prepared for emergencies."

"This definitely qualifies as an emergency. We have to lose him. Go into the back compartment, take out one of the ekti canisters, and rig it for detonation. We should have small triggers in the spare-parts locker."

The little compy left the piloting deck, though he seemed hesitant. "My training is not necessarily appropriate for this activity."

"The ship's database should have all the information you need."

"I will do my best."

"You'll do fine, DD. Just get it ready, and I'll do the blowing-up part. Meanwhile, I'll keep this nutcase occupied."

"Perhaps he will see reason if you explain the situation to him," DD said.

"I wouldn't hold my breath—I'm just stalling for time so you can rig the canister." Orli opened a channel, and he appeared on the screen. "Look, Mr. Rom, let me make a bargain with you. I can give you the complete history of an alien race, the architecture of that space city, the full records of clan Reeves, full documentation of the disease and its progress."

Even as Tom Rom raced after them, his expression remained placid. He didn't look angry, didn't smile. "Very well, I will accept those records as adjunct information. Transmit them. They may be useful in the overall characterization of the disease—but my employer has very specific needs. I am required to take a blood and tissue sample."

Orli saw red at the fringes of her vision. "And you're not listening to me. Every person aboard that station died of the plague—one hundred percent mortality rate! It has to end here. I can't let anyone else be exposed."

Tom Rom seemed unimpressed. "I have adequate quarantine measures. The organism will remain safely contained. There is no need for concern."

She muted the comm when DD returned to the pilot deck. "It's prepared, Orli. What is our next step?"

"We'll jettison the canister and detonate it. Can you rig the signal through my station?"

"I have already done so, Orli."

"This may be our last chance."

The compy moved to the rear of the *Proud Mary* and inserted the ekti canister into the disposal bay.

Orli reopened contact with her pursuer. "I don't know what kind of sick hobbies your boss has, but you don't get a sample of this disease." She leaned closer to the screen, hoping to impress her determination upon Tom Rom. "Look, this plague is going to kill me, and it'll be a long and horrible end. I saw the bodies of the other victims. Between you and me, I'd rather just self-destruct here—quick, clean, a final flash of glory."

Tom Rom seemed surprised by that. "You don't appear to show any symptoms. You can't be so eager to die."

"Who said I was eager? But I'm looking at the big picture."

"You are bluffing," Tom Rom said.

On the screen, DD signaled that he was ready. Orli's hand raced across the control panel. "Am I?"

She jettisoned the ekti canister, and two seconds later she pressed the detonation signal. The fuel tank exploded in a bright flash, sufficient to blind Tom Rom's sensors, to startle him . . . and maybe, she hoped, confuse him. She only needed a few seconds.

Orli instantly changed course, not caring how much fuel she burned. She shot off at maximum acceleration along the course she had already laid. The *Proud Mary* plunged down like a launched projectile. Orli shut off all her engines, all lights, every external power source.

Her ship hurtled along in dark silence under its own momentum, leaving Tom Rom's vessel behind. With his sensors blinded, he wouldn't be able to see where she had gone.

The *Proud Mary* slipped into the expanding, simmering debris cloud. Her pursuer would never find them in the glowing thunderstorm of wreckage and radiation.

DD returned to the pilot deck. "Did it work, Orli?"

"Well enough—I think." Her pulse was racing, and she felt feverish. Before she could catch herself, she vomited on the deck. Maybe it was just the tension, a response to the terror, the adrenaline rush.

But probably not.

She wiped her mouth while DD hurried to find a cleanup kit for the mess on the deck.

"Now we sit here and wait for him to go away," Orli said. "This isn't exactly how I had hoped to spend my last days."

AELIN

No one in the ekti-extraction field objected when Aelin asked to use an inspection pod so he could see the strange nodules up close. The controls were simple enough, and he accessed information from the worldforest. The bloaters called to him, a powerful, weighty presence that seemed to promise so much more. He wondered why no one else could sense it. . . .

He left the industrial complex, with its cold metal decks and artificial light, and headed toward the majesty of the drifting cluster. The thrumming sensation in the back of his mind indicated a presence greater than and different from the huge tapestry of the verdani mind—possibly only a hint of something even more vast.

He needed to comprehend it better. The bloaters were much more than mere space plankton. He wished he could have shared this experience with Shelud, even if only through telink before his brother died of the plague. . . .

Now he tried to recapture his sense of wonder so that it brightened his shadowy depression. He had never felt like this before. Aelin always had dreams, always looked to the sky and imagined places beyond the worldforest, but now that he had ventured far out into the Spiral Arm, he had not found what he expected. Neither had Shelud.

The inspection pod was cramped, built for only one person; it had external arms and manipulator tools for servicing space equipment. Aelin set his potted treeling beside him and flew forward, paying little attention to the lights of other Iswander ships and facilities.

Hundreds of bloaters had been drained of ekti and the cluster was diminished by half. The remaining nodules continued to drift toward the nearest star, which grew brighter every day.

The pod approached the greenish tan spheres. He touched the treeling, opened his thoughts as a green priest, but the phantom half-entity he sensed out there had nothing to do with the verdani mind. In fact, the looming presence seemed to make the stars themselves insignificant.

Suddenly an alert notice skittered across the comm channels, and the ekti-field workers withdrew. Extraction operations raised their shields. Alarms began to ring.

Aelin barely knew how to work the pod controls, and he didn't understand what was happening until he saw one of the distant bloaters glow, then a closer one responded with a bright flash, followed by a flare from the nucleus of a third bloater. The floating spheres lit up like scattered firecrackers in a staccato pattern.

So quickly that it seemed instantaneous, Aelin felt a tingle through his skin, a flicker in the treeling beneath his fingertips. He looked out at the gentle curve of the swollen nodule drifting right in front of him—

A chain lightning of mysterious signals ricocheted from one bloater to another, and the one directly before Aelin lit up with an explosive flash. It sent a surge through telink, an avalanche of light that continued to build as other bloaters flared, spark after spark.

He gasped, and his mind ignited. The flash was entirely inside of him, behind his eyes, throughout his mind. An overwhelming flood filled him with awe and ecstasy . . . and continued to build.

The flash was over in an instant, but Aelin could barely see. He tried to focus again, but the light was everywhere. He saw that his treeling had died, burned out in the pot beside him. His pod reeled, tumbling end over end.

Within him, the flare grew brighter and brighter, and Aelin had no way to stop it. Even retreating into unconsciousness was not enough. He couldn't get the light out of his head.

ONE HUNDRED

JESS TAMBLYN

Inside the hollow comet of Academ, streams of energized wental water poured from the walls and pooled into the spherical zero-gravity ocean. The water thundered in from all directions, aerating the pool, and droplets orbited in sparkling rings.

Academ's air was rich with mist, and residual wental energy added a glow to the walls. Jess drifted outside the fringes of the water as he watched a group of students at their exercise time, jetting through the water, launching themselves through the surface tension. Their activities were monitored by three Governess compies, who hovered like overprotective hawks.

Seth Reeves joined his classmates in an enthusiastic game of tag that had questionable and inconsistent rules. Jess had noticed that the boy missed his father even more than most of the children here did, because Garrison was all he had left, but Seth had thrived here in the classes. He truly loved being at Academ.

Sadly, a few days ago, Seth's father had sent the terrible news about clan Reeves and how their new Okiah colony, including the young students withdrawn from Academ, had perished from the alien plague. All of them.

Jess had been there when Seth received the message. The boy had shifted from side to side, clearly not sure how to react. "I didn't really know them," he mumbled. "I only met my grandfather once, and . . . well, they should never have left Rendezvous. They wanted us to go with them. And if we had—"

Tears stung Jess's eyes when he thought of Jamie and Scott Reeves, rambunctious boys with overactive imaginations. But he couldn't control the Guiding Star that other Roamers might see. . . .

Cesca drifted up to him in the zero gravity, maneuvering with a compressed-air pack. She bumped against him and slipped her arm around his waist. Back when they had both been possessed with wental energy, he had been able to sense Cesca from star systems away; now they were just normal human beings again, although occasionally the water elementals initiated a flash of contact.

Jess and Cesca remained quiet, watching the students, remembering how they themselves had once played, overjoyed in the sharing of their bodies. Maybe as a residual effect of the wental energy, they had not aged much in the twenty years since losing the elementals inside them. Cesca's dark brown hair, high cheekbones, and generous mouth were exactly as he remembered when he had first fallen in love with her.

Now, though, her fine dark brows drew together. "Do you sense it, Jess?" When he took her hand, he instinctively felt the tingle that the electric elemental touch used to have. "The wentals seem uneasy."

Jess looked at the glowing comet walls. Though the wentals had lost the ability to communicate with them in clear words and concepts, he did feel a throbbing of buried turmoil. "Yes. I don't sense any imminent danger to Academ. But . . . something's changing, something big—out in the Spiral Arm."

Their conversation was interrupted when a strange woman jetted across the open sky, heading like an aimed projectile toward the splashing children. Two Roamer teachers followed her, looking flustered, but the woman knew exactly where she meant to go. Her brown hair had highlights of gold and her brittle expression diminished her natural beauty. She wore normal business clothes, not traditional Roamer garb, and Jess noted an insignia on her jacket—Iswander Industries.

He and Cesca moved to intercept her, and she sped directly up to them, using a compressed-air pack to kill her forward momentum. "My name is Elisa Enturi. My son is Seth Reeves. You have him here."

Cesca tried to stall. "Seth?" The boy was playing with his classmates and hadn't noticed the woman yet.

Jess asked, "You're Elisa Reeves?"

"*Enturi.* Seth's father kidnapped him and placed him here without my knowledge or consent. He let me think my son was dead! I will initiate legal proceedings soon enough, but for now I need to take Seth to safety."

"But he's perfectly safe here," Jess said. "Everyone thought you died in an explosion. Seth said he saw it himself. I know Garrison believes you're dead."

"I am obviously very much alive, and I am the boy's mother. His father stole him, placed him in extreme danger—" She calmed herself with a visible effort. "I am relieved my child is unharmed. Thank you for watching over him, but I will take him. Now."

"I don't think he'll want to go. He's doing very well among the other students," Cesca said.

Two Roamer teachers finally caught up with Elisa, looking breathless. "Sorry, Jess. She docked here and just barged in! She says she's taking one of our students away."

"She's Seth's mother," Cesca said.

Elisa looked toward the children playing in the water, narrowing her eyes as if she were doing a deep scan, until she spotted her son. She jetted forward. "Seth!"

The Governess compies broke up a squabble when a quick game of splashing got out of hand. Seth dove out, rose above the water, shaking droplets off of him and rubbing his eyes.

Then he saw his mother, and Jess saw his expression change—more to confusion than delight. "Mother? You're alive!" He stared for a moment and then started to cry.

"That explosion . . . your father never should have taken you out there. He put you in harm's way. You could have died."

"But . . . but you fired the shot—"

Elisa intercepted the boy, took his arm, and held on—not a warm and motherly embrace but more like a capture. "I was trying to protect you."

Seth seemed cowed. He didn't cling to his mother, but said, "I'm glad you're alive. I was so scared when all those bloaters exploded. . . ."

Cesca said, "We'd better send a message to Garrison. He's at Earth, so it'll take him a few days to get here. In the meantime—"

"I'm taking custody of my boy now."

Jess felt a knot in his stomach. "Seth *asked* to be here. He's doing well in his studies and has a good life with the other Roamer children. Let's discuss this like adults."

"If Garrison acted like an adult, he wouldn't have tried to kill my son," Elisa snapped.

Alarmed, Seth found the courage to say, "Dad always protected me!"

Cesca said, "Your version differs significantly from the account that we received, Ms. Enturi."

Elisa was adamant. "You cannot prevent me from taking my own son."

Jess and Cesca both felt a pang, especially after the domineering Olaf Reeves had withdrawn Retroamer children from Academ and taken them with his clan out to deep space; now they were all dead. But Academ operated under certain rules. Even Garrison had signed the agreement that any parent could remove their child from the school.

Cesca's voice was cold. "Come with us to the administration office, Ms. Enturi. If you insist on taking him without letting his father have input, we'll require documentation. . . ."

Seth was well behaved, clearly disappointed, but he did as his mother told him. "I'd rather stay here," he muttered.

Inside the administration office, Cesca called up the files on the screen. "We need to know where you're taking him. There has to be some way for us to contact the boy."

"After Garrison stole my boy and hid him from me?" Elisa said. "I'm afraid not. Seth will be just fine. I have everything he needs. I'll see that his education continues properly."

Jess wished he saw more warmth in her and less possessiveness. He unsealed a locker in his desk and withdrew a small vial filled with a sample of wental water. A keepsake. Handing it to Seth, he said, "Take this as a souvenir of your time here."

Seth placed it in his palm, looking with wonder. "What is it?"

"Wental water, just like what you played in. It's special."

Cesca shot Jess a quick glance; she knew what he was doing, but didn't say anything.

"As long as it's not harmful," Elisa said, then hurried through the rest of the paperwork. Before she took the boy with her, she remembered to thank Jess and Cesca for their efforts. "I'm sorry to put you in the middle of this."

After they departed, Jess felt very uneasy. Cesca's eyes shone with unshed tears, and he hugged her. "We should send a message through the green priest at Newstation. We've got to let Garrison know what happened."

KING PETER

Unannounced, the *Kutuzov* and part of the CDF battle group careened into the Theroc system so swiftly that the verdani battleships prepared to defend against an attack.

General Keah broadcast on the emergency frequency, requesting an immediate meeting with King Peter. "This can't wait, Sire. It seems we're at war, and we didn't even know it. Wait until you see these images."

CDF warships filled the skies above the worldforest, many of them battered and damaged. Her flagship Juggernaut and fifteen Manta cruisers had managed to limp back from the disastrous confrontation at Plumas that should have been a simple war game with the Solar Navy.

King Peter was deeply disturbed to see the wounded battle group. "General, what happened to the rest of your ships?"

On the screen, Keah wiped a hand across her brow. "I sent many of them directly to Earth for full refit and repairs, Sire. Admirals Handies, Harvard, and Haroun escorted the ships to the LOC, but I won't lie to you—we lost a hell of a lot of ships in that mess."

His brow furrowed. "We'll need your report, General, as soon as you can get down here."

Queen Estarra contacted governmental staff throughout the fungus-reef complex, calling Roamer clan representatives, Confederation delegates, and any planetary ambassadors who happened to be on Theroc. Inside the throne-room chamber, technical officers scurried to rig the image-relay screens, unrolling and applying them to the soft fungus walls. Everyone was still abuzz with questions when General Keah's shuttle arrived. A Roamer man in a clean, but well-worn jumpsuit accompanied her: Ron Tamblyn, who had escaped from the Plumas water mines with nothing more than the clothes on his back.

Keah spoke without being introduced, without calling the meeting to order. "We were attacked, Sire. For the test exercises, I had three full battle groups, plus the *Kutuzov*—and we still barely made it out alive." She shook her head as the techs powered up the relay screen. "Without Adar Zan'nh, I wouldn't be making this report—you'd be wondering why you lost fifty of your best ships."

The wallscreens displayed images of the attacking black robot ships, and Peter felt a chill to see them again. "Those are more black robots than you chased at Dhula."

"Worse than that," General Keah said. "The bugbots have allied themselves with the Shana Rei. Creatures of darkness straight out of Ildiran legend." The dramatic images showed the boiling shadow cloud that opened up like a stain in empty space, disgorging first the robot ships and then enormous hexagonal cylinders.

Keah looked uncharacteristically agitated. "We didn't know how to fight them. Our weapons did nothing."

Estarra asked, "We understand that the Klikiss robots have a grudge against us, but we've never encountered the Shana Rei. How did we become their enemies?"

"I don't have a molecule of an idea. One of the robots communicated with us, said that their combined goal was to exterminate all intelligent life, all vestiges of civilization." The listeners in the room fell into a stunned silence. "In my opinion, your Majesties, that doesn't leave much room for negotiation." Keah switched to another file. "Watch these images of Plumas. The Shana Rei just *crushed* the whole ice moon!"

Ron Tamblyn stepped forward. "My clan lost everything—the Plumas water mines, our trading operations, fifteen tankers. We're still counting the number of casualties."

Sheri Sandoval, the Confederation's representative from the Roamers, looked shell-shocked at the task before her. "How many survivors do you have, Mr. Tamblyn? Our ships can take you to Newstation."

"That's exactly where I want to go," Tamblyn said. "I've got family there. My cousin Jess is at Academ."

Peter said, "We'll make sure your refugees get the help they need."

Estarra sat straight in her ornate chair. "General Keah, we'll want a full report on the damage to your ships and which weapons were most effective. How do we fight these things that have declared war on us?"

"In my professional assessment, Queen Estarra, our jazers and relativistic projectiles did *squat*. We destroyed quite a few bugbot ships, but no matter how evil the robots are, I believe the Shana Rei are far worse. They consider the robots nothing more than cannon fodder. Whenever our ships got close to those giant Shana Rei hexagon vessels, our systems started to malfunction and break down. Adar Zan'nh sent me information the Ildiran rememberers retrieved from their old historical records. Apparently, the Shana Rei are composed of entropy itself, chaos. Even physics doesn't work right in their vicinity."

The dour representative from the planet Ramah said, "Then what hope do we have of fighting them?"

A small smile curved the edges of Keah's lips. "There is a bit of a silver lining. The Solar Navy found some ancient weapons designs and tested out their prototypes. Laser missiles and sun bombs—they both showed some promise. The Solar Navy will share the designs with us, and we'd better get them into production yesterday." Keah crossed her arms.

King Peter rose from his chair, and Estarra stood beside him. "Now, more than ever before, the Ildiran Empire and the Confederation need to work together as allies. Prince Reynald is currently a guest in Mijistra, but it's time that the Queen and I go there to meet with the Mage-Imperator. This is a crisis." He glanced at Estarra. "We'll depart for Ildira as soon as possible."

SHAREEN FITZKELLUM

Shareen's brother liked to get muddy, so he volunteered to work with the crews in the plankton skimming operations on Kuivahr. Most distillery laborers wore full-body films and goggles to protect themselves from the splashing muck. Toff liked to strap on a life-preserver bladder belt and wade right into the slurry with his buckets and skimmers, tracking down colorful blooms of plankton. He would return to the distillery, oozing and dripping and smelling like rotted vegetation, and he laughed as the other workers hosed him off.

At least it distracted Shareen's brother from bothering her and Howard, so they had time alone. As soon as Toff had detected that she liked Howard, he became a curious pest, as only a younger brother could be. He hovered nearby until he saw them snatching a private moment, then he made certain to interrupt their conversation. Howard, already quiet and shy, seemed embarrassed, and Shareen would chase Toff away, overreacting with enough defensiveness that she often felt embarrassed, too.

Howard surprised her with a reassuring smile. "Don't worry about it, Shareen. He's not so bad. My own brothers used to set up practical jokes and damaged some of my school projects because they were jealous. It's rough to be the studious, practical one in a rambunctious family."

"Tell me about it!" She laughed. "Not that I'm really studious."

"Toff is just teasing," Howard said. "I doubt he's ever seen you with a boyfriend before."

Shareen's heart skipped a beat, but she clumsily deflated the situation with her automatic reply. "Oh, so you're my boyfriend?" *Wrong tone!* She felt like kicking herself.

Howard flushed. "Maybe it was just a hypothetical comment."

"Or maybe not." Feeling as if gravity had just decreased, she nudged him with her elbow. Maybe she *would* have to pay more attention to her appearance, as her grandfather had suggested, at least give her hair another look.

Shareen signed out a mudskimmer, marking on the log that the two of them were on a "kelp bed mapping and assessment expedition." In truth, she wanted to get Howard away from the refinery and out onto the open water for a change. It was going to be a fun day.

With the tide at midlevel, most of the dangerous reefs would be submerged, and the larger ones were clearly marked on the charts so she could avoid them. Howard was content to sit beside her as she piloted the mudskimmer. She wasn't shy about using the accelerator as they bounded away from the distillery tower, sending up spray behind them. Even Howard started laughing as the wind picked up, and she enjoyed showing off for him.

Shareen swung the skimmer past the outcropping where the ancient Klikiss transportal sat up out of the water. After anchoring the craft against the rocks, they picked their way up the moss-slick black stones to stand before the transportal wall. The alien transportation network had always fascinated her, all those gateways to other planets. Though Roamers traveled widely, and Shareen had seen many places, there was something amazing about the flat trapezoidal wall with its coordinate tiles that offered the prospect of stepping through and instantaneously appearing parsecs away.

Now she and Howard stared at the alien wall, feeling the weight of mystery. She slipped her hand into his, and he pretended not to notice, but returned the grip. Roamers and the Confederation used the transportal walls for mundane transportation needs, but that didn't stop her from marveling at what could be on the other side if she pushed a random coordinate tile. Not because she was dissatisfied with her life, but because she was curious. "Want to take a trip with me, Howard? Set foot on some other planet? We could go farther than a few kelp beds."

"If we did that, we would be wise to tell someone where we're going." He looked surprised, but she noticed he didn't let go of her hand. "Are you trying to run away from home?"

She chuckled. "Maybe if they tried to send me back to that academy on Earth! But no, not today. Someday. There's so much to see." The transportal looked like a sheet of stone, but the implanted circuits were connected to powerful engines and energy fields that could open a passageway from one planet to another. She shivered, but it was a good thrill.

Howard said, "I thought we were mapping and assessing Kuivahr kelp beds."

"Yes, I suppose we are. Does that sound exciting to you?"

He responded with a small but intriguing smile. "If I'm doing it with you."

She laughed. "Well then, on with the excitement!" They made their way back to the mudskimmer.

Because Kuivahr's kelp rafts drifted, charts could not keep track of their locations, and the cloud cover made it impossible for satellites to follow the migrating islands that moved in the shallow tidal exchange zone.

Pretending to know where she was going, Shareen piloted the skimmer. The clouds parted to let sunlight play golden beams on the steel-gray water, then closed up again. Howard kept his eyes on the water ahead and pointed off to the distance. "That dark spot—it's a kelp raft. Let's go see."

Shareen adjusted course toward the seaweed patch. As they drew closer, she saw olive-green fronds swirling like tongues in the sea around them.

Ildiran swimmer kithmen darted beneath the water, trying to keep up with the mudskimmer; some of them surfaced and splashed ahead. Shareen slowed the engines to give them a chance, then zoomed ahead to race them to the kelp island. The Ildirans enjoyed the game, streaking under the water, and showing off. When Shareen accelerated the skimmer, she and Howard both got drenched with spray.

A group of swimmers appeared on the kelp island, waving their webbed hands in invitation. Their large eyes were bright, their sleek skin glistened with moisture. Shareen glanced at Howard. "Looks like they're welcoming us. Should we stay for a visit? Be good neighbors?"

"All part of the learning process." He shaded his eyes. "I think they're as interested in us as we are in them."

Swimmers came alongside the mudskimmer and guided the vehicle through a cleared channel in the morass of kelp fronds; one took the guy line and tied it to a thick seaweed trunk. They looked so sleek, so comfortable in the water; even though they were from Ildira, they had entirely adapted to Kuivahr.

"Humans do not often come out to visit us," said one of the swimmers.

"This is our first time," Howard said. "We'd like to see how you live."

The kelp raft had an uneven surface of woven fronds and bladder nodules. It looked wet and squishy, with uncertain footing. Confident in his balance, Howard swung out of the mudskimmer and climbed onto the kelp, arms out at his sides, wobbling and testing each step before he rested his weight.

Not to be outdone, Shareen bounded onto the kelp, and one foot promptly slid between fronds and into the water. She flailed, grabbed on to Howard's arm, and pulled him down with her. They both fell into the water, clambering over each other, pulling themselves up through the thick weeds. Shareen tried to help him, but he sputtered and flung water from his eyes, and "accidentally" dunked her. The swimmers laughed and steadied both of them, dragging them onto the raft.

One young male swimmer came up and inspected their two dripping forms with something like satisfaction. "I am Tora'm. I met you when we delivered kelp flowers to your big structure. I was intrigued by you then."

Shareen recognized him by the distinctive speckle pattern on his cheeks. "Oh, I remember you. We were less of a mess then." She nudged Howard.

"Yes, my friend wasn't so clumsy," Howard said.

"Careful, or I'll pull you into the water again."

"That would be acceptable, if you'd like to swim with us," Tora'm said. "We were made for the water. You two . . . perhaps not. Come, we can relax where it is less wet."

Tora'm guided Shareen and Howard to a cluster of stretched-fabric awnings on metal poles, which offered shelter against intermittent sun or intermittent rain. The swimmer kith didn't seem bothered, regardless.

Swimmer families walked across the matted island, stooping to cut fronds and harvest whatever the kelp raft and the oceans had to offer. "Fish, plankton, shells . . . all we could ask for," Tora'm said. "Kuivahr has bounty for all of us. This is a good splinter colony. Other Ildirans aren't so fortunate." He smiled, showing tiny pointed teeth. "Even our brothers on Ildira itself don't have such a beautiful ocean."

Other groups sliced open bladder nodules to drain the liquid from them. Tora'm said the liquor inside was intoxicating, though it tasted foul to Shareen when she sipped it.

"We range far. We watch the seas. We help your distillery when we can, we help ourselves when we wish. Most of all, we help Tamo'l in her sanctuary domes. That is the main reason we came here. This is a perfect refuge for the misbreeds." He grinned again. "And of course, the Kuivahr ocean is perfect for swimmer kith. A hundred volunteers came at first, and we do not miss the light of the seven suns. We were made for the water."

Shareen and Howard had a chance to dry off as they moved about the floating island. The swimmers obviously enjoyed living on the organic rafts, which drifted from place to place, currents taking them in slow circles around the tidal areas.

For their guests, the Ildirans sang an eerie thrumming song that was hypnotic and disturbing at the same time. Tora'm insisted the music would sound better under the water, but they performed it on the surface so Shareen and Howard could hear it.

The two stayed for hours, intrigued by the swimmer kith and glad to be with each other. While the swimmers gathered close to listen, Tora'm asked Shareen and Howard about the distillery, then about skymines, then about human culture, which the swimmers found both funny and fascinating. Shareen enjoyed herself so much among the strange folk that she lost track of how late it was. When the gray drizzly skies darkened, she realized that someone might grow worried about them back at the distillery.

"We better go, Howard." She rose to her feet and immediately lost her balance on the squishy platform, but Howard caught her by the wrist. Although it was unnecessary, he also slipped an arm around her waist to steady her. They made their way back to the mudskimmer, helping each other.

Tora'm dove over the side of the kelp cluster, plunged into the water, and bobbed back to the surface. After the two visitors were aboard, a few swimmers detached the mudskimmer and towed the craft away from the kelp island.

As Shareen started the thrumming engines, Tora'm struck out ahead of them, swimming at top speed. "I'll guide you back!"

Shareen chuckled. "Our boat goes a lot faster than you can swim."

Tora'm seemed to take that as a challenge. "Remember, I was made for the water." He stroked away furiously.

Shareen gunned the engines and set off, cutting across the water. The swimmer surprised them by keeping up the entire way back to the distillery.

ORLI COVITZ

For more than a day the *Proud Mary* drifted in silence among the cooling debris of the alien space city. Orli didn't want to take any chances. Rather than sending out pings, which Tom Rom might detect, she used passive scanners to keep watch for the other ship, but there was so much radiation and dissipating gases that the resolution was poor. Even with DD double-checking the readings, Orli had little confidence in the results.

She had very little confidence in anything at all right now.

"The best way to be certain we are alone is to extend a full-range active scan in the vicinity," the compy suggested. "His ship will display a reflective signature and energy readings—if you would like to be sure."

"I'd like to be sure, DD—but if we do that and he *is* still here, he'll notice us as well."

The exploding ekti canister had made a bright flash, a diversion, but a hunter as determined as Tom Rom would never be fooled by a decoy. She hoped he had concluded that she had activated her stardrive and streaked away. But if he thought the *Proud Mary* was still hiding . . .

As her ship drifted among the half-melted shards of the Onthos city, the wreckage tumbled and reflected the distant starlight. With its external systems shut down and engines giving off no heat or energy signature, the *Proud Mary* should look like just another piece of metal rubble.

This helpless waiting, though, was maddening—especially as the plague took hold.

Orli spent time reviewing the records that BO had provided them, studying the last messages from clan Reeves, as well as the green priest's translations of the Onthos records, and the progress of the alien disease that she felt in her body. And no, it wasn't her imagination.

As Orli reviewed how the epidemic spread among the poor Retroamers, she hoped with all her heart that something might be different in her, that she wouldn't react the same way as those other victims had. *One hundred percent mortality.*

The progression of her symptoms was different after all, but not in a good way. The effects manifested much faster in Orli than in the other victims. Her nausea increased, accompanied by dizziness and a rising fever. Maybe the constant surge of adrenaline had accelerated the progress of the virus.

When she saw the first dark discolorations appear on her forearm and her face, she knew they would soon turn into black splotches from subcutaneous hemorrhages. Her time was running out. Orli looked out at the space wreckage drifting around her and said to DD, "This isn't going to end well."

"I am happy to assist you in any way possible."

"You already know what you'll have to do, and you won't like it. Maybe I should just have you set our power blocks for a chain-reaction discharge and vaporize the *Proud Mary* now. Get this over with."

"My programming precludes that, Orli," the compy said. "You are still alive. And we have not yet delivered the scientific information that you said was priceless."

Orli grimaced as another bout of nausea raced through her. She clenched her jaw, fought it down. "I know all about your damned programming, but I don't like to put something off until tomorrow that I can do today."

"You are still alive, Orli Covitz," DD insisted, sounding like a stern Teacher compy. "My response is not because of my programming or the paradox choice of having to let you die to save other human lives."

"Well, what is it, then?"

"I will not let you give up on hope."

Frustrated, Orli powered up the *Proud Mary*'s systems and activated the engines. "We've waited long enough, and I'm tired of just sitting here. You're right. We have to get to a human settlement, so I can disseminate this information. *Then* I can rest in peace."

First, she would head down into the asteroid belt where she could plot her course and make sure Tom Rom couldn't follow her. She wasn't clear which human settlement was closest. Clan Reeves—and the Onthos refugees before them—had not chosen a very populated section of the Spiral Arm.

She eased the *Proud Mary* away from the expanding debris cloud under low acceleration with running lights off. DD sent out an active scan to search the area, but could detect no sign of Tom Rom.

Orli guided her ship down toward the asteroid field. She blinked hard, and rubbed her eyes. She was having difficulty focusing her vision, and she felt weak. When she could not hold back the nausea anymore, Orli staggered out of the cockpit to be sick in the reclamation chamber. DD took over the controls.

After Orli washed her face and dragged herself back into the padded captain's seat, she nodded her thanks to the Friendly compy. "You're a good copilot, DD—and a good friend. Thank you for your help and for being here with me." It wrenched her heart to think that she had nobody else.

Not exactly the way she had imagined her last days . . .

The asteroid field was like a snowstorm of rocks, large and small. "When we get in there, you're going to have to pilot. I don't trust myself."

Since they had detonated one of their spare ekti canisters, they had a smaller fuel reserve than Orli would have liked, but she wasn't planning to go far. In fact, she was losing patience—and time. She looked at a darkening splotch on her arm.

Tom Rom's ship came from nowhere, streaking down toward them at the edge of the asteroid field. He must have been lying in wait, watching, silent.

He flashed past the *Proud Mary* and opened fire without warning. DD nudged the ship just enough so that the blast didn't destroy their engines, merely damaged one of the three.

Alarm lights danced across the control panel. Orli snapped back to full concentration and leaned into the controls. She took over for

DD and hit the engine acceleration, and the ship careened toward the randomly tumbling rocks.

DD said, "I'm sorry I didn't detect him, Orli."

"Not your fault. He seems to be good at this." She was already queasy, and now the tumbling ship nearly made her vomit again, but she squeezed the chair's padded arm and closed her eyes so tightly that tears trickled out from under her lids. She commanded the pain, "Not . . . now!"

Tom Rom's ship swooped in, and his weapons lanced out. Another impact struck their hull, doing external damage and causing a slow atmospheric leak, but at least two of her engines still functioned.

Nevertheless, the *Proud Mary* was a smaller, slower ship than Tom Rom's. Even before she had lost an engine, she wouldn't have been able to outrun him in a straight-up race.

As they bolted into the asteroid field, DD grew more alarmed. "Orli, the safety parameters won't let us go close to those rocks. The margins are not adequate."

"We're going to have to adjust the margins," she said. "*I'm* flying."

"But you informed me you were too weak, that your concentration—"

"My concentration's just fine right now. There's nothing like facing a madman to focus your thoughts."

The pursuer kept after them, ominous and silent. Orli was oddly thankful for that.

They streaked past an outlying asteroid, the first jagged chunk of rubble rolling overhead in a silent pirouette. The field may have looked dense from a distance, but the rocks were separated by many kilometers. Orli picked her course one step at a time, weaving among the rocks, looping over them, hiding behind and then around one, hoping to block herself from view.

But Tom Rom kept coming after her.

She could dodge the largest fragments, and DD helped her by scanning ahead and identifying intercept courses. The smaller rocks, though, proved the most troublesome and damaging. The *Proud Mary* was constantly pelted by a hail of sand and gravel, which wore down the shields.

"We are sustaining damage, Orli," DD reported.

"I can tell. If we ever find some safe haven in the asteroid field, you're going to have to complete the repairs yourself—I won't be able to." Then Orli caught herself, realizing what she had said. "All the instructions are in the database. Upload them into your personal memory now, so you have the full background as a starship mechanic."

"That would be a useful skill, Orli, but I hope you help me do the repairs."

"Just upload the skill module."

That would also give DD all the specs he needed to trigger a power-block overload in the *Proud Mary* when it was time. That would vaporize everything, including the compy. Maybe she would tell him to exit the ship before it blew up. He could remain functioning on an airless asteroid . . . like a castaway on a deserted island. No, Orli wouldn't do that to DD.

She swerved around another asteroid, dove among three that orbited around a common center of mass, then changed course abruptly. Tom Rom's ship was bigger and faster, but that wasn't necessarily an advantage here. She burned a great deal of fuel, but managed to stay ahead of him in the cat-and-mouse game.

She always had the option of just ramming into an asteroid now—and she would do it if Tom Rom got too close. She studied the screens, looked for any traces of his ship. She had left him behind at least five minutes earlier.

She kept leapfrogging from one asteroid to another. Finally, as she pulled around to the dark side of a potato-shaped rock, she found a cozy crater where she could set the *Proud Mary* down, a place where DD could repair the ship.

Or a place where she could die.

GARRISON REEVES

When the job-transfer approval came in from his LOC supervisor, Milli Torino, Garrison wasn't surprised. His skill set qualified him for much more than debris-survey flights along the Moon's old orbit. He had decided it was time to do more than just "run around in circles"—and all the damaged CDF warships crowding the repair docks now fundamentally changed the orbital complex. There was work to do.

With the unexpected threat of the allied Shana Rei and black robots, the Confederation was in a tense state, gearing up for a possible, yet incomprehensible, war. Everyone at the Lunar Orbital Complex, both civilian and military, had seen General Keah's report about the devastating shadow cloud at Plumas—stunning destruction inflicted upon the CDF, the Solar Navy, and Roamers alike.

But for Garrison, the shock and sadness struck closer to home. The deaths of clan Reeves had hit him hard—Dale, Sendra, even his father—and made him think of lost possibilities and diverging courses in life. He should have tried harder to find common ground, to talk his father out of his impetuous decision to fly to a space city in the middle of nowhere . . . but changing Olaf Reeves's mind would have been like altering the course of stars, and that had never been within Garrison's ability.

Even so, the knowledge made him assess his own situation. Elisa always had enough ambitions for both of them, while Garrison remained content with his job at Sheol so he could be with his wife and son, choosing *family* success over career or financial success. For years he had focused on escaping his backward clan, running *away from* rather than *toward* something. After losing his wife in the bloater explosion and sending his son off to Academ, he had withdrawn, convincing himself he was just recovering.

But he was taking too damn long, and it was time he opened his eyes and looked for his Guiding Star again. So he applied for a transfer and a promotion at the LOC. Even though his prickly supervisor had never given him particular kudos, barely even noticed his performance among the LOC crew workers, she approved his transfer within a day.

After Plumas, numerous battered battleships now overloaded the orbiting shipyards, industrial processing facilities, and the military training yard. The damage was extensive on the battleships, particularly to Admiral Haroun's Juggernaut.

Scientists combed over the marks left by Klikiss robot weapons as well as the bizarre shadow creatures that no one seemed to understand. They hoped to find clues that would allow them to develop new defenses or weapons. King Peter and Queen Estarra were heading to meet with the Mage-Imperator to retrieve plans for ancient Ildiran weapons that might prove effective. Garrison thought they might be better off turning the Roamer genius Kotto Okiah loose on the problem in Fireheart Station.

Now that the Confederation was facing a new enemy, the CDF's operational mission dramatically changed. Even if he had not asked for a new assignment, Garrison would have found himself doing other work, since mapping and shepherding lunar rubble was no longer going to be a high priority.

Torino assigned him to a metals-processing station where he supervised a crew that manufactured spare parts needed for the repair work. It was a typical Roamer operation, run mostly by experienced clan members. He had no trouble overseeing their operations because they were Roamers and knew what they were doing.

Thanks to his efficient coworkers, Garrison easily did his job, and the station produced the needed Manta spare parts faster than they could be installed. Now that the routine ran smoothly, he was surprised when Milli Torino pulled him from his duties one day and assigned him to escort Deputy Eldred Cain on a tour of the LOC shipyards and industrial facilities.

"I can certainly show him around, ma'am, and give him all the details he needs, but I don't have any protocol background." Cain was possibly the most important man on Earth. "Perhaps you'd be more suited—"

"I couldn't agree more, but I have many duties that keep me busy," she said in a clipped voice. "Besides, Deputy Cain requested someone with hands-on experience, preferably a Roamer."

Garrison understood. Torino very much wanted the job, but Cain had turned her down, which put him in an awkward position. Elisa would have agonized over the politics of it all, but Garrison just said, "I'll do my best."

His supervisor looked intense, as if blaming him for something. He knew that Milli Torino was recently divorced, and apparently it had not been pleasant. From his few meetings with her, Garrison couldn't imagine that the marriage itself had been pleasant either. . . .

She said, "Emphasize how dramatically we've stepped up production in only a week. I want him to know that we're ready for full-scale ship assembly, should the CDF need to go into emergency operations. And as soon as we receive the Ildiran sun bomb plans, our weapons engineers are ready to duplicate them."

"I'll do that, ma'am."

During the day-long tour around the sprawling orbital complex, he found Deputy Cain to be an intelligent, soft-spoken, and interesting individual. In the *Prodigal Son,* they flew from facility to facility visiting the various operations. Garrison briefed Cain on how the metals were extracted from the lunar rubble field, how the Roamer operations (particularly his own team) produced components that the military ships needed for repair. Cain seemed comfortable with Garrison's knowledge and his apparent disinterest in politics.

He took the Deputy to the LOC civilian complex for a final debrief. Milli Torino provided summaries of the different operations, as well as repair estimates for the damaged Mantas in the spacedocks, while the largest ships remained parked or tethered to nearby rubble, awaiting their turn.

Cain frowned. "Shouldn't priority be given to the Juggernauts? They're our most powerful warships."

The question jarred her train of thought, and she visibly worked to control her annoyed expression. "There's a bottleneck, Mr. Deputy. A Juggernaut is so big, only one of our spacedocks is adequate to accommodate the repairs. Six of our docks can work on Mantas. We're repairing Admiral Harvard's ship now, because it can be placed back into service the quickest."

Garrison spoke up. "Also, sir, Juggernaut components are more specialized, and my team is manufacturing them as swiftly as possible. Even if we had all three Juggernauts in the dock, we wouldn't have enough replacement parts. Yet. Trust me, this schedule allows the greatest number of battleships to be repaired in the shortest possible time."

Deputy Cain tapped his fingers on the desktop. "I'll accept that, Mr. Reeves."

They were interrupted when the green priest Lubai came to Torino's office and insisted on speaking with Garrison. Now his supervisor looked particularly upset. "We are in an important meeting here. Mr. Reeves can take care of personal matters on his own time."

The green priest would not be budged. "I have urgent news, a message just received through the worldforest network from Academ. It's about his son."

Garrison was on his feet immediately. "Is he all right?"

"A woman claiming to be the boy's mother withdrew him from the Roamer school. Jess Tamblyn and Cesca Peroni were unable to stop her."

Garrison tried to wrap his mind around the revelation. "His *mother*? But she's dead."

"Her identity was confirmed as Elisa Reeves, although she called herself Elisa Enturi."

Her unmarried name? "Elisa's . . . alive." He had to say it aloud to help himself believe it. He turned quickly. "And she took Seth?"

"They departed from Academ. Jess and Cesca insisted that you be informed right away."

Garrison was already moving toward the door of the conference room, casting his apologies to Deputy Cain and the supervisor. "I have to go. Right now."

Milli Torino was indignant. "You can't just leave! You're responsible for important shipyard operations here—"

"I said I have to go." He understood that the Roamers at the fabrication complex could do their work just fine without him, and he had to get to Academ right away.

Deputy Cain's expression was more understanding. "Go, Mr. Reeves. No need to worry about having your job back when you return to Earth."

Rushing into the corridor, Garrison paused, surprised by the comment. "Thank you, Mr. Deputy." But in his mind, that was the last thing in the universe he was worried about.

He flew the *Prodigal Son* directly to Academ without stopping at the main inhabited ring of Newstation. He passed through the access zone and rushed to the school offices in the walls of the hollowed-out comet.

When Jess and Cesca joined him, their expressions showed concern. Jess said, "There was nothing we could do. Legally, any parent has the right—"

Garrison held up his hand. "I'm not blaming you. I . . . I just can't believe Elisa's still alive."

"Apparently, she didn't know that you and Seth had survived, either," Cesca said. "She was rather upset when she learned it."

"Do you know where she took my son? I heard Lee Iswander has some massive secret ekti operations—no doubt Elisa's gone back to him." He clenched his fist. "That's no place for a boy. Seth should be here at Academ with other Roamer students."

"She wouldn't tell us where she was going," Cesca said. "In fact, she made a point of refusing."

He had hardly been able to think during the swift flight from Earth to Newstation, and now he knew his next step would be to track down Iswander's ekti operations. Even after the industrialist's disgrace at Sheol, Garrison knew that Elisa would stick with him. She might ignore her son and resent her husband, but she would never, ever abandon Lee Iswander.

Still, he had no idea where to look.

"We have a way to track him down," Jess said with a smile. "I gave your son a vial of wental water as a souvenir—on purpose. We hoped you would come."

Garrison was confused. "What good will a vial of wental water do? They can't protect him . . . can they?"

"The wentals are mostly dormant. But, even though they rarely communicate with us anymore, we can still sense them," Jess said.

Cesca smiled. "That means we know where that vial of wental water is. We've already gathered the coordinates for you. But it's very strange. . . ."

Garrison was not concerned about esoteric details. He was ready to rush off. "Strange how?"

"The wentals can sense something huge and slumbering there," Jess added. "We think Iswander is awakening it . . . or harming it. We don't know."

LEE ISWANDER

Out in the industrial complex, the ekti-extraction workers scrambled through a damage assessment after the particularly severe series of bloater flashes. The pumping stations reset their power trains after the overload. All systems checked in, and the production facilities finally came back online.

It was an hour before anyone even noticed the missing green priest, the silent drifting inspection pod.

Iswander couldn't figure out what had happened. Apparently, after the flashes, Aelin's pod had spun out of control, its systems dead, life support shutting down, no propulsion. Inside, the green priest was unconscious, perhaps comatose. Alec Pannebaker led a swift retrieval operation to bring the pod back into the modular complex. They dragged the limp green priest out onto the cold deck in the hangar bay.

Iswander tried to control his anger. "Is he alive at least?"

One of the station doctors checked the motionless form. "Barely, sir."

After Sheol, Iswander could not afford another foolish industrial accident—especially one that the entire green priest network would know about. Inspection pods were supposed to be taken out only for external repairs on the ships and refinery facilities, not for sightseeing—and Aelin had gone out alone with almost no training, without even an environment suit for extra protection. How stupid!

Though the pod's air was mostly gone and the interior temperature had plunged, Aelin remained in some kind of coma, his metabolism extremely low. His potted treeling, however, had not survived: it was withered, its fronds curled up, as if burned from within.

As they carried him away to the medical module, Aelin's eyes flickered open, and he stared without seeing anything around him. His hand reached out, questing in the empty air as if trying to grasp something. He grabbed Iswander's forearm, clutched him desperately. His sudden grin chilled Iswander to the core.

"My mind is filled with colors! Thoughts that not even the verdani could hold . . ." His voice rattled as he drew a long breath. "I can see eons in my head, and I hear the voice of God. Or maybe it's God's God."

Iswander frowned at the medical team. "He's having hallucinations. Do what you can for him."

His son Arden hurried into the hangar, worried about his tutor. "Is he all right? Will he recover?"

"I think he suffered a brain injury," Iswander said. "We don't know yet if he'll be able to teach you anymore."

Later, Iswander met with Pannebaker and three of his crew chiefs in the conference chamber. "I want to know how dangerous those flashes are. I can't afford any more stupid accidents like what happened to the green priest."

One of the crew chiefs called up data and displayed it for the meeting. "Here's a record of the flashes over the past several weeks. We're draining a substantial number of bloaters, so the cluster is significantly smaller, yet other outlier bloaters seem to be drifting in from deep space. The frequency of the flashes is increasing."

"Could it be some response to our extraction operations?" asked a second chief. "As if the bloaters are alarmed . . . or in pain?"

Iswander frowned. "They're just gas bags. Are you implying it's some kind of distress signal?"

The second chief looked embarrassed. "I wasn't implying anything. Just asking a question."

Alec Pannebaker called up his own projection that charted the path of the bloater cluster and showed how it had been accelerating toward the distant star system. "Maybe the cluster is growing more active as it gets closer to that sun."

. . .

As if she had won a prize, Elisa Enturi showed off her son when she returned to the bloater-extraction field. She held the boy's shoulder as she led him into the admin module. "This is Seth. He'll be staying here. I'll make sure he doesn't get in the way."

Iswander nodded, glad to have Elisa back. "I'm pleased everything worked out for the best. Any problems?"

"None whatsoever. And Seth is glad to be with us now."

The boy nodded without any noticeable enthusiasm, but he did seem fascinated by the cluster of bloaters and all the extraction operations. He tried to get a better look through one of the windowports, but Elisa held him close.

"I've seen the bloaters before," Seth said. "My dad and I found the first ones." His comment provoked a sharp glance from his mother.

Iswander watched her. Without a doubt, Elisa was his best employee, but she had been focused on family problems for some time, her emotions erratic: angry with Garrison, then hurt because she thought he and her son were dead, then indignant when she learned she'd been deceived. Well, now that she had the boy in her safekeeping, Iswander hoped Elisa could concentrate on her work and devote herself to the ekti operations. He needed her.

To help, he called his family into the admin module and introduced them to the boy. Maybe Elisa's son and Arden would become friends. "This is Seth Reeves, our newest member of the team. Make him feel welcome."

Londa seemed delighted. "We'll take care of him. It will be so good for Arden to have someone close to his own age here." She gave Seth a warm smile. "This will be different from Academ, but Arden enjoys it here. You will, too."

Now that she had gotten what she wanted, Elisa seemed anxious to get back to work. "And you and I can be together, Seth. I'll see you after my shift."

Elisa followed Iswander to the medical module. Aelin lay on a bunk, connected to monitoring apparatus. The two staff doctors wore expressions of consternation.

Aelin's face looked gaunt; his green skin had a more ashen color.

His mouth hung slack, but it seemed to wear a hint of a smile, as if he understood something mysterious and incomprehensible. His eyes were open, staring, and glassy. But as soon as the two entered, he became lucid. He turned his head to face Iswander. "I have seen it!"

Elisa was skeptical. "What have you seen?"

The green priest jerked his head toward her. "Wonders that even my soul can't contain. I hear the thundering thoughts." He squeezed his eyes shut. "And I still see flashes behind my eyes, inside my soul." Aelin tried to sit up, but the doctors had put him in restraints.

Iswander frowned. The poor man was likely insane—but the accident was the green priest's own fault, not something the industrialist could be blamed for.

"I have a warning for you, Mr. Iswander! You are spilling the blood of the cosmos—and the shadow is coming." Aelin struggled against his restraints.

Both doctors were worried. "We don't know what to do, sir. Our treatment options are limited."

The second doctor said, "He should be transferred to a larger medical facility, maybe taken back to Theroc where green priests can care for him."

Iswander shook his head. "No, he stays here. Do what you can." He paused, then added, "And you'd better sedate him. He's delirious."

O S I R A ' H

Osira'h awoke in terror. From the raw burning in her throat, she realized she must have screamed. In her mind's eye she could still see the echoes of blackness, the images burned into her thoughts.

She sensed the strands of *thism* throughout the universe, a glorious web that strengthened and bound the Ildiran people—but in her nightmare it had become a tangled tapestry. She saw intersection points, frayed and weak strands beginning to turn black, darkening, tightening.

The Shana Rei could strike in more insidious ways than the gigantic hex cylinders they had used at Plumas. . . .

Before going to bed, Osira'h had spent an enjoyable hour with Prince Reyn. He was having a good day and seemed strong and engaged. Even though Osira'h watched him closely, she barely saw any signs of his illness.

They sat with a dozen quiet and fascinated Ildirans in a storyteller's bowl, a small sunken theater ringed with seats. In the center, a mound of rough-cut orange fuel crystals glowed, shedding warm light on the audience.

Rememberer Dyvo'sh and the human scholar Anton Colicos told a story they had recently resurrected from the document crypts. Taking turns, Anton Colicos and Dyvo'sh talked about a small Ildiran splinter colony on Carii, which was due to have an eclipse. Ildiran astronomers had staked out a camp in the path of totality, an hour's flight from the main city, ready to take measurements as the planet's moon slid in front of the sun. The total eclipse lasted less than four minutes.

In that brief span of time, the Shana Rei emerged—manifesting out of the shadow and swallowing the astronomers. Even though the scientist kith remained in contact with the Carii colonists in the main city, the *thism* strands were knotted, then severed. And when the eclipse was over, everything in their camp was gone: astronomers, equipment, and records. The trees themselves were black and lifeless. . . .

The tale chilled the audience in the storyteller's bowl. The story reminded Osira'h of her brother Gale'nh, all alone aboard the dark-shrouded *Kolpraxa*.

Reyn leaned close to her and said, "If the rememberers are searching old records to find useful information about the Shana Rei, what can we learn from that story to help us defend ourselves?"

"Maybe the lesson is that we should avoid eclipses."

When they each retired to their quarters, Osira'h drifted off to sleep, thinking warm thoughts of how much she enjoyed being with Reyn. She had hoped to have dreams of Reynald. Instead, the blackness struck at Osira'h through her dreams.

She heard shouts and pounding at her chamber door before guard kithmen forced themselves inside. Still shuddering, she climbed to her feet, trying to push away the nightmare. One of the guards looked around, crystal sword drawn. "We heard you cry out—are you in danger?"

The words caught in her throat. Maybe they were all in danger, Ildirans and humans. But apparently the others hadn't felt it. She drew a deep breath before answering. She gestured around her, trying to sound aloof. "I'm unharmed. As you can see, there's no threat."

Rod'h burst into the room, his eyes flashing. "Osira'h?" He was normally haughty and confident, but she saw a gray tinge of fear on his face. With her enhanced telepathy, she could feel his thoughts reverberating through the *thism*.

"Yes, I felt it," she said. "I saw darkening strands of *thism*. I saw the network tangled and broken." She thought about the perfectly normal Ildirans who had suddenly turned on her mother during the birthday procession, trying to assassinate her.

"I think the Shana Rei are poisoning the *thism*," Rod'h said. "They're trying to attack Ildirans from the inside, by striking at the very thing that binds us together." He straightened. "It may be up to us again, dear sister, to find a way to fight it."

"I'm worried about Gale'nh," she said. "If he felt it too . . ."

The guard kith accompanied them as they hurried to their brother's quarters in the Prism Palace. Gale'nh was awake. Ever since his rescue from the *Kolpraxa,* he had been wan and pale, but now he looked full of dread.

Their warrior sister Muree'n stood next to him, breathless. "I came to protect Gale'nh. I had the nightmare too. I knew something was wrong."

Osira'h looked at her siblings. "We must see the Mage-Imperator—all of us."

They found Jora'h in his contemplation chamber where the walls of crimson crystal let in a dark and brooding light. Blazers illuminated the private chamber, but the Mage-Imperator was alone with his thoughts, his concerns.

Seeing how haggard and weary her father looked, Osira'h wondered if he had experienced the terrible dread as well. Was he afraid to sleep? With the thoughts of all Ildirans thrumming through his mind, he, too, must have been sensitive to the shadow, the darkening strands of racial telepathy. Somehow the Shana Rei had infiltrated their racial network.

"Father, we all felt the nightmare," Osira'h said.

"Nightmare . . . or maybe it was a message," Rod'h interrupted. "The *thism* is growing dark. The Shana Rei are looking for weak points."

Jora'h lifted his head, squared his shoulders. "*I* am the Mage-Imperator. *I* am the heart of the *thism.* I need to defend our race against all threats."

In a rough voice, Gale'nh said, "We know the stories of how the Shana Rei attacked—not only by physically destroying worlds but also through subtle and insidious ways. How can Ildirans be strong enough to fight it?"

The Mage-Imperator rose to his feet. "Come to the rooftop. I need to be in the sunlight when we speak of this."

They followed him to the top of the highest minaret tower where mirrors and lenses bathed the deck in rainbows. Jora'h sounded tired as he confessed, "I thought I was just experiencing nightmares, but they may be a manifestation of a more tangible darkness . . . something inside of me."

"If it is inside of you, then it is in all Ildirans," Muree'n said.

Gale'nh added, "You are the Mage-Imperator. You are the soulfire of our race."

"And I am—I *must* be—strong enough to save us all," Jora'h said.

Osira'h watched her father, listened to his voice, observed the determination in his eyes. He raised a hand to wipe the perspiration from his brow. For an instant—just a startlingly quick flicker—the veins on the back of his hand were highlighted by a tracery of black, then they returned to normal.

She grabbed his hand, touched his skin with her fingertips, but she could find no sign. He smiled at her, squeezed her hand, and Osira'h wasn't sure she had seen anything at all.

TOM ROM

She was out there. He knew it.

Tom Rom extended his ship's sensors, scanned for lingering exhaust particles or, more likely, residue leaking from the damaged engines. He knew he had scored at least one solid hit during the chase.

The *Proud Mary* was limping along, and the desperate pilot maneuvered as best she could, making suicidal moves and surviving them. The woman on that plague ship must be an extraordinarily talented flyer—or maybe just desperate enough to have no inhibitions or limitations.

Tom Rom would have admired that if she wasn't causing him so much trouble.

Under normal circumstances, she would never have been able to elude him, but during the pursuit, Tom Rom was startled when his superior ship failed to respond as expected. His engines were sluggish; several minor systems failed, while others lit up with alarm indicators.

Then he realized his disadvantage. He had made only stopgap fixes after the Roamer pirates damaged his ship on Vaconda. Ideally, he would have had all repairs completed back at Pergamus, the engines primed, power blocks recharged, hull integrity checked. But he hadn't taken the time to restore his ship to full operational status.

After hearing the news of the Onthos space city and the fascinating plague, he had raced off too quickly. No, he thought, not *too quickly*, since he'd arrived just in time. Even an hour later, and the *Proud Mary* would have been long gone with the only remaining vestiges of the fascinating microorganism.

Even so, his ship wasn't ready for this. His systems weren't capable of the full power he needed, which was a disappointing setback.

Now his ship prowled among the asteroids. He doubted Orli Covitz had any plan; she was simply reacting, making random course changes, trying to hide. She was good at that. Tom Rom drifted along, his ship's systems alert for any trace, and he also kept his *eyes* open. Over the years, he had found that his own senses were just as reliable as artificial sensors. He had good instincts.

During the first chase, the desperate woman had jettisoned and detonated an ekti canister to distract him. The maneuver, though expected, had been effective. The soup of gases and reflective bodies in the expanding cloud of debris gave her camouflage among the roiling energy signatures. The flash from her exploding fuel canister had blinded him just long enough to let her dive into that briarpatch, and she'd hidden there like a rabbit, waiting. A smart move.

But Tom Rom was smarter. Sooner or later she would have to come out.

While he had hung there in silence, waiting for her to venture out of hiding in the debris cloud, he scoured his databases to learn what he could about his quarry. According to records, the *Proud Mary* was a trading vessel piloted by a pinch-faced woman named Mary Coven who always traveled alone. That image didn't match the younger woman he had seen on his screens. Digging deeper, he found a recent notice that the piloting registration had been transferred to someone named Orli Covitz, and this flight must have been one of her first missions. An extraordinary way to start . . .

Hiding in the debris cloud, Orli Covitz lasted six hours longer than he had estimated, but he eventually saw the *Proud Mary* reactivate and ease out of the field. Covitz would be cautious, watching for any sign of him, but he had to let her get far enough from the debris cloud that it was no longer a viable hiding place. Then he set off in pursuit.

He opened fire without warning, hoping to cripple her ship so he could force his way aboard. All he needed was a blood and tissue sample, easy and efficient, but in the event that Orli refused to cooperate, he could take his sample with a hatchet, if necessary.

He chased the *Proud Mary* into the asteroid field, trying to match her maneuvers. She slipped through a group of tumbling rocks, but Tom Rom's ship was larger and less graceful. A rough chunk of rock caromed off his hull; the shields were sufficient to protect him, but the ship went into a spin.

By the time he reoriented himself, Orli Covitz had lost herself among the rubble. He continued his pursuit, picking what he thought was her most obvious route. He tried to think the way she would think, see the opportunities as she would see them.

Unfortunately, he guessed wrong.

Maybe the disease was affecting Orli Covitz's brain, and she was becoming increasingly irrational. Her flight pattern was erratic. When he finally gave up and doubled back, he studied her path, trying to discern a pattern. He picked up his own trail, but it didn't lead him back to the *Proud Mary*. Tom Rom felt himself growing angry, but that could not be allowed. Zoe was counting on him.

His greatest fear was that Orli would just let herself die, or that she would self-destruct the ship—before he could get a sample of the disease. Then Zoe would lose that valuable item for her library, perhaps a vital organism.

He realized he should not have been so aggressive initially. Even without being pressed, the woman had offered to give him the data she had compiled. He should have accepted her files so that at least he had something to bring back to Pergamus. Then he could have found a way to take her blood as well.

It did no good to second-guess what he should have done.

He continued to scour the asteroid field. The disease would be worsening. Orli Covitz was going to die soon, and Tom Rom had to find her.

ARITA

Arita used Sarein's isolated hiveworm dwelling as a base and spent her days wandering out in the Wild, collecting samples, exploring—and leaving her reclusive aunt alone. The more time they spent together, though, the more intriguing and mysterious Arita found her.

Sarein still didn't know how to react to having a stranger living with her. Arita had come over to the Wild fully intending to work in solitude, but she had hoped to hear her aunt's stories about the Hansa and the Elemental War. Sarein had actually been a Theron ambassador trying to build bridges between the isolated and independent forest world and the Terran Hanseatic League!

Arita sensed that if she talked too much, Sarein would ask her to leave. Her aunt seemed to be looking for an excuse to grow annoyed with her, so Arita did not give her one. In the evenings, after coming back from her explorations, Arita didn't ask questions or try to strike up conversations.

Every day she ranged farther and farther, returning to the hiveworm nest and the small sleeping area Sarein allowed her. As if inspired by her visitor, Sarein had turned her focus to her writing with a renewed vigor, adding extensive sections to her chronicle/confession. Sometimes after dark Sarein went back to her input pad and wrote for hours, glancing up occasionally at Arita as she catalogued her daily samples. Twice, Arita even heard Sarein humming while preoccupied, before the older woman caught herself and fell silent again, turning back to her writing.

One night Arita sat on the branch balcony outside the hiveworm nest and listened to the chirping, humming, simmering sounds of the worldforest after dark. She saw skirling lights, like a mobile constellation, and realized it was a small firefly swarm moving in an intricate ballet; some flew straight up through a gap in the trees, like shooting stars in reverse.

She was startled when Sarein came out to sit on the branch next to her and stared up at the sky visible through the high ceiling of fronds. "There's so much out there, so many planets. . . . But I'm happy to be here now."

Arita longed to start a conversation, but wasn't sure whether or not she'd be successful. "I've been to many worlds myself, but I tend to choose isolated ones where I can do my work. On Eljiid, there were Klikiss ruins and a species of cactus that seemed to communicate. They're called Whistlers."

Sarein nodded. "When I was your age, I wanted to go away from Theroc too, but I set my sights on Earth. Theron was backward then—I was embarrassed by my own home. We had our green priests and forests, but Father Idriss and Mother Alexa refused to allow trading with the Hansa. I wanted to change all that. I thought it would benefit everyone if we could open commerce—sell worldforest products in Hansa markets, and welcome traders, settlers, visitors, tourists. On Earth, I'd seen the Hansa headquarters, the Whisper Palace, the Chairman himself. Back then, I had so much power, such influence. . . ."

Sarein frowned. "In the end, I achieved everything I wanted, but success wasn't all I thought it would be." She continued to stare at the stars. "And when I understood myself better, it brought me back here, full circle." Though Sarein's face was in shadow, Arita could see a wistful, forlorn look. Her aunt's voice was barely a whisper. "Ah, Basil, I'm not even sure how I feel about you anymore."

Sarein caught herself and stood up quickly. She looked disturbed by her thoughts. "I'm tired. You can stay out here longer, if you like."

Arita was sure she had broken a thin barrier. Maybe from now on her aunt would give less clipped answers to general questions. Maybe she'd even enjoy Arita's company, after a fashion. . . .

Before Sarein went to bed, Arita called to her, "Is that why you're letting me stay here? Because I remind you of yourself when you were my age?"

Sarein answered with an odd laugh. "No. It's because you don't."

ONE HUNDRED AND NINE

KING PETER

The *Kutuzov* and five other CDF ships arrived at Ildira, where they were met by Solar Navy warliners. General Keah's flagship had been fully repaired by ambitious crewmembers during the flight carrying King Peter and Queen Estarra, though the hull still showed scarring from the robot and Shana Rei attacks at Plumas. Peter suspected that Keah viewed the marks as a matter of pride, and he noted that some of the colorful Ildiran battleships also showed signs of the recent combat.

On the Juggernaut's bridge, General Keah turned to Peter and Estarra. "Once the Solar Navy delivers the designs for their sun bombs and laser missiles, I'll make sure our weapons engineers put them into production at the Lunar Orbital Complex. Maybe our scientists can modify them, intensify them. But they'll be starting the manufacturing from scratch."

"Let's hope we have them ready before the Shana Rei show themselves again," Peter said.

"I'd rather they didn't show themselves at all, Sire," Keah said with a hard smile. "I suppose that's not an option. We don't have enough data yet to understand how to fight those things."

"The Ildirans have more historical records," Estarra said. "We'll learn everything we can."

The General lifted her chin. "You two and the Mage-Imperator can discuss the background and the ramifications. Adar Zan'nh and I will come up with a strategy."

As their shuttle left the orbiting *Kutuzov* and descended through the bright atmosphere, forty-nine small streamers zipped past them in a flashy escort. One of the giant warliners even accompanied them down toward the Prism Palace. "The Ildirans always manage to find time for pomp and ceremony," Peter said with a wry smile.

Keah opened the comm and said conversationally, "You're such a showoff, Z."

"Merely demonstrating our capabilities, General. Welcome to Ildira."

When their shuttle landed at the Prism Palace, the escort streamers looped up and away, performing aerial acrobatics, their reflective hulls glittering in the sunshine. Adar Zan'nh emerged from his streamer and stood ready to accompany them. "When we begin our conversations, only essential personnel will be present," he said, then lowered his voice. "And guards. We have had recent . . . security issues."

Through the green priest network, Peter and Estarra knew about the bizarre assassination attempts against Nira. General Keah piped up, "We'll have our own security detail as well. Just to be sure."

Soldier kith marched out in a grand parade, and Ildiran nobles and bureaucrats ushered them through the crystal arches into the Prism Palace. Peter saw (but was not surprised) that the "essential personnel" included nearly seventy courtiers, military officers, trade ministers, rememberers, and some Ildiran kiths he could not identify, as well as Mage-Imperator Jora'h, the green priest Nira, and the scholar Anton Colicos. Numerous armed guard kith stood at attention, alert for danger . . . and seemed to be watching one another just as closely, as if they didn't know where the threat might arise.

Estarra glanced around the crowded meeting room. "I was hoping we'd see Prince Reynald."

Nira answered, "He and Osira'h may join us soon."

Mage-Imperator Jora'h sat in his chrysalis chair, ignoring the gathered attendees and addressing the King and Queen. "You are our allies, and we face an enemy that may be greater than both of our civilizations combined. We need to share old fragments of our history that we thought—or hoped—were nothing more than legends. Our rememberers have been trying to learn as much as possible about the Shana Rei—where they come from and how they attack."

General Keah, sitting at the table to the left of King Peter, said, "If I may, Sire? We know that one of those shadow clouds appeared near the Dhula moon after we discovered the Klikiss robot infestation. Something similar erupted from the clouds of Golgen and destroyed a Roamer skymine *after defeating the hydrogues there.*" She let the significance of that hang for a moment; everyone remembered how nearly invincible the hydrogues had been. "Another shadow cloud appeared at Plumas and kicked our butts. We don't know what other targets they might have hit."

Adar Zan'nh added, "Our exploration ship *Kolpraxa* also encountered the Shana Rei. Every crewmember was lost—except for Tal Gale'nh."

He indicated a strikingly pale young man who sat quietly at one of the discussion tables. His vibrant and colorful Solar Navy uniform only seemed to emphasize his unnatural pallor. His drained appearance sent a shiver down Peter's spine.

Mage-Imperator Jora'h said, "We do not know exactly how he survived. Gale'nh is a halfbreed, Nira's son by Adar Kori'nh. His mind is different from any Ildiran's or human's."

"We encountered the Shana Rei in the emptiness and they engulfed my ship," said the pale officer. "Something pushed them out of their dark void, and now they are coming back to find us."

"Worse, they've teamed up with the bugbots," General Keah said, disgust heavy in her voice. "Their stated goal is to exterminate all sentient life in the Spiral Arm."

Peter looked around, trying to focus the meeting. "I'm afraid we need to begin with even more basic information. Where do the Shana Rei come from, and why do they hate Ildirans so much? What initiated this conflict?" He knew all too well how humans had accidentally provoked the hydrogues.

Jora'h said, "Rememberer Anton Colicos, please enlighten us."

The human historian wore rememberer robes. He cleared his throat, nervously brushing a hand through his gray-flecked hair. "That's an ironic turn of phrase, Mage-Imperator. I'll *enlighten* you about the creatures of darkness." He grinned at his joke but no one laughed.

"Rememberers have been inventorying sealed chambers filled with ancient records." He rearranged crystalline sheets on the table surface and pulled up an image on filmpaper. It was strange and surrealistic, a Rorschach blot of black ink in the center of which gleamed a baleful eye. "This is how the Shana Rei are depicted in the old documents we recently uncovered." He showed it around, and the Ildirans muttered with great unease.

Anton continued with growing excitement. "Recently we made a remarkable discovery, uncovering an entire archive of prior weapon developments and tests from ancient times. We call it the Vault of Failures—records of every design that Ildiran scientists tried and discarded during the previous conflict. Some ingenious ideas there."

Zan'nh frowned. "If they are all failures, how is that a useful discovery?"

Keah understood, though. "It saves us the trouble of doing all the development. We can avoid dead ends, maybe modify some of the experiments. That gives us a big head start. We have the sun bombs, but this might lead to something different. Maybe better."

Anton nodded. "Yes, that's what I thought. The vault is filled with meticulous records, years and years worth of research, designs, tests, data. When the Shana Rei were defeated, a later Mage-Imperator buried all that information, assuming it was too frightening and no longer relevant. But *we* can use it. I've got five rememberers in the vault now, cataloguing and sorting."

"The CDF could use copies of everything," General Keah said. "Let's get up to speed even while we build an arsenal of those sun bombs."

"But how were you able to defeat the Shana Rei before?" King Peter asked.

Anton said, "The Ildirans formed an alliance with the faeros. A Mage-Imperator had resorted to extreme measures to get their attention."

"How do you get the attention of the faeros?" General Keah asked. "By banging on pots and pans?"

Jora'h answered in a grim voice. "Mage-Imperator Xiba'h burned himself alive, and his dying scream through the *thism* was enough to draw them."

"Oh."

"I can summon the faeros—I think."

Peter turned to see an exotic young woman enter the chamber.

"Sometimes I communicate with them."

Nira smiled and said, "Our daughter Osira'h."

Prince Reyn accompanied the young woman, and Estarra sat up straighter when she saw her son. Peter thought Reyn looked tired and weak.

Osira'h joined them at the discussion table. "I can open myself up to them. Maybe they will remember the Shana Rei from before."

Her halfbreed brother Rod'h entered the chamber, close on his sister's heels. "I could summon the faeros as well. I have the same power."

He seemed to be challenging Osira'h, but she smiled at him. "We can do it together."

When the Mage-Imperator declared a break so they could be served a meal, Reyn came over to his parents wearing an uncertain smile. Osira'h walked close beside him, brushing against his arm.

Estarra gave her son a hug and drew back. "We've missed you, Reyn . . . but you don't look well. Are you tired?"

Peter had noticed a lack of energy in his son for the past several months, but his weariness now looked more pronounced. "I think you're homesick. We need to get you back to Theroc, where you can recover."

Reyn seemed nervous, as if he had something important to say, and Osira'h gave him an encouraging nod.

"I'm not homesick . . . and it's not caused by anything here. I've already seen the best medical experts on Theroc, Earth, and Ildira. I wanted a different answer before I said anything, but now . . ."

Osira'h leaned closer to him.

Reyn said, "I've got something to tell you."

ORLI COVITZ

Orli's will to survive had nothing to do with logic. The Onthos plague raged through her body, and new dark blotches appeared on her skin. Her fever remained high, and she felt as if a halo of mist surrounded her, closing in on her peripheral vision so that she saw only a clear central tunnel with blurred edges. She was nauseated most of the time. Her hands shook so badly that she could barely operate the *Proud Mary*'s controls.

But now the ship rested at the base of a large crater in a tumbling asteroid.

Orli knew she couldn't possibly have more than a few days left. She also knew that Tom Rom was probably still hunting for her. She began to doubt she would ever find a chance to transmit the vital historical and biological records that she kept.

Given that, logically, she should just self-destruct the ship right now, erase all trace of herself and the disease—and DD. But Orli was a fighter, and she was still alive. She couldn't bear the thought of her loved ones spending the rest of their lives wondering what had happened to her—Rlinda Kett, even Matthew (although he was a turd, she had to find a way to send word). Not to mention the treasure trove of scientific data about the Onthos and about the plague itself. It might give researchers some starting point if the disease ever appeared again.

And . . . she wanted to live.

"One step at a time," she said. "We don't have many options, DD, but we're not going anywhere unless we get our engines repaired." She turned to the Friendly compy. "You downloaded all that information about repairing starship engines. Time to put it to use. Get the toolkit and go outside to work on the external damage."

The isolated crater had high walls, and the *Proud Mary* should be stable and undetectable, at least long enough for DD to finish. For the past day Orli had been too tired and weak to do anything but rest, hide, and wait. But her condition was growing worse, and she knew that if she didn't do something now, she would lose her last chance.

Carrying the toolkit, the compy looked like an undersized but eager repairman. He went to the airlock hatch. "I have the complete maintenance record for the *Proud Mary*. I hope I don't let you down, Orli."

"You'll do fine, DD."

After he cycled through the airlock chamber, Orli remained in the padded pilot's chair that had seen so many years of use. The worn chair enfolded her like a comfortable blanket. She lost track of time . . . and was startled when DD reentered through the airlock. On the chronometer, she saw that the better part of an hour had passed.

"The damage is extensive, Orli. According to our inventory, I have the spare parts I need to make the *Proud Mary* function, but I will have to disassemble the outer casing and remove part of the hull. It will take me several hours. Are you sure you wouldn't rather have me stay here to keep you company?"

"I'd love your company, DD, but you're the only one who can fix the engines."

"Yes, I am." He fetched the requisite components, then cycled back through the airlock.

Orli struggled with the pain inside her. When she was a little girl, she and her father had lived from hand to mouth, chasing one get-rich-quick scheme after another. She had survived a Klikiss invasion and black robot massacres, and in the years afterward she'd made a good name for herself, built a business rescuing unwanted compies, married a man who should have been perfect for her. But life was messy and had taken her in unexpected directions. Rlinda Kett had given her a chance to start fresh, but in spite of all that, Orli was going to die alone in a crater on an unnamed asteroid in an uncatalogued system.

No, not alone. She still had DD.

Orli dozed again, and she awoke, confused. Her body felt cramped and achy, and she realized that DD's voice had roused her, but the cockpit remained empty. The *Proud Mary* was quiet and dim, conserving energy.

DD's urgent voice burst across the comm speakers. "Orli! He found us. His ship landed nearby, but our engines are dismantled, and we can't escape!"

As if swimming through a soup of black static, Orli forced herself into awareness. She felt dizzy. Her head pounded. "What do you mean he—"

Through the windowport she saw Tom Rom's ship on the crater floor not far away. A tall figure in a silvery environment suit already strode toward her ship. In the asteroid's low gravity, he seemed to dance, light-footed as he crossed the distance in large bounds.

"Orli, he's almost to the hatch! I transmitted a stern warning for him to stay away, but he doesn't respond."

Orli doubted stern warnings would have any effect.

She felt so groggy, so helpless, and when she shook her head the throbbing only grew more intense. Given the option, she would have detonated the *Proud Mary* now, but the ship wasn't designed with a series of scuttling charges. "DD, you have to stop him. Do anything you can. *Anything*. You know what'll happen if he gets what he wants."

"I will try, Orli." The compy sounded panicked. "Margaret and Louis Colicos gave me the same instructions when the Klikiss robots were attacking . . . but I failed there."

"So now you've had practice. Don't fail this time."

The Friendly compy was only four feet tall, and he was not a combat model. He had no weapons, except perhaps his repair tools, but strict compy programming would preclude him from harming a human. He could not attack Tom Rom.

Orli forced herself out of the pilot's seat, swayed, and fought back the dark unconsciousness fluttering around her. If her ship had possessed weapons, she could have opened fire on the other landed vessel, maybe vaporized the spacesuited figure, but she didn't have that option.

Outside the windowport, DD stepped in front of the man, looking small and nonthreatening, but very brave. He refused to move. Tom Rom grabbed the compy, lifted him, and simply tossed him like a lightweight ball all the way across the crater. DD flailed as he flew, tumbling, until he hit the steep far wall.

A few moments later Orli heard the *Proud Mary*'s outer airlock activating.

DD's voice came over the comm. "I tried to stop him, Orli. I am hurrying back to you as fast as I can."

The ship's outer airlock hatch sealed, and the chamber began to fill with air.

Orli applied a voice-command lock that scrambled the controls, hoping that would prevent Tom Rom from entering the main cabin. She staggered back to the captain's locker and rummaged around. Everything was in disarray, the contents tossed about during her evasive maneuvers. Toward the bottom of the paraphernalia, she found the small hand jazer.

The airlock controls hummed with the frenetic flashing of lights. Tom Rom was scrambling them somehow.

As the heavy door slid open, Orli faced him with the weapon, trying to hold it steady, but the discharge tip wavered in a jagged pattern. She set the intensity to Stun. As Tom Rom's suited form stepped out of the airlock, she fired.

The jazer blast crackled around his silvery suit. He paused, then continued forward. She fired twice more, but his suit insulated him. Orli increased the intensity to Kill level—which still didn't stop him.

"Stay away!" she cried.

Tom Rom reached her, and she fired one more ineffective shot, even though he was less than a meter away. He grasped the hand jazer and wrenched it from her grip. Orli was too weak and shaky to resist.

He took the weapon in his gloved hand, glanced at it, and adjusted the setting back down to Stun. He turned the hand jazer on Orli. She had nearly depleted the power pack, but even the minimal Stun blast was enough to send her toppling backward into blackness. . . .

· · ·

She didn't remain unconscious for long—but it was long enough. When she struggled back to wakefulness, Tom Rom was already wrapping up his work. Her arm was sore and bleeding. From the inside of her right elbow, he had withdrawn several glass vials of her infected blood. Still in his protective suit, he packed the vials away and sealed them into an insulated pouch at his waist.

She struggled to focus her thoughts, touched her bleeding arm. She meant to scream at him, but her words came out only as a hoarse gasp. "You bastard. You know how deadly that plague is. Why are you doing this?" She felt a sick horror. "Are you a terrorist? Are you going to turn this loose on whole populations?"

He turned the curved front of his helmet toward her. Through the reflective coating, she could see only a ghost of his features. His brow furrowed. "No. I don't intend to release the plague at all. We will use every possible decontamination and quarantine procedure. Rest assured, it is completely safe. There was no need for you to be so concerned."

"Then why?" Orli said.

"Because my employer is interested in it as part of her collection."

For a moment Orli thought he was going to thank her or wish her well, but he made no such insipid statements. Now that he'd gotten what he wanted, Tom Rom had no further use for her. He went to the airlock and cycled back through.

GARRISON REEVES

After refueling the *Prodigal Son* at Newstation, Garrison followed the coordinates Jess and Cesca had given him. He couldn't understand why Elisa would take Seth so far out into uninhabited space, with no nearby planets or moons. That wasn't like her. What possible operations could Lee Iswander have established out here?

Garrison had heard of the man's lucrative new stardrive fuel business. The CDF had purchased a great deal of ekti-X for their fleet, provided by Iswander Industries. He had paid attention only because of Iswander's name.

When the *Prodigal Son* arrived at the obscure coordinates, Garrison looked around in astonishment at another grouping of bloaters, just like the cluster he and Seth had discovered out in the emptiness between the stars. Like the one that had exploded in such a titanic detonation . . .

What did Elisa—and Lee Iswander—want with the strange nodules?

As he eased the ship nearer to the cluster, he noticed the artificial lights. At higher magnification he spotted the dispersed industrial complex: vessels, tankers, modular habitats, loading platforms, pumping facilities—all bearing the logo of Iswander Industries.

He remembered how the bloaters had exploded, the flame front, the shock wave, the devastating fire. The drifting sacks were filled with some volatile substance . . . and now an industrial operation had been set up here?

Garrison narrowed his eyes and put the pieces together as he saw pumping stations connected to the bloater spheres like giant mosquitoes. Beyond the lights of the complex he saw drifting deflated membranes. Elisa must have told the industrialist about the bloaters after the Sheol catastrophe, and he had built a factory complex out here where no one could find him.

Lee Iswander had found a tremendous source of stardrive fuel.

And Elisa had brought Seth to another dangerous place. Hadn't she learned? Hadn't *Iswander* learned?

As anger welled up inside him, Garrison flew in toward the operations. Even if Iswander had taken a lesson from Sheol and improved his safety systems, Garrison didn't want his son there. Not with Elisa, not with Iswander, not with those explosive things. . . .

He flew in close before announcing himself. By now, someone must have picked up his ship, but there was substantial traffic in the vicinity, and the *Prodigal Son* was a typical cargo vessel. In fact, the ship's ID beacon might still be in the Iswander Industries database, since he'd taken the craft from the Sheol yards.

He flipped on the comm. "This is Garrison Reeves, and you have something of mine." He didn't care about the bloaters or the ekti-extraction operations, and he doubted Lee Iswander would fight to keep a ten-year-old boy in his operations. Elisa liked the *idea* of winning, of taking the boy away from him, but business operations would preoccupy her. Garrison hoped he could just take his son and leave— but he knew that hope was naïve.

He heard a buzz of garbled chatter on the comm, scrambled transmissions. Five ships raced toward him, closing in and surrounding him. A voice came over his comm. "This is Iswander Security. Mr. Reeves, you are trespassing."

"I didn't see any signs posted," he said. "And you have my boy."

After another flurry of chatter, he recognized the voice of Alec Pannebaker. "Garrison, we wish you hadn't come here. I have orders from Mr. Iswander to bring you to the admin module."

"Good, that's where I wanted to go anyway."

The ships flanking him were not exactly security vessels. Garrison doubted they were even armed, but they made sure he flew toward the docking module. Garrison realized, with a pang of sadness, they were the same design of modules he had bought from Iswander for his clan's use at Rendezvous, the ones Olaf Reeves had discarded.

After he landed the *Prodigal Son* inside a bay, his heart was pounding. Lee Iswander stood there waiting for him. He wore business attire, kept his hands at his sides; his expression was more disappointed than angry, as if this was the last problem he wanted to deal with today. "Mr. Reeves, I see you're well. You must be relieved that you got away from Sheol before the disaster happened."

"I'd be more relieved if you had listened to me back there," he said. "More than fifteen hundred people would still be alive."

"I can't argue with your point, Mr. Reeves. Believe me, I've suffered from it, and my conscience still weighs heavy on me, but we have to move on. You saw these ekti-extraction operations. I have implemented thorough safety procedures, believe me."

"I'm not here about your operations. I came to retrieve my son. I intend to take him and leave."

Iswander frowned. "I'm afraid that may be problematic."

Garrison felt suddenly cold. "Why? Has something happened to Seth?"

"Not the boy, Mr. Reeves—it's you. It's this place. It's what you've seen. Follow me."

Garrison followed him through a connector into the main admin module. The first thing he saw was Seth standing with an older boy and a woman he believed to be Iswander's wife.

Seth's face lit up. "Dad! I hoped you would come!" He bounded off the deck and shot toward Garrison in the minimal gravity. Iswander's wife reached out, trying to grab Seth's shoulder, but he slipped away. He careened into his father like a cannonball.

Garrison wrapped his arms around his son. They both caught their balance.

"As you can see, the boy is unharmed," Iswander said.

Garrison held on to his son. They were going to have to pry Seth away from him. "A child belongs with his family—in a safe place."

Elisa swept onto the admin deck like a thunderstorm. "How dare you suggest I would hurt my son!"

"Good," Iswander said with an odd smile. "I see we're fundamentally in agreement." He looked at her as if he expected her to agree automatically.

"You should never have found this place, Garrison," Elisa said. "We can't let you leave."

Iswander was trying to calm them both. "No need to be melodramatic, Elisa. I'm interested in a clear solution. There's got to be an answer that works best for everybody, so let's solve this. Garrison has shown himself to be a good worker, and he is technically still an employee of Iswander Industries. He could stay here, work the ekti operations, live in our habitation module—separate quarters, of course, unless you manage to reconcile?" She made a low angry noise. "And that way you can both be with your boy. No need to tear a family apart."

Garrison didn't like that idea at all, but Seth wore a hopeful expression.

Iswander continued. "And unlike the lava-processing facility on Sheol, these are just simple ekti operations. Despite the volatility of the bloaters, we have solid safety procedures in place. It's all perfectly safe." He seemed pleased to have solved the problem.

Then alarms began to ring. Sensor screens in the admin deck lit up, and the ops crewmembers hurried to respond.

Elisa snapped, "I bet he led someone here! Who is it, Garrison? Roamers? CDF? Mercenaries?"

"I came alone."

Wide-eyed, Seth stood close to his father. Then with a yelp he pawed at his pocket and yanked out a small vial—the sample of wental water Jess and Cesca had given him. Now it glowed bright, flaring with a pale blue illumination. "It's hot and cold at the same time!"

He let go of it and stared down at his tingling fingers. The vial fell gradually in the module's minimal gravity. The contained wental light flared bright, then went out like a snuffed candle just before the vial clinked onto the deck and bounced back up in a slow ricochet.

One of the sensor techs hunched over a screen. "This doesn't make any sense! The stars are disappearing—it's like a crack in space. A dark nebula."

Garrison's eyes widened. Through the broad windowports of the admin module, he watched a shadow cloud unfold as something emerged— huge, black hexagonal cylinders, like ebony crystals extruded from a poisoned seed of night. Having seen the report of the disastrous CDF engagement at Plumas, he knew exactly what this was.

"Please listen to me this time, Mr. Iswander! You have to evacuate," Garrison said. "That's a shadow cloud. The Shana Rei. The last one devastated both the CDF and the Solar Navy, then crushed the entire ice moon of Plumas, wiped out clan Tamblyn's water mines there. They'll do the same here!"

More alarms sounded throughout the ekti-extraction facilities. The dark nebula expanded, exploding blackness across space.

ANTON COLICOS

From the thousands of revealed documents in the Vault of Failures, Anton hoped he could gain some insight into the Shana Rei. This new chamber definitely showed great promise. The sheer number of weapons and experiments the normally stodgy Ildirans had tried when they first faced the creatures of darkness indicated just how terrible an enemy the Shana Rei must be.

In the hours after the war-strategy meeting, he and Dyvo'sh returned to the newly unsealed chamber, where a special table had been set up for them in the anteroom of the main vault. Piles of sorted documents waited for his inspection, and the light from blazers reflecting off the crystal sheets was bright, enough to make Anton's eyes hurt.

Inside the expanded Vault of Failures, five rememberers continued to inventory and triage the ancient, fragile documents from sealed shelves. There were countless records scribed by scientist kith, warrior kith, lens kith, medical kith, describing defensive systems, test results— everything the ancient Mage-Imperator Xiba'h had tried during his most desperate times before he chose his final solution. They knew about the sun bombs, but nothing else had proved effective. Now, the Solar Navy would reassess all these records and discuss with the various powerful Ildiran kiths that might help, but Anton had higher hopes that the CDF could take the designs and run with them. *Something* had to work.

Three ferocious-looking guard kith stood just inside the vault. Anton hated having the guards looming there all the time, but Yazra'h insisted on extra security after the attempted assassination of Nira. Yazra'h had always been overprotective of him, but he supposed he couldn't blame her.

Yazra'h and her ever-present protégée Muree'n arrived at the Vault of Failures, to find out if there had been any results and also to check on him. Anton was alarmed to see that both women sported obvious bruises. "Did you get into another fight?"

"We got into *training*," Yazra'h said with a laugh.

Anton frowned. "It doesn't inspire much confidence to see that my special bodyguards are battered and bruised before any danger even occurs."

With all seriousness, Muree'n said, "I apologize for damaging her."

Yazra'h arched her eyebrows. "These few scuffs only loosened me up." She glanced down at the stack of crystal sheets, though she had never shown any real interest in reading. "Ildirans tried those ideas already. We need new ones."

"Sometimes failures show us how to succeed. They might spark new concepts."

Muree'n's response was gruff. "I would rather succeed the first time. I'm not afraid to fight."

Yazra'h grasped the younger girl by the shoulder. "Neither of us is afraid, but we do not want to waste our efforts. I am confident Rememberer Anton will find a way for us to strike a mortal blow."

Anton lifted a crystal sheet. "It may be in here somewhere. The team inside the vault is organizing all of those old records."

Dyvo'sh spoke up, "We should request more rememberers to be assigned to the task."

Muree'n looked approvingly at the young assistant. "It will be done—if I have to drag them here myself."

Anton said, "Oh, I think they'll come without having to be dragged. There may not be much time, if the Shana Rei are increasing their attacks."

Osira'h and Prince Reyn joined them, and Anton greeted the young man, remembering his last visit to Theroc. "Prince Reyn—I mean, *Reyn*. Sorry I haven't had a chance to welcome you on your visit, despite my best intentions. This task is all-consuming." He gestured into the vault, where five rememberers removed archive after archive from the dusty shelves and sorted them into ever-growing piles. "I can't believe the worldforest has no clear knowledge of the Shana Rei, if the ancient war was so terrible. Any hints, Reyn?"

"I . . . I am not a green priest."

Suddenly Anton heard a clatter of crystal plaques, then loud crashing sounds from inside the vault. Oddly, the three intimidating guards at the entrance stood immobile and uncaring. They did not react even as the racket continued.

Anton stepped into the doorway to see that the five rememberers had stopped their meticulous cataloguing. Instead, they yanked fragile crystal sheets by handfuls from alcoves and shelves, and without speaking, smashed one document after another onto the floor.

"What the hell? Those are priceless historical records!" Anton bounded into the vault, and an astonished Dyvo'sh rushed in after him. The armed guards remained frozen, as if in a trance.

Anton grabbed one rememberer by the shoulder, trying to stop him from destroying more crystal sheets. The Ildiran looked at him with eerily blank eyes. Dropping the stack of records, he placed his hand against Anton's chest and shoved with surprising strength. Anton was hurled against the wall, knocking down even more crystal sheets. Blackness swam around his eyes. He shook his head, tried to focus.

He heard shouts from the anteroom. At the vault doorway, one of the three guard kithmen finally began to move, drawing his crystal katana and marching toward Anton. He yelped and rolled out of the way as the guard thrust a crystal spear at him, missed, and then stabbed again.

Suddenly the guard froze, jittering, as a jagged blade sprouted from the center of his chest. His katana fell from limp fingers.

Yazra'h yanked her weapon out of the attacking guard's back and shoved his body to the ground. "Rememberer Anton, keep yourself safe!"

Dazed and in pain, he tried to fight his shock. What was happening? "I . . . I'll do my best."

The other two guards swayed, then turned with a singular focus toward Osira'h and Reyn in the anteroom. Reyn grabbed Osira'h's arm and drew her behind the meager shelter of the small table.

Yelling, Muree'n threw herself at the two guards, but the nearer one backhanded her with incredible strength. Her reflexes jerked her head backward, and she barely avoided a blow that would have snapped her neck, but struck her shoulder instead. She crashed hard onto the floor and skidded against the wall with a cry more of indignation than of pain.

The two possessed guards lunged toward Osira'h and Reyn again, obviously intending to kill them. But Osira'h drew herself up and seemed to armor herself with her own strength and telepathy. Her eyes were wide, pearlescent, and she *stared* at the guards with tangible force. Her jaw clenched, her teeth ground together, and she forced words between them. "I have brought hydrogues and faeros to their knees—I can stop *you!*"

One of the two guards reeled away, as if derailed, but the other stood anchored, pressing himself forward as if against a hurricane. He inched closer, raising his katana. Osira'h strained, until the blood vessels stood out on her temples, on her neck.

With a wordless cry, Reyn shot forward, waist bent, head low, and rammed the guard at waist level, knocking him backward. The kithman clattered to the floor, his weapon skimming aside. The guard flailed, as if he couldn't control his muscles. Reyn staggered, caught his balance again.

Inside the vault, the other possessed rememberers were sluggish and no match for Yazra'h when she dove among them. In moments she was spattered with blood.

Panting, Anton wondered if he had broken a rib or two when the rememberer hurled him against the wall. He'd never broken a rib before. Anton had heard about the inexplicable flashes of violence against Nira, but he couldn't understand why any rememberer would destroy *history!*

Again, sounds of fighting came from the anteroom. "Go save them," he told Yazra'h. "I'll be safe here with Dyvo'sh."

As if in a trance, Dyvo'sh bent over the body of the first dead guard. He looked stunned.

In the anteroom, Muree'n threw herself back at a possessed guard, snatching his katana from the floor and driving it into his chest. The long crystal blade snapped off in his sternum.

The remaining guard came to himself for a moment, fighting with an invisible force. His eyes flashed, and he held on to the staff of his katana as if wrestling with a demon. Directing an anguished gaze at Osira'h, Reyn, and Muree'n—all of whom he was supposed to protect—he righted the katana staff, pressed the butt end against the floor. In a brief moment of triumph, he launched himself forward— onto the katana blade, snapped the shaft, and collapsed to the ground.

Still breathing heavily and leaning against the vault wall, Anton turned to Dyvo'sh to ask if he had suggestions. But when his young assistant rose from the dead guard's body, his eyes were blank, and he held the crystal dagger he had yanked from the armor. Dyvo'sh's face was a placid mask, yet he raised the crystal dagger and slashed.

Anton dodged, felt a sharp pain in his back and side—indeed, he must have broken some ribs—and Dyvo'sh drove in again, trying to stab him. Anton deflected a blow from the dagger with a crystal document sheet, and the document shattered in his hand.

Yazra'h bounded back into the vault to protect Anton. She swung her bloody katana before he could yell for her to wait. He cried out in anguish as her razor-edged blade cleaved Dyvo'sh nearly in half, and his young assistant fell dead on the cluttered floor.

Anton was horrified and confused, unable to understand any of this. "You didn't have to kill him! It wasn't his fault. He wasn't in control."

She stood over his assistant's body, satisfied but not triumphant. "I know that, Rememberer Anton, but he was tainted. They were all tainted."

Muree'n entered the vault to stand next to her. "We would never have been able to trust them again. They were vulnerable." The girl looked exhausted as well. Her mane of hair was wet with splashed blood.

Reyn and Osira'h joined them, both covered with red spray as well. Osira'h said, "The Shana Rei must have invaded through the *thism*. They found these weak points, these people, and controlled them. Made them try to kill."

Yazra'h faced Anton. She had always been haughty and overconfident, not affected by anything. He had never seen such a depth of emotion on her face as he saw now.

"Rememberer Anton, I cannot protect you anymore—not against threats like this. You must leave Ildira. Go with the King and Queen when they return to Theroc." She cocked her head toward Osira'h and Reyn. "You too, Prince Reynald. You must all go."

ORLI COVITZ

Orli had never felt such despair. After Tom Rom left her in the *Proud Mary*, she fumbled with the med kit and slapped a pad of coagulant gauze on the inside of her arm where he'd been so rough taking his blood and tissue samples.

Her mind was filled with recriminations. She never should have given him the chance to come near her. She knew that Tom Rom was a relentless extremist, and he had explained what he wanted from her. She should have taken the time to rig her ship for self-destruct when he'd first started to pursue her.

BO and the other clan Reeves compies in the derelict city had been so brave. DD would have been just as brave. The thought of sending a final message to Rlinda, of delivering all that valuable scientific data—those had just been excuses. Excuses! And now that madman was in possession of the deadly alien plague. She had clung to a last few days of life, and now that decision might cost billions of lives if the disease ever got loose.

She hauled herself to the cockpit, barely able to stay on her feet, and collapsed into the pilot chair. She stared across the shadowed crater and watched the lights on the other ship brighten as Tom Rom went back inside with his prize. The stardrive engines glowed, and with a graceful leap the ship lifted from the crater floor and rose away from the asteroid. It ducked over the foreshortened horizon and streaked off, dwindling until it became lost among the other stars.

Orli slumped back, sobbing. Tom Rom was gone. He had vials of the plague. What sort of twisted employer would take such extraordinary actions to obtain a deadly microorganism, if he or she had no intention of using it? A collector?

It was too late.

She heard the outer airlock door activate and the hatch slide aside. Instantly alert, she scrambled for her hand jazer . . . but Tom Rom had taken the weapon as well. Orli felt yet another degree of helplessness. But when the inner hatch opened, it was only DD stepping into the main compartment.

The compy looked scuffed and covered with grit from tumbling against the crater wall and then trudging across the loose crater floor. His polymer body was also smudged with soot and charred lubricant from his repair work on the *Proud Mary*.

She nearly collapsed with relief, and he seemed just as pleased to see her. "Orli, I am so glad that man didn't kill you. I was concerned."

"He didn't need me dead because the plague is going to kill me in another few days. Maybe he left me alive because he knows there's absolutely nothing I can do about him. Bastard!"

She lifted herself from the pilot chair and staggered over to the compy like a little girl seeking comfort. She needed DD like this more often than she wanted to remember, and he had always been there to soothe her. The last time she'd cried on his shoulder was when Matthew had told her he was leaving. Now, that seemed like such a trivial thing to cry about.

Seeing her sway on her feet, DD met her halfway, put his polymer-coated arms around her waist, and hugged her close. Her tears now flowed in full streams. "It's all right, DD. You tried. Don't feel guilty that you couldn't stop him."

"Would this be a good time for me to tell you good news, Orli?" DD said.

She sniffled and laughed, but it was an odd almost hysterical sound. "Yes, now would be a good time for that."

"You instructed me to stop Tom Rom. You told me to find *any* way. I was not able to fight him physically. So I found another way."

Orli stared at the compy. "What did you do?"

"Earlier, you had me download the full module of starship engine design and principles. While Tom Rom was in here with you, I accessed his ship's engines from outside and made several important modifications to them."

Orli blinked. "You . . . sabotaged his ship?"

"According to my context database, 'sabotage' has negative connotations. I believe what I did was a good thing. Once he took off, a silent timer was activated that will build a feedback loop in the exhaust system and pipe the heat back into his ekti-reactor chamber. Once the process begins, he cannot stop it. I believe I succeeded in locking his diagnostic sensors so they will continue to display optimal readings, regardless of the actual measurements. The overload should be well under way by the time he detects anything out of the ordinary."

Orli felt dizzy. Her head pounded, and she hoped she wasn't hallucinating. "What will that do? Will it shut down his engines? Strand him in space?"

"No, Orli, it will cause the engines to explode. His ship and everything aboard will be sterilized. Including the plague vials."

Orli couldn't believe what she had heard. "So the explosion will kill him?"

"That would be the obvious consequence of the ship vaporizing."

"How did your programming even allow you to consider that? Your core routines don't allow you to harm a human."

"It was an extreme conundrum, Orli, but I ran an analysis of the situation. My core programming forbids me to harm a human. These strictures also require that I not allow a human to come to harm through my own inactions. In the end, I was able to apply context. If I allowed Tom Rom to escape with viable samples of a disease that is known to be one hundred percent fatal to human beings, I concluded that my *inaction* would result in far more deaths than my *action* would. I did the calculations and I made the proper choice."

Orli went back into her piloting chair and collapsed into it. She felt as if her bones had turned to water.

DD came to stand beside her chair. He looked concerned, even shy. "Did I do a good job, Orli?"

She laughed with relief. "Yes, DD. You did a good job."

TOM ROM

Tom Rom never patted himself on the back to celebrate his own success. He did a job and took satisfaction in his work, glad that he had not let Zoe down. He would never let her be disappointed in him.

After returning to his ship on the crater floor, he stripped off his environment suit and quickly set the glass sample vials in a temporary bin on the counter inside the self-contained isolation chamber. The glass tubes had been sterilized, of course, and he would do the full isolation lockdown during the flight back to Pergamus.

First, though, he had to get away from the asteroid with all possible speed. He didn't trust that woman. There was something about Orli's eyes, the determination on her dying face. She was desperate enough, resourceful enough that she just might do something unexpected. Her ship's damaged engine was dismantled, and once he left the asteroid she couldn't come after him—at least not soon enough to catch him. She had nothing.

And yet . . .

He guided his ship out of the asteroid field and set course for Pergamus, where he would make sure that the repairs and upgrades to his ship were completed this time. Back at the research facility, he would happily endure the many hours of successive decontamination procedures so he could spend time with Zoe. Finally, he would stay long enough that they could have a meal together, talk about life, maybe about their past, maybe about their future.

Tom Rom would say little, and even Zoe would keep the conversation to a minimum, but they would be together—just as they had been in their last few years of caring for the dying Adam Alakis at the watchtower station on Vaconda. At least he would provide genuine companionship, a small reminder to help Zoe hold on to her humanity.

When he was safely on course with the autopilot secured, he went into the isolation chamber to inspect the sample vials. Orli Covitz's blood looked as red as any normal blood, but he knew it was swarming with deadly microorganisms, possibly the last specimens of their kind in existence. Zoe and her research teams would be ecstatic. Within a few days he would be back at Pergamus.

The ship sailed on . . . but something didn't feel right. He knew the ship's vibration. His instincts were attuned to its lifeblood, its rhythms, the *unscientific feel* of its systems. He returned to the cockpit and studied the control panels. According to readings from the engines, the exhaust train, the power blocks, the numbers were exactly as expected. Before takeoff, he had done a cursory check out of habit and noted no anomalies.

Now he sat perfectly still, let his eyes fall half closed, and walked backward into his memory, trying to recall precisely what the readings had said. It was an exercise he had learned long ago.

His breaths were shallow, his focus complete, and at last he remembered the numbers. They were exactly the same as what showed now. All of them. Very unlikely. There should have been some variation between takeoff and now, hours later.

He touched fingertips against the control panel, drew deeper breaths as if trying to connect telepathically with his ship. There had been slight differences after the temporary repairs he had made on Vaconda, as if the engines were a fraction out of tune . . . but the vibrations felt different and were increasing in intensity.

He pressed his hands flat on the panel and thought he sensed the vibration jumping. The sound of the engines was too loud, but the diagnostic screens read exactly as they should. Exactly—like a textbook. He purged the diagnostics, reset the sensors, and took new readings.

That's when he discovered an overload was imminent.

Automated alarms rattled through the cockpit. He muted them immediately so he could concentrate. The ship's systems were damaged. The exhaust train was dumping massive amounts of thermal energy back into the reactor, and the containment was nearing collapse. Temperature spikes had already caused several systems to fail.

His fingers flew over the controls, trying to shut down or at least reroute the failures, but the ship's controls were nonresponsive. The damage was already too great. The overload was building to critical levels.

His mouth went dry, and he froze with just a moment of indecision, which was completely unlike him. This could not possibly be the result of normal damage.

Sabotage.

Somehow Orli Covitz had rigged an overload in his engines . . . but she had never left the *Proud Mary.* How could she possibly . . . ?

The compy must have done it.

Seconds after understanding what was going wrong, he concluded that he would be unable to stop it. Overload and vaporization would occur in less than two minutes.

Tom Rom disengaged the stardrive, dropping the ship out of light-speed to increase his chances of survival, then took a moment at the controls to perform a data backup, dumping all his records into the secondary systems. This took fifteen seconds longer than expected, and he watched the thermal spikes.

If his vessel had been fully repaired, the systems might have been stable enough to give him an extra minute, but they were breaking down. When he saw a suddenly increasing gamma cascade, he knew the reactor was failing.

He dove into the isolation chamber. The self-contained compartment would also serve as a lifepod. It was his only chance. He triggered the emergency launch, bypassed all safety systems.

The hatch slammed shut with the speed of a falling guillotine blade. It would have amputated his legs if he had been an instant slower. The explosive bolts severed the connectors from the main ship, flinging hull plates away. Tom Rom threw himself against the wall and held on as the escape engines ignited, launching him like a rock from a catapult.

Then the main ship exploded. The shock wave struck the escape pod like a vicious slap, sending it tumbling. The pod's engines valiantly struggled to outrace the detonation—but they could not. A wash of light, radiation, and high-velocity debris battered the pod.

In theory, the containment chamber's shielding would be sufficient to protect him against the external radiation bath. Even more important, he didn't want the samples of the plague virus to be destroyed by a bombardment of X-rays and gamma radiation.

The pod continued to reel out of control in open space. Disoriented, hand over hand, he pulled himself along until he found the inset control panel and activated the stabilization thrusters. Finally, he turned on the artificial gravity.

Debris inside the escape pod tumbled down to what was now defined as the deck. As weight returned, he felt sharp pains in his body. He had been battered, and he took a moment to touch the sore spots, flex his arms and legs, press against his ribs. Taking inventory. He determined that nothing was, in fact, broken.

The containment chamber had its own short-range stardrive. Once he recalculated his position using navigational interpolation, he could make his way to a nearby system, acquire other transportation. He had planned for emergencies such as this. His ship had everything he needed in the short term, until he could limp back to Pergamus and present Zoe with an extremely valuable item for her collection.

With a start, he recalled that he had left the vials of Orli's blood in the open bin on the counter. Unsecured items had flown in all directions during the buffeting.

He scrounged around, looking for the three vials. He found loose records, an empty specimen pack, then one of the vials, still intact and sealed, which he retrieved and placed in the cabinet where it should have gone in the first place.

Under a tumbled analysis tray and a pair of protective gloves, he found the second vial, also sealed. But the third proved elusive. As the evacuation pod continued to stabilize itself and the automated navigation sensors mapped the stars around him to determine his position, Tom Rom scoured the chamber.

He looked in corners, in between storage and analysis decks. Two rectangular system boxes had shifted apart during the explosion, leaving a narrow gap, and as Tom Rom crouched he saw a glint of the blunt end of a sample tube. He reached into the cranny to pull out the last vial, but when his fingers touched it, he felt the tiny bite of broken glass, a jagged edge.

He pulled the tube out. His fingers were covered with blood—Orli's spilled blood, and his own from a small cut. With a detached analysis that was parsecs away from panic, he realized he was also infected now.

He was going to have much less time to get back to Zoe Alakis than he had expected.

EXXOS

Exxos relished the fact that humans and Ildirans knew they would soon become an extinct species. Impatient, he wished the Shana Rei would simply unfold and strike huge population centers, destroy Ildira and the traitorous Mage-Imperator, crush the human capital, and then methodically wipe out one settlement after another. For the creatures of darkness, it should be as simple as snuffing out candle flames. Extinguishing the clamorous disruption of intelligent life bit by bit would ease their pain.

But the chaotic inkblot creatures chose their own targets and rarely listened to Exxos. The Shana Rei refused to explain why they had chosen to manifest a shadow cloud out here, so far from any known inhabited system. Why worry about a minor industrial outpost, when they could be destroying Ildira instead? What could be interesting about this place?

But when he objected, the pulsing inkblots turned their singular, glowing eyes toward him. "It calls us."

"What calls you?" Exxos asked. "What is here? I demand to know."

The Shana Rei did not answer for a long moment, then the voices echoed around him in the entropy bubble, a thrumming cacophony. "We do not know."

The creatures of darkness had their own goals. They were uncontrollable, unpredictable. Exxos knew that would be problematic once they finished the extended plan to exterminate all intelligent life. What if they reneged on their promise to create a pocket universe for the robots to inhabit and rule? Would the Shana Rei turn against the black robots?

Of course they would.

Exxos and his comrades had already pooled their calculating power. Planning, always planning, they began to consider alternatives for how they might defeat the creatures of darkness. Fortunately, they would have plenty of time. The annihilation of all other life would take time.

As they emerged into the normal universe again, the Shana Rei pulled matter out of nothingness in order to create their hex battleships. The effort caused them enormous agony, as if they were flagellating themselves by creating matter—yet they endured, so they could continue to destroy. A paradox.

When the shadow cloud began its attack on the ekti-extraction field, Exxos and his companions experienced a wrench of disorientation. Then they found themselves on the control decks of their re-created fighting ships. Several of their enhanced war vessels had been destroyed at Plumas, but the Shana Rei simply remade them now, as if nothing had happened.

Individual robots could not be replaced. The memories of those unmade by the Shana Rei were already lost, but the stored experiences of the remaining ones could be duplicated and shared. As their numbers dwindled, Exxos commanded that all of his companions act as backup for one another, with himself as a primary repository of their existence. He designated himself as the baseline entity.

Now the gigantic hex ships emerged from the cloud. Even Exxos did not know what sort of weapons the ebony vessels possessed. They projected an entropic field that disrupted or destroyed technological systems, but that was a passive weapon. He hoped the Shana Rei would cease to be passive.

When the attack began, Exxos commanded the newly manifested robot ships to launch out and destroy, but he was curious to discover what had drawn the Shana Rei to this particular place. He had to understand, had to stay one step ahead of the creatures of darkness, if he intended to continue his bluff.

He observed the island of strange nodules, the flurry of human activity, bright facilities and equipment that drifted among the cluster. Not impressive. The human population here would be small, and Exxos would annihilate them easily—another wasteful exercise, not sufficiently important, in his opinion, to merit the effort. If the Shana

Rei suffered so to create their ships for this particular attack, why would they consider the tiny outpost a worthwhile target?

What was here?

He had never seen anything like the strange nodules, an odd anomaly, and the humans were exploiting them somehow. The operations had drained and discarded hundreds of the sacks, while continuing to work on the hundreds that remained.

The ebony Shana Rei ships hung over the largest complex, but did not move, as if something caused them to hesitate. The creatures of darkness didn't attack, even though the human ships flurried in a seemingly disorganized evacuation. Many were escaping, but the Shana Rei did not seem concerned.

Knowing he couldn't count on the shadow creatures to do what was necessary, Exxos transmitted an order to his robots. "Commence full attack!" Like a flock of black vultures, they streaked into the industrial complex.

G A R R I S O N   R E E V E S

The shadow cloud swelled near the Iswander ekti-extraction complex like smoke ripping through the fabric of space. Utterly silent, the black nebula reached toward the cluster of bloaters.

Lee Iswander's face was markedly pale when he turned to Garrison. "I didn't listen to your warnings at Sheol—I hesitated too long before I evacuated. I won't make that mistake again." He turned to the frightened-looking techs at the admin stations. "Signal our operations to evacuate immediately. All ships out of there! Follow emergency procedures."

Elisa was angry. "We can't give up without a fight, sir. You banked everything on this. It is your chance—"

"No, Elisa. We'll pick up the pieces later." He raised his voice, transmitted over the open channel, "All work crews, find the nearest escape vessel and get away from that cloud."

The intercom echoed with distress calls, confused shouts. Evacuation alarms rattled through the connected modules. Ships at docking hatches and in landing bays were quickly crowded with people and launched out into the open, heading away from the bloater-extraction fields in every direction.

Alec Pannebaker called from the industrial yards, "But, Chief, this ekti hauler is fully loaded. I'm taking it up and out of here. That way, we'll salvage something at least."

"Only if you can do it safely. The facilities can be replaced—and we know there are other bloater clusters." He turned to his wife and son. "I will not lose personnel again. Fifteen forty-three . . . that was enough."

Garrison was relieved. "Thank you, sir. Seth, come with me to the ship. We'll get as many aboard as possible. Mr. Iswander, we have room for your wife and son. Elisa, are you coming?"

Elisa placed herself at the doorway. "You're not taking Seth away from me again."

"I'm not taking him away from *you*. There's no time for your nonsense. We're getting out of here. You're welcome to come with us."

Iswander surprised him by interjecting in a firm, commanding tone, "Elisa, I need you to cooperate. Go with Mr. Reeves and your son, see that my family gets to safety."

She blinked, taken aback that he would side against her. She rallied visibly, then turned to Iswander. "Yes, sir. You need to leave, too."

He shook his head. "No. I'm staying here to wrap up. I can get away in my own cruiser, but I don't want to worry about you. Mr. Reeves, thank you for your offer to take a few extra passengers. I am indebted to you."

Arden said, "No. You have to come with us!"

Iswander frowned. "I have other responsibilities first, and *your* duty is to do as you're told."

Nodding to the industrialist, Garrison put a hand on his son's shoulder and said, "Come on, everyone, let's *go*!"

Elisa hesitated. Iswander said to her, "Leave! That is an order."

The huge refinery vessels were gathering momentum, lumbering away from the bloater cluster. One panicked cargo ship accelerated blindly, slammed into a group of deflated bloater sacks, and exploded.

Around the extraction field, ships flew about like enraged insects from a stirred-up hive. Another evacuating ekti hauler had raced off without securing its cargo, and the heavy tanks of stardrive fuel tumbled out, spoiling the vessel's weight distribution and sending it into a spin, which ejected even more ekti canisters. They spread out like unaimed projectiles, and one struck a small ship flying away from an extraction station that was still connected to a flaccid bloater. The tank exploded, ripping open the fleeing ship.

As he ran into the landing bay where the *Prodigal Son* waited, Garrison saw the explosion and expected the shock wave to ignite the bloater, which would cause another chain-reaction explosion . . . but they got lucky. The deflated sack did not catch fire.

Elisa grabbed Seth's hand and hurried him into the *Prodigal Son*. When Londa and Arden were also safely aboard, Garrison headed for the cockpit while the others strapped in. In less than a minute, he had primed the engines and launched from the bay into the dubious safety of open space.

AELIN

With emergency evacuation alarms hammering through the Iswander complex, the green priest prepared his escape. Aelin didn't know what was happening out there, nor did he care. Everything else was insignificant to what he knew now.

The song of the cosmos continued to play in his head, deafening him with blinding colors, filling the backs of his eyes with incomprehensible words. He tasted music at the back of his tongue.

Ever since being exposed to the revelatory bloater flash, Aelin had felt the surreal symphony inside his mind. He never wanted it to stop, and his heart ached to know that he had dipped only a single droplet out of an infinite ocean.

How he wished he could have shared this with his poor brother. . . .

Since his rescue, he had been comatose off and on, but Aelin did not mind. While unconscious and drifting, he found that he was able to bask in all the wonders that filled his head. When he woke, though, he felt dull and stupid, his perceptions fuzzy, his vision limited. His treeling was dead—withered by the overload of the flash—but the mind that now encompassed him was orders of magnitude greater than even the verdani.

He had come back to himself in the Iswander Industries medical center, swimming up through the murk of sedatives that the doctors gave him, only to find that the modular station was in the midst of a turbulent evacuation. Frantic people rushed through the corridors. A crewman ran by, shouting into the doorway, "Another ship leaves in two minutes. Better be gone before the shadow kills us all!"

In the adjoining room, two doctors were helping an injured ekti worker who had suffered a mishap at one of the pumping stations.

One of the doctors looked up at him. "Good, you're awake—prepare to evacuate!" He quick-released the unnecessary restraints that had held Aelin down. "You'll have to walk on your own. Hurry!"

People scurried toward evacuation hatches and landing bays. The doctors guided the other patient into the corridor, and Aelin eased himself out of his infirmary bed. He felt weak, as if his muscles had forgotten how to function.

But he didn't want to evacuate—in fact, he had no intention of leaving the bloaters. He had a plan.

Aelin made his way to a small garment closet, unfolded the door, and slipped inside, closing it behind him. Several minutes later the doctors returned, looking for him. "Where the hell did the green priest go?"

"Everybody's evacuating. Somebody must have taken him." Grumbling, the doctors left.

Aelin let out a long sigh. Evacuation alarms continued, but by now most of the people had departed from the station.

He emerged from the closet and tore off his loose infirmary gown. He was a green priest; he needed no clothing other than his traditional loincloth. He worked his way through the well-lit corridors, creeping along, ready to hide if he heard someone coming. The station seemed empty.

In the loading bay, Aelin found one of the inspection pods still sitting there. The small ship was too slow for anyone to use it for escape, but it suited him just fine. He did not wish to get away. Whatever the crisis might be, it did not interest him.

With his mind so vast and open, it took him considerable effort to limit his thoughts to mundane matters, such as operating the controls of the pod. This was *important*. He felt the pull of that presence out there.

As the inspection pod drifted away from the station, he saw the ominous shadow cloud looming above the extraction operations like a cosmic thunderstorm. Iswander ships rushed everywhere, scrambling for safety. With his newfound sensitivity, Aelin could sense the angry chaos of the Shana Rei, but the bloaters beckoned him.

He flew out into the emptiness.

OSIRA'H

After the attack in the archives, Prince Reyn and his parents were kept in secure quarters as the King and Queen prepared to depart for Theroc. Osira'h would travel with them to the supposed safety of the worldforest planet, although she suspected the Shana Rei could reach wherever they liked. She could not forget the shadowy blankness in those possessed Ildirans who had tried to kill them in the Vault of Failures. . . .

Gale'nh was also distraught about the incident. "I should have felt it," he told her, hanging his head. "I watched the black nebula engulf the *Kolpraxa*—but this type of darkness strikes through the *thism,* as it did on our mother's birthday. Yet I was unprepared. It can take hold of anyone, anywhere."

"But *you* resisted it," she pointed out as they walked toward Rod'h's quarters in the Prism Palace. "Maybe I can, too. Maybe all of the halfbreeds can."

Because she would be departing for Theroc in a day, she wanted to say goodbye to her siblings. As she and Gale'nh approached the closed door to Rod'h's chamber, though, Osira'h felt a thrum of pain like a dagger jab. It came from Rod'h.

Gale'nh felt it as well. He pushed forward and hurled open the chamber door, prepared to fight, ready to save his brother.

Startled by the interruption, Rod'h yanked his hand away from the open flames in a bowl of contained fire. His eyes sparkled with a sheen of pain. Embarrassed, he snapped, "You shouldn't have interrupted me. I nearly succeeded!" He stared at his burned hand, then held it close to his chest.

Osira'h ran to him, reaching for his arm. When he resisted, she tugged harder, pulling his hand toward her so she could look at the blisters on his palm. "You held your hand in the fire!" The reflectorized bowl continued to shimmer as flames ate at the fuel crystals, building higher with intense white fire.

Rod'h was defensive. "The faeros are out there, but they don't care. I was using the fire to call them, to demand that they listen to me. I *needed* to feel it burn."

Osira'h suddenly understood and chided him. "The faeros listen because they wish to—not because you inflict pain on yourself."

Rod'h shook his head. "I know the story of Mage-Imperator Xiba'h. He went into the center of Mijistra, stood before his people, doused himself with fuel—then ignited his body, burned his flesh from his bones. And that was enough." Rod'h clenched his fist, ignoring the pain. "It was enough!" He closed his eyes and turned away from the bowl of bright fire. "I need to do *something*! Why do I have these powers if not to use them? Why was I born?"

Osira'h was guarded. "The faeros are capricious. I have communicated with them, in a fashion . . . but they also destroyed many of our worlds. They leveled Mijistra. Do not be so eager to rouse them."

"Unless there is no other way," Gale'nh said.

He stood fixated, staring at the bowl of fire. He extended his hand toward the bright white flames, hesitant at first and then steady. Reaching his fingers into the fire, he touched the heart of the fuel crystals.

As soon as Gale'nh touched them, the flames went out.

He lifted his hand away, flexed the fingers. "We may need more than fire this time."

Alone in her quarters, having packed for her trip to Theroc, Osira'h sat meditating. She had lit a small bowl of fuel crystals. The flames were tiny, flickering fingers.

Even after the end of the Elemental War, she had been among the faeros, had felt their volatile thoughts, incomprehensible emotions of joy and energy, of rage and defeat. Osira'h knew the fiery elementals were afraid of her, and furious with her, but considered her *different*, an intriguing anomaly.

Could she call them? Maybe they would listen—but only if they wanted to. She had to make them *want* to. She had to make them notice her.

She reached into the bright flame and touched the fire. She flinched from the pain, yanked her fingers back. The white flames danced as if laughing at her.

She forced her fingers into the fire again, reaching out with her mind. Far away, she felt the faeros, sensed them stir. At the back of her thoughts she held the awful echoing image of Mage-Imperator Xiba'h standing in his own pyre.

Osira'h kept her hand in the fire for as long as she could endure the burn, then yanked it away. In a distant part of her mind she felt a tremor, a surge of bright heat. The faeros had noticed her.

LEE ISWANDER

The horrific shadow cloud loomed over the extraction field, the harvesting equipment, the bloaters, and their deflated husks. Black hexagonal ships emerged and were joined by another squad of ominous vessels: Klikiss robot ships!

Alone in the admin module, Lee Iswander transmitted over the main comm, "All ships head down into the star system and regroup." He remembered those last hours on Sheol, when he had been unable to save his people at the lava-processing facility. Here, instead of being surrounded by magma plumes and thermal spikes, his operations were in the cold dark of space—and the shadow cloud was the coldest and darkest of all.

Iswander clenched his jaw. This time, he would make certain his people got away. He had no room in his conscience for further blame. The Sheol disaster had been caused by bad luck, overconfidence, and poor planning. Here, though—how could he ever have planned for the Shana Rei and the Klikiss robots?

Outside, Alec Pannebaker drove a bulky cargo ship filled with ekti cylinders. He accelerated at full power, but the load was so massive he gained little speed. An obvious target, he seemed to be daring the Shana Rei to notice him. Pannebaker headed up and away from the bloaters, trying to outrun the shadow cloud. Over the comm, he let out a whoop of triumph, as if he did this sort of thing for fun.

As the robot ships blasted at the evacuating ships, Iswander watched the bloaters, holding his breath. He had seen images of how Elisa "accidentally" ignited the ekti-filled bags in the first cluster—with disastrous consequences. Knowing how volatile the bloaters were, Iswander had taken tremendous precautions, providing shielding and insulation to dampen any ignition source in the ekti-extraction field. Still one stray spark could cause another chain-reaction explosion.

Iswander narrowed his eyes. Maybe that's what he needed.

The extraction yard was not a military installation, and he could not fight an enemy that had trounced the CDF and the Solar Navy, a dark force so terrible that it could crush an entire planetoid. But with the explosive bloaters . . . Once his people got to a safe distance, maybe Iswander could fire a shot to ignite the remaining bloaters. It was the only defensive possibility he could think of. That might be sufficient to scatter the black robot attackers, repel the shadow cloud.

Maybe, just maybe, his admin module was far enough away to survive the shock wave. But not likely . . .

As he tensed, running the options through his mind, debating how much he was willing to risk and how valuable the sacrifice would be, Iswander saw a tiny inspection pod leave the admin module. And the pod was flying *toward* the bloaters, where it would surely be engulfed by the blast.

By now all personnel should have been evacuated. "Damm it!" Fifteen hundred forty-three was more than enough . . . and he had already lost some people in this mad scramble of an evacuation. He was rapidly losing his chance to inflict damage on the shadow cloud and the robot ships, though. He had to decide.

It was going to be a debacle either way.

Just then, the shadow cloud clenched and began to *change*.

EXXOS

With their attack gaining momentum, the robot ships careened into the chaotic evacuation activities. Exxos would demonstrate their abilities to destroy, prove the worth of the robots. Success here would ease the pain of the Shana Rei, impress the creatures of darkness, and the robots would benefit from it as well.

Suddenly his ship lurched to a halt, as if a giant invisible hand had wrapped around it. His engines rattled and roared as he fought to charge into the fray; the hull groaned with the unexpected strain. The robots on the bridge struggled to maintain their balance on clusters of finger-legs.

"What is happening?" he demanded, but none of the robots could give him a report. "Is this a weapon the humans are using?"

The ship's control systems winked out and plunged them into darkness. None of the robot attack vessels could move. Their weapons went dead. Exxos's crimson optical sensors flared brighter.

The blackness on his bridge turned into static, and Exxos felt himself falling as the universe dissolved around him. . . .

He reappeared in the entropy bubble with the Shana Rei glaring down at him with their singular eyes. "Your attack has been aborted," one of the inkblots said. "We are done in this place."

"We could have wrecked this outpost," Exxos replied. "All of it, killed all the humans."

The pulsing inkblots hummed. "We no longer want this place destroyed."

Exxos hadn't understood the choice of this target in the first place, and now he was even more confused. "Why?"

"We comprehend additional details now," the Shana Rei answered.

The vagueness of their response angered Exxos. Retreat was foolish and unnecessary. "But we agreed to destroy all life. That is our plan. We cannot be selective. We are here: let us finish our mission."

"No—they do our work." The shadows refused to explain further.

"But we must fight," Exxos insisted. "We have many enemies to destroy. Trust me to envision the long-term plan."

The shadows were not swayed, though. "We continue our methodical eradication of the hydrogues through transgates into their gas giants. We access and attack Ildirans through their *thism*." The shadow cloud began to collapse out of space and into the dark passages behind the universe.

"For now, we will withdraw from here. We have chosen a more significant target." The Shana Rei paused as if conferring, then added, "We will go to Theroc and destroy the new heart of the worldforest. The verdani are powerful and cause us great pain. We have a way to starve them without destroying ourselves."

Though frustrated, Exxos decided it was expedient to approve. Theroc was indeed far more significant than a minor human industrial operation in an isolated system. "Yes, that is a preferable target," he conceded. "We will help you fight the worldforest."

Through shifting reality around him, he could feel that the shadow cloud was once again on the move.

AELIN

Of all the humans at the ekti-processing station, only Aelin understood the sheer power residing in the bloater conglomeration. As he flew the pod toward them, he saw several nodules sparkle and felt a growing hunger in his mind. He wanted to embrace it all, wanted to drown in it.

He paid very little attention to the shadow cloud, believing that even such darkness was irrelevant to him. As he approached the floating nodules, the gigantic hexagonal ships retracted into the uncertain boundaries of the nebula, which folded up around them. It was not his concern. The inspection pod continued toward the nearest bloater.

After the shadow cloud collapsed and then vanished into empty space, he heard a buzz of distracting voices cross his comm system. The evacuated Iswander Industries ships hovered at a distance, far from the extraction equipment. Lee Iswander remained in the main admin module, still in contact with his ships. Some of the more daring vessels cautiously returned, while others continued down into the distant star system, waiting to receive the all-clear.

Aelin, though, had no intention of going back. His pod descended toward one of the swollen spheres. A bloater sparked off in the distance, and others flickered in some kind of sympathetic rest response. He felt the residual ecstasy of the mental surge he had experienced. He longed to feel it again.

He maneuvered the pod up to the bloater, ignoring the background babble of comm transmissions until a message blared out of the speakers, directed at him. "Who's in that pod? What are you doing?" It was Lee Iswander's voice.

"This is Aelin, Mr. Iswander." Beyond that, he could not explain what the industrialist was not equipped to understand. "I am among the bloaters. I need to . . . comprehend."

He muted the comm and applied gentle thrust to maneuver the pod's main hatch directly against the membrane. The soft bloater skin shifted around the hull like a mouth forming a kiss, embedding the pod.

Iswander overrode the comm block, and his voice broke through again. The transmission was rough and staticky. "Green priest, withdraw—back that pod away from the bloater."

Aelin had no intention of obeying. He felt giddy with the certainty that he *must* know what was inside these nodules.

He disengaged the locking mechanisms, stepped in front of the pod's hatch, and, without hesitating, opened it.

He faced the exposed membrane. It exuded an intoxicating smell, like oily electricity. The air vibrated with a powerful summons. He stood there, his eyes half open, letting the bloater know he was there and who he was.

They had already touched once before. With an ecstatic smile, Aelin plunged through the membrane and into the crackling soup of exotic protoplasm. The blood of the cosmos.

In the admin module, Lee Iswander lost all contact with the pod.

ONE HUNDRED AND TWENTY-TWO

MAGE-IMPERATOR JORA'H

After the King and Queen left Ildira, taking the others to safety—including Osira'h—Jora'h felt that he *should* relax. But the sense of brooding, dread, and danger did not diminish.

Hoping to find some solution to his inner turmoil, he consulted four lens kithmen. Perhaps the large-eyed philosophers, known for their connection to the Lightsource, would have the answers he lacked. Focused on that higher plane of existence above even the *thism* network, members of the lens kith often had a soothing effect on those around them. Each wore a faceted crystal pendant, which they used to reflect flashes of sunlight into their eyes.

They sat together under the open sky near a light fountain. "You are the Mage-Imperator," said one. "You control the *thism*. You have the most direct path to the Lightsource."

Jora'h wanted to take comfort from the words, but they could not strengthen him. "And if the Mage-Imperator loses control of the *thism*, what then? Twice now the Shana Rei have insinuated themselves into our thoughts, coercing good Ildiran people to do terrible things. I did not sense it. I was unable to protect my people from them. And I do not know how to stop it from happening again."

The lens kithmen turned their faceted pendants toward him, splashing reflections across his robes. "Draw upon the Lightsource, Liege. Pull greater illumination into the *thism*. Shadows disappear when light shines upon them."

"Bright lights also cast sharp shadows," he said.

Finding no help in their answers, he rose to his feet, exhausted to the core. Jora'h had felt sick inside ever since the assassination attempts against Nira, and then against the human scholar, the Confederation

Prince, and his own daughters in the Vault of Failures. He needed sleep. Perhaps next to Nira, touching her soft green skin, he could find a few hours of peace to recharge his own soulfire. . . .

Knowing he was troubled, Nira did her best to support him. She always did. Even though she couldn't feel the *thism*, she understood. Their private chambers were lit with colored light. Four spindly young worldtrees, each taller than Nira, stood around the room. Nira often communed with the worldtrees, tapping into the thoughts of the verdani mind before she went to sleep. But now she gave her full attention to Jora'h. "My shoulders may be strong enough to lift some of the weight from yours, my love."

"It is not weight that I fear, Nira. It is *darkness*."

"Then close your eyes and dream about the light."

She kissed his eyelids, and he lay back, pretending that he didn't feel the cold shadow inside of him. But the more he wished for peaceful dreams, the more harshly his body and mind reacted.

In the human enclave, shopkeepers opened their doors, set out their wares, and prepared for the day's business. Blondie cooked meals for her human customers. Crisp, savory aromas of frying onions and spattering grease wafted from the sizzling griddle. The coffee-shop owner brewed a new batch.

The artist who made mirrored wind spinners and colorful dreamcatchers hung out new creations that she had made the previous day, and now they turned in the faint breeze, reflecting light. The dulcimer maker propped up one of his new instruments, crafted from a combination of rosewood and imported black pine. Taking the soft hammers, he began to tap out lovely ethereal music, but he couldn't seem to find the tune.

The writer sat at his usual place at an outdoor table drinking a second cup of coffee, which tasted just as bitter as the first one. He couldn't concentrate on words to put down in his tablet.

The coffee-shop owner took a seat next to him with a foamy cup of cappuccino. She looked out at the quiet city of Mijistra, which seemed to be holding its breath to the point of suffocation.

Blondie came over, wearing an apron tied across her skirt. The heavyset woman brought two large cinnamon rolls drizzled with white frosting. "These were leftover from yesterday. If they don't get eaten today, they'll be wasted."

The coffee-shop owner said, "I don't feel welcome here anymore. I'm considering packing up and moving back to Ramah."

A gust of wind rippled through the enclave, twirling the dream-catchers and wind spinners. Suddenly, they fell still. The dulcimer player stopped his music and looked around. The hush deepened.

The writer glanced up to see a group of Ildirans coming down the streets toward the shop district of the human enclave.

Blondie set forks next to each cinnamon roll. "Looks like we might have customers after all."

The writer kept staring at the approaching Ildirans. His brow fur-rowed, and he slid aside his coffee cup. He had not touched the cinna-mon roll. "I'm not sure they're here as customers."

The Ildirans came from all kiths, judging by the mixture of cloth-ing and body types, but they moved as if choreographed into a single unit. Their steps were somnolent, their expressions affectless.

The dulcimer maker put on his performance smile and played sev-eral notes before falling silent. Other humans came out of their shops and homes to watch.

The Ildiran crowd revealed clubs and crystal-bladed weapons. Without increasing speed, without yelling or showing any emotion at all, they began to smash and attack everything in sight.

Jora'h found no pathway to the Lightsource from within his night-mares. He dreamed of the lens kith, who smiled and gave him advice in a language he didn't understand. They appeared one after another in a circle around him, and he spun around, desperate to learn what they were saying.

But every time he turned his back on one, the lens kithmen drew a dagger and stabbed him between the shoulder blades. When he whirled, trying to get away, a different lens kithman stabbed him. Each jolt of pain thrummed out through the *thism,* and made the stain grow.

One of the lens kith handed him a large round lens. "Peer through this, Liege, and you will see what truly awaits."

But when Jora'h stared through the lens, it merely painted the whole world black.

The humans in the enclave tried to defend themselves. The writer fought with a chair. Blondie returned with cutting knives and heavy pans.

The marching Ildirans fell upon the dulcimer shop, smashing and jangling the instruments. When the musician tried to stop them, they smashed his skull to a pulp and stomped on his ribs until his body was a broken pool of flesh.

They set fire to Blondie's diner, and the flames and black smoke rose high.

The writer and the dreamcatcher artist barricaded themselves inside a home, but the structure was not defensible for long. Ildirans smashed the windows, broke down the door, and pushed their way inside with clubs and crystal blades. Eight Ildirans managed to fit into the small home, and they closed on the cornered victims. Each one took a turn at the stabbing.

The massacre continued. All the artwork, signs, businesses, and homes were vandalized, desecrated. The fire began to spread. They slaughtered every human, dragging some out from bolt-holes and cutting them to pieces in the streets. Others were simply locked inside their dwellings and burned alive.

Throughout it all, the mob made no sound. When they were finished and every human was murdered, the Ildirans reawakened and became aware of who they were.

Looking around at the bloodshed and destruction they had caused, they began to wail. Their return to consciousness was no mercy, though, but a brief revelation so they could know despair at what they had done.

Then, like harvested grain, every one of them fell dead in the bloody streets.

When Jora'h tore himself out of sleep, he was screaming. Nira shook him, held him against his thrashing. She shouted his name.

He stared at her and finally his eyes focused.

Nira put her arms around him. "I'm here. It'll be all right."

But he knew that it was far from all right. He dreaded going out into Mijistra to discover exactly what had just occurred.

KING PETER

During the *Kutuzov*'s return to Theroc from the Ildiran Empire, the mood aboard was somber, not like a celebratory homecoming.

King Peter had already been aware that the shadow clouds were immensely destructive—General Keah's encounters proved that, as did the obliteration of the Golgen skymine. But in Mijistra, he and Estarra had also seen how the darkness infected random Ildirans like a murderous poison. The Shana Rei were a far more insidious enemy than he had imagined.

If the creatures of darkness had declared war on *intelligent life itself*, human and Ildiran, there could be no reasoning with them, no negotiation. The Shana Rei and the Klikiss robots would have to be fought, defeated, destroyed.

He and Estarra were glad to have their son back, though dismayed to learn of Reyn's debilitating medical condition, which he had hidden from them. He had revealed his illness to Osira'h—and to Arita, months ago—before telling his parents. Peter was shocked that he hadn't recognized the signs. The clues seemed so obvious now.

And just when Reyn had finally decided to accept all the help that others could offer, the Spiral Arm might be at war again with an enemy more terrible than they could comprehend. As the Confederation's King, Peter had to defend all of his worlds, but as a father he couldn't help worrying about his son. . . .

As the *Kutuzov* arrived at Theroc, General Keah stood on the bridge, regarding the ferocious verdani battleships and the heavily armed Manta cruisers placed in orbit to protect the planet. She propped her hands on her hips and shook her head. "Under normal circumstances, I'd tell you we're safe now, Sire, but these aren't exactly normal circumstances. We have the Solar Navy's sun bomb designs, and I intend to have our armaments industries at the LOC manufacture them at top speed."

Peter looked out at the thorny verdani treeships as the Juggernaut glided past. Osira'h and Reyn watched the forward viewscreens together; the two seemed inseparable. The halfbreed girl tilted her head, and her brow furrowed. Her feathery hair twitched just slightly. "Do the treeships always feel so . . . uneasy?"

"That's a question for the green priests," Estarra said. "I'm just glad we're all home."

While General Keah remained aboard her flagship, the rest of them returned to the fungus reef. Reyn seemed glad for the opportunity to show Osira'h the wonders of the worldforest, though he was disappointed to learn that his sister was off by herself in the Wild. He wanted Osira'h and Arita to meet.

Anton Colicos joined them, bringing a thick stack of documents with him. Though shaken by the assassination attempt and the death of his assistant, he refused to abandon his work. Even on Theroc, he would continue to study forgotten tales about the Shana Rei, while rememberers on Ildira did further translations.

Inside the throne room of the fungus-reef, Peter picked up on the tension in the air that Osira'h had detected. He whispered to Estarra, "I can feel it. Something's not right."

The Queen's dark eyes were troubled. "I thought it was just my imagination after what happened on Ildira, but . . . I agree."

Documents and obligations had piled up while they were away. The business of the Confederation continued as usual. Space traffic and trade to Theroc remained undeterred, and planetary representatives met inside large conference-room chambers.

A delegation of green priests insisted on seeing Mother Estarra and Father Peter; they pushed their way to the front of the schedule, much to the annoyance of a shipping company and an allied planetary cluster that wished to formalize an extended trade agreement.

The four green priests stood close together, two women, two men. A slender female said in a warning voice, "The worldforest is deeply disturbed. The trees sense a terrible force coming here."

The throne room's wallscreens activated, their blank dullness replaced by an image of General Keah. "Something's going on out here, Sire! The tree battleships are shaking." She glanced up quickly as one of her bridge officers gave her an urgent message, and Keah's eyes widened. "There's a disturbance in space, sensors going wild . . . aww, shit, it's one of those damn shadow clouds!" She squared her uniformed shoulders, deadly serious. "The CDF will do everything possible to defend Theroc, Sire. You can count on the *Kutuzov* and all my Mantas."

Estarra said, "That may not be enough. You saw what they did at Plumas."

"We're still going to fight—we don't have any of those Ildiran sun bombs yet, but we'll try everything else in our arsenal."

Everyone in the throne room watched the wallscreens as an inky stain bled out of a rip in the universe into the starry openness of space. Three enormous hexagons emerged from the tear, cylindrical vessels that looked like blunted spears.

Peter felt cold inside, as if the Shana Rei had found some way to leak a shadow into his body.

Estarra turned to the delegation of green priests. "We'll need the verdani battleships to help defend us."

The orbiting treeships spread their thorny branches and swelled into a defensive line. Peter had seen them wrap those massive boughs around hydrogue warglobes and crush them. Maybe they could fight back against the Shana Rei hex ships.

When the Mantas attacked, jazers did little more than make a darker scratch on the ebony surface of the hexagon ships. Each time a CDF vessel approached the Shana Rei vessels, their systems were scrambled, and many of the shots missed.

Out of arrogance, or maybe because they simply didn't care, the Shana Rei ignored the provocation. Instead, the black hex cylinders aligned themselves at the edge of the widening shadow cloud, but did not approach.

Peter ordered General Keah to back off and take a defensive position. "Don't lose any more ships until we find a better way to fight."

As a desperate alterative, he and Estarra tried to open communications with the creatures of darkness. "Shana Rei, this is King Peter, leader of the human Confederation. We have no desire for war. What have we done to provoke you?"

At the beginning of the Elemental War, when the hydrogues began to attack human settlements, the Terran Hanseatic League had no idea what they had done to incite the deep-core aliens . . . and by the time they had learned the answer, it was much too late.

Peter and Estarra sent message after message to the Shana Rei, but received no response. The gigantic black ships just hung there, directing the flat ends of the hexagonal cylinders toward the forested planet. The continuing silence was a void in itself.

Then something changed on the dark battleships. A thin slice of the hexagonal end separated from the main cylinder and twirled away. Identical slices peeled off the ends of the other two cylinders and hexagonal plates spun off into space—toward Theroc.

Slice after slice produced plates that flew together until they took up position high above the verdani battleships. One hexagon linked to a second, edge to edge, and a third nestled in like a piece of a puzzle. Another hex, then another. More slices continued to spin away from the black cylinders, connecting to the other plates.

Piece by piece, they began to construct a wall in space.

On the comm General Keah shouted to her weapons officer, "Full bombardment! Knock that structure apart."

The CDF ships launched jazers and high-velocity railgun projectiles against the growing barricade. The most concentrated explosions broke some of the hexagonal plates apart, but the hexes drifted back together as if they were magnetically bound.

Hanging motionless above Theroc, nested in their shadow cloud, the Shana Rei cylinders continued to split off plate after plate, piece after piece, by the thousands, which did not even seem to diminish the size of the gigantic ships. The hexagonal components locked together and spread the barricade wider.

Peter was the first to recognize what it was. "It's an occultation barrier—to create an artificial eclipse over Theroc. Without even coming closer, they can block out the sun."

Estarra put it more bluntly, "All of the worldtrees will wither and die."

TOM ROM

After half an hour of processing, Tom Rom's navigation interpolation systems managed to pinpoint where he was. He had dropped out of lightspeed somewhere between the stars, reeling out of control in the escape pod, but the computers were able to map the brightest points, the closest stars, and determine his position, then suggest alternatives of where he could go.

When designing the ship, he had tried to ensure that he could survive any emergency. His escape pod contained extended life-support capabilities and minimal engines. He had food and air for a long voyage, supplemental power blocks, enough to be self-sufficient for quite a while, whatever it might take for him to get back to civilization.

Now that he had been exposed to the plague, though, what Tom Rom did not have was *time*. He no longer needed to worry about preserving the vials of Orli's infected blood for Zoe Alakis. He himself was a walking specimen—but he had to survive long enough to get back to Zoe, and he was far from any hope of rescue.

He studied his engine-thrust capacity, the ekti levels that remained. He reviewed all available information about any inhabited systems in the vicinity. Pergamus was much too far away. The nearest possibility was a small, obscure transfer station with a Klikiss transportal node. Vuoral.

He just might make it there. It was his only chance.

According to his most optimistic calculations, he would never live to reach the next closest planet on the list, not to mention survive the journey back to Pergamus from there, provided he could arrange transportation. He wanted to see Zoe one more time.

The Vuoral transfer station had its advantages. He'd be able to find one or two ships there, while avoiding questions that might delay him.

Tom Rom needed to be meticulous. Although his desire to deliver the alien microorganism to Zoe was paramount, he also had to make sure that the plague did not spread. That was not, nor would it ever be, his intention. The deadly disease had to be properly contained; Orli Covitz had been correct in that respect.

He set course and ignited the pod's engines, applying full thrust with the stardrive and burning his fuel at a rapid clip. No sense in conserving ekti if he could shave an hour or two off of his ETA. Tom Rom would have at most two or three days before the plague symptoms became obvious to anyone who glanced at him. And an infected captain would raise suspicions and complicate the rest of his plan.

Vuoral proved to be as unremarkable as expected, but he hadn't come here as a tourist. Because of the transportal on the planet's surface, pioneers had taken the Hansa's early colonization initiative bonus, but the small colony had practically fallen off the map.

Tom Rom could not go down to the surface, because that would release the plague. He had to find some other ship—and soon.

Fortunately, as he approached Vuoral he spotted a small independent trading ship in orbit, one of the unaffiliated vessels that eked out a living by working niche routes and serving out-of-the-way places, sometimes making a profit, sometimes suffering a loss.

Yes, the ship would serve his purposes nicely.

He had already developed his story, and he began transmitting a distress beacon directly toward the trader. "Declaring an emergency—I need help. Life support is failing, stardrive fuel almost gone. This escape pod is all that's left of my ship, and it's not holding together. Please pick me up!"

It was like casting bait into a lake. He didn't see any other ships at Vuoral, so there was only one option, and the trader ship responded as he had known it would. A distress call must be answered: few things were so ingrained in the mind of anyone who flew aboard a spaceship.

The response came immediately. "This is the *Pigeon*. We're on our way. What's your status?"

"Surviving—for now. But hurry."

After a quick check, he found that the ship's hatches were compatible with his own, so Tom Rom knew he could transfer across. He prepared himself, gathered the few things he needed, then set the timer aboard the escape pod. He had to clean up the mess behind him, leave no trace.

While the ships maneuvered into position, the other captain chatted over the comm. The *Pigeon* was a courier vessel that had arrived at Vuoral en route to a succession of other planets that Tom Rom had never heard of. He was a plump and kindly older man with long gray hair and a beard. He said he was retired and doing this for fun with his wife (who was even plumper); she looked thirty years his junior, but she adored him.

Despite his supposed experience, the *Pigeon*'s captain was clumsy, and it took him four tries to match up the hatches. Tom Rom began to grow nervous, looking at the countdown in his pod. By now he could feel the fever coursing through him, the tremors, the nausea.

When the hatches cycled open, Tom Rom pulled himself across, and sealed his own pod behind him. Entering the *Pigeon,* he felt weary, but he squared his shoulders and summoned the additional strength he would need for the next few minutes. Everything had to be done properly.

The supportive captain and his wife looked worried for him. "What happened to your ship," asked the wife. "How did you end up out here?"

"It exploded," Tom Rom said. "Engine overload. Sabotage I think."

"You're safe now," the old man said. "Was it piracy? Some kind of attack? You'll need to report this. We could drop you down at Vuoral, and you can go through the Klikiss transportal network back to civilization. Or you can hitch a ride with us to our next destination."

"We'll help in whatever way we can," said the wife.

Behind them, he heard his escape pod automatically detach from the *Pigeon* and tumble away with a small burst of thrusters. The couple was startled. "Your pod just broke loose!"

"I detached it. I won't need it anymore. I have your ship now."

The captain and his wife were confused. They seemed to think Tom Rom was not thinking straight.

After ten seconds the countdown ended, and the small explosive charges destroyed the escape pod and all the virus inside it. The shock waves jolted the *Pigeon* sideways, and the captain grabbed his wife for stability. "What the heck?"

Tom Rom removed his hand weapon and shot them both dead. There was no point in wasting time. He needed their vessel. Besides, he had exposed them to the plague. From the moment he stepped aboard, the bearded captain and his plump young wife had been as good as dead. Tom Rom had simply skipped to the inevitable outcome. It was the most efficient way to solve a problem.

While he still had the strength, he hauled the bodies into the airlock chamber. He glanced at the woman's face; her startled expression made her look like a little girl. He ejected the two bodies into space, though he could just as well have kept them in storage aboard the *Pigeon*. He always thought out second- and third-order consequences, and he decided that getting rid of the bodies would raise fewer questions than keeping them.

The courier ship had only one deck, two cabins, a common area, and a cockpit. Everything had small homey touches, colorful bouquets painted on the walls, even the sweet flowery scent of potpourri added to the ventilators.

Tom Rom studied the pilot controls and was disappointed by the engine speed. For a courier ship, the *Pigeon* wasn't very fast. He input the coordinates for Pergamus and ran three different routines, using a few tricks to minimize the flight time. He could feel the progress of the plague through his body; the virus had settled into his tissues and was eating away at him. Black blotches would soon start to show.

When he activated the stardrive, the acceleration pressed him back into the pilot's chair. He raced off at the *Pigeon*'s top speed, determined to get back to Zoe Alakis before it was too late.

ORLI COVITZ

After Tom Rom's ship flew away, DD went back outside to finish his work on the *Proud Mary*'s damaged engines. The little compy was determined to accomplish his task and fly away from the asteroid field before Orli died.

She curled up in her bunk with the intercom on because DD kept up a polite and friendly conversation, chatting about which components he was replacing and how many more hours he thought it would take. She could barely respond, drifting in and out of sleep, but it was a comfort just to hear his voice and know he was there.

Even before her symptoms began, Orli had studied the records of the Onthos disease. She knew exactly how her body would break down, and now she followed each stage like a grim blueprint. But she didn't need those records to tell her when she was in the final phase— she could figure that much from the crushing weight of pain throughout her nerves, her head, her thoughts.

Her memories became tinged with delirious echoes, but she tried to hold on. Orli Covitz did not give up.

The vibration of the ship and the rumble of engines penetrated her dream, and she felt the *Proud Mary* lurch away from the crater floor and up into space. She fought her way to consciousness to see DD at the piloting controls. He looked very small sitting in the worn cockpit seat designed for Mary Coven. He could barely reach the controls.

Seeing her awake, he said, "I'm sorry I disturbed you, Orli."

She eased herself into a sitting position on the bunk, then struggled to her feet. "That's all right, DD." When she reached the cockpit, she grasped the back of the pilot chair to keep her balance. "You fixed everything by yourself."

"I was aware of your wishes. I wasn't able to restore the *Proud Mary* to its full pristine capabilities, but it should be sufficient to take us to a place where we can transmit our data."

"Where is the closest inhabited settlement?" Orli asked. *And will we make it there before I die?*

"I am not precisely certain. I set course for a nearby star system, even though our records don't indicate any human or Ildiran colonies there." He paused. "But it is the only place we can reach within the appropriate time frame."

"All right, let's have a look then."

The compy swiveled out of the pilot chair so that Orli could take his place. "If we don't find a settlement there, you know what to do."

"Yes, Orli, I know what to do."

Even if she died, DD would fly the *Proud Mary* to a known human outpost, transmit the priceless records, and then like the brave compies that had disrupted the reactors of the Onthos city, DD would detonate the ship to erase any last sign of the virus.

"I'm glad you're here, DD," she said.

"My duty has always been to serve, to provide companionship and guidance when possible. I have had several extremely kind masters, but I think you were the best."

Orli's eyes filled with tears.

As the *Proud Mary* flew on, she tried to decide whether she regretted where she was. She could have stayed on Relleker, tended the orphan compies that came in . . . or she could have traveled to the Ikbir colony with LU, MO, and her other compies. Matthew could have been with Orli in her last days, out of some sort of guilt or obligation, but that would not have been more comforting to her. She could have had a long uneventful life if she hadn't bothered to *do* anything. She had wanted more adventures . . . but this one had a tragic ending.

They reached the next solar system with a bright white star and no interesting planets, according to the star atlas. As they cruised in, DD studied the sensor readings for any sign of habitation or activity, scanned the territory around the sun—and was surprised to spot energy readings. "Orli, there appears to be an industrial outpost on the outskirts of the system. It's far outside any planetary orbit, but is moving down toward the star."

Orli shook her head and had to think about what he said. "A human outpost?"

"It appears so. I picked up communications transmissions, and they are speaking trade standard."

"That'll have to do. Adjust course. Let's fly close enough to introduce ourselves."

The *Proud Mary* arrived among ships, habitation modules, storage tanks, pumping stations—and a cluster of strange inflated sacks that drifted through space.

"From markings on the structures, this appears to be an outpost of Iswander Industries," DD said.

"As long as they're willing to receive our information, I don't care who they are." She adjusted course, shut down the engines, and used reverse thrusters to slow the ship as she drifted to the perimeter of the industrial operations.

"Three ships are approaching us, Orli. We have been detected. They are asking us to identify ourselves."

They didn't look like military ships. Orli couldn't tell if they even had weapons. Her fingers shook as she remembered how Tom Rom had stalked and attacked her. She fumbled with the comm controls before finally managing to activate the system. "This is *Proud Mary*, under quarantine. We are a plague ship, and I'm dying from an alien disease. Please do not approach."

The security ships hesitated, circling her vessel. "We have limited medical facilities, *Proud Mary*. We certainly don't have the capability for full quarantine."

"Not asking for that." She hardened her voice. "But if you don't back off, I'm prepared to destroy my ship rather than let you come aboard."

She glanced at the little compy. DD gave a silent nod. This time, they had prepared for an easy initiation of the self-destruct sequence.

The pause was long enough that she guessed there must have been an intense discussion on secure channels, and no small amount of consternation. The three Iswander Security ships backed off and held their position. "What is your intention, *Proud Mary*? What do you need?"

Orli took a deep breath. "I need to transmit a database of vital information—scientific, archaeological, anthropological, and medical data. I also have final messages for a few friends." Her voice hitched. "I need your promise that they'll be delivered."

She stared at the screen and knew she must look haggard, her eyes red, her skin covered with dark blotches. "And then I just need to be left alone so I can die in peace."

GARRISON REEVES

It was going to get ugly, Garrison knew it.

He and Seth had avoided the catastrophe on Sheol; they had escaped from the exploding bloater cluster out in empty space; they had even, by a miracle, survived the Shana Rei shadow cloud.

But now that the Iswander ships had returned to the ekti-extraction field, assessed the damage, and counted the casualties, Garrison knew that Elisa was going to fight him over Seth. Though Lee Iswander made no threats, he impounded the *Prodigal Son* so that Garrison couldn't leave.

During the panicked scramble to evacuate, thirty-seven people had lost their lives through mishaps and the brief robot attack. But Garrison had watched the industrialist during the crisis, how he had responded. Iswander had stayed behind and saved as many of his workers as possible—maybe he had learned his lesson after Sheol. Garrison couldn't exactly blame the man for not preparing against the Shana Rei. It wasn't something any operation would have planned for. In fact, no one could understand how they had escaped total obliteration. The Shana Rei had just . . . left.

But that didn't solve Garrison's personal problem.

"Once everything gets back to normal, we'll figure this out," said Iswander. "For now, you can stay here with your son."

"As a prisoner, you mean."

Iswander folded his hands together, serious, businesslike. "I've checked on you. I know what you've been doing since you left my employ—minor and unfulfilling work in the lunar rubble around Earth. You're better than that. Don't you want something exciting, engaging, and on par with your abilities?"

He didn't wait for an answer, but continued, "If you're willing to set the past aside, I'll wipe your personnel record clean. A second chance for both of us. I could use another good man on my crews here—work any part of the ekti processing you like. That way, you and Elisa both get to stay with your son, so the boy isn't in the middle of a tug-of-war. Besides, I keep Elisa as a happy and undistracted employee, and I don't have to worry about you keeping these operations secret. Everybody wins." He smiled. "You have to agree, it's the best possible solution. No need for the situation to get any messier."

"You make it sound so simple," Garrison said.

Iswander shrugged. "I've run the numbers."

Grudgingly, Garrison said he would review the list of possible jobs at the extraction field, though he was careful not to give a final answer. He knew Seth wanted to stay with him, but would never say he *wanted* to leave his mother. Garrison wouldn't force the boy to choose.

Elisa ignored him, as if she assumed the problem was solved. Meanwhile, he spent time with Seth, but that didn't mean he wanted to be here. He had seen bloaters explode, and he knew they were dangerous— even the green priest had demonstrated that.

During the chaotic evacuation, Aelin had flown to one of the bloaters, following some siren's song only he could hear. He had immersed himself in it—and then climbed back out of the protoplasm into the inspection pod. He sealed the hatch and somehow found the presence of mind to operate the craft.

Aelin flew back to the modular complex and landed the pod in an available hangar in front of an astonished crowd. The green priest glowed with warmth and an expression of blissful wonder. Now, whenever Aelin looked at any individual, his eyes seemed to have a hypnotic power.

"I have been baptized in the blood of the cosmos. I am rejuvenated." He didn't resist as the two flustered doctors led him back to the infirmary. . . .

The following day, Iswander Security forces detected another intruder at the bloater-extraction field and raced out to intercept an unidentified ship. As soon as the unexpected pilot began transmitting, Garrison knew she was no spy come to uncover the secret ekti operations. From the quiet admin module, Garrison and Seth watched the drama unfold. The woman was dying from a plague.

When Orli Covitz introduced herself, Seth lit up with surprise. "That's the compy lady! Don't you remember her?"

Seth was right. Although her face was haggard and sickly, Garrison recognized the compy researcher from Relleker who had done so much crusading to support compies. Seth, who watched many of her reports, often showed them to his father in hopes of convincing him to pick up one of her misfit compies. Garrison remembered how beautiful, how intense and animated Orli had been when she spoke in the video recordings about her compies.

Garrison had never expected to find her out here on the edge of a far-flung star system. Yet here she was, with a Friendly compy beside her in the cockpit.

Orli transmitted the files of medical data about the disease, the alien race, the lost derelict city . . . and the dead Roamer clan. Garrison felt a chill as he realized that this was the same plague that had killed clan Reeves.

He went over to the comm screen. "I need to talk with her. She was at the derelict city where my whole family died."

The technician frowned at the interruption, but Lee Iswander gave a quick nod, and Garrison nudged the comm officer aside. When he told Orli that Olaf Reeves was his father, that he and Seth were possibly the last survivors of clan Reeves, he watched her expression fall. "I'm sorry," she said. "They were all dead when I arrived, but I have recordings from your father and some of the other clan members." Orli's eyes drooped, and her head swayed. She was clearly in pain. "Olaf Reeves did everything he could to prevent the spread of the plague. The derelict city should have been vaporized before I got there, but it was just bad luck and bad timing. The sickness ends with me. Here."

Garrison planned to review the records, listen to Olaf's last words. Though he doubted he would hear any apology, it was still his obligation to listen to what his father had to say. He leaned closer to the screen, and his voice was hoarse. "Thank you for bringing this back."

When Garrison looked at Orli, everyone else in the admin center seemed to fade away. He concentrated on her, felt her intensity.

"I need you to do me a favor, Garrison Reeves," she said. "There's a woman, Rlinda Kett—tell her I'm sorry about losing her ship. I should have just stayed on Relleker." She heaved a breath, her shoulders shuddered.

Joining his father at the comm, Seth spoke to her. "I like compies. We listen to your reports sometimes. I always wanted to meet you." Then he smiled. "Is that DD?"

The Friendly compy perked up. "Yes, I am DD."

Garrison asked, "Why did you leave there in the first place? You had your compy work."

Tears filled her eyes. "My husband, Matthew . . . everything broke apart and it was too painful to stay. I wanted something else. I guess I should have picked a different midlife crisis." Orli let out a bitter chuckle. "It won't be long now. DD is ready to self-destruct the *Proud Mary*. He has his orders."

"Don't give up yet!"

"That's what I've been telling myself for days."

Seth's brows drew together, and he spoke urgently to DD. "A good compy takes care of his master. DD, you need to take care of Orli."

The little compy turned his optical sensors at the screen. "I promise, I am doing all I possibly can."

Orli said, "There's nothing DD or I can do. And I refuse to let anyone else catch this plague. Nothing can cure me."

Garrison ignored everyone else in the admin module. "We can talk as long as you like. We'll keep the comm channel open. I'll be here." He didn't even notice the silence that fell in the admin module followed by startled whispers.

The green priest came up to stand between Seth and Garrison. Aelin had a warm smile and bright, intense eyes. "I can cure her. It's simple."

MAGE-IMPERATOR JORA'H

As the leader of the Ildiran Empire, the heart of the *thism,* and the focus of his people, Jora'h could not waver. His personal strength had to be an anchor for all Ildirans. Despite his resolve, a cold blade of fear lanced him as he went with Nira and Tal Gale'nh to the site of the massacre in the human enclave. Yazra'h and Muree'n insisted on accompanying them, armed and armored, alert and angry; they had made it clear they trusted no one else to keep the Mage-Imperator safe.

Jora'h had not wanted Nira to join the group, since she had already been the target of an assassination attempt, but she insisted. "Bring extra guards. I will be safe enough."

"We will keep you safe, Mother," Muree'n vowed, and Jora'h didn't doubt her.

He felt sickened even before he saw the first body—and there were many bodies. The guard kithmen formed a loose protective cordon around him, crystal katanas raised, fearing some other unexpected attack.

But what if his *own guards* became tainted like those in the Vault of Failures? How could he make sure Nira was safe anywhere? Maybe Muree'n and Yazra'h should remain at her side at all times. To be safe, he should have sent Nira back to Theroc with their daughter Osira'h, but Ildira was her home now and had been for years. Nira made it clear she had no intention of staying inside the Prism Palace when all of the human expatriates had been slaughtered.

And Jora'h knew that she strengthened him. With Nira here at his side, he was a more powerful leader.

The flames in the human enclave had been extinguished, but

greasy smoke still curled into the sky like escaping shadows. *His own people* had caused this. Peaceful everyday Ildirans from various kiths had turned into mad butchers, slaying every human who had come here to share their culture.

The human bodies on the ground were burned and mangled, but not unrecognizable. Jora'h remembered them: businesspeople, craftsmen, café owners, artists. And all around, like toppled pieces on a game board, lay their dead Ildiran attackers. Of those attackers—more than a hundred of them—not one was marked save for the blood spatters. And it was not their blood. After committing their brutality, they had all simply fallen dead. Each of the corpses wore a frozen expression of horror.

Yazra'h and Muree'n regarded the massacre, grim and assessing. Both of them had their weapons drawn.

Gale'nh stared, as if he had received a stunning blow. His fingers extended, and he reached out a tentative hand, as if to save these people but much too late. He let his arm fall to his side.

Nira shuddered beside Jora'h, her breath hitching raggedly. She began sobbing and knelt beside one of the fallen humans, whose face was battered to a shapeless mass. From the apron and the dark skirt, Jora'h knew it must be Blondie, the diner owner.

"Why?" Nira turned her eyes up to him. "Why . . . why would they do this?" She seemed to think he could give her an answer.

Through the *thism*, the Mage-Imperator understood the threads of thought and emotion that bound his people together . . . but this, he couldn't understand at all.

Accompanied by uniformed Solar Navy soldiers, Adar Zan'nh arrived in response to the news. Gale'nh stood beside the Adar, as if falling into ranks. Zan'nh inspected the scene grimly. "Liege, my soldiers are here to help defend you."

Yazra'h and Muree'n stiffened, but they did not insist that they would be sufficient. "The Mage-Imperator cannot have too much protection."

"This was not any sort of attack we know how to defend against," Jora'h said.

Gale'nh was pale and shaken. "I sensed tension and uneasiness, but it was murky. Maybe it was through my connection, my scars . . .

but my *thism* is not strong." He looked at the Mage-Imperator, as if Jora'h had let him down. "You hold all the *thism* within you, Liege. Why did you not know?"

"It . . . eluded me," Jora'h answered, but he knew it was a weak excuse. "I was sleeping when all this happened."

Nira rose to her feet. She had not touched the diner owner's body, but somehow she was covered with blood. "You did feel it, Jora'h— the nightmares told you."

He didn't want to voice the growing suspicion and dread within him. What if this were worse than just him sensing a dark manipulation in the *thism*? What if he himself had become a conduit for the Shana Rei, and the shadows emanated through him? What if through his subconscious he had actually *allowed* this?

Nira walked through the wreckage, and the guards kept up with her. She made a point of staring at each of the bodies, closing her eyes as if in silent prayer.

Jora'h had felt nothing from the attacking Ildirans; once possessed, they had been erased from his telepathic tapestry. Adar Zan'nh and Tal Gale'nh followed close. Uniformed Solar Navy soldiers flanked the Adar, wary, possibly even suspicious of the guard kithmen.

Zan'nh gave his report. "We will fight the Shana Rei in traditional combat. Our industries are manufacturing as many sun bombs as possible. General Keah and the Confederation Defense Forces also have the designs. We will be able to fight back much more effectively in our next encounter." He paused and just stared at the slaughter around him. "But this . . . how can we fight against *this*? This is not an enemy— this is *ourselves*."

"This is not a battle the Solar Navy can undertake alone," the Mage-Imperator said. "The Shana Rei attack us with more than warships. They also strike through the *thism*."

At the thought, a chill rushed through his body. What if the mesh of racial telepathy that made Ildirans so powerful and unique became their greatest vulnerability? What if the only way to defend against this kind of insidious darkness was to sever them all from the *thism* network? If that happened, would they still be Ildirans after all?

Nira was weeping, and Jora'h held her, giving strength and drawing strength back. He refused to acknowledge any feelings of despair, because then all Ildirans would feel it. They had to remain strong, and so he had to remain strong.

King Peter and Queen Estarra needed to know about these human deaths, these poor settlers who loved Ildiran culture and merely wanted to share their own. The Mage-Imperator had promised the expatriates they would be safe in Mijistra. Now he wondered if anyone was safe—humans or Ildirans. He didn't know how to protect them.

At least Osira'h had gone to Theroc.

He straightened, forced resolve upon himself. "We cannot fight what we do not understand. Therefore we must understand. These humans were not at fault. Our own people fell prey to a kind of madness. We must learn how they became vulnerable, and how we can stop it from happening again."

He turned to the guard kith and the Solar Navy soldiers. "Gather the bodies of these fallen Ildirans and bring them to our medical kithmen so they can test and dissect and analyze until they tell me how to defend against the shadow." He turned to Zan'nh. "Meanwhile, Adar, continue to arm the Solar Navy. Wherever the battle may come, Ildira must be prepared."

ARITA

After the Shana Rei darkness settled over Theroc, the unnatural night did not end.

When Arita had gone out exploring that afternoon, she felt a definite stirring among the worldtrees, heard whispers in the back of her mind, sensed a real tension in the air. It was not normal. She closed her eyes and pressed her hands against the gold-scaled bark of a towering worldtree, pushing so hard that the bark scales left deep indentations in her skin. "Tell me what is happening."

But the verdani refused to answer her.

She felt the cold, darkness encroaching from above, the daylight growing dimmer through the thick canopy overhead. Hurrying back to Sarein's hiveworm nest, she broke through to a meadow with a clear view of the sky. She shaded her eyes, squinted—and saw that a bite had been taken out of the sun, a black chunk that covered an increasing portion of the solar disk.

When she reached Sarein's tree and scrambled up, she found her aunt intense and concerned as she listened to broadcasts from the main fungus-reef in the capital city. When she glanced at Arita, Sarein's thin face was more drawn than usual; lines showed around her lips. "Theroc is under attack," she announced, as if glad for someone to tell. "A shadow cloud has appeared—and Klikiss robots. They're working to create some kind of eclipse. The King and Queen are trying to command a defense." She turned back to the portable comm system. "But the reports don't sound promising."

Sarein expanded the screen so Arita could join her, scanning transmissions until she found a direct feed from the CDF battleships. In an image from space, Arita got her first glimpse of the Shana Rei occultation barrier.

Hexagon slices continued to peel from the ends of the long black cylinders. The thin, opaque plates twirled across space to line up with adjacent hexes, building the black gridwork larger and larger. As it grew, the barrier blocked out more of the sun and expanded the eclipse shadow across Theroc.

The flagship Juggernaut and twenty Manta cruisers attacked the growing "nightshade" with flamboyant energy displays and exploding weapons, but to little effect. Even when the CDF scored major strikes and shattered off numerous hexes, the segments simply re-aligned and reattached themselves.

Several reckless Manta cruisers had gone on direct attack runs against the gigantic Shana Rei cylinders. Four cruisers had already been destroyed, though it wasn't clear to Arita exactly how the shadow creatures were fighting them.

And the nightshade grew, widening the eclipse across the forest.

"They can blot out the sun and kill the worldforest," Arita said. "They don't even have to approach the planet." She turned to her aunt. "Kennebar and his green priests can tap into the verdani mind. Maybe they know more about what's happening." She suddenly wanted to find Collin.

Sarein frowned. "We have the comm here. We can listen to reports." That seemed to be good enough.

She and Sarein sat inside the hiveworm nest, both fascinated and horrified to hear the reports. They spoke little, though occasionally they would send grim glances to each other.

Over the hours, the diameter of the nightshade grew, cutting off more and more sunlight. The forest was restless, and the insects began humming, confused as to when they should make their nighttime music. Clinging to normal routines, Sarein lit several lamps outside. Arita could see the glitter of numerous species of firefly leaving their forest mulch nests.

And when the giant occultation plate in orbit finally blotted out the sun entirely and drenched the Wild in shadow, an abrupt smothering night fell without the gentle transition of twilight.

Arita shivered as the temperature dropped. Breezes picked up in an angry stirring of fronds. Even the glow of scattered atmospheric light faded, and bright stars appeared at the periphery of the nightshade's giant hole in the sky.

Predatory night moths took flight, swooping through the fronds to devour other insects. The forest wildlife seemed on the verge of panic, as if they could smell the smoke of an approaching wildfire, but this was worse.

Sarein finally agreed to go. The darkness elicited a primal uneasiness even in her, and she decided she didn't want to be here alone after all. Arita took her packs and her hand lights; Sarein had a brighter portable lantern. The two climbed down from her tree and trudged off through the dark and restless forest. Arita wanted to find her landed flyer. It was time to return to the main continent, her parents . . . even Reyn had just come back home.

"I don't usually wander the forest at night," Sarein muttered. Arita could tell that her aunt was frightened.

"I'm not sure when morning is going to come again," Arita said. "We have to go now."

They moved through the underbrush, dodging branches and finding their way through the light of phosphorescent fungi. Arita wasn't surprised when an alarmed-looking Collin dropped down from the trees and landed gently on his bare feet. "The worldtrees were watching you. I knew you were coming."

"We're going back to the capital city," Arita said. "We'll have more options there, more protection, and we can flee off-planet if necessary. You should come along with us."

Collin looked horrified. "We can't just leave the trees! This darkness will smother them—they'll die."

They looked up to see the other green priests sitting among the fronds above, touching the trees with their fingertips, their eyes closed.

Arita turned to Collin. "What are the Shana Rei? Can the verdani tell us anything? Why are they attacking here?"

He shook his head. "The trees are afraid of them. They know how terrible the Shana Rei are, but they can't remember. There's a gap in the worldforest's memory. As a green priest, I have searched . . . but there's nothing, as if that part of the memory has died."

Sarein said, "How can there be a gap in the verdani mind?"

"Some part of them was erased long ago," Collin said. "That past is gone in their memory." Above them, Kennebar's green priests muttered to one another, making shorthand comments, not deigning to explain to Arita or Sarein.

Arita heard Kennebar say aloud, "General Keah lost two more vessels. The verdani battleships are gathering their strength for an assault."

A second green priest added, "They are moving toward the nightshade now. Their boughs are spread wide for combat."

Arita imagined the titanic trees extending long thorns like impenetrable spears. The verdani hurled themselves against the growing occultation plate, stretching out branches, trying to tear away the hexes.

Collin bent to a tree, tapped into telink. "The treeships are attacking the Shana Rei—they have no choice. They have to stop more plates from launching off. Others are hurling themselves against the growing barrier, stretching out branches, trying to tear away the hexes." He winced. "But . . . there's something about the shadow. It's like acid. Their boughs are shriveling."

In unison, the green priests winced and gasped. "The fronds are blackening! The trees are fighting, tearing . . . and withering." Several priests stopped using words altogether and just let out moans and cries of pain.

Shaking, Collin heaved several breaths, removed his fingertips from the worldtree. "The verdani battleships have dropped away from the nightshade. They tore away a section of the occultation plate, but it won't last. Already more hexes are flying into place to fill the gaps." He shook his head. "The Shana Rei have succeeded. This night will not end until all life is smothered on Theroc."

Arita was sure the forest air had grown colder. The breezes rustled branches with a sound like a death rattle. The false night went on.

The trees would weaken, the plants would die, and the sun would never again rise on the Theron worldforest.

OSIRA'H

In the smothering blindness of the continuing eclipse, the stars around the black blot in space gave no comfort. The cold dark had a stranglehold on the worldforest that tightened, day after day. For Osira'h, with her Ildiran blood, the gathering psychic shadow was even worse.

The fungus-reef capital was lit with supplemental bright panels. Overhead, racks of spotlights shone down over the settled area, which provided enough illumination to give Osira'h strength.

The green priests refused to leave the planet, but Peter and Estarra issued orders for offworld diplomats to evacuate. The Ildiran trade ministers and ambassadors slipped away on the first ship, and the green priests had spread word of the crisis throughout the Confederation, even to the Ildiran Empire.

Osira'h insisted on remaining with Reyn, even though he begged her to go. She was just as worried about him as he was about her. His sister was off on another continent, but they had word that Arita was as safe as any of them were.

But none of them were safe.

Three times in the past several days, black robot ships had launched from the shadow cloud on a sortie against the CDF defenses, but it was mere harassment. The robot ships swooped in and opened fire, paying little attention to their own safety. Two verdani battleships surprised a pair of robot vessels, opening powerful thorny branches to embrace them, crush them, and tear them into ragged debris, while the rest of the robot ships retreated.

The main attack on Theroc, however, was simply the *darkness*. By blocking off all sunlight and engulfing the world in endless night, the Shana Rei were crippling and starving the great worldtrees. An impressive tactical plan, too, Osira'h realized—it allowed the Shana Rei to obliterate the powerful verdani mind at very little cost to themselves. To her, that meant the worldtrees must pose a threat, and the Shana Rei were weak enough to fear them. But the nightshade would do the work of crippling the verdani for them.

Rlinda Kett had remained on Theroc, supposedly to watch over her Arbor restaurant. She made herself visible and available, bringing fresh meals down into the main fungus-reef. She and her maître d' Zachary Wisskoff delivered a cart laden with soup tureens and spicy fruit salads she had made from the supplies in her kitchens. The maître d' looked gaunt and skittish, but he refused to evacuate, perhaps so he could sneer at the situation.

Reyn had introduced Osira'h to the hearty Rlinda, who embraced the young man with an all-enfolding hug. "Glad to see you, Raindrop, but also sorry you're here." She lowered her voice. "Any progress? Did you find what you needed?"

"I've been to see more doctors, and I have tests, but no answers. Lots of people are working on it, though. Oh, and I did tell my parents. They know how sick I am."

"About time. They'll do everything they can to get this figured out."

"Osira'h has helped me a lot, too." He slipped an arm around Osira'h's waist, which seemed to thrill Rlinda more than anything.

"Now that's the kind of help you need." She opened the tureen of soup, sniffed as she stirred. "Mr. Wisskoff, did you bring the good bowls?"

"Not at all, ma'am. Just recyclable ones. Or did you expect me to wash them? Most of our staff departed on the first evacuation ships."

With an extravagant sigh, Rlinda found serviceable bowls and presented soup to Reyn and Osira'h. "The flavor should be enough to command your attention."

Wisskoff served food around the table in the main meeting room, where the King and Queen were studying reports. Peter thanked them. Wisskoff muttered, "Will those be on separate checks?"

Rlinda gave him a withering glance. "Do it for the gratitude."

"I'll be sure to inform our creditors that we will be paying all future invoices with 'gratitude,' ma'am."

Osira'h didn't entirely understand their teasing banter, but she

sensed that they were hiding their worry by keeping busy and contributing their support in the best way they knew how. Reyn still kept his
arm around Osira'h, who leaned closer against him; they seemed to
generate strength for each other just by being in close proximity.

Inside the meeting chamber, several green priests looked frail as
they huddled over their treelings, touched the verdani mind, and tried
to prepare for the worst. The whole worldforest was weakening—and
no effort on a human scale could save them.

"It happened before, and we survived," said one of the priests in
the throne room. "All but the smallest portion of the worldforest was
wiped out, and yet the trees survived to thrive again."

Queen Estarra wore her traditional garments, like the ones her
mother Alexa had worn. "Much of Theroc was devastated, but the
trees came back."

The green priest shook his head. "That was the recent war. I was
referring to something much worse—a battle far, far in the past." He
touched the treeling again, and his brow furrowed in puzzlement.
"Theroc is not the original home of the worldforest. That was destroyed, and the . . . *Gardeners* were made extinct." He looked up, surprised by what he had just discovered. A stir rippled through his fellow
green priests as they realized the new hint of information that had just
been revealed to them.

"Who were the Gardeners?" Peter asked. "Can you tell us more
about that battle?"

"Long before humans became green priests, there were . . . others.
Gone now. Smothered by the Shana Rei."

Listening, Osira'h looked at Prince Reyn. "The Shana Rei nearly
destroyed the Ildiran Empire as well. Fear of them is etched deep
within us, a permanent scar on our psyches." Her eyes flashed as she
drew herself up, and she felt her feathery strands of hair twitch with
energy as her determination grew. "But we are in a different situation
now. We have new skills. We have *me*." She gasped Reyn's hand. "Take
me to the treetops. I need to see the sky, look out at the stars, and focus
my thoughts." She flexed her hand, felt the still-tender burns on her
fingers, focused on the pain. "Maybe I can summon the help we need
to solve this problem."

Curious, Reyn took her above the fungus-reef city, and they

emerged onto the dense polymerized canopy. A few evacuating ships still glinted in the sky, hot exhaust trails rising to orbit. Osira'h sat with him in the soft, spongy embrace of interlocked worldtree fronds. Deprived of nourishing sunlight for days, the leaflets drooped, the color washed out of them.

Reyn looked worried, with a faint sheen of sweat on his face. "All the Shana Rei have to do is wait. This darkness will be the death of the worldtrees."

"Not necessarily." Osira'h had never been able to feel the trees the way her green priest mother did, but she was aware of the verdani presence. Now, as she looked up at the mocking stars, she used her telepathic powers and her understanding of the great forces of the universe to call upon other entities.

Osira'h summoned the faeros, begged them. With her open mind, she showed them the threat, called upon her past connection with them. Though she couldn't see into the thoughts of the fiery elementals, she felt the awakening, the awareness, the response. The sparks grew brighter in her mind.

She turned to Reyn. "They are coming."

Osira'h asked him to stay with her, and they sat together for hours in the deepening cold of the continuous night. They watched the dark sky until she saw bright lights like distant fireflies drawing closer. She rose to her feet, and Reyn stood with her, his face filled with questions.

Before long, dozens of the fireballs appeared, blazing ellipsoids that rolled along spouting a corona of flames. They roared across the Theron sky, crackling and sending out waves of palpable heat. Like miniature suns, they shone their light over the darkened forest.

Green priests ran to the canopy, shouting in fear and confusion. Osira'h, though, was not afraid. "The faeros aren't here to attack," she assured Reyn. "I asked them to help us."

The fireballs drifted over the canopy as if to acknowledge Osira'h's presence, then together they swooped upward and hurtled out into space.

ZOE ALAKIS

Zoe waited inside her sterile dome on Pergamus—and waited, and waited—hoping for word from Tom Rom. She checked with her system perimeter sentries, the picket-line ships. Nothing. She began to grow very concerned.

She had good reason to worry about him, especially after his recent encounter with the Roamer pirates on Vaconda. Though he was more competent than any other person she knew, Tom Rom put himself in dangerous situations—to do as Zoe asked—and she dreaded the day when he would not come back.

Finally, though, a small, unrecognized courier ship arrived at Pergamus, burning the last of its fuel in a red-line deceleration. Her picket security ships went on alert, racing out to defend the medical research station, but she could see that this tiny courier vessel posed no conceivable threat. One or two blasts could vaporize the ship before it even entered orbit.

Then Tom Rom transmitted a security code, and his voice came through, rich and familiar. "Zoe, prepare an available ORS, full lockdown and quarantine setup. I've . . . brought you the alien plague for your library."

She found herself grinning like a teenage girl. Just hearing his voice made everything all right, but she found it odd that he hadn't transmitted his image. She wanted to see him. Zoe responded quickly, using a priority override to break through the usual signals of the security ships and the receiving crews. She had a wealth of questions.

"I don't recognize that vessel—what happened to your own ship? Why didn't you send a message? You're five days late, and I was worried. . . ." She let out a nervous laugh. "Go through the full decon routines and meet me here in the main dome. We'll have time for the whole story. It must have been quite an adventure."

Tom Rom maintained an audio-only transmission. "Zoe, use secure channel five." Then he switched off.

She frowned. That meant he had a private message for her that he didn't want even her most dedicated personnel to overhear. Something that could not wait. She tapped the controls on her desktop and opened a new window, piped in through several layers of security access.

When Tom Rom's face appeared on the screen, she gasped in dismay. His face looked ravaged and discolored, as if thugs had held him down and beaten him . . . but Zoe could see the blotches were not mere bruises.

"I brought you the alien microorganism, Zoe, as promised. It's inside me. I'll take samples of my own blood, seal them in sterile packages, and arrange to transfer them to a designated Orbital Research Sphere. I don't want this to go into any surface dome, no matter how many precautions you take. This may be the deadliest disease we have ever studied. I have only a few days left."

Zoe shook her head, trying to deny what she saw. "I'll put you in one of the ORS labs. I'll use all of our facilities and researchers— everything Pergamus has. We'll find a way to treat you."

Tom Rom had never denied her before, but now he shook his head. "This is incurable, Zoe: one hundred percent mortality. You can't risk it. Every person aboard the alien space city died."

Zoe refused to listen. "Those other victims didn't have my resources, my experts, my database. I'll take care of you—I promise."

"You will get the disease sample for your library, but anything else is too dangerous. I can't let this disease get near you, Zoe. Once the specimens have been placed in a safe orbital station, I will need to be neutralized."

Growing angry, she leaned closer to the screen. "That's not going to happen, and you know it."

"I insist," he said.

"Insist all you like. I'm going to ignore it. You've always listened to me, done as I asked. You *swore*—and now I'm going to hold you to your word."

"Then I'll destroy this ship myself, just to be sure."

Zoe snorted. "No, you won't, because you haven't given me the sample yet."

She called up records on screens across her table surface. "Take your ship directly to ORS Twelve. It's empty—recently sterilized and decontaminated. Our best team just finished refitting it for research."

"Dr. Hannig's lab?"

"Yes. Hannig made a mistake, and I cleaned it up. We can take care of you there."

Tom Rom looked deeply disturbed, but she had found a loophole and she knew it. "You have to do this for me," she said. "Let us put the Pergamus facilities to good use. You know I'll take the proper precautions. I will assign a team of doctors, every one of them in a sterilization suit. The ORS is completely isolated."

"Too risky."

Now she hardened her expression because Tom Rom needed to see her resolve. "You know me. If anything goes wrong, if there's even the slightest chance of a release, I'll vaporize it all rather than risk contamination."

He seemed amused by that. "Even with me aboard?"

"Yes, dammit! Even with you aboard. You know I will."

He let out a rattling sigh. "Yes. I know you will." She could see Tom Rom was too weak and too ill to argue, and he accepted defeat with as much grace as he could manage. "If nothing else, you'll learn quite a bit by monitoring and testing me as the disease progresses. I'll allow myself to become your specimen."

He guided his stolen courier vessel toward the necklace of research spheres that orbited above the planet. Security escort ships followed him in, unaware of what was happening. They simply believed Tom Rom carried an extremely valuable and dangerous specimen—which he did, but they didn't need any more information.

Her pulse racing, Zoe called up the records of her research teams, scanned their areas of expertise. She knew little about the alien disease, so she would put her best scientists on it. *All* of them. Other work on Pergamus would grind to a halt, and she didn't care.

Tom Rom continued to talk to her in his ragged voice. He transmitted a summary that he had compiled on his journey, but many of the sentences were aimless or incomplete. He had trouble focusing his thoughts, which chilled Zoe to her core. She had never known Tom Rom's mind to be anything but sharp and organized.

She couldn't lose him!

This exotic and deadly plague was a Klikiss-borne disease that had infected another, previously unknown alien race, then also spread to humans as well. It might have opportunistically shifted its genetic structure to adapt. A disease that could cross species lines was amazing and terrifying—Zoe needed to study it. In her war against the unseen world of germs and diseases, this was like a super weapon.

She understood Tom Rom's determination to get the specimen here, but she couldn't imagine how he had been so careless as to become infected. He simply did not make mistakes.

Though she struggled to remain calm, panic rose within her. Seeing him, knowing he was dying, made her feel helpless again—just as when her father was in the last stages of Heidegger's Syndrome. Adam Alakis had died because no medical research teams had bothered to devote resources to curing an obscure disease, and Zoe refused to let that happen to Tom Rom. To save him, she would devote the full resources of Pergamus: people, equipment, finances, and knowledge.

She handpicked her top doctors for the ORS 12 research team and powered up the sphere's life-support systems.

She wanted to keep talking to Tom Rom, because she didn't dare lose a second of what remained of his life. He looked as if he'd grown sicker in just the few minutes while she'd been busy making arrangements.

She said, "Do not underestimate me."

His smile was weak but genuine. "Zoe, I never underestimate you."

ORLI COVITZ

Orli didn't want to get her hopes up. Depending too much on unrealistic hope was what had made her hesitate while Tom Rom was pursuing her.

But the green priest said he had a way to cure her. On screen, Aelin wore an expression not of arrogance, but of unwavering confidence that he knew *everything,* even though he could only share the tiniest fraction of it.

"What have you got to lose?" asked Garrison Reeves, who looked earnest on the screen as he talked with her from the admin module.

And Orli realized that she did not in fact have anything to lose.

Though they had never spoken before, she felt a connection with Garrison. He and his son were both familiar with her compy work. And she knew something about Garrison too, having watched the sad last messages of clan Reeves, including the farewells spoken by Olaf, Dale, Sendra.

He seemed different from the Retroamers, though, an independent man who had not wanted to isolate himself from the rest of the Confederation. From his obvious compassion, she could tell he was not at all like Matthew. Orli wished she could have had a chance to know him better. It was a cruel irony to meet someone like that when she was in the last stages of a terminal disease. . . .

DD contributed his opinion about the green priest's offer. "I encourage you to pursue any option of a cure, Orli. I would find it difficult to force you if you decided to resist—but I would still make the attempt."

Orli looked at the Friendly compy, struggled to focus her eyes. Her head pounded, every part of her felt indescribably awful. She doubted she had the energy to fight off even little DD. "Why would you force me?"

"My programming requires me to save you. I cannot allow you to come to harm through inaction—mine or yours. If you refuse to try the only possible cure, then I would not allow *your* inaction."

She responded with a weak, rattling laugh. "That's an interesting contortion of logic. I'd like to stay alive, even if just to study that further." She turned back to the concerned audience that watched her from Iswander's admin module. "All right, so what exactly am I supposed to do?"

The green priest said in a calm voice, "Do what I did. Go to one of the bloater nodules and pass through the membrane. Inside is the universe's primordial sea—life itself, and everything. Immerse yourself."

"I thought the bloaters were filled with ekti. Won't I just drown in stardrive fuel?"

"You will bathe in the blood of the cosmos," said the green priest. "You are not like me. You don't have telink, so the effect will not be as pronounced, but I am confident you will find the cleansing you need."

"I'm glad somebody's confident," Orli muttered.

Without being told, DD operated the piloting controls and eased the *Proud Mary* toward the bloater cluster. Far below, the system's bright white sun looked intense and alone. Nodules drifted toward the star, followed by the extraction ships and equipment.

Iswander Security flanked her, as if to make sure Orli didn't try to escape, but that was the farthest thing from her mind. With blurred vision, she looked at the industrial operations, the cargo ships flying about, the dark and deflated husks that drifted loose in space—and the remaining bloaters, spherical, silent, except for an occasional flash that sparkled from a nucleus.

Orli indicated a bloater that drifted outside the main mass of nodules. "Fly me to that one, DD. Get as close as you can." She still didn't really believe the green priest had a solution, but—as Garrison said—what did she have to lose?

It took her three tries to push herself out of the pilot chair. DD decreased the artificial gravity aboard so she had an easier time moving. She would need an environment suit, at least until she was submerged inside the bloater. She dreaded the effort that donning the suit would require, but she knew she had to do it.

Orli tugged on the slick fabric. She hadn't had many occasions to use a spacesuit in recent years, but the safety systems were helpful. The fastenings sealed themselves. Her left foot was maddeningly uncooperative, and she couldn't seem to get it seated properly in the integrated boot.

When DD came to offer his assistance, Orli almost wept with gratitude. Like a prim butler, he adjusted her fingers in the gloves, sealed the remaining components, repositioned her foot in the boot, then activated the suit's life-support systems.

"I have piloted the *Proud Mary* up against the bloater membrane," he said.

She sank down onto a bench so she was low enough for the compy to fasten her helmet. "Thank you, DD." Then it was time to go.

With weaving steps, she moved to the airlock. Through the windowports, she could see the bloater's mottled membrane so close. The thing was both intimidating and majestic. Standing at the airlock hatch, she turned back to the little compy. "Even if this works, I can't come back aboard the ship. The *Proud Mary* is contaminated. Nobody else can come aboard. Ever."

"I already have my instructions, Orli. I have prepared the ship's self-destruct systems." He paused and added, "BO and the other clan Reeves compies provided an example that I intend to emulate."

Orli stepped into the airlock, then turned back. "I'm modifying your instructions, DD. Once I'm inside the bloater, take the *Proud Mary* a safe distance from the Iswander operations and set the destruct timer. Transmit your coordinates, and then exit through the airlock into open space. You'll be adrift in hard vacuum, but someone will retrieve you soon enough."

"So, to clarify—you do not wish for me to be aboard during the self-destruct sequence?"

"No, DD, I don't wish that at all. The plague organism won't survive exposure to open space. It can't."

DD hesitated. "Are you certain?"

"Dead certain. Once they retrieve you, the industrial crew will keep you isolated and put you through every possible decontamination routine they can think of just to be sure."

"Just to be sure," DD echoed.

If nothing else, she imagined that DD could become the companion of young Seth Reeves. She was sure the boy and the Friendly compy would get along well together.

Before DD could argue with her, she closed the airlock hatch, sealed her helmet faceplate. After the air was purged and the outer airlock door opened, Orli faced the oddly gelatinous membrane of the bloater. She extended her gloved hand, touched the surface, and patted it. It felt as if the bloater were made of a kind of stiff jelly.

With a shove, she inserted her arm all the way up to the elbow. The density and texture inside eluded her, but the pain in her body did not. If she died, the plague would die with her. DD would destroy the *Proud Mary* as planned. But if she didn't die . . .

"What have I got to lose?"

Orli ducked her head and plunged into the bloater, where she found herself drifting in an invisible, intangible embrace. *Baptized in the blood of the cosmos.* Orli didn't know what to do with the green priest's mysticism, but all she had left was trust and hope.

Pushing aside any vestiges of hesitation, she opened the faceplate of her helmet.

Bloater protoplasm flooded her helmet, her suit; it poured into her eyes and ears and nose. Instinctively, she drew a last breath and sucked the impossible substance into her lungs. It raced everywhere, saturating her cells.

Orli Covitz felt reborn.

GENERAL NALANI KEAH

As commander of the Confederation Defense Forces, Nalani Keah knew when the battle was lost, whether or not she wanted to admit it. But leading the CDF involved more than just numbers and analyses. She had a heart, too, and fiery passion, and she knew damn well she was never going to give up.

The roiling shadow cloud hung in space like a stain on the universe. Even though the gigantic Shana Rei cylinders did not move, they seemed to pulse out waves of chaos and disaster.

Two verdani battleships again hurled themselves against the ever-growing nightshade, but the obsidian hex plates were more than just opaque: the darkness seemed to drain life itself from the huge treeships.

And the eclipse barrier continued to drown the whole planet in darkness. The worldforest was dying.

Klikiss robot vessels streaked out from the dark nebula like attack dogs. On the *Kutuzov*'s bridge, Keah sounded battle stations and summoned her scrappy Manta cruisers into defense formations. "The bugbots are after our asses again—let's show them what scrap metal looks like."

The rattling call to arms made the pulse pound faster, the adrenaline flow.

The black robots attacked at random points, caused whatever destruction they could, and then retreated into the shelter of the shadow cloud. The CDF had destroyed dozens of the enemy ships, but they kept coming! How many armored vessels did the damned bugbots have? Did they keep replenishing somehow?

Standard CDF weapons did little or nothing against the hexagonal plates or the Shana Rei cylinders, but at least the robots were an enemy her people could fight. It did her soldiers good to blow up a few bad guys every once in a while.

"Mr. Patton, power up the magnetic fields on our railguns. Let's get rid of some of those spare projectiles we've been hauling around."

The weapons officer grinned. "My pleasure, General."

The *Kutuzov* thrummed as a blizzard of high-velocity projectiles sprayed across space, turning three oncoming robot ships into metal confetti. The other enemy vessels spread out in evasive courses that— because they were robots—were not quite random enough to fool Keah's tactical team. They anticipated the paths of the robot ships and sent out another spray of projectiles.

Yes, it was good to blow up a few bad guys every once in a while.

Keah's green priest looked up from his treeling with a horror-stricken grimace on his face. "General, I think the worldforest is under attack!"

"That's old news, Mr. Nadd."

"Not the Shana Rei—it's . . . faeros!"

The *Kutuzov*'s imagers were focused on the nightshade, the Shana Rei shadow cloud, the attacking robot ships, but when the General scanned down at Theroc, she saw a cluster of shooting stars roaring *toward* her from below, streaks of fire like the ones that had caused horrific devastation during the Elemental War. They had hammered the worldforest, caused tremendous destruction to Ildira, and shattered the Earth's Moon into a million fragments.

"Oh, crap. I could have gone my whole day without seeing them again," she said. "All ships, prepare to defend against the faeros!"

"But . . . *how,* General?" asked the first officer.

Good question.

Like fiery comets, the faeros hurtled out of the Theron atmosphere, leaving sooty trails behind them as they rushed toward the defensive line.

"They're coming right at us, General," yelled Tac Officer Voecks.

"Brace yourselves!" Keah said.

At his treeling, however, Nadd's expression changed from terror to confusion. "Wait, General, they're not . . . attacking. Something happened down there—none of the green priests can understand it." He blinked in surprise. "Prince Reyn says the faeros are here to *help.*"

The molten cannonballs rocketed past the CDF battleships as if they weren't there and headed straight for the gigantic nightshade blocking sunlight from Theroc.

The first two fireballs splattered against the interlocked black hexes, and the impact spread across the eclipse barrier like napalm. Even though CDF ships had been bombarding the nightshade without success for days, the faeros shattered some of the hexes. Dazzling cracks began to show between the plates, as long-blocked sunlight streamed through the gaps.

Another fireball slammed into the eclipse plate near where the weakening verdani treeships had been trying to rip it apart. The force was sufficient to dismantle a wide segment of the occultation barrier. Even more sunlight flooded through, carving a bright blade of daylight across the night-smothered planet.

In response to the unexpected threat, the black Shana Rei cylinders finally began to move. The huge battleships spilled out dozens more hex plates that twirled in to rebuild the nightshade as fast as the faeros could destroy it.

An explosion shook the *Kutuzov,* and Keah held on to her command chair to keep from being thrown to the deck. An attacking robot warship soared past, launching another volley of weapons at them.

"No significant damage, General."

"That'll teach me to drop my guard," she grumbled. "Now let's teach that bugbot a lesson of our own. You soldiers aren't getting paid to watch the faeros do our fighting for us—come on."

Mr. Patton wore a hard grin as he aimed the railgun launchers. He fired a projectile right up the exhaust port of the escaping robot ship, which blossomed into wreckage. The bridge crew cheered. More Manta cruisers chased after the remaining black robot ships as they scrambled back toward the shadow cloud like a child hiding behind its mother's skirts.

Her sensor chief cleared his throat. "General, this is probably the last thing you want to hear, but I'm detecting a large group of inbound ships. Are we expecting company?"

"Not unless one of my Grid Admirals is acting independently." General Keah had not called for any CDF reinforcements, which would have proved useless. "How many ships?"

Lieutenant Saliba ran a quick analysis. "Forty-nine, sir."

"Then there's your answer." She felt a palpable relief.

After Mr. Aragao opened a comm channel on the standard Solar Navy frequency, Keah leaned forward. "Z, I think you've been watching old Earth cavalry movies. I'm pleased you can surprise me after all."

Adar Zan'nh's face appeared on her screen. "The Mage-Imperator's consort told us Theroc was under attack. As you've said many times, General, a good military needs to practice in order to remain in peak fighting condition."

"Practice away, Z! I hope you brought more than one functional sun bomb this time."

Zan'nh nodded. "Each warliner is equipped with ten. Do you think that will be sufficient?"

"One way to find out," she said.

The faeros fireballs continued pounding the nightshade. Looking oddly out of place, the gaudy Solar Navy warliners cruised ahead with angular fins extended. When the Ildirans launched their sun bombs, the result was like a re-creation of the Big Bang. The *Kutuzov*'s screen filters dimmed protectively as one small nova after another erupted against the flat expanse of black plates.

The forty-nine warliners launched their second rounds even before the first had finished exploding. Sun bomb after sun bomb exploded against the occultation barrier, and at last the opaque wall fell apart into thousands of individual hexagons, which tumbled loose through space. The substantiated matter of the hexes dissolved back into nothingness, like shadows vanishing in the dawn.

As soon as the nightshade began to crumble, the faeros fireballs sensed that part of the burden had been lifted from them. They flew away from the broken barrier, but rather than flitting off into open space, they streaked toward the shadow cloud. The hex battleships were already diminished by the ruin of their nightshade.

As the flaming ellipsoids provoked them, the Shana Rei launched the first active weapons that Keah had seen. A mouth opened at the flat end of the hexagonal shafts to vomit out a gout of black static.

The manifested shadow struck and engulfed the first faeros, wrapping around the fireball like a shroud, coalescing and darkening. The black cocoon cracked and trembled. Dark orange lines shivered through the inky skin as the faeros struggled, but gradually it died like a candle flame starved of oxygen.

Another gout of black static engulfed a second faeros, but with each weapon launched, the Shana Rei hex ships seemed to diminish further, as if creating the darkness required immense effort and energy.

And then many more faeros swarmed toward them.

The fiery ellipsoids pursued the retreating hexagon ships into the shadow cloud. Streaking in, the fireballs intensified, as if about to go supernova, inspired by the Ildiran sun bombs.

Klikiss robot ships buzzed around before wheeling back to the safety of the shadow cloud. The dark nebula contracted like a folding fist, and the last of the robot battleships disappeared into it.

The Shana Rei retreated into the tear in space, slipping between dimensions, and the remnants of the shadow cloud swirled like smoke being sucked into an exhaust vent. Then they were gone from the Theron system.

The last remnants of the nightshade crumbled and vanished, ending the eclipse. The surviving faeros flitted about like sparks in an updraft before they shot away into space.

"Guess they didn't want to stay for the victory party," Keah muttered, then raised her voice. "But we sure as hell are going to have one!"

Nadd the green priest wept openly. Even the Ildirans aboard the Solar Navy ships were excited. The comm officer was already relaying a congratulatory message from King Peter and Queen Estarra.

General Keah wanted to make some kind of inspirational victorious comment on their victory, but it was unnecessary. Her crew kept yelling and cheering. She decided that she owed Adar Zan'nh another one of her historical ship models. In fact, after today he could take them all.

ONE HUNDRED AND THIRTY-THREE

MAGE-IMPERATOR JORA'H

The Mijistra medical research center was staffed by thousands of doctors who trained among their greatest sages before being transferred to serve throughout the Empire.

Every member of their kith was predisposed to practice medicine. Some became proficient surgeons, while others were diagnosticians, pharmaceutical specialists, first-aid technicians, or skilled biochemists. Others performed intensive research, like those investigating Reynald's disease. The medical kith members who would gather in the quarantine chamber today were those who specialized in autopsies.

Jora'h and Nira watched the proceedings through a rectangular observation window made of thick crystal. Gale'nh stood with them, silent and curious, insisting that he might notice a detail because of his own encounter with the Shana Rei. Open to any insights, the Mage-Imperator agreed.

The walls of the autopsy chamber were smooth and seamless, molded from a continuous shell of polymer metal. The diagnostic equipment and power sources were all self-contained.

"This is dangerous work, Liege," Gale'nh pointed out. "What if the darkness is still within them, some residue of their possession?"

"We hope to learn the answer, Tal," Jora'h said. "And we must take risks before we can learn."

Nira's expression was hard. "I want to know what turned those people into monsters."

Gale'nh straightened. "I will submit myself to analysis if it would help . . . vivisection, if necessary. Prove that they are not still within me."

"No!" Nira said.

"It will not be necessary," Jora'h said in a tone that allowed no argument. "Let us learn from those we have lost."

The analytical specialists entered the chamber through three layers of security hatches, each of which sealed behind them. The randomly selected bodies for inspection had already been brought in, and when the dissection team was in place, the chamber was locked and secured. Banks of ceiling blazers shone down upon every surface; the bright light could be increased a millionfold in an instant, should extreme sterilization precautions become necessary.

Inside the chamber, five cadavers lay on the tables, chosen from the participants in the mob massacre. Four members of the medical kith were ready to proceed, the lead autopsy specialist, Enda'f, and three assistants.

"We will extract every possible answer from these specimens, Liege," said Enda'f. He tugged gloves onto his long-fingered hands.

One of the lesser medical kith mounted a set of magnifying goggles and a high-resolution projector onto the doctor's head. A second doctor laid out an array of tools, as well as devices for performing automated chemical and spectral analyses and a cabinet for holding specimens.

The third medical kith prepared a body, a long-limbed female who lay naked on the table, her skin a dull gray-green. She was a member of the teacher kith; perhaps in death, her body would teach them important information.

"We have one hundred seven total specimens, Liege," the autopsy specialist said. He did not even remark on how appalling the number was. "If we do not make any breakthroughs with these first cadavers, I promise you I will dissect and test every one until I have the answers you require."

Nira held Jora'h's hand. "We should have done this with the attackers that tried to kill me. If we'd learned the cause then, maybe we could have prevented this slaughter."

Following that assassination attempt, Jora'h had ordered the tainted Ildirans incinerated in a solar furnace. He had been disturbed by what they represented, and afraid that even after death their corruption might linger. Although he understood the necessity now, he still felt gravely uneasy as he peered down at the otherwise healthy-looking bodies in the autopsy chamber. He felt a chill to know that a hundred more remained in storage.

How many times would this insidious violence happen again? Had there been other instances on splinter colonies that he was not aware of?

"You should have studied me as soon as I came back from the *Kolpraxa*," Gale'nh said. "I do not believe that any of the poison remains inside me . . . but how could I know?"

"The worldforest is also fighting the Shana Rei on Theroc," Nira said with a shiver. "How many places can they strike at once?"

The Solar Navy had rushed to help as soon as the worldtrees informed them of the nightshade there. "I hope Adar Zan'nh has been able to assist Theroc," Jora'h said. That would be only a small consolation after what his ravening people did to the poor human settlers in Mijistra.

They peered through the thick window into the chamber below. Three autopsy assistants leaned close to the dead female cadaver, running their fingertips over her face, shoulders, breasts, ribs. Their deep scans covered the entire surface of her body.

Enda'f scrutinized the images projected on a holographic screen in front of him, not missing a detail. When the intense scans were complete, he shook his head. "No apparent external cause of death. No marks, no injuries. She just . . . died."

Gale'nh said to Jora'h and Nira, "The taint that killed them—and drove them to kill—is *inside*."

Using crystal knives to make seven access incisions, the assistants and the autopsy specialist cut open the female's body, peeled away the skin, and studied the muscle fibers, the blood vessels, the body cavity. They removed the internal organs one at a time, frowning—first curious and then fearful.

The images zoomed closer. Among the wet slime and cold blood, a black substance oozed like oil, curling behind the heart, permeating the lungs and blood vessels.

"A peculiar contamination," said Enda'f. "Like a black stain that ebbs and flows." He poked with forceps, but could not obtain a sample.

He used a syringe, but the cylinder came away filled with only normal-looking blood.

The assistants shifted the remaining internal organs as if to catch an escaping serpent, but they were also unsuccessful.

The autopsy specialist stood up from the cadaver, his gloves bloody. "I cannot locate the source, Liege, or where it resides now." He made a notation, consulted with his assistants, then moved on to open the cranium.

Jora'h said, "It is in the *thism* itself."

After the team removed the top of the female cadaver's head to expose the brain, the autopsy specialist inserted probes to test the convoluted brain matter. "Ah, there's the blackness—it has burrowed deep within the cerebral tissue."

Gale'nh looked deeply uneasy. "It is still there. . . ."

Enda'f removed a long, thin knife from the tray. Turning it so that the light from the blazers gleamed on its crystalline edge, he cut into the brain.

Darkness exploded outward like an erupting geyser. Oily black static sprayed from the opening in the cadaver's head. More of the tangible shadows lunged out of the chest cavity.

The assistants recoiled, scrambling away and knocking over the tray of instruments. The autopsy specialist caught the black eruption full in the face and chest. He screamed and writhed backward in agony.

It wasn't a black liquid—just an oily intangible substance that filled the air, pouring from the dead body. It engulfed another assistant who collapsed on the smooth floor, thrashing and twitching. The remaining two assistants rushed toward the hatch, but the interlock seals had already snapped into place.

The blackness swarmed over them, suffocating them. The room continued to fill with a roiling black shadow cloud. Gale'nh howled, covered his face with one arm.

Nira let out an astonished cry, and Jora'h pulled her away from the observation window just as an exterior armor plate dropped into place, shielding them before the incineration blazers released an instant vaporization burst.

The light of a thousand suns swallowed the autopsy room. Even the hair-fine line of light that showed through the window covering was searing enough to blind him momentarily.

Jora'h could only hope that the emergency system had been swift and intense enough to cleanse that horrific darkness in time.

Shareen Fitzkellum

Even on the isolated, tide-swirled planet of Kuivahr, they heard about the Shana Rei attacking Theroc. The black stain vomiting out of Golgen's clouds had only been one of the first encounters with the creatures of darkness. Shareen was not looking forward to another one.

When a Kett Shipping vessel arrived to take a load of kirae to Ildira (including one special bottle designated for the Mage-Imperator himself), the pilot told about the massive shadow cloud that had appeared at Theroc. As the crates of kirae were loaded aboard his ship, the pilot seemed uneasy about going to Ildira as well. "Odd reports coming out of there, too—mass hysteria, mob violence. The Ildirans say it's also the work of the Shana Rei."

Shareen remembered the quicksilver form of the hydrogue that had appeared on the Golgen skymine with blackness welling up inside its body, and how the shadow itself had flooded through the clouds of the gas giant. "Sounds like we were lucky to get away from Golgen when we did."

"We lost a whole skymine, by damn! I wouldn't call that lucky," Del Kellum said. "Except I'm lucky that you're all here with me now."

Her father added, "I have no interest in a galactic war. Done that already."

While Toff devoted his days to racing around in mudskimmers, Shareen and Howard worked in the distillery. They had already made improvements to increase production and shorten the fermentation time, but otherwise they didn't have specific job assignments yet—this wasn't exactly the skymine work-study routine Howard had signed up for.

Shareen enjoyed his company, though, and he didn't get tired of her ideas. Howard turned to her with a serious expression. "You have some very thought-provoking concepts."

"Then why are you so quiet after I tell you about them? You don't say that much."

"Because I'm thinking about them. That's what *thought-provoking* means."

They sat together on the outside upper deck under the cloudy skies, dangling their legs several stories above the muddy water. Del came out to join them, letting Marius Denva and other line supervisors handle the operations.

"Thought I'd find you here."

"Are we that predictable?" Shareen asked.

"No, I just looked everywhere else." Del made a great effort easing himself down and adjusting his legs precariously close to the edge, but he seemed comfortable enough. He gazed out toward the horizon in silence, which was unusual for him. Shareen didn't break the spell, and all three of them just sat thinking, listening.

Del finally spoke up. "I've seen enough of the Spiral Arm, operated facilities on half a dozen planets, served as Speaker for the Roamer clans. There's so much out there . . . but for me, this distillery is just enough. There was a time when *my* Shareen and I had plans to operate skymines on different gas giants. We were going to invest in a luxury spaceliner that would take tourists to the most amazing places—and we'd charge them through the nose each step of the way. She and I even talked about what we'd do when we retired together."

Shareen saw tears sparkling in his eyes, and when he took a deep breath she heard a slight hitch in his throat. "Even if we didn't retire, I still thought we'd be *together*. Sometimes the universe rises up and bites you right in the butt."

She had heard many stories about her grandfather's lost love Shareen Pasternak. It sounded like a truly epic romance, and she wondered if Del had exaggerated a little, but she was glad he had those stories and those memories, anyway. Coming back to himself, he looked at his granddaughter and reached over to tousle her hair.

"You two deserve more than spending your best years here. You're too important for this. I expect great things from you, Shareen."

She didn't know what to say to that, except to thank him.

Howard included himself as well. "We'll do our best with the op-portunities we have, sir."

"That's the problem right now—not many opportunities here. That has to change. I've already called in a few favors for you." He drew a deep satisfied breath, then made quite a production of getting back to his feet. "I'll have some news tonight at dinner—it's a sur-prise."

Shareen knew she was supposed to be excited, and she wondered what sort of odd scheme her grandfather had come up with.

Clan Kellum ate their meals family style, and Howard was consid-ered an adopted member of the family. He sat next to Shareen as they shared whatever seafood stew or shellfish concoction the commis-sary sent over.

Patrick took care of feeding Rex, who played with his food and jabbered about each item. Toff talked about the adventures he'd had (which sounded like the same thing he did every day, but Shareen had long ago learned how to tune out her pesky brother).

Zhett served herself and passed the pot down to Howard, while Del took his place at the head of the table. The big man cleared his throat and called them to attention. "I want you to know I've figured out what's best for my granddaughter."

Zhett bit her tongue with a visible effort.

"She needs something more challenging than this distillery has to offer. At the Golgen skymine she could have met her potential, taken over a major clan business, but not here. It's not grand enough for her. You know where she belongs?" Del looked over at Shareen.

"Do you want me to guess?" she asked.

He chuckled. "Shareen—and Howard, of course—belong at *Fire-heart Station*!" He grinned into the sudden silence, waiting for the reaction.

Patrick ventured, "That's where Kotto Okiah is working. There could be worse places. Unless she wants to go back to the private school on Earth?"

"No!" Shareen said quickly.

Del continued in a rush, not wanting anyone to steal his thunder. "I made arrangements. I'm going to escort Shareen, and Howard—if his parents agree—to Fireheart Station, make sure they arrive safely." He turned to Zhett. "Meanwhile, my sweet, you and Marius Denva can handle the distillery operations." He hooked his thumbs in his waistband and waited for someone to hand him a dish of food. "In fact, I may just stay at Fireheart for a while."

Zhett remained skeptical. "You're just handing your distillery over to us, Dad?"

Del sniffed. "You're my daughter, and you lost your gainful employment when the Golgen skymine was destroyed. You can handle these operations better than I can."

Patrick was too quick to agree. "Sounds like a good deal to me." He intercepted Rex from throwing food on the deck.

"Good," Del said. "It's decided then."

Shareen straightened in her chair. "Wait, nobody bothered to ask me."

Her grandfather just rolled his eyes. "Oh? Are you telling me you don't want to go to Fireheart Station?"

Shareen looked away, but not before she glimpsed the excitement on Howard's face. "What I *want* is to be consulted beforehand."

Del said, "All right, then I'm consulting you. You want to go to Fireheart Station?"

Shareen grinned as she imagined the giant glowing nebula, the processing stations, the huge experimental superconducting ring that Kotto Okiah was building, all the special films bathed in stellar radiation to be used in power blocks . . . and a thousand other innovative scientific projects that she hadn't even heard of yet.

"Absolutely," she said.

"Then you two better pack up. I'm ready to take you right away."

EXXOS

Sealed inside the entropy bubble after the Shana Rei retreat from Theroc, Exxos and his black robots assessed their losses. Though each of them had synchronized their memory cores to a stable parallel with Exxos, the rate of attrition was highly disturbing. So many ships had been destroyed.

A thousand Klikiss robots had hidden in the ice moon of Dhula to wait for the return of their comrades, but that had not happened. They had suffered setback after setback in what should have been a glorious victory. The universe itself seemed to want to destroy them. Since their reemergence, Exxos had lost three quarters of his robots. As far as he knew, these were the last Klikiss robots in existence.

Accidentally encountering the Shana Rei might be their greatest opportunity, or their ultimate devastation. Now the black robots were trapped among them, allies or prisoners ... depending on how well Exxos could convince the creatures of darkness. The Shana Rei were insane.

Now, as the shadow creatures retreated into the folds of the universe, Exxos could sense the fury and accompanying agony of the Shana Rei, and he knew that he was about to lose more of his comrades. No doubt about it. He hoped at least some of them would survive. And himself, at all costs.

Exxos had forged a dangerous alliance with the Shana Rei—it had seemed the only way to survive—and now the robots could not escape. At Theroc, the Shana Rei had insisted on killing the planet with their nightshade, while they remained at a safe distance from the still-formidable worldforest. That was much too time-consuming! Exxos and his robots were ready to attack any vestige of humans anywhere, and would have preferred a more direct and active role in destroying the world and the trees. But the Shana Rei had not been willing to engage in outright battle against the verdani. The world-forest was too powerful.

With the eclipse darkening and the landscape and sentient trees beginning to weaken and wither, the robots had satisfied themselves with destroying numerous human vessels: battleships, small fighters, larger cruisers. Exxos was able to test new modifications that the Shana Rei had implemented when they manifested the new robot ships.

Theroc should have died in the dark, thereby extinguishing part of the shrill agony the Shana Rei experienced from the verdani. The robots would have moved ahead with their own extermination agenda.

Exxos had never expected such a crushing defeat.

The Confederation military had caused no serious harm to the Shana Rei, and even the verdani battleships were not strong enough to tear apart the nightshade, but the faeros and the Ildiran sun bombs tore apart the Shana Rei's plans and forced a full retreat. The creatures of darkness abandoned the matter they had ripped into existence, and their gigantic hex ships were heavily damaged.

The agony of the Shana Rei was now like jabbering madness, and Exxos could barely stand it. They lashed out, making indescribable sounds. And they needed something to blame.

"Your failure!" the nearest inkblot said. "You robots are not as powerful as you promised. The tree mind fought back, and now our pain is greater."

Three black robots drifting in the emptiness of the entropy bubble were whisked upward, twirled about, and slowly ripped apart, dismantled piece by piece until they were nothing more than atoms.

The thunderous shadow voice continued. "And now the faeros have been awakened and turned against us—the fire that defeated us before!"

More black robots were separated from the group and surrounded by entropy bubbles. Exxos could still view his hapless comrades, but all transmission and communication cut off as soon as their bubbles sealed. The Shana Rei collapsed the entropy bubbles, and the robots winked out of existence.

They intended to erase all of the robots, one by one. "We are your

allies!" Exxos insisted. "Without us, the Shana Rei would fight alone."
But he knew his bluff had failed.

"You created great pain," said the pulsing black blot. "Additional pain."

"The *humans* created great pain. The *Ildirans* create pain. The verdani and the faeros create pain. We robots are your only allies. Only we understand what is at stake."

"You say you understand," the Shana Rei said, and the central eye glowed brighter. "But you do not feel our pain. If you fail, we will make your robots feel our agony—a hundredfold!"

More robots were torn apart in front of Exxos, and he was helpless to prevent it.

He knew that the Shana Rei were afraid of the tremendous enemy that was awakening in the universe, the mysterious but powerful force that had driven them out of the dark corners of the cosmos.

Despite his fear, Exxos began to make contingency plans. Perhaps the black robots would have to find this other mysterious enemy, switch sides, and help destroy the Shana Rei.

If any robots survived at all . . .

ONE HUNDRED AND THIRTY-SIX

ZOE ALAKIS

Though Tom Rom was so sick he could barely move, he made his way to the quarantine-only airlock at ORS 12. All alone, he cycled through the airlock into the quarantine chamber, while Zoe rushed her handpicked team up to the orbiting laboratory.

The researchers arrived in full decontamination suits and crowded into the spherical station, twice as many scientists as on Dr. Hannig's team. Zoe took no chances, wanting her most talented researchers there. All scientists who weren't assigned to ORS 12 would work on the problem from their own labs. Nothing was a higher priority at Pergamus.

On the edge of consciousness, using his last strength, Tom Rom gave them a verbal summary of his current physical status. During the trip in the stolen courier ship from Vuoral, he had taken meticulous notes of his symptoms, temperature, blood pressure, and pulse in hopes the data would give them something to work with.

To buy time, the medical team placed him in an induced coma, used precision robotic arms to take samples, sealed his body into the quarantine module's coldchamber, and dropped the temperature to bare survival levels. But still the disease progressed. . . .

Trapped in her sterilized dome on the planetary surface, Zoe felt very alone. She watched the screens, read updates, and insisted that one or more cameras in the ORS be focused on Tom Rom at all times, so she could keep looking at his face.

He was gaunt, his mahogany skin discolored by hemorrhagic bruises, but since his eyes were closed she tried to believe that he looked peaceful. With every second that passed, she knew he was one step closer to dying.

She hated the disease. Hated all diseases. Wanted to destroy them. Pergamus was supposed to be her invincible fortress, her arsenal. Now, all the data and samples she had collected, all the sophisticated researchers were being put to the test.

She had never doubted the dedication of her researchers; she studied each person's background before offering them employment at Pergamus. But Tom Rom's illness made her so desperate that she needed to give them additional incentive. She wanted no excuses, only a cure.

At first, she considered infecting the researchers so they would all live, or all die. *Incentive.* The advantage would be that they could then discard their cumbersome decontamination suits, which would facilitate easier work. But the progress of the disease was swift, and they would quickly deteriorate. She needed them at their best.

Instead, she told them that if they failed to find a cure for Tom Rom, she would consider the disease too dangerous even for her most extreme precautions, and she would be forced to destroy ORS 12 with the entire team aboard. She ordered her well-armed sentry ships to stand guard in orbit just in case one of the scientists found a way to escape the lab sphere.

The researchers were not overly cheered by her ultimatum, but they continued to work, regardless. Zoe couldn't tell if they worked with greater intensity once they knew how much was at stake, but she felt better knowing she had done everything possible to encourage them.

During the interminable wait, Zoe felt as if she herself were dying. Giving in to uncharacteristic nostalgia, she unlocked the old and secret recordings of her journals as a young woman at the watchtower station on Vaconda. She saw images of a younger, but somehow unchanged, Tom Rom working with the specimen-collection teams, helping to repair high windows that had cracked after a furious pelting storm, returning from offworld supply runs, repairing a weather satellite in orbit.

She found one image of Tom Rom deftly applying ointments and bandages to the numerous small bites she had received when the hummers broke into their tower station and swarmed into the chambers. Her father had been badly injured, but Tom Rom tenderly took care of her first.

"If it weren't for you, Tom Rom, I would have died long ago," she murmured to herself, then sighed. "Probably a hundred times over."

There were images of Adam Alakis, too, and she smiled to see her father when he'd been healthy, his eyes alert, his conversation brisk. The pain of losing him to Heidegger's Syndrome was long healed, the scars faded. Could she ever endure such pain again?

But Tom Rom was still alive—for now.

She checked hourly with the team aboard ORS 12, demanding to know what progress they had made. Then she made successive inquiries among the groundside domes where researchers worked on the problem independently, asking for their ideas, their insights. Teams scoured the entire Pergamus database, looking at every disease on record from any planet, trying to match the symptoms and possible effective drugs, but they could do only so much. This plague had originated in the Klikiss race, then mutated to kill Onthos, then humans; very little was comparable in the library of known diseases.

Even when they suggested long-shot drugs, the potential side effects were severe, and the various possibilities appeared to be fatally contradictory. If one treatment failed, they couldn't try another. Tom Rom would be dead.

Zoe was unable to sleep and didn't want to eat. She pestered the ORS 12 research team so mercilessly that finally the lead scientist scolded her, "You are distracting us, Ms. Alakis. We're under enough pressure, thanks to your threat, and you could cause us to make mistakes. We will inform you the moment anything changes." He switched off the comm.

Zoe felt so offended that she wanted to scream, then forced calm upon herself as she realized he was right. She sat sobbing by herself inside the sterile dome. . . .

In the end, her scientists did not let her down.

Pulling the possible cures and treatments of every recorded malady, deconstructing the genome of the alien virus and following the pathways of infection, one of her independent teams working in a groundside dome made the proper connection by suggesting that a cure might be obtained from a distillate of the Klikiss royal jelly Tom Rom had harvested from Eljiid. Her researchers showed that something about

Klikiss physiology rendered them immune to the virus. Therefore the royal Jelly might hold a key.

With racing pulse, Zoe listened to the research team's reports, watched the glacial progress, felt the work as a frantic race against her friend's degeneration, even as he lay in an enforced coma. The time it took to produce the royal-jelly distillate was maddening; after it was administered, the delay was more maddening still.

Zoe's eyes were bloodshot and scratchy. She felt haggard, weak, and feverish, as if she had somehow become infected by her very obsession with the disease. It was eleven hours before the team on ORS 12 was able to report with confidence that the patient had turned a corner and his condition was *ever-so-slightly* improved.

Fortunately, on his acquisition trip to Eljiid, Tom Rom had collected enough of the royal jelly to produce effective vaccinations for every member of the research team in the orbiting sphere. As Tom Rom slept and slowly regained his strength, Zoe commanded the research team members to remove their decontamination outfits, expose themselves to the disease, and inoculate themselves.

"We have to be certain," she said. "I want to see you stand by your own cure."

Some of the scientists took offense at being treated as guinea pigs, but they eventually acceded. After being exposed and vaccinated, they monitored themselves for three days and finally concluded that the treatment worked and that they themselves were not infected by the plague.

Then they revived Tom Rom from his induced coma.

Zoe, who had wrestled with the decision throughout the ordeal, at last found the courage and strength—to change her life.

She gave herself the inoculation, then called a small one-person ship to dock against her sterile central dome. Drawing a deep breath, digging deep to find long-buried reservoirs of courage, she exited through five layers of protective decontamination zones, boarded the one-person ship, and flew up to ORS 12.

Tom Rom was awake and aware when she cycled through the airlock and entered the spherical lab. The researchers gaped at Zoe in amazement. None of them had ever seen her in person before—very few people had.

The smells of the processed air were strange to her, the proximity of other human beings was intimidating. Zoe fought back her nervousness, though, and came forward.

Tom Rom stared at her, as if trying to convince himself this was not a hallucination. "You can't take this risk."

"I can, and I did. You're too weak to leave the lab yet. I could see you needed strength. Let me give it to you."

At his bedside, she touched his skin, felt the warm reassurance there that was so foreign to her. It had been at least fifteen years since she had touched another human being—even Tom Rom.

But now she slid her fingers down his forearm, took his hand in hers, and squeezed. "I'm here," she said.

NIRA

After the autopsy-chamber disaster, the remaining Ildiran bodies were spread out in the expansive arena normally used for the mirror ballet. Mage-Imperator Jora'h could not dispose of them quickly enough.

No audience was allowed to gather, but Nira remained with him. They had both seen the horrific eruption of darkness in the sealed chamber, but thanks to the protective systems every vestige of the contaminated corpses, the autopsy specialists, and the rising shadow had been incinerated in the tremendous discharge of intense solar light.

Jora'h would take no chances with the remaining cadavers. One hundred and two of them. The shadow stain must still be pooled inside the bodies, so they would all have to be disintegrated, flash-cremated. Lens kithmen insisted that the light of the seven suns was blessed. Maybe that light would be potent enough to erase the stain and achieve one small victory, to push the Shana Rei back.

Under general supervision, workers had laid out the dead participants of the massacre mob—a variety of Ildiran kiths and body types—stripped away their garments and incinerated the clothing in solar furnaces. Cremation workers moved from one cadaver to the next, carrying containers of a gray metallic paste—a photothermic cream used for funeral purposes—which they slathered over the skin, like a potter working clay. Jora'h had commanded the cremation workers to work as swiftly as possible.

Nira and Jora'h were alone in the primary observation box. This was no celebration, no spectacle of lights and colors. For a long time, neither spoke, although they shared their silent thoughts and feelings. Nira noted the troubled look in his eyes, how his long braid twitched with anxiety.

Finally, he turned to her. "I feel greater dread with each second. If the shadow should escape here and flood out into Mijistra . . ."

"But you know the shadow is already here." She thought of how easily it could infiltrate the Ildirans through the *thism*—as it had before. She remembered feeling uneasiness among the crowds that had come out for her birthday procession, when perfectly normal Ildirans had suddenly turned into wild killers.

Now the stadium was utterly still except for the quiet movements of the cremation workers. Outside, a full contingent of guard kithmen kept the curious away from the entrances.

Word had spread through the city of the horrors committed in the human enclave, how Ildirans had slaughtered all those people. They knew about the assassination attempts on Nira's birthday and the attacks in the Vault of Failures. Even though no one could understand the true cause of the violence, Ildirans whispered about the Shana Rei—and Jora'h could offer them no comfort.

"These people aren't at fault. They are victims, too," she said, looking down at all those bodies. "Will the families be allowed to have funerals for their loved ones?"

"We will give them wrapped effigies. They will have their ceremony and their time of grieving, but we won't make a spectacle of what their people did. . . ." He dropped his voice and said much more quietly, "It is my fault. I let them down. I allowed the weakness to seep inside."

Nira turned to face him. "The Shana Rei did this, not you."

"But they may have used me to do this." He straightened. "What if *I* am the weak point that makes our race vulnerable? I am the heart of the *thism,* and I must be the first line of defense."

She took his hand. "Then I'll make you stronger."

All the reflection plates, lasers, and prisms from the mirror ballet had been commandeered. Illumination physicists retooled them, intensified the parabolic lenses, used laser tracers to map out the full carpet of cremation. Every component had been tested. Jora'h insisted on incinerating all the bodies at once, fearing that if they did one at a time, the shadows might have time to retaliate.

The cremation workers finished covering the bodies with the thick gray paste, and they scurried away. Jora'h stared down at the corpses.

A messenger rushed into the box. "Liege, the illumination physicists are prepared. The dome can be opened."

"Then bring down the light," Jora'h said.

"We need to bring down a great deal of it," Nira added quietly.

They both applied filmgoggles and adjusted them to the densest settings. The louvered awnings in the arena ceiling tilted downward to reveal polished rectangular mirrors. The mirrors gathered sunlight from every portion of the Ildiran sky, reflected it, and flashed it down into collector bowls. Lenses intensified the searing light, and it gained strength and brightness in a flash.

Solar light poured onto the covered bodies, activating the photothermal cream, which blazed for an instant with a brightness more powerful than the core of a star. The flame incinerated every vestige of the bodies, vaporizing them so swiftly that the black taint trapped inside them was also boiled into bright nothingness. . . .

Nira was glad to know that the Shana Rei had been defeated at Theroc by the faeros as well as Ildiran sun bombs. Adar Zan'nh was on his way back, more than victorious, and confident that the Solar Navy weapons would have some effect against the creatures of darkness. The Confederation Defense Forces would also be building many of the weapons.

But even as these contaminated bodies were flash-cremated, and knowing the nightshade had been destroyed above Theroc, Nira could not feel relieved. "We may have hurt them, Jora'h, but the Shana Rei will be back."

He continued to watch the light bombardment until it was finally over. The louvered mirrors tilted again, closing off the ceiling and reflecting the sunlight back into the sky. He removed his eye protection and stared at the still-smoking ground of the mirror ballet arena. Only a smear of soot remained, shaped in vaguely humanoid forms . . . like permanent shadows of the fallen.

"You're right. You said they may already be here," Jora'h said.

"Your people can fight them if they are strong," she said. Jora'h looked uncertain, but she wouldn't back down; she pressed him again. "And they *will* be strong if you tell them to be strong. They'll be hopeful if you tell them to be hopeful."

"Yes, I can tell them that." He squared his shoulders and stood tall and strong—the powerful Mage-Imperator she had fallen in love with so many years ago. "I can tell them that, and they may even believe it." Then his voice dropped. "But the darkness is still closing in."

GARRISON REEVES

Even from a distance, Garrison could see that Orli was very near death from the ravages of the alien plague that had killed the rest of his clan. Aelin's suggestion for a miracle cure seemed ridiculous, but Orli obviously needed a miracle.

After Orli plunged through the bloater membrane as the green priest had directed, her compy detached the *Proud Mary* and flew it to a safe distance above the ekti-extraction operations. Garrison anxiously watched for some kind of signal from the dying woman. He could sense that no one really expected her to survive, though Aelin smiled with eager fascination. Garrison wished he had the same confidence.

He wanted to go retrieve her himself, but Lee Iswander sent Alec Pannebaker instead. Pannebaker flew the inspection pod over to the drifting nodule. He arrived just as a thin, spacesuited form pulled herself back out through the bloater wall similar to a child being born, then floated like driftwood in the vacuum.

Pannebaker transmitted, "I'll fetch her—and I just saw her move. Hard to believe, but she's still alive!"

Garrison's heart skipped a beat.

Then, unexpectedly, the *Proud Mary* exploded. The fireball expanded, flared brighter, and vanished. All traces of the plague-ridden ship were gone.

Seth began to cry. "DD was aboard!"

Garrison put his arm around his son's shoulder, sad for the loss of the compy, though he could not tear his gaze away from Orli's rescue. His joy at learning she was still alive was entirely out of proportion given that he barely knew her.

Pannebaker snagged the spacesuited form with the pod's manipulator arms, spun the vessel, and raced back to the cluster of modules. "What are your instructions, Chief? We still have to follow quarantine measures."

"That will not be necessary," Aelin said. "She is cleansed, healthy . . . restored. The plague will be gone from her." His eyes had a strange sheen of utter conviction like a fanatic. Unfortunately, fanatics could be wrong.

"We're not taking any chances," Iswander said. "Set up an isolated module so that we can observe her. We'll keep her completely separate from any other workers until we can confirm that all signs of the disease are gone."

"We need to be quick about it, Chief," Pannebaker replied. "I don't dare take her aboard my pod, and she's got limited air in her suit."

Iswander ordered a small group of workers to move out of a new habitation module, which was then sealed off. Pannebaker raced the pod to the designated hatch and deposited Orli's suited form in the makeshift quarantine module.

"She'll be all alone," Garrison said. "She'll have to take care of herself."

"She was doing that already," Iswander pointed out.

Just then the station's comm received a faint signal. "Per the instructions of my master, Orli Covitz, I am requesting a retrieval. I am just drifting in space. If anyone is listening, I would sincerely appreciate your assistance."

Seth brightened and looked at his father. "DD's still alive!"

The compy continued. "Before self-destructing the *Proud Mary,* I subjected my body to four full levels of decontamination. Now after several hours in hard vacuum, I am confident that all traces of the microorganism have been destroyed." The compy paused. "I will understand, however, if you still wish to disintegrate me. Just to be certain."

"No!" Seth cried.

Pannebaker was still out in his inspection pod. "What do you want me to do, Chief?"

Iswander looked at Elisa, then at Seth. "Bring the compy back and put him in quarantine with the woman."

Pannebaker sped off to pick up DD.

Once inside the newly evacuated module, Orli removed her hel-met and heaved great breaths. She wore an astonished, disbelieving look—and Garrison immediately saw on the screen that her face was free of the discolorations and blemishes that had been so prominent before. Stripping out of her environment suit, Orli looked drained but strangely rejuvenated. Her shipclothes were drenched with per-spiration.

Inside the admin module, Aelin beamed. "I told you. The blood of the cosmos purged the disease and left her fresh and whole."

During the next day, DD nursed her back to health. Orli was raven-ous, and made a remarkable recovery.

While in quarantine, she also spent a great deal of time face-to-face on the comm with Garrison. They talked about their lives, the chain of events that had brought them to this wasteland on the out-skirts of an unnamed star system. Orli regaled him with her adven-tures growing up, and Garrison talked about the Retroamers and the impossible dream of rebuilding Rendezvous.

Meanwhile, Iswander increased his ekti-extraction operations to a frenzy, worried that the shadow cloud might reappear at any time. His workers had already drained two-thirds of the bloaters, filling numerous surplus silos with stardrive fuel to be sold through their new arrangement with Kett Shipping. Meanwhile, the cluster floated closer to the bright white star.

After the regular crew, including Elisa, went back to work, Garri-son had more time alone with Orli, face-to-face on the screen. Iswan-der still didn't want to risk direct exposure. She talked about Matthew and how her life path had not gone the direction she expected. Hesi-tantly, Garrison talked about Elisa and said the same thing. And they talked about nothing at all.

He wanted to know Orli. He had so many questions for her, *about* her. Despite her ordeal, she appeared strengthened by it. She seemed lost—not aimless, but searching—and glad to have him to talk to.

Garrison realized he was in a similar situation. Ever since the Shana Rei's inexplicable withdrawal from the bloater field, followed by Orli's unexpected arrival in the plague ship, he had set aside the questions of where he and Seth should go—or *if* they should go.

When at last even the most skeptical doctor agreed that Orli was cured, that all symptoms were gone, that her blood tests were negative, and that she and the compy posed no further threat, Garrison was allowed to go into the module. He had Seth remain outside, and safe, for now.

It was their first meeting in person, although Garrison felt as if he had known her for a long time. Inside the quiet module, he came forward and gave Orli a hug. Oddly, he felt closer to her than he'd felt to Elisa in a long time.

Aelin joined them, eager to share his experience. Orli seemed energetic and alert now, but she did not have the intense euphoria that the green priest exhibited after his exposure. "The conduit of telink allowed me to receive so much more," he said, sounding disappointed. "All the glory and wonder were not available to you. I knew it wouldn't be the same, and I'm sorry for you."

Orli did not seem disturbed, however. "I'm *alive,* thanks to you. I never expected that to happen. That's all I could ask for."

Her attention, though, was on Garrison. "I thought about what you said—about the importance of my work with the compies. The Spiral Arm has plenty of traders and spaceship pilots, but not everyone can do what I do. I should have focused my efforts and skills on doing what I do best . . . *my* skills, not just as a shadow of Matthew's."

DD piped up, "That is my opinion as well. Most of the compies we distributed from Relleker have been transferred to a new colony on Ikbir."

"Never heard of the place," Garrison said. "What's it like?"

Orli flushed. "I have no idea."

He laughed. "Sounds like a well-considered plan then."

"We could go there," DD said. "I am sure they'd be glad to have her. Orli Covitz is a very useful person. And she can continue her work there."

Now she frowned. "I don't know how I'd get there, though. I seem to have lost my ship."

DD swiveled his head. "You gave me instructions to destroy the *Proud Mary,* Orli. Perhaps you don't recall—"

"I remember, DD. Just trying to solve a problem."

To Garrison, going with Orli to a Confederation colony sounded like a much better idea than staying at the ekti-extraction operations or even going back to the LOC—better for him, and better for Seth to be in a place where there were colonist children his age. Or maybe the boy would go back to Academ. And of course there would be DD. The boy had grown quite fond of the Friendly compy in a very short time.

And Orli would be there too.

He said, "I could give you and DD a lift in the *Prodigal Son*." On the comm, he asked, "Seth, would you like to go to Ikbir, at least to have a look around?" The boy couldn't agree quickly enough.

Now all they had to do was convince Elisa.

In the admin module, Elisa was preparing the manifest for a large shipment of ekti to the Ulio transfer station. She planned to be gone for several weeks, negotiating to buy salvage vessels that could be shipped out to the bloater cluster and reconfigured as pumping and filtering barges. She simply assumed Garrison would take care of their son whenever she went away.

But he had to focus on what was best for the boy, not let himself be buffeted by Elisa's capricious priorities. He announced, "Seth and I are going to check out a colony called Ikbir, maybe settle there if it looks good. I'll leave the coordinates, and you'll be able to contact me anytime you like."

Elisa's eyes flashed. "I didn't agree to that. My son is staying here where he's safe."

"Safe?" Garrison said.

Even Lee Iswander gave her a sidelong look. "Perhaps it's best if he takes the boy to a stable settlement, Ms. Enturi—this family squabble needs to end."

She visibly fought to contain her anger. "Custody is not just a squabble, sir."

"Indeed not, but I'm thinking of everyone's best interests. What if I were to expand your duties here? Your responsibility to Iswander Industries would require your time and attention . . . but if you prefer, I can give you a less stressful job, so you have more spare time to manage your personal life. Mr. Pannebaker is my alternate choice."

Elisa's face hardened. She looked at Seth and Garrison, as if she were being pulled by an intense gravitational force, but it took her little time to make up her mind. "You can count on me, sir. You've always known my reliability and my dedication to Iswander Industries." She glanced back at Garrison, as if she didn't even see Seth standing there. "He's still my son."

"He's still *our* son."

They were interrupted when Aelin entered the admin module, looking ecstatic. He spread his arms and tilted his chin. "Can you feel it? It'll happen soon now!"

One of Iswander's techs frowned at her readings, refreshed the screen, then stared out at the bloater cluster. The nodules were pulling away from the extraction operations. "The cluster is accelerating, Mr. Iswander."

The drifting bloaters had been picking up speed as they approached the nearby star, but the industrial operations had kept pace. Now, though, the remnants of the cluster—still hundreds of bloaters, despite the wreckage the ekti operations had deposited in their wake—drew ahead and left the complex behind.

The green priest closed his eyes, lifted his hands palms up, splayed his fingers. "Can you *feel* it? Something beautiful is happening!"

Flashes sparked through the bloater nuclei like fireworks, a random pattern that increased in intensity and speed as the bloaters plunged toward the star.

"All those flashes—it's like they're communicating," Garrison said.

Orli stood beside him, watching intently. "Or a chain reaction."

Inside the admin module, monitoring screens switched to higher magnification as the bloaters drew farther and farther away. The huge nodules shifted, flattened, and then swelled. Their elastic shapes contracted in the middle and began to spread out. Still swelling and stretching, the nodules *fissioned*, each sphere dividing into two bloaters.

Orli's voice was husky with awe. "It's like mitosis—cells dividing."

Each new sphere inflated to the size of the original nodule, until there were twice as many of them. The bloaters continued to shimmer, flashing signals, pulsing, squirming, swelling.

Within an hour, before the Iswander operations managed to catch up with them, the bloaters fissioned once more, restoring the numbers in the strange cluster to more than they were before.

Tears streamed down Aelin's face. "And they're not finished yet!"

The metamorphosis continued. The newborn bloaters squashed and expanded, becoming disklike and elongated until broad fleshy wings with membranous surfaces extended from their body cores, making the nodules look like huge space mantas.

The broad wings gathered the bright light of the nearby star, absorbing energy, and they swooped forward, accelerating until they circled the white sun. The transformed bloaters reveled in their new forms like butterflies emerging from a chrysalis. Their body cores sparkled, as if their flickering conversation had increased in intensity.

Everyone inside the admin module stared, struck dumb with wonder. The glorious creatures moved like a single flock, riding the solar wind. Picking up speed, they came back around and soared out past the Iswander extraction operations.

Then the bloaters flashed away, heading out into empty untracked space.

RLINDA KETT

On Theroc, the flood of sunlight rejuvenated the worldforest. As the trees strengthened, the green priests rejoiced. People bustled about the fungus-reef city, barely able to believe they had escaped the deadly impenetrable night.

Rlinda Kett met the new day with great joy, announcing that Arbor would be open for all customers. She was already planning great feasts to celebrate the bounty available from the thriving forest.

As day dawned again—a *real* dawn—and the atmosphere warmed, winds whipped up, stirring the worldtrees. Capricious rainstorms appeared as weather patterns readjusted, but even the rain seemed like a wonderful gift. Rlinda stood out on the open forest canopy next to her restaurant, while others ran for shelter. She just smiled and enjoyed the sparkle of raindrops on her skin.

Stepping back inside, dripping wet, she announced, "Mr. Wisskoff, we will be providing klee for all customers, fresh, hot, and free. It's time to give back." She slurped from her own cup of the rich beverage, felt the energy of ground worldtree seeds seep into her bloodstream.

"Free? Wonderful." The maître d' sniffed. "Perhaps I could simply open our pantries and refrigeration units, toss all of our food out into the meadows? Spread the bounty far and wide by flinging it from the branches?" His pinched face tightened at the very idea.

In the end, she allowed him to talk her into limiting the offer to "one day only." The maître d' brightened slightly. "While others are celebrating their salvation, I will celebrate you coming to your senses, ma'am. Briefly."

Rlinda and Wisskoff took a portable dispenser and made their way to the main fungus-reef. A small ship had flown in from the Wild and landed on one of the canopy decks. Arita emerged from the landed vessel, accompanied by her aunt Sarein, who had lived as a veritable hermit for years. Although Sarein gave Rlinda a cool reception, because of their many interactions during the Elemental War, Arita ran forward to hug her. "Where's Reyn? Is he here?"

Rlinda smiled. "Oh, he's here, and safe—with an Ildiran girl he seems quite fond of." She brushed aside the impatient Wisskoff, who didn't seem happy to be wherever he was, at any time. "Follow us. They're all meeting with your parents and General Keah."

"And we are delighted to offer free cups of klee for everyone," Wisskoff said without enthusiasm.

When they reached the fungus-reef's main meeting chamber, Arita ran to her brother, who seemed shy as he introduced Osira'h. Arita warmed to her as soon as she noticed the attraction between Reyn and the Mage-Imperator's daughter. "Oh! I'm very pleased to meet you." Arita's knowing grin embarrassed her brother.

Rlinda moved throughout the room, supposedly trying to be unobtrusive but not at all successful. During her many years as trade minister before moving on to Kett Shipping and her restaurants, she had formed a habit of keeping her eyes open and her finger on the pulse of society.

Sarein seemed out of place, but she took a seat at the table and waited for the meeting to continue, as if she were an integral part of the discussions. "Please don't allow us to interrupt," she said.

Several advisers and Confederation representatives were in the room along with General Keah, who wore her full dress uniform and was seated next to four Manta captains, whom she had handpicked after their performance during the nightshade crisis. Rlinda handed them all cups of steaming klee, whether they asked for one or not.

Keah put her elbows on the table, and continued. "As I was saying—first off, we need to get our butts in gear. Adar Zan'nh gave us the Solar Navy plans for sun bombs and laser missiles, but who knows when the Shana Rei will strike again?"

Peter said, "The factories at the Lunar Orbital Complex are ready for full-scale production. I received a report from Deputy Cain this morning. We should have sun bombs for CDF ships within the coming weeks."

"Yes, Sire, but those are the standard-issue sun bombs. Ildirans being what they are, I'm sure the weapons were from old plans that hadn't been changed in thousands of years. We can do better. The CDF will add some finesse, increase the intensity, and show the Ildirans how it's done. It's a matter of pride."

Sitting next to Reyn, Osira'h said, "The faeros came because I called them, but they suffered losses, too. I tried to thank them, but it's difficult to know if they understood. There's no guarantee that they'll respond again if I call them. They are unpredictable. We need to be prepared to fight the Shana Rei even without the faeros."

"I still find it difficult to trust the faeros," said Queen Estarra, "after what they did to the worldforest."

"Therefore, more sun bombs." General Keah took the klee Rlinda handed her and slammed it down as if it were a shot of whiskey.

Three green priests sat in the room, each with a potted treeling. All at once, they sat upright, turning to one another and then back to the King and Queen. "The verdani battleships are reacting. Something is coming."

Keah leaped to her feet as did the Manta pilots. Touching the comm on her shoulder, she said, "Keah to *Kutuzov*—battle stations! Full sensor sweep." She activated the screens inside the chamber.

Rlinda paused to stare, then moved out of the way so others could see the screens. The *Kutuzov* and the armed Mantas remained on high alert, poised in a widespread defensive formation. The huge verdani battleships spread apart, their thorny boughs now green and powerful again, recovered from the battle against the nightshade.

Sensor Chief Saliba transmitted from the *Kutuzov*, "General, our deep scans detect a flurry of incoming ships—small unidentified vessels."

Keah said, "Is it the Solar Navy?"

"Definitely not, sir. They're too small—and there's an accurate count, not a multiple of seven. Ildiran ships always travel in multiples of seven."

"At least you're learning, Lieutenant Saliba," she said. "How many then?"

"Ninety-nine."

The small vessels streaked in like shotgun pellets. The CDF ships raised their shields, stood in defensive formations. The weapons officer called, "Should we open fire, General?"

Glancing at the General, Queen Estarra shook her head, keeping her eyes on the curious expressions of the green priests. "Let's wait and see."

Peter added, "We can't just shoot at anything that approaches Theroc."

"Agreed," Keah said, though she didn't sound happy about it. "Hold your fire, Mr. Patton. But keep your fingers on the firing controls, just in case."

The verdani battleships spread out, leaving obvious gaps for the incoming ships to pass through. One of the green priests said, "The treeship pilots . . . know them."

"Who are they?" Peter asked.

The *Kutuzov*'s comm officer said, "The unidentified ships don't respond to any transmissions."

As the flurry of small vessels streaked past the picket line of CDF Mantas, the long-range imagers resolved details: the strange ships were small, featureless ovoids like armored seedpods. They bore no markings, no external lights—and, thankfully, no weapons ports.

The ninety-nine ships cruised past, wove their way among the restless verdani battleships, then dropped through the cloudy Theron atmosphere to the heart of the worldforest.

The green priests looked up from their treelings and rose to their feet. "The Gardeners have returned. We should welcome them."

Everyone in the chamber left the fungus-reef to head outside and watch. Wisskoff started to gather up the klee service, but Rlinda was already moving out. The maître d' said, "I suppose you'll be wanting to offer a free banquet to all our new visitors, as well?"

"Let's see if they're hungry first," she said. "And what they eat."

Outside, the podships poured down through the sky like shooting stars. Each craft was no larger than a cargo shuttle. Finding gaps in the worldforest canopy, they landed in the expansive meadow like armored raindrops.

The teardrop-shaped podships settled down on their wide, rounded ends, with the narrower portions tilted upward. Seams appeared in their polished hulls, which split into triangular sections, unfolding like the petals of a large artificial flower.

Each podship held several creatures crowded together: small-statured and smooth-skinned, with rounded heads and heavy brows. They belonged to no race Rlinda had ever seen before, though they looked vaguely familiar.

King Peter and Queen Estarra stood together as the strange aliens emerged, beings that the green priests called Gardeners. Hundreds of them stepped out of the opening podships, filling the meadows in the forest, standing in the clearings between trees. They were eerily silent and looked gentle, contemplative.

Now the worldtrees trembled, and the green priests tapped into the verdani mind but found confusion rather than information. It was as if the worldforest were reaching for memories only to find them missing.

One of the silent creatures walked over to the nearest tree, ignoring the crowd of observers. The Gardener touched the gold-scaled bark, closed its eyes, and let out a long sigh, as if finally reconnecting with an energy source. The other aliens scurried forward to touch the trees as well, gathering information from the worldforest mind—and adding information as well.

Once the aliens made contact, the gathered green priests looked startled, their eyes open wide. Finally, the strange creatures turned, now identifying Estarra and Peter as the leaders. After drawing the information they needed from the verdani mind, they spoke in perfectly comprehensible trade standard.

"We are the last survivors of the Onthos. We are also called the Gardeners—though we have not been able to tend the blessed trees for thousands of years."

As more and more of the Onthos tapped into the worldforest network, they acquired knowledge, language, and the details of history over a vast gulf of time. They seemed overwhelmed by their new situation . . . but more than anything, relieved.

"We were the first tenders of the worldtrees, the original worldforest that thrived on our world," said the Onthos who had initially spoken. "That forest was entirely destroyed by the Shana Rei. In doing so, they carved out and extinguished all of those memories from the verdani mind. No one remembers . . . but us."

The green priests in the meadow buzzed with excitement.

Amazed, Arita looked at her mother. "Where could they have been for so long?"

The Gardener heard her question. "Darkness engulfed our world, killing all of the worldtrees. We did manage to scatter some treelings before it was too late . . . and those remnants have grown into the current worldforest." The little aliens spread their hands in a strange unison. "It has been centuries . . . millennia since we had treelings of our own. We have nothing. We are the last refugees from the Shana Rei."

In a choreographed pattern, the Onthos bowed, and turned to face the King and Queen. "We ask to live here with the forest in peace, to become Gardeners once again. We beg sanctuary from the creatures of darkness."

GLOSSARY

ACADEM: Roamer school inside a hollowed-out comet, near the Roamer complex of Newstation. The school is run by Jess Tamblyn and Cesca Peroni.

ADAM, PRINCE: failed candidate to replace old King Frederick of the Hansa.

ADAR: highest military rank in Ildiran Solar Navy.

AELIN: green priest, brother of Shelud.

AGUERRA, RAYMOND: original name of King Peter.

AHLAR: Ildiran splinter colony, site of an ancient Shana Rei attack.

ALAKIS, ADAM: researcher on Vaconda, father of Zoe Alakis, died of Heidegger's Syndrome.

ALAKIS, EVELYN: researcher on Vaconda, mother of Zoe Alakis, killed in a flyer crash when Zoe was young.

ALAKIS, ZOE: wealthy head of the Pergamus medical research facility.

ALEXA, MOTHER: wife of Idriss, former ruler of Theroc.

ARAGAO, OCTAVIO: communications officer aboard the *Kutuzov.*

ARBOR: Rlinda Kett's restaurant on Theroc.

ARITA, PRINCESS: daughter of King Peter and Queen Estarra, a budding naturalist.

ATTENDER: servile Ildiran kith.

AURIDIA: sparsely inhabited planet over which Newstation and Academ orbit. Auridia contains a Klikiss transportal for access into the transportal network.

AZZAR: Klikiss robot.

BALI'NH, ADAR: historical Ildiran commander, first Ildiran to contact human generation ships.

BEBOB: Rlinda Kett's pet name for Branson Roberts, her favorite ex-husband.

BEKH: Ildiran curse.

BENETO: green priest brother of Estarra, killed by the hydrogues.

BIG GOOSE: deprecating name for the former Terran Hanseatic League.

BIG RING: Kotto Okiah's large experimental accelerator under construction at Fireheart Station.

BJORN: spaceship engineer in clan Reeves.

BLACK ROBOTS: intelligent and evil beetlelike robots built by the Klikiss race; most of them were wiped out in the Elemental War.

BLIND FAITH: ship flown by Captain Branson Roberts.

BLOATERS: strange organic nodules found in deep, empty space.

BLONDIE: diner owner in the human enclave in Mijistra.

BO: Teacher compy from Academ, tasked to teach Roamer children from clan Reeves.

BOLAM, DENNIS: administrator of the Eljiid research camp.

BOONE'S CROSSING: former Hansa colony, wiped out by a hydrogue attack in the Elemental War.

BREEDEX: central mind of the Klikiss.

BRIA'NH, TAL: historical Ildiran commander, one of the first to combat the Shana Rei.

BRINDLE, ROBB: administrator of Kett Shipping, married to Tasia Tamblyn, father of Xander.

BRINDLE, XANDER: one of the pilots of Kett Shipping vessel *Verne*, son of Robb Brindle and Tasia Tamblyn.

BUGBOT: deprecating slang term for a Klikiss robot.

BUZZBEETLE: Theron insect.

CAILLIÉ: generation ship from Earth whose passengers colonized Theroc.

CAIN, DEPUTY ELDRED: former deputy of the Terran Hanseatic League, now an administrator of Earth loyal to the Confederation.

CARII: Ildiran splinter colony, site of an ancient Shana Rei attack during an eclipse.

CARLIN, REESE: Retroamer.

CELLI: green priest, married to Solimar, who tends a terrarium dome in Fireheart Station. Celli is the sister of Estarra and Sarein.

CHAIRMAN: true leader of the Terran Hanseatic League.

CHIAR'H: Ildiran woman of the noble kith, volunteer worker on the Kuivahr sanctuary domes, married to human Shawn Fennis.

CHRYSALIS CHAIR: reclining throne of the Mage-Imperator.

COLICOS, ANTON: historian, known for his work with Ildiran records, first to translate portions of the Saga of Seven Suns; the son of famed xeno-archaeologists Margaret and Louis Colicos.

COLICOS, LOUIS: xeno-archaeologist, husband of Margaret Colicos, specializing in ancient Klikiss artifacts, killed by Klikiss robots at Rheindic Co.

COLICOS, MARGARET: xeno-archaeologist, wife of Louis Colicos, spent much of Elemental War as prisoner of the Klikiss. She and her son Anton collated the only known Klikiss history, *The Song of the Breedex.*

COLLIN: young green priest, friend of Arita's.

COMPETENT COMPUTERIZED COMPANION: intelligent servant robot, also called a compy, available in Friendly, Teacher, Governess, Listener, Worker, and other models.

COMPY: nickname for competent computerized companion.

CONFEDERATION: new human government replacing the Terran Hanseatic League, loose alliance among Roamer clans, independent planets, and remnants of the Hansa. Ruled by King Peter and Queen Estarra, capital on Theroc.

CORRIBUS: colony where Orli Covitz once lived, devastated by Klikiss robot attack during the Elemental War.

COVEN, MARY: former pilot of the *Proud Mary*.

COVITZ, ORLI: compy scientist, strong advocate for compies, married to Matthew Freling. She is the owner of DD.

DANIEL, PRINCE: former candidate to replace King Peter in the Hansa.

DARO'H, PRIME DESIGNATE: successor to Mage-Imperator Jora'h.

DAYM: blue supergiant star, one of the "seven suns" in the Ildiran sky.

DD: Friendly compy owned by Orli Covitz.

DENVA, MARIUS: line supervisor at Del Kellum's distillery on Kuivahr.

DETEMER: Roamer clan.

DHULA: gas-giant planet on the edge of the Ildiran Empire.

DOBRO: Ildiran splinter colony, former home of the secret breeding program where many humans were held captive.

DOLUS: famous twenty-first-century Earth artist.

DREMEN: cloudy planet, former home of Orli Covitz.

DROGUE: nickname for hydrogues.

DUGGAN, ANDREA: artist suffering from Heidegger's Syndrome.

DUGGAN, JAMES: husband of Andrea Duggan.

DURRIS: trinary star in the Horizon Cluster, three of the "seven suns" in the Ildiran sky.

DYVO'SH: young Ildiran rememberer, assistant to Anton Colicos.

EARTH DEFENSE FORCES (EDF): former military for the Terran Hanseatic League, precursor to the Confederation Defense Forces.

EKTI: exotic allotrope of hydrogen used to fuel Ildiran stardrives.

EKTI-X: stardrive fuel with higher energy potential than traditional ekti.

ELEMENTAL WAR: conflict across the Spiral Arm involving the human race, Ildiran Empire, the hydrogues, faeros, wentals, verdani, as well as the Klikiss and their black robots.

ELJIID: abandoned Klikiss world where Margaret Colicos is buried.

ENDA'F: Ildiran autopsy specialist.

ENTURI, ELISA: wife of Garrison Reeves and mother of Seth, deputy of Lee Iswander at the Sheol lava mines. Also goes by her married name of Elisa Reeves.

ESTARRA, QUEEN: ruler of Confederation, married to King Peter, with two children, Reynald and Arita.

EXXOS: leader of surviving Klikiss robots.

FAEROS: sentient fire entities dwelling within stars.

FENNIS, SHAWN: human born on Dobro, volunteer worker at the Kuiv-ahr sanctuary domes, married to Ildiran woman Chiar'h.

FILMGOGGLES: eye protection used on Ildira.

FIREHEART STATION: Roamer research and industrial station at the heart of a nebula, specializing in energized films. Site of Kotto Oki-ah's current large-scale experiment.

FITZKELLUM, KRISTOF: thirteen-year-old son of Zhett Kellum and Patrick Fitzpatrick III, also called Toff.

FITZKELLUM, REX: two-year-old son of Zhett Kellum and Patrick Fitzpatrick III.

FITZKELLUM, SHAREEN: seventeen-year-old daughter of Zhett Kellum and Patrick Fitzpatrick III.

FITZPATRICK III, PATRICK: husband of Zhett Kellum, one of the managers of the Kellum skymine on Golgen.

FREDERICK, KING: predecessor to King Peter, killed by hydrogues.

FRELING, MATTHEW: compy scientist, husband of Orli Covitz.

FUNGUS-REEF: large inhabited fungal growth on the worldtrees of Theroc.

GALE'NH, TAL: halfbreed son of the green priest Nira and Ildiran war hero Adar Kori'nh, a tal in the Ildiran Solar Navy. Gale'nh is the captain of the exploration ship *Kolpraxa*.

GANN, HENNA: mistress of Matthew Freling.

GARDENERS: ancient, original tenders of the worldforest.

GOLGEN: gas-giant planet, home of the Kellum skymine.

GREAT KINGS: the Kings of the Terran Hanseatic League, figurehead leaders.

GREEN PRIEST: servant of the worldforest, able to use worldtrees for instantaneous communication.

GUIDING STAR: Roamer philosophy and religion, a guiding force in a person's life.

HALL OF REMEMBERERS: headquarters and historical archives of the Ildiran rememberer kith, where the Saga of Seven Suns is maintained.

HANDIES, ADMIRAL EDGAR: CDF Admiral, head of Grid 0, one of the "Three H's."

HANDON, TERRY: one of the pilots of Kett Shipping vessel *Verne*, partner of Xander Brindle.

HANNIG, KLAUS: medical researcher on Pergamus.

HANSA: Terran Hanseatic League.

HAPPINESS: closed-off former Klikiss planet, inhabited by neo-Amish settlers.

HAROUN, ADMIRAL SHIMAL: CDF Admiral, head of Grid 6, one of the "Three H's."

HARVARD, ADMIRAL PETROV: CDF Admiral, head of Grid 11, one of the "Three H's."

HEIDEGGER'S SYNDROME: fatal degenerative neurological disease, thought to be incurable. Adam Alakis died of Heidegger's Syndrome.

HORIZON CLUSTER: star cluster in which the Ildiran Empire is located.

HUMMERS: voracious locustlike insects from Vaconda.

HYDROGUES: alien race that dwells within gas-giant planets, the main destructive antagonists in the Elemental War.

HYRILLKA: Ildiran planet, site of several battles in the Elemental War; the Klikiss robots were originally discovered on one of Hyrillka's moons.

IDRISS, FATHER: former ruler of Theroc, father of Estarra.

IKBIR: Confederation colony world.

ILDIRA: home planet of the Ildiran Empire, under the light of seven suns.

ILDIRAN EMPIRE: large alien empire, the only other major civilization in the Spiral Arm.

ILDIRAN SOLAR NAVY: space military fleet of the Ildiran Empire, commanded by Adar Zan'nh.

ILDIRANS: humanoid alien race with many different breeds, or kiths; they are able to interbreed with humans.

ISWANDER, ARDEN: thirteen-year-old son of Lee Iswander.

ISWANDER, LEE: Roamer industrialist with numerous operations, including the Sheol lava mines.

ISWANDER, LONDA: wife of Lee Iswander.

ISWANDER INDUSTRIES: company owned by Lee Iswander with numerous high-risk operations, including the Sheol lava mines.

JAZER: energy weapon used by Confederation Defense Forces.

JORA'H: Mage-Imperator of the Ildiran Empire. He is the father of numerous important Ildirans, including Adar Zan'nh and the halfbreed telepath Osira'h. His consort is the green priest Nira.

JUGGERNAUT: largest battleship class in the Confederation Defense Forces.

KANAKA: one of the old Earth generation ships, origin of the Roamer clans.

KEAH, GENERAL NALANI: commander of the Confederation Defense Forces.

KELLUM, DEL: former Speaker of the Roamer clans, successor to Cesca Peroni. Father of Zhett Kellum. He now runs a distillery on the Ildiran ocean planet of Kuivahr.

KELLUM, ZHETT: daughter of Del Kellum, married to Patrick Fitzpatrick III. She runs a large skymine on Golgen. She and Patrick have three children, Shareen, Kristof, and Rex.

KENNEBAR: leader of an isolationist faction of green priests on Theroc.

KETT, RLINDA: trader and former trade minister of the Confederation, now owner of Kett Shipping. She also owns several high-end restaurants.

KETT SHIPPING: Rlinda Kett's shipping company, managed by Robb Brindle and Tasia Tamblyn.

KHANDUL: colony planet near Vaconda.

KIRAE: intoxicating drink enjoyed by Ildirans, although humans find it distasteful.

KLANEK, TONY: space traffic controller at Newstation.

KLEE: a hot beverage made from ground worldtree seeds, a specialty of Theroc.

KLIKISS: ancient insectlike race, long vanished from the Spiral Arm, leaving only their empty cities. After their resurgence in the Elemental War, they departed through their transportal network and are considered lost or extinct.

KLIKISS ROBOTS: intelligent and evil beetlelike robots built by the Klikiss race; most of them were wiped out in the Elemental War. Also called black robots.

KOLPRAXA: new-design Ildiran exploration ship to go beyond the Spiral Arm, led by Tal Gale'nh.

KORI'NH, ADAR: great Ildiran military hero from the Elemental War, father of Gale'nh.

KO'SH, REMEMBERER: Ildiran historian assigned aboard the *Kolpraxa*.

KUIVAHR: Ildiran planet with shallow seas and strong tides, site of Tamo'l's sanctuary domes for misbreeds and Del Kellum's distillery.

KUTUZOV: flagship Juggernaut of the Confederation Defense Forces.

LENS KITH: one of the Ildiran breeds, religious philosophers.

LIGHTSOURCE: higher plane of existence above normal life, an Ildiran version of heaven.

LU: Listener compy at Orli Covitz's compy laboratory.

LUBAI: green priest serving at the Lunar Orbital Complex.

LUNAR ORBITAL COMPLEX: military and civilian base established in the rubble of Earth's Moon.

MAGE-IMPERATOR: the god-emperor of the Ildiran Empire.

MANTA: cruiser-class battleship in Confederation Defense Forces.

MEDUSA: large cephalopod from Rhejak; its meat is considered a delicacy.

MIJISTRA: Ildiran capital city.

MO: Domestic compy at Orli Covitz's compy laboratory.

MOSBACH, PROFESSOR MICHAELA: one of Shareen Fitzkellum's teachers on Earth.

MUREE'N: halfbreed daughter of Nira and a warrior kithman, a skilled fighter, student of Yazra'h.

NADD: green priest serving aboard the *Kutuzov*.

NEW PORTUGAL: Confederation planet, home of a university and also known for its wines.

NEWSTATION: large orbiting station above planet Auridia, the new Roamer center of government. The Roamer school Academ is also nearby.

NIGHTSHADE: Shana Rei occultation barrier.

NIRA: green priest consort of Mage-Imperator Jora'h, mother of five halfbreed children: Osira'h, Rod'h, Gale'nh, Tamo'l, and Muree'n.

OK: compy owned by Xander Brindle.

OKIAH: name given to derelict space city inhabited by clan Reeves.

OKIAH, KOTTO: renowned but eccentric Roamer scientist.

ONTHOS: alien race, builders of derelict space city claimed by clan Reeves.

ORBITAL RESEARCH SPHERE (ORS): isolated medical research satellite orbiting Pergamus.

ORFINO: architectural specialist working on Eljiid.

OSIRA'H: daughter of Nira and Jora'h, bred to have unusual telepathic abilities.

OSQUIVEL: ringed gas giant, former site of Kellum shipyards.

PANNEBAKER, ALEC: one of Lee Iswander's deputies at the Sheol lava-processing facility.

PAOLUS, DR. BENJAMIN: foremost neurological researcher on Earth.

PASTERNAK, SHAREEN: lost love of Del Kellum, killed by hydrogues on a skymine. Shareen Fitzkellum is named after her.

PATTON, DILLON: weapons officer aboard the *Kutuzov*.

PELLIERI, KAM: desert geologist working on Eljiid.

PEPPERFLOWER TEA: Roamer beverage.

PERGAMUS: secure medical research facility owned and managed by Zoe Alakis.

PERONI, CESCA: former Roamer Speaker, wife of Jess Tamblyn; together they run the Academ school complex for Roamer children.

PETER, KING: ruler of Confederation, married to Queen Estarra, with two children, Reynald and Arita.

PIGEON: small trading ship at Vuoral.

PLUMAS: frozen moon with deep liquid oceans, site of Tamblyn clan water industry.

POWER BLOCK: energy source made of a charged film, folded and packed inside a shell.

PRIME DESIGNATE: eldest noble-born son of the Mage-Imperator, and successor.

PRIMORDIAL OOZE: trade name of one of Del Kellum's distillations from Kuivahr.

PRISDIAMOND: rare precious gem found on several Confederation planets.

PRISM PALACE: crystalline palace of the Ildiran Mage-Imperator.

PRODIGAL SON: Garrison Reeves's ship, formerly an Iswander Industries vessel.

PROUD MARY: Kett Shipping vessel formerly piloted by Mary Coven.

QORLISS: Confederation planet.

QRONHA: binary star in the Horizon Cluster, two of the "seven suns" in the Ildiran sky.

RAINDROP: Rlinda Kett's pet name for Reyn.

RAMAH: Confederation planet.

REEVES, DALE: brother of Garrison, second son of Olaf Reeves.

REEVES, ELISA: wife of Garrison and mother of Seth, deputy of Lee Iswander at the Sheol lava mines. Also goes by her maiden name of Elisa Enturi.

REEVES, GARRISON: Roamer worker at the Sheol lava-processing facility. He is married to Elisa, father of Seth. He is the son of clan head Olaf Reeves, brother of Dale.

REEVES, INDIRA: Retroamer.

REEVES, JAMIE: young son of Dale Reeves.

REEVES, OLAF: gruff clan head, leader of the "Retroamers," isolationist Roamers who are trying to rebuild the wreckage of Rendezvous. Father of Garrison and Dale.

REEVES, SCOTT: young son of Dale Reeves.

REEVES, SENDRA: wife of Dale Reeves, formerly Sendra Detemer.

REEVES, SETH: ten-year-old son of Garrison Reeves.

RELLEKER: Terran colony planet, home of Orli Covitz's compy laboratory.

REMORA: small attack ship in Confederation Defense Forces.

RENDEZVOUS: asteroid cluster, former center of Roamer government. Destroyed by the Earth Defense Forces, but clan Reeves attempted reconstruction for years.

RETROAMERS: mocking term for the isolationist clan Reeves.

REYN, PRINCE: son of King Peter and Queen Estarra, in line to be the Confederation's next King. His full name is Reynald.

RHEINDIC CO: Klikiss world, serves as a nexus for humans using the Klikiss transportal network for travel among planets.

RHEJAK: watery planet with habitable reefs, known for large cephalopods called medusas.

RICKS, SAM: candidate for Speaker of the Roamer clans.

ROAMERS: loose confederation of independent humans, primary producers of ekti stardrive fuel, often disparagingly called "space gypsies."

ROBERTS, BRANSON: Rlinda Kett's favorite ex-husband, affectionately called BeBob.

ROD'H: older halfbreed son of Nira, fathered by Dobro Designate Udru'h as part of the secret breeding program.

ROHANDAS, HOWARD: fellow student with Shareen Fitzkellum on Earth.

SAGA OF SEVEN SUNS: historical and legendary epic of the Ildiran civilization.

SALIBA, SHARON: sensor technician aboard the *Kutuzov.*

SANDOVAL, SHERI: representative from the Roamers to the Confederation.

SAREIN: sister of Estarra and Celli, lives in self-imposed exile in the Wild.

SEPTA: small battle group of seven ships in the Ildiran Solar Navy.

SEWARD, ISHA: retiring Speaker for the Roamer clans, successor to Del Kellum.

SHANA REI: fearsome creatures of darkness that preyed upon the Ildiran Empire long ago.

SHELUD: green priest, brother of Aelin.

SHEOL: binary planet under heavy tidal stresses, site of lava-mining operations led by Lee Iswander.

SHIZZ: Roamer curse.

SKYMINE: ekti-harvesting facility in the clouds of a gas giant planet, usually operated by Roamers.

SKYSPHERE: audience chamber of the Prism Palace.

SOLIMAR: green priest, married to Celli, who tends a terrarium dome in Fireheart Station.

SONG OF THE BREEDEX, THE: Klikiss historical chronicle transcribed and translated by Anton and Margaret Colicos.

SPEAKER: Roamer leader.

SPIRAL ARM: the section of the Milky Way Galaxy settled by the Ildiran Empire and Terran colonies.

SWIMMER: otterlike Ildiran kith that spend most of their time in the ocean.

SWOOPER: small skybike used around skymining operations.

TAIT, MATTHEW: navigator aboard the *Kutuzov*.

TAL: military rank in Ildiran Solar Navy, cohort commander.

TAMBLYN, JESS: one of the heads of Academ school, married to Cesca Peroni.

TAMBLYN, TASIA: administrator of Kett Shipping, married to Robb Brindle, father of Xander.

TAMBORR'S DEMENTIA: disease being studied on Pergamus.

TAMO'L: one of Nira's halfbreed children, daughter of a lens kithman. She runs sanctuary domes for misbreeds on the planet Kuivahr.

TARKER: architectural specialist working on Eljiid.

TELINK: instantaneous communication used by green priests via the worldtrees.

TERITHA: Roamer colony, site of a disaster caused by failed life support.

TERRAN HANSEATIC LEAGUE: former commerce-based government of Earth and Terran colonies, dissolved after the death of Chairman Basil Wenceslas at the end of the Elemental War. Also called the Hansa.

THEROC: forested planet, home of the sentient worldtrees.

THERON: a native of Theroc.

THISM: faint racial telepathic network, centered on the Mage-Imperator, that binds all Ildiran people.

THREE H'S: Admirals Handies, Harvard, and Haroun in the CDF.

TOM ROM: guardian and majordomo of Zoe Alakis.

TORA'M: Ildiran swimmer kithman on Kuivahr.

TORINO, MILLI: Garrison's supervisor at the Lunar Orbital Complex.

TRANSPORTAL: Klikiss instantaneous transportation network.

ULDO'NH, QUL: maniple commander in the Ildiran Solar Navy.

ULIO: large trading complex in open space, frequented by traders of all sorts.

ULIO, MARIA: founder of the Ulio transfer hub.

VACONDA: wilderness planet, site of the Alakis forest watchtower station.

VANH, LARA: Klikiss researcher on Eljiid.

VAULT OF FAILURES: document crypt in Mijistra containing ancient discarded weapons designs developed for use against the Shana Rei.

VERDANI: organic-based sentience, manifested as the Theron worldforest.

VERNE: cargo ship flown by Xander Brindle and Terry Handon.

VOECKS, ALAN: tactical officer aboard the *Kutuzov*.

VORACIOUS CURIOSITY: Rlinda Kett's private ship.

VUORAL: small, obscure Confederation settlement on the Klikiss trans-portal network.

WARGLOBE: crystalline sphere used by hydrogues.

WARLINER: largest class of Ildiran battleship.

WENCESLAS, CHAIRMAN BASIL: former leader of the Terran Hanseatic League.

WENTALS: sentient water-based creatures.

WHISPER PALACE: traditional seat of power in the Terran Hanseatic League, where the figurehead Great Kings ruled.

WHISTLERS: possibly sentient cacti on Eljiid.

WILD, THE: unexplored continent on Theroc.

WINGO, MERCER: first officer aboard the *Kutuzov*.

WISSKOFF, ZACHARY: manager and maître d' of Rlinda Kett's Arbor restaurant.

WORLDFOREST: the interconnected, semisentient forest based on Theroc.

WORLDTREE: a separate tree in the interconnected, semisentient forest based on Theroc.

WULFTON: active star, home of numerous faeros.

YAZRA'H: daughter of the Mage-Imperator, skilled warrior and body-guard. She is the mentor of Muree'n.

ZAN'NH, ADAR: Ildiran military officer, eldest son of Mage-Imperator Jora'h, Adar of the Ildiran Solar Navy.

BRANCH	DATE
LY	08/14